# *Fae of Rewyth*

## THE COMPLETED SERIES

EMILY BLACKWOOD

*authoremilyblackwood.com*



Omnibus Cover Design by MerryBookRound

Created with Vellum

# House of Lies and Sorrow

BOOK 1

*For the readers who get bored with normal.*

# CHAPTER 1
## Jade

"How do you think he'll kill you?" Tessa asked me.

I continued focusing on the knot that I was tying, even though I was certain the blood had rushed from my face. "I'm not really sure. I haven't thought about it," I lied.

Of course I had thought about how I was going to die.

I had pictured all the ways he could end my meaningless life.

Would it be as simple as a dagger to the chest?

Or something less merciful?

But my sister never saw me as weak. She wasn't about to start now. I put a joking smile on my face before I added, "I wonder if he'll do it himself, or if he'll send someone else to finish his dirty work."

Tessa leaned in with the same grin she always wore while gossiping. At least my upcoming death was important news to her. "Hopefully he does it himself. I heard he's handsome as sin."

I playfully shoved her away. "You've been listening to too many rumors, little sister. Those big ears of yours will get you into trouble. We both know nobody knows anything about the Prince of Shadows."

Tessa didn't respond. She looked down at her own knot she was tying, studying it closely. Except she wasn't still tying it, either. She had dropped the rope into her lap and had begun picking at her fingernails. The silence grew heavier with every second.

"You never know, Jade. Maybe he'll end up really liking you. Maybe he'll fall madly in love, and he'll protect you with his life." Her voice took a turn from light and playful to serious and emotional. "You have to try. You have to *try* to survive. Promise me you'll try to make him like you? That you'll fight?"

Her large, deep eyes searched my face for an answer. They searched for any slither of hope that I wasn't being sent to my imminent death.

But I knew the truth. I was being sent into the fae lands to marry one of the fae princes.

And if that wasn't bad enough, I was going to marry the Prince of Shadows. The merciless, deadly prince who waltzed through this world with no consequences.

And like every human wife he had before me, I was going to be killed.

Any other scenario would be a useless attempt at having hope.

There was no way around it. I was going to die.

But nonetheless, I smiled at my sister. "Of course, I'll try, Tessa. I'll do everything I can. You know I'm not one to give up easily."

She seemed pleased with my words, and she quickly resumed tending to her own knot.

Tessa was a worrier. I knew that's why my father had chosen me, along with many other things.

She was softer. She was likable. She didn't have sharp edges and scars. She didn't come with damage. She was *perfect*.

I, on the other hand, was not even close to perfect. I was damaged.

I was easily expendable. Which was why I was being sent to my death.

Okay, I was being sent to my marriage. But what was the difference?

"Give me that," I demanded after watching her fumble with the rope a few times. She gave it to me without hesitating and watched in awe as I tied the perfect knot in a matter of seconds. "Here," I said, handing it back to her. "You're going to have to learn this type of thing when I'm gone. We all know father isn't any help."

She giggled again, but it didn't quite reach her eyes. "I know, I know. I wish you could stay a little longer to help me."

"I wish I could stay longer, too. Unfortunately for us, time is not our friend. We've put this off for long enough."

"I still don't understand why it has to be you!" Tessa said, her emotions seeping into every word. Thick tears began welling in her eyes. "Why can't someone else marry the fae prince? Why does it have to be you?"

I dropped the knot and pulled her into my arms. She didn't know the details about the deal my father had made with the fae king. I took a deep breath and told myself to calm down. Just thinking about it made my blood boil. How could he be so reckless? Of course he had gotten caught. And when the king learned that he had two daughters, they made a deal.

My life for his.

Of course, it wasn't me that they wanted. I was just the one Father picked. To nobody's surprise, either.

But Tessa didn't know that part, and I certainly was not about to tell her. It's not like she would jump up to take my place or anything, but she would at least feel guilty.

Well, I hoped she would.

But even if Tessa was ignorant, useless, skinny, and slightly selfish, I was determined to keep her safe. She had experienced enough hardships in this life, even though I had done everything in my power to protect her.

And if this was going to help protect her, I would do it with a smile on my face. A fake smile, at least.

"It's getting dark," I said after a few minutes. "I'm going for one more hunt before tomorrow. I won't be long. Go inside and make sure Father is asleep by the time I get back."

"Okay," she agreed, rolling her eyes. "Be careful out there!"

"I always am," I said before grabbing the rest of our rope and throwing it over my shoulder, bending down to kiss her cheek before turning my back on our cottage and heading toward the tree line.

My mind was racing. From the day I learned of the deal my father had made with the fae king, I knew I would die for his mistakes. I just always thought I would have more time.

Now, I had only a handful of hours left in my life.

But there wasn't time to panic. Tessa needed food. My biggest fear wasn't dying. It wasn't marrying one of the most evil creatures on the planet, and it wasn't traveling to the fae lands.

My biggest fear was Tessa dying because of me.

If I died—when I died—Tessa would have nothing. I had tried to prepare her for this, but there was only so much I could do. My father was nothing but a drunken burden. He was no provider. He was no father. Ever since I could carry a knife, I would wander into the forest and gather food for Tessa and me. Without it, we certainly would have starved to death. Not like that was rare in the human lands, but still.

I was all Tessa had. I wasn't going to let her die, too.

I buried my emotions and focused on the land around me. We were lucky to live close enough to so much empty land, making it easier to hunt for food instead of paying for meat at the markets.

Saints, everyone knew we didn't have the money for that.

I never caught anything too big. Mostly rabbits with snares that Tessa and I would make. But it kept us alive. It kept us fed, which was better than most people who lived in these lands. It wasn't rare to see children so skinny that you could count every bone. It also wasn't rare to be killed over a loaf of bread if a family was desperate enough.

Tessa would need as much as possible after I left if she was going to make it.

The ground turned from the plowed dirt path to the full, leafy forest that surrounded our land. Walking my familiar path deep into the woods, I approached the snares I had set up yesterday.

*Please have something,* I silently pleaded. *Anything.*

My old, worn boots crunched on every dead leaf and broken branch beneath me. Those were the sounds that had grown to comfort me all these years later. This was the place I learned to find my peace.

Relief flooded my body once I saw the dead rabbit I had caught.

I wasn't leaving empty handed. That was something.

There were many nights when I hadn't been so lucky. I pushed away the memories of Tessa crying from hunger, my father screaming that I was no good.

I began releasing the prey from the trap, pushing away any emotions that came with it.

I was nine when I made my first kill. My father had forced me with him on one of his hunts. He used to love hunting. That was before my mother died, of course.

The only thing he loved now was drinking.

*They don't deserve to live more than you do*, he said. *They die or your sister will starve to death. Pick one.*

I'd shot an arrow through its tiny body and cried for the rest of the day. How cruel life was, to create something so fragile and give it no chance at surviving.

A deep growl rumbled the air around me, piercing through the silence. The hair on the back of my neck stuck up. A few feet away stood the largest wolf I had ever seen, eyeing the rabbit that he had thought was his.

He was going to attack me.

Perhaps this was how I was going to die. I had to admit, it sounded better than marriage.

"Easy there," I whispered under my breath. "Is this what you want?" I held the rabbit out between us, trying to draw the wolf's attention from me to the meat.

The wolf bared his teeth and growled again.

I guess he was really pissed.

"Take it and go," I whispered again, as if he could understand what I was saying. Every inch of my body was telling me to run. But I was no fool.

And I knew that wolves never traveled alone.

Human footsteps on the forest floor approached from behind me, but I didn't dare take my eyes off the creature. It wasn't all that rare for other hunters to run into me out here. If I was lucky, whoever it was would scare the wolf away.

"What in the Saints are you doing?" a deep male voice made me jump.

"Stop! Don't move!" I hissed, whipping my gaze between the towering wolf and the strange, hooded man behind me. He stood with his hands in his pockets, clearly not a threat.

"Whatever you say," he said in a casual tone that made me even angrier than I already was.

I focused back on the wolf. If I could get his attention onto the rabbit, I could throw it into the trees and get out of here. But then I would be empty handed. Tessa would be hungry. All of this would be for nothing.

"It's you or me," I said to the hungry beast, "and I'm afraid I have a family to feed." I tucked the rabbit into my satchel and backed away slowly.

Which only made the wolf let out a deep, blood-curdling howl toward the sky.

Low laughter filled the air behind me. "I think you've angered him," the man said.

I kept stepping backward away from the wolf and in the direction of the man. I didn't care. I had dealt with many men in my life. They were nothing compared to a hungry pack of wolves.

Although they often liked to think otherwise.

"Shut up," I mumbled in his direction. The wolf stepped forward, following my every move.

And then another wolf followed behind it.

*Shit.*

There had to be more hiding in the bushes, and they were no longer interested in the rabbit.

They were interested in me.

The man behind me knew it, too. He let out a quiet noise of satisfaction.

I unsheathed the knife, holding it out in front of me.

"Come on then," I urged the wolf, loud enough for my audience to hear. "If you're going to kill me, do it already!"

I didn't care that I sounded crazy. This was my last night alive, anyway. If the wolf decided to attack, I at least had a chance at killing one of them before they killed me.

At least my death wouldn't be for nothing.

"You should probably get behind me," the man said. "Unless you want to be dinner for about five wolves."

"Get away from me," I snapped, continuing to step backward. I knew I was just a few feet from him. The wolves were pushing me closer and closer.

I took another step backward. Then another.

When I took one more step, I found myself pressed against the man's chest.

He didn't touch me, though. Just laughed silently. I could tell by the way his body shook against my back.

The wolves didn't seem to pay him any attention. He wasn't the one who had stolen their dinner.

A third wolf came into view, snapping its jaw just inches from my legs. I jumped back on instinct, further into the stranger's body.

*Coward,* I thought to myself. I twisted the knife in my hand, gripping tightly. Would it be enough? If these wolves lunged, would my knife protect me? By the looks of it, it would require much more than that to take one of them down.

Seconds later, I had no choice.

The wolf in front of me lunged, and my body reacted without my permission. I didn't cower this time. I propelled myself forward, blade out, aiming for the wolf's throat.

A mixture of limbs, fur, and claws hit the forest floor. I was waiting for the piercing pain of teeth to impale me, but it never came.

And my knife never made contact, either.

An aggressive, alpha growl rumbled through the still air right before strong hands pulled me from the floor, dragging me backward. My knife slipped from my grip, but the hands kept dragging me away.

And the wolves didn't follow.

"Are you out of your damn mind?" the stranger hissed into my ear, dropping me to the ground. "You're going to get yourself killed!"

I scrambled to my feet, ready to fight with my bare hands if I needed to. That knife wouldn't have helped much, anyway.

"They're going to—" I started, then froze.

The wolves, who had been mere seconds away from ripping me apart, were now backing away. Each of their heads bowed and their tails were now tucked between their legs.

Not because of me, though. No, they were all focused on the man to my left.

I had never seen anything like it.

As soon as the animals turned their attention onto him, the energy in the forest changed.

What was he doing?

He stepped forward once, and the wolves scattered completely. He must have known some secret to deter the wolves that I didn't. That was the only explanation.

That, or the fact that the man was an absolute giant.

I was of average height, but this man towered over me. And his wide shoulders told me that he was certainly strong enough to fight one of the beasts if given the opportunity.

"What was that?" I asked. I hated the way my heart was pounding in my chest. I was too close to death to be afraid of it. "What did you do?"

The man turned to me, and I saw his face for the first time. He didn't look much older than me, but he had sharp, mature features that matched the clear leanness of his body. His dark hair stuck out under his hood, even blacker than my own.

I was certain I had never seen him before. I would have remembered.

"What makes you think you can take on a pack of wolves with your bare hands?" he asked, his voice dripping with anger.

"That's none of your business. And it wasn't with my bare hands. I was armed," I said, crossing my arms.

The man laughed. "Right. You're lucky I was here, or you would have been slaughtered."

"Excuse me?"

"What? You think that sad excuse for a dagger was going to save you? I've seen a pack of wolves much smaller than that take down an entire lioness, sweetheart. Don't bite off more than you can chew next time."

I was actually speechless. Who the Saints did this guy think he was? He knew nothing about me or my experience with hunting.

He continued anyway. "A lady should not be wandering the forest alone after the sun goes down," he said. "It's dangerous, as I'm sure you know by now." He was still standing way too close to me, but I didn't back away. He was trying to intimidate me, and by the smirk he wore on his face, he knew it.

"Do not speak down to me," I said, rolling my shoulders backward. "I am not a child. My family needs food, and I am providing it. You can mind your own business next time."

He laughed and shook his head. "That's a lot of confidence coming from someone who just nearly died. You're welcome, by the way."

"I don't need your help," I spat. The darkness hid the embarrassment rising to my cheeks. I hoped so, at least.

I turned away from the stranger and began walking toward the edge of the forest. Returning for my knife would have been no use. I wouldn't need it anymore, anyway. Not after tomorrow.

"You provide food for your entire family?" he asked, catching up beside me.

I don't know why I felt the need to answer him, but I did. "My sister, Tessa. My dad's a useless drunk. Someone has to put food on the table."

A flash of something crossed his dark features, but it passed before I could identify it.

"Did you make that rabbit trap yourself?" he asked, continuing the interrogation.

How long had he been watching me? Annoyance crept into my body. Was he serious? Following me into the forest to embarrass me, taunt me, and start casual conversation as if we were friends?

"Look," I said, stopping and turning to face him, "I don't know who you are or what you're doing out here, but it's probably best for both of us if you go home and leave me alone. And if you're a creep who thinks he can take advantage of a young woman, just know that that knife isn't just for rabbits. And it wouldn't be the first time I've used it on a man."

I was angry. My heart was beating into my ears.

But the man merely smiled in amusement, crossing his arms over his chest and leaning on a nearby tree.

"Okay, Jade," he said. "I'll leave you be, then. My apologies for interrupting your clearly under control hunting trip."

"How do you know my name?" I demanded, stepping forward. "Who are you?"

He paused in thought, as if he were debating on whether or not to answer me.

"I know your name because you are marrying the Prince of Shadows tomorrow. Everyone knows your name, Jade Farrow."

"That's not true," I argued. My heart sank to my stomach, dread creeping into my senses. "Nobody knows about that."

"You're very wrong," he said. "It's all anyone's been speaking about for weeks."

"You're not from around here. I've never seen you before. How did you find out about my marriage?"

He smiled in amusement again.

He was taller than any man in my village, stronger than any of them, and a complete stranger.

A chill ran through me. Could he be a fae? In the human lands?

I shook my head. No. It was impossible. He didn't even have wings. The darkness hid most of his features, but I didn't see pointed ears, either. They looked normal, with a small silver piercing on his left ear.

"Nervous about something?" he asked. His calmness and cockiness were doing nothing to help my growing agitation.

"Yes," I answered. "I'm nervous about how damn creepy you're being. If you won't answer my questions, then I suppose I'll be on my way. It was *not* nice to meet you, stranger."

I turned to continue walking, but he pushed himself off the tree and blocked my path.

"You're being sent to marry a fae prince," he repeated. *It wasn't a question.*

I lifted my chin. My mind swarmed with possibilities of what he could want from me. Did he need me for leverage? Or did he hate the fae so much he wanted to kill anyone associated? This man might have been a stranger, but I was not going to show him fear. Not on my last day alive.

"No," I said with all the confidence and power I could muster. "I'm being sent to be *killed* by a fae prince. Not much of a difference, though."

For the first time during this entire interaction, the man looked shocked.

"What, you're surprised?" I asked. "If you know enough to know that I am being married off, then you should know that every human who marries the mysterious Prince of Shadows ends up dead."

"Those are rumors," he said, suddenly defensive.

"Maybe," I replied. "But rumors start from somewhere."

"I have a good feeling about this. You will not die tomorrow, Jade Farrow. I wish you a long and happy marriage to your mysterious Prince of Shadows."

His words were respectful and cordial, but I nearly laughed in his face. A marriage to the Prince of Shadows had no hope of being happy. *I* had no hope.

Death would be easier.

"Sure," I said after a few seconds. "Whatever you say..."

"Mal. My name's Mal."

"Well, *Mal,* I should get going. Big day tomorrow and all."

I'm not sure why I was expecting him to protest, but the tiniest amount of disappointment crept into my chest when he nodded his head and moved away so I could pass.

"I'm sure I will see you again soon, Jade," he said as I walked away.

I ignored the butterflies that ignited in my stomach, likely from the sudden nerves about the realization of what would happen tomorrow.

*Mal was never going to see me again. Tonight was my last night alive.*

# CHAPTER 2
## Jade

My father was awake when I made it back to the house.

*Not good.*

His slurred, temperamental voice carried into the street, followed by Tessa's crying. I changed my pace into a run.

"What's going on?" I demanded, storming through the front door. My father, clearly drunk, was pacing in the kitchen. Tessa had cowered herself into a corner, arms across her body and tears streaming down her face.

If he laid a hand on her, even a finger, I was going to kill him.

"Are you okay?" I asked Tessa, running over to her and blocking her line of sight with my body. "Did he hit you?"

She shook her head.

"Then what's going on?"

She opened her mouth to speak, but the only thing that came out was a stifled sob.

My father shattered something behind me, mumbling something I couldn't understand.

I turned my back to Tessa but made sure to keep her protected.

"You should be asleep!" I yelled to him. He staggered forward, shirtless, and nearly tripped over nothing.

"Don't tell me what to do, girl," he slurred as he caught himself on the kitchen table. "I'm your father. I'll go to bed when I please."

My body stiffened. "You're drunk. It's late."

"I know how late it is. I am not an idiot, despite what you believe. You look down on me, treat me like garbage. But I am the leader of this household. Show some respect, both of you!"

Tessa was still crying behind me. "Go to your room," I whispered to her, making sure my father wasn't paying attention as she slipped by in a hurry.

I hated that she saw him this way. I hated that she had to endure his behavior, and I hated that after tomorrow I wouldn't be here to help her.

My father reached for a mug of ale that likely came home with him from whatever tavern he had wasted away inside of all day. I grabbed the mug from his hand and slammed it back onto the kitchen table, causing liquid to splash over the both of us.

"That's enough," I seethed.

"It's enough when I say it's enough," he responded, but his words strung together.

"Just go to sleep!" I said, feeling my temper unraveling. "Isn't it bad enough that you scared Tessa? Can you just for once be a good father and not ruin everything?"

He considered me for a moment, then clenched his jaw. "You disrespectful brat. After everything I've done for you, too."

"Everything you've *done* for me?" I asked. "Please enlighten me on all of the great things you've done for me. I'm dying to know. Especially after I've kept this family alive all these years."

"*You've* kept us alive?" he spat. "You would be nothing without me. Nothing! I taught you everything you know, child!"

"You taught me what a deadbeat father looks like. You taught me that I have nobody in this life to count on but myself. And when I die tomorrow, which I will, it will be *your* fault. So thank you, father, for everything you've done. I apologize that I have not been more grateful." I took a step toward my bedroom.

"You are marrying a prince, Jade. A prince! You *should* be thanking me!"

"Thanking you? You want me to thank you for ruining my life?"

Before I could back away in time, my father slapped me hard across my face.

It wasn't the first time he had hit me. But it was going to be the last.

The taste of copper filled my mouth.

I straightened, touching a finger to my lip and surveying the blood that dripped from it. My father didn't budge.

"You've always despised me," I said, lifting my chin to face him once more. The man standing in front of me, sloppy and drunk and barely alive, was a stranger to me. He was nothing. Certainly, no father. "I'm not surprised at all that you made this deal to save your own skin. Just do yourself a favor and leave Tessa alone when I'm gone. It's the least you could do after ruining my life."

I didn't wait for him to respond. He grunted something behind me, but I ignored him and continued to my room, shutting the door firmly behind me.

Anger pounded through my ears. I rested my forehead on the wooden door and tried to breathe.

"We won't survive without you, Jade," Tessa whispered from our bed.

She and I shared a room in our small, broken-down cottage. I didn't mind it most nights, especially when my father was as temperamental and uncontrollable as he was. I could keep her safe this way.

"You will," I said to her. "You will survive because you have no choice. He won't help you, so you have to do this yourself." I walked to the bed and ripped off my old, torn boots. "You have food. Save as much money as possible. As soon as you're old enough, you marry one of the nice boys in town and he'll take care of you. Do you understand?"

My voice was harsh, but I didn't care. Tessa had been coddled her entire life, even in this cursed town.

She was about to face a fierce reality.

She nodded, eyes red from tears.

"Good," I said. It was the last thing I said to her for the rest of the night.

She curled into the bed beside me, sniffling silently as she drifted off to sleep. I stayed awake, however. Thinking about all of the things I would have rather done on my last day alive.

Pounding on the front door jolted me from my restless sleep.

"Go away!" my father yelled in a sluggish, half-awake voice from somewhere within the house.

My body was already buzzing with energy. I knew exactly who was at the door.

It was the fae prince's help coming to collect his human bride.

"Jade Farrow," a young man yelled. "We're here to take you to the compound."

*The compound*. The magnificent fae palace sounded more like prison confinement.

I was already sitting up and pulling on the same torn up boots I wore every day.

"No." Tessa stirred awake next to me. "No, not yet! It's too early! I thought we would have the morning!"

I looked at her and placed a hand on each of her shoulders. "You have to be strong now, Tessa. Your future is up to you now. Do you understand?" She nodded silently. "Good. You know what to do. I'll survive; you know I will." A lie. "I'll write to you as soon as I can, okay? And if I'm allowed to come back for you, I will. I'll find a way to keep you safe Tessa, but you have to hang on until then. Can you do that?"

Tears welled in her giant, childish eyes.

"Don't cry," I said sternly before I pulled her into a quick, tight hug. "Don't cry."

"I love you," she whispered into my shoulder.

Now it was my turn to blink away tears. "I love you too, bug."

"Jade Farrow!" the voice from the door yelled again.

"Coming!" I hollered back, the small slither of peace from hugging Tessa now gone.

I stood up, not bothering to grab a change of clothes, and walked to the front door. I didn't look for my father. I didn't look back at my sister. They were on their own now, and so was I.

My hand froze on the doorknob, just for a moment. This was it. This was the moment my entire life's downfall began. From this moment forward, I was no longer in control. The guards would take me to the fae lands, and I would never be coming back.

It had been a long seventeen years. Life had been a stubborn bitch, I'd have to give her that.

Before I could cry, I swung the door open.

"You really can't let a woman sleep in on her wedding day?" I sneered, taking in the four guards that stood at my door.

No wings. No sparkling skin, no magical powers. They were human. That was a surprise.

"Apologies, miss," the younger man responded, hand over his chest. He couldn't have been more than a few years older than myself. "His Majesty likes to follow a strict schedule. We wouldn't want to be late."

"No," I huffed, shoving past him and stepping toward the carriage that was bound to be the gossip of the entire village for the next decade. "We certainly wouldn't want that."

One of the guards opened the small golden door to the carriage. It was quite a show, that was certain. I grabbed his hand, about to step inside when my father stumbled out the door behind me.

"Stop!" he yelled, more coherent than I had ever seen him. His voice cracked as he continued, "Stop! That is my daughter! You can't take her!"

"Father—" I started.

The young guard stepped in front of him, blocking his path to me. "You wish to go back on the deal you made with His Majesty?"

My father froze.

*No,* I thought. *He can't go back on his deal.* That would mean death for him, and he was much too selfish to ever do something like that.

But then my father looked at me, a look of pure helplessness strung across his tired features. "Jade," he mouthed.

"I'll be okay," I said with a straight face. "Take care of Tessa."

Tessa chose that moment to exit the house, grabbing my father's arm.

"No!" my father yelled again, anger flooding through the air. "Jade, don't go! Please! I'm so sorry. I'm so sorry, I'm so sorry, I'm so sorry," he was babbling now, lowering himself to his knees in a plea. Tessa was the one to comfort him this time.

Tears streamed down my father's face. I never expected this from him. From the day he informed me about the deal he made with the fae king, I was certain he had never cared about me.

Apparently, I had been wrong.

Nonetheless, I turned my back on my family, stepping into the gilded carriage. I didn't look back. Not as the rest of the guards mounted their horses. Not as the carriage jolted into motion. And not as my father screamed for me to come back.

It wasn't until we were miles away from my house, from everything I had ever loved, and from everything I was being ripped away from, that I let the first tear fall. I didn't care that the guard across from me in the carriage saw. I didn't care if he thought I was weak or foolish. I was walking into my death. I didn't really care about anything anymore.

"Your family loves you very much," the man across from me remarked.

I scoffed. "Don't pretend you know anything about my life. And we don't have to play nice, either."

He straightened. "You are going to be the new bride to the prince. The least I can do is make your acquaintance, Lady Farrow."

"The prince," I repeated, playing with the name on the end of my tongue. "So, tell me..."

"Serefin."

"Tell me, Serefin, are the rumors true? Will I be dying today?"

He paused. "Don't believe everything you hear, Lady Farrow. The Royal Family is very complicated. Your prince in particular. I think you'll find much of what you've heard about the fae to be just that. Rumors."

I considered his words.

"How did you come to work for them?" I asked Serefin. "How did you enter the fae lands?"

A wicked smile crossed his face. "You believe me to be human, Lady Farrow?"

My heart pounded in my chest. It was impossible. He looked exactly like a human. There was nothing strange about him. Nothing peculiar. Nothing *fae.*

"You're fae?" I asked, not able to keep the shock out of my voice.

Serefin nodded.

"But you look..."

"Glamour," he replied. "His Majesty did not want to frighten you on your wedding day. He suggested we use glamour to keep our appearances... human-like."

"He doesn't want to scare me, huh?" I continued. "Very hypocritical coming from a man who is rumored to kill all of his human wives."

"You'll be safe, Jade," Serefin said, losing his calm and collected composure. "Your husband... well, let's just say that he doesn't like it when people touch his things. You will be safe. Please do not worry yourself with believing anything other than that."

A certain edge to his voice caused me to reconsider any argument I might have had. I had no idea what I was walking into, and the things Serefin said were not helping that situation.

My husband, one of the cruel and ruthless fae princes of Rewyth, was going to protect me?

I nearly laughed out loud.

"I hate to do this, Lady Farrow, but His Majesty insists that you are asleep for the trip to Rewyth. Would you mind?" he asked politely, handing me a small vial of liquid.

"Is this going to kill me?" I asked skeptically.

Serefin laughed. "I sure hope not. A lot of people are looking forward to this wedding of yours."

I closed my eyes and dumped the vial of liquid into my mouth, swallowing it all. "It wouldn't be the worst thing in the world if it did though, would it?" I asked him, passing the empty vial back. "If it killed me?" I didn't care if I sounded weak or pitiful. I was dreading whatever came next. To die in my sleep would be a mercy.

It might have been the sudden sluggishness I felt in my senses, but I could have sworn I saw his brows furrowed in concern as my own eyes drifted shut, the sound of the horse's hooves pounding repeatedly on the ground lulling me back to sleep.

I was in a bed when I woke up. Correction, I was in the biggest damn bed I had ever seen in my entire life.

"Oh good!" A woman, not much older than me, sat in a chair opposite the bed. "You're awake! Good thing, because we have a lot of work to do. No offense, of course."

"Where are we?" I asked, rubbing my pounding temples. "How long was I out?"

"Just a couple of hours. The wedding starts soon, though, so up, up!" she chirped, clapping her hands and pulling the blanket away from my body. "I'm Adeline, by the way. It's a pleasure to meet you."

I shook the small hand she held out for me. Adeline was beautiful, perhaps the most beautiful woman I had ever seen. She had bright red hair that cascaded in perfect curls to her waist, contrasting against her porcelain-white skin.

"You're..."

"Fae, yes," she said, already knowing my question. "I'm also your soon-to-be sister-in-law. I insisted on helping you get ready today, mostly because these maids have no sense of style. But also because you and I are going to be best friends!"

I smiled as best I could to be polite, but this was all too much. Adeline was fae, too? So far, none of the fae I had met were monstrous, evil creatures. Serefin and Adeline were both kind to me. Unless of course this was all a façade.

"I'm marrying your brother?" I asked as she pulled me into the bathroom. "Please tell me everything I've heard about the fae princes isn't true."

Adeline didn't even try to hide the pity she felt for me. "Sweetie, there's a lot to learn about my brothers. If I told you everything, we would be here for weeks on end. But I'll tell you this much," she said, guiding me to a chair and sitting me in front of a large mirror. "My brother isn't everything he seems on the surface. Give him a chance. He really might surprise you."

"Great," I mumbled. "I can't wait."

She grabbed a brush and picked up my long black hair, running it through her fingers. "He'll love this too, you know."

I scoffed. "No offense, but I hardly care about whether or not my new captor likes the way I look."

"Captor?" she repeated. "Rewyth has to be a step up from the human lands at least, no?"

I shook my head slowly, fighting the sudden urge to cry. "I left my sister behind. She'll die without me. She'll starve."

"My brother will take care of your family. The fae aren't as cruel as the humans might have told you, you know."

She spoke matter-of-factly, but I wasn't entirely sure I could trust her. I wasn't sure I could trust any of them.

"Well, one good thing about Rewyth is the drinks, so please drink up. We both know you're going to need it," she sang, passing me a crystal glass of clear, bubbly liquid. I had never been into drinking, mostly because of my father. But today, I would be an idiot to object. "Here's a piece of advice, though," she continued. "This is the same liquor you have in the human lands, but don't drink anything else tonight. The fae have special drinks that will be way too... potent for you. So, stick to this stuff."

"Thank you," I said to her, noting her warning. "Really, thank you for being nice to me."

"Of course, darling. You've been through enough already. Now, let's make you beautiful. It is your day, after all." She winked and tapped her glass against mine.

I took a small sip of my drink. The liquid was sweet and light. It burned in my stomach, but it was better than the ball of nerves I had been trying to ignore.

Adeline worked through my hair for what felt like hours before moving to my face. Her touch was gentle, which I was grateful for. She didn't ask me about the scars on my back or the recent bruise on my face, although her hands worked extra carefully when she addressed those areas. She spoke to me about the traditions of weddings in Rewyth and about everything I should be expecting today.

She didn't mention the fact that I might die. I didn't ask.

Hours later, I stared at myself in the mirror. I hardly recognized myself. Adeline definitely possessed magic after all. My hair looked just as perfect as hers, jet-black instead of her fiery red. My skin was spotless. I was still pale, but she had covered every flaw. Hidden every scar. I looked... pretty.

And my dress was more magnificent than anything I could have imagined. It was pure gold, not white like I had expected. The silk fabric hung to my thin curves, a tight corset giving me a figure I never knew existed. I had to admit, with the exposed back and low neckline, I was showing more skin than I ever had in my life. But as Adeline had said, the fae world was different. She had actually called this dress *modest.*

"One last touch," she remarked, walking toward me with a white gift box. "This is for you. From your future husband."

My stomach sank. "How generous," I mocked, lifting the lid to the box. My jaw nearly dropped when I saw what was inside.

It was a knife. A black, perfectly welded steel knife with a delicate, artistic handle.

Emotion rumbled in my chest.

"You like it?" Adeline asked.

"It's perfect. Absolutely perfect."

And I meant that. I didn't realize how exposed I would feel without the knife I had lost with the wolves last night. This was a massive upgrade.

"Well, I suppose I can't send you to the vipers without some form of protection. Just promise me you won't use it on me!" she joked.

I laughed with her and hiked up my dress. Adeline helped me strap it to the inside of my thigh. As if a simple blade would protect me from the fae.

I took a deep, shaky breath.

"You ready?" she chirped. "I'm sure everyone is dying to meet you!"

I smiled and nodded. "Am I allowed to say no?"

She laughed and hooked her arm through mine. "You'll be fine," she insisted. "But a piece of sisterly advice? Don't trust the other brothers. I love my family, but the boys have minds of their own. Especially when it comes to wives."

That last part I knew.

"Serefin said the prince would keep me safe. Is that true?" I asked.

She thought for a moment before answering. "If my brother is around, you'll be the safest human in the kingdom."

I let go of the breath I was holding. Adeline seemed genuine enough. If she was warning me against the other princes, at least she wasn't entirely full of shit.

"Can I ask something of you, Adeline?"

"Of course you can, honey. What is it?"

"If this goes badly... if I die today... will you take care of my sister? My family, I mean. They need food, they need money, they—"

"Yes, Jade. Of course, I will. You mustn't worry about it anymore, okay? You have my word. Besides, everything will go perfectly."

I blinked once. "I hope you're right."

We walked through the massive stone hallways, our heels clicking the porcelain floors in dreadful unison.

I tried not to stare at the pure magnificence of the compound. The walls, which were so tall I had to bend my neck to view the top, were covered in artistically crafted black molding and green vines. Every detail was created with perfection. The vines weaved across the walls as we walked, arching around every massive window that let in a perfect amount of sunlight.

It was beautiful.

*Beautifully horrific,* I reminded myself. These walls were my jail cell, as gorgeous as they may be. This compound was no haven. It was filled with evil and torture and malice. It housed the worst family in the entire kingdom.

These beautiful details were no more than a façade.

Adeline walked me to a pair of massive black doors. My future husband and the rest of the fae were on the other side, I could feel it in my bones. I took a deep breath and rolled my shoulders back. If the Prince of Rewyth thought he was going to get another ignorant human wife who would kneel before him and thank him for killing her, he was terribly wrong.

I wasn't going out that easily.

The massive doors swung open.

"You'll be fine," Adeline whispered to me. "I'll find you after the ceremony."

I nodded at her, but I was frozen where I stood. Hundreds of people filled the ballroom, everyone now staring directly at me.

I forced myself not to shiver, now very aware of how much skin I was showing.

I kept my eyes on the floor directly in front of me. The room was silent. I was certain everyone could hear how fast my heart was pounding. Fae could hear that stuff, right?

It didn't matter. *Keep moving forward*, I told myself. *Move forward and stay alive.*

I walked down the aisle, my gold dress flowing behind me, until I arrived at the front.

"Well, come up here, girl. We don't have all day," one of the men at the altar said.

Eventually, I had to look. I had to lift my head and lay eyes on the fae prince that was going to ruin my life. But not yet.

"Jade," a softer, familiar voice said.

This caused me to finally lift my gaze. *I had heard that voice before.*

When I met his eyes, I nearly vomited.

Standing in front of me, waiting for me to arrive at the end of the aisle, was Mal.

No. Not Mal. The Prince of Rewyth. The Prince of Shadows.

*My soon-to-be husband.*

# CHAPTER 3
## *Jade*

The king and queen sat on a pair of thrones next to us. This was a guess, but considering the golden crowns they wore, I assumed it was a pretty good guess.

"Prince Malachi," the king growled from his throne, "please take your beloved by both hands."

My heart was racing. Mal was Prince Malachi? Mal—Prince Malachi—was fae?

Not just any fae. A fae prince. *My* fae prince. The Prince of Shadows.

"Don't worry," Malachi whispered with a smile, clearly noticing my hesitation. "It will be over soon."

Over soon? Was he talking about the ceremony, or my life?

He held his hands out, inviting me to take them. If I declined, they would certainly kill me on the spot. The way the king was looking at me confirmed it. Like he was waiting for me to make a mistake so he could end my useless, human life.

I took Malachi's hands.

They weren't as cold as I had expected. They were large and warm, and he held me gently, as if he wanted to give me some space.

I tried to keep my hands still but couldn't stop the mild shaking.

His respect was a façade. I knew enough to know that the fae, however kind they may seem on the surface, were creatures of malice.

Especially the Prince of Shadows.

"Jade Farrow," The king said, standing from his throne and approaching us. Malachi's hands tightened around mine, just barely. His shoulders stiffened as his father approached. "Let me be the first one to formally welcome you to Rewyth. As I'm sure you've heard, these lands are precious to us. Generations of fae have lived and died to protect the very ground you stand on today."

I held back an eyeroll. If he really intended to preach to me on how noble the fae of Rewyth were, he could hold his breath. I knew better than to listen to any of them.

"You are not the first human to enter the compound and likely will not be the last," he continued. "Yet my son remains in need of a wife. A human wife, who will bring together our lands and create peace across all of Rewyth. Your duty here is not just that of Prince Malachi's wife, but as a leader to our people."

One of the men standing behind Malachi, his brother I assumed, laughed. I turned my attention to the brothers. They looked nothing like Malachi. He was tall and sculpted, with dark hair and brooding shoulders. His siblings were lighter, in both color and muscle. They looked young, and based on their inappropriate laughter, I assumed they were just as immature as they looked.

"Prince Malachi," the king said, turning my attention back to him. "Jade Farrow stands here to become your wife. It is your duty to protect her with your life. It is your duty to honor her as you would your own, and it is your duty to fulfill these vows as long as you both live."

More laughter erupted from behind us. Heat flushed my cheeks.

The king continued.

"Do you agree to uphold these vows for the future of Rewyth?" he asked.

"Yes," Malachi responded without a second of hesitation.

The king turned to me. His eyes were an electric blue, almost shocking to look at. But there was something cold in his gaze. Something... *fae.*

A chill ran down my spine.

"Lady Farrow," he addressed me, "as wife to Prince Malachi and princess of Rewyth, it is your duty to honor and protect Prince Malachi, it is your duty to honor this wedding agreement, and it is your duty to lead our people as you would your own for as long as you both live."

My heart was pounding in my chest.

This was all happening too fast.

"Do you agree to uphold these vows?"

I looked away from the king and back to Mal. Back to *Prince Malachi*. My soon-to-be husband.

He was shockingly handsome. That much I could not deny. But his gaze was harsh and evil. He had seen and done terrible things. He would do terrible things again, and he would likely do terrible things to me.

But I had made it all the way here. I had to do this for Tessa, I reminded myself.

And frankly, I had no choice. Any one of these fae could kill me in a heartbeat.

I blushed when I realized I had been staring, but I did not look away. He smirked as if he knew what I was thinking. I was not going to show him weakness. He wanted a scared, submissive human that would bow down at anything these fae said.

I was not going to be that wife. I was not going to be that human.

"Yes," I said strongly. Malachi looked almost... shocked.

I didn't move a muscle. I kept my chin high, even as the brothers continued to giggle and snicker. I saw the way they stared at the exposed skin on my body, yet I did not move to cover it.

I was not going to die as a weak little girl.

"Excellent," the king said, pulling a small knife and grabbing Malachi's closest hand from mine.

The king roughly sliced Malachi's skin, blood rushing to the surface. He grabbed my hand next, skin cold as ice, and did the same. Despite my best efforts, I flinched as the pain stung my hand. The blood pooled in my palm, and the king clasped both of our hands together. The blood flowed together, down our fingertips and onto the floor.

"Jade Farrow, Princess, welcome to Rewyth," the king said.

Before I could object, he grabbed my face with both hands and planted a harsh, nasty kiss onto my cheek.

I was frozen. Bile rose in my throat. If this was any type of wedding tradition that the fae followed, I was not a fan. Especially when his wandering hands found the skin on my bare back.

Just before panic began to set in, Malachi grabbed my shoulders and pulled me backward, away from the king's grasp. I opened my mouth to object to whatever the Saints had just happened, but Malachi squeezed my shoulder. A warning.

"You must learn to share, Father," Malachi said. This elicited more laughter from the brothers, but something dark and hateful laced each of his words. I dared a glance at the queen, who sat silently with a bored look on her face.

The king laughed. "You can't blame a man for noticing beauty," he retorted. "And you should be thanking me for finding you such a stunning human this time."

*This time.*

"Now, Prince Malachi," he said, gathering his composure once more. "Kiss your wife, and let the party begin!"

I could still feel the king's lips on my skin. I couldn't do it again. I couldn't let them defile me this way.

But Prince Malachi was my husband now. This kiss was going to be the least of my worries. Malachi stepped forward, coming mere inches from my face. I prepared myself for the worst but felt relieved when he simply placed a quick, featherlight kiss on my lips.

I supposed it was better than the king's kiss, but I could still feel my cheeks flushing pink.

Cheers of applause erupted in the room. I had completely forgotten about the hundreds of fae witnessing the ceremony. Certainly, they were all here for the food and booze the fae were rumored to indulge in.

Malachi placed a hand on my lower back. "Stay by my side," he whispered close to my ear, loud enough for only me to hear. I gave him a small nod of acknowledgement and let him guide me back down the aisle I had just come from.

Except now, I was not just a human girl in the fae world.

I was the wife of Rewyth's Prince of Shadows.

Had the other wives survived this long? Or was this when they all were killed?

It didn't matter. There was nothing I could do here with hundreds of fae surrounding me. I held my chin high and kept a straight face as Malachi led us through the crowd and out the giant doors. As the doors were closing, I heard the king make a muffled announcement, which cued a loud chorus of music and even more cheers from the crowd.

The doors boomed shut behind us.

We were alone in the hallway.

He dropped his hand from my back and paced to the large window near us, running his hands through his dark hair.

I assessed the situation.

The knife was still strapped to my thigh. If I aimed perfectly, I had a chance at stabbing his heart.

But would it kill him?

I doubted it. And it wasn't worth the risk. I had to survive the night, and then I would make my escape.

But what about Tessa? Our deal would be broken if I ran away. She could starve if I didn't make it home alive.

No. There was only one way to survive this. And it was to be the damned human Princess of Rewyth.

"Mal," I said, breaking the silence. He spun around to face me, leaning against the window ledge. *Do not be afraid,* I told myself. "You came to see me yesterday. Why? Why didn't you tell me who you were?"

His eyes scanned my body, pausing at the busted lip Adeline had poorly attempted to conceal. "What happened?" he hissed. The fierceness in his voice almost made me step back. I fought the urge to cover my lip.

"Nothing," I said, touching a finger to the painful area. I wasn't about to unload what happened with my father last night. I had larger issues here.

His eyes squinted like he was about to call me out for the lie.

I spoke before he had the chance and asked, "Answer my question. Why were you in the forest yesterday? Fae aren't supposed to be in the human lands."

His eyes scanned my body once before meeting my own. "I am not allowed to see my wife before I marry her?"

Heat creeped up my neck at the way he stared at me.

"I assumed you wouldn't care much either way," I said. I hated how weak it sounded, but I stood my ground anyway. If I was going to die tonight, I wanted to dig up as much information as possible. "Your wives have never lived that long anyway, right? How long until you tire of me, too?"

His eyes grew dark, and he pushed himself off the window ledge, coming so close I could feel his breath on my cheek. It was the same dominance I saw from him in the forest yesterday against the wolves.

"Let me get one thing straight here, *Princess*. My other wives have been killed, yes, but not by me."

My eyes widened.

"Shocked?" he challenged. *Yes*. "Surprised that the deadly, feral Prince of Shadows is not killing each of his wives after they are wed?" A low, evil laugh rumbled in his chest. "You have a lot to learn, Jade. And we're about to spend the evening with hundreds of drunk, idiotic fae who haven't seen a human in decades."

If he was trying to scare me, it was working.

"So do yourself a favor and stay by my side. Don't trust any of them, and hold onto that little toy strapped to your leg," he said, eyes flickering down my dress once more. "You're not safe here, Princess. But I'm not losing another wife. I don't care how many fae assholes it costs me."

He stopped talking but didn't back away. I stood there, staring into his dark, passionate eyes.

"That's good to know," I admitted after a few awkward seconds. I couldn't believe he was talking about the other fae—his family—this way. From what I could tell, he despised them. Especially his brothers.

Malachi broke our gaze first, walking back to the massive doors of the ballroom. When he held his hand out to me, I took it.

"A bit of advice," he said. "Don't drink anything."

Malachi pushed the large doors open once more, and we were greeted by the same group of fae.

Except things had certainly gotten rowdy in the few minutes we were out of the room.

Music flowed through the massive ballroom, echoing off the stone walls. The reserved audience from earlier was now standing, dancing, and drinking away. Never-ending tables of food lined the perimeter of the room, and servants walked around with trays of drinks for every guest.

Malachi navigated us through the crowd. The others had a large level of respect for him, bowing their heads as he passed. Part of me wondered if they were just as afraid of him as the humans were.

What had he done to gain his reputation? How many people had he killed? Tortured? Tormented?

I shook my head. None of that mattered now. What mattered was getting out of here alive, and Malachi was my best chance at that. I squeezed his hand tighter, hoping he didn't realize how nervous I was. I was the only human in this entire room, perhaps even this entire compound.

I was going to find out just how much fae hated humans, after all.

# CHAPTER 4
# Malachi

I KNEW TWO THINGS TO BE TRUE:

One. Someone was attempting to murder Jade tonight.

Two. I was going to rip the head off anyone who tried.

I knew both of those two things to be true the first time I laid eyes on her.

Besides, I was sick of people *touching my things.*

We just had to make it through this party. And then I could protect her. But here, with hundreds of fae around us…

It would be nearly impossible.

There were dozens of reasons for numerous different people to want her dead.

Correction: They wanted *me* to be an unmarried, desperate, brooding bastard. They didn't give a damn about whether Jade lived or died. I didn't trust a single one of those snakes.

Jade's grip on my hand tightened as we walked through the sea of drunk, dancing guests. She had never seen fae before. Not that she realized, anyway. Surely this was overwhelming for her.

I don't know why I cared. I *didn't* care. But we were going to survive the night. *That* is what I cared about.

Not her. I wasn't stupid enough to let myself care about a human.

Not again. *Never* again.

I pulled her toward the front of the room, nodding at my brothers who sat at the end of the massive stone table.

And no, I didn't trust them either.

But they knew better than to even look in our direction as Jade awkwardly sat down in the seat beside me.

Her eyes were massive, darting around the room at every movement. Her face was stone, but those eyes gave everything away. She may not have been afraid, but she was alert.

*Good girl.*

I let go of her hand but draped my arm around the back of her chair. "As soon as everyone's drunk, we can leave," I whispered to her. "Shouldn't take long."

She stiffened, and I knew it was at the feel of my breath against her ear.

Jade hated me. Like all humans, she hated fae and anyone who had to do with the fae. She likely hated me even more because she recognized me as the man from the forest last night.

But I couldn't tell her why I had come to see her in the forest.

Especially with all the annoyingly large fae ears lingering around.

"Your fourth wedding," Lucien, one of my brothers, announced from the end of the table. A certain stillness filled the air, but I could tell by his boldness alone that Lucien was drunk.

Absolutely plastered.

"You're a lucky man," he continued, "to have not one, not two, not even three... but four parties thrown in your favor. Truly, what an honor, Prince of Shadows."

"Watch it," I growled casually. Lucien's only warning, and he knew it.

The other brothers' relationship didn't bother me. When I was younger, I had been jealous. Of course I had been. But I was stupid and arrogant back then. I didn't understand why they hated me. I didn't understand why they were desperate to get ahead every step of the way.

But now, I understood. After learning that I was the one and only true heir to the fae throne, I understood.

My mother had been the true Queen to Rewyth. She still was. But after my father remarried and had four sons, things got complicated.

They would never stand a chance. All four of them.

So, they hated me for it. For decades, they had taunted me and envied me. But I never really cared. Not after those first initial years, after I had learned what type of people they really were.

What type of men they really were.

I was never going to be anything like them, and they hated me because of it.

"What?" I blinked at Jade, realizing she had asked me a question.

"Are you going to eat?" she repeated, clearly pleased by my level of distraction.

"You're hungry?" I asked. *Idiot.* She was obviously starving, likely hadn't eaten a single thing since we dragged her from her home, and *I* had dragged her in here through the crowd of food without offering her anything.

She had been starving herself so her sister could have food. I *knew* that. I had seen it firsthand.

"Stay here," I commanded, forcing down the wave of anger that rushed forward at the single thought of Jade providing for her ungrateful family. "I'll grab you some food. Don't move."

She nodded in acceptance. I did my best not to stare at the exposed skin on her chest as I stood from the chair and walked toward the crowd of guests.

It didn't take more than a few seconds before Kara approached me in the sea, wrapping her skinny arm around my own.

"If you want a real party," she purred, flicking her tongue across her red lipstick, "you know where I'll be."

"Not tonight, Kara," I insisted. "I'm a married man. That's over." *However long that would last.*

The disappointment on her face didn't go unnoticed, but I couldn't bring myself to give a shit. I had told Kara many times that I wasn't interested.

But I guess I couldn't blame her for trying.

I wasn't that person anymore. There was a time when I would have jumped at any chance to get absolutely trashed with the other fae and sleep with someone like Kara, but not anymore.

I had a duty to uphold. A vow to keep.

Kara shook her head but didn't remove her hand from my arm.

"I mean it," I warned. "That's enough."

"You know you'll grow tired of her," she muttered. "I can keep you happy, Malachi. I can—"

I snapped, taking her hand off my arm and gripping it so hard I knew it hurt her. I let my power rumble, just enough for her to sense it was there. "Don't make me repeat myself. This is already embarrassing enough for you. Now get your things and go."

Her brows furrowed before she snatched her hand from mine. She mumbled something under her breath and stalked away. I didn't bother giving her a second glance.

Kara was nice. Sometimes. But even if I wasn't destined to marry a human, things would have never worked out with her. Kara was a spitting image of what the humans hated so much when it came to the fae: selfish, materialistic, ignorant, and naive.

Still, I couldn't help but wonder if it was her own fault or this warped reality we had been living for the past few decades. We sat in this castle pretending nothing else existed outside of it.

Like I said. Ignorant.

I brought my attention back to the food I was searching for.

My father—the king—was standing just a few feet away. I could have turned around, tried to avoid him, but that would no doubt result in some sort of punishment later.

And right now, I needed him on my side.

Especially if Jade Farrow was going to survive the night.

"Thank you for all of this," I said, throwing the *grateful son* smile on my face as I approached my father. "It's a beautiful party."

His companions nodded and found themselves busy with other conversation as I approached.

"It's not every day that your firstborn son gets married! Although, it might be every few years. Perhaps we should keep the decor for next time, yes?"

It was a joke, but my temper flared. I clenched my fists, trying to keep my cool.

"Relax, son. Your wife seems to be a fighter. No doubt this one will be different!" Every word was a lie. "Besides... fourth time's the charm, right?" he said, stumbling over his words and sloshing the liquid from his cup as he leaned toward me.

"You're drunk already?" I asked. "With so much of the night left ahead?"

He took another drink. "It's a party, boy. You should enjoy it while you can."

"Not much to enjoy when my wife is in danger," I admitted through gritted teeth.

My father's face grew serious. "You're married not even an hour and she already has you running around for her own protection!" he laughed. "You really don't think you can trust this room full of your closest friends and family?"

I looked around the room. Strangers. That's who these people were to me. They weren't friends, and they certainly weren't family.

"I thought I could trust them the last three times, and look where that got us."

My father's eyes darkened. "Your wife is safe, Malachi. Don't be a fool. Not a single person in this room wishes harm on her."

A small slice of anger laced his words. Was he really pissed that I didn't trust this room full of drunk, selfish fae? Or was he more pissed off because I was actually taking a stance and protecting my wife?

I wanted nothing more than to stand up to him. His power was no match for mine, and we both knew that.

But my father had leverage. That one piece of information that forced me to obey his every command, his every wish.

I held his gaze until I heard Jade's laugh echo in the room behind me.

"Excuse me, *my wife* is waiting," I mumbled to my father before turning around, *without* any food, and returning to the table.

One glimpse of my brother's white hair and I knew exactly what had made Jade so cheerful. My brother Lucien had moved his chair a few feet closer to Jade's, separating himself from the others and leaning in to fill her ear with nothing but nonsense, I was sure.

Jade's demeanor had flipped entirely since I had walked away. She sat at the table with both elbows propping her head up, tossing her chin back and laughing at something Lucien was saying.

*Lucien.* Certainly, the least trustworthy of my brothers. But Jade didn't know that. And Lucien was clever enough to ensure she thought the exact opposite.

"I leave for two minutes, and you start having fun without me?" I chirped, sliding back into my seat.

Jade hardly glanced in my direction, her long black hair spilling over her shoulder.

"Your brother here was just filling me in on exactly what type of family I've married myself into," Jade said with a smile still plastered on her face.

"Is that so?" I asked.

Lucien nodded, his dark eyes drinking up every second of her attention. "Nothing too terrible yet, brother. We must ease her into these types of things. But I did inform your beautiful bride here that of all the idiot Rewyth princes, you may be the only one who has managed to set the castle on fire." A wicked grin played on his lips.

I pretended to be amused by the memory, but I knew what Lucien was doing.

He was trying to piss me off.

We both knew that I wasn't the one who set the castle on fire. I was just the one who got blamed.

Like I was blamed for everything else growing up.

Lucien leaned in to whisper into Jade's ear again, now just inches from Jade's face. His eyes flickered over every one of her features.

I draped my arm across Jade's shoulders, squeezing lightly. A clear display to my brothers, to Lucien, to back off. "I'm sure Jade's heard enough," I interjected, trying my best to sound as bored as possible.

Jade whipped her head toward me. "He was just telling me–"

"I said *enough*!" I boomed. I didn't care that the words came out too strong. I didn't care that she flinched at my voice.

Lucien needed to learn. And frankly, so did Jade.

Lucien held my gaze a second longer before he sat up and returned to his original position at the table.

I didn't take my arm off Jade's shoulders but did my best to touch as little of her as possible. As if that would help. Any type of relaxation she was displaying just seconds ago was gone now, replaced by the strong look of a woman who wanted to survive.

The thought of Lucien getting so close to Jade with that look on his face made me want to throw him across the ballroom.

But then people would think I cared. Which I didn't.

I had expected the snakes to come out of the swamp at this wedding. I should have expected my brothers to be four of them.

And like I said, I was tired of people touching my things.

# CHAPTER 5
## *Jade*

"What a beautiful bride!" Adeline gushed as she approached our table that was apparently reserved for family... and myself.

"Thank you, Adeline," I said. "Although, a bit more fabric would have been nice."

"Malachi, she is simply gorgeous," Adeline continued, ignoring my comment.

Malachi looked at me sideways and raised an eyebrow. "Yes," he said, causing me to fight a blush. "She is, isn't she?"

I was shocked that he would admit a compliment so easily. But I was his wife, after all. I supposed it wasn't the worst thing in the world if he agreed that I wasn't hideous.

Not like I cared.

Malachi relaxed back into his chair, sprawling his legs in front of him in a nonchalant demeanor. His arm still rested around my shoulders. A predator staking claim on his prey.

A shiver shuttered through me.

The rest of the princes, Malachi's brothers, busied themselves with whispering and giggling, no doubt talking about their *new sister*.

They stole glances at Malachi every few seconds, but he didn't seem to spend a single moment thinking about any of them. After my conversation with Lucien, I was skeptical. Although he seemed friendly enough, Malachi didn't trust him. I could tell by the way he sat next to me, tense and tracking every movement his brother made.

Malachi didn't even trust his family around me. *Noted.*

"Everyone is here?" Malachi asked Adeline in a low voice as she took a seat at the table.

She nodded. "Including the King of Paseocan."

A low growl escaped Malachi's throat at the name. I tuned in, suddenly interested in whatever quarrel they may have that would make Malachi react this way to him.

The killer of his past wives, perhaps?

If there was one thing I would listen to Malachi about, it was not to trust anyone. Not a single one of these wicked fae were off my list, which meant my guard was up. Even if I had to pretend to be the stupid human who would laugh at any of their jokes.

Malachi shifted in his seat, and his leg brushed mine. If he noticed, he didn't seem to care. Or react.

He whispered something to Adeline, most likely about the King of Paseocan they had mentioned, and her eyes glanced over me once before she stood from the table and lost herself in the sea of guests.

"Something wrong?" I asked, hiding my nerves with strong words.

"Nothing you need to worry about," he said. Spoken like a true asshole, assuming I was too dumb to know anything of value.

But I bit my tongue.

Malachi moved to whisper in my ear, coming so close that his lips nearly brushed my skin. "What did I tell you about my brothers?" he asked.

I didn't back away as I turned my head slightly and replied, "I don't take orders from you, *Prince.*" If Malachi were to move an inch, his forehead would be touching mine. But he stilled where he was, challenging me with the darkness in his eyes, before finally leaning back in his chair once more.

This action alone drew dozens of eyes our direction, including a few looks of jealousy from a couple different women around the room.

Impressive.

I didn't miss the way he interacted with the beautiful blonde fae as he was walking around the room earlier. But Malachi was the most powerful prince in Rewyth. Surely, he had women throwing themselves at him for any chance at power.

And surely, he had taken them up on their offers from time to time.

I kept my gaze anywhere other than Malachi's brothers, especially Lucien, but I knew they could sense how nervous I was. I was sure they could hear every heartbeat. I was sure they could smell the sweat that glistened on my brow.

I was sure Malachi could, as well.

But my efforts to ignore the brothers didn't last long.

"Care for a dance, *sister*?" one of the princes said, rising from his chair and extending a pale hand in my direction.

I hesitated. After Malachi's warning, this was bold. But he didn't say a word, and everyone at the table locked their gaze onto me. It was a test, I was sure of it. The stupid human girl would be too terrified to dance with fae. Let alone a fae prince.

But like I said. I wasn't going to be that human. And my *husband* wasn't going to boss me around like I was his property.

"I must warn you," I said as I rose from my chair and took his hand. I could have sworn I heard Malachi growl once more, or maybe I had just imagined it. "I'm an awful dancer."

The rest of the brothers wore their shock on their faces. Even Lucien had a wicked grin of satisfaction from where he sat at the table. They were not expecting me to say yes.

"Then we must teach you the ways of the fae," the prince said mischievously before leading me to the dance floor.

Tessa and I had learned to dance together, each of us taking turns on who was the boy and who was the girl. It had never come in handy for me, not until this moment. I was hoping, however, that Tessa could use the skills to seduce herself into a rich husband and get out of the burning pit that was our home.

She was always better than I was, I had to admit. But the fae prince—*not* my husband—tugged my body to his and led me into a long, graceful waltz.

"My name is Adonis, by the way," he whispered, each word tumbling off of his perfectly rounded lips. He was just as handsome as Malachi, each feature crafted with perfection. And he knew it.

"It's nice to officially meet you, Adonis," I replied. He turned us around the ballroom, and his grip tightened on my hip when I nearly lost my footing.

"Relax," he said. "I'm not going to hurt you."

I tensed in his grip. "What makes you think I am afraid of you?"

He smirked. "I am sure you have heard the rumors by now. Are you not curious as to who your enemies are in this very room?"

I looked over his shoulder, stealing a few glances at the wandering eyes that were practically gawking at us on the dance floor.

Gawking at me.

"I suppose I have been curious, yes. Although I haven't yet crossed any of you off the list."

"Smart girl," he purred.

Looks aside, he was nothing like Malachi. Lucien hadn't been, either. That much was obvious. All the princes had an annoying arrogance to them, but Adonis had something beneath his eyes that made my skin crawl. I was very aware of his cold skin touching my bare back.

I was also very aware of the knife that rested at my thigh.

"Why waste such a beautiful party if I am just going to be killed tonight, then?" I asked Adonis quietly.

He laughed under his breath. "My dear brother doesn't plan on his wives being killed, Lady Farrow. Besides, I think you might be his favorite," he said with a wink.

I scoffed. "Surely an entire ballroom full of capable, powerful fae would know who has assassinated not one, but three newlywed princesses." My words were bold, but my nerves had finally settled. I was desperate for answers now.

I needed a plan.

The music changed, and Adonis pulled me closer to his chest as he transitioned into the next dance. I was close enough to feel his breath on my face, but I wasn't going to back away. They wanted me to be afraid. They wanted me to back down.

That sure as Saints wasn't going to happen.

I lifted my chin to face him, finding nothing but amusement strung across his face.

"Am I wrong?" I urged.

"Careful, Lady Farrow," he whispered in my ear. "You're in a room full of men who won't like what you're implying."

"And what am I implying, exactly, Adonis?"

A flash of something crossed his face. Anger? Annoyance? But it quickly disappeared. "You want to look out for yourself. I understand that," he said. "It's respectable. Especially in a house full of fae. But every time Malachi is wed, his wife is assassinated. If we knew who was doing it, we would stop it. Malachi would stop it. I don't think he quite likes weddings enough to repeat them every few years, to be honest with you."

I glanced back to our table to find Malachi staring at us, watching our every move. Watching Adonis's every move.

I returned my gaze to his brother. I didn't trust him, but he knew something. I could see it in his eyes.

"I like you, Lady Farrow," he continued. My eyes widened. "The other humans have been so... boring. And it's been a while since we've had some excitement in this castle. So, I'm going to help you."

My eyes nearly rolled out of my head. "And how can you help me?"

"Three doors to the right from here, there's an unlocked room. Meet me there at midnight and I'll tell you everything I know."

My heart was pounding. Adonis kept tugging me across the dance floor. "But what about Malachi?"

Adonis glanced at his brother before returning his gaze to me. "I know you think you can trust him, but be very careful. You don't trust me," he said, "and that's a wise choice. You shouldn't. You shouldn't trust anyone in this room, Lady Farrow."

"You tell me not to trust you, yet you expect me to mysteriously meet you at midnight?"

He smiled. "Someone is going to try to kill you tonight. I think it might be your only option."

If Adonis noticed the chill that ran down my back, he didn't show it. As he continued guiding me across the dance floor through the sea of people I couldn't trust, I began to realize the depth of the situation.

I couldn't trust a single person here. Not the person I was dancing with. Not Adeline, who had been so nice to me.

*And not even my husband.*

# CHAPTER 6
# Malachi

"It's not polite to stare," Adeline scolded. She bounced back toward the table and took Jade's empty seat next to me.

"I'm not staring, I'm observing," I corrected.

"Well, it's creepy. Adonis won't do anything to her, and you know that," she said in a low voice so only I could hear.

"I'm not too sure about that," I replied, mostly to myself. "Did you find anything?"

Adeline took a long drink from her glass and tossed a glance at my brothers, who were still lingering at the table.

She leaned toward me and whispered, "Just like you thought, Mal. Apparently our dearest father hand-picked each guard on duty tonight. The same guards will be guarding your rooms later tonight, as well."

She didn't say anything else. She didn't have to. Everything she was saying confirmed what I had been thinking all along.

My father was anticipating Jade's assassination just as much as I was. All that talk about being able to trust my family... what shit.

My father didn't trust them, either.

"It's going to be okay," Adeline said after a few moments. "We'll keep her safe. I don't care if I have to stay up all night."

I smiled. Adeline was one of the only people in this world I trusted with my life. With Jade's life, as well.

Trust was a rare quality in Rewyth. Adeline had been by my side since we were kids. Except she didn't act any different when she learned that I was going to inherit the throne. Perhaps it was because as a female fae, it was impossible for her to take the throne anyway. The others saw me as competition. Without me, Lucien would have the throne.

Since my title was announced, my brothers pushed me away. Although it didn't help that our father adores them all yet finds me absolutely mortifying.

"I saw that little conversation you had with Kara," Adeline whispered. "What was that all about?"

I rolled my eyes. "Don't worry about it," I said.

"Well, I am worried about it. You have a wife, Malachi. You can't keep entertaining her like you're a bachelor in Rewyth."

"You know that's not what this is."

"Don't I?" she scoffed and leaned back in her seat. "You're blind, brother. Always seeing people for their best qualities and ignoring the worst."

"I see who she is. Trust me, she's not an issue."

Adeline just shook her head. "You'd better be telling the truth. Jade's been through enough as it is. You don't need a jealous ex in the mix making things worse."

"I'm next!" one of the twins shouted, pointing to where Adonis and Jade still flowed through the dance floor.

This earned a roar of laughter from the others.

"You should get married more often, brother," Lucien announced. "It really brings some excitement to the family!"

"You're all pigs," Adeline sneered. "Jade is not a prize to be passed around, she's your new sister. And princess, might I add."

"Yeah? For how long?" Lucien retorted. I stood so fast my chair fell to the ground behind me.

I left them all at the table, Adeline yelling after me, as I stormed onto the dance floor to find my wife.

Jade stared at me with wide eyes as I approached.

"Do you mind?" I asked Adonis. He had always been the most mature of my brothers, and there had been times when I really wanted to trust him. I really wanted to believe he was different from the others.

But loyalty was expensive. And it wasn't a risk I was willing to take tonight.

Adonis gave a respectful nod and passed Jade's hand to mine. Unlike Lucien, Adonis would never disrespect me in front of everyone. In private, maybe, but not here.

Whatever walls Jade had dropped when she was dancing with Adonis were up again. Her face was blank, and her posture was stiff, no doubt tracking each one of my movements as I took her small hand and led her slowly through the crowd of dancers.

"You seem to be getting along with my brothers," I said. She missed a small step, stumbling over my foot and nearly falling. I caught her around the waist as she fell into my chest. "And it also seems you were not lying about your dancing skills."

Jade huffed as she straightened. "No, *Prince*, I was not lying. And your brothers have been... entertaining."

There was more to that, but I didn't push. Although, my curiosity was at an all-time high. Perhaps she needed more of a warning. Did she think I warned her from my brothers out of my own jealousy?

"Lucien is a hothead," I admitted. "He's relentless with women, and he'll pretty much say anything to get whatever he wants from you."

"And you think I'm the type to be easily manipulated by a few funny jokes or superficial compliments?"

Her jaw was sharp, matching her perfectly sculpted cheekbones. With her face this close to me, I could see every flash of emotion in her eyes. Even as she kept her expression composed.

Those eyes were daggers. Her sharpest weapon.

"I don't know," I replied. "I don't really know anything about you."

"Really? Stalking me in the forest didn't show you everything you needed to know?"

"Careful, Princess," I whispered, very aware of the wandering ears around us. I tugged her closer to me, just an inch, and leaned down to her ear. "You don't want to give away all my secrets, do you?"

She tensed but didn't back away. I continued talking.

"Adonis has always been my favorite brother. He's smart. He's respectful. But his loyalties are questionable."

"And what about you?" she asked. "Where do your loyalties lie?"

"My loyalties lie with myself, my future kingdom, and my wife," I said. The words came out harsh, but they were truthful. Jade had to know that.

There were hundreds of rumors circling the human lands about me; I wasn't naive. But Jade had to know that she could trust me. She had to believe that I would do anything to protect her, and she had to believe that everything I did was for the future of my kingdom.

*Everything.*

Whoever was responsible for killing my wives wasn't going to get away with it again.

If the guards weren't going to catch whoever tried, I would do so myself.

"Your brothers don't seem to like you very much," she said.

Her voice had softened, and she stepped close enough that her chest nearly touched my own as another song stopped and started again. Her hand moved from my shoulder to the base of my neck, taunting me.

Was she doing that on purpose?

I rolled my eyes. "You're very observant."

"You practically ignored them at the table. It was hardly an observation. Not to mention the fact that I never heard the end of Lucien's story."

"I am the heir to the throne. I am my mother's only son. I've been put in situations they could never understand. I've been asked to take on things they could never take on. They've done nothing but indulge in what royalty has to offer them. I quit being their brother years ago."

She studied me closely, as if she was looking for a lie in my words.

"Adeline seems nice. Is that all fake, too?" she asked.

I smiled. It felt like the first time all day. "No, it's not fake. You can trust Adeline. She just might hate this just as much as I do."

"Hate what?"

"The parties. The royalty. The façade. It's all just a game to these people. They never step foot into the real world. They live here in this bubble and don't care about what happens to the others."

"And you're so different?"

I clicked my tongue. "You're very inquisitive, Princess."

"It seems I have a lot to learn, *Prince*, and if history tells us anything, I may not have much time to learn it all."

"You're also stubborn."

"So I've been told."

When the song was over, Jade stepped away. "You should get back to your party. I'm going to find something to eat," she said.

Shit. I had totally forgotten about the food I was supposed to find for her. "Do you want me to find something for you?"

"No," she answered sharply. "I can handle myself, thank you."

I nodded and watched her walk away, back into the pit of vipers.

# CHAPTER 7
## Jade

I KNEW HE WAS WATCHING ME. I KNEW HE WASN'T GOING TO TAKE HIS eyes off me for the entire evening.

But I had to find a way to meet Adonis at midnight.

I was skeptical at first, but he was right. I didn't have any options. Malachi wasn't exactly forthcoming with information about who I should be on the lookout for. And Malachi seemed to respect Adonis enough.

Not like I trusted Malachi's judgment, but still. It was better than nothing.

I kept my head down as I weaved through the crowd. Most of the fae ignored me completely. Only a few were brave enough to raise their heads and meet my eyes. Malachi's reputation had seen to that, I was sure.

Whatever reputation he had with the fae was beyond me. But whatever it was, it hadn't been all rumors. Or else his brothers wouldn't have banded against him like that.

Perhaps the rumors I had heard about my dear husband held some truth.

I continued walking the perimeter of the ballroom, but I found myself drawn into the pure magnificence of the building. I had never seen anything like it. Back home, the houses were built with nothing more than wooden scraps. Even the wealthier families had struggled with building anything out of the ordinary.

But this... this was more than I had ever imagined. Even in the grand room, the space felt inviting. The walls were not just bare stone but covered with vines and greenery that moved with the structure. Each doorway was large enough to fit four people at any given time, and the ceilings were arched with an opaque glass that allowed me to see through and into the now dark sky.

Someone bumped my shoulder, nearly knocking me off my feet, but I caught myself against the wall. I turned, half expecting to be confronted by another fae, but the culprit just mumbled an apology and kept moving.

"Having a good time?" a woman's voice approached from my left.

I snapped my head in her direction, only to find myself staring directly at the gorgeous blonde fae who had been speaking to Malachi earlier.

Great.

I forced a smile and rolled my shoulders back. "As good as possible, I suppose."

The girl grinned and stepped closer. "The fae love their parties. I suppose of all the rumors that live in the human lands, that one is likely the most truthful. I'm Kara by the way."

I studied her face for any ounce of malice but found nothing. Every word that came from her mouth felt genuine. But if what I saw between her and Malachi earlier was what I thought it was, Kara was just pretending to be nice to me. If anything existed in both the fae and human lands, it was jealousy.

"It's nice to meet you, Kara. And yes, this party certainly does not disappoint after everything I've heard," I said, matching her politeness.

"This must be quite a change from home," she continued. "I can't imagine leaving fae and continuing life in the human lands."

Was that a diss? Or was she being genuine?

"The human lands weren't much, but they were home."

Kara took a sip of her drink and flipped her long hair over her shoulder. Her dress was even more scandalous than my own, exposing most of her tanned skin. "Rewyth can be tough at times, but it's home. If you find yourself needing a friend here, I'm never too far."

I hid my shock as much as possible. Not only was she a fae interacting with a human, but she clearly had some sort of past with Malachi. Nonetheless, I needed as many allies as possible.

"That's very kind of you, thank you. Although, I'm not entirely sure how much freedom I'll be permitted here," I said.

Kara laughed. "Malachi can be possessive, that much is true. But you're a smart girl, Jade. I can tell. You'll figure it out."

Now it was my turn to laugh. "You sound pretty confident for someone who just met me."

Kara leaned in to whisper, "You remind me a lot of myself, Jade. But I must warn you—Malachi isn't the brooding, obedient prince everyone takes him for. He's a crack of lightning in the middle of a thunderstorm. Be very careful."

I didn't have time to question what she meant. She winked at me and disappeared into the crowd, her dress flowing on the ground behind her.

Okay, this night was getting weird.

What in the Saints did that mean? Adeline had told me I could trust Malachi, but Kara was telling me the opposite?

I caught myself frowning and straightened immediately, replacing the slip of emotions with a delighted, ignorant mask.

Kara wasn't going to mess with my head. I knew what I was doing. I took a few steps toward the massive doorways. It was almost midnight. Adonis would be waiting for me, and after the conversation I'd just had with Kara, I was desperate.

Nobody seemed to be paying attention. Everyone was busy dancing or drinking until they passed out. I dipped my head and slipped through the doorway, into the dark hallway.

A few rings of laughter echoed against the stone walls. I froze, but nobody approached. I kept my ears peeled for any sign of approaching footsteps.

Saints. Would I even be able to hear a fae if one tried to sneak up on me?

I walked slowly, but my shoes still clicked on the floor. I knelt down and slid them both off. My plan wasn't about to get ruined because of some stupid high heels.

The floor was cold against my feet, but it was refreshing. It was like a wave of cool water rushing through me, electrifying my senses.

I didn't so much as breathe as I snaked through the shadows, counting the doorways as I passed them. Adonis would be waiting here. I just had to make it a few more feet until—

A strong hand grabbed my arm and yanked me sideways, sucking me into a shadow-filled doorway. I would have gasped if it weren't for a strong hand covering my mouth and forcing away any scream for help.

I fought to get free in the dark hallway we were pulled into, but the arm that wasn't covering my mouth pinned my arms to my sides and forced me against a male body.

"Be quiet, dammit!" Malachi's voice whispered roughly in my ear.

I needed to scream. I needed to get free. I needed to do something—anything. Because I wasn't going to die here. I wasn't going to let him ruin my entire plan.

I was seconds away from biting his hand to scream for help when a group of footsteps rushed into the hallway.

"Where is she?" a man asked. No, I knew that voice. It was Adonis.

"She came this way, I swear!" one of the other brothers chirped.

"I told her to meet us here at midnight," Adonis's voice echoed through the hallway. I stiffened. Mal's hand didn't leave my mouth.

They were talking about me.

"Maybe she's not quite as stupid as the others," another one of the brothers asked.

This earned a laugh from the rest of them.

Were all of the brothers out there looking for me?

"Do you think she told Malachi what you said?" the brother asked.

"I doubt it. She doesn't trust a soul right now, and after I was done talking to her, she practically reeked of fear. She won't tell Malachi anything."

Now it was Malachi's turn to tense behind me.

Okay. If I wasn't dead earlier, I was definitely dead now.

The footsteps approached us, and I was prepared for them to walk into the same dark room as us. But they passed us by, echoing into the distance until they eventually grew silent.

My husband released the death grip he held on me, and I let out a long breath.

"What was that?" I breathed, whirling to face him. "Why are you hiding from them?"

He grabbed my shoulders and shoved my back against the wall, pinning me there. "What did he tell you?" he demanded, his dark eyes piercing into me. I hesitated. Malachi saw it, too. "I can smell lies, Princess, so think wisely about what you're about to say."

I debated my options. Malachi clearly had reasons not to trust his brothers. Did that mean that I shouldn't, either?

After what I had just heard, I wasn't so sure meeting with Adonis was going to help me at all.

Malachi's body was inches from mine, and he pressed a hand on the wall on either side of my head. The room was too dark to see anything, but I could feel his breath on my cheek.

I knew he could see me, though. I knew he was tracking every emotion that flickered across my face. And he was furious.

The truth might be my only way out of this situation alive.

"Fine," I admitted. "Adonis told me I couldn't trust you. He said he would meet me out here at midnight and that he could help me."

"Help you?"

"That's what he said." Malachi backed away and ran a hand through his hair. "Were those the rest of your brothers with him?" I asked.

He took a long breath before mumbling, "Yeah. Yeah, it was."

"What do you think they were doing? Why would all of them try to meet with me alone in an empty room?"

"I don't know, dammit!" Malachi said, temper clearly unraveling. He clenched his fists as he paced back and forth in the dark room. "If you would have just stayed by my side like I ordered you to do, we wouldn't be in this situation. You knowingly put yourself in danger, Jade!"

"Excuse me? Like you *ordered* me?"

"You are my wife, Jade Farrow. If I tell you to do something, it's an *order*."

I couldn't believe what I was hearing. I pushed myself off the wall, heart pounding in my chest.

"If you think I'm just another one of your stupid human wives who will let you boss them around, you're wrong. And I'm sorry your family is messed up and your brothers are clearly not very supportive, but grow up. It's not my fault someone wants me dead. You seem to care enough about me to not kill me yourself, which somehow doesn't make me feel any better. We've all got issues, Malachi. Don't think for a second you can boss me around and treat me like trash just because I'm not fae."

My voice had grown to a yell, but I didn't back away.

Malachi took a step closer. "Then let me get one thing straight, *wife*. You think I care about you? That's cute. I don't care. I don't care about your past, and I certainly don't care about your future."

He spoke in a way that shook my bones. It was pure power. Pure anger.

"But someone wants you dead. That creates a few problems for me, and the main problem is that someone close to me has been betraying me. I'm going to find out who that is, which will be impossible if you walk away from me and get yourself killed before I find out! So, when I order you to stay by my side, you stay by my side next time. Got it?"

I clenched my jaw. How stupid was I to think Malachi was actually an honorable man who wanted to keep his wife safe? Who wanted to uphold his vows. *Dammit, Jade.* Of course he didn't care about me. I was *human*.

I was nothing but a temporary toy to the fae.

In this case, I was nothing but a tool for Malachi's master plan.

I had to remember what my goal was. Tessa would starve if I died. I was here for a reason, and I had to survive. If that meant going along with whatever plan Malachi had, then so be it.

Even if it absolutely killed me to admit it.

"Fine," I said after a few seconds. "I'm sorry I left you. It won't happen again."

He considered my words for a moment, and I could feel him examining my face in the darkness. I shivered.

"No," he growled. "It *won't* happen again."

Before I could protest, he grabbed my wrist and walked out of the room, dragging me behind him.

Except he didn't take us back to the ballroom.

"Where are we going?" I asked.

His steps were fast and aggressive. I had to jog so I wouldn't fall straight on my face.

As we snaked through the cascading hallways of the castle, it dawned on me where Malachi was going to take me.

It was his wedding night. *Our* wedding night. He was taking me to his bedroom.

The pit that formed in my stomach was confirmation enough. I had expected this. From the moment my father told me I was being sent to marry the fae prince, I expected this moment. Prepared for it mentally.

But Malachi was pissed. That wasn't exactly helping my nerves.

He didn't say anything else. Just continued dragging me through the castle in silence.

When we rounded the last corner, we weren't alone in the hallway. I rolled my shoulders back and lifted my chin as Malachi approached the guard that stood in front of what I assumed to be his bedroom door.

I had seen that guard before. His dark skin contrasted with the white stone walls. He was tall but still held a comforting posture. He turned to us as we approached, and his face came into view. He was the man who took me from my home.

Serefin.

"My lord," Serefin greeted Malachi as we approached. He gave me a small nod of acknowledgment before returning his attention to Malachi. "I believe congratulations are now in order."

I half expected Malachi to yell, but he merely clasped Serefin on the shoulder and laughed, finally letting go of my wrist.

"If you even think about it, I'll kill you," Malachi joked.

The two of them chuckled, and I found myself surprised that the Prince of Shadows interacted with anyone this way. It was intimate and personal; they had clearly been friends for quite some time.

He added, "You're lucky you get to miss stupid parties like that."

I rolled my eyes behind him. Of course he would describe the biggest and worst day of my life as a *stupid party.*

But I was merely a human. My life was expendable to him.

"Something wrong?" Serefin asked, calling me out. I supposed my annoyance wasn't as subtle as I expected it to be.

"Nothing's wrong," I replied, but the words somehow added to the fuel of my anger. Malachi turned to face me, eyebrow arched. "Being dragged out of my house before dawn this morning only to have my entire life ruined by a *stupid party* full of people who may or may not want to kill me is exactly how I imagined this day. Thanks for asking, Serefin."

He didn't respond. Just gave Malachi a glance that said *good luck with that*.

"My wife has had quite a day," Malachi said. "But I have a feeling the night is far from over. Are you on guard all night?"

Serefin checked that the hallways were empty before answering, "So far, yes. I had to bribe Darcy to switch posts with me, though. He was a bit hesitant, I guess your father has everyone on pretty strict orders tonight."

Malachi sighed and tilted his head back, eyes closed. "I wish I could say that was surprising," he said.

"You think the king has something to do with this?" Serefin whispered.

Mal clenched his jaw, then moved to open the bedroom door. "Let's talk in here," he said. Serefin nodded, and the three of us entered Malachi's bedroom.

I did my best to appear relaxed and confident, but as soon as I walked through the door, I was amazed. What was I expecting? Skulls and black everything? *Yes.*

Malachi's room was spectacular. The ceiling was nearly transparent, similar to the ceiling in the ballroom. Greenery and vines twisted their way around the dark stone of the walls, and a large four-poster bed with black silk sheets sat anchored in the center of the room. A bathroom in the back of the room consisted of a waterfall-like structure, the greenery and stones mimicking nature almost to perfection.

Serefin and Malachi were oblivious to my reaction, which saved me a decent amount of embarrassment. They walked into the room as I lingered by the door.

"My father was insistent on me trusting everyone at the party. He practically told me not to worry about Jade's safety," Malachi said.

"So, you think he wants Jade's safety to be compromised? Maybe he's just a prick and didn't want his ego to take a hit by you not trusting his guards."

"Perhaps, but I also found my *brothers* looking for Jade in the hallway earlier. Adonis wanted to meet with her *alone*."

"What?" Serefin exclaimed, spinning to look at me. "Why? What did he want?"

I lifted my hands in defeat. If I knew, I wouldn't have gone to meet him like an idiot.

"You can't trust them," Serefin warned me. He looked between Malachi and me. "You told her she can't trust them, right?"

"That seems to be a common warning around here," I mumbled.

"You don't think they have anything to do with the murders, do you?"

"I don't know. I can't be sure about anything anymore."

Serefin nodded. "I'll be on guard all night. I'll let you know if I run into any problems."

"Thanks, Ser," Mal replied. "This is going to be a long night. Nobody's laying a hand on her."

"Indeed," Serefin said.

An unsaid agreement crossed between them. I could tell Serefin meant it. He was loyal to Malachi. I might not have trusted a single soul in the castle, but Serefin trusted Malachi, and Serefin might have been the only person that Malachi actually trusted.

Either way, I knew Serefin would do his best to keep his word. Even if I wasn't sure I could depend on Malachi yet.

Serefin moved to open the door but paused and looked at me. "By the way, you make a beautiful bride, Jade," he said.

Heat rushed to my face, but he was already out of the room, closing the door behind him.

Leaving Malachi and I alone in his bedroom.

## CHAPTER 8

# Malachi

"You're welcome to stand there all night, but it might get a bit uncomfortable," I said. Jade had been standing there for the past five minutes as if that was going to somehow protect her.

She rolled her eyes and stepped away from her spot near the door.

"Is anyone going to miss us at the party?" she asked.

I huffed and shrugged off my thick jacket. "That event wasn't for us. It was just an excuse to get drunk and party all night. They won't be stopping anytime soon."

"That's reassuring," she muttered. Her words were strong, but she crossed her arms over her chest and refused to look at me. She looked at the bed, the couch, the walls. Anywhere but me.

It hadn't dawned on me that Jade would be nervous about sleeping in here. After all the rumors she had heard about me before, certainly she expected something to come from tonight.

I wanted to reassure her but stopped myself before I opened my mouth. Jade *should* be afraid. It was good that she had her guard up. None of my other wives had made it this far into the night. That might have been because we all over-indulged in the fae wine each time.

"We'll both have to stay here the whole night," I said, forcing myself to say *something*. "If you sleep in another room, I won't be able to protect you. This is the best option."

"I understand," she said, walking over and sitting on the edge of my bed.

"Besides," I continued, "I already get enough shit from my father. I don't need to give them any more reasons to doubt me."

She opened her mouth like she was about to say something but closed it again.

My chest tightened. She really *was* terrified. It was surprising, I had to admit. This was the same girl who launched herself at a wolf over a tiny dead rabbit, and she was afraid to be in a room with me.

She wasn't the least bit afraid of me in the woods. Granted, she didn't know I was fae.

A tiny shiver rumbled down her spine, one that she tried to hide.

"You're cold?" I asked.

She shook her head. *Liar.*

I walked over to my closet and pulled out a shirt and pants. They would be huge on her, but it was better than wearing the gold wedding dress all night.

The dress I was sure Adeline had something to do with.

"Here," I said, tossing them into her lap. She looked relieved when she realized what it was. "Bathroom's that way. Use whatever you need."

She stood and walked toward the bathroom with her head down but then paused and turned around. "You're not going to kill me while I'm in the shower, are you?"

I laughed. "If I wanted to kill you, Princess, you'd be dead right now."

She offered a sarcastic smile before mumbling under her breath and walking into the bathroom.

I took a long breath. We had made it this far, which was a good sign. But something was definitely going on with my brothers.

And Jade had actually trusted Adonis over me. I knew she wasn't going to trust me right away, but trusting one of them was going to be more dangerous for her than anything.

My brothers never had my best interests in mind. *Never.*

I listened to the bathroom until I heard Jade step under the stream of water. My mind wandered to the thought of her standing there, water trickling over her perfect black hair. She was beautiful, that much was true. She was different from the other humans who had been sent to marry me, somehow owing a debt to my father and thinking this would make up for it.

Jade was defiant. She wasn't planning on listening to anything I said. I still wasn't entirely convinced that she was actually afraid of the fae, but maybe she was at least pretending to be afraid for her own safety. She had survival instincts. When I saw her for the first time in the forest with the wolves, I knew she would be hard for anyone to try and kill. Jade had a certain fire to her that annoyed me to no end.

If she would just trust me, keeping her alive would be a lot easier.

But what was I supposed to say? I couldn't tell her that the rumors weren't true. I couldn't tell her that I wasn't the horrific, violent Prince of Shadows she had heard about. I couldn't tell her those things because they weren't true.

The things I did to survive were less than admirable. But Jade had those same instincts. Maybe she would understand.

Or maybe she would hate me for everything I had done. She probably already did. I couldn't ask her what she had heard about me. Saints, did I even care? People had been spreading rumors about me longer than Jade had been alive. For years, I had heard about the Prince of Shadows who could kill an entire room of fae with just a look. I had heard about the Saint-cursed fae with black wings who was touched by the demons. I had heard about the slave of the king who carried out his assassinations with ease and delight.

The stories had gotten so ridiculous, Serefin and I had often sat down and joked about how twisted they became. But that's the thing about rumors: Truth is usually mixed in there somewhere.

"How's it going in there?" I asked.

"I am very capable of taking showers without the need for you to check up on me, thanks," she yelled from the bathroom.

*Great.*

I tugged my shirt off and threw it into my closet, lying back on the bed. The stars were bright tonight. That was one thing I actually admired about Rewyth: the stars. They were brighter here than anything else I had ever seen. It was why half the castle was built with transparent ceilings. The view was too beautiful to ignore.

It was a view I would fight for.

Amongst other things.

My thoughts were interrupted when Jade stepped out of the bathroom. Wearing my clothes. With dripping-wet hair.

*Saints save me.*

"Nice shower," she remarked.

I nodded, trying not to stare. "Our ancestors wanted us to be connected to nature. I like it. Reminds me of where we come from."

"And where's that?" she asked.

"You have a lot to learn about the history of fae. We didn't always reside here. The fae had to fight for this land. There was a time when fae weren't at all powerful. We were the weakest of creatures, in fact. We fought for decades to claim our power. To claim our lands."

She listened as I talked.

"Many fae used to believe we drew our power from the elements. It's not practiced as much anymore, but it used to be. Fae would partner with witches and warlocks to strengthen their gifts."

"Gifts?" She raised a brow.

I nodded. "Some fae have special gifts. Magic, I guess. But not everyone."

Jade walked around the bed and sat on the edge, as far away from me as possible. Her eyes flickered to my bare chest.

"I won't bite, you know. You may think whatever you'd like about me, but I'm not going to touch you."

She nodded but didn't move. Clearly, she didn't trust me. It made me wonder if another man had ever hurt her before. And that made me want to storm right back to the human lands and rip the head off anyone who did.

Jade interrupted my thoughts. "Can I ask you a question, Malachi?"

"Depends on the question."

"You don't look like fae. None of you do. On the way here, Serefin told me you used..."

"Glamour?" I finished for her. "We all do. It's simple magic to make us appear normal."

"But why? You're in your own castle, so why wouldn't you just be yourself?"

The question made me smile. "It's a simple trick so you would feel more relaxed. It's bad enough that we drag a young woman into our castle and force her to marry. Better not scare you with our looks."

She scoffed. "How noble of you."

A feral sense of competition creeped into me. Jade was challenging me. She was challenging my words. Stupid, stubborn human. I rolled off the bed and walked around to her side, inches from where she sat. "Would you like to see what the fae really look like, Princess?"

She swallowed once.

"Or are you afraid?"

"I'm not afraid," she answered quickly.

I stepped closer, looking down to where she sat on the bed. "No?" I teased.

Jade lifted her chin and stared at me with those big, endless eyes. "Let me see," she said.

I couldn't tell if it was fake confidence or simple arrogance.

But I didn't care. If Jade was going to survive the night, she was going to have to learn what she was up against.

With a single breath, I dropped the glamour that was concealing my fae characteristics. The glamour that hid my large, uniquely black wings. The glamour that hid the points to my ears.

Jade's eyes widened. I growled and spread my wings, nearly covering us both with the sheer size.

"Well?" I asked. "What do you think?"

Her eyes dragged across my torso and drank up every new detail. She wasn't afraid like I had expected her to be.

No, she was feeling something else. She stood from where she sat on the edge of the bed, her head just meeting the top of my chest despite the fact that she was tall for a human.

Slowly, Jade smiled. Wicked curiosity washed over her face. "They call you the Prince of Shadows for a reason, I see."

"They call me that because of more than just the color of my wings, Princess."

Her eyes snapped to mine. "Don't call me that."

"Why not? Like it or not, that's what you are now. Princess of Rewyth."

"Let's just worry about surviving the night first."

"You doubt my abilities to protect you?"

"I doubt my safety in the presence of fae."

The silence that rang though the air said more than I could form with words.

Jade still didn't trust me. I guessed that was fair.

But we had a few hours to go until sunrise, and it was her and I in this room alone until then.

I moved my wings in a motion that blew her hair across her face.

She gasped and scrambled to get it out of her eyes while I laughed.

"You think this is funny?" she snapped "You really have fun toying with worthless humans, don't you?"

"Calm down, Princess. We're both in a shitty situation here. You might as well lighten up."

"You can't be serious."

"Serious as ever."

"Please explain to me, Prince, how this could possibly be a shitty situation for you? You basically get hand-delivered a wife, a party thrown in your favor, and eligibility for your own kingdom. What part of that is shitty for you?"

I stepped back, finally putting some distance in between us. "It's complicated," was all I had the energy to say.

"Right, because your dumb human of a wife can't understand anything complicated."

"You really should get some sleep," I sighed, walking to the other side of the room. "I'll wake you if I hear anything."

To my surprise, Jade actually got back into bed. It had to be from pure exhaustion, because Jade was too stubborn to do anything I suggested.

I listened to her breathing as it slowed.

It was only after I was sure she was asleep that I turned around to look at her.

I smiled when I saw her curled up in my bed, clutching the knife I had gifted her as if it were her only hope in this world.

## CHAPTER 9
# Jade

I WOKE UP IN A PANIC. SWEAT DAMPENED MY FOREHEAD. FALLING ASLEEP was certainly not part of the plan, especially when my life was at risk. But I was still holding my weapon, *my wedding gift*, which was a good sign.

Perhaps Malachi let me keep it in case we *were* really attacked here tonight. Or maybe it was because my little knife was nothing against a fae. Maybe he knew I wasn't even a threat against him with it.

I sat up and caught him already staring at me from the chair across the room. "You snore," he grumbled.

Ignoring him, I flung the blankets off my legs and stood up. Although I didn't remember getting under the blankets in the first place.

"It's been quiet so far," Malachi continued. "No sign of anything unusual. Serefin is still outside the door. Nothing from him, either."

I nodded and folded my arms across my chest. Malachi was still shirtless, and his black wings hung casually off each side of the large sofa. Part of me was grateful that he had waited to show me until we were alone. I was certain I had looked like an idiot, mouth gaping and everything.

But if I was being honest, Malachi looked terrifying with those things. I had heard the stories about the Prince of Shadows and his dark wings, which obviously stood out in a fae land with predominantly silver wings. But I wasn't going to ask about them.

Malachi's ego was big enough already.

I looked away before he caught me staring.

I walked over to the large glass window, staring up at the stars that littered the sky.

"Careful," Malachi warned. "You don't want an arrow in the chest because you're admiring the stars."

I blushed, as if somehow Mal realizing what I was doing made me appear weak.

"You really think someone will try to kill me while I'm with you?"

"Yes," he said without hesitating. His dark eyes seemed to grow even darker, swarming with emotion and exhaustion. "I do."

I ran my hands through my hair and let out a long breath. "How were they killed?" I asked, crossing the room to sit next to him on the long sofa. "Your wives, I mean."

"I know what you meant," he said quietly. His eyes remained somewhere in the distance. "We found my first wife with a slit throat in the hallway during the party," he said. "Nobody saw, nobody knew anything. We had all continued to drink like idiots. Who knows how long she had been dead?"

I remained silent.

"My second wife was strangled while I slept next to her. Someone had drugged my drinks. I didn't find her until I woke up nearly a day later."

More silence.

"My third wife didn't even make it to the ceremony. I guess that doesn't technically make her a wife, but it all meant the same."

I hid my shock.

"Who would want your wives dead?" I asked, careful with my choice of tone.

"That list is very long, Princess. I've earned quite a few enemies in my days."

I thought for a moment. Each of his wives had died long before now. Why was someone waiting so long to make an attempt on me?

As if on cue, Malachi's pointed ears flickered up. I opened my mouth to ask what he was hearing, but the look he gave me made me close my mouth.

I double checked the knife I had strapped back to my thigh. Someone was here.

"Act like we're still having a normal conversation," he whispered.

I nodded and smiled. "Okay," I said. I didn't risk looking out the window.

Malachi reached his arm up and over, placing it around my shoulder. He moved his body, so I was tucked into his side.

"Is everything okay?" I murmured when he was close enough.

He picked up a strand of my hair and leaned in. To anyone watching from the window, it would look like he was kissing my neck.

Still, every single one of my senses was aware of his every move.

"When I say go, I want you to roll under the bed," he whispered, lips brushing my ear. "And don't come out until I come get you."

I let him lean over me, pushing my torso back and reclining both of us until his entire body was covering my own on the couch.

I couldn't speak. I merely nodded.

He slid a hand up my thigh, finding the knife that he had gifted me. My skin lit up under his touch.

"I hope you know how to use that thing, Princess," he mumbled. He was so close, I was certain he was going to kiss me again.

His eyes moved to my lips, only for a split second, before the sound of shattering glass erupted in the air.

"NOW!" Malachi yelled, launching into action. Before I could even sit up, Mal was across the room. Two fae, dressed head to toe in black, concealing armor busted through the window.

Malachi dropped on them in seconds. He held a small dagger in each hand.

Where had he been keeping those? He dodged each advance with little effort, towering over both of his attackers by at least a foot.

I was still cowered on the couch like an idiot.

*Under the bed, Jade. Get under the bed.*

Saints, where was Serefin?

I rolled sideways and crawled on all fours toward the bed. I had almost made it, too, when rough hands grabbed me by the ankles and dragged me backward.

I screamed and kicked as hard as I could, but my attacker just launched himself on top of me, pinning me to the ground.

I searched for Malachi in the dark room but saw him fighting hand to hand with the other attacker.

A rough hand grabbed my hair, pulling my head backward.

"Please don't," I begged. "I have a family to take care of!"

The man laughed. It was rough and ugly. "Unfortunately for you, so do I."

I felt the cold steel of a blade against my neck.

This was it. I hadn't fought hard enough. I didn't try hard enough.

I was going to die.

Warm liquid poured over my back, and my attacker went still.

"Are you okay?" Malachi huffed.

My heart pounded. I waited for the weight to lift off my back before I turned over.

Both attackers were dead.

And Malachi held a severed head.

I couldn't talk. I could barely breathe. I backed up slowly, scooting away from the pool of blood that I was now covered with. It dripped down my back, still hot.

Serefin kicked through the bedroom door. He took one glance at Malachi, holding the severed head, and cursed. It was then that I noticed Serefin also splattered with blood, his sword already drawn.

"We're okay," Malachi informed him. "Two of them came through the window. They didn't even wait until I was asleep."

"Bastards," Serefin cursed. He walked to the body that was still intact and rolled it over. Malachi had stabbed him in the chest. "There was one in the hallway. He ran off after I landed a blow, but I heard Jade's scream."

"Do you recognize them?" Malachi asked.

Serefin shook his head. "Someone in this castle will, though."

He stood up and looked at me. I cowered into the corner, my entire body still shaking from what just happened.

"You okay, Princess?" Malachi asked again, finally dropping the head he had been holding. It rolled to the side with a sickening thump.

I nodded, but I was sure they knew I was lying. I should be dead right now. What Malachi just did, the speed at which he moved... it wasn't possible.

Malachi had ripped that man's head off within a second.

It was purely feral behavior. Pure predator.

Serefin and Malachi exchanged a knowing glance.

Mal walked over and knelt beside me, lifting my chin with a finger.

"People want you dead, Jade. They want you dead so badly that they'd risk fighting against me to get to you."

His eyes were intense, and I sat in silence as his focus moved from my face down to my throat. He reached out and rubbed a thumb against my skin. It stung, but I didn't flinch. I hardly felt it.

When he pulled away, his thumb dripped with my blood.

His wings flared once more, and he drew his eyebrows together in an intense expression that nearly made me look away.

"You're hurt," he said. It wasn't a question.

"I'm fine." My words sounded foreign.

"Don't tell me you're fine. You're bleeding."

He balled his hand into a fist and stood up slowly, looking between me and Serefin.

"Those bastards drew blood," he announced. "The people in this room are the only people we tell about this. Nobody else finds out until we know who we can trust."

Serefin nodded.

"If anyone so much as lifts a finger toward Jade, I will kill them. And I'll have *fun* ripping their heads from their useless bodies."

# CHAPTER 10
# *Malachi*

"WHAT ABOUT YOUR FATHER?" SEREFIN ASKED.

"Someone expects Jade to be dead. Get rid of the bodies. Let's go see who's surprised when they see her alive and well," I said.

The next few hours mixed together in a blur of rage and fear.

Serefin took care of the bodies, but Jade didn't take her eyes off the severed head until our attackers were out of view.

I couldn't even look at her. She was covered in blood, most of it not her own. Her black hair was matted with it, and the shirt of mine she wore had ripped at the torso during her struggle.

He never should have touched her. I should have stopped it.

But here we were.

Serefin had left a few minutes ago, but Jade still hadn't moved from the floor.

"You have to eat something," I said in an attempt to break the silence in the room.

She pulled her knees to her chest and wrapped her arms around them.

"Jade," I said again. "You faced an entire pack of wolves over a dead rabbit in the woods. Certainly, a couple of rogue men aren't that bad."

I tested the waters, trying to get any reaction out of her. Anything to let me know she was actually alive in there.

"What was that?" she asked. "You didn't even touch them and they..."

"It's a special gift of mine. I can inflict severe pain on anyone with a single thought. It takes focus, but it comes in handy."

She nodded.

Her dark eyes snapped to mine. "That can't happen again," she said, her voice barely a whisper, and I tried not to react when it cracked.

"No," I replied quietly. "It can't, and it won't."

She wouldn't even look at me. I wasn't sure if she had been talking about the attack or me.

"So, what do we do? We don't know who wants me dead. We don't even know who those people were who..."

"From now on, you'll either be with me or Serefin at all times. It would take an entire army to kill one of us, Princess. You're safe. It might not feel like it, but you're safe."

She pushed herself from the ground and stood up. "I want to see my sister," she said.

I waited for a second for her to add something to that statement.

But she just stared at me.

"Absolutely not," I answered.

She scowled and crossed her arms. "She expected me to die last night. I expected to die. I have to tell her I'm okay."

"You're covered in blood, and you're cut. You're not going anywhere, especially when we don't know who wants you dead. You're not okay."

I watched her chest rise and fall. If she wasn't in shock yet, she would be soon.

But based on the amount of blood she had yet to wash off, she wasn't handling this well.

"If you take me to see my sister, I'll help you find out who did this. We both want the same thing. Me alive. Do this one thing for me, and I'll help you."

Any other day, I would have said no. I would have said Saints no. But even covered in her attackers' blood, Jade was the most stubborn human I had ever met.

That was going to be dangerous. But it could also be useful in the fae court.

I looked at her from head to toe. Her bare feet looked so small against the stone tile of the floor. Her exposed legs were tan, something I was sure she had earned from hunting outside all the time. She was skinny. Too skinny. I was going to have to strengthen her up if she was going to fight off a fae.

And she still held that knife. Her knuckles were white from her grip.

"Fine," I said. I didn't know if it was a lie, or if I was actually giving in. "I'll take you back to your house. But you do everything I tell you, no arguing anymore. And you have to actually trust me if you want to survive in Rewyth, princess. And I decide when we leave, so don't go bugging me about it every day. You're staying here for now."

Her eyes lit up, but she kept her face still. "Don't call me princess," she repeated as she walked past me and into the bathroom. "And quit looking at me like I'm fresh meat. It's not a good look on you."

I waited until I heard her step underneath the water again before I let out the breath I was holding.

Her sass would have annoyed me to no end any other day, but today, I found myself smiling. She had seen me rip a man's head from his body and yet she was still able to crack jokes. That was a good start.

But we had a long way to go if Jade was going to stay alive.

# CHAPTER 11
# Jade

MALACHI HAD BEEN GONE FOR HOURS. I SPENT A MAJORITY OF THE night trying to sleep, but it was impossible.

Everything I thought I knew was wrong, and Malachi had power that I had only heard about in ancient legends.

My mind was spinning. I remembered every single rumor I had ever heard about the Prince of Shadows, and I tried to decipher the truth.

The truth about my husband. The truth about my new life.

My stomach grumbled. What was he out there doing? Where did he go? To find whoever did this, I hoped. But Malachi seemed to have his own agenda. He seemed to have his own ideas about who was behind this attack.

And he wasn't sharing anything with me.

The door had been locked. I checked as soon as Malachi left. I wasn't surprised. After what happened, he wasn't going to let me out of here. I was as good as dead.

"I know you're out there!" I yelled through the door. My forehead felt hot as I laid in against the surface of the door. "You can't just leave me in here and expect me to sit quietly. I'm hungry!"

I heard movement before Serefin responded, "Just wait a few more hours. I'm sure the prince will be back soon."

My stomach sank. "Hours? You really want me to sit in here alone every day just waiting for Malachi to come home?" I took a deep breath and tried to calm my emotions, but my throat was stinging. "I didn't survive this far to sit here and rot in a bedroom that isn't even mine."

Tears threatened my eyes. I placed both palms against the door and imagined bursting through it, bursting all the way out of this damn castle. My words were true. I didn't survive longer than any human wife before me to just sit here and rot like some sort of prisoner.

I was Malachi's wife. I was a princess of Rewyth. I hated that title, but I sure as Saints was going to use it to my advantage if I had to.

Before I could open my mouth to plead with Serefin once more, the door handle began rattling.

I backed away as Serefin entered, shutting the door behind him.

"I can't let you leave," he said. His eyes assessed the situation, and I saw the tiniest bit of pity in them.

"You feel sorry for me?" I asked.

"I would feel sorry for anyone who's going through what you're going through. Nobody should have to live here against their will."

I laughed. "Even a retched, useless human? Aren't all fae supposed to hate us, anyway? What makes you so different?"

Serefin walked over to my open window and pushed it shut. He turned to face me before answering, "Not all fae think that way, Jade. That would be like you thinking all fae are evil, malicious beings. And you don't think that, do you?"

I held his gaze. Serefin was nearly as tall as Malachi, with now-visible silver wings that tucked tightly behind his shoulder blades. His black guard uniform was perfectly aligned to his slim body. Serefin wasn't my enemy. If anything, Serefin had been kind to me when he had no reason to be. He had shown me mercy.

I took a seat on the large sofa, but Serefin didn't move from the window. "I don't think you're evil, no," I answered with caution.

Serefin smiled. "Good. Then we're off to a good start, Princess."

I tossed my head back and groaned.

"What?" he asked. "You don't want to be a princess?"

"That's a joke, right?" I replied. "In what world would I want to be a princess in a place where everyone wants me dead?"

Serefin paused as if he were debating whether or not to stay. But after a few seconds, he sighed and came to sit with me on the sofa.

"Malachi's not so bad, you know," he said.

This forced another groan from me. "Yeah, and everyone seems to keep reminding me of that. But he's still the Prince of Shadows, Serefin." I shook my head, remembering the way he killed those men in the blink of an eye. "He's dangerous."

"But he's a great ally," Serefin argued.

My head was spinning. "What type of ally would lock me in a bedroom for an unknown amount of time?"

"You know he just wants to protect you."

"This isn't protecting me," I snapped. "I'm a sitting duck here. If anything, this is more dangerous than the alternative."

"The alternative?" Serefin questioned. "You mean it's more dangerous than following Malachi around the kingdom to handle his court business? You really want to do that?"

I thought about it for a moment. "What type of court business does Malachi do, anyway?"

Serefin stood up and walked toward the door. "If you want to know so badly," he said, "then you should probably ask your husband." He grinned, and I caught myself wondering how old Serefin really was. He didn't look much older than me, but fae lived for centuries; they were nearly immortal.

Serefin could have been hundreds of years older than me. And Malachi, for that matter.

"It's a little hard to ask him anything when he leaves me locked in here."

Serefin turned toward the door and opened it. "You'd better hurry up then," he asked. "We're going to get dinner."

# CHAPTER 12
# Malachi

My heart was pounding. It hadn't stopped pounding since the almost deadly attack on Jade.

That had been too close. The fact that blood had been drawn was already too much.

I had slept in an empty bedroom across the hall the past couple of nights, but it didn't stop my mind from wandering to Jade's wet hair from the shower, the way she looked at me when I showed her my wings.

Saints help me.

I walked down the empty hallway to my father's quarters. I had spent hours debating whether or not to trust him with the incident, and my mind was still shouting warnings at me.

My father wasn't going to help me.

He didn't help me with any of my other wives. Not even Laura. So, there was no way he was going to help me now.

Laugh in my face? Maybe. Help me? Not a chance.

But this castle was a snake pit. At the end of the day, my father was the king. If I wanted to stay alive, I had to play by their rules.

"Malachi!" A female voice echoed through the empty hallway. "Wait up!"

I turned around and found Kara running toward me.

A sigh escaped me. "Not now, Kara," I said, turning around and continuing toward my father's quarters.

"Your wife seems like a nice girl," she continued. "I'd love to get to know her more one day."

I stopped dead in my tracks. "You talked to Jade?"

She caught up with me, her blonde hair bouncing as she jogged the last few feet.

"At your wedding, yeah," she said. Another breath escaped me, but my heart was still pounding. "She's pretty, too. Although for a human, she's awfully—"

"If I were you, I would be very careful about what you say next, Kara."

She looked at me in awe, then scoffed. "I can't believe this. You're really going to drop everything we have for another human. I thought you were done with that. After what happened with Laura, I figured you had learned your lesson."

Kara was stupid, but not that stupid. She was trying to make me angry.

I turned and continued walking, but she grabbed my arm. It took every ounce of my strength to resist throwing her small body to the ground.

"What lesson is that, exactly?" I growled.

Kara smiled, but it was calculated. "That what you need is right here, Malachi. You don't have to keep doing this."

"Doing what, Kara?" I ripped my arm from her grip. "I'm not the one deciding I should get married to a human again and again. I'm not the one making those decisions."

Anger flashed across her face. If I had learned one thing about Kara, it was that she couldn't hide her emotions. That type of flaw was deadly in Rewyth.

"You're more powerful than them. You know you are. If you decided what to do with your own life, they would have no choice but to listen."

I shook my head. Kara, just like everyone else, had no idea what they were talking about. They didn't know the power my father had over me. Of course I was stronger than him. I was stronger than everyone. I could kill any one of them with my power, but then what?

My mother needed me.

My father was my only link to her.

"Leave me alone," I snapped. "You have no clue what you're talking about."

She didn't follow me as I stormed away, but that didn't stop her from yelling, "She'll never belong here, Malachi!"

My vision darkened, and my fists clenched.

Jade belonged wherever I said she did.

I pushed my father's door open before my anger forced me to turn back around.

He sat alone, drinking from a golden mug in his massive study. "Malachi!" he cheered. "What a pleasant surprise!"

I shut the door behind me and continued inside the room. His guards didn't move an inch.

They were smarter than him.

"I haven't seen you in a few days," I started. "Anything new I should be aware of?"

He stood from the long wooden table.

"Nothing comes to mind."

"Really? Anything regarding my mother, perhaps?" I leaned against the wooden frame of the door.

My father shook his head. "You know the deal, Malachi."

"The deal was that I do what you ask. Well, I married the human. Again. So, I think it's about time you hold up your side of this bargain. Where is my mother?"

"Patience, boy," he chided, standing from his chair. "Marrying the girl is not the end of the road. You should know that more than anyone."

Anger rumbled in my chest. I urged my power back to its core, reining it in.

"How long are we going to play this game?" I asked.

My father just laughed. "It's no game, son. I'm running a kingdom here. You'll understand one day. You'll understand all the sacrifices I've made for you. And you'll come back to thank me."

It was my turn to laugh. "Thank you?" I repeated. "For what, exactly?"

"For protecting you. There are hundreds if not thousands of people who will enslave you and use your power for their own will. Are you not aware of the war happening across the sea?"

"They'd have to catch me first." I crossed my arms over my chest.

He took a step closer to me and shook his head. "You're just like her. Defiant. Arrogant."

My mother. I couldn't even remember what she looked like. It had been that long since he hid her away, claiming to protect her. I had spent decades obeying his every order in the hopes that he would eventually tell me where she was.

And we had gotten nowhere.

"I'll tell you everything you want to know soon. But I need you to trust me." He placed his hand on my shoulder and squeezed. It wasn't often that I saw this side of him.

He hadn't always been terrible. It was hard to believe, but it was true.

"Fine," I said after a while. "But leave Jade alone. She has no part in this."

He nodded in agreement, and I was out the door.

It took a few seconds for my breathing to slow down.

My father knew exactly what he was doing. Saints, I might have done the same thing. But to my own son? That was a stretch.

One step after another, my feet pounded the stone floor of the compound. How many times had I walked these stupid halls, reporting to my father what mission had been successful? How many of his enemies had I killed? How many wars had I won for him?

And how much information had he given me about what happened to my mother?

I shook my head. This wasn't the time for anger. I had to play this one smart. If he had anything to do with Jade's attack, he would attack again.

And soon.

I heard her before I saw her.

Jade's voice echoed through the stone walls of the dining hall. My feet moved toward her like I had no choice.

What in the Saints was she doing down here?

I turned the corner just in time to see her tossing her head back in laughter, that red line on her throat still visible. She was sitting next to Serefin, which instantly made me relax.

But it wasn't Serefin and Jade that concerned me. It was everyone else.

"This has to be some sort of record," my brother Eli said to her. Nobody looked at me as I approached, lurking as far back as possible.

Jade smiled, but her eyes remained focused. "Are you surprised, dear brother?"

The way she spoke to him made my stomach flip. It was bold for any human to talk to a fae that way. Even if that human was my wife.

Eli sat back in his chair, and the rest of my brothers laughed. The dining room was filled with spectators. Nobody would dare make a move here, but still. Serefin was tense, his eyes tracked every single one of my brother's movements.

I trusted him with my life. I had no doubt that he would keep Jade safe.

But why the Saints would he bring her here? Sitting around, waiting for an attack?

Kara entered the room, trotting over to the table as if she owned the place. She pulled up a seat on the other side of Serefin and beckoned one of the servants for a plate of food.

I took a step back, ensuring I was hidden in the shadows of the hallway.

"What have I missed?" she sneered. How had I not noticed how annoying her voice was?

My brothers were still laughing amongst themselves, but Adonis leaned forward. "We're just making the acquaintance of our dear sister. Someone attempted to take her life the other day. Did you know about it?" he said, loud enough for everyone to hear.

I watched Kara's eyes as they darkened. "You're kidding," she gasped. "Who was it?"

Adonis shook his head. "Nobody knows. Isn't that right, Ser? Nobody knows who tried to kill our dear princess."

Jade stiffened, but the coy look on her face was unmoving.

"We're working on it," Serefin answered.

Adonis stared at him for another second before saying, "I heard Malachi did quite the damage. There wasn't even a body to bury, was there?"

Serefin's jaw tightened.

Adonis shifted his attention to Jade. "Did you see it?" he asked her. "Did you see him rip the head off the man's body? It's quite intense, really. Malachi has a gift." He eyed Jade, sizing up her every reaction.

I wanted to rush to the table. I wanted to shut them all up.

But I also wanted to see how Jade acted when I wasn't around. Jade didn't have to like me. But she was my wife. I hoped that she had at least a tiny ounce of loyalty.

After all, I did save her life.

"He really does have a gift, doesn't he?" Jade added casually. "It's really no wonder he's going to be king. With all that power, he could take down any kingdom. Don't you agree?"

Every muscle in my body froze. I watched as Adonis stared at her, unblinking, like a stunned rabbit.

Kara's mouth had fallen open, and the rest of my brothers were too busy snickering to pay any attention.

"You seem to know a lot about my attack," she added. She leaned over the wooden table, propping her chin on her elbows. "Careful, brother. You don't want to get yourself into any trouble," she said with a wink.

Serefin choked next to her.

"It's been a while since we've seen you," Kara interjected, cutting the tension in the room. "I suppose that's your husband's doing?"

"Malachi and I have been very busy," Jade said. *Busy.* The way she said it made my skin crawl.

Kara smiled, but I knew her enough to know it was full of malice. "I'm sure you have," she said. "It's quite a shame, you know. I'm used to seeing so much more of him."

Jade smiled, but Serefin leaned in and whispered something in her ear. Whatever he said made her brows furrow.

"I suppose we'll have to learn to share," Kara said quietly.

Jade ignored Serefin's ongoing warnings and snapped her head to Kara.

"It's really a shame that my husband chose a human over a fae. That must be really hard for you, Kara. I sympathize with you, truly."

Kara growled, but my stomach flipped.

Jade was jealous.

And I liked it.

"Have your fun while it lasts, Princess. It doesn't matter how deep you pierce your claws into him. He'll always be one of us."

Serefin was whispering to Jade again, and I saw him motioning for them to leave.

As if my wife had to go back to her room and hide from all of this.

I took a deep breath. Like I said, I was tired of people touching my things.

My feet didn't make a sound as I approached. In fact, nobody noticed me until I was standing directly behind Jade.

"I see I've been missing out on all the fun," I announced.

Kara stiffened, but my brothers didn't move an inch.

"Prince Malachi," Serefin greeted. "We were just leaving." He stood from his chair and moved to help Jade do the same.

"No need," I replied. "Jade has hardly eaten. I'm sure she'd like to enjoy the rest of her dinner. Right, Jade?" I picked up a piece of her long hair and let it fall through my fingers.

Her throat bobbed as she swallowed, but she didn't look at me. "Right," she answered.

"Perfect," I said, taking Serefin's seat next to her.

Kara moved as if she, too, were about to leave. My brothers followed.

"Stop," I yelled. "Everyone can sit here until my wife is done eating."

My brothers laughed. "Yeah, we're not doing that," Lucien sneered. This won a laugh from Kara.

As much as I hated hurting my brothers, there was a power in me that was hungry for more. It was always there, always waiting to be unleashed.

Perhaps I would give it a small taste.

I blinked at Lucien, envisioning a black tendril of smoke circling his chest and tightening.

Lucien dropped to his knees, gasping for air.

I cleared my vision, taking a deep breath as the hunger for power subsided. A taste was all it needed.

And it was enough to keep the others from leaving the table.

Lucien scrambled back to his seat.

"You're a coward for that," he said through gritted teeth.

I laughed. We all knew I could kill them all right here if I wanted to. We all knew the type of power I had access to, the type of power they would never wield.

Jade stared across the table at Lucien with a straight face, but I saw a small glisten of amusement in her eyes.

I didn't stop the smile that spread across my face.

"So where were we? Talking about me, weren't you?" I asked.

Kara spoke next. "Only that we heard about the attack on Jade. It's terrible news, Malachi. If there's anything we can do to help you, please just ask."

She placed a hand on my shoulder, and Jade's eyes followed it. She flinched, only for a second, before replacing her mask.

"That's very kind of you, Kara," she said. Something told me Jade had a lot of practice with shoving hatred aside, burning it deep down and replacing it with a façade.

I should know. I had been doing the same for decades.

I didn't move Kara's hand from my shoulder. Instead, I placed my hand on Jade's thigh. It was a small movement, but I could feel the eyes of everyone. I could feel the amusement from my brothers and the annoyance from Kara.

But Jade didn't move.

At least she didn't recoil. That much was a relief.

Kara slowly moved her hand, placing it back in her lap. I left my hand on Jade's thigh as she picked up her fork.

"That's thoughtful of you, Kara, but Serefin and I have everything under control. Besides, I have reason to suspect our attacker might be someone within our walls. But I'm sure you all know that by now."

"What makes you say that?" my brother Eli asked.

I eyed him carefully before answering, "A few different things. I don't see how someone could have gotten into the castle without being seen, for one."

"Surely the guards would have noticed someone," Kara added.

"During the ceremony? There was so much going on, anyone could have snuck in," Adonis said.

I remembered how close Jade was to getting caught by them that night. They had wanted to meet up with her. They were trying to get her alone.

"You're right," I replied, keeping my composure. "Many things can happen in the chaos of the wedding ceremony. I'm only glad I was there to protect Jade from the threats this time."

I squeezed Jade's thigh lightly, and she dropped her fork.

"Sorry," she stammered. "It, uh, slipped."

I looked up to find Kara staring at my hand. And she was done hiding her emotions. "You should be more careful, Jade. One mistake will get you killed in Rewyth. Your husband should have warned you of that. Humans aren't supposed to be here."

Jade opened her mouth, but I spoke first. "Is that a threat, Kara?"

Kara knew better than to challenge me, but jealousy was a great motivator. "I'm just making sure Jade knows what she's getting into. If you're so worried about her safety, maybe she shouldn't be here."

I stood from the table. "Are you questioning my ability to keep Jade safe? Because I assure you, I am more than capable of eliminating any threat. *Any* threat."

Kara shook her head in disgust. "For a human?"

I motioned for Jade to stand next to me, and I wrapped an arm around her waist. "For my *wife*," I growled. "Let's go, Jade."

She nodded and followed me out of the room. I didn't let go of her until we were alone in the hallway. Surprisingly, she played along until we were alone, then shoved me away.

"This is your game now?" she hissed. "You ignore me for days, then show up to be a possessive asshole?"

I held in my laughter. Jade looked wild. Her long black hair was messy and unhinged. Her clothes hung awkwardly off her body, and her eyes seemed larger than the last time I had seen them.

Saints, I had missed her. I had actually *missed* her these past few days. Although I was never going to admit that.

"Possessive asshole?" I repeated. "You forget I am the next king. They should respect you more."

"I can handle myself, thanks," she replied.

"Oh really? You seemed to be doing a great job out there. Serefin shouldn't have let you leave."

"Because I'm your prisoner, right? I'm supposed to sit in my room like your property and not leave until you tell me to? Is that right?"

I opened my mouth to reply but couldn't speak. Yeah, that was right. That was exactly what I wanted from her. Because she wasn't safe here. Even my bedroom wasn't safe, but at least I knew where she was. At least I knew what she was doing.

"I can't risk you waltzing around the castle. You're a target."

She gave a 'who cares' motion with her arms and let them fall to her sides. Her big eyes glistened, but the rest of her face was drenched in anger. "I don't want to be here," she said, taking a step closer to me. "I can't just sit in there and watch my life waste away."

My chest tightened, but I didn't budge. "It isn't safe, Jade." *I'm sorry*, I almost added. But I stopped myself. I wasn't sorry for protecting her. I wasn't sorry for wanting to keep her alive.

A single tear fell from her eye, but she didn't look away. "I want my life back," she said.

She was pleading with me. I knew that. This was probably the closest thing to begging that Jade would ever do.

But it didn't make a difference. I didn't care. Giving into her meant risking her life.

I opened my bedroom door and motioned for her to enter. Her jaw clenched, and her nostrils flared. I knew she was holding back her emotions. Her mask was cracking. But hope was deadly in Rewyth, and Jade was holding onto a life she would never return to.

I leaned in close to her as I whispered in her ear, "What life, Princess?"

And I shut the door, locking Jade in.

"I wasn't going to let them hurt her," Serefin said from behind me.

"I know you weren't."

He smiled. "Although you sure know how to put on a show."

"You think they had anything to do with this?" I asked him.

He shook his head. "I don't know, but they seem to know more than everyone else about the attack. And Kara's trouble. We both know that."

I agreed. "I'm only keeping her in here until I know she'll be safe," I explained. I don't know why I felt the need to explain myself to Serefin. He was never the type to question my decisions. He would follow me anywhere, do anything I asked him to do.

But still. Something in his expression made me continue, "As soon as I find out who's trying to kill her, she'll be free to roam the castle."

"I know, brother," Ser replied. "I get it."

I nodded and started to walk away.

"You can't keep her safe from everything," he yelled after me. "A human will always be a target in Rewyth. As much as we wish that weren't true."

I didn't turn around. I didn't acknowledge his words.

But Saints, he was right. I knew he was. Jade had a lot to learn if she was going to survive in Rewyth.

# CHAPTER 13
# *Jade*

TWO HUNDRED DAYS WENT BY.

Okay, it was only four days. But it felt like two hundred.

The water couldn't get my skin clean enough. I stayed under the steam until I was sure I was going to melt away and float into the river myself. But it didn't matter how many times I rinsed my hair or how hard I scrubbed my skin; I couldn't forget the feeling of Malachi touching my thigh.

Holding my waist

Leaning in close.

I shook my head. It was ridiculous. It was *pathetic.*

My brain even resorted to dreaming about him. As if I needed to think about him any more than I already had.

My thoughts were interrupted by a knock on the bathroom door.

"Go away, Malachi," I yelled.

But it wasn't Malachi who entered anyway, seating themself on the edge of the sink.

It was Adeline.

"Adeline!" I shrieked. "What are you doing in here? I'm kind of naked right now!"

"Oh, please," she said, flipping her long hair over her shoulder. "Humans are so prude. Mal thought you might be losing your mind in here or something. You know, if you stay under the water too long, it causes wrinkles."

"I'm fine!" I yelled.

"Yeah, he also said you would say that. And he told me it probably wasn't true."

I cursed under my breath.

"Heard that," Adeline chirped.

*These damn fae.*

I stepped out of the water and wrapped myself in one of the pristinely white towels Malachi had. The fact that they weren't all already stained with blood was impressive.

"I'm really fine, Adeline. I don't need a babysitter."

She squinted her eyes. "You should be dead right now. And that cut still looks bad."

I glanced in the steamy mirror and tried not to cringe. Right in the middle of my throat, a bright red cut was nearly halfway healed.

A reminder of how close my assassin had gotten to succeeding.

No wonder Malachi was so pissed.

"I'm alive, which is better than I could have asked for."

"Yeah, but we have to *keep* you alive. And your will to live is a slightly important factor there."

I rolled my eyes. "I'm not going to do anything stupid, Adeline. I already told Malachi I would listen to him from now on."

Adeline glanced toward the bathroom door before hopping off the counter and stepping closer to me. "Mal can be... possessive. He doesn't like that someone laid a hand on you, Jade. And this is the first time he's been able to make some headway on whoever has been killing his wives. He's going to protect you no matter what. You understand that, don't you?"

I let my head rest on the wall behind me. "I'm willing to do whatever it takes to stay alive. If that means living, acting, and breathing like a damn faerie, then so be it. But I can't stay locked up like this. I can't just sit in here like I'm nothing. I can protect myself."

I realized after I said the words that they may have been stupid, but when I looked at Adeline, she had a giant grin on her face.

"You have no idea how happy I am to hear that," she beamed, nearly jumping with excitement. "Now put these clothes on. I'm taking you somewhere."

I didn't have time to ask questions. Adeline was gone, leaving a stack of clothes on the counter.

After getting dressed, I had to admit I was impressed. Adeline hadn't picked out a ridiculous, revealing fae outfit. Instead, she brought me simple slacks and a basic tunic.

I could actually move freely. And I wasn't covered in blood or wearing Malachi's clothes.

Consider me grateful.

After a few minutes of walking, Adeline and I found ourselves leaving the castle and heading into the jungle-like woods that encapsulated the entire back half of the estate.

"Does Malachi know we're heading into the woods?" I asked Adeline.

She rolled her eyes and groaned. "What Mal doesn't know won't kill him. Besides, it can be really beautiful out here. He would just ruin it."

I followed her down a narrow stone path, the light around us slowly diminishing even though the sun had just fully risen.

She wasn't lying. The beauty of the castle should have been a huge indication as to how beautiful the forest was going to be. Even so, the castle hardly compared. Thick vines weaved through massive trees, filling the space with a variety of greenery.

Moss covered the stones we walked on, silencing every step we took further into the woods. The sound of water pouring in the distance grew stronger and stronger as we continued.

I was about to tell Adeline to stop when we entered a clearing, revealing a small waterfall that was almost hidden in the vast stone structure behind it.

Hidden. Like it was here just for Adeline. Just for us.

"Saints," I mumbled. "This is what you dragged me out here for? It's gorgeous, Adeline."

She gave me a knowing smile and trotted forward, perching herself onto a bench-like structure I assumed she was responsible for.

"See?" she said. "It's not so terrible here, is it? You're a fighter, Jade. I knew that as soon as I met you. You're going to stick around, I just know it. So, you might as well not absolutely hate this place while you're here!"

I couldn't help but smile. This was undoubtedly the nicest thing anyone had done for me. Granted, nobody ever did nice things for me at home, and all Adeline did was drag me into the woods, but it was still true.

I couldn't believe it.

"I'm assuming this is where you hide while your brothers continue whatever feud they have going on."

"You have no idea, honey. I feel like I've spent years out here with all the fighting they do. But family is complicated. Mal knows that. I'm sure you'll learn about all of their silly politics soon enough."

Now it was my turn to groan. "I feel like I've learned enough already."

Adeline's eyes were full of pity when she looked at me. "I know this must be hard for you, Jade. You don't know who to trust, and you don't know what to believe about us. After what happened..."

"It's really okay—"

"Mal can be terrifying," she interrupted. "I could smell the blood the second I walked into that room, Jade, and that was after they had cleaned it all up. I've seen him kill. I've seen him slaughter people dozens of times. Just because I'm fae doesn't mean I'm heartless, despite what you humans may think."

I shoved her shoulder playfully, then she continued.

"This world can be daunting, and Malachi has been through a lot. He's had to turn into someone he doesn't want to be."

"He seemed pretty proud of himself after ripping that man's head off."

"For nearly killing you! I would have done the same thing!"

I took a deep breath. This was all too much to process. I was starting to believe everything I had been told about Malachi, despite Adeline's confusing claims. "How am I supposed to believe he'll protect me when he has the reputation he does? I'm only human. I'm nothing here."

"You're not nothing, Jade. You're Malachi's wife. That makes you untouchable."

"Well, his last wives were pretty touchable."

She gave me a look of pity. "This is going to be a never-ending cycle, Jade. The facts are that you're Mal's wife now, and you're also a Rewyth princess."

"I'm not a princess," I muttered.

"But you are. And you can either live here in fear every day, or you can do something about it. I know you're trying to help Mal find out who's been doing this. I don't have to tell you to be careful. You already know that."

I nodded, unsure of what else to say.

So, I changed the subject. "Do you know Kara?" I asked.

Adeline groaned. "Please don't tell me she's bothering you. I've had enough of her to last me two lifetimes."

I smiled at her reaction. "She seems very attached to Malachi."

"Yeah, she has been for decades. Literally. Malachi had some fun with her, but it was never serious. Kara wants power. She's a snake, and we all know it. Even Malachi."

I scoffed. "I don't know. He seems to put up with her more than anyone else. If other people talked to him the way she does, they would be dead."

"I think Malachi feels bad for her. I do, anyway. She wasn't always this terrible. We actually used to be friends a long time ago."

"Really?" I asked. "You and Kara?"

Adeline nodded. "But that was before her obsession with my brother."

I thought about her words. "You don't think she would be killing Malachi's wives out of jealousy, do you?"

"The thought has crossed my mind, I'll admit. But Kara is harmless. She is jealous, yes, and you should avoid her at all costs. But she doesn't have it in her to actually kill someone out of cold blood."

I nodded. Adeline confirmed what I had been thinking. Kara was a spiteful brat, but I had known girls like her. They were all talk. Kara was used to getting her way, and I was an obstacle.

Although, I couldn't say I liked the way she acted toward Malachi.

"Okay!" Adeline sighed. "Enough of this serious stuff. I brought you here to show you how beautiful faerie can be, so come on!" She stood from the bench and kicked off her shoes.

"What are you doing?!" I yelled.

I was answered by the sound of her splashing into the water.

"What?" she called from the water. "It feels so nice!"

I laughed. It was a real laugh, and it somehow felt wrong, like I didn't deserve to be enjoying myself.

Tessa was probably freaking out right now. For all she knew, I had been killed.

I had to go see her. Mal had to take me there.

And I had to help Malachi.

Adeline splashed a handful of water in my direction. "Are you jumping in, or are you staying out there like a big baby?" she taunted.

I always loved swimming. Back home, I used to spend every morning swimming in the pond near our house. But that was before I spent every day fighting for survival. For food. For Tessa.

That felt like ages ago.

But this was a new life. This was a new home. And as much as I hated to admit it, this was my new reality.

Adeline was right. Rewyth, as despicable as I might have thought it to be, did have a few benefits.

A gorgeous waterfall in the middle of the woods was definitely one of them.

Adeline clapped her hands with excitement as I stood from the bench, kicking my own shoes off and jumping in.

The water beneath the waterfall was a welcoming, luxurious pool of bliss. Okay, maybe that was an exaggeration. But it was absolutely amazing.

I held my breath and dunked beneath the water, letting the weightlessness of my body drift.

"I knew you'd love it!" Adeline said a few feet away.

The water hardly covered my chest when I stood on the rocks that rested at the bottom.

"My sister would love it here," I said to her. "She usually hates the outdoors... but this..."

"Welcome to Rewyth, Princess Jade. This is just the beginning."

I opened my mouth to respond, to object to the princess title once more, but Adeline's eyes had settled on something behind me.

I didn't turn around. I froze as I heard what she was hearing.

Footsteps in the woods headed straight toward us.

# CHAPTER 14
# *Malachi*

I WAS GOING TO KILL ADELINE.

She had seriously taken Jade into the forest? After what had just happened? After I explicitly told her to keep an eye on her in my bedroom, not parade her around to the most dangerous part of Rewyth?

I normally trusted Adeline, but there were times when she acted like a stupid teenage girl. Part of me didn't blame her. Like the rest of us, her childhood had been ripped away from her. There was no time for fun and games in the Royal Family, and Adeline had always had a hard time making friends.

It was hard to know who you could trust when everyone in Faerie was a greedy asshole who wanted something from you.

But I knew Adeline would like Jade, although I was surprised to learn Jade had been reciprocating those feelings.

No, I didn't care about what I had said to Jade last night. I didn't care about the look on her face as I locked her in that room again. I shoved those thoughts aside. She was going to have to learn what she was up against, and if that meant making her hate me any more than she already did, then so be it.

If it meant keeping her alive...

If it meant figuring out who had tried to kill her...

It was worth it.

I had learned very little about the identity of our attackers. Kara and my brothers were gossips, but someone else in the castle had to know something. Had to have seen something.

Someone in this castle thought they could outsmart me. Thought they could kill my wife.

I just had to find out who was behind this, and I would throw a celebration around their deaths.

But it's not like I could go around asking questions. I couldn't trust anyone.

Every single fae in this damned castle was a suspect in my eyes. Even family. Even guards.

I heard their voices and took a sharp turn, toward the lagoon. I should have guessed it. This had been Adeline's favorite spot since we were children.

The sound of laughter nearly made me pause. It was warm and full of life, something I wasn't used to.

Most people were cold around me, and I didn't blame them.

When I stomped through the trees and into the clearing, I froze in my tracks.

And then Jade screamed.

A massive tiger, one that had likely been stalking them this whole time, lunged toward Jade. It splashed as its body hit the water, and they both went under.

Adeline yelled and threw herself toward Jade and the tiger.

I was already moving.

The next few moments were a blur of water, blood, screaming, and limbs flailing in the lagoon.

I gripped the tiger from behind and threw myself backward, taking it with me.

Jade gasped as she resurfaced, but the tiger thrashed in my arms.

"Adeline!" I yelled. "Get her out of here!"

Adeline moved toward Jade, but so did the tiger.

It was too slippery. The massive animal twisted from my grasp.

But Adeline was there. She had her hands around the tiger in an instant, stopping it in its tracks. She screamed as she fought, squeezing hard on its large neck.

The tiger whimpered. I moved to help Adeline, and together we threw it from the pond.

Its wet body landed on the ground, but it wasn't dead.

Not yet.

The tiger stood and looked at us. For a moment, I thought it was going to lunge again. I regained control and pictured black smoke surrounding us, protecting us from the tiger.

Jade couldn't see it. Adeline couldn't see it. But animals had always been able to sense my power.

The tiger shook its head and backed away before darting back into the forest.

All three of us stood in the shoulder-deep water, panting.

I was the first one to speak. "I hope you both have a very good explanation for this."

My sister swallowed. "I'm sorry, Mal, I was just trying to—"

"Stop," I interrupted. "I don't want your apology right now. You both would be dead right now if I hadn't come looking for you."

"I would have stopped it!" Adeline argued.

"Really?" I asked. "You really think you're in the position to fight off a grown tiger that's likely twice your size, all while protecting Jade at the same time?"

Adeline stammered, looking for her next words. But Jade interrupted. "She was trying to help me, Malachi."

"And what exactly was she helping you with? You're this desperate to get yourself killed?"

"She was trying to get me out of that prison," Jade replied. Her voice shook, likely from the adrenaline of what just happened, but she still held her chin high. "It's not our fault there was a massive animal waiting to attack us out here. How were we supposed to know that?"

"You and I will talk about this later," I snapped to Adeline. "Let's go, Jade."

The girls looked at each other, and Jade scoffed before the three of us crawled out of the lagoon. Jade's breaths were still coming out in short bursts.

"I trusted you, Adeline," I said quietly.

She lowered her head. "I know. I'm sorry. I'm sorry, Jade."

Jade grabbed Adeline's hand. "Don't apologize. Thank you for bringing me here. It really is gorgeous."

Adeline looked up and smiled shyly before walking back to the castle, leaving Jade and I alone.

# CHAPTER 15
## *Jade*

Malachi didn't say a single word to me as we walked back through the jungle toward the castle.

And the way he had spoken to Adeline...

He had crushed her. I could see the way Adeline physically shrank at the way he didn't trust her. At the way he ridiculed her. Adeline had looked up to him, had tried to help me, had made me laugh for the first time in what seemed like decades, and he had put her down because of it.

Like I said. *Ignorant bastard.*

Once I was certain my voice wasn't going to shake, I spoke up. "She was just trying to help me," I said as we approached the large castle. My stomach dropped at the sight of it, like my body knew I wouldn't be leaving again anytime soon.

Malachi shook his head in front of me. He hadn't released the tension in his fists for the entire time we had been walking, and his muscles had been flexing nonstop under his thin shirt that was now plastered to his body with water.

Not like I had been looking.

"She knows better than to disobey me," he growled without turning to face me.

The words alone were enough to make me laugh out loud. "Okay, *Father,*" I spat. I was playing with fire, but I didn't care. Malachi had made it very clear that he could kill anyone he wanted to, yet here I was. Alive.

Malachi stopped walking so abruptly, I almost bumped into his back.

When he turned to face me, his eyes were swarming with emotion.

"Don't ever talk to me like that," he seethed, pointing a finger at my chest. "And don't pretend like you know anything about my family or what goes on here. You know nothing about this court, and you know nothing about me."

"Because you won't tell me anything," I pushed. "And you've been ignoring me for days!"

He laughed, but it chilled me to my bones. I crossed my arms over my chest and tried not to shiver. "If you knew everything, you would run like the Saints as far as you could to get away from here. So don't ask for something you can't handle, Princess."

I debated his words for a second. He had turned and continued walking, but as I followed after him, I added, "I want to learn how to fight."

"To fight?"

"I want to learn how to protect myself," I said, trying and failing to keep my voice from breaking. "I don't want to be afraid. I want to have a fighting chance at survival. You've made it very clear that I'm as good as useless here."

He hesitated, and for the second time today I thought he was going to apologize, but he didn't.

"Fine," he said after a few awkward moments. "I think we could all benefit from you knowing how to protect yourself against the fae."

The fae. He said the words as if he wasn't one himself. I nodded in response but said nothing else. The conversation was over.

I followed him as he entered the castle, completely ignoring everyone who seemed to be gawking at him. I copied his movements, keeping my head down as we weaved through the maze of the hallways.

Something on my leg was burning, but I didn't dare to look. Adrenaline had been pulsing through my body since the tiger had attacked, and I hadn't thought to check if I had been injured in the crossfire.

I certainly wasn't going to check in front of Malachi. He didn't need any more reason to keep me locked away.

I was still dripping wet. My hair was leaving a trail of water on the white flooring, but Malachi didn't seem to notice. Or care.

Probably the latter.

Malachi turned another corner and tensed immediately.

I lifted my head for the first time since we entered the castle, only to be standing in front of the King of Rewyth himself and all five of his sons.

# CHAPTER 16

# Malachi

I WANTED TO GRAB JADE AND DRAG HER BACK INTO MY BEDROOM, where I could lock my door and keep her there, away from the monstrosities of my family.

But it was too late. I had successfully avoided the bastards since our discussion the other day, and now it was time to confront them.

My father and my brothers stood just a few feet away. Every single pair of eyes fell on me. And then I watched as every single pair of eyes shifted to the dripping-wet girl standing behind me.

My *wife.*

"Well, well, well," my father said, stepping forward. "The lovely prince and princess. It's quite a pleasure to see you doing so well!"

He meant *alive*. It was a pleasure to see Jade alive.

I wasn't buying it. "We were just heading back to my quarters," I said as I reached a hand back to Jade. She grabbed it without hesitating, which nearly made me sigh in relief after the fight we just had.

*Smart girl.*

I wondered if she could feel how tense I was. How important it was for her to play along here.

My father eyed us both up and down, his gaze lingering on Jade's wet clothes for a few seconds too long before saying, "I'm calling a court meeting this evening. I suggest you attend and bring your new... wife."

The way he said it had me clenching my jaw, but I plastered a smile on my face. "I'll see if I can fit it in," I said through gritted teeth.

Jade kept her mouth shut beside me, which was surprising. Especially as my father kept staring at her.

"Anything else?" I said after a few moments of silence. Adonis whispered something to Lucien, and they both laughed. I felt my composure crumbling. "Care to share with the group?" I pushed.

I couldn't help it. After what happened with Jade last night, I wasn't taking anyone's bullshit. People had been pushing me to the limits for far too long.

Perhaps they had forgotten why I was called the Prince of Shadows.

Adonis squared his shoulders before responding, "Oh, we were just admiring your wife's appropriate court attire. I supposed none of us prepared for her to be around long enough to need her own tailor, right?"

They laughed again.

The power building in my body was almost enough to become tangible. They knew who they were messing with. They knew what the consequences would be. I snarled at him before my father held up a hand.

"Enough, Malachi," he said, sounding as bored as ever. Was he serious? They talk about my wife, the Princess of Rewyth that way, and he takes their side? "I'm tired of these immature games you all play. We'll see you this evening for the court meeting. We can discuss the politics of this arrangement then."

He didn't look at us again as he walked past, sauntering out of the hallway with his posse of princes trailing behind him.

Jade exhaled loudly as soon as we were alone in the hallway. "Shit," she mumbled, crossing her arms over her body once more. "No offense, but your family is a bunch of assholes."

I smiled quickly before the reality of the situation hit me.

Jade had actually survived her first few nights in Rewyth. And now she was going to have to survive a court meeting. This might be an even more difficult task than the first.

"Let's go," I said, guiding her back down the hallway toward my room. "Things are about to get very interesting."

"Because they were so boring already," she muttered under her breath.

I clenched my fists. "You realize fae can hear every dumb thing you say under your breath, right?"

Jade merely smiled and flipped her wet hair over her shoulder. "Good, you were meant to." She strutted past me and continued walking to my bedroom.

*Our* bedroom.

Did she not understand how serious this was? Did she not know the dangers of the situation she was about to be in?

I followed her in and shut the door behind me. Jade just perched herself on the sofa, completely ignoring the fact that her hair was still dripping water.

"We need to talk," I said, pacing past her. "I need you to do everything I tell you to do tonight."

Jade tensed but maintained her calm expression. "For the court meeting?"

"Yep."

"Do you think someone there wants me dead?"

Her face was blank.

"I don't know."

Silence.

It was only a couple seconds, but it felt like hours.

"Okay," she said finally. "What do you need me to do?"

I did a double take. Definitely did not expect her to say that. But I was relieved, nonetheless.

I leaned against the wall as I gathered my thoughts. What did I need her to do? Saints, I had no idea. The wedding was bad enough, and we had barely survived that. This was something different. The public eye wasn't here to keep my family's behavior in line. These court meetings got ugly, and few of them ended without any bloodshed.

Whether it's from my idiot brothers punching each other or worse.

"First, you'll need new clothes. Court clothes. I'll have Adeline bring some for you."

She nodded.

"And you'll have to stay quiet. Actually quiet this time. My brothers will... They'll try to start something. They always do. There's no telling what they have in mind, considering there's never been a wife at any of these meetings."

"None of your brothers are married?"

"Nope. Apparently, I'm the only one my father hates enough for that."

She cringed at my words, and I immediately wanted to take them back.

But Jade just lifted her chin and said, "I guess that makes two of us, then."

I met her eyes from across the room. Jade had been a surprise, indeed. The fact that she hated the fae so much but still wanted to defend Adeline said everything I needed to know about her. Jade had a soft spot underneath her badass, rock-solid demeanor.

But in Rewyth, that was as good as a death sentence.

Show no weakness. Yield no mercy.

"You know how to use that thing, right?" I asked her regarding her knife. I assumed she could wield a weapon, but in the two times she had been attacked here in Rewyth, she hadn't used it.

Something dark hardened her expression.

"I've used it before," she said. I fought the urge to ask her when.

"Good," I replied, pulling an iron knife of my own from my hip. "Because fae are strong. Much stronger than any human. And you've seen the animals in the forest now. That tiger was the least of your worries out there. You have to be ready."

"For what, exactly? For your father to try and kill me? Sorry, but I'm not sure I'd have any chance against that. Dagger or not."

"Let me show you," I said as I pushed myself away from the wall. I didn't think, just acted.

She stood up slowly, but fear crept into her features. I know she was thinking about how I held the knife to her throat and probably how the assassin had done the same hours earlier.

"Relax," I soothed. "I'm not going to hurt you."

She snapped her gaze to me. "Great, it's so nice to know my husband isn't going to kill me, despite how much he likes threatening everyone else."

My breath stalled.

"I didn't mean to scare you," I said. I wasn't sure which incident I was even talking about.

She simply nodded. "This is my new life, isn't it? Fight to survive?"

"You're human, Jade. Hasn't it always been that way?"

She stiffened again. "Just because I'm not fae, just because I don't live in a fancy castle or party with rich court members every day, doesn't mean I've been fighting for survival every day."

I considered her words. "When I saw you in the forest, I could have guessed differently."

"I was fighting for my family."

"Quite a family you have."

"Likewise."

I froze. Jade stared me down. Her and I were different. I knew that. Jade was a human who was living off scraps, hunting her own food.

I was a prince of Rewyth. In fact, I was the most feared prince in the kingdom. And it wasn't for no reason.

But Jade didn't need to know that just yet.

I held the knife to my side, pushing those thoughts away. "The quickest way to harm a fae is a blade to the heart. It might not kill them, but it will hurt them enough for you to run and get help."

She held her own knife, examining it as if it were the only thing keeping her from death.

"Try to stab me," I said.

"What?"

"You heard me."

"I'm not going to stab you," she sneered.

"No," I agreed. "You're not. But you can try."

Her brows furrowed. "Are all fae as cocky as you?"

I smirked. I couldn't help it. "Not all fae are the heir to the kingdom."

"And not all fae are the Prince of Shadows."

"Also correct," I said.

Jade's hair was beginning to dry, curling slightly at the ends where the long locks hit her waist. She was thin, thinner than she was in the forest the first time I had seen her.

She wasn't strong enough to fight off a fae.

As if she could read my thoughts, Jade lunched forward, dagger in hand and aimed directly at my chest.

Her form was decent, but I easily batted her away with my hand.

"Try again."

She huffed, clenching her fists. It was good if she was getting angry. Anger would give her strength. Adrenaline.

She lunged again, this time with a grunt of frustration.

I grabbed her arm and twisted. Her weapon clattered to the floor.

"Are you even trying?" I asked.

She backed away and ran her hands over her face. "This is stupid. I'm not fast enough."

"You have to be, Jade. And if you can't be faster, you have to be smarter."

"Smarter than who, exactly? The dozens of fae who may or may not want me dead?"

I rolled my eyes. She might not have been trying to be difficult, but we were stuck in an endless cycle.

"Are you done feeling sorry for yourself?" I demanded.

"Excuse me?"

"Look," I said, "I get that you're in a shit situation, but your attitude really isn't helping."

"My attitude?" she repeated. I just nodded in response. "I'm sorry that I can't be happy and helpful all the time when my sister might be freaking out, your brothers may want to kill me, you ripped off someone's head on our wedding night, and now we might be walking into some sort of testosterone bomb. Apologies, my prince."

I chose my next words carefully. "You know that's not what I meant."

She just nodded, the tough walls of her composure slowly crumbling behind her deep eyes. Part of me wanted to comfort her, but I didn't.

"You have no idea what it's like," she said. "None of you do. You don't know what it's like to starve for days because your father was too drunk to come home and bring food. And when he finally showed up, he had spent the rest of our money on drinking. You don't know how it feels to have to hunt and steal for food just so your little sister doesn't starve. And you certainly don't know what it feels like to have your coward of a father ship you to the fae because he can't pay his own debt. So, I think the next time you have an opinion on my attitude, or anything about me for that matter, you can respectfully shove it."

I merely nodded. "Okay."

She looked shocked, like she had expected me to fight back. "Okay," she repeated, picking up the dagger. "So, teach me how to use this."

"I thought you said you've used it before. On men, if I'm not mistaken," I said, repeating her words from the first night I met her.

A wicked smile spread across her face. One that almost made me smile in response. "Stories for another time, husband. I need to know how to use this against the fae."

I nodded. We would definitely have to come back to that. "The facts are that you won't be stronger or faster than a fae. Probably ever. So you'll have to use other advantages."

"Like what?"

"You're human. Nobody's going to expect you to fight back. Surprise is going to be your best bet. Just keep that thing where you can grab it easily, somewhere nobody is going to see it."

"You had a pretty easy time knowing I had this at the wedding."

"Maybe, but nobody else should be looking at you that closely."

Jade blushed, but I didn't back down. Something primal inside of me wouldn't allow it.

"Your brother seemed to be looking just as closely as you," she said, a smirk on her face and a hand on her hip. She was taunting me. I didn't stop the growl that rumbled in my chest. Jade's eyes only widened. "Does that bother you?"

She held my gaze, testing me. She was brave, that much was certain. But I had already told her I wouldn't hurt her.

Maybe she was getting too confident.

In one second, I grabbed her around her waist and hurled her against the wall, pinning her there with my arms.

"I could kill you right now," I growled.

She lifted her chin in silent defiance. "Then why don't you?" she whispered.

The feeling of her breath on my cheek made me shiver. I held her there for a few more seconds, pressing her body against the wall, staring into her eyes. She wasn't going to back away. She knew I wouldn't kill her.

Saints. This girl was going to get me killed.

The sharp, copper smell of blood distracted me. "Are you bleeding?" I asked, backing away from the wall and looking her up and down.

Jade took a deep breath and looked down at her leg. Her trousers were black, but I could now see the thick coat of blood that covered them, dripping down to the floor.

How had I not noticed that before?

"It's not that bad," she mumbled. "I can barely even feel it."

"That's because you're stubborn," I replied. I didn't wait for Jade to protest before putting an arm under her knees and picking her up, carrying her to the bed.

"It's seriously fine!" she protested as I knelt before her and rolled up her pant leg.

Jade hissed in pain. "You should have told me you were hurt," I whispered.

I grabbed my shirt and ripped a strip of fabric from the bottom.

Jade went still as my fingers traced up her leg, just above her knee, where the slice of a claw began.

"You shouldn't have been out there," I sighed. She didn't respond. I began tying the fabric over her wound, aware of every single time my skin brushed against hers.

Jade was silent. When I finished tying the knot, I looked up at her. And I immediately wished I hadn't.

She was staring at me with the same longing that I was feeling. The same longing that neither of us could act on.

My hand lingered under her calf. I slid it up, just an inch, and waited for Jade's reaction.

She inhaled sharply, as if my touch affected her just as badly as hers affected me.

"I should get ready for the court meeting," she insisted.

I cleared my throat.

"Right," I said. I stood up and backed away from the bed. "Of course."

"But thank you, Malachi. And thank you for saving my life today. Again."

"Anytime," I replied.

Jade smiled at me before heading to the bathroom, leaving me alone.

# CHAPTER 17
# Jade

"How does it look?" I asked Malachi.

He was standing in the corner of the room, his massive black wings tucked behind each shoulder blade. He had changed into a sleek black royal outfit, which matched his wings and hair.

A Prince of Shadows, indeed.

"You look fine," he said, although I could tell he didn't even bother glancing at me. Since our encounter earlier, he had been ignoring me completely.

But maybe that was for the best.

I had let myself forget who Malachi really was. I had let myself fall for his soft touch on my leg.

Saints, I had nearly *kissed* him.

Malachi might have been my husband, but he was still fae. And I was still trying to survive.

I looked at myself in the mirror, smoothing down my black corset and matching skirt that fell past my feet. "How the saints am I supposed to fight off an attacker in a skirt like this?"

His shoulders shook in laughter in the mirror's reflection, but he still didn't meet my gaze. "Your five minutes of training won't help much anyway, Princess."

*Jackass.*

The nerves in my stomach were enough to make me want to vomit, but I didn't dare tell Malachi that.

Show no weakness, as he said. Yield no mercy.

These fae weren't about to see me cower.

I took a deep breath and let go of the nerves. I was a survivor. A fighter. "Let's get this over with," I said, turning from the mirror.

Malachi looked up for the first time since I got dressed. His expression was blank, which made me more nervous than if he were pissed off. "Don't forget what I told you," he said in a low voice. "Keep quiet."

Warning laced every word. I nodded.

He looked at me, eyes finally moving from my face, landing on my new dress. I had never worn something like this. My gown at the wedding had been a singular piece of fabric that flowed with my body. This dress was thick and structured, and I couldn't take a deep breath without my chest nearly spilling from the top.

He opened his mouth like he was about to say something, but we were both interrupted when the bedroom door creaked open.

Serefin.

"I'm here to escort you, my lord," he said in an unusually polite voice. Malachi nodded, as if the two of them had done this dozens of times before.

Whatever softness that had lingered in his gaze disappeared. "Let's go, Jade," he said in a voice that was rumbling with power. He didn't wait to see if I followed him before storming out of the room and into the hallway.

"You look beautiful," Serefin whispered to me as I forced my feet to move. "Don't worry. Everything will be fine."

Was he talking to himself? Or to me?

I didn't dare ask. Just kept my mouth shut as Serefin guided me behind Malachi, his prince and my husband, the heavy pit of dread in my stomach growing with every step.

Malachi

The scent of Jade's fear was about to rip me apart. She knew just as well as I did that if the people in this room wanted her dead, they just might be able to succeed.

Every ounce of my body was on alert. I wasn't going to let anything surprise me. Prepare for the worst, always prepare for the worst.

For all I knew, we were walking into a death trap.

I couldn't even look at her, but I heard her and Serefin's footsteps echoing behind me until we were standing right outside of the solar. I could hear the voices of the others already inside.

We were the last to arrive.

I closed my eyes and took a deep breath. It wasn't going to happen again. I was going to protect her.

I had to.

Without thinking, I slipped my hand into Jade's. We had to appear united in front of the court. We had to at least pretend to act like a couple.

Jade just stood next to me, a quick flash of shock on her face before she covered it up. Burying it deep down where it couldn't hurt her.

Good. She couldn't afford to feel anything. Neither could I.

I balled my free hand into a fist, nearly piercing the skin on my palm. Serefin nodded at me once before pushing open the doors.

My brothers were seated in the center of the room around my father. They didn't even glance at us as we walked inside.

Ignorant bastards.

The other members of the court, however, weren't as obtuse.

"The man of the hour," Carlyle said to me, walking forward and holding out his hand.

I smiled in relief. "Isn't it past your bedtime, old man?"

He laughed before turning his attention to Jade. "And I believe congratulations are in order. It's a pleasure to have you in this court, Lady Farrow," he said, bending down to kiss her knuckles.

He was always such a flirt. If he wasn't triple my age, I might have kicked his ass for it.

But Carlyle had always been good to me. He had pure intentions, which was a rarity for the fae, I had to admit.

It was decades ago when I met him. My father had sent me as a last resort during a war between our countries. He had sent me as a weapon, but I had returned as Carlyle's ally.

And friend.

A dull ache threatened my chest, but I cleared my throat and buried that memory.

Jade was doing her best to look confident, but she was clearly out of her element, staring at Carlyle like he was some sort of Saint.

"Thank you," she finally responded to him. "Although, I can't say everyone has been as welcoming as you."

She'd better watch it. Everything we said would be heard by dozens of ears. Ears that would pay millions to watch me burn.

To watch *us* burn.

And what better way to watch a man suffer than to torture his wife?

No. They didn't know I cared about her. Saints, I *didn't* care about her. But they had to believe that, too. At least here.

"Shall we?" I said, guiding Jade with a hand on her back. We maneuvered through the sea of whispering fae and found our seats at the head of the table.

Right next to my father.

I simply nodded at him, not trusting my mouth to not say something stupid.

"Princess Jade," Adonis said. "You're looking well. It's a pleasure to see you again so soon."

A feral growl filled the room, and it took me a second to realize it was from me.

Adonis looked at me as if I were unhinged.

Maybe I was.

"What?" he asked. "Am I not allowed to speak to your wife?"

Jade opened her mouth like she was going to answer for herself, but I cut her off. "This is a court meeting, and Jade knows nothing of the court, so it's best if you don't address her at all today. She already has enough to think about. Right, Jade?"

Anger pulsed through my body with every heartbeat.

"As a matter of fact," I said to the room, very aware of my father sitting mere feet away from me, "nobody in this room speaks to Jade. If you would like to address something, you can speak to me about it."

The twins snickered before one of them, Eli, said, "Well, what if we want to tell her that she looks expensive? How much are human whores worth these days anyway?" He could hardly contain his laughter.

Jade stiffened. The room silenced.

That was all I needed.

I didn't draw my sword. I didn't need it. My black wings cast a shadow around me as I stepped forward toward my brother.

His face straightened. He had never seen me this way before. Most of them hadn't.

This was the Prince of Shadows everyone talked about. This was the prince that was a weapon to Rewyth.

The ground began to rumble. "Control yourself, Malachi," my father warned, but I pushed his words aside. I kept my focus on Eli, on the words he'd said.

I didn't care if it hurt Jade, but disrespect to Jade was disrespect to me.

Perhaps they had forgotten. I was going to make them remember.

Power rumbled through the air. *My* power. The same power that could kill with a single thought. The same power that made the entire kingdom fear me. That made my father use me as a weapon all this time.

I wasn't planning on killing my brother, but I would scare him just enough. He would be the example of what would happen if anyone messed with Jade again.

"Mal, stop," Jade's voice cut through the air.

Normally, I would have ignored it, but her voice was strained. The tiniest smell of fear filled the air. It was enough to stop me in my tracks, to stop any amount of power that was building up inside me.

I blinked a few times, now very aware of the fact that I had pinned my brother against the wall, arm against his neck hard enough that he was fighting to breathe.

I dropped him and backed away.

The entire room was staring at me in awe. Including my father. Including Jade.

"Malachi," my father boomed from his chair. "Are you able to keep your temper intact? Or must we excuse you from this court meeting?"

I clenched my fists. "I'll be fine." One look at Eli, who was now cowering against the wall, told me he was done with his snide comments.

And everyone else was now too stunned to speak.

"Very well, then," my father announced to the room. "Now that the drama has subsided, it's best we go ahead and get started. Everyone, take your seats."

We all did as we were told. Jade ended up sitting between myself and Lucien, who apparently was having a hard time keeping his eyes off her.

I made a mental note to teach him a lesson later, as well.

Part of me wanted to lean toward Jade and ask her if she was okay. I wanted to tell her she didn't need to be afraid of me, that I wasn't going to let people speak about her that way.

But not now. Not in front of a room full of fae who were looking for weaknesses in me.

Certainly not in front of my father.

My father cleared his throat with a sound that made me want to gag. "We have a few topics to discuss today," he started, "but I would like to begin by welcoming our dear princess, Jade Farrow, to the meeting today." Jade stiffened next to me, but she forced a small smile onto her face. "Jade's role as Malachi's wife will serve Rewyth in many ways, the first and foremost being to unite the human and fae lands once and for all."

I blinked. What was he talking about?

"How is a human supposed to unite our lands?" one of the elders asked. The elders were usually the ones to voice concern during our court meetings, especially when something was changing. Having a human in this room was the biggest change of all. "She can hardly be in a room of fae without reeking of fear. No offense intended, dear," he said.

I glanced at Jade, half expecting some sort of sassy retort. But her expression was unchanging, as if the man's words did nothing but bore her.

"Your concerns are something we have thought long and hard about," my father responded. I nearly laughed out loud. How ridiculous was that? My father hardly thought about any humans, let alone bringing peace to their lands. "It is no secret that the humans and the fae have been in a feud for centuries, but for what? What started as a petty war years and years ago has now led the humans to famine and poverty. They're starving to death every day, and our dear princess here can attest to that."

Dozens of eyes turned to my wife. She blinked a few times, as if she were just processing what my father had said.

I took a deep breath and asked, "What specifically are you hoping to achieve from this union, Father?"

He turned to me with a smile big enough to show his rotting teeth. "Thank you for asking, son. This brings me to our first agenda item today." I stiffened, bracing for his next words. I sensed Jade doing the same. "You and your wife are being sent to govern your own lands, where fae and humans will live together in one place."

The room erupted into chaos.

# CHAPTER 18
# *Jade*

My ears were ringing, but that didn't stop me from hearing the stream of profanity that left Malachi's mouth as he stood from the chair.

"Everyone, calm down!" the king yelled. His voice was barely audible over the crowd of fae yelling questions of their own.

"And when were you planning on sharing this plan with me, Father?" Malachi demanded. His face was red, and I wondered if it was from anger or embarrassment.

"I'm sharing it with you now," his father boomed. "Now sit down."

Malachi huffed and, to my surprise, sat back down in his chair.

I guess the beast could be tamed, after all.

After a few seconds, the room began to silence, all eyes locked on the king.

Including mine.

"This has been a plan of mine for quite some time," he started. "And it is in Rewyth's best interests to eventually unite the humans and fae."

"Why?" someone shouted. "What could we possibly want from them?"

As much as I hated to admit it, I was actually thinking the same thing. The fae lived in wealth and riches in Rewyth. And the humans? We were scum. We were poor and sick. We had nothing.

We had nothing to offer the fae.

Which means the king had something else in mind.

Malachi must have realized that too. His eyes filled with anger, curiosity, and stubbornness as he stared down his father.

"The humans have something we don't have. They may be poor. They may be sick. They may be disgusting creatures that can't take care of themselves..."

I rolled my eyes.

"...but they have safety."

Now it was my turn to look confused. What could he possibly be talking about? Compared to the fae, humans were the furthest thing from safe. We didn't have to worry about our enemies, because we were too busy worried about if we were going to starve to death or not.

"He's talking about Trithen," Malachi mumbled to himself, just loud enough for me to hear.

Trithen... it sounded familiar.

"Because of the old treaties between the fae and the human lands, the fae are forbidden to attack any lands where humans reside. Or they risk punishment from the Paragon."

The room collectively began absorbing his words, some even nodding along.

I wanted to ask Malachi what the Saints they were talking about, but I resisted, biting the inside of my cheek as he continued.

The king stood up and began pacing the room. "The humans, however, conveniently reside in the land that is separating Rewyth from our sister kingdom, Fearford."

Adonis was the one who spoke next. "So, you think the Paragon will allow you to move fae into the human lands? Won't there be riots?"

"Not if we do this correctly. You see, this union proves that fae and humans can live peacefully together. Especially when the new prince and princess are madly in love."

"The humans won't accept this," Malachi argued.

"They will if we stop them from starving. We'll share our resources in exchange for sharing their land."

I couldn't believe what I was hearing. He actually wanted to make a deal with the humans?

"So, you'll give away our food and money for a chance at positioning some of our fae closer to Fearford?"

"Exactly."

The room erupted in a low murmur of voices.

I didn't realize Lucien was leaning into my ear until he began whispering, "Better buckle up, sweetheart. The humans might not hate you yet, but they're sure about to."

"Shut up, Lucien," Malachi snapped before I had the chance. My head was spinning. It was all too much information to absorb. I placed my elbows on the large wooden table and rested my head on my wrists, rubbing my temples lightly.

"Are you sure the princess is up for it?" a new voice yelled from the corner of the room. "She doesn't seem too fit for the challenge."

I couldn't stay quiet. I know Malachi had warned me, but I had to say something.

"What do you all know about the humans, anyway?" I said without lifting my head. "We starve. We beg. We suffer. You will never last in the human lands."

The entire room went silent. Even Malachi.

When I finally lifted my head, the king was the only one smiling. "You underestimate your own union, child," he said. "This is your duty. You and Malachi will make this happen. This is the sole purpose of this union, so it's in your and your family's best interests to make this happen. Do you understand?"

I forced myself to nod but couldn't stop the way my teeth clenched and my nostrils flared.

Malachi put a hand on my knee, likely in an attempt to stop the rush of anger that was now bubbling to the surface.

His fingers tightened. I sat back in my chair.

"And why me? Why can't you have Adonis marry a human and move to Fearford?" Malachi asked.

This earned a snicker from Adonis, but Malachi shot him a death glare that almost made me shiver.

That shut Adonis up.

"You're the heir to the kingdom, Malachi. Who better to unite our species?"

Malachi snorted, crossing his arms and leaning back in his chair.

Of course, nobody was going to ask my opinion on the matter. I was just the dumb human along for the ride.

"Any questions?" the king asked.

The room was silent. My heart was pounding in my chest, definitely loud enough for all of these annoying fae ears to hear.

"Great," he said. "Then this meeting is over. Malachi, prepare to move to Fearford by the end of the week."

I could barely stand as I followed my husband out of the room. I half-begged my body to hold it together, to wait until we were alone to have a meltdown.

Malachi and I were being sent away to rule human lands. I hadn't decided if this was a death sentence or the best thing that had happened since I married the Prince of Shadows.

# CHAPTER 19
# Malachi

Jade hadn't spoken since we left the court meeting. I made sure to get her out of there as fast as possible once it was over, but she still hadn't uttered a word.

It was concerning.

"You understand what this means, right?" I said after a few minutes of silence. Jade had laid on the bed, staring into the ceiling above her. Completely emotionless.

"I understand," was all she replied.

Her silence was killing me. Couldn't she be angry? Couldn't she come up with some snarky comment or bash my father for such a dumb idea?

Jade sat up, supporting herself on her elbow as she finally looked me in the eyes. "I want to go home," she said.

"Okay," I said carefully. "Once we get to Fearford, it should be easy to—"

"No," she interrupted. "Tonight. I want you to take me home tonight."

"Tonight?" I repeated. The sun was already down. Leaving Rewyth and crossing into the human lands would take weeks of planning, maybe more. Especially without my father knowing. "That's impossible, Jade. We can't just leave."

She stared at me, not even blinking. Not a flicker of emotion crossed her features. Had her cheekbones gotten sharper since she had been here?

"Tonight," she demanded. "Or I won't go to Fearford with you."

I didn't stop myself from laughing that time. "You think you have a choice, Princess? Do you think either of us have a choice?"

She dropped herself from her elbows and fell back on the bed. I stayed where I was with my back against the wall.

"I'm not trying to be an ass," I said as I attempted to quiet my voice.

"Could have fooled me," she mumbled. Whatever fiery spirit she had keeping her emotions locked in was slowly deteriorating. Melancholy began swimming in her features, leaking into her voice.

Saints. I couldn't believe I was actually considering this.

"We can attempt it," I said. "But a single ounce of trouble, and we turn around."

She sat up, head snapping in my direction. "Really?" she asked. I couldn't help but smile at her childlike excitement. How long had it been since I'd felt that?

I tossed my hands up in defeat. "I guess we all have death wishes."

She crawled off the bed and crossed the room within seconds, throwing her arms around my neck. "Thank you, thank you, thank you!" she squeaked. "I'll be very good. I'll listen to everything you say, I promise!"

I lightly wrapped my arms around her, trying not to notice how perfectly her body fit against mine. "You might want to change out of this dress. I'll run it by Serefin. We have a long journey ahead of us tonight if we want to pull this off."

She pulled away too soon. "It'll be worth it," she said as she walked to the bathroom.

I really hoped she was right.

# CHAPTER 20
## Jade

My dark hair paired well with my all-black clothing.

Good. The more we blended into the dark night around us, the better.

My clothes were casual and clung tightly to my body. I strapped my dagger to the outside of my thigh, a perfect position in case I needed it. I didn't think about Malachi. I didn't think about the power that rumbled from him in that room. I didn't think about how afraid everyone was as they stared at him.

Okay, maybe my mind had wandered in that direction a little bit.

And maybe I was confused because I wasn't afraid of him. Malachi, the Prince of Shadows and the killer of hundreds, did not scare me.

Malachi and Serefin were whispering to each other when I emerged from the bathroom, but both of their eyes landed on me as soon as I stepped into sight.

"What?" I asked.

They both responded in unison, "Nothing," before turning back to their hushed conversation.

"You sure you want to do this?" Serefin asked me after a moment. Even in the darkness of the room, I could see the genuine concern in his eyes. Or perhaps he was concerned for himself. Because we were about to directly disobey the king.

"I have to see Tessa," I explained. "I'll be the princess. I'll move to Fearford. I'll do anything you want. I just have to tell Tessa I'm okay first."

He gritted his teeth and passed a look of understanding to Malachi, who merely shrugged.

"Don't look at me," he said. "It was her idea."

I knew Malachi was sticking his neck out for me, but it couldn't be that hard to sneak into the human lands.

He had done it before, after all.

I shook away the memory of seeing him in the forest before our wedding and walked toward them. "Okay, so what's the plan? You have to drug me again so I don't expose all of the mysterious fae secrets?"

Serefin laughed. "Unfortunately for you, we need you conscious this time. We don't have a carriage, and we won't be traveling on main roads. The passageways through the wall can be dangerous. We need you on high alert."

A chill ran down my spine. "What kind of dangers?"

Malachi looked at me and said, "The kind we really hope you never have to see for yourself."

Enough said.

After a few minutes of Mal and Serefin debating which route to take, we were out of the castle and on the road.

Nobody saw us leaving the castle. That was the easy part.

I stared into the dark abyss that surrounded us. The fae had no problem seeing in the dark. To them, this was probably just like looking into the forest during the day.

But to me?

I hated the dark. I had my fair share of lessons learned after the sun had set back home.

But here I was, willingly stepping into it for the sake of my sister.

"You coming?" Malachi whispered. I could barely make out the hand that he held backward, likely after he realized how visually impaired I would be out here.

I accepted it. "Thanks," I mumbled.

"No thanks necessary. The faster we get this over with, the better," he said.

"You really hate humans that much?" I asked.

Malachi huffed. "I don't hate humans, Jade."

I stopped in my tracks. "You're kidding, right?"

Malachi also stopped and turned to face me. "What? You think that because I'm fae I automatically hate all humans?"

"Actually, yes."

Malachi turned back around and tugged me forward with him, nearly causing me to stumble in the darkness.

"I thought you were smarter than that. Not all fae hate humans. Just because you grew up in a place that whispered all the evil doings of fae doesn't mean they're true."

"So, the fae haven't massacred entire towns of people? They haven't used their power to manipulate humans before? I've heard you were involved in quite a few of those doings, dark fae."

Malachi stiffened.

"What's the matter?" I pushed. I knew I should have stopped, but I couldn't help it. He was trying to tell me that all the poverty, pain, and suffering the humans have gone through wasn't because of the fae? "Tell me I'm wrong and I'll shut up. But you can't, because I'm not."

"Do you ever stop talking?" he spat. "Or do you just like the sound of your own voice?"

I was about to demand that he answer my question when Serefin stopped dead in his tracks a few paces ahead.

We had only been walking for an hour at most.

"You hear that?" Serefin whispered.

Malachi's wings tucked even tighter behind his shoulder blades. It was still so dark, but my eyes were beginning to adjust enough so that I could see the figures of both of them standing in front of me.

I tightened my grip on Malachi's hand. He didn't seem to notice.

"Don't say a word," Malachi whispered, barely audible. "And don't let go of me."

I nodded. Fear began creeping into my limps, taking over my heartbeat and pumping adrenaline into every inch of my body. I wanted to reach for my knife, but something told me to stand as still as possible beside Malachi.

So, I did.

Not even two seconds later, trees began rustling to our right. Serefin and Malachi both crouched down in the brush, with Malachi pulling me along with him.

I swallowed the urge to ask Malachi what it was. I was too afraid to speak. But the way every muscle in Malachi's arm tightened told me he was ready for it. He was prepared for a fight.

Two figures stepped into the brush just a few feet away from Serefin. He motioned silently to Malachi, who nodded.

The figures were moving slow. Abnormally slow. Eerily slow.

Malachi turned to face me, almost as if he wanted to say something, but he couldn't. Whatever they were, they were too close to us. They would hear anything he said.

But he didn't turn his head. For the few seconds we were crouched in the brush, Malachi's breath blended with mine. He was close enough that I could see the shadows of his eyelashes. He didn't look away. Neither did I.

Malachi slowly removed his hand from mine, sliding it up my back. We were close enough, even crouched to the ground, that he could wrap his entire arm around me.

Whatever he was doing, I was sure he had a plan. I stayed as still as humanly possible, but I felt like my heart was going to pound out of my chest.

And then one of the creatures shrieked, lunging at Serefin.

Malachi jumped and threw me to the side. I landed hard on the ground a few feet away.

The sound of metal in flesh was the only thing I heard after that.

The entire fight may have lasted ten seconds.

"You okay?" Malachi asked Serefin.

"Yeah, I'm good. But we need to get out of here. Where there's two deadlings, there are more."

"Agreed," Malachi said. He walked back over to me and knelt next to where I was still lying on the forest floor. "Sorry, but I didn't want you caught in the crossfire."

I pushed myself to my feet and brushed the twigs off my pants. "That might be the first time you've ever apologized to me."

I couldn't see Malachi's smile, but I knew it was there. "Then maybe we should run into more deadlings. It brings out my chivalrous side."

My breath caught in my throat. Was he... flirting with me?

Serefin coughed behind us, and we both began walking again.

It wasn't the first time I had been nearly attacked by creatures in the darkness, but as I stepped over the mangled bodies, I had to remind myself to stay calm.

"Saints," I mumbled. "What are those things?"

Dark, skinny figures that almost resembled human children were lying on the forest floor. In the darkness, I even thought I saw fangs.

"Deadlings," Malachi answered. "They're savage creatures that want nothing more than to dig their dirty little teeth into flesh. They've been in these parts for centuries, but they're almost impossible to eradicate."

He said it so casually, like seeing these things was a daily occurrence. It was disturbing, to say the least.

"How many more of these are out there?" I asked.

"Are you referring to the deadlings or to mythical creatures that humans have no clue exist?" Serefin answered.

"Um, both."

Malachi jumped over a massive log, then reached back to help me over it. I nodded my thanks and turned my attention back to Serefin.

He took a deep breath before saying, "There are many creatures in the woods. More than you could likely ever fathom."

"Great," I sighed. "That makes me feel much better."

"It's better if you just don't think about it. The wall isn't just to keep the fae out of the human lands, you know."

"Well, that's probably good considering it doesn't stop you at all."

Serefin laughed.

"Let's keep moving," Malachi interrupted in a voice that made me shiver. "We have a lot of ground to cover before we cross the wall."

# CHAPTER 21
## Malachi

I HAD NO IDEA HOW SEREFIN AND JADE WERE BEING SO CALM.

They were talking and laughing as we walked in the darkness. I couldn't even breathe too loudly. I didn't want to hear the sound of an approaching predator or another creature that lurked in the fae forests.

If we came all this way just for a damned deadling to murder Jade, I was going to be pissed.

"We're approaching the vines," Serefin called back to me.

"The vines?" Jade questioned.

"You'll see," I said to her. Serefin and I now led the way, and I kept my eyes open for the beginning of the massive greenery that would soon make it nearly impossible to walk.

"Are we getting close to the wall?" Jade asked.

"Closer," I replied. "But the wall is covered for its own protection. The forest blocks almost any creature from even being able to lay eyes on it. We'll get as close as we can before we have to fly."

Jade cursed under her breath.

"What?" I teased. "Afraid of heights?"

"Nope," Jade replied. I heard the attitude in her voice. "Just afraid of falling to my death. There's a difference."

Serefin laughed ahead of us.

"Trust me, Princess, I didn't come all this way for you to fall to your death. You have nothing to worry about."

She grunted next to me.

It took us no more than ten minutes before we were jumping over giant vines and weaving through the impossibly thick greenery.

"Alright," Serefin announced. "This is where we begin to climb."

"Climb?" Jade sputtered. Her breathing was heavy, and she propped her hands on her hips while she caught her breath. "You mean we have to climb up these things?"

She looked toward the sky, where the vines crawled and ducked around each other at an incline for as far as we could see.

Although I knew Jade couldn't even see that much in the darkness.

"Yep," I added. "But if you'd like to turn back instead, just let us know."

Jade cocked her head sideways. "I'm ready to climb!" she chirped.

Serefin gave me a sideways look as Jade moved forward and jumped on top of a large vine.

The vines were my favorite place to mess around as a kid. Deep in the forest, this place was a mystical playground. The vines were thick enough to stand on, but one misstep would send you plummeting to the ground below.

I didn't bother telling Jade that part.

"You really think this is a good idea?" Serefin asked me as Jade jumped from one vine to another, slowly beginning the ascension to the massive wall that separated us from the human lands.

"Saints, no," I replied. "But I don't think that's stopping anyone."

"Hey!" she yelled. "Are you boys coming, or are you just planning on sitting back all day while I do this alone?"

Serefin clapped me on the shoulder. "Good luck with that, brother."

I cursed under my breath before following after Jade, easily leaping from vine to vine.

Jade was slower, of course. As fae, Ser and I had an easy advantage. But we slowed our pace down, giving Jade enough space to lead the way.

The vines slowly transformed from large, thick logs to smaller vines. Jade noticed this, too, and began crawling on all fours as she used her hands to swing across.

She didn't look down once.

"You're actually not bad at this, Princess," I commented as she easily leapt from one vine to another.

Jade tossed her hair behind her back and laughed. "Did you expect otherwise, Prince?"

"I can't imagine humans have much experience with foliage like this. Certainly not in that forest of yours."

Jade shook her head. "You have no idea what I've had to do to survive. Hunting in that forest was just the beginning."

I shut up as we moved forward. For whatever reason, thinking of Jade struggling in the human lands put a knot in my stomach. I knew the humans were suffering, but there was more that Jade wasn't telling me. There was more that she wasn't comfortable telling me. And I didn't like that one bit.

Yes, she had to hunt so she wouldn't starve to death. It was messed up that a young woman would have to do something as dangerous as that to feed her family. But from what I had heard, her father was the opposite of help.

Jade's foot slipped, and she let out a scream as her body slammed against the thick vine beneath us.

I jumped forward, easily grabbing her wrist and securing her to the branch. I waited a few seconds before hauling her up to her feet, keeping a hand on her back until she steadied herself.

"Thanks," she breathed, inches from my face.

I smiled. "I think it's about time for you to face your fear of heights, Princess."

"Now? I can't even see the wall yet."

"That's because you're human," Serefin answered from behind me. "You can't see it. It's glamoured."

She lifted her chin. The hands she placed on my shoulders to get her balance remained there. "Fine," she said. "But if you drop me, I'll be pissed."

A small growl escaped me. I couldn't resist. I scooped her in my arms as she secured an arm around my neck. Jade was stiff with nerves, but I couldn't tell if it was from me holding her or from us about to launch into the air.

I hoped it was the latter one.

Serefin jumped first, his wings spreading tightly around him as he navigated his way through the maze of small branches above us.

"Hold on tight, Princess," I breathed into her ear. And then I jumped.

Jade squealed as my wings surrounded us, hauling us higher and higher into the night sky. It was a good thing Jade couldn't see in the dark. Because the wall was tall, and we rarely flew this high.

But she didn't say a word, just buried her head into my neck as Ser and I made the silent ascension into the sky.

The wall was difficult for most people to see, even the fae. The humans, of course, would never be able to find it on their own, and they sure as Saints would never be able to cross it. This wasn't the only way through the wall, but it was the best way to not get caught.

Getting caught wasn't an option. Especially for the Prince of Shadows and his new human wife.

I lost track of how long Serefin and I had been flying. It wasn't long until Ser and I peaked the wall, shimmering in glamour, and began our descent into the human lands.

# CHAPTER 22
# Malachi

I never understood humans. I didn't hate them, but I didn't understand them. I remembered that as we entered Jade's old residence. The smell alone was enough to keep any fae away.

But I didn't tell her that.

She walked in front of Ser and I, just enough that I could watch the bounce in each step as she trotted up the main path to her house. It was dark. Everything was dark, but she didn't need our help to see anymore. Something told me she had likely walked this path at night hundreds of times.

My chest tightened thinking about her walking all alone at night, scavenging for something to feed her sister with. I shook my head. What was I thinking? Jade was perfectly capable of taking care of herself in the human lands.

Saints, she had survived long enough in the fae lands that I was starting to think she could take care of herself there, too.

Jade turned, walking up to the front door of probably the smallest house on the entire path. Not a single light remained on, but I knew it was Jade's house.

One, because her scent still lingered here,

And two, because I hadn't taken my eyes off her that night in the forest until I had watched her get inside.

Something in me wouldn't let me look away.

"Wait here," she demanded as she grabbed the doorknob and pushed it open.

Serefin glanced at me, as if he was wondering whether I would listen to Jade or not.

"I'm staying out here because I want to," I clarified. "Not because she told me to."

"Sure, you are." He stifled a laugh, but we both remained at the front door as Jade closed it behind her.

## JADE

"Tessa?" I whispered into the darkness. The house was just as I remembered it, only with the chill of winter just around the corner, it was much colder. And messier. As if that were possible.

"Tessa?" I asked again, a little louder.

A thump from her bedroom, followed by thudding footsteps on the floor answered me.

"Jade, is that you?" she called out.

I could have dropped to my knees in happiness right then and there. Tessa was still here.

I didn't have time to answer her question before she jumped into my arms, almost tackling me backwards. I hadn't been gone for more than a week, but Saints. Was she getting taller already?

"How are you alive?" she whispered in my embrace. "What happened? Did you get married? How are you here?"

Her questions rambled on in a continuous flow, and I couldn't stop myself from laughing.

"It's not funny!" she replied, finally pulling away. Although I could hear the laughter forming in her words, too. "You better start explaining yourself!"

"Okay, okay," I said. "I'll tell you anything you want to know. Where's Father?"

Tessa rolled her eyes. "I haven't seen him in a couple of days. He'll be back, though. You know how it is."

My heart warmed and tightened at the same time. Tessa was never one to worry about our father's whereabouts. It was always me. But with me gone, she had to step up.

And I hated that. Even though I was so proud of her.

"Who cares about him, though. What about you?"

Tessa grabbed my hand and tugged me back into our bedroom. She sat on the edge of the bed and motioned for me to join her, exactly how we used to sit and exchange stories almost every night growing up.

I guess some things never changed.

I folded my hands in my lap, unsure of where to rest them. I took a deep breath before I said, "I got married. It was giant and beautiful and there were hundreds of fae."

"Tell me everything!" she pushed.

But I knew I couldn't do that. I couldn't tell her how much danger I had been in. I couldn't tell her that I had almost been killed, or that I was risking my life by even being here. She couldn't know.

"It turns out Malachi wasn't the one killing his wives. It was all rumored."

"Malachi," Tessa repeated slowly. I became very aware of how the two fae outside the door were likely listening to every word of this. "Is he nice? Is he handsome? Please tell me he's handsome!"

I laughed, and I was very grateful a wooden door separated Malachi from me. But I wanted Tessa to believe the fairytale. I wanted her to think I was okay.

My cheeks heated as I said, "Oh yes, he's very handsome." Tessa clapped her hands in excitement. "He's tall and has long black hair. And he's strong, one of the strongest fae in the kingdom. He has giant black wings, and he's the only one I've seen with black wings. Everyone else has white or silver. It's amazing."

Tessa was drinking every detail. I didn't care that Malachi was listening to this. All I cared about was making her happy.

"And he protects me. He's the reason I'm still alive."

"Are the other fae nice to you?"

I thought about her question. "Some of them, yes. But some are hard to figure out. Just like humans, I guess."

She nodded. "And they just let you come here? How often can you visit?"

I turned my body to face hers and grabbed her hands in mind. "Here's the thing, Tessa. I'm not sure when I'll be able to come back. Malachi and I have a lot of work to do now, and we might be moving far away from here."

"What? What do you mean? They can't just keep you prisoner, Jade! I need you!"

"I know," I said as I tried to keep my voice from shaking. "But I'll send you money, and I'll try to write you as much as I can."

"No!" she yelled. "No, Jade! You survived. You were supposed to die, and you survived! You should be able to at least visit me!"

Tears welled in my eyes. "Trust me, I want that more than anything in this world."

"GET OFF MY DAMNED PROPERTY!" Our father's voice echoed through the entire house, loud enough that Tessa and I both jumped to our feet and ran to the door.

"Stay here," I demanded, knowing she wouldn't listen as I swung the front door open.

My father, clearly drunk once again, was stumbling up the pathway to our house. Malachi and Serefin didn't even flinch, but in the dim lantern light, I could see Malachi's face. I had seen that look before. He was pissed off.

"I SAID GET!" he yelled again. "You have no business being here!"

"Father, calm down. They're with me," I interrupted. I walked past Serefin and Malachi to stand in between them and my father. Tessa stood still as night in the doorway.

Did he know they were fae? They were using glamour to hide their wings, at least. There was no way it was that obvious.

"I know who they are," he spat. "And I want you to leave. All of you."

I knew he was drunk. I don't even know why I cared. But I clenched my fists at my sides, hard enough that my fingernails could have pierced my skin. "We came to visit Tessa," I said strongly.

Malachi moved behind me, but I didn't take my eyes off my father. My skinny, old, drunken father.

"I don't care why you came back here," he mumbled. "Do you understand me? You aren't one of us any longer. Get back to where you came from."

I couldn't believe he was saying this. Where was the father that nearly begged me to stay not even a week ago?

"Father, I—"

"I DON'T WANT YOU HERE!" he yelled, but he wasn't talking to the fae.

His eyes were locked on mine.

I was too stunned to move. How many times had my father said something like that? How many times had he sworn he hated me or told me to leave this house? His words didn't bother me. They were only a reminder of how much the man could drink.

But now? Every word sliced me like a sword.

"I thought you would be happy to see me," I said. I tried to whisper, but I knew Malachi could hear.

My father laughed. Actually laughed. In fact, he laughed so hard he nearly fell over.

"You're pathetic," he sneered. "You're pathetic, and you're nothing but useless, used garbage—"

The next few moments played out in slow motion. Malachi moved with a flash, fast enough that I couldn't even react before he had my father on the ground, a foot on his chest and a sword at his throat.

"Say that again," Malachi growled at him. I moved to stop him, but Serefin wrapped his arms around me, holding me back.

"Malachi, don't!" I pleaded.

Malachi didn't flinch. He stared at my father, who now cowered on the ground like a child.

"I said, say that again. Tell me that Jade—my wife—is useless, used garbage."

The ground rumbled under my feet. Any glamour he had been using to hide his wings was long gone. His massive, and black feathers towered around him.

My father stammered but said nothing. There was no way he would say a word with Malachi's sword touching his throat.

Tessa's cry of terror filled the air. This finally made Malachi back away, leaving my father panting on the ground in front of us.

I turned and ran to Tessa, surprised that Serefin had let me. "Tessa, don't be—"

"Stop!" she yelled, holding her hands up to stop me. "Don't get any closer!"

"What? Tessa, I—"

"I SAID STOP!" Her voice was filled with fear and something else.

Disgust.

I looked over my shoulder at Malachi, who just stood with a blank face.

"I think you should go," Tessa muttered. I had never heard her use a tone like that. "I think you should go and not come back."

My whole body was shaking. Was she serious? Did she think I was going to hurt her? Did she think they were?

But Tessa's eyes were wild as they darted between Malachi and me. I wanted her to believe she was safe. I wanted her to believe Malachi wouldn't hurt her, that he was just trying to protect me.

How could I explain all of that? Half the things I learned about the fae over the last week would be impossible for her to believe. She was like me. She was stubborn and naïve, and she had grown up believing all the lies about the evil fae who wanted to kill humans.

Plus, she had just seen firsthand how deadly they could be. How deadly the dark fae prince could be.

"Fine," I said after a few moments. "If you really want me to leave, I'll leave."

A sob wrecked through her, and I wanted to wrap her in my arms and never let go.

But instead, I backed away from the door and nodded. If she wanted me gone, I would give her that. I had come here so that she knew I was alive.

I supposed I had at least accomplished that.

"Jade," Malachi's voice boomed behind me. "Let's go."

This time, I listened.

# CHAPTER 23
## Malachi

Nobody had said a word in hours. Serefin didn't speak, but every few paces he shot me a glare. There was no way I was going to apologize to Jade. Not when she was just letting him talk to her that way. Jade was my wife, and her father was nothing more than human scum.

By the time we walked back to my bedroom, the tension was practically dripping from Jade.

"Good luck with that." Ser nodded before I closed the bedroom door.

I stayed there for a second, resting my head against the solid door, before taking a deep breath and mustering the strength to face Jade.

She slapped me straight across the face.

"You selfish, stupid, big-headed son of a bitch!" she sneered. Her face was flushed, and her heart was racing.

Maybe I deserved that. After watching Tessa, the only person Jade truly loved in her life, cower away from Jade, I understood why Jade was pissed at me.

But even so...

"Did you just slap me?" I asked slowly. Her eyes widened, like she just realized the extent of what she had done.

"You deserve far worse," she said, but her words didn't match her actions as she took a step backward. "You shouldn't have done that, Malachi! Saints, what were you thinking?"

"I was thinking your father is an asshole."

"Well, so is yours!" she yelled, "And you don't see me nearly killing him in front of your sister!"

Her face flushed, and her chest rose and fell with every deep pant of breath.

"It wasn't supposed to happen like that," she said, shaking her head in disbelief. "That wasn't supposed to happen."

I couldn't respond. I was watching her unravel completely, but I could do nothing but stand by and watch.

Jade's eyes glossed over. "She hates me. She hates me, and she never wants to see me again."

Because of me. Tessa hated her because of me.

"All I wanted to do was let her know that I was okay," she continued. Her voice had dropped to barely a whisper. "And now she never wants to see me again." Jade stood there, just a few feet away from me, staring at her hands.

I wished I knew what she was thinking. I wished I could fix everything. I really wished I could rip the head off that piece of shit father of hers.

But she was here. I could at least make her think that this place was better than that wretched home of hers.

I don't know what came over me, but the sudden urge to make her smile washed over me.

"Tell me what you want," I whispered, stepping closer to her. "Tell me what you want, and I'll make it happen."

She stared at me with those dark, glossy eyes. As if she couldn't believe what I was saying.

"I want none of this to have happened," she breathed. "I want to be back in bed with Tessa and my drunk father yelling nonsense in the kitchen. I want to be hunting for our food in the forest. I want to be free again," she said. Her voice grew stronger with every word.

"Then be free," I pushed.

"You know I can't." She rolled her eyes. "We both know that."

"But why not? We are about to be the rulers of our own kingdom."

"A kingdom your father, the king, still oversees."

I took a deep breath. "My father has been in charge of me for far too long. I'm not really in the mood to keep answering to him."

"Do you have a choice?" she challenged.

"Don't we all?" I replied.

I wasn't sure when we had gotten so close to each other, but I was standing no more than a few inches away from her. Close enough to smell the cinnamon on her hair. Close enough to see the golden flecks in her eyes.

"This is a chance to get away, Jade. This is our chance at freedom."

She huffed in frustration. "You mean it's your chance? They're never going to stop wanting to kill me, Malachi. They want me dead. Everyone does. And now that I'm the human who married the fae prince, even more people are going to want me dead. Are people even going to accept us as their prince and princess?" She stared at me for a beat longer before looking down and saying, "Saints, I don't even know how to be a princess."

"I guess we haven't really talked about that," I admitted. "I'm sure ruling your own kingdom wasn't in your plans of things to do this week."

She giggled for the first time all day. "No, fighting for my life pretty much took up all my time."

I smiled then, and I wasn't sure if it was because of her words or the familiar spark that had returned to her eyes. "I know you think I'm a monster," I said, "but I don't want us to be enemies."

I fought the urge to step closer to her, to comfort her.

She looked me in the eye and said, "I don't think you're a monster, Malachi."

"I could have ripped his head off," I mumbled. I didn't have to explain who I was talking about.

"I know," she breathed. Had she stepped closer to me?

"Good," I breathed back. Or was that me that stepped closer to her? "I would kill anyone who touches you, Jade. I would end anyone who mistreats you."

My words were harsh, but they were true.

A faint smile spread across her lips. "I know that, too."

"Good," I repeated.

My hand wandered to her bare arm, tracing the skin from her wrist up to her shoulder, then pausing there.

"Do you want to kiss me?" she asked me. Her eyes were wide, but she did not look away. I leaned forward, our lips nearly touching in the dim light of the bedroom. "I can smell lies, Prince," she teased, repeating my words from earlier. "So be careful about what you say next."

A low growl escaped my throat. Jade was testing me, challenging me. And she knew it.

"If I wanted to kiss you, Jade Farrow, I would do it."

"Is that so?" she pushed. "Then why haven't you?"

"You're the one who thinks I'm handsome, protective, kind—" I began repeating from her conversation with her sister.

She punched me in the arm, but I caught her wrist and pulled her body into mine until our chests were touching.

We stayed there for a few moments, our breaths blending, our hearts pounding.

Until I quit resisting, and I gave in to Jade Farrow.

# CHAPTER 24
# Jade

Malachi kissed me like I was the only thing that had ever mattered.

His mouth crashed into mine in a deep, unbreakable hunger.

My body pressed against his, but I still needed more. I needed to feel more of him. He was holding back. I knew him well enough to know that.

I traced my hands up his back, avoiding the large, feathered wings that shadowed around us.

Malachi's arms wrapped around my waist, around my entire body, and pulled me closer to him. Our mouths moved together like they belonged there, like they were destined to be together.

He picked me up in one swift motion and carried me to the bed, leaning over me as he laid me down.

My heart pounded in my chest as he pulled away, just enough to look at me. "I knew you would cave," he said before kissing me again.

I pulled away this time. "Me?" I asked. "Weren't you the one who swore you didn't care about me?"

Our mouths crashed together once more as a laugh rumbled in his chest.

I never wanted this moment to end.

The sound of knocking on Malachi's bedroom door made me freeze.

Although Malachi didn't seem too distracted.

"Go away," he mumbled without taking his mouth from mine. I laughed as I felt the vibrations.

The knocking just repeated. "Malachi, I need to talk to you," Adeline said from the door.

*Shit.*

Malachi's disappointment echoed in his exhale. "Don't think I'll forget about this, Princess," he purred before pulling away, leaving me paralyzed on his bed.

## MALACHI

I cracked the door open just enough to see Adeline's face in the hallway.

And enough to see her eyes darting between me and Jade, who was still lying on the bed.

"What?" I asked. It came out harsher than I meant it to, and it showed on her face.

"Father wants to see you," she said, her eyes darting to Jade and back one more time. "Alone."

I ignored the dread that immediately flooded my stomach.

"Did he say why?" I asked. There was no way he knew we had left. I was careful. Serefin was careful. He had no idea.

"No," she responded. "But he didn't look happy. I would hurry if I were you."

I glanced down the hallway, to where Serefin was usually on guard. "Where's Ser?" I asked.

"He asked to see Serefin, too. He's already there."

Adeline was terrible at hiding her expressions. She always was. I could see the subtle fear all over her face.

"I'll stay with Jade," she added, as if she knew exactly what I was thinking. "We'll be right here the entire time, I swear it."

I took one deep breath, letting go of all the fear that was threatening to take over.

"Fine," I said, stepping back to allow her into the room. "But I don't like this. Not at all."

She shot me a glare that said she didn't, either.

"Adeline?" Jade exclaimed from across the room. "What are you doing here?"

"Don't let her leave your sight," I whispered in my sister's ear before slipping out the door and storming off to find my father.

## JADE

"What was that about?" I asked, sitting up in the bed. Malachi had left the room as fast as he could, leaving Adeline and I alone.

She waved her hand toward the door. "Just politics, I'm sure. He'll be back in just a few minutes."

I shook my head, not entirely convinced.

"Don't think I can't tell what you two were just up to," she said, mischief filling every word. She pranced over and jumped on the bed, lying on her side next to me.

"What are you talking about?"

But I knew what she was talking about. I was certain she could hear my heart racing, even now. I was also sure she could see my ruffled hair, my swollen lips.

Traces of Malachi were all over me.

Adeline just laughed, throwing her head back.

"You humans aren't very good liars," she said. "Did you know that?"

"Oh, shut up!" I joked. "He's my husband, after all. I could think of worse things."

"So, I guess you've changed your mind about him then?"

"Not entirely."

"Mmmmhm," she teased. "I can see that. Why don't you just go ahead and admit that he wasn't as terrible as you had expected?"

"Adeline, he—" I stopped myself before I told her that he had nearly killed my father, and he had certainly terrified my sister enough to never talk to me again. "He still has a temper," I said finally. "And a past. And motives I don't understand."

"We all have ugly pasts, Jade. We've all done ugly things to survive. Even the humans."

Her crystal-blue eyes blared into mine like she knew something more than she was saying.

"That doesn't mean your brother can't be a complete asshole," I added.

"Please," she said. "I would be an idiot if I tried to argue that he wasn't an asshole."

I smiled. "Good, because I really wouldn't believe you if you did."

She moved her body closer to mine and lowered her voice to a whisper, "This might be a bad idea, but do you want to go eavesdrop?"

"On Malachi?"

Adeline nodded in excitement. "Growing up, there was never too much entertainment here in the castle. But Malachi getting his ass handed to him by our father was one of the more common forms of it."

"You can't be serious," I said, but my smile grew.

"Come on!" she said, jumping to her feet. "We have to have at least some fun here, right? And from the look on my father's face, he's really pissed about something."

I had to admit, I was curious as to what had Malachi running out of here so quickly.

"Fine," I said, "but if we get in trouble, I'm blaming you."

"Totally understood." She winked. "I'm used to it, anyway."

Adeline led us out the bedroom door, where two new guards had apparently been waiting.

"Where are you heading?" they asked Adeline without even glancing at me. Classic.

"Official court business," she answered. She flicked her long hair over her shoulder and batted her dark eyelashes.

*Damn*, I thought. Even I would have fallen for that.

The two guards looked at each other and exchanged a knowing glance before looking back at us.

"Fine," they said. "But make it quick."

Adeline strung her fingers through mine and blew a kiss to the guards. "Thank you, gentlemen," she sang.

And continued to prance down the hallway.

"Won't Malachi be mad if he knows we left the room?" I asked. He certainly wasn't happy about us swimming in the lagoon.

"My brother gets mad about everything," she said. "I try not to take any of it personally. Like you said, he's an asshole."

I nodded my agreement as she pulled me around the corner and up a grand, spiral staircase. Just like everything else in the castle, it was covered in vines and greenery. And like every other time we had walked the halls of the castle, the other fae completely avoided eye contact.

"Why don't they look at us?" I whispered. "Nobody ever looks at us when we're walking through this castle."

Adeline gave me a knowing smile. "It's because they know who they'll answer to if we ever find a problem with them."

That made sense. "The king?"

She laughed quietly. "Your husband, princess."

I let her words sink in. Nobody ever looked at us because they were afraid of what Malachi might do?

"If Malachi is so big and tough, why does he let your father boss him around like that?"

Adeline rolled her eyes. "See for yourself."

We turned the corner, and I nearly dropped to my stomach.

Because we were literally on a balcony, overseeing the same meeting room we had all been in yesterday. Malachi was standing in the middle of the room, with the king sitting on his throne like the leader he was.

"Don't worry, they can't see us," she whispered.

"But can't they hear us?"

"Not unless they're trying to. And since they don't know we're here..."

"Fine, fine, fine," I said. "Let's just be quiet."

Adeline nodded and we inched closer to the balcony ledge, hiding ourselves from sight as the king's voice echoed off the walls.

"You didn't seem too pleased about my announcement yesterday," he said.

I couldn't see Malachi, but I could almost picture him rolling his shoulders back and lifting his chin before he responded, "What makes you say that?"

The king laughed. It was low and ugly. The type of laugh that made you want to bite your own tongue.

"I know my own son, and I know when he's not pleased with me."

"Is that not what you want?" Malachi challenged. "Does it not please you to have your own son unhappy?"

"I've done plenty to make you happy, boy. I would remember that before you go mouthing off if I were you."

"Mouthing off?" Malachi laughed. "Is that what this is to you? If I remember correctly, it was you who called me here, Father. If you would like me to leave, then please just say so."

The amount of silence that followed was enough to send chills down my arms. Adeline and I both froze.

"I want to know what was so important that you and your new wife had to leave Rewyth last night," the king finally said.

*Shit.*

Adeline snapped her eyes to me, but I just shook my head.

*Not now.*

"It was personal business for Jade," Malachi replied in a bored tone.

"And what makes you so interested in your wife's personal business?" he asked.

"Probably the fact that she is my *wife*, Father. I made vows to her. And she to I."

"And those vows somehow make you break the treaty we have with the humans?"

Malachi released a long breath. "We did not interfere with the treaty in any—"

"But you did!" the king yelled. Adeline flinched next to me at the sharpness of his voice. "You knew I would not allow you to cross the wall, so you did so without my permission. Is this correct?"

The ground rumbled, or maybe I had imagined it.

"That's correct," he answered after a few painful moments.

Adeline's eyes were wild as they stared into mine. Was this normal for them to be fighting like this? Was the king usually this mad at Malachi?

I wondered how many other times Malachi had snuck into the human lands. And how many times he had gotten caught.

Something told me this wasn't the first time.

"You continue to disobey me after I give you everything. I've given you a life. I've given you a wife. And now I've given you a kingdom. When does it end? When does the disrespect end?"

Malachi took a breath. "I respect you, Father. This has nothing to do with that."

"Doesn't it?" he asked. "I think this has everything to do with respect, son. Your brothers have no problem obeying me. They never have. Perhaps one of them should inherit the kingdom, no?"

"We both know I'm the best one to rule the kingdom," Malachi responded, his temper began to unravel. "I've done everything you've asked of me, Father! You asked me to get married not once but four times, and I obliged happily every time. You ask me to do your dirty work, and again, I oblige. Every. Time. No questions asked. You sit around and use me as your weapon, and I let it happen. Happily. Because you are my father, and you are the king. My wife asked me to go to the human lands, and I obliged, because she is my wife, and she has given up everything to be here with me!"

"Given up? You really think that human scum had a better life in her human lands? This is an honor for her, Malachi. This was an honor for each of them, even if the first three weren't strong enough to survive here!"

"How dare you talk about them that way."

"They are weak! Humans are weak! Has your past not proved that to you enough?"

"You know who killed them," Malachi demanded. "I know you do. You have spies everywhere in this castle. Certainly, you know who is to blame for their deaths."

I froze. Even if we had suspected that the king knew something, it was bold to accuse him this way. Especially when he was already pissed off.

Adeline must have known this too. She reached her hand across to mine and gave me a 'let's go' type of look, but I couldn't move. I couldn't leave without knowing how this conversation ended.

I shook my head at Adeline.

"You accuse me of murder in my own kingdom?" the king asked.

Malachi paused, as if he actually wasn't't sure how to answer for once. "I just want to ensure the safety of my wife. That's all."

"You're willing to do a lot for this girl, Malachi. I have to say I don't like where this is heading."

My heart was pounding in my chest.

"She has nothing to do with this," he responded. "I simply want to know who I can and cannot trust in my own home."

"You still assume the attacks are coming from within the castle?" the king asked. His voice was cold. The fake ignorance made me want to jump down there and kill him myself.

"I don't assume anything," Malachi answered. "But there has been no evidence of break ins from outside the castle, so the obvious answer is that these murderers are from the inside. And I know plenty of people who may want my wives dead."

"Like whom?"

"Like your other sons, for one. I'm sure they don't like seeing me as the heir."

The king laughed again, but it was humorless.

"The rest of my sons have no problem obeying their orders. They know their time is coming. You are supposed to be setting an example, Malachi. Yet for some reason it has been so hard for you to just do as you are told, even with your mother on the line."

This time, Malachi did not respond.

"My punishments for you do not seem to be taking effect. Perhaps we should adjust so you'll learn this time?" the king asked.

Again, Malachi did not respond. Adeline's hand found mine and squeezed. Because we both knew where this was going.

The king turned his attention to the guards. "Go find Malachi's *precious* wife."

# CHAPTER 25
# *Malachi*

Uncontrollable rage pulsed through my body in one second.

Nobody was going to touch Jade.

*Nobody.*

My father sent the guards away, leaving him and I alone in the room.

Except we weren't really alone. The sweet cinnamon scent of Jade's hair hit me as soon as her and Adeline crawled in here.

Not to mention the sound of her heart racing.

I knew she was still on the balcony, listening to every word. But my father didn't know that. For all he knew, Jade was still locked away in my bedroom.

"You really think harming my wife is going to make me obey you?" I challenged. My wings inched wider with every second. A predator's defense.

"I think she is your weakness, Malachi. As every wife of yours has been before this one. When are you going to learn? I've tried to make you learn, I really have. You weren't meant to be like the others. You were meant for power. Can't you see it?"

"Jade is not a weakness." I kept my voice as flat as possible.

My father smirked. "I saw the way you defended her yesterday in the court meeting. Against your own brother, too."

"I was defending myself."

"You lie!" he yelled. "You have grown *soft!* You are not the boy I raised, Malachi. I raised you to be a weapon. A killer!"

I couldn't take any more. I had spent *decades* obeying my father in the hopes that he would eventually tell me where my mother was. I had waited and waited like an idiot. But now he was using Jade was leverage, too?

My blood boiled in my veins.

"You want me to be a killer, Father?" I asked through gritted teeth. My heart pounding was the only thing I could hear. "Then you should have just said so."

One of the guards entered the room, and I didn't hesitate. I flashed across the room, unsheathing my sword and slicing the back of his legs. He dropped to his knees in an instant, and I grabbed him by the hair, exposing his neck.

"Is this what you wanted?" I yelled at my father. "You want me to be tough?"

My father's eyes widened, just slightly. Enough to let me know that he hadn't expected that.

Good.

Because he underestimated me. He *always* underestimated me.

"Malachi, I—"

I sliced the guard's throat before he could finish objecting.

"Is that enough for you, Father? Is this the man you always hoped I would be?"

"Control yourself," he boomed. "Or there will be consequences."

"I'm tired of controlling myself, Father. I'm tired of being told what to do. You want me to be powerful? You want me to be the Prince of Shadows that everyone has hoped for? Then fine."

I stepped over the body in front of me, heading toward my father. Ready to fight him if I needed to. Ready to defend myself and my wife from this monster.

I *was* tired of controlling myself. I was sick of it all. My power rumbled through my body. My wings sent shadows across the floor, a reminder of how strong I really was.

How *powerful* I really was.

*The Prince of Shadows.*

"I wouldn't do that if I were you," my father said in a rushed voice. He held his hands out in front of him, as if that would stop me.

As if *anything* could stop me.

"And why is that?"

His eyes moved from me to something behind me.

I turned to see what he was looking at, and my stomach dropped.

Two guards dragged Jade into the room and threw her to her knees in front of me.

# CHAPTER 26
## Jade

"DON'T HURT HER," MALACHI SEETHED. "IF YOU EVEN THINK ABOUT touching her, I'll kill all of you." The power in his voice boomed across the room, but the guards didn't budge.

I should have been ready. How stupid was I to think sneaking around the castle was safe for me?

Adeline had tried to fight them, but it was no use. The guards had trained every single day for combat.

A female fae was no match.

She could do nothing but watch as they dragged me away.

"Malachi, I'm okay," I said to him. But I knew he would do anything to protect me.

I also knew this was a test. The king was testing Malachi to see exactly how far he would go.

All for me.

"You claim she's so important to you, Malachi. If you disobey me, she'll get hurt. And you'll never find your mother. Do you understand?"

Malachi's hands were fists at his side. The fact that his father pushed him this far was astonishing to me. Did he not think Malachi could kill him?

*Would* Malachi kill him? Was he capable of killing his own father?

My eyes darted to the body on the floor just a few feet away. Fresh blood pooled around it, slowly leaking onto the stone floor.

"I understand," he said through gritted teeth, but the darkness in his eyes said something else. They promised retribution. They promised death.

"Good," his father said. I let out a breath I didn't know I was holding. "But just in case..."

Blinding pain splintered across my back. I gasped for air, but my lungs were frozen. I fell forward, catching myself with my hands before another lash of pain whipped through me.

"Enough!" Malachi yelled. He moved to attack the guards behind me, but his father stepped between them.

Pain was pulsing through me. I could hardly keep my eyes open, but I heard the king say, "Take her and go. I can't even look at you right now."

And then Malachi was next to me, lifting me, darkness swarming all around us. Malachi was whispering something, and then we were moving, but I couldn't stay awake any longer. Pain was splintering through me with every ragged breath that hit my lungs. And I was tired. So incredibly tired.

Malachi's wings spreading around us was the last thing I saw.

# CHAPTER 27
# Malachi

THE ONLY THING THAT WAS STOPPING ME FROM RIPPING MY OWN father's head off was Jade.

I had to get her to safety. I had to get her out of here.

And then I would come back and kill every single one of them.

"Stay with me," I repeated. "Don't fall asleep. Stay awake, Jade. Come on," I urged as I ran down the hallway.

Serefin was waiting outside my room, and his wings immediately flexed at the sight of Jade in my arms.

"What happened?" he asked. I rushed past him and into my bedroom. He followed close behind me.

"We're getting out of here," I said, lying Jade down on the bed. Her eyes flickered open, but they shut again without coming into focus.

She didn't resist as I rolled her to her stomach and ripped the torn shirt away from her sliced skin.

"Saints," Serefin exclaimed. We both froze, just for a moment, as the reality of what had just happened sunk in.

My father's guards had whipped Jade.

And they were still living.

My power flared, and the floor rumbled under my feet.

"Go find Adeline," I demanded to Ser. "Bring her here and tell her it's an emergency. Don't say anything else."

Serefin left without another word.

I surveyed Jade's back. The two lashes were bleeding, but they weren't too deep. It would still take days to begin healing without any help, especially for a human.

I couldn't believe I'd let this happen. Jade wasn't supposed to get hurt.

She was alive, but at what cost?

Were we supposed to continue living in fear, doing whatever my father commanded?

*No.* I was done with it. I was done with this life. We were getting out of here.

I picked up Jade's hair and moved it away from her tear-stained face. "Just hang on a little longer," I whispered. "We're getting out of here. Tonight."

Serefin opened the door, and Adeline pushed past him, "What in the Saints happened?" she yelled. "Is Jade—" She froze in her tracks when she saw her on the bed. "Is she...?"

"Still breathing. For now," I responded.

Anger flashed across her face. She moved to my bathroom, grabbing a cloth and running the water.

"What do you need?" Serefin asked me. "What can we do?"

"You can start by killing my father."

Serefin paused. It was dangerous to talk this way in the castle. People were sentenced to death for treason for far less.

And my father clearly had it out for me. And my wife.

Adeline returned to the room and began cleaning the blood from Jade's back.

"We're leaving," I whispered to Ser. "Tonight. As soon as Jade can walk, we're out of here. I don't care if I have to carry her the whole way."

"To go where? Fearford?"

I nodded. "I can't think of a better place. At least we'll be away from here. My father's uncontrollable. He wants me to suffer, and he'll do whatever it takes to obtain that."

"You think he'll kill Jade?"

I shook my head. "I don't think there's any limit to what he'll do to punish me. He knows we crossed the wall to the human lands, and he knows he can hold Jade over my head. He probably has spies in this castle tracking our every move."

"But you think you'll be safe traveling to Fearford? You need guards, Malachi. You need food and shelter and a planned route. That's days of travel, maybe more. Jade won't be able to make the trip with an injury on her back like that."

I ran my hands through my hair, pacing the room. I was desperate. I hated that I couldn't control this. Every day that Jade stayed here was another day that we risked her life.

I was no longer willing to put her life at risk.

"Fine," Serefin sighed, like he knew what I was thinking. "But I'm coming with you."

My head snapped in his direction. Serefin was loyal, I knew that much. But this would be considered treason, even if he was simply assisting me in my journey to Fearford.

I nodded. "We leave before the morning. Adeline, get her cleaned up as well as you can. I don't want any infections."

Adeline nodded without looking away from her work. Her eyes welled with tears as she stared down at Jade. Adeline would be able to heal her wound enough for travel. That was at least one small perk of being in fae lands.

I placed a hand on my sister's shoulder. "Thank you," I whispered. "And thank you for being kind to Jade. I know she appreciated it."

Adeline shook her head and tears fell down her cheeks. "I didn't mean for any of this to happen. I just want a normal family, Mal. This is so messed up. Jade was... different. She didn't deserve any of this."

"I know."

Adeline looked at me with pure determination in her eyes. "You'd better take her far away from here, Mal. And don't let those bastards lay another finger on what's yours."

# CHAPTER 28
# *Jade*

"CAN YOU STAND UP?" MALACHI WHISPERED. EVERYTHING HURT, BUT he had an urgency in his voice that told me to push past it.

Adeline sensed it, stating, "Don't push her, Mal. Maybe you should wait until—"

"No," I interrupted. "I'm fine. Really."

I placed my feet on the ground and stood up, feeling the shooting pain of ripped skin on my back.

Adeline had wrapped me in bandages and given me a new shirt. My last one had been torn from my body in shreds.

Malachi's hand was at my waist. "Only if you're ready," he said.

I saw the pain that flickered through his features as he surveyed my body. He was blaming himself for this.

He would have killed them all if it weren't for me. I knew that too.

"I'll make sure the coast is clear," Adeline announced before taking off with Serefin, leaving Mal and I alone in the room.

"I'm so sorry Jade," he said. "I swore to protect you, and I failed. I failed you, and I'm sorry."

"Don't talk like that," I chided. I moved my hand to the back of his neck and rested my forehead against his. I didn't care that it was an intimate touch, nor that I was nearly on his lap at this point. "We're in this together, Malachi. And I don't blame you for your shit family. You can't control that."

He shook his head, not looking me in the eyes. "You shouldn't have to put up with this, Jade. Any of this."

"Neither should you." I moved my hand to the side of his face and forced him to look at me. "But there's nothing we can do about it now, Malachi. Your father is uncontrollable. Let's get the Saints out of here before he changes his mind about letting us go."

He nodded in understanding and helped me stand up, careful about not touching the bandages on my back.

I hissed in pain and squinted as my vision blurred, but I kept moving. If we stayed, it would be a death sentence. For both of us.

"Serefin and Adeline are coming with us?" I asked.

Malachi smiled. "It would be impossible to keep them away."

"Loyal sons of bitches," I joked. "At least we'll have backup."

A few minutes later, we were outside of the castle near the horse stables.

"Can you ride?" Malachi asked. I nodded, knowing damn well I had never ridden a horse before. But we were desperate. And it couldn't be that hard, right?

Serefin and Adeline were strapping bags of food onto their own horses.

"Are you sure about that?" he pressed. "Because you look nervous."

"I'm nervous because we're about to go on a multiple-day trek to a kingdom we've never stepped foot in. A kingdom that may want us dead. All while running from a king who may or may not want us dead, as well."

Malachi scoffed. "That's nothing, Princess. Piece of cake."

We walked over to a massive white horse. Easily the biggest horse I had ever seen, but it's not like we had many horses back home.

"Alright," Mal started. "Hop on."

It was a test to see if I actually knew how to ride. He stood with his arms crossed, watching me expectantly.

I rolled my eyes and moved to grab the saddle, ignoring the screaming pain that followed every movement. I placed my foot in the stirrup that was nearly as high as my hip.

And I stopped. What the Saints was I thinking? I couldn't ride a horse. I couldn't even get on a horse. Even if I was completely healthy and my back didn't have gaping wounds, this would be a near impossible task.

Plus, I would just slow us down.

"Something wrong, Princess?" he asked, raising an eyebrow.

"Oh, shut up," I scoffed, brushing his shoulder with my own as I walked past him to the horse he had claimed as his own.

Malachi laughed quietly. "It's not a bad thing to admit you need some help," he teased.

"Perhaps you should take your own advice."

Malachi ignored my comment but gripped my waist lightly, helping me onto the saddle. His hands lingered for a moment as I settled in, adjusting the seat, before he hauled himself on the saddle behind me.

"Remind me why we can't just fly there with all of your wings and magic?" I asked.

"It's a three-day trip, and we might need our strength when we reach Fearford. We have no idea what's waiting for us there. Plus, Adeline's wings aren't as strong as ours. We'll be faster on horses."

I pretended not to notice the feeling of our bodies pressed together. Malachi was my husband. This shouldn't be weird... right? He had likely done this before with dozens of people. This was nothing.

My body was stiff. I tried to keep as much distance between us as possible, but as soon as the horse started moving toward Serefin and Adeline, my back couldn't take it.

"I don't bite," Malachi whispered in my ear. He was close enough to feel the chill that jolted down my spine, but he didn't acknowledge that.

Normally, I would have fought him. But I was exhausted. And in pain. Plus, Malachi was a warm, safe surface behind me.

So, I let myself relax with every step of the horse.

"We're getting out of here, Princess," Malachi whispered after a few minutes. I couldn't tell if he was talking to me or to himself. "And let's pray we don't have to come back."

# CHAPTER 29
# Malachi

JADE FOUGHT TO STAY AWAKE. SHE DIDN'T HAVE TO SAY IT. I COULD feel her body needing more and more support as we rode in silence for hours.

"We need a break," I announced to Ser and Adeline. "Jade won't be able to ride much longer."

She attempted to lift her head when she heard her name but quickly let it fall back on my shoulder.

"This should be a good enough spot for the night," Serefin said. "As long as we keep away from the main path and stay alert."

Adeline agreed, and the three of us steered our horses through a small clearing in the thick forest.

It eased my mind that there were so many dangers out here. It would prevent any spies from following us.

The ones that wanted to live, anyway.

"Where are we?" Jade asked as soon as the horse stopped moving.

"We're stopping here for the night. You need rest, and Adeline can check your wounds."

Adeline jumped off her horse and hurried over to us so she could help Jade. She grumbled something of a response, but we ignored her as she slid off the saddle.

"You really think this is a good idea?" Adeline whispered.

I shrugged. "If you have any other ideas, I'm all ears."

My sister stared at me for a second before helping Jade to a small log. Serefin was already busy with a fire. It was risky, and he knew that. But Jade wasn't going to make the journey if she was injured, hungry, and freezing.

## JADE

Tessa held my hand as we walked through the field of flowers.

"You're leaving me?" she asked.

I shook my head. "Never, bug. I'll never leave you. You know that."

She smiled and kicked the tall grass ahead of her. "Good. I don't know what I would do without you."

My sister was beautiful. She had always been the better looking of us two. Her long brown hair stopped at her waist, and her tan skin glistened under the sun as she knelt down to pick up a flower.

"You know he's coming for you, right?" she asked.

I eyed my sister carefully. "Who is, Tessa? What do you mean?"

"You don't have much time."

"What are you talking about?"

She stood up to hand me the flower that she had plucked from the ground.

Except she wasn't holding a flower anymore.

Her hands were cupped in front of her, and they were covered in blood.

"Tessa!" I yelled. I closed the gap between us as she dropped to her knees. "What's wrong? Are you hurt?"

But Tessa didn't respond. She looked at me with a blank face. Her big, beautiful eyes were empty, gone somewhere I could never follow.

"Tessa!" I yelled, shaking her hands. "Tessa!"

But it was too late. Tears ran down my face as I screamed her name again and again. I had to get her home. If I could just get her home, someone could help us.

I picked her up and began walking, but the field of flowers had been replaced by an endless body of water, growing deeper and deeper with each passing second.

"No!" I yelled. "NO!" I used all of my energy to keep us above the water, but it was rising too quickly. The ground under my feet disappeared completely, leaving my sister and I in the water.

Leaving us both to die.

My limbs were burning. My lungs were on fire. I held on as long as I could for Tessa's sake.

But it would never be long enough.

"Jade, wake up," Malachi whispered. He shook my shoulders lightly, and I was no longer on a horse. I was lying on a blanket on the forest floor. "Jade," he repeated.

"What's going on?" I asked. "Where are we?"

I sat up and took in as much as I could. I wasn't in water. Tessa wasn't here. All three horses were with us, but Adeline and Serefin were gone. Malachi and I were alone, and the sun was rising.

"You've been sleeping for a few hours. We took a break so you could rest."

I nodded, unsure whether I could trust myself to say anything else.

Malachi eyed me carefully. "What were you dreaming about?" he asked.

I squeezed my eyes shut and tried to forget. Tessa was fine. She was home, safe with my father. Nothing was going to happen to her. But when I opened my eyes, Malachi's eyes were still locked into mine.

"Nothing," I answered. "It was nothing."

"It was Tessa, wasn't it?"

I pulled my knees to my chest and ran my hands over my face. I couldn't afford to think about her right now. Not when so much was already at risk.

My lips cracked as I spoke, "Where are the others?"

"They went to scout the path ahead, but they haven't come back yet."

He sounded confident, but concern was darkening his features as he glanced between me and the forest path. "I think I'm going to go check it out and make sure everything's okay."

I sat up, ready to stand and follow him.

"No, no, no," he insisted, stopping me with a hand on my shoulder. "You should stay here. You're too weak to move, and it's safer for you here. You have your knife, right?"

I nodded and reached for the knife that was still strapped to my body.

"Good. Use it if you need to. And Saints, Jade," he said in a voice that put a knot in my stomach, "please do not leave."

My voice was breathless as I responded, "I won't. I promise."

Malachi squinted, like he was deciding whether going after the others was going to be worth it.

"Go," I insisted. "I'll be right here when you get back."

Without another word, he stood and stormed off, leaving me alone in the forest.

The brutal stinging sensation in my back had faded to a dull throbbing, but it was a pain that radiated through my entire body.

I sat up and reached for a loaf of bread that had been left out. I ripped off a piece and chewed it slowly, thinking about all the times I had shared a loaf like this with Tessa.

*Tessa*. My stomach dropped at the memory, and I nearly gagged on my food.

She would come around. I would see her again. I *had* to see her again. As soon as she figured out that she would always be safe with Malachi, she would understand.

Tears threatened my eyes. I was absolutely exhausted. And now here I was, in the middle of the forest, all alone, heading to rule over human lands with the dark fae prince. Things were just going to get worse from here. We were nowhere near the finish line.

I couldn't help but smile at the way Malachi had defended me. All this time I had assumed he wanted me alive to prove a point to his father or to use me as a way of drawing out his enemies from the castle, but I was starting to believe it was more than that. Malachi was more than the Prince of Shadows I had been forced to marry. Over the past few weeks, he had turned into something more. Somewhere in the dark nights and the lonely glances, I had seen a version of Malachi I never expected.

And I didn't hate it.

I shook my head. I couldn't think about that stuff right now. I couldn't think about Malachi in any other way than as the Prince of Shadows.

Saints. He was my *husband*. Perhaps it wasn't entirely uncalled for if I thought about him that way.

The morning passed painfully slowly. I tried to catch up on sleep, but my mind raced through every detail I could remember from the day before. If Malachi thought we were safest in Fearford, then I had good reason to trust him. But hiding in the place that his father told us to go? It didn't make much sense to me.

What was stopping his father from marching straight there and finishing what he started?

Footsteps in the distance caught my attention. "Malachi?" I asked quietly. "Is that you?"

The footsteps continued approaching, but Malachi never responded.

My instincts kicked in. I reached for the knife at my thigh and crouched behind one of the large trees around us. My heart was racing, fueling my body with adrenaline with each passing second.

Who would be out here? Who would know where to find us? Granted, I had been asleep for most of the journey so far, but I was sure the three fae would have noticed if someone was following us.

Perhaps it was just a traveler or someone passing through.

I didn't loosen my grip on my knife. Not when the footsteps were approaching quicker.

And it sounded like more than one person.

I wanted to call out for Malachi, but it would be a dead giveaway of my hiding spot. Although when our visitors found the camp, it wasn't going to take them long to find me, as well.

"Jade," a male voice cooed in the silence of the forest. Not Malachi and not Serefin.

But I had heard that voice before.

It was Lucien.

"Come out, come out, wherever you are," he continued.

Saints. If Malachi's brothers were here for us, for *me*, it wasn't good. Especially after we left so abruptly. Had their father sent them to finally kill me off? Had we finally pushed him over the edge?

"I can hear your heart beating, Princess," another male voice added. Adonis. I would recognize that cold voice anywhere. "Come on, we won't hurt you."

*Lies.*

I didn't move a muscle. Not like it was going to help, though. Not if they could hear my heart beating. Not if they could smell the blood from my open wounds.

I was about to lunge out from my hiding space and slice my knife towards Lucien's head when a pair of hands grabbed me from behind, shoving me into the ground.

"You really thought you could hide from us?" one of the twins laughed. Saints. All four brothers had come for me.

And here we were.

I struggled under the cold grasp of the twins, but it was no use. Eli easily twisted the knife from my grasp. Even if I was completely healthy, it wouldn't have been a fight. I was an injured female human up against four strong, healthy fae males.

The fight was already over.

"What do you want?" I hissed. The twins picked me up and carried me to the center of our camp, where Adonis and Lucien were waiting expectantly.

If Malachi didn't kill these bastards, I was going to do it myself. If I survived whatever this was, of course.

Adonis walked over and knelt next to me, tucking a piece of my hair behind my ear. I flinched away in disgust, which only made him laugh.

"We hate to break up this fun little trip of yours, Princess, but you're going to come with us."

"What's going on?" I asked. "What did you do with Malachi?"

"Your friends are fine for now," Lucien responded. "Although they aren't going to be too happy when they come back and you're gone. Which is kind of the point."

I took a deep breath, trying to weigh my options. My back was now screaming with pain, the wounds ripped open during my struggle.

"He'll kill you," I grunted. "He'll hunt you down and kill you."

"Oh, we know he'll come for you, Princess. That's the whole point. Plus, we couldn't turn down some quality time with our dear sister, right guys?" Adonis said. The others muttered agreements.

I couldn't believe I had been so stupid as to believe we would be safe. Of course the king wasn't just going to let us leave. He had no intention of letting us make it all the way to Fearford.

I didn't speak as the brothers tied my hands behind my body. They didn't have any horses with them, which meant they had either walked all the way here or flown. I was guessing the latter.

The thought alone made my stomach drop.

"Ready to get out of here, dear sister?" Adonis asked, walking toward me.

I shook my head and spit in his face, anger flooding my body. He was going to take me out of here. He was going to take me far away from anywhere Malachi could find me.

He would have no idea where I went. He would have no idea what happened.

But I had no choice. I had to stay alive. That was all I had to focus on.

Adonis laughed and wiped his face clean. "You want to play dirty?" he asked. He wrapped his arms around me and jumped into the sky without waiting another second. I sucked in a sharp breath. "What?" he taunted. "Afraid I'll drop you?"

Once we were just above the tree line, Adonis did just that. I couldn't stop the scream of terror that escaped me as I left his arms, plummeting to the ground.

Except Lucien caught me before I could hit the grass, flying me back up into the sky with a wicked, satisfied laughter.

Fury, terror, and hatred were swarming my mind. I couldn't think straight. Not when my heart was racing so quickly. Not when I could die at any moment. These brothers didn't care if I lived or died. All they cared about was hating Malachi. And I was a perfect accessory.

I didn't cry. I wasn't going to give them that satisfaction. I spent the next few minutes thinking about every single way Malachi was going to torture these idiots as we flew.

And kept flying. And kept flying.

# CHAPTER 30
# *Jade*

THEY DIDN'T TAKE ME BACK TO THE COMPOUND.

After what felt like hours of lying in Lucien's arms, we eventually landed in what appeared to be some sort of ancient ruins. I had no idea how far we were from Malachi, nor how he would find me.

But I couldn't think about that right now. I had to focus on surviving. Keep myself alive, and the rest would come later.

*If there was a later.*

"Here we are, Princess," Lucien sang as he dropped me onto the concrete ground. The structure wasn't complete, and four partially crumbling walls surrounded us.

I ignored the pain from the wounds on my back and scrambled to my feet. Dread filled my stomach. "Where are we? What are we doing here?"

The twins whispered something to each other before they turned around and left, leaving Lucien, Adonis, and I in the abandoned structure. "So many questions, Princess. All you need to do is sit tight and look pretty. We'll handle the rest," Adonis said.

"What does your father want with Malachi?" I asked. My voice shook, but I didn't look away.

"He wants what we all want, Princess. He wants Malachi to step in line."

I scoffed. "You're all just jealous of him. You'll never be a better leader than Malachi. It's not possible."

"Watch what you say. Wouldn't want you getting hurt before your big, bad husband has time to come watch," Lucien snarled.

My stomach dropped. Adonis grabbed my arm and roughly dragged me to the corner of the abandoned building, shoving me onto the ground. "Sit here and don't move a muscle. If you try anything stupid, Lucien here will kill you. And he'll enjoy doing it."

One look at Lucien, who was lounging against the crumbling wall across the structure, told me Adonis was telling the truth.

"You're the ones who tried to kill me the night of the wedding, aren't you?" I demanded.

Adonis laughed. "Come on, Princess. Who else would want Malachi's wives dead?"

I couldn't say I was surprised. "You would do that to your own brother? Why?"

Lucien and Adonis exchanged a glance. "Malachi is no brother of ours."

"But why? What has he ever done to you?"

Lucien pushed himself off the wall and stalked over to me. I tried not to cower away from his fast approach.

"Malachi has been the golden boy of Rewyth for as long as we can remember. It all started with those damned black wings. He's always thought to be better than us. He was always our father's favorite. Our father sent him on every mission, every political tour. He was feared by everyone. And for good reason."

I straightened, trying not to look surprised. "But what does that have to do with you?"

Adonis huffed. "You really don't get it, do you? You humans are so stupid. It's no wonder you can hardly feed yourselves."

I bit my tongue.

"Malachi has it all," Lucien continued. "Yet he thinks our father is cruel and unfair. What's unfair is how spoiled he's been. He's the oldest. The strongest. His power is so rare, he's known across kingdoms. It isn't fair, Jade. We're done with it."

"And your father just allows this to happen?"

"Our father would never publicly denounce Malachi. He knows Malachi could kill him if he really wanted to. It's a balance of power. Make Malachi strong enough to be useful, but keep him weak enough to stay submissive."

My body was shaking. I couldn't believe they were admitting this to me now after all this time.

But it made sense. Malachi had mentioned doing work for his father a few times. He was obviously powerful enough to kill anyone who threatened him, yet he let his father live.

All because his father kept him weak.

And his brothers had been helping him.

Malachi was right to not trust them. How did I not see this coming? Malachi had practically admitted that his brothers hated him. I should have paid more attention.

"He'll kill you," I spat. "He'll kill every single one of you for this. You know that."

Lucien tossed his head back and laughed. A cold laughter, the kind that sent a chill down my spine. "He can try. He's sure tried before. But at the end of the day, Malachi isn't as tough as he looks. That's his weakness, Princess. He cares too much."

"About who? *You?* I seriously doubt that."

Lucien's smile turned to a growl. "You humans all think you're so smart. You know nothing. You've known Malachi for weeks, but I've lived with him for decades. I've seen him kill. I've seen him slaughter entire villages. But at the end of the day, we're his family. We're the only ones who have been here when everyone else turns their back on him."

Now it was my turn to laugh. "You really think you have his back? This is your version of family?"

"And what would you know about family?" he retorted.

I tightened my jaw. "I know enough."

He smiled again and said, "Of course you do, Princess. Why don't you do us both a favor and just be quiet for now."

"What are we waiting for?"

He took a second before responding, "We're waiting for somebody important."

# CHAPTER 31
# Malachi

**Something was wrong.**

I tracked Serefin and Adeline for miles until I found them both at what looked like another campsite.

"What's going on?" I asked them. "I thought you both were dead. You were supposed to be back by now."

"Check this out," Adeline said, gesturing to the site. "Somebody's been here. Recently, too."

The hair on my neck stood up. "Who?"

Serefin sighed and answered, "We can't tell. No markings anywhere, no personal belongings. Just this leftover fire and the blanket."

I surveyed the area around us. We were pretty far from our own campsite. It could have just been a coincidence.

But this far into the forest?

My hand moved to the pommel of my sword strapped to my hip. "Adeline, come with me to get Jade. Serefin, stay here for another hour, and if nobody shows up, come find us. Let's hope these people are smart enough to leave us alone."

"What do you want me to do if they come back?" Serefin asked.

"If they're simple travelers, let them go."

I clenched my jaw and let my mind wander to what could happen if we were found. What if my father had sent people after us? What if there was a bounty on Jade's head?

"And if they're looking for us, kill them all."

I knew Serefin understood. He would do whatever it took to keep us safe.

He nodded, and Adeline and I turned to head back to our campsite. She followed behind me without saying a single word.

"You can tell me what you're thinking, you know," I said after a few minutes.

She exhaled a large breath. "I'm just worried. I hope you have a plan for all of this, Mal. The humans won't be welcoming of us."

"They'll be welcoming of Jade. She's one of them."

"Not anymore. She's your wife. She's made an alliance with the enemy. They'll hate her just as much as they hate us."

Adeline had a point, but it wasn't something I had time to worry about. Jade in the human lands was far safer than Jade in the fae lands. Adeline, Serefin, and I could take care of ourselves.

"We'll figure something out," I said.

She went back to silence, step after step, for nearly the entire walk back to our campsite. It would have been quicker to fly, but flying over the trees would draw attention to anyone around us.

We'd had enough of that already.

"What about your mother?" she asked.

The words rumbled through me. "What are you talking about?"

"You know damn well what I'm talking about, Mal. Father has been keeping her whereabouts hidden from you. Are you just going to give up? Are you leaving here for good?"

I shook my head and clenched my fists. "I can't keep holding onto something that isn't real, Adeline. I don't even know if she's alive. For all I know, he's been lying to me this whole time."

She nodded in agreement. "As long as you're okay with it."

"I can't keep worrying about everyone else. It has to end at some point."

"You're right."

I crossed the last few steps to our campsite and stopped dead in my tracks.

"What is it?" Adeline asked. "What's wrong?"

"Someone's been here," I said. I could smell the presence of multiple fae.

My brothers.

A growl escaped me, my power rumbling through my body and pulsing at my fingertips.

"They took Jade," I seethed. "They took her."

Adeline immediately ran around the campsite, checking for any signs of her. But I already knew what happened.

Just when we thought we were free, my father had sent them to kill her.

"I'll kill them," I promised Adeline. I didn't recognize my own voice. I didn't care. "I'll kill every single one of them if I have to. They're not getting away with this again."

Adeline looked at me with a fierceness I had never seen from her before. "We have to find her," she said. "We find them, and we get Jade back."

## CHAPTER 32

# Jade

My consciousness was fading. I had to stay awake. Just a little longer, and they would find me. They had to find me.

I had no choice.

Lucien threw a small rock in my direction, making me snap back to my surroundings.

"Wakey, wakey, Princess," he teased. "If you fall asleep, you might miss all the fun."

My head rested on the stone wall behind me. "You say that as if spending this time with you isn't the highlight of my night."

Lucien stepped closer. "I've always envied Malachi and his wives, you know."

"Really? You don't quite strike me as the marriage type," I joked. Every word took more energy than I had left.

"You flatter me," he responded, still stepping closer with each tiny, torturous step.

I glanced around. Surely there was some way to escape. Some way to defend myself. But aside from a few rocks, there was nothing.

When I got out of here, I was sure as Saints going to learn how to fight.

"Something wrong?" Lucien asked. "I can hear your heartrate increasing."

"Just thinking about all the things Mal will do to you when he finds us. It really gets me excited," I responded. I meant for the words to sound strong and sassy, but they were hardly audible. I was too weak.

Lucien took another step, just an arm's length away from where I sat on the floor, and knelt down. His sharp ears and bright silver wings blocked my vision from anything but him.

"Did you think you would be different?" Lucien asked. "Did you think you would be the one human to survive?"

With Lucien this close to my face, I could have sworn I saw fangs.

"That was the plan," I spat.

Lucien smirked. "You really think you can survive against us? Against me?"

I rolled my eyes. "It would have been a lot easier if you weren't all giant assholes."

Lucien didn't laugh this time. "How about this, Princess. I'll untie you and I'll give you a head start. You can run as far as your little human legs can carry you, but I'll still find you. Because you're just a human. You're prey. Do you understand that?"

Now my heart really was racing. But I didn't say a word. I lifted my chin, staring Lucien directly in the eye.

"Killing you will be fun. Hunting you will be even more thrilling," he growled before ripping the ropes off my arms with a single movement. "Better get going, Princess. The clock's ticking."

I waited another second, just to make sure this wasn't some sort of sick ploy to kill me even sooner. But Lucien just waited for me to move.

So, with all the energy I had left, I climbed to my feet and bolted.

# CHAPTER 33
# *Jade*

I RAN UNTIL THE BOTTOMS OF MY FEET BLED ON THE FOREST FLOOR.

Dying hadn't been something I was necessarily afraid of. Even when I left to marry Malachi, I wasn't afraid of dying.

But somehow, this was different. In the weeks I had spent here in Rewyth, something changed. I no longer felt content at the idea.

I had to survive, and it wasn't just for my sister. It was for myself.

I stopped running and dropped to my knees. Who was I kidding? If Lucien wanted to find me, he would. Running like the dumb human I was wasn't going to stop anyone.

Malachi *had* to find me. They *had* to be close. I could feel it.

And that was my only chance at living to see another day.

My breathing was loud, and my heart raced in my ears. I hadn't run like this in ages. I hadn't *run away* from something in ages. I had typically been the stand and fight type of girl.

But that was the reckless version of me. That was the version of me who didn't care what happened to her.

Footsteps crunched on the dead leaves to my left.

But I was out of fuel. My feet were numb from the pain. My mouth was cotton dry, and the healing wound on my back had split open.

I rubbed the sweat and tears from my face with my dirty hands. If these bastards were going to kill me, I couldn't do a single damn thing to stop them.

"Come here," a voice said. But it wasn't Lucien. It was a woman.

I snapped my head in her direction and was surprised to see a middle-aged woman, also barefoot, summoning me.

"What?" I breathed. "Who are you?"

She shook her head. "It doesn't matter. I'll tell you all that later, darling. I know where Malachi is. You have to follow me if you want to live."

She smiled as she spoke, as if she were happy to see me for some reason.

Frankly, I didn't care. I was out of options.

I flinched as I stood, and the woman took my hand in hers. Warmth radiated from her. A long braid fell down the middle of her back.

"Where are we going?" I asked.

"Not much further," she said. She did not sulk or whisper as if she were hiding. She stood tall and held her chin high.

She didn't look fae. Her ears weren't pointed, and she didn't have wings. Although, it could have been the glamour that Serefin and Malachi had been using before.

My thoughts were interrupted when a pair of footsteps approached us.

My heart raced. If this woman had just led me to my death, I was going to be pissed.

"What is this?" I asked her.

She smiled at me and stopped walking.

Right when Malachi stepped into view.

"Saints," I whispered. I moved to step toward him, to throw my arms around him, to let him know I was sorry and that I didn't mean to leave.

But Malachi stopped dead in his tracks and drew his sword.

The woman shoved me to my knees and pressed a blade against my throat.

# CHAPTER 34
## Malachi

"If I so much as smell a *drop* of blood spilt from her skin, you won't have time to take a single breath before your life has ended," I warned. "Think wisely."

"If you were going to kill me, I would be dead," the woman responded.

She held herself with a confidence I recognized only in myself.

Who in the Saints was she?

Power pulsed through my body. Death *wanted* her.

At a single thought, she could drop to her knees in pain, and I could end her life.

But the blade was touching Jade. It was too risky.

Jade was covered in dirt and blood. Saints, she looked awful. Her eyes were wild, and her chest heaved with every breath.

"What do you want with her?" I growled. Serefin and Adeline had their swords drawn behind me, waiting for my command and watching the woman's every move.

At my command, they would kill for me.

But the woman simply smiled. "I want us all to be friends," she said.

Jade's eyes were blaring into me, but I didn't meet them. I couldn't. One look at her and I would burn the entire damned forest to the ground.

"And what makes you think we can be friends after you lay your hands on my wife?"

Without moving the blade, the woman took her free hand and placed it atop Jade's head.

"Because," she said, "she is my daughter now, too."

My head spun. The familiar voice. The familiar smile.

I knew this woman.

"Malachi," she continued. Her features softened as she continued to stare at me. "It's been so long."

Power rippled in the air around us. I reminded myself to take a deep breath before daring to say anything. "My mother has been held captive by the king. There's no way you would be out here. It isn't possible."

She wasn't my mother. She *wasn't*.

The woman rolled her eyes. "Of course he's been telling you that, boy. How else would he control that special power of yours? He used you as a weapon this entire time. He had no idea where I was, Malachi. He only made you believe he did."

Words escaped me.

The woman—my mother—released her grip on Jade. Jade fell to the ground, catching herself with her hands. Adeline was beside her in a flash, picking her up and returning to stand behind me.

I lowered my sword. "Why are you here? Why do you have Jade?"

"Your brothers," Jade managed to say from behind me. Her voice broke as she continued, "They're looking for me."

As if on cue, Lucien dropped from the sky.

I didn't wait this time. He would pay for what he did to her. I flashed across the forest, teeth baring at my brother's throat.

But he was ready. He gripped my shoulders and flipped me, and the two of us plummeted to the ground.

I let my power release, sending pain through every ounce of Lucien's being.

He shrieked and released his grip on me.

But I didn't stop. I let my power flow into his body, breaking him down from the inside out. And I wasn't going to halt it. I wasn't going to rein in my power. My brothers had done enough. They had disrespected me time and time again, but my wife?

"Enough, Malachi!" my mother yelled.

I was on my hands and knees, but Lucien was on the ground in front of me. He had no chance at fighting my power.

*Nobody* did.

"ENOUGH!" my mother repeated. "It's not what you think! He's been working with me!"

"You better start explaining," I growled, "Or you're both dead."

My mother took a deep breath but didn't move any closer. "Look," she started, "your father has been killing your wives. We all know that. If you don't know that by now, Malachi, you're blind to his ways. I knew he wouldn't let me contact you. I also knew he had spies all over the castle, dead set on following your every move. I also knew that you would be marrying Jade Farrow."

"What does that have to do with anything?"

"You don't have to believe me, Malachi, but Jade is special. I have very powerful friends who have told me to protect her with my life. I couldn't let your father kill her. Not when so much was at stake."

I glanced at Jade, who looked just as confused as I was. What in the Saints was she talking about?

She continued before I could ask any questions. "Your brothers were the obvious path of information on you. They were allowed close enough to know everything about you and Jade, but your father had no interest in keeping spies on their tail. It's not what you think, Malachi."

Adonis stepped out of the forest. "He's right, brother."

"You are no brothers of mine," I spat. "We were *never* family. You think I believe a word any of you say? It's been decades. *Decades*. And I'm supposed to believe you actually want to help keep Jade alive?"

"We all have our reasons to distrust Father," Lucien said as he finally recouped from the ground.

"You knew my mother was alive and living in Rewyth?" I demanded.

Adonis nodded. "We wanted to tell you. Honestly, we did. But it was too risky." He shook his head. "We never had anything to do with your wives, Malachi. After Laura died, I wanted to tell you. But your mother had us swear a blood oath."

*A blood oath.*

I took a breath and tried to calm the power pulsing through me. A blood oath could never be broken. If they were telling the truth, it would have been impossible for them to tell me.

"You were going to kill me!" Jade yelled from behind, pointing a finger at Lucien.

He just smiled. "I have to protect you, Jade. That doesn't mean I suddenly have a love for humans now. You can't blame a guy for having some fun."

I released my power again, sending Lucien to his knees in pain once more.

"We can talk about all of this later," my mother interrupted. "But the king will come looking for us soon enough. We have to go."

"Go where, exactly?" Adeline asked.

She looked back and smiled at me. "To your new kingdom, of course. We're heading to Fearford."

# Bonus Scene

*The following scene is an additional, alternative scene between Jade and Malachi in House of Lies and Sorrow. This scene takes place on Jade and Malachi's wedding night, immediately following the assassination attempt on Jade.*

# CHAPTER 35
# *Jade*

"TELL ME YOU'RE OKAY," MALACHI ORDERED FROM THE DOOR OF THE bathroom.

Was he *insane*? Someone just tried to *kill* me! Of course I wasn't okay! But this was predator territory. I had to remind myself that I was the only human in this entire kingdom. They expected me to cower; they expected me to fall apart. Showing any weakness would get me killed even quicker.

"I'm fine!" I yelled, letting only a fraction of my shaking voice bleed through. "Can you leave me alone to wash this blood off my body? I don't need a bodyguard!"

I waited in the bathroom, standing under the hot falling water and basking in the rare warmth as Malachi and Serefin did whatever they did to the dead bodies around here. Burned them? Buried them? I didn't want to know. As long as that bastard didn't touch me again, I didn't care.

The blood from my attacker still stained my skin, red and warm, as it fell onto the stone floor beneath.

My eyes fell shut as I placed a hand over my chest, settling my racing heart. *Calm down, Jade,* I reminded myself. That would be the first of many, many attempts on my life here in Rewyth. It was nothing special, anyway. I was used to fighting for my life, was used to surviving.

This was simply surviving with a new enemy.

I snapped my eyes open as the sound of Mal's footsteps filled the steamy room. He entered, his large body filling up nearly all the empty space outside the shower as he looked at me with dark, serious eyes.

"Excuse me!" I snapped, covering what I could of my exposed body with my hands. "Privacy, please! Saints!"

To my surprise, Malachi's eyes didn't leave mine. Not for a second. "We need to talk," he said, his jaw tightening, "about what happened tonight."

"You mean, the fact that one of your fae maniac friends tried to kill me? Not a topic I'd like to discuss, actually, but thanks. Now get out." I tried to cover my panic with spite.

Malachi crossed his arms over his chest and leaned back, using the bathroom wall to support himself. "You're angry."

I scoffed. "Really? You think so? Why would I possibly be angry?"

Malachi cocked his head to the side. "Because you were taken from your home, because you hate the fae, because you don't want to be here with me. I don't take it that marrying a fae and leaving your home was first up on your to do list."

"Fighting for survival is nothing new," I admitted. "But at least in the human lands, I actually had a chance." I hated how weak I sounded, hated how vulnerable I was here. Naked in Malachi's bathroom with water washing off the blood of my attacker, I was nothing. I had no fighting chance, no upper hand.

Mal stayed silent for a moment, as if he were really listening to my words. I guess he had surprised me recently. He wasn't the arrogant prick I thought he was, at least not all the time.

And the way he killed that man for touching me...

His speed, his strength, his pure dominance. Malachi was a predator, one that could and would kill anyone who tried to hurt me. One that *would.*

I wasn't used to it. I wasn't used to blatant protection, and I certainly didn't expect it from a fae prince. Malachi was the heir to the fae throne. He was brutal and rough. But I saw another layer of him, too. One that protected and saved. One that begged for mercy.

Heat warmed my lower stomach before I snapped my thoughts away, but my mind wandered right back to that torturous, forbidden place as Malachi stepped forward, walking closer to me.

"Okay," I sneered, backing further into the shower. "I don't know how you people do it in the fae lands, but where I'm from, people don't typically like to have important conversations while they are naked in the bathroom."

The corner of Mal's mouth flickered upward as he leaned forward, placing a still-bloodied hand on the edge of the shower wall. "Even your husband?"

"You are not my husband," I snapped. "Not as far as I'm concerned, anyway."

He stepped forward, coming dangerously close to the wall of falling water that covered my body. "Would it be so terrible?" he pushed. "Someone to protect you, someone to look after you?"

"I don't need protection," I lied, feeling the sting in every word. "And I certainly wouldn't want it to come from you."

He stepped forward again, fully clothed, entering the stream of water. My arms still covered my chest, but it didn't matter. He was inches from me now, staring down at my face as if it consumed all of his attention. Water dripped down this thick hair, traveling across his chiseled features and fell down his chin.

"You forget that I'm a fae," he whispered. He lifted a finger to pick up a wet strand of my black hair from my shoulder. "I can hear your heartbeat, Jade. I can hear how fast it beats when I do something like this," he said, dragging that same finger down the side of my jaw.

I gasped before quickly recovering. "That doesn't mean I like you," I argued. "It only means I want you to get out of here." I silently willed my heart to slow, but it was impossible when he stood so damn close to me. *It wasn't because I liked him, right?* It was because I hated him. That had to be the reason. The water falling down his body made his shirt cling to his sculpted chest. The blood washed from his skin, too.

"Really?" he teased, tracing his rough fingers along the side of my neck. "If you want me to go, Jade, I'll go. But I don't think that's what you really want."

I swallowed, but I didn't move away. I didn't stop his hand from grazing my skin, either. "You do not know what I want."

"I think I do," he answered. "I think I know you pretty well, actually."

I dropped my arm from my chest, feeling a brand new wave of courage as I leaned into him. He would not have all the power here. He would not back me into a wall and intimidate me, no matter how fast it made my heart race. *Two could play this game.*

"Please," I pushed. "Do continue."

Mal's jaw clenched before he took a quick glance at my chest. It was the only sign that he was mildly affected by my presence here, but just as quickly as the mask fell, it was right back up, covering each of his sharp features in a blanket of cold, fae arrogance.

"You're used to taking care of everyone. You're used to fighting ruthlessly for everything in your life, for everything you've been through. Your father didn't give a shit about you, and clearly, your sister cannot take care of herself. You've never let yourself relax." His hand scattered across my collarbone before running down my bare arm.

Even in the water's warmth, I shivered. "I relax," I breathed.

"Do you?" he questioned. "When's the last time you let someone take care of you, Jade?"

My bare chest touched his, I wasn't sure if it was me leaning forward or him.

He could hear my heart beat. He could hear the lie before it even came out of my mouth. I swallowed my answer instead, not wanting to admit that he was right. *Saints,* he was right about it all.

"You're a fae," I said. "I'm supposed to hate you."

He smiled, and *damn,* it was a good smile. "We're on the same team here, Jade," he said. His touch paused at my wrist. "We don't have to be enemies."

I hated that his words made sense. I hated it even more than I wanted him, wanted *much* more than these subtle touches.

I wanted Mal to take care of me, to protect me. Even if I didn't want to admit it.

"I guess I would be dead already if it weren't for you," I admitted.

Malachi's laugh echoed off the wet stone. "That's twice I've saved your life if we're keeping count."

The small, hidden crack in my chest ached, and I knew I was about to break. I lifted my chin anyway. "Fine. You can keep me alive, but that doesn't mean I have to like you."

His hand flickered over to my waist, pausing. He would not touch me unless I wanted it. I knew that. Even his eyes seemed to be fighting not to drop again, even though I could tell it took restraint.

And Saints, that satisfied me.

"We can hate each other," he whispered, leaning dangerously close to my mouth. "You can hate me and my species. You can hate who I am. That's fine."

"I do hate you," I replied, but the words came out in a rugged gasp. "I hate you so much."

He leaned so close to me now, all I had to do was lift my chin, and his mouth would be on mine. This was intentional, of course. He wanted me to make the move, wanted me to be in control.

In a world where I was nothing, Malachi was giving me the power.

"You're so damn sexy when you lie to me," he whispered, equally as breathless.

As if the last string of restraint finally snapped inside of me, I gave in. I lifted my chin and crashed against him, covering his mouth with mine and throwing my arms around his wet shoulders. He responded with an equal amount of energy, scooping me up in his arms and holding my body to him while he kissed me back, pushing us against the stone wall of the shower. The heated water fell around us, only adding to the heat that now cascaded through my body, pooling between my thighs.

"This changes nothing," I gasped as his mouth dragged down my jaw, my neck, sucking and biting on the sensitive skin just above my shoulder. "You still aren't my husband."

He laughed quietly, and the vibrations through his chest spread to mine. "I can be whatever you need me to be."

Yeah, I wanted him. I wanted him right here, and I didn't give a shit who he was. Fae or not, husband or not. None of that mattered as his hands slid across my skin, sending every ounce of my being ablaze.

I tugged at the bottom of his soaking wet shirt, peeling the fabric away from his skin. He got the hint, ripping it away in one swift motion.

I had never been with a man before. It wasn't exactly a priority of mine back home, especially when finding food for dinner each evening took up my entire day.

But this? This was instinctual. I didn't have to think. Didn't have to second-guess any of my movements. My body led the way, pulling me to Malachi like we were meant to be doing this, like all of it was so, so right.

His mouth found mine again as he pulled my naked chest against his. His hands slid up my back, cupping my waist gently yet firmly as the rough pad of his thumb brushed the underside of my breast.

A quiet moan escaped me, which only seemed to excite him further. I never imagined a fae, much less a fae prince, would want me like this, but he did. It was so damn obvious that he did, and the heat in my chest swelled even further at the thought.

"I may not be your husband," he mumbled against my mouth as he nearly lifted me from my feet. "But you are my wife, Jade Weyland. You will be mine until the day I die, and I'll protect you with my life if I have to."

I kissed him back harder, biting his lower lip and pulling it into my mouth. Somewhere along the way, the gentleness of our touches morphed, changing into hungry and desperate kisses and grasps. Malachi lifted me by the waist. I wrapped my legs around him, not caring that I was naked and soaking wet. I could feel him beneath me, could feel how much he wanted this, too.

He carried me out of the shower and back to the bedroom without lifting his mouth from mine. His hands traveled from my waist to my back before lowering slowly and gripping my ass.

This time, it was Malachi who moaned.

He pulled away slightly and lowered me onto the bed, covering my body with his. His hair was a wet mess now, loose strands dripping down his forehead and water beading off his bare chest. His black wings tapered tightly behind his shoulder blades, as if wanting nothing more than to stay out of his way.

Malachi propped himself up and gazed down at me, his chest rising and falling in unison with mine.

"Can you hear my heartbeat now?" I asked. "What does it tell you?"

He leaned in to place one more needy, desperate kiss on my mouth before he answered, "It tells me you're mine now, princess. And this," he picked up my hand and placed it on his bare chest, "this tells me I'm yours, too. No matter how much you want to deny it."

This time, I didn't object.

Mine.

His.

I could see the darkness in his eyes, the same darkness that I had lived alone with for years now.

Now, I didn't have to be alone in it.

For the rest of the night, I opened my darkness to him. I let him see it, let him share it. Something deep within me felt *whole* at the way he touched me, the way he took care of me. Tears threatened my eyes as I let the feeling of him take over. I had never felt that before, had never felt... *not* alone.

Part of me knew this was my home now, even if I didn't want to admit it. Not in Rewyth, but here in Malachi's arms, sharing his bed.

The darkness wasn't mine to carry alone anymore.

# *Prince of Sins and Shadows*

BOOK 2

# CHAPTER 1
# *Jade*

HUNGER HAD NEVER BEEN A STRANGER.

When I was ten years old, my kid sister Tessa and I had wandered our boney, exhausted bodies to the nearest market in town to steal food. It had been days since we had eaten anything but bread crumbs, and our father was nowhere to be found.

Tessa was still a child. We both were, really. But one of us had to grow up if we were going to survive.

It wasn't unusual for us to go hungry. It wasn't unusual for any humans to be on the verge of starving. It still wasn't. But we had never suffered that long before.

We dragged ourselves the multiple miles to the market and smiled kindly at everyone we passed.

Our feet bled from the rough road and the summer sun scorched our skin. Tessa nearly fainted more than once, and I remember thinking she wasn't going to make it. But she did. She was always stronger than I gave her credit for, even back then.

When we got there, though, we were told to leave. *We can't help you*, the older man had said. *Come back with your parents or come back with some money.*

They didn't know we didn't have money. They didn't know we didn't have a parent worth mentioning. They took one look at us and guessed.

It was an accurate guess.

Tessa didn't cry, but I knew the hunger hurt her. It hurt me, too.

It wasn't the usual dull ache from lack of a solid meal. It was a special pain that only came with extreme emptiness. It was a pain that gave us little reason to keep going. Little hope. After a couple of days, though, you don't notice the pain. You don't notice the lack of hope. If you have any chance of surviving, you *can't* notice those things.

On our way home that day, during the endless hours that I spent thinking about every possible way to feed myself and my sister, we came across a small deer.

The deer was alone, just standing in a field of tall grass, out in the open. Up until then, I had seen only a handful of deer in my lifetime, and never that close to me.

Never that calm. She was gorgeous, I remembered thinking that. And she stared at us, chewing on her food, like we were her friends.

She trusted us. She knew we would not hurt her.

But Saints, we were *so hungry*.

And I remembered how to hunt. My father had dragged me with him a handful of times by that point, before he had started drinking again.

"Do it," Tessa had whispered, tugging on my hand. Her eyes were big and desperate, likely mirrors of mine. I was surprised that she would even suggest it, she was always one to love animals.

Tessa had stayed put as I approached the deer, just close enough so I could throw the knife I had taken from our father's things. I remembered how fast my heart was beating. This was our last chance, I thought.

It was this, or starving to death.

Tessa dropped to her knees in relief when my blade sliced the animal's skin, sinking deep into its flesh.

I nearly did, too. It was the one and only time I had ever managed to kill a deer that way.

We did not cry as the animal's blood covered our hands. We did not cry as we dragged it the last mile to our cottage. We did not cry as we worked together to slice it apart, piece by piece, and roast the delicate meat over our fire.

We did not cry.

It wasn't until Tessa was deep asleep, and I had scrubbed our hands dry of any blood and any small memory of the beautiful creature, that I let myself grieve.

Not for the deer, although I felt bad about what I had to do.

No, I grieved for myself. Because a part of me died that day, too.

I had pushed the memory away for so long. I didn't want to remember all the horrid things I had done to survive. It was easy to forget those things when I was living in Rewyth.

When I was living in *luxury*.

But in the two days I had been in Fearford, living with the humans like mere scum on the bottom of the fae's shoe again, I remembered every last detail.

We were so exhausted by the time we made it to Fearford that I didn't care to even glance around. I ate the poor excuse of a dinner served to me and I happily let someone lead me to an open structure where I had nearly passed out on a cot next to dozens of other girls. Even if Malachi argued about it the entire time.

He had nothing to worry about here. We were humans, after all.

But now, after who knows how many hours of laying in the corner, I was curious to see where exactly we ended up.

"Good," a voice said as soon as I began sitting up. "You're up. We have a lot to cover today, and your nap time is about over, so let's get going."

"Excuse me?" I asked. My voice was groggy and I had to squint through the morning sunlight to see the dark-haired woman sitting on the cot next to me, clearly waiting on me to wake up. How long had she been there?

Where was Malachi?

She rolled her eyes, as if my confusion was somehow an inconvenience.

"You've been sleeping for days, and we have some questions about you and your friends. Let's go. He doesn't like to wait."

I massaged my temples with my fingertips and squeezed my eyes shut. "Who's 'he'?"

"The boss man around here. He was kind enough to let you sleep it off, but if I were you—" she leaned closer to me and glanced around us before finishing, "—I would get your ass moving, sunshine."

She stood up and headed for the door. My body resisted every movement as I pulled myself to my feet. The cracked skin on my back was healing, but every ounce of my body still ached. I didn't even want to know if I looked as wounded as I felt.

Step by step, I walked past dozens of cots filled with girls who stared curiously at me. I ignored the murmurs and whispers as I followed the dark-haired girl out of the building and into the blinding sunlight.

I knew Fearford would be poor. I knew it would be dirty and the people would be hungry. I wasn't expecting anything more than a shithole of poverty.

This was a city of humans, after all.

On the way here, Malachi's sister, Adeline, had filled me in on most of the politics I needed to know. She told me that all the humans used to live together in poverty, and that Fearford had separated themselves in hopes of coming out on top. They were flanked by two of the biggest fae kingdoms, Rewyth and Trithen.

How these humans thought that would benefit them was beyond me. It's not like the fae were just going to give their goods and resources to humans.

But here, on the complete opposite side of Rewyth, was Fearford. A large shithole of hunger, poverty, and powerlessness.

"I'm Sadie, by the way," she said. "You're Jade, right?"

I looked at her again. She seemed to be about my age. Her shoulder-length, dark hair had small braids throughout, and her shirt exposed her long, toned arms. She looked like a fighter. A survivor.

Anyone who lived here would have to be.

"That's right," I sighed.

We walked past numerous shacks that looked as if they would tumble down any second. Only a few other humans nodded acknowledgements at us, but for the most part, they kept their heads down.

Fearford was bigger than I expected, I had to give it that much. Rows and rows of tents and makeshift housing spanned as far as I could see.

It reminded me of home, it truly did. Only Tessa wasn't here. My father wasn't here. As if either of them would come to see me, anyway.

Was it even possible to get back home?

"Where is everyone else?" I asked.

"The fae, you mean?" Sadie asked. I couldn't decipher any emotion in her voice. "They're still here, don't worry. Your big bad army of freaks wouldn't leave without you."

I let out a breath. I don't know why it surprised me that they stayed. The fae hated humans so much, why would they accept help from them?

But part of me also knew Malachi wasn't going anywhere if I was here. And after finding his own mother with me in the forest...

We had a lot to discuss.

Sadie caught me staring at the makeshift homes around us and stopped walking. "Not as glamorous as the fae castle, I imagine," she said.

I shook my head. "Maybe not," I said. "But at least everyone here doesn't want me dead."

Sadie took a deep breath and kept walking. "I wouldn't be too sure about that," she mumbled.

"What? I'm awake here for a few minutes and people already hate me?"

She slowed down so I could catch up to her pace. "It's not that people hate you specifically," she said. "But the fae aren't welcome here. If it wasn't for your prince's mother, you all would have never stepped foot inside of Fearford. She's the one that convinced us it would be okay. Without her, you would be out of luck."

I held back a laugh. If the fae wanted to enter Fearford, these humans couldn't stop them. Her confidence was inspiring, though.

"Mal's mother...how long has she lived here? Why does she want us here so badly?"

Sadie glanced at me and rolled her eyes. "You have a lot to learn, Jade. Maybe save those questions for her. I'm sure she'd just *love* to talk to you about it."

"But what does that have to do with me? I'm human, not fae. Nobody should have a problem with me being here."

"You're kidding, right?"

I waited for her to continue.

"You're married to the Prince. How do you think that makes you look, Jade? You might be human, but to everyone else here, you're one of them."

I didn't expect to feel embarrassed, but I did.

Yes, I was married to Malachi. But it wasn't because I wanted to be. I had no choice but to marry Malachi.

How much did they know about all of that? Had Malachi told them everything? Had his mother?

I decided not to argue, and stayed silent as Sadie led us to the others through the small city of Fearford. By the time we got there, even though it was just a few minutes of walking through tents and wooden structures, sweat was beading off my forehead and dripping down my neck.

I followed her through a thick steel door into what looked like the only substantial building in Fearford. I was immediately greeted by thick, stale air and the smell of more sweat.

*Great.*

"Welcome, Jade," a sugary, young man's voice chirped. "We've been waiting for you to awaken. I trust you slept well, then?"

My eyes adjusted to the dim lighting of the room. Dark steel constructed four thick walls, enclosing the space with barely enough light to see. A makeshift desk stood in the middle of the room, and the thin, sun-kissed man who greeted me sat behind it.

"Well enough," I responded. He looked younger than I expected, just like Sadie. Definitely too young to be the sole leader of Fearford. "Where's everyone else?" I asked. *Where was Malachi?*

"They'll be here," he replied. He closed some sort of book he was holding and stood slowly from the desk. "We've heard quite a lot about you, Jade Weyland."

"It's Jade Farrow," I corrected. I might be married in the eyes of the fae, but I was still Jade Farrow. "Not Weyland."

"Really?" he questioned. "Does your *husband* know that?"

My stomach dropped. I fought to keep still. "Maybe you should ask him that question..."

"Isaiah," he finished.

"*Isaiah*," I repeated.

"I can't say he's been entirely forthcoming with information since your arrival," Isaiah continued, walking around the desk. "None of them have, despite Esther's best efforts."

"Esther?" I questioned.

"Malachi's mother," he answered.

I crossed my arms over my chest and smiled. My instincts told me not to show him weakness. Not to show him confusion. I ignored that bomb and continued, "Our people hate each other. Fearford is a dump compared to Rewyth, and I'm sure my friends are expecting you to kick them out at any minute. So yeah, I bet they've been *real* forthcoming. Where is *Esther*, anyway? What's going on?"

Isaiah's eyes dragged down my body as he stood there, leaned against his desk, with a smug look on his face. If it weren't for the exhaustion I felt, I might've slapped the look off him myself. But I let it slide this one time.

Malachi was going to *hate* this guy.

"They've been staying in a separate location. The other citizens haven't been too happy about our guests. I'm sure you understand. It was a bit of a surprise, after all. We don't have many guests here. Especially not fae."

"You had to have known we were coming," I said.

Surprise flashed across his face before he quickly covered it. "What makes you think that?"

"The King didn't tell you? He sent us here," I chose each word carefully.

Isaiah laughed. "The King of Rewyth hasn't spoken to us in years. We have no contact with your people, darling."

My people? Darling? Who the Saints did this guy think he was? I took a deep, calming breath. My mind raced through all the possible things to say to him when the door swung open again.

"She's not your darling," Malachi's voice boomed as he waltzed into the room. It only took him two strides to cross the room and stand next to me, so close that his bare shoulder brushed against mine. He was in the same clothes he had been wearing on our journey here, only now, they were ripped and blood-stained. "And I suggest you watch the way you speak to my wife."

## CHAPTER 2
# *Jade*

Malachi's mother followed behind him, and the solid door shut behind them once more.

I pushed away the butterflies I felt by being so close to him again. I hated that he did this to me.

He was *fae*. I was *forced* to marry him.

Yet, here I was, absolutely obsessed by how close he was standing to me.

We had bigger things at stake here.

Malachi glanced at me, and I quickly looked away from his dark eyes and focused my attention on his wrists.

On the chained restraints that cuffed them.

"Chains?" I asked Isaiah. "Are you kidding me? You can't actually believe that those are doing anything."

"They do enough," Isaiah responded. His relaxed demeanor was gone. It had changed into a broad-chested, stiff one to match Malachi's presence. Very different than the boyish presence he had just moments ago. "It's more of a formality for the others, anyway. Malachi knows we're on the same team here."

*As if he stood a chance.*

I looked back at Malachi. "Those things really stop you? You can't break out?"

Malachi's gaze lingered on me, as if he were drinking up every feature. I couldn't look away. I was frozen.

Without saying a word, Malachi flexed his wrists, just once, and broke out of the small iron cuffs.

Even as they clattered to the floor, he didn't break our gaze.

Sadie snickered, and Malachi's mother mumbled some sort of warning.

I broke our stare first, turning my attention back to Isaiah and Sadie. "See?" I gestured. "What was the point of that? Are they supposed to be prisoners here?"

"Not prisoners," Malachi's mother, Esther, spoke up. "You all are our guests."

Malachi shifted on his feet next to me but didn't speak up. "Yet you put your own *son* in chains," I retorted.

Now that I knew this woman was Malachi's mother, I saw the resemblance. They had similar eyes, eyes that filled with power. On the journey to Fearford, I hadn't had the energy to ask the woman any questions.

Now, however, I felt particularly well-rested.

"I know I might have missed some things while I was asleep," I continued, unable to keep the growing attitude out of my voice, "so why don't you go ahead and fill me in on what the Saints is going on?"

Malachi and Esther glanced at each other but didn't say anything.

It appeared that everyone knew more than they were letting on.

I wasn't in the mood.

"If anyone has some crazy shit to tell me, like what we're doing here and why Malachi was in chains, then I suggest you start talking."

"Yes," Malachi continued, focusing his attention on Isaiah. "Why don't you tell her why I'm in chains here."

"Don't be dramatic," Esther chimed in. "It's just a safety measure."

"And where have you been?" I asked her. "You show up in those woods with no warning and put a knife to my throat? You have Malachi's brothers nearly kill me? I think I deserve an explanation."

Her soft smile disappeared. Malachi took the smallest step toward me.

"Listen up, child," she started. "I don't owe you anything. Certainly not an explanation. I saved your life on multiple occasions, times when you didn't even know you were in trouble." She paused and examined my face. It took everything in me to stay silent. "You have a loud mouth for someone in the presence of the Prince of Shadows. Has she always been this way, son?"

Malachi rolled his shoulders back and clenched his fists. I waited for him to yell, to lose his temper. But instead, he laughed, low and eerie.

When I built the courage to meet his face, he was already staring at me.

Malachi, the man who could never keep his mouth shut, was at a loss for words.

A lot more had changed since I had been sleeping than I thought.

"Are we done here?" I said to Isaiah. "Because my *husband* and I need to have a little chat."

"That's the thing, Jade," he responded. "I know you think the King of Rewyth sent you here, but it's not that simple." He glanced at Malachi, then back to me. "The humans won't like it. Not at all."

"Why?" I asked. "I'm human. I'm one of them."

Malachi's mom shook her head and mumbled under her breath.

"Not to them, you're not," he said, repeating Sadie's words from earlier. "They'll view you as a traitor."

"That doesn't make any sense. This union doesn't hurt them, it helps them. With Mal's connections we can bargain for food and other goods. That's the whole reason we came here!"

"Not the only reason," Mal's mom chimed in. "Which is what we need to talk about. All of us."

My heart sank to my stomach. I had a feeling something was waiting for us in Fearford. It was never going to be as simple as the King had let on.

"Did you know about this?" I asked Mal, keeping my voice low.

He took a deep breath. "They told me while you were asleep. We didn't want to wake you."

"Great," I mumbled back. "I missed all the fun, it seems."

"Fun is an interesting choice of words, but yes. We have a lot to talk about."

"Start talking then," I responded. Annoyance dripped from my voice.

"As you know," Mal started before shifting uncomfortably, "for decades now, I believed that my father was holding my mother hostage somewhere, in an unknown location, so that I would continue to cooperate. It was his way of keeping my power in check, because power like mine is incredibly rare and incredibly powerful. After talking to Esther here, I learned that that was not the case at all. Esther left Rewyth long ago, after she discovered how cruel my father could be."

"You just left? How is that even possible?"

"I have very powerful friends," she said. "And very powerful ancestors. It made things easier, and the King knew better than to come looking for me. Besides, it was embarrassing enough already. He had no problem moving on after I left, as you can tell by Malachi's siblings."

"You were working with Malachi's brothers? Why? And how?"

"It was difficult at first," she explained. "Finding ways to send messages back and forth was tricky, but it became easier over time. The boys eventually agreed to a blood oath, which made things much easier. Once I learned of the wedding, we made our plan to protect you. We *had* to protect you, Jade."

My mind was racing. "Hold on," I said, holding up my hands. "Everyone is just okay with this? Your mother tells you that her and your brothers have been conspiring behind your back, and you're okay with it?"

"They were saving your life, Jade."

"Why? Why me?"

Mal glanced at Esther, who stepped forward.

"Because I was told to."

"By who?"

Malachi stepped forward and grabbed my hand. "Jade," he whispered.

"No!" I blurted. "Stop treating me like I can't understand."

"Fine. Tell her," Malachi said, looking at Esther again. "She'll find out eventually."

A few painful seconds passed.

"You know I'm not fae," Mal's mother said. "But I'm not exactly human, either."

The words were a confirmation of what I already believed. I clenched my teeth and tried to control my breathing while she continued.

"I'm sure you've heard about witches that used to live with the fae. My bloodline is one of the eldest of the witches. One of the most powerful."

The shaking in my voice betrayed me as I asked, "You're a witch?"

"My bloodline has been going extinct for many reasons, but the lack of magic is one of the main reasons. Magic is like water, you see. Especially to us witches. It comes and goes, as natural as the wind. But a few decades ago, the magic us witches possessed began to retract. It became more and more difficult to use our power, until eventually it was entirely impossible without a sacrifice."

"So you used to have magic, but not anymore? How is that different from magic the fae possesses?"

"The fae are gifted, Jade. By the Saints or whomever you pray to. For whatever reason, the Saints have chosen them as worthy to carry their magic. We had a feeling this might be the case, though."

I waited for her to continue, ignoring the sick feeling growing in my gut. Esther stepped closer to me and lowered her voice.

"Our elder at the time told us of an ancient prophecy. She had said that a human would be the turning point for us, joining the fae magic with the magic of witches. That this human would return magic to its original form, back to the fae and the witches both to use freely without sacrifice."

Malachi stiffened next to me. He must not have known, either. "And what makes you think this human is me?"

The room seemed to be getting smaller, walls inching closer and closer to me with every passing second.

My mind was spinning. Esther didn't answer me, she just continued to stare at me with those large, green eyes.

Pity. That's what I saw in her. She pitied me, no matter how hard she tried to hide it.

My heart was racing, and I suddenly became very aware of the sweat now dripping down my back.

"I think I'm going to be sick," I said. I didn't wait for anyone to respond to me. I shoved through the front door, past Sadie and Malachi's mother, and back into the blazing sunlight.

My stomach flipped over and over as I kept walking.

I took five more steps before I dropped to my knees and vomited.

Nothing made sense. I had lived my entire life in the human lands, and now I find out that I was somehow related to this witch's prophecy?

I vomited until my stomach was empty, and continued to heave with every breath.

The door slammed again in the distance. I knew it was Mal. I could feel his presence before he even said a word.

"Saints, Jade," he mumbled, rushing to my side and kneeling next to me. He placed a large hand on my back, a simple gesture that sent a shiver down my spine, even in the heat of day. "Are you alright?"

Tears and snot both dripped from my face. "No, definitely not. None of this is okay. None of this is normal."

"It's a lot to hear all at once," he said.

"Did you know?" I asked. "Did you know that I was different? That I was being protected?"

"No," he answered sternly. "I swear I didn't know. Did I think it was a miracle that you were still alive? Yes. Did I know my mother was behind it? No. And I definitely didn't know any of that crazy shit about the prophecy, or whatever my mother called it."

Tears dropped from my chin. Malachi studied my face for a moment, then caressed it with both of his hands, wiping my tears with his thumbs. "I'm still going to protect you, Jade. They might not like it, but you're still my wife."

A harsh laugh erupted from me. "I thought you were supposed to rule here. What happened to that plan?"

He sighed, cracking a smile himself. "Plans change, princess."

"And your mother?" I asked. Malachi just raised an eyebrow. "Aren't you supposed to be, like, traumatized or super pissed off or something? I mean, she left you. She's been gone all this time and you thought she was somewhere being tortured by your father."

He shook his head. "I can't even think about that right now. If I let myself get pissed, this entire city might burn."

"Wow," I replied. "Is it crazy that I've actually missed that temper of yours?"

"A little bit."

I smiled and let him press his forehead against mine.

"The humans might not respect our marriage, but we'll be out of here soon. We'll figure this out. And in the meantime, I'll protect you. Always," he said, his breath tickling my cheek.

"It might not be that simple," I said.

"I don't care. I don't care what I have to do. Shit, I don't care if I have to hide in a bunker until all of this is over. It'll end soon, and we'll get out of here."

"To go where? Rewyth?"

A smile spread across his face. "Anywhere we want."

"Fine," I whispered. "That better be a promise."

His hand still cradled my face, his thumb tracing my cheek lightly.

I wanted to kiss him. I wanted to do more than kiss him. I wanted to get out of here, away from his mother and all the other ridiculous people here in Fearford.

But Malachi was *fae*. He was dangerous, and here, he was trouble.

Isaiah had made that very clear.

Malachi inched closer, just a touch. Close enough for me to realize that his eyes, framed by black walls of thick lashes, had small specks of gold in them.

How hadn't I noticed that before?

The doors slammed open behind us again, and any tension that was lingering between us vanished.

I stood up before Malachi and put a few paces between us.

"There you are," Sadie chirped. I quickly wiped my face dry and turned to face her. "Look," she said. "There's a party tonight, it happens every full moon." Her gaze shifted to Mal. "Come. Show the humans they can trust you. It might be worth a shot."

"That doesn't sound like a good idea," I said.

She raised her hands in a lazy shrug. "Do whatever you want, I honestly don't care. But it's not just you two in the picture. Your fae friends will have a hard time if the entire kingdom fears you two."

"Where are they? Serefin and Adeline?"

"They're fine," Mal said. "I'll take you to them. Follow me."

Sadie stepped forward and added, "I have to warn you, though. You might not like what you see. The humans and the fae have a strange relationship here in Fearford. You should brace yourselves."

"Brace ourselves for what? What do you mean?" I asked.

Sadie didn't answer. Just turned her back and walked away, her feet crunching on the ground with every step.

I glanced at Malachi, but he just shrugged his shoulders. He didn't know what she meant, either. And he didn't seem to care.

If one more person in this damned kingdom didn't answer my questions, I was really going to lose my mind.

Mal began walking away, mumbling something under his breath and leaving me to scramble behind him.

My mind was racing. Malachi hadn't really talked about what had been going on between us. We didn't have the time. He was my husband, after all. Didn't that answer any question I might have?

And Sadie had a good point. It wasn't just Malachi and I against the world. We had friends to take care of. And all of the humans hating us would not help.

Malachi's shoulders were wide. I imagined what his wings would look like if he dropped his glamour. It was Esther's idea to hide the fae wings. We were supposed to ease into the human lands, not march in with our wings out. Did it take energy to hold the glamour? Did it exhaust him to hide his fae features in the human lands?

I guess it didn't matter. Malachi was the enemy in the human lands, and while he could easily drop any rival who raised an arm against him, it would be a sign of war.

A war without his father's backing. A war with no army.

It wouldn't be humans against fae or fae against humans, it would be Malachi against the world.

And I would be forced to fight with him.

"Can you slow down?" I yelled from behind him. "Not all of us are seven feet tall with wings."

Malachi slowed enough for me to catch up, but didn't turn to face me.

"Hey!" I stomped forward and grabbed his arm, spinning him around to face me. He grabbed me by the arms, gripping tightly like he was still deciding what to do with me.

His eyes were wild and his chest rose and fell with shallow breaths.

"Don't walk away from me like that," I spat. He smiled amusingly, baring his teeth.

His eyes dropped to my lips and lingered there for a few seconds.

We hadn't talked about what we were doing with our *relationship*. There hadn't been time. Both of us were too busy trying to stay alive.

But with the entire human race despising our union, we had to figure it out. Soon.

His hands still gripped each of my arms. I was close to him. The closest I had been in a while. Did he feel the same way?

He tugged on my arms, causing me to slam into his chest.

"I'm not leaving you, Jade," he whispered close to my lips.

"Okay," was all I could manage to respond. "I don't plan on leaving you, either. I don't need to give the King of Rewyth any more reason to want me dead."

"Really?" He teased, a small smile on his lips. "Is that the only reason you don't want to leave me?"

His hands moved from my arms to my back, and I found myself placing my hands on his shoulders and around his neck.

I nodded once. "Yes," I breathed. "That's the only reason."

His hands moved to caress my side, dropping dangerously low.

"You swear?" he asked. A noise I didn't recognize escaped my mouth.

This time I couldn't bring myself to respond.

Malachi brought his mouth so close to mine that our lips touched, just barely, as we both breathed the same, electrified air.

"You're mine, princess," he spoke into my lips. "Whether you like it or not."

Malachi slammed his mouth into mine. The kiss wasn't gentle or exploring. It was rough and needy. He kissed me like I was the only thing keeping him alive, like I was his only hope at survival.

And I kissed him back.

My chest pumped adrenaline through my body as my hands splayed through Malachi's hair. I pressed my body against his as tightly as I could, not wanting a single inch of distance between us.

Malachi kissed me deeply, pulling me to him and dragging his hands across my body. His touch left a trail of fire, and I longed for him in ways I would never admit aloud.

Somewhere in our tangle of limbs and mouths, I realized what we were doing.

"Stop," I mumbled, pulling away enough to look at his face. What the Saints was I doing? "Stop, we can't do this. Someone will see us."

A devious look crossed his features. I knew that look. That was the look of someone who wanted to be caught. He wanted to cause trouble.

That was the look of the Prince of Shadows.

Malachi leaned in again, ready to continue where we left off, when Serefin shoved out of the door directly next to us and stepped into the sun.

"Someone already has," he announced.

I found myself scrambling away from Malachi and straightening my tunic that was now shoved up my back.

"There you are," Malachi said to Serefin. "We were looking for you."

"Really?" Serefin teased. "And where exactly did you think I was?"

Malachi glanced at me, clearly amused by my embarrassment.

"Would you like to answer that, Jade?" He smirked at me.

"No. I would not. Nice to see you again, Serefin. We have a lot to discuss."

"Indeed, we do, Lady Farrow."

I brushed past him and into the room he exited from.

My eyes adjusted to the darkness, and my jaw hit the floor.

## CHAPTER 3
# Malachi

"What's going on?" Jade asked. I had been dreading this moment. The moment Jade had to see how her *beloved* humans were treating the *monstrous* fae.

Part of me was curious to see her reaction. To see if she cared or not. To see if she would pity the fae or take the side of the humans.

*The side.* Is that what we were now? The enemy in these lands?

Adeline rushed forward and threw her arms around Jade. Jade staggered backward, but hugged her back.

"I'm so glad you're okay," Adeline whispered. I looked away, letting them have their moment as I surveyed the others.

*My brothers.*

If I could even call them that anymore. I had come so close to killing Lucien, so close to ending his useless life. I told him what would happen if anyone laid a finger on Jade. Lucien was chaotic and disobedient, he always had been.

Yet he was still alive.

I took a deep breath and reminded myself that none of that mattered now. With all the information my mother had given me and with the blood oath she made them take...

Nothing mattered now except that Jade was different. *Actually* different, and not just in the way I felt about her.

My mother seemed to think Jade was part of some sort of prophecy. Now that she was here and talking about it all, I remembered how my mother used to be. How crazy she had been about prophecies of all sorts. I didn't have many memories of my mother, but many of the ones I did have showcased her mania and obsession with these stories other villagers would tell her.

I even remembered being dragged by her into the villages when I was a child. She would listen to anyone who could tell her old stories about the mysterious girl who would either end their suffering once and for all or ruin the world with her failures.

Of course, I never listened to her. What would be considered suffering for us? We were fae royalty. But back then, my mother was just as respected as the eldest fae in Rewyth, if not more so because of her lineage.

Everyone bent a knee to her without hesitating. My father was different, though. People knelt before him because of fear. Not because of respect.

The entire kingdom grieved for years when she left. My father and I were some of the only ones who knew she was still alive. Although I had to admit, I had my doubts over the decades.

If only I could trust her...

It's not that I *didn't* trust my mother, but something wasn't right. Why would she stay hidden all this time? The numerous wives I had that had been murdered by my father... she knew about them. She knew about them all and did nothing.

She stepped in to save Jade, and she let each of the others die at my father's hand.

Who cared about the prophecy? I had been tormented time and time again by my father, and the whole time I had looked for an assassin. An outside enemy.

And the whole time, it had been the King.

While I suffered for decades.

When I went to talk to her late last night, while Jade and the others were still asleep, she had little information to give me. *I tried to help them*, she had said. *I tried to help them but your father moved too quickly.*

Did I believe her? Saints, no. My mother had manipulated all of my four brothers to swear a blood oath to her. Adonis, Lucien, Fynn, and Eli. They wouldn't have done that willingly. A blood oath was serious, even to fae.

Esther was a powerful woman. If she wanted to save the lives of mere humans who were forced to marry me, she could have easily done it.

But no. Only Jade was spared. Only appearing after all these years.

"Good to see you again, brother," Adonis mumbled. Jade pulled away from Adeline and turned her attention to Adonis. To him and the chains that were loosely linked around his wrists and ankles.

"More chains?" She questioned. "Really?"

Adonis held his wrists up to show her. "Why just your brothers?" she asked me.

"Isaiah wanted to assure the humans that the *dangerous fae* were locked up."

She laughed. "And they let you stay out here?"

I caught myself smiling at Jade's bubbly laugh and I cleared my throat.

"It's more of an insurance policy. And I'm sure big bad Isaiah wants us to know who's in charge." I explained.

"But why?" She asked. Her big brown eyes looked at me. "Something's strange here. I can't tell exactly what, but something doesn't feel right."

I shook my head, quickly brushing off her words.

Mostly because they were true, but I didn't want her worrying about that. "It's fine." I said. "Nothing we can't handle. Once we get the annoying politics out of the way we might really like it here."

She looked around the room. "And you're all okay with this? With slumming it in Fearford while the fae live like royalty in Rewyth?"

It was my turn to laugh. I let my glamour drop, my wings flared out to my sides.

Jade's lips parted in surprise and her eyes drank up every inch. I couldn't deny that it thrilled me, knowing Jade *liked* how we looked as fae.

I would have never thought a human would like our flashy wings and pointed ears.

I rolled my shoulders back and said, "We are royalty, princess. I don't give a damn where we're at. Nobody tops us. Nobody."

She nodded slowly, but I swore I saw her lips curl slightly in the corners.

"Besides," I said. "This is just temporary."

"Oh yeah?" Lucien chimed in. "Because you think our father is just going to graciously change his mind? He'll kill her the second he gets his hands on her. You know that."

My fists clenched at the thought. Yeah, I did know that. Just like all my previous wives, my father wanted Jade dead. It was his display of control over me, time and time again. Now that the truth was out about exactly who was killing them, he would stop at nothing to make sure he was successful.

I also knew that *anyone* who touched Jade would deal with *me*. Father or not.

"We'll make a plan," I said. "Let's just get through this night first to make Isaiah happy."

"And since when do you care about making humans happy?" Adonis asked. "You're supposed to be the leader of Fearford, Mal. You're supposed to be their *king*. Our father declared as much when he sent you here. Jade's changing you for the worse, huh?"

A low growl rumbled the room around us. It took me a moment to realize it was coming from me.

"Relax, brother," he said. "I'm only kidding. If you want us to play nice with humans, we will. But Isaiah is arrogant. I don't like arrogant. I could rip that skinny man to shreds in two seconds if I wanted to."

"Get over yourself," Adeline said. "Isaiah has been the leader of this place, it has to be hard for him. He lost his father and he's trying his best to rule. You see what they have to work with here. It's not much. Why don't you at least try to show some respect."

Adonis smirked but didn't respond. Adeline always had a talent for shutting our brothers up.

"You can't actually think we're all going to that stupid human party tonight," one of the twins, Eli, said.

"If Esther wants us to make an appearance, that's what we'll do," I replied.

"You heard what they said. Something strange is happening at that thing. I don't want to be there when it goes down," Lucien added.

"Afraid of humans, Lucien?" I teased. Lucien frowned but kept his mouth shut, crossing his arms over his chest and leaning back onto the wall. "It will be nothing. Whatever weird party this is, we can handle it. It's just one night."

"Wait," Jade interrupted. "You're actually going to this party?"

"Why do you look surprised?" I asked.

She shook her head, biting her cheeks to hide her smile. She still failed. "No reason," she started. "I just didn't really take you for a human party type of person."

"We're going strictly for business," I said. "I'm not staying long. One appearance and that's it."

"Great," she said. "I'll see you tonight then."

I watched her walk away, fighting every urge to follow her out that door. To never let her out of my sight.

But Jade could take care of herself here. I had to believe that.

"Yes you will," I mumbled after she was too far away to hear me.

The door closed behind me, and I was left with my family and Serefin.

Everyone stared at me like I was a stranger in front of them.

"What?" My voice echoed off the walls.

Everyone diverted their gaze then, quick to shuffle around the room in an effort to appear occupied.

Lucien was the only one that continued looking at me, chuckling silently while he shook his head. "You are a lion in a field of mice right now, brother," he said. "Don't starve yourself because you're too busy making friends."

# CHAPTER 4

# *Jade*

It was stupid that I was excited.

Stupid and naive and ignorant.

It was a stupid party that we were nearly *required* to attend as guests here. If anything, the night would test whether there was any hope for the humans and the fae getting along.

Was that Esther's plan? To see how quickly we would fail?

But it had been so long since I *actually* had a fun time. And even back home, I never hung out with other people. Besides Tessa, anyway.

My stomach tightened at the thought of my sister. If she knew what I was trying to do, would she hate me even more than she already did?

Shit... what *was* I trying to do?

Play *house* with Malachi? The Prince of Shadows?

My mind hadn't stopped wandering to his lips on mine. His hands wandering my body.

It had only been our second kiss, third if you want to count our wedding. But it felt so *right*. It felt *natural*.

I shook my head and kept walking. Where? I wasn't sure. Just being in this kingdom brought me a strange level of comfort. Walking through the rows of beat-down tents and half-built cottages.

These people didn't know luxury. They were fighters.

They were humans.

"You're not wearing that," Sadie said, interrupting my thoughts as she stepped into my path. She dragged her eyes up and down my tattered, dirty clothes.

Was she serious?

"I don't really have much to choose from, so this is the best it's going to get."

She stared at me for another second before clicking her tongue and saying, "Alright, this is the only time I'm going to do this. Follow me."

Sadie turned around and sauntered away before I could protest. I scrambled to keep up after her. I was decently fit, I would admit. Hours of running, hunting, and climbing back home kept me healthy and agile.

But Sadie was tall and she had at least four inches on me. Her strides were wide and graceful over the dirt ground.

We passed the run-down, makeshift tents of families one by one until we approached the end of the row. I almost thought we had passed it, or that Sadie had absolutely lost her mind, but right at the last second, she stopped and turned into a wooden shed.

I had to duck my head to step inside, but once we were in, it wasn't so bad. Sadie had clearly spent a lot of time and effort making this small area of dirt and wood feel like home.

I didn't blame her. Part of me even envied the small, carefully placed trinkets and items she held close to her heart. There had been times where I would have killed for a place like this, no matter how small or dirty.

A place that was *mine*.

Sadie crossed the room in two steps and began tugging on a large trunk, sliding it out of place to reveal a small hole in the ground.

"If you tell anyone about this," she warned when she caught me staring, "I'll kill you. I mean that."

She didn't mean it, but I nodded anyway.

"I can't imagine you have many safe-spaces around here," I responded, keeping my voice soft. I didn't want Sadie to be my enemy.

I knew exactly who she was.

She was just like me. Only she wasn't forced to marry the Prince of Shadows.

"Put this on," she said, throwing me a fresh pair of black clothes. "No arguing."

I held the clothes to my chest. "Why are you being nice to me?" I asked. "I figured you all hated the girl who married a fae."

Sadie shook her head. "We aren't stupid, Jade. We know about your father. We know he owed a debt to the King and that's why you were sent away to marry the Prince."

I couldn't hide the shock that was undoubtedly clouding my features. "What? How? Nobody knows about that," I said. *Not even Tessa.*

Tessa knew that I had to marry him, of course. She just didn't know the reasoning behind it. That my father had ruined everything for us, gambling and cheating until he had nothing left to give.

Nothing except me. But that was hardly an improvement.

"Fearford is one of the largest human cities. We have spies that give us intel. That little gem of information just happened to be some of it."

I couldn't believe it. Sadie knew that my dad had owed a debt to the King and that I was the one who repaid it.

Which meant Isaiah also knew.

"Don't worry," she interrupted, reading my thoughts. "Isaiah keeps his mouth shut. Nobody here cares, anyway. It's obvious that your Prince is totally obsessed with you. They might hate fae, but they can root for a love like that."

I scoffed. "No, no," I said. "It's not like that. He's saved my life a few times, that's it. Our marriage is political."

She squinted her eyes. "Right. That's why he was completely ballistic when we separated you two after you arrived."

Why didn't I remember that?

"I'm his wife in the eyes of the Paragon. He made a vow to protect me. Of course, he would be worried."

"Mmhm," she said. "We'll see how he reacts tonight when he sees you wearing something other than bloody rags. Now get changed. Use that bucket there to wash the dirt off yourself."

I could feel the heat of my blushing cheeks. I listened to her and quickly got moving while she turned her back to give me some privacy.

The clothes I was wearing practically peeled off my dirt-coated skin.

I removed layer by layer until they were nothing but a nasty pile on the floor. The bucket of water Sadie had gestured to looked clean. Not like I would complain, anyway. I had done this type of thing hundreds of times back home.

It was a far cry from the running water they had in Rewyth. The showers. The luxury.

But this is how us humans lived. I didn't make a sound as I quickly scrubbed my arms and legs, cleaning as much dirt off as possible.

By the time I was done, the water was nearly black. And I could actually see my skin again.

"Can I ask you something?" I asked her, breaking the growing silence between us.

She replied without turning around. "Sure."

I picked up the clothes she gave me and began stepping into them. "You said something earlier, about tonight's bonfire. That the fae here are treated differently or something like that. What did you mean?"

Sadie took a long, deep breath. She was hiding something. Hiding it, or keeping it inside of her because she didn't know how to let it out. One or the other.

"Esther has power, as you know. She's been part of this community since before I was ever born. I grew up knowing her, loving her. Supporting her. Her sacrifices never meant much to me."

"Sacrifices?" I asked, recalling my earlier conversation with Esther. She had mentioned something about sacrificing. "What does she sacrifice? Will that be tonight?"

"It will be tonight, yes." I watched her shake her head from behind. "Esther will kill me if I tell you."

My heart sank to my stomach. "It's me, isn't it?" I asked. "Esther saved my life because she wants to sacrifice me."

Sadie spun around to face me. Thank the Saints I had just finished putting the shirt on. "Seriously?" she asked. "You really think Esther would drag you all the way here to kill you?"

A sigh of relief escaped me. "I mean, I don't know! Plenty of weirder things have happened to me these past few weeks. And I don't know Esther like you do. I know her as the woman who abandoned Malachi, and as the woman who held a knife to my throat just days ago." I ran a hand over my neck.

Sadie relaxed an inch. "You're safe here, trust me," she mumbled. "But your friends should be careful."

"Why?" I asked. Desperation for answers began creeping into my voice. "What's she planning to do with them, Sadie? What happens at these parties?"

"As long as they keep their mouths shut, nothing will happen. Really. I already told you the humans hate the fae. It wouldn't surprise me if Esther tried to use this event as some sort of power beacon. That's all."

My head spun. "So as long as my friends lay low, they'll be fine?" Sadie shrugged, as if she truly didn't know either way.

"I'm just trying to help you out," she admitted. "Human to human."

Sadie had a certain quality that made me want to trust her, but she also had a certain darkness that kept me wary. "Fine," I said. "I believe you."

"Besides," she added. "I think your fae are plenty capable of protecting themselves. This is a human kingdom, remember?"

I nearly laughed. "How could I forget?"

Sadie took a step back and turned her attention to the clothes I was wearing.

They were different than anything I had ever worn, back home or in Rewyth. The style in Rewyth had certainly been more formal than I was used to, but this...

My trousers were nearly form-fitted to my legs, leaving almost nothing to the imagination. My black blouse flowed around my arms, giving me plenty of room to breathe in the heat of the desert but exposing just enough skin at my chest to be flattering.

At least I thought so, anyway. But if Adeline had taught me anything, it was that I had no sense of style whatsoever.

"Well?" I asked her. "How does it look?"

*I don't care. I don't care. I don't care.*

I waited for her response.

*I cared.*

"Damn, girl," she said. "Now I can see why you drive the Prince of Shadows crazy."

My stomach flipped, but I kept my features as straight as possible.

Nerves fluttered through every inch of my body.

What if the humans hated him? Not just him...what if they hated Adeline and Serefin? What if Mal's mother wasn't enough to convince them that we could stay? What if this entire thing was just a setup and Malachi's father would come for us any day?

This was supposed to be Malachi's kingdom. Not Isaiah's.

Then again, we weren't supposed to be here at all.

Sadie and I spent the rest of the day together, preparing for the night's event.

Keeping Malachi off my mind was entirely impossible, even with the strange pit in my stomach that told me something dreadful was coming.

# CHAPTER 5
# *Malachi*

"Why are we doing this?" Adonis asked me. "We could take over this kingdom right now without even breaking a sweat. Yet you're letting that Isaiah idiot talk to you like you're nothing."

"We have a plan, Adonis," my mother answered. "We should try getting along with the humans first. If we take over, your father will just invade and this will be another branch of Rewyth. We'll accomplish nothing, Malachi will wait ten more decades for a kingdom of his own, and this will all have been a waste. Besides, we need to keep Jade safe. We need the humans on our side."

Adonis rolled his eyes and Lucien let out a groan. I let my power flare in response, just enough to let them know I was still here.

My mother's eyes snapped to me. "Careful with that, son. If the humans know you possess that power, it won't help your case. Humans fear what they don't know. It's their nature."

"I don't need them to like me. I need them to like Jade. As long as she's safe here, I couldn't care less."

She shook her head. "You might be married legally, but it won't be enough. They need to believe that you two love each other if they're ever going to think that humans and fae can get along."

"I'm sure everyone already knows this was a setup. We won't fool them all. There's no logical way to explain how Jade possibly ended up married to me and wants to stay that way."

Adeline stepped forward. "They don't all know," she interjected. "That the wedding was forced, I mean. I heard a few humans talking earlier and they were completely shaken that Jade would choose to marry you. They have no idea that it wasn't her choice."

I reminded myself not to clench my fists.

"Either way, we stick with the plan," I said. "I won't just march into a city and take over like I run the place."

"But you do run the place, Mal," Serefin said from the back of the room. "This is your kingdom. Your father ordered you to rule."

"And I will. With time and in peace."

"You've grown soft," Adonis sneered. "This will never work. We don't have time."

"Show some respect," my mother interjected. "Your brother is making the right choice."

"Says who?" He spat. "You? No offense, *witch*, but that doesn't mean much to me."

Tension thickened the air. The ground grumbled beneath us, and this time, it wasn't from me. I looked to my mother, whose typically forest-green eyes had now turned black as night.

My attention turned to the ground beneath our feet, where the grass was dying inch by inch around my mother.

I could have sworn the air around her darkened, too.

Magic. She was using magic.

"Now," my mother said. "Your job is to go out there and make the humans like you. That's it. So don't screw this up for us, got it?"

My brothers nodded, but I knew they didn't have a choice. They had sworn a blood oath to my mother. They might not have been her sons, but she owned them.

I had only heard of a few other occasions when blood oaths had been taken. They were rare, requiring a powerful witch like my mother to be effective. Decades ago, there used to be rumors about entire armies who were sworn to one witch, everyone obeying the witch's every command. Those were just stories, but it could be entirely possible.

As long as the individual willingly took the blood oath, there was nothing that could be done to break it.

The blood oath would remain until the witch who originated it released them from the oath. It would be physically impossible to do anything against the oath swearer's will.

If it was her wish for them to obey tonight, they would have no choice but to oblige.

Saints, that made me happy.

"Hurry up now," my mother said. "The sun is already down and we don't want to keep them waiting. I'm sure everyone is dying to meet the mysterious fae."

"Right," I mumbled. "I'm sure they're just ecstatic."

I followed suit as she led the way, Adeline and Serefin staying close behind me.

I had never been one to care if others liked me or not. The Prince of Shadows had an entirely different reputation. Did the humans know that about me? Did they know I was the one their children feared? Had nightmares about?

Did they know I had killed hundreds of humans? That it took me less than a thought to drop a grown fae male to his knees with my power alone?

I doubted it. If they did, they would be fearing for their lives.

Not throwing a party.

We all had our wings hidden with glamour, just like the first time Jade had met us.

No need to scare them even more. *We were one of them*, my mother had said. *We were similar.*

And we were supposed to act that way tonight.

The deep vibration of music began creeping into the earth under my feet.

I wasn't a huge fan of music in the past. Music meant emotions. Emotions meant memories.

I couldn't afford memories.

But this music was accompanied by laughter and cheers. Dozens of voices chattered in the distance.

Adeline squealed in excitement. "Relax," I reminded her. "We might not even make it to the bonfire before we are forced out of here."

"Speak for yourself," she said. "Everyone likes me and you know it. And if they really hate the fae, I'll just lie and say I'm one of them." She flipped her hair over her shoulder and trotted forward toward the party.

"Your loyalty is astonishing, dear sister," I yelled after her.

Serefin put a hand on my shoulder as we continued to walk. "I can't say I have a good feeling about this," he whispered. "We're walking into a city of people who want us dead. That's never ended well for us."

"The difference is, Ser, these people don't stand a chance against us. We'll play along to give them what we want, and then we'll figure out how to get back at my father."

He nodded, and I knew he understood. Serefin always had my back, even if he knew I was being an idiot.

Which was more frequent than I'd like to admit.

We followed the small path of lanterns that lit a walkway to a large, open field. A massive fire, likely burning dozens of trees at the same time, illuminated the party ahead.

Makeshift tables and chairs scattered around the perimeter, making plenty of room for the humans to sit, talk, mingle. Food and drinks were being passed around freely, and it looked as if nearly the entire Kingdom of Fearford was already here.

I scanned the scene again, looking for any type of threat.

But all I saw was a chaotic, drunk group of humans.

And then I saw her.

Jade.

She was commanding the attention of everyone around her, whether she wanted to or not.

Jade was sitting on the end of a bench with a red drink in her hand. The glow of the nearby fire lit up her face as she talked and smiled. A few other girls sat around her, listening to every single word she said.

A couple of boys, probably Jade's age, stood behind them with the same level of concentration on Jade.

Only they had something else all over their faces, too.

I took a step forward.

"Don't," Ser said from behind me. "You heard your mother. You'll scare them."

"They're looking at her like she's a new toy."

"She's your wife, Mal. Not theirs. She can take care of herself."

Ser was right. I took a long, calming breath. If I stormed over there and shut them all up, the humans would hate me. My mother would despise me. And the night would be ruined.

I kept my mouth shut, clenched my jaw, and kept following Ser to the other side of the bonfire. The side where Isaiah sat with Sadie and a few others.

"Welcome!" Isaiah said as he saw us. "Welcome friends! Thank you for coming!"

"Did we have a choice?" I responded.

I walked around the wooden table and took the seat right next to him, giving me a perfect view of the fire.

And of Jade, who was still oblivious to our arrival.

"We all have a choice," he continued. The others, including my brothers, took their seats at the same table. "But you made the right one. These parties are what the people of Fearford look forward to."

"What for?" I asked. "To sit around and stare at a fire?"

"Esther has been living with us since before I was even born. We have routines here. Rituals. There are other witches here who look up to her for peace and for guidance. They look up to both of us," he said.

"You're saying this is one of the witchy rituals?" I asked. I looked around again, but didn't see anything out of the ordinary.

"Don't make your arrogant judgements until you see it for yourself."

"Great," I mumbled to Ser. "I can't wait."

Isaiah chuckled coldly and took a long swig of his drink. "We might not be living in a palace, *Prince*, but humans do know how to have fun. Perhaps your wife can remind you sometime."

Hot anger rolled up my neck. "Don't talk about Jade," I growled. "You don't know anything about her."

"And you do?"

"Yes. I do."

He shook his head and smiled. He looked just as juvenile as he acted. His eyes were shallow and ignorant. He may be living in poverty. He may struggle to feed his people. But he hadn't known real hardship.

He hadn't known real war.

I had known men like Isaiah my entire life. Men that thought they had everything figured out. Men that said a few words and expected the crowd to drink up every word. Men that had been handed their position in the world.

Men that had no idea what was coming.

"If I can have everyone's attention please!" He announced.

The humans obliged without another thought, ending their conversations and turning their attention toward Isaiah.

"Thank you, thank you. We've been hosting these parties once a month for years now, and I could not be happier that I get to continue on my father's legacy with the same traditions." The crowd fell into still silence. "But we have recently been given the chance to carry on something that my father always wanted. To unite the humans and fae."

I looked through the crowd of orange glowing humans. Some of them made sounds of disgust, others sat quietly and continued to stare at Isaiah as if he were their savior.

When my eyes fell on Jade, she was already staring at me. Her brows were drawn together, and I could tell that she had tightened the grip on her drink.

I didn't break eye contact as Isaiah continued. "As some of you may have heard, we have had a few guests stop by. Malachi, will you please stand up."

"It's *Prince* Malachi," Serefin yelled from the table, which caused a roar of hollers from the crowd.

I ignored them all and stood, letting the humans know who their enemy was. What we looked like.

"For centuries," he continued, "the humans and the fae have been rivals. The humans have starved while the fae have feasted. We, as humans, have nothing to offer. Nothing to give. Not to them."

Hundreds of human eyes stared at me. I did not move.

"Prince Malachi and his friends are fae from Rewyth. They come here to unite our lands, bring us riches, and save us from poverty," he preached, pure confidence lacing every word.

I physically flinched at his words. How *idiotic* they were.

My father had no intentions of following up with this deal. Even I could see that. The humans had spent centuries in suffering, and that wasn't going to change just because I waltzed in here with a human.

"But Prince Malachi has come to help us. He has come to finally put a stop to this ridiculous feud between human and fae."

"How?" someone yelled. "How will he be able to help us?"

Isaiah turned to me as he answered. "That's what our friends are here to help us discover, isn't that right?"

I clenched my jaw. If I opened my mouth to respond, he wouldn't like what would come out.

"Enjoy yourselves!" he continued after a couple of seconds. He turned back to the crowd and raised a drink. "Eat, drink, dance. We're one family here at Fearford, so let's make our guests feel welcome!"

Isaiah was quickly pulled to the side, talking to the dozens of people that practically begged for his attention.

And with that, the music started up again. Any hatred the humans had felt toward us seemed to dissipate as everyone moved around the fire, swaying to the beats of the music.

A sharp pang of envy bolted through my chest. It had been decades since I had fun like that. Saints, it was an entire other lifetime.

Before the wars. Before the guilt. Before the marriages.

And before all the death.

If these people knew all the things I had done, they wouldn't let their guard down around me. Around any of the fae, for that matter.

Serefin handed me another drink. It was obviously nothing compared to the drinks we had for the fae in Rewyth, but perhaps if I drank enough it would eventually take the edge off.

If that were even possible.

"How long do you think he'll keep that act up?" Serefin asked when I sat back down.

"What act?"

"The act where he thinks he's in charge."

I choked down a laugh. "We've known plenty of men just like him. He'll do anything he can to appear like he's in charge, but when shit starts going in the hole, he'll be looking for someone else the people can blame. I'm not sure what his angle is here, but I don't like it."

"Yeah. Me either."

"He wants something with Jade. I can feel it. I just don't know what."

Serefin considered my words. "Would your mother know?"

I shook my head. "Even if she did, she wouldn't tell me. She acts like she's loyal to us, but she's lived with these humans for decades now. We have to keep our eyes open."

"Agreed, brother."

We both relaxed in our seats and observed the scene of the bonfire. My other brothers seemed to be doing the same.

Adeline rushed up to me and Serefin. It was then that I realized she had stepped away at some point. Her hair blew all over the place as she approached, and she had a look on her face that made me think she was actually enjoying herself.

"Come dance!" she said, rushing up to Serefin and I and grabbing each of us by the arm. "Come dance with me!"

"Absolutely not," I answered as Serefin mumbled his own declining words.

"Come on!" she whined. "It's a party! You all look so grumpy over here sitting by yourselves. Everyone's having fun!"

"Dancing with the humans isn't fun, Adeline," Adonis chimed in from behind me. "It's embarrassing."

Adeline brushed his comment off with the wave of her hand.

"Fine," she said. "I'll make Jade dance with me."

Nobody responded, but the hair on my neck stood up at the mention of Jade's name.

Adeline trotted away, through the crowd, until she was out of sight. Serefin kept his eyes glued on the crowd, too. Ready to interfere if needed.

Always protecting Jade.

"At least one of us can be friendly," I muttered to Ser.

He laughed and took another drink. "Your sister could solve the entire nation's problems in one afternoon. I'm certain of it."

I laughed with him but couldn't get past the growing pit in my stomach. I scanned the crowd, looking for that familiar black hair of hers. Why did I even let her out of my sight in the first place?

But she would be fine with Adeline.

These were just humans, after all. Nothing was going to happen to her.

I needed to relax.

Just as I was about to turn around and give up on the entire idiotic party with the humans, Jade's laugh rippled through the air.

Every muscle in my body tensed.

Adeline held tightly to her hands as she swung her around a small circle. A few other humans circled them, laughing and drinking as they moved to the beats of the music.

Serefin laughed quietly next to me.

"What?" I asked, snapping out of my trance.

"You're in big trouble, brother."

I shook my head. "I don't know what you're talking about."

Ser leaned in, placing his elbows on his knees, and said, "You know exactly what I'm talking about. You can't forget that she's a human. I get that you wanted to save her life before, and that made you protective. She might be your wife in Rewyth, but the humans might not see it the same way."

"I've never cared about what the humans think."

"I know that. But you care about Jade. It's obvious to anyone who pays attention to the way you two look at each other. All I'm saying is that humans will look at this union as an abuse of power."

"Adeline said the humans supported our union."

Ser shook his head and leaned back in his chair. He had an aloof appearance, and only I knew him well enough to know it was a facade. Serefin might look relaxed and laid back, but he was watching every single person at this party.

He had been watching me, too. And Jade.

I trusted Serefin. I trusted what he had to say to me.

"Adeline hasn't been watching them the same way I have. Look over there," he said, pointing to the darker edge of the clearing.

I followed Serefin's gaze and my power immediately rumbled in my body, letting me know it was still there. A group of men, now including Isaiah, were huddled in a small circle, heads down, whispering. Their tense body language and clenched fists told me everything I needed to know. For whatever reason, they weren't happy.

One individual in particular pointed his finger at Isaiah, yelling something I couldn't hear over the pounding music.

"Those are the type of people we have to look out for. Not the ones laughing and dancing."

I nodded. Serefin was right. We weren't looking in the right places.

"Should we go over there and see what's going on?" I asked.

"Absolutely not. But your call," he answered.

I moved to stand from my chair but was immediately cut off by a small group of girls running up to where my brothers and I were sitting.

"Come dance!" they chirped. One of the tall, blonde humans grabbed my brothers Eli and Fynn by the wrists and pulled them to their feet. If it weren't for her shockingly low-cut shirt, I'm sure they would have objected. But instead, they let the cluster of girls pull them to dance in the crowd.

As the moon rose in the sky, people began to let loose. More and more men added to the song of flutes and fiddles. Laughs became louder and more carefree. The energy electrified, a palpable tension in the air.

My other brothers were next. In the swarm of the crowd, they had little choice in the matter. After a few objections, they also were swallowed into the sea of dancers.

I scanned the crowd, looking for Adeline. She had to be up to this.

Ser looked to me for help when two girls grabbed each of his arms, but I only shrugged.

They wanted us to mingle with the humans, anyway.

The girls cheered and clapped as he, too, rose to his feet and followed them into the sea.

But nobody grabbed me. Nobody tried to convince me to dance.

*Smart humans.* Perhaps they *did* have an idea of who I was.

I scanned the crowd again, almost laughing at how awkward Serefin looked as the crowd tried to get him to move his hips from left and right.

"You're missing all the fun," Jade's voice made me jump.

"Who says watching isn't the best part?" I replied.

Jade smiled. She was breathing heavily, probably from running and cheering with the crowd. Her eyes looked differently than I had seen them before.

They looked alive.

"What?" she asked, stepping closer. "You're too good to have a fun time?" She stood directly in front of me, almost close enough to touch. "It's a party, Malachi."

She leaned forward, placing an arm on either side of me. I could smell the liquor on her breath, warm and sharp. "Don't you want to come dance with me?"

Now she was definitely close enough to touch. Close enough that I could cover her mouth with mine in a second.

But I didn't budge. Didn't blink.

"No," I answered, even though my body was telling me something different. "I don't want to dance."

"Really?" she asked. Her eyes flickered down to my lips, lingering for only a moment. "You won't come dance with me? Your wife?"

"Dancing isn't really my thing."

She nodded and stood back up, allowing me to finally take a breath.

"Fine," she said. "Suit yourself."

And with that, Jade Farrow walked away, back into the sea of humans. I watched her until she was too deep in the crowd, but every inch of me could still feel her presence.

And every inch of me needed more.

# CHAPTER 6
## Jade

DAMN. I HADN'T DRANK THIS MUCH IN A *VERY* LONG TIME.

Like, *ever*.

I knew I was teasing Malachi. But I also knew he liked it.

And that was addicting.

Even if he wouldn't come dance with me.

The music moved through my body, commanding each of my movements. The summer sun had set long ago, but the heat of the crowd sent beads of sweat rolling down my neck.

I didn't care if I looked like an idiot. I closed my eyes and tilted my head backward, letting the beat of the drums hit the deepest parts of my soul.

I wasn't the only one, either. Dozens of humans were doing the exact same thing, either alone or in the arms of their loved ones. Two bodies melded into one.

It was euphoric.

Bodies bumped into mine from every direction, but I didn't mind. Not as we all moved however the music wanted.

When two large hands grabbed me around the waist from behind, I stepped forward slightly. I didn't turn around. I figured my body language was clear enough.

Apparently I was wrong.

The hands grabbed me again, pulling me backward against a sweaty male body.

And it wasn't Malachi.

"Come on, baby," he whispered in my ear. His breath reeked of liquor and smoke. "A girl like you doesn't need to dance alone."

I shoved the hands away once again, saying, "Not interested."

It wasn't until the grimy hands grabbed me *again* that I became pissed off.

But when I turned to shove the loser one last time, my jaw dropped.

Malachi's power rumbled through the ground, although I'm sure the humans were too drunk to notice anything out of the ordinary. He was on the loser within a second, grabbing his shirt collar and holding tightly. "You're done here," was all he said.

The grabby man's face changed entirely as he stared at Malachi with wide eyes.

"I wasn't doing anything, man," he muttered.

"You touched my wife," Malachi growled. "You should be happy that you still have your hands. And I'm not your *man*."

I would have said something. I would have intervened, I would have told Malachi to put the guy down. But I was frozen in place.

Me and everyone else who was now watching.

Malachi must have realized this, too. He let go of the man, who staggered backward in fear, and rolled his shoulders back.

The music still played, but everyone was staring at us.

At Malachi.

"You really know how to cause a scene," I said.

Malachi shrugged. "He shouldn't have done that."

"He just wanted to dance."

"He wanted a lot more than *a dance,* princess."

Heat creeped up my cheeks. I glanced at the faces around us, most of which had small hints of fear written all over them.

Malach's outburst was going to ruin the entire plan.

I held out my hand to him. "I suppose you'll have to take his place, then," I teased.

My heart was pounding in my ears. I had been drinking, yes, but that was no worse than the usual effect Malachi had on me. Combining the two, though, was going to be dangerous.

But right now, I didn't care one bit.

He mumbled something under his breath before stepping forward, but he didn't take my hand. He yanked my wrist firmly and sent my body stumbling into his.

Malachi caught me around the waist and I wrapped my arms around his neck to support myself.

"Fine," he whispered, close enough for only me to hear. "But just one dance."

A few people around us snickered and giggled before returning to their own dance movements, adjusting their paces to the now slower beat of the music.

"You can't go around scaring the shit out of people, you know," I said. "It's not a great way to make friends."

Malachi took a deep breath, his chest touching mine as it rose and fell.

"What if I don't want to make friends?"

"I don't think your mother would like that very much."

"And what if I don't care about what my mother thinks?"

The intensity in his gaze made me shut my mouth. I had been this close to Malachi a handful of times now, but my body reacted like it was the first. His hand on my waist slid to my lower back, his fingers brushing the exposed skin in a gentle touch.

"Do you really think this plan will work?" I asked, breathing heavily and desperate to distract myself from his touch.

Malachi smirked. "I don't know. I've never spent time with humans before. I have no idea what they will or will not fall for."

"Like a fae and a human actually getting along?"

"Right," he said. "Like that."

"Well they're all watching us now," I teased. I unclasped my hands from around his neck and twirled a finger through his thick, curly hair. My heart was beating faster. Stronger. "We could convince them."

Malachi stiffened at my touch. For a second, I thought he was going to pull away. His eyes darkened, but his grip on my waist didn't falter.

"Are you sure this is a good idea?" he asked.

With my next words, I was certain I was drunk.

"What? You've kissed me before. I even thought you liked it, too."

The corner of Malachi's mouth turned upward, but he quickly recovered. "And what if I did?"

"Then I suppose humans and fae can get along, after all."

We spun in circle after circle, dancing more intimately than I had ever danced with anyone before.

Malachi took a deep breath and turned his attention up to the night sky. His throat bobbed once, and when he returned his gaze, his eyes had changed entirely.

Something like desire dripped heavily over every feature.

A look that made my stomach flip.

Malachi leaned down, close enough that our lips barely brushed when he whispered, "If you want me to kiss you in front of all these people, princess, you'll have to ask me nicely."

My breath hitched. Another bead of sweat rolled down my chest. "You want me to ask you to kiss me?"

"Mmmhm," he hummed. He no longer hid his amusement.

"Fine," I hummed back, lifting my chin so my eyes met his. "Will you kiss me, dear husband?"

Malachi laughed quietly, and the vibrations of it erupted through my body.

"Anything you desire will be yours, dear wife," he whispered, and before I could take another breath, his mouth crashed into mine.

Our bodies moved together under the night sky of Fearford. The music still blared around us, but the only thing I could hear was the sound of my own heartbeat as Malachi kissed me, deep and passionate. His hands didn't leave my body, only held me tighter against him as if he would never let go.

And I didn't want him to let go.

I kissed him back, letting my hands wander from his hair to his shoulders to his back, where strong black wings should have been. I wished then that he wasn't using glamour, that I could see the wings that had been wrapped around us before.

Malachi smiled against my mouth.

"What?" I mumbled as I pulled back just enough to look at his face.

"I know what you're thinking," he breathed.

"Oh yeah? And what's that?"

Malachi glanced around us, as if he were checking to see who was looking, before he dropped his glamour. It was a bold move. His dark wings were tucked in tightly, but they were still massive as I looked up at them.

"I was right, wasn't I?" he said, moving in to place his hot mouth against my neck, my collarbone.

I closed my eyes again and held onto him tightly as he continued to move us to the beat of the music.

I felt...I felt carefree. I felt giddy. I didn't remember the last time I had felt this happy. I certainly never expected to feel happy with him.

With the Prince of Shadows.

But here we were.

Malachi pressed his forehead against mine, our breaths blending together as we danced through the crowd.

Until a blood-curdling scream split through the air.

# CHAPTER 7
## *Jade*

The music stopped playing immediately. Malachi and I jumped apart, ready for whatever problem we were about to face.

"What's going on?" I asked.

Panic crept into my chest as I looked at the crowd around us. Well, looked *back* at the crowd around us.

Everyone had stopped what they were doing and now stared at Malachi, whose massive black wings still flared around his body.

They hadn't seen fae wings before. They certainly hadn't seen Malachi's wings before. And they looked mortified.

"They're just wings," I announced. My desperation to resolve the situation only increased with every passing second.

Malachi's glamour was back in an instant, covering any trace of a fae appearance that had slipped through.

"Demon," one of them muttered. My blood ran cold.

"Don't be ridiculous," Malachi replied. "They're just wings."

"Black wings," another person mumbled from the depths of the crowd.

"You knew we were fae," he continued. "What did you expect?"

I wanted to reach a hand out to him, to tell everyone he wasn't someone they should fear.

But who would I be then? Just moments ago, I was kissing him in the crowd. But this was the same fae I had been forced to marry. The same fae who had killed thousands.

He might have been my husband. But he was still a stranger to them.

"Let's just go," I said, stepping toward him and lowering my voice.

"No," another voice chimed in. Malachi's mother. "Don't leave. You are our guests here." She emerged slowly from the fae end of the crowd. The people shifted to make way for her as she walked toward us.

Her eyes blared into Malachi with the look of a disappointed mother. I wanted to laugh in her face.

I knew that look all too well. And I also knew when it wasn't deserved.

"It was my fault," I interrupted. "I made him do it. I didn't think anyone was paying attention."

Malachi's mother only shook her head. "It's nobody's fault, dear. The fae deserve to be themselves. They shouldn't have to hide who they really are, especially here. Right?" she asked.

Most of the humans just stared at each other in awe, others still looked at Malachi in disgust.

"Show them," she said to Malachi, and now to his brothers who were approaching from their own spots in the crowd. "Show them what you all really look like."

Malachi began to object, but Lucien, who had been lurking this entire time, beat him to it. He dropped his glamour, revealing the wicked silver wings I had grown to resent.

The same wings that carried me through the sky just a few nights ago. I hadn't forgotten.

The crowd gasped as soon as they realized what they were looking at.

Adonis followed, and so did the twins. Serefin and Adeline now stood behind Malachi, though, waiting for his move.

"It's okay, son," Mal's mother cooed. "Show them who you are."

Malachi's throat bobbed. I knew he didn't care about what these humans thought, but he would try. *For me.*

He would try to get the humans to like him.

Which meant they couldn't fear him.

Malachi's eyes shifted to mine. Those beautiful, dark eyes. The eyes that held decades of secrets, secrets that I would never unearth from the depths.

Malachi didn't care about the humans' opinions. He cared about mine. I was now his window into the human world.

I nodded once.

And his midnight black wings reappeared.

The crowd collectively gasped again. A child screamed in the distance.

You would have thought they were staring straight into the face of a monster.

Maybe they were.

"Why are they black?" an older woman asked. "Your wings?"

Malachi opened his mouth to respond, but his mother answered for him. "We don't know," she said. "They were like that when he was born."

The older woman, with white hair and wrinkles around her eyes, smiled slyly. How many lifetimes had these fae lived? When all us humans had was this one, precious life? "It can't be good, boy. It can't be a good omen."

She stepped forward toward Malachi, causing me to step back so she would have room. She placed a hand on his shoulder. He stiffened, although I was probably the only one who noticed.

The crowd silenced as everyone waited for her next words. But she leaned in close to Malachi, who graciously bowed so he could hear, and whispered.

It could have only been a sentence or two.

But Malachi's entire posture changed.

The woman turned, and I thought she was going to walk back into the crowd. But she stopped directly in front of me.

Malachi acted as if he would interfere, but nobody moved an inch.

"You," she hissed, pointing a curved finger at my chest. "You are the one. Your mother told us you would be coming soon."

"What?" I whispered to her.

"The peacemaker. We've been waiting for you."

Peacemaker? My head was spinning. How many drinks had this woman had?

"My mother is dead," I whispered. "You must be thinking of someone else."

The woman looked to Malachi's mother, who just gave her a knowing glance. "You should have brought her here sooner," she said. Esther simply bowed her head.

What in the Saints was she talking about?

I looked to Malachi for any inkling of help, but he looked equally as lost.

Gratefully, however, the woman had lost interest. She walked back into the crowd, which parted like she was fire. And she didn't look back.

Adeline was the one who spoke next. "You don't need to be afraid," she yelled. "We aren't here to harm any of you. We just want peace!"

I cringed internally. They would never believe that. Saints, *I* would have never believed that. It had taken the fae saving my life multiple times for me to believe that they didn't actually want every single human being dead.

It took me getting to know Adeline and Serefin.

And Malachi.

I still wasn't so sure about Malachi's brothers, especially Lucien.

The humans didn't have that same chance that I did. They weren't forced to move to Rewyth and see it all for themselves. They simply had to take the fae's word for it.

The word of their enemy.

"Adeline," I said, stepping forward. Her sharp ears stuck out of her long, bouncy hair. She wanted them to like her. I knew that. But they were never going to give her a chance.

And somewhere deep inside of my heart, that hurt. It hurt for her.

"No, Jade," she said, emotion leaking into every word. "They need to understand. We came here to help. Malachi came here to help."

"Then let her go!" another stranger shouted.

My heart was pounding again, but this time I knew it wasn't from the liquor.

"She's not a captive!" Adeline shouted back. "She's Malachi's wife!"

"Only because you forced her into it!" the voice persisted.

Malachi was at a loss for words. His brothers weren't much help, either, as they snickered in the background.

Because it was the truth. There was nothing they could say.

"Jade?" Adeline asked, tears swelling in her eyes. I opened my mouth to say something but nothing came out. What could I possibly say, anyway? That they were wrong? That I willingly entered this marriage?

I couldn't say any of that.

I shook my head at Adeline, mouth wide open. The look of disappointment and hurt on her face was one I would never forget.

"Well," Esther interrupted. "Since we're all here, I suppose we should get the real event of the evening started. Isaiah?"

Isaiah appeared in the crowd, and a small clearing formed around him.

It was then that I noticed a small, makeshift altar at one of the vacant wooden tables.

As if it were even possible, the silence of the crowd increased.

"Come here," she demanded, power dripping from her every move. Her usual lightness had been replaced. She was nearly unrecognizable. The energy between us all darkened instantly, and only continued to darken as the four brothers moved toward Esther, unable to disobey.

Did the others know they had sworn a blood oath?

Esther was wielding a power so strong, these four fae men could not even look away. Neither could I, I noticed. It was as if we were all entranced, watching this interaction.

The twins made it to her first, stopping in unison before her with Lucien and Adonis behind them.

Malachi was a statue beside me, his radiating body heat the only indication that he was still there.

"Many of you know about us witches and our rituals, but I'll give a quick history lesson for our new guests," she started. "We witches have been losing our power for many decades now. This isn't news to anyone."

A few people in the crowd nodded. How many of them were witches?

"What is new," she continued, "is the recent finding that small sacrifices can protect our magic, even if it is just temporary."

I didn't dare move. I didn't even risk a glance at Malachi. If he was feeling an inch of the dread I was feeling, his face would break me.

"This small sacrifice is something we have been doing every few months for decades now. And today," she motioned to the brothers, "with the help of these men, our magic will be protected once again."

The only sign of resistance was Lucien's clenched fists. Did they know this would be part of the oath? Was this the first time they had been used for a sacrifice?

"Your hand, please," she said. One by one, the brothers stepped forward.

And one by one, she sliced a small blade across their palms, squeezing drops of blood onto the makeshift altar.

"Did you know this was happening?" I whispered to Malachi, not sure if he could even hear me.

He mumbled something in response but it was barely audible over the ringing in my ears.

"You are all very generous for your sacrifices," Esther said to the boys. "And the Saints will thank you for this."

The fire cracked and spewed behind us, making me jump.

"It's done, then," Isaiah said eventually, clapping his hands. "Once again, Esther graces us with protection. Because of this sacrifice, we can all rest our heads this evening knowing that the Saints are on our side."

"Saints, save us," the crowd murmured in one demonic, unified voice.

Malachi leaned down and whispered in my ear. In my drunken state, I even thought I imagined it.

"Saints, save us."

# CHAPTER 8
## *Malachi*

ADONIS AVOIDED EYE CONTACT, STARING DOWN AT HIS DUSTY SHOES. He wasn't usually one to keep his mouth shut.

He must've learned a thing or two.

"If you have something to say just spit it out already," I spat. We had been sitting in this dark, musty room for half an hour now. Esther demanded we meet with her in private, but that was before she left to talk to her *beloved* Isaiah.

Whom I was becoming increasingly less fond of.

Adonis shook his head and turned his eyes toward the ceiling, smiling to himself. "You just had to ruin it for us, didn't you?" he asked.

"Ruin what, exactly? Esther's genius plan to save us all?"

He leaned forward, staring at me with hidden anger in his eyes. An anger that he and I shared. "She's trying to help us. You can't get over yourself long enough to look past your mommy issues. Esther is the only one that can bring down our father."

"You have to believe her," I argued. "You swore a blood oath, remember? Are we going to pretend that the *ritual* tonight was normal?"

"A blood oath makes me obey her commands, idiot. Not believe everything she says. If Esther thinks a stupid ceremony with our blood is going to keep this entire kingdom safe, so be it."

"I can't believe we came here," I mumbled. "This isn't going to help anything."

"There you go again, not seeing the bigger picture. Esther has a point. You have to be patient, brother. We might be stuck here kissing the ass of a bunch of humans, but this gives us time. Time to wait for our father to screw up. To make mistakes. He'll be going absolutely ballistic without us soon. And as soon as he lashes out..."

"We make a move."

Adonis nodded.

"But do you really think he won't just march here and kill us? Or send assassins, at least?"

Adonis shook his head again. "Doubtful. He'll be sitting in Rewyth, waiting for the day we all come walking back in there."

"He sent me to rule this kingdom for a reason, Adonis. He has to know something we don't."

Esther's voice trailed in from outside the door. Adonis stiffened in his chair before whispering, "And that is where your mother comes in. Try listening for once."

I clenched my fists to keep from lashing out again. Adonis was the smarter of my brothers. If he wanted me to listen to what Esther had to say, I could at least try.

After decades of spying on my family, she better have some decent insight. Especially after using my brothers' blood for a *sacrifice*.

She mumbled something else outside before opening the door, her long, gray, hair blowing across her face as she shut it behind her.

"Thank you boys for your patience," she said. "Busy night."

"Indeed," Adonis mumbled back. I stayed quiet.

"I think that went quite well, actually," she said, "despite the little scene toward the end."

"You mean despite the humans freaking out? Or despite you cutting each of my brothers for their blood?" I spoke up.

"You can't judge them for fearing the unknown," she continued, ignoring my second statement. "It's human nature."

"And how would you know that," I pushed. "Considering you're clearly not human."

Esther paused where she stood near the wall and simply tilted her chin. "You're angry," she stated.

I rolled my eyes. Of course I was angry. I was royally *pissed*. I had been forced out of Rewyth, turned into a damned spectacle, and walked all over by this Isaiah guy who thought he ran the place.

Shit was going to change around here. And soon.

"Yes," I started. "I am angry. And I'm getting tired of these humans treating us like we can't kill them all in five seconds."

"Threats aren't going to help you," she said.

"I think my rule over Fearford would be much more... effective."

"Why?" she asked. "Because you have a great gift? Because your wings are black?"

"Because I'm the heir to the throne," I reminded her.

"Yes," she continued. "The fae throne. Not the human throne."

I could have laughed out loud. Everyone knew the humans didn't have a throne. Not a real one, anyway. They were fighting to survive every single day. What seat did they have at the table of war, trading, and politics?

"Then what are we doing here? My father sent me here to rule. He *gave* me this kingdom."

Esther began pacing. "Honestly, Malachi, if you really think forcing these humans into submission and using them as servants will help you get anywhere in this life, be my guest. But you're not thinking clearly. Your father wants this land. He sent you here because he thought you would fail."

I took a deep breath and tried to calm down. "That's ridiculous. He knows I won't fail."

"He was counting on it!" she replied. For the first time since I had seen my mother again, she was losing her temper. "He sent you here because he knew the humans would fear you. He knew you would force them all to submit and it would be more proof that the humans and the fae cannot get along."

"Why would he care? He just wants this land for himself without punishment from the Paragon."

"Exactly," she continued. "If you force the humans into submission and the Paragon hears about this, you're the one that gets punished. Not him."

My mind raced through each of her words.

"But if we can get the humans to like you, to live peacefully with you and possibly even accept you into their community..."

"The Paragon will never know."

"The Paragon will never know," she repeated.

Shit. I didn't dare look at Adonis. I knew he would have that arrogant look splattered all over his face.

He was right. Esther did know what she was doing.

"And Jade?" I asked. "What about her?"

Esther and Adonis locked eyes for a second before she answered. "Jade will not be harmed."

"Well I would seriously hope not," I boomed. "But I'm glad that's cleared up."

Esther stepped forward and finally took a seat with Adonis and me. "Look," she started. "I know you heard what that elder said at the party. About Jade being the peacemaker."

I eyed my mother. "Was I supposed to believe anything that woman said?" I asked.

"Maybe not from her, but you should listen to me. Jade is special. I told you this before and I meant it. She's written in dozens of scriptures from the Saints. We've been waiting on her for decades now, Malachi."

"You're kidding, right? Jade's just a human. Her father is a drunk. She's not part of any crazy story the elders might have told you."

"She's special, Malachi. There's a reason these boys are sworn to protect her." I opened my mouth to respond but quickly shut it. My brothers had taken blood oaths to protect Jade. But that didn't mean that she was some special descendent of the Saints or the girl the elders had been waiting on.

Adonis spoke next. "Listen to her, Malachi. She's telling the truth."

"Is this what you wanted to talk to me about?" I asked. "You both wanted to corner me here to tell me that my wife isn't the person I think she is? Do you hear how ridiculous that sounds?"

"She might look like a regular human to you now, Malachi, but she isn't. Let me talk to her. Let me work with her. I can figure out if my elders were right about everything."

It sounded absurd. It sounded like Esther had absolutely lost her mind and was taking my brothers with her.

"Have you talked to Jade about any of this? Does she know?"

Esther sighed. "She knows I saved her life. And she's a smart girl. She has to know something."

Jade wasn't going to take this well. She wanted her life back. She had made that very clear to me even before hearing my mother's conspiracies. She was surviving for now, but I knew she would leave at the first chance she had to get back to her family.

If they would take her back, that is.

"Fine," I said, standing from my chair. "Do whatever you want. I can't make the humans like me if they already have their minds made up."

"Just lay low for a while," she said. "I'll handle it."

I nodded once to Adonis and left the room, back into the night.

Saints. What was happening? What had this all come to? Two months ago, I would have been living another boring, ignorant day in Rewyth, doing whatever my father asked of me. I was fine.

And then Jade changed everything.

I had no idea where she stood with her feelings for me. Tonight had been fun, but how would she feel in the morning? Would she still accept me in front of all the humans in the daylight?

"Brother, wait up!" Adonis yelled from behind me. He jogged to catch up with me, and I didn't slow a single step. "We need to talk," he started.

"I think we've talked enough," I mumbled.

"No," he said, grabbing my arm and forcing me to stop walking. "We need to talk about the King. We need to talk about our father."

That interested me. "What about him?"

Adonis looked at our surroundings and pulled me further into the darkness of the path we were walking before he whispered. "We know you want to kill him."

My stomach dropped. "Saints, Adonis, you can't just go around saying shit like that."

"We want to help you, Malachi."

"Even having this conversation could get us killed for treason. You know we can't kill him," I said, even though I had been dreaming about this very thing since we left Rewyth.

Since he allowed his guards to harm Jade.

I stopped myself from shivering as memories of Jade's ripped up back flashed through my mind.

They had whipped her. Yes, they were all going to die.

"Why would you want to help me, anyway?" I asked.

"We have our reasons," he stated.

"We?"

"Us, your brothers."

I wanted to believe Adonis. I really did. But decades of lying and sneaking around with my father had taught me to be smarter than that.

"If you want to kill our father, go right ahead," I said. This conversation had already gone on too long.

"We need your help," he called after me. "You know we have to do this together, brother."

"We should be happy if he lets us all live," I sneered. "Especially after you've been working with *her*."

"He'll never know. He has no way of suspecting that we're working with Esther."

"And you can be sure about that?"

Adonis closed his eyes and shook his head. "No," he answered. "I can't be sure about anything. But we're not just going to sit back and let him run our kingdom to ruins."

I had to admit, I had never seen Adonis so passionate about Rewyth. In fact, I never thought that any of my brothers actually cared about the kingdom.

I wanted to believe him, but my instincts told me to keep my guard up.

"Fine," I answered. "I'll help you. But I still don't trust her. And nobody else can know about this."

He smiled. "Agreed."

And with that, Adonis was gone.

Leaving me with a nauseating wave of dread.

I should have gone straight to bed. I shouldn't have pushed the boundaries any further.

But my mind wasn't going to rest until I talked to Jade.

I waited until Adonis was entirely out of sight before taking a left turn, straight toward where I knew Jade was staying.

# CHAPTER 9
# *Jade*

I was almost back to my poor excuse of a housing facility when I heard strong footsteps following me in the darkness.

"Not now," I yelled toward whoever it was. "I'm not in the mood!"

"I didn't mean to make things difficult for you," a voice said. *Isaiah's voice.*

I stopped walking and turned around. After the tension at the party and the blood sacrifice, I wasn't in the mood for this. "What do you want, Isaiah?"

He held his hands out in defense. "I just want to talk," he said.

"Can it wait until tomorrow?" I asked. My body was exhausted from the evening, and I wanted nothing more than to slip into bed and sleep for three days straight.

"It will be quick," he insisted. "I promise."

"Fine," I stated. "What's this about?" My words came out sassier than I wanted them to, but I didn't have the strength to care.

"Just checking in," he said. He clasped his hands behind his back and walked toward me slowly, his boots grinding on the dirt beneath our feet. "Tonight didn't go exactly as planned."

A long breath escaped me. "No," I agreed. "It didn't."

"Is Malachi always this...aggressive?"

The question alone sent a rush of emotion through my body. "Malachi is the Prince of Shadows. I believe he can act however he likes."

"Fair enough," he answered carefully. "But still. I can't help but wonder how scary that must be for you."

*What was he getting at?*

"It's not scary at all, actually," I said, suddenly feeling defensive. "People who fear him just don't know who they're dealing with. He would never hurt me."

"Right," Isaiah continued. "Of course he wouldn't."

"What's that supposed to mean?"

Isaiah stepped closer. He was close enough now that I could see the golden freckles that spotted his tan skin.

"What I'm trying to say is that you're safe here, Jade. You don't have to pretend. We can protect you from *them*. From the fae. If you want protection, that is."

I shook my head. "They have never hurt me, Isaiah." *Most of them, anyway.* "Malachi has saved my life on more than one occasion."

"But you're still married," he continued.

"Yes," I breathed.

"And you didn't want to get married, did you, Jade?"

My heart was pounding in my chest, so loud Isaiah could likely hear it. Of course I hadn't wanted to get married. Getting married to Malachi had been my worst nightmare just a few weeks ago. But why? Because I thought he would kill me? Because I thought they would take Tessa if I didn't go? Because I had a family to look out for? A selfish father to save?

I shook my head. I hadn't wanted to get married. But this marriage had turned into something I could have never expected.

Something that felt terrifyingly real.

"Look," Isaiah continued after I failed to respond to his question, "I know you're in a tough situation. But I know what you really want, Jade. I can help you."

"Oh really?" I laughed. "And what is it that I really want?"

Isaiah took another step closer. I stepped back, but my body hit the wall of the building behind me. I took a deep breath and reminded myself not to panic. Isaiah wasn't the enemy.

*Right?*

"You want freedom. You want to go home to your sister and your father, and you want to forget about all of this."

Well, he was right about some of it.

I would kill to go back to Tessa. To apologize. To let her know that I was still the same person and that I would do anything to protect her.

She was the only family I had, and after our last interaction, she was afraid. Of Malachi or of me, it didn't matter.

It all just seemed too far out of reach.

"You can't help me with that," I sighed. "Nobody can."

"And that's where you're wrong, Jade," Isaiah said. His eyes were wide and wild. Isaiah looked manic, like he would lose his mind at any second.

I didn't want to hear what he had to say. I didn't want this conversation to happen at all. Not with him.

"Back up," I said after a moment. "I need some space."

But he didn't move. Instead, he reached forward and grabbed my hand, holding it with both of his. "We would be unstoppable, Jade. If you help me here in Fearford, I can guarantee you get back to your sister. You would both be safe."

My breath came out in shallow pants. My vision became narrow, and everything around me suddenly didn't feel real at all. I didn't trust Isaiah. I didn't like him one bit.

But why was he saying this? Why now?

Malachi's voice booming from the distance snapped me out of my trance. "You two look cozy," he said as he approached. "I hate to break up your party, but I believe Jade told you to back up."

Isaiah dropped my hand and obeyed Malachi. I took a long, deep breath of the cool night air and leaned my head on the wall behind me. My legs shook under the weight of my body.

"We were just talking," Isaiah protested.

"You're done now," he growled. "Go home, Isaiah." Isaiah might not have noticed the way Malachi's fists were clenched tightly at his sides, but I did. I also noticed the tightness of his jaw that indicated he wasn't just mad.

He was absolutely outraged.

"Just go," I added, desperate to prevent whatever confrontation was about to happen. "We'll talk tomorrow."

Isaiah's face lit up at my words, but he didn't say anything else. Just bowed his head in my direction, then Malachi's, and stormed off toward his quarters.

But Malachi didn't come any closer. Didn't try to argue. Didn't yell. He just stood at a distance and crossed his arms over his chest, shaking his head at the ground.

"I came to make sure you were alright," he mumbled without looking at me.

I sighed, and suddenly felt the need to fight back tears. "Well, I'm not," I answered. The crack in my voice must have made Malachi look at me. "And I haven't been for a while. But thank you for checking," I answered.

My eyes burned. Malachi uncrossed his arms and stepped closer. "Jade–"

"Don't," I insisted. "Don't try to apologize."

"Fine," he said, taking another step toward me. "I won't apologize."

I couldn't hold the tears back any longer. My throat was on fire, and the hot tears spilled from my eyes. I was so damned tired. I didn't want to talk about Isaiah. I didn't want to talk about the bullshit he just spilled. I didn't want to talk about Tessa or Esther.

"I know this arrangement isn't what you wanted," he said. He took another step toward me and held my face with both his hands, using his thumb to wipe my tears. "And when this is all over, when we no longer have to fear for our lives because of my idiotic father, I'll do everything I can to make you happy, Jade. Even if that means letting you go."

It wasn't an apology. It was everything that I had been feeling between us put into words.

A harsh sob escaped my body, and my legs would have given out beneath me if it weren't for his strong arms wrapping around my waist, holding me to his chest.

"I just don't want to do this anymore," I managed to say.

"I know, princess," he whispered into my hair. "I know you don't."

Any other day I would have been pissed at the nickname, but not today. Not now.

"Will you take me somewhere?" I asked him. "Just for a while? Somewhere we can forget about this disaster."

I heard the smile in his voice when he answered, "I thought you'd never ask."

Malachi scooped me into his arms and jumped into the air. My stomach dropped, but I buried my face into his neck as he carried us through the night.

"Won't people see us?" I asked.

"You forget that my wings are as black as the night," he laughed. "Nobody will see a thing."

"I think you scared everyone here enough already," I added.

Malachi let us drop a few feet in the air, causing me to tighten my grip on his shirt. "Saints!" I yelled. "Don't do that!"

He only laughed. "What?" he teased. "You don't like it?"

"Let's just land in one piece, thank you," I replied.

After a few minutes of flying in the darkness, Malachi obliged. He returned us to the ground in one smooth motion.

We were still in a field outside of the forest. Tall grass surrounded us, just short enough that I could barely see over it. Malachi beat his wings a few times, causing the grass around us to scatter so we had enough room.

"How about this for an escape?" he asked.

I sat down in the grass, extending my legs out in front of me. "It beats Fearford, that's certain."

"Oh, come on," he said. "It's not that bad here."

"I preferred being in danger in Rewyth. At least there I *knew* who my enemies were."

Malachi settled in the field next to me.

"This will all be over soon," he said. His tone had darkened in a way I couldn't explain. "All of it."

"Did Esther care to explain why she thought she could use your brother's blood as a sacrifice?"

"We didn't exactly get to that, no," he replied. "But at this point, that's the least of my problems."

I shook my head. "Do you think we can trust what she says about this prophecy?"

Malachi looked up at the sky. "I don't know. But I have a feeling this isn't the last we're going to hear about it."

I let my body lay back onto the field, staring up at the sky. Stars littered the black, endless void above us.

"Do you ever wonder what it would be like to just...leave? To escape and run away and never return?" I whispered.

Malachi took a long breath, but eventually reclined himself so he was lying next to me. "Sleep, Jade," is all he said. "You're safe with me."

It wasn't an answer. Saints, it wasn't even close. But it was exactly what I needed at the time. My eyelids were heavy, fighting to stay open with every blink.

I listened to the sound of Malachi's breath, steady and slow, until my eyes fluttered closed, and I drifted into that dark abyss.

# CHAPTER 10
# Malachi

"Saints," a man's voice jolted me awake. Jade woke at the same time, scrambling away from me on the grassy ground. The sun was rising quickly in the distance.

I jumped up, ready to confront our visitor, but it was only Serefin and the human girl. Sadie, I think her name was.

"We've been looking for you two everywhere," he continued. Sadie had her hands on her hips, a very annoyed look on her face.

"What's going on?" I asked. Jade brushed her clothes off behind me.

"Messengers came from Trithen. They're demanding to speak with the Prince of Shadows and his human bride."

My blood ran cold.

Hearing anything from Trithen was bad news. Messengers that came just for Jade and I? Serefin gave me a look that told me he knew what I was thinking.

"Trithen?" Jade asked. "As in Rewyth's enemy kingdom?"

"One of them, yes," I answered. Rewyth didn't have a great reputation amongst the other fae kingdoms, but Trithen and Rewyth had gone to war on more than one occasion in the past few centuries.

War was never forgotten.

"Let's go," I insisted. "How in the Saints did you find us here, anyway?" I asked.

Serefin smirked. "It wasn't hard to guess, brother," he answered. Jade blushed and mumbled something under her breath, but it didn't stop me from picking her up again and launching the two of us into the air. Serefin followed with Sadie behind me.

"That was humiliating," she said when we got far enough from Ser and Sadie.

"Why?" I teased. "You think they had bad ideas about why we slept in the middle of nowhere all night long?"

"Saints," she mumbled. "At least it was Serefin and not one of the others."

"You can trust him, princess," I replied.

"I know I can, but what about Sadie? This can't be helping my reputation."

"Your reputation?" I asked. "As my wife, you mean?"

"Yes," she answered firmly. "Exactly."

A few moments later, I was lowering us to the ground inside the front gates of Fearford.

Esther was the first to greet us. "Where have you two been!" she yelled. "You can't just go off like that without telling anybody! We thought you..."

"Left this damned place?" I finished for her. "Not yet, but don't give us any ideas."

Jade stiffened as Esther rushed forward and hugged her.

It looked like a completely normal action for Esther, but Jade looked as if she had never been hugged before.

"Are you alright?" she asked Jade. "Are you hurt?"

"No," Jade answered. "I'm fine."

It was odd watching my mother care for someone. Part of me wondered if she worried about Jade's wellbeing or if this had more to do with the fact that Jade was somehow special to Esther.

Time would tell.

"Where are they?" I interrupted. "The messengers from Trithen?"

"This way," Sadie spoke, charging in front of us and leading the way. Jade, Serefin and I followed behind her.

Nobody spoke. Not as Sadie led us to an open, unoccupied wooden structure in Fearford and not as she held the door open for us to walk inside.

I had been nervous before in my lifetime.

There were countless times that my father had sent me into life-or-death situations. Did I really care? Maybe not. But those situations were the same ones that made your palms sweaty. That made you double count your breath before you walked inside.

Those were the situations that made you feel alive, also.

"There you are," a voice greeted us as we walked through the door. "It's about time," it continued.

My eyes adjusted to the dim light of the room, and I waited until I felt Serefin and Jade's presence behind me before I answered, "What do you want?"

"Is that how you welcome all your guests to your new kingdom, Malachi Weyland?" the man asked.

I bit my tongue. "Who are you and why are you here?" I asked. "Who sent you?"

"Easy now," one of the messengers said. His slicked back, blonde hair was annoying enough. His boots had been freshly cleaned, and there wasn't a flaw to be seen on his uniform.

Total prick.

"We heard the infamous Prince of Shadows had taken up residence in one of the human colonies. We just came to see if it was true or not, that's all."

"You're lying," I answered. Jade stood still as stone behind me.

"You're right," the other messenger said. "We are lying. Our king sent us to find out what was really going on here. Fae taking over human lands is prohibited. We could have the Paragon here within days."

My anger flared, and it took everything in me to keep my temper cool enough so that my power didn't lose control. Of course they came here to rat on us to the Paragon. I'm sure the first thing my father did was tell everyone that fae were taking over Fearford.

It was his insurance policy.

Unless Trithen wanted something else from us.

My mind spun, trying to find anything to say to the bastards.

Jade took her chance and spoke up next. "That won't be necessary," she said. "The fae aren't taking over anything here. They're breaking no treaty. Fearford has welcomed them here as guests."

"Is that so?" the blonde one asked. "And who is this pretty lady?"

Jade opened her mouth to answer but I cut her off. I didn't need these strangers knowing who my wife was. "That's none of your concern," I growled. "You're speaking to me."

Serefin stepped forward next. "Did you come all this way to threaten the heir to the fae throne, gentleman?"

I choked back a smile. Serefin always had a respectful tone, but there was also an edge to him that surprised even me from time to time.

Blondie's friend stepped forward. "Look," he said. "Our king heard there were fae living here. We also heard the Prince of Shadows hasn't been seen in Rewyth for a bit of time now. We took a wild guess, and now we see that it's true. But we didn't just come here to verify our suspicions."

"Oh really?" I taunted.

He rolled his eyes but continued. "We come with an invitation. Bring yourselves to Trithen to speak with our king in person, and we won't report whatever the Saints is happening here to the Paragon."

My fists clenched. The air around me shook, barely noticeable. "Calm down," Jade whispered. It didn't work.

"You have one week. Bring the humans, too. Our king wants to know how much of this arrangement is mutually beneficial." And as quickly as those Trithen bastards appeared here, they were gone.

"I'm going to find Isaiah," Sadie said before she rushed out the door.

I couldn't move. I couldn't think. I had yet to process what just happened.

"The Paragon can't actually punish you for this, can they? You're only here because your father ordered you to come." Serefin asked.

I shook my head. Yes, my father had ordered me to come here. But that wasn't the whole story.

Trithen knew very little about what had happened the last few weeks, if anything at all. Unless they had spies in Rewyth, which wouldn't exactly be surprising to anybody.

"What does that mean?" Jade whispered to me. "That they'll report you?"

"The fae have plenty of rules we have to follow, although it may not always seem like it," I replied. "The Paragon is a group of powerful fae and witches both. They draw the line. Centuries ago, they drew up a few treaties. Basically commands that we have to live by to keep us in line. It's vague stuff, really, and they usually don't bother following through with any punishments, anyway. But the threat is still there."

"Why?" she asked. "For just being here? For just living with humans for a few days?"

"I guess so," I replied. "There's an old treaty stating that the fae cannot invade human lands. Fearford is a human territory, and, well, here we are."

"But they don't mind that you're married to a human? Wouldn't that break some sort of treaty that you have?"

I shrugged. "Yes and no. But like I said, they usually don't care what we do either way. It's rare for them to show up in any of our business. I haven't heard from the Paragon in a decade or two."

She shook her head, as if she were just letting the weight of the situation hit her.

"But if they do come for you..." she started.

"Don't worry," Serefin interrupted. "Mal isn't doing anything wrong. Trithen is just blowing their horns at this point. They have no pull with the Paragon, it's all a bluff."

Jade nodded and took a deep breath. "What makes them so powerful?" she asked. "Why is everyone afraid of them?"

I exchanged a glance with Ser.

"Hey," Jade interrupted. "I know that look. You guys have to tell me. I'll find out eventually, you know I will."

It's not like I wanted to hide things from Jade. She had learned a lot today, and she had enough problems to deal with between my mother and this crazy prophecy she insisted Jade was part of.

The truth was, the Paragon and I didn't always have a great relationship. Yes, it had been decades since I had heard from them. But it felt like a calm before chaos. The Paragon had never been out of my life for that long. They had always been right around the corner, watching my every move.

Waiting for me to make a mistake.

Saints. Maybe today was that day.

"Some of them have powers like Mal," Ser answered slowly. "The witches are powerful, more powerful than Esther. The fae are ruthless. They possess gifts some people have only heard about in stories. They'll enforce any rule they wish to on anyone they see fit. There's simply no match to their power. That's why they are feared."

Jade nodded. I relaxed a small amount.

"You're not telling me something," she said after a second.

This damned girl.

"They were impressed by my *special* gifts when they learned of them. Let's just leave it at that," I said.

Jade's eyes lit up. "Really? What did they want from you?"

"The same thing everyone wants, princess. Power. They see my gift as a threat and they want to use it for themselves."

It was easy to talk about now, but that hadn't always been the case.

"Fine," Jade said after a few seconds, taking the hint. "What do we do about it? Go there and walk into an ambush?"

Jade didn't know what I knew about Trithen.

Serefin caught my eye but I shook my head, just enough for him to see. Nobody else would find out what we knew.

"There won't be an ambush," I said. "But if they're true about reporting to the Paragon, it's in our best interest to not call their bluff."

Jade nodded, although I could tell from the look she gave me that she would be asking me about this later.

Sadie and Isaiah broke into the room, Isaiah was out of breath. "What did I miss?" he asked.

"Pack your bag, champ," I said. "We're being summoned to Trithen."

"Trithen as in the largest fae territory?" he asked.

"That's arguable," Serefin chimed in. "Largest behind Rewyth, of course."

"Right," Isaiah said. "That one."

"We don't really have a choice," I added. "Your presence was requested, too."

"You didn't think to tell me when messengers arrived? Isn't that something I should know?"

"They weren't exactly waiting around for you," I said. "And nothing you would have done would have stopped them."

"This is my kingdom," Isaiah spat. "If fae are trespassing, I need to know about it."

"Why?" Jade asked him. Her tone was purely inquisitive, but the way she crossed her arms over her chest was dominant.

I didn't try to hide my smile.

Isaiah looked at her like it was the first time he had ever laid eyes on her. "Why?" he repeated. "Why would I want to know about two fae breaking the treaty?"

"What would you do about it?" she asked. "Stop them?"

Isaiah clenched his fists. I could have predicted each of his next moves down to the second. I had seen it hundreds of times. He was a young man fighting for power where he had none.

"Don't pretend like you're in charge here, Isaiah," I said calmly. "Our presence is being requested in Trithen, and we're going."

"Sounds like you're not in charge here either, then, *Prince of Shadows.*"

"Unless we all want to die, we'll go," I said. My words were harsh enough to be final.

And they were true. If it was true that the Paragon was going to be involved, we had to comply.

Where the Paragon was involved, death was always close by.

## CHAPTER 11
# *Jade*

I HADN'T HEARD THE WORD *PARAGON* AT ALL IN MY NEARLY EIGHTEEN years of life until I had moved to Rewyth.

Now, however, the word alone shook me to my core.

The Paragon were the ultimate punishers of the fae. Sure, there were different fae kingdoms. But they each answered to the Paragon.

And with Rewyth being the most powerful fae kingdom, they had a special eye on the Prince of Shadows.

My husband.

Adeline had taken the time to explain to me that the Paragon didn't mind when a fae married a human as long as the human went willingly, or there was a deal agreed on by both parties.

Until now, they weren't doing anything wrong.

But with Malachi and the others staying in Fearford, it caused some problems.

This was all speculation, of course. Those messengers from Trithen could have been making it all up just to get us to do what they wanted.

We couldn't risk not believing them.

"Are you ready for this?" Adeline asked. She had joined me with Sadie to prepare for our trip. Sadie didn't have much, but compared to what we had brought to Fearford, she had everything. She let Adeline and I both borrow a spare change of clothes, consisting of simple trousers and a light jacket.

It was hot enough to sweat through multiple layers, but Adeline insisted we would need protection where we were going.

We didn't argue.

"Am I allowed to say no?" I asked. Adeline finished zipping her backpack. She had a long, tight braid that flowed down her back.

"It won't be anything to worry about," she replied. "Just politics. This type of thing happens all the time."

"Really?" Sadie interrupted. "Other fae really threaten to report you to this Paragon thing frequently?"

Adeline hesitated. "Well–"

"Right," Sadie replied. "That's what I thought."

Sadie and Adeline were complete opposites. Adeline was tall, classy and elegant. Sadie had short, dark hair and had an arm full of tattoos.

Still. I think Adeline was happy to have the company.

Sadie on the other hand...

"You've never left Fearford?" I asked her, attempting to change the conversation.

"Never had to. This place has provided for us enough, although you all might not think so."

"I didn't choose to come here, Sadie. Neither did Adeline," I said. Adeline didn't need my backup, but I somehow felt the need to defend her.

Sadie exhaled a long breath before flinging her own bag over her shoulder. "I know. This is just all very different, and I can't say anything good has happened since fae showed up in Fearford."

Adeline raised an eyebrow.

"Yeah," I admitted. "I have a feeling that streak will only continue."

"They're probably waiting for us," Adeline said. "We should probably get going."

She trotted out the door, leaving Sadie and I behind.

"You can stay here, you know. The fae in Trithen would never know," I said.

Sadie shook her head. "If Isaiah's going, I'm going. He'll never make it without me. Besides, I'd like a chance to get outside these walls. As comfortable as they may be."

*That* I understood.

"So, you and Isaiah..." I led on.

Sadie quickly shut it down. "Never. You know how it is. He likes to pretend to be in charge, to call all the shots. But at the end of the day, when he needs advice, it's me he comes running to. That's how it's always been. I've known the guy my whole life."

"You're a good friend to him," I admitted.

Sadie smiled. It made me think that I hadn't seen her smile like that much at all. She wasn't as tough of a badass as she looked.

"Let's go," she said, pink rushing to her cheeks. "We're going to be late."

I couldn't help but smile as I followed Sadie out of her room.

The sun was beating down. I squinted my eyes and immediately wished I could cut off half of my hair. It was longer now, hitting almost to my waist. Adeline had twisted it into a braid similar to hers, but the thickness of it still sat heavy on my neck.

"You princesses ready to go?" Lucien yelled from across the clearing. "We've been waiting all morning."

"Don't call me that," we replied in unison.

That earned a laugh from us both.

"Ignore him," I whispered to her. "He's terrible and crude and has no redeeming qualities."

"And any of the fae do?" she replied.

Now it was my turn to blush. "You'll see," was all I could manage to say.

The group of us looked like we were prepared for a six month adventure. Isaiah and Sadie were the two humans joining the group, other than myself. Then we had the fae, which included Malachi, Adeline of course, and the brothers– Adonis, Lucien, and the twins. Serefin refused to stay here while Malachi went, so he was tagging along, too.

And then there was Esther.

Nobody wanted her to come. Saints. I have no idea why *she* even wanted to come. Her relationship with Malachi's brothers freaked me out. It was weird, to say the least. They had all sworn a blood oath to her and nobody seemed to want to talk about that, or why they would do something like that in the first place.

But I wasn't about to start asking questions. I knew Malachi was thinking all of the same things. And she was his mother, after all.

"Horses?" I asked. "We aren't just flying there?"

Malachi laughed. "As much as we would love to carry you humans across an entire kingdom, this is the safest option."

I nodded, remembering what he had said about some fae being stronger flyers than others.

"Fine," I replied. "But I get my own horse."

And I regretted those words as soon as I said them.

There weren't enough horses for all of us.

And Malachi was technically my husband, which meant they probably expected us to ride together.

Malachi knew it, too. He leaned against the massive white stallion with his arms crossed over his chest, a smirk on his mouth as he chewed on a small twig.

"Don't look at me like that," I said to him as I passed him, shoving his shoulder with my own.

"Like what?" he replied. "This is my normal look."

"No," I responded. "It's not. Your normal look is the one where everyone you talk to thinks you're about to kill them."

"And you're saying this isn't that look?" he said, smiling again.

I rolled my eyes.

A bead of sweat was already forming at my temple.

"How long of a trip is this, anyway?" I asked.

"It will only take two days if we keep moving," Adonis replied.

"Three days is more reasonable," Isaiah chimed in.

"Yeah?" Lucien sneered. "And how would you know? Have you been to Trithen before?"

Isaiah's jaw tightened. The obvious answer was no.

"No fighting, please," Esther yelled from her own horse. "We have plenty of time for that on the road."

That seemed to shut everyone up.

We spent the next few minutes packing the bags onto the horses. Isaiah and Sadie spent their time digging through maps and planning a clear route.

But the fae did no such thing.

"Are you not the least bit concerned that we'll get lost out there?" I asked.

"Why?" Malachi answered as he finished feeding the white stallion a large apple. "Are you?"

"You know what I mean," I said. "Just answer the question."

He took a deep breath before answering, "It's a straight shot, princess. Getting lost isn't the thing we need to worry about out there."

Serefin walked up next to him.

My blood ran cold.

"You don't mean..."

"More deadlings?" Serefin answered for me. "You bet. And we'll get lucky if that's all we'll see."

Saints. How stupid was I to assume that the dangers in the woods were only between Rewyth and the walls to my own human lands? Of course they would be everywhere. There was a reason these walls existed.

"Do they know?" I asked, pointing to Isaiah and Sadie.

Mal shrugged, and gave Serefin a knowing look. "They'll find out soon enough. No need to scare them."

I sighed and wiped the sweat from my forehead with the back of my hand. I couldn't believe I agreed with that. We could be walking into a death trap, and yet...

Trithen could be a death trap of its own. Isaiah and Sadie knew the risks.

And here they were.

"Fine," I said. "But any weird, mythical creature tries to attack me, I'm throwing you between us," I said to Malachi. "And I mean it."

Malachi just laughed. "I would be disappointed if you didn't."

He locked eyes on me, and his expression alone made my stomach flip. Serefin left to get settled on his own horse, following the rest of the group as they exited through the narrow entryway of Fearford's walls.

Malachi held out his hand. "Your turn, princess."

"I can get on a horse by myself, thank you," I replied.

"Really?" he teased. "That's not how I remembered it last time."

"I wasn't in riding condition last time, was I?" I asked. A flash of emotion crossed his features, but I ignored it. The last time Malachi had seen me attempt getting on a horse, I had just been whipped by his father's men. The memory was fresh in my mind, and I could imagine it was even fresher in Malachi's.

"I'll kill them, you know," he whispered as I turned to get on the saddle. He picked up a loose strand of my hair that had fallen out of my braid. "I'll kill them for what they did to you that day."

He didn't have to say it. I knew he would get his vengeance one day.

"I know," I whispered back.

We stayed there for a moment, looking at each other in the blazing heat of the sun.

Until Malachi cleared his throat and turned to help me on the saddle.

"Alright," he said. "Jump on and move forward."

I did what I was told, grateful that the heat covered the blood rushing to my face.

My body rested easily on the saddle, much different from the last time I had ridden. Malachi was behind me within a second, effortlessly throwing himself onto the back of the horse.

"You sure you don't want to fly?" I asked him. His arms settled around mine as he grabbed the reins.

"Why?" he asked, his breath against my ear sent a chill down my spine. "Are you afraid?"

I rolled my eyes, but the edge in his voice sent a warmth through my body.

Malachi laughed behind me, sending vibrations through my back. I kept my spine stiff, but Malachi was clearly making no effort to keep his distance on the saddle. His legs tapped against mine with every step the massive horse took, and his chest pressed tightly against my back as we moved into a steady walk at the back of the group.

"Just like old times," he whispered. "Let's hope this trip goes differently than that one."

"At least we don't have to worry about your brothers killing me this time."

"That's true," he agreed. "But I wouldn't be so trusting of the group."

My interest peaked. "Why?" I asked. "You don't trust them?"

He took a deep breath. "I don't trust anyone so easily, princess. Neither should you. Keep your guard up, even with Sadie. We don't know what they really want."

"And your mother?"

"Her too."

I nodded, and Malachi and I fell into a silent trot for hours. His body against mine became more and more comfortable as the journey continued. He didn't make any annoying comments as I let my body relax into his, leaning on him for support.

The forest was beautiful. With the sun blazing down, it was easy to see all the different life out here. It wasn't terrifying and disastrous. It was peaceful, with a certain darkness that would lure you in if you weren't too careful.

It felt familiar.

Massive trees towered around us, and they became thicker and thicker as we advanced forward. Humidity increased, too. Within the next hour, nearly my entire shirt had been soaked with sweat.

"You'd be a lot cooler if you just took that off, you know," Malachi whispered in my ear when he saw me fidgeting. I elbowed him in the ribs.

"Ow!" he exclaimed. "I was just trying to help!"

I was about to come up with any insult I could think of when Isaiah stopped at the front of the group.

"There's water here," he said. "Let's stop for a break."

Nobody objected, and the group of us brought our horses around a small clearing near the river we had been following through the forest.

Sweat covered every inch of my skin. Malachi's, too, as he swung himself off the horse. He reached up and grabbed my waist to help me down, his fingers brushing under my shirt and sliding against my skin.

"Thanks," I mumbled before quickly straightening and turning to the others.

It's not that I was embarrassed to show affection. I wasn't. I had just never shown affection publicly before. And Malachi was *complicated*.

Nobody seemed to be paying us any attention, though. Everyone tied their horses to a nearby tree and gathered around the water.

I knelt on the ground, dipping my hands into the stream. It was cool water, covered by the shade of the massive trees. I cupped my hands and threw water over my face, letting it drip down my neck. I threw another handful on my back.

We all looked ridiculous, as if we had already been riding for days.

This was definitely going to be a long trip.

Esther knelt next to me, mimicking my movements. "It's amazing, isn't it?" she asked.

"What is?"

"That the forest gives us what we need." She cupped her hands and took a long drink of the river water.

"Yeah," I suggested. Even though Esther had a strange way of talking. "I guess so."

"How are you feeling, girl?" she asked.

"Fine."

She eyed me suspiciously, as if she didn't fully believe my answer. "That will change, you know," she said.

"What?" I asked. "What will change?"

"How you're feeling. Things are going to start changing for you very soon."

"What do you mean? I'm going to get sick?"

She took a moment before responding, "Not sick, child. Just different. You and I have a lot to discuss."

Now it was my turn to eye her. I hadn't noticed before, but her long, silver hair was littered with small beads and gems. She definitely looked older, yet her skin had an olive glow that radiated youth.

Esther hadn't been explicitly rude to me, she was just strange.

And after Malachi told me what she had been planning for me...

"What do you plan to do when we return from Trithen?" I asked her in a hushed voice that only she could hear.

"What I've always done," she responded.

"And what is that? What does the mother of the fae heir do while she hides from everyone she abandoned?"

The sudden wave of emotion surprised me, but Esther didn't look the slightest bit troubled. "I know you think I am cruel. For leaving Malachi."

"I don't think much of anything about you, actually," I responded.

"But you'll get to know me more I hope. I would like it very much if you and I were friends."

"Why?" I asked. "Because you need something from me?"

"No, I am trying to help you, Jade."

My name felt *powerful* when she said it. It sounded strong.

Something inside of me stirred.

"You *are* a witch, aren't you?" I asked, hoping she would confirm the rumors.

"Something like that, yes."

"So that makes Malachi only half fae?" I whispered.

Esther released a long breath, eyeing the water instead of holding eye contact with me. "That is a very long story, Jade. A story for another time, maybe."

I got the feeling it was a story we would need to know sooner rather than later, but I let the subject go.

Next to us, Isaiah peeled his shirt off and jumped into the water, splashing everyone. Sadie let out a squeal when he shoved a wave of water into her face.

"What!" he exclaimed. "It feels amazing! You all should give it a shot!"

"No thanks," Adeline responded. "You have no clue what you're swimming with in there. It could be nasty!"

"Or dangerous," Adonis added.

I glanced at him and quickly looked away. The less time I spent talking with Malachi's brothers, the better.

"What about you, Jade? Care to join me for a swim?"

Malachi snorted a laugh behind me, but turned and followed his brothers and Adeline back to our camp.

It was so incredibly hot, and the cool water felt amazing on my skin.

"You know what?" I replied, standing from my knelt position by the river. "A swim sounds great."

Isaiah looked at me in shock as I kicked my boots off and jumped in, fully clothed.

The water was deeper than I expected. I sank a few feet before kicking my legs, sending my body toward the blue surface.

The current was soft, gently trickling around my body.

Isaiah roared in laughter as I broke through the surface. "Wow, I really didn't think you had that in you," he said.

"You think I'm some sort of Saint?" I asked.

Isaiah splashed a handful of water in my direction. "Hey!" I yelled.

"What?" he teased. "Afraid of water now?"

He splashed again, but I didn't flinch away this time. Instead, dipped my head under water, swam toward him, and yanked him underneath with me.

I almost choked on my own laughter as we both surfaced, Isaiah gasping for air.

"Oh, you really want to play that game?" he teased. I laughed again and moved to swim away, but Isaiah's arms caught me and yanked me under again before I could get out of reach.

He let go quickly, and we both resurfaced seconds later. "Okay!" I yelled, out of breath from the water and the laughter. "Okay, we're even now!"

Isaiah looked different. He wasn't the annoying, broody leader of Fearford. He was just a boy. A young one at that. I caught myself wondering how I would act if I had an entire kingdom in my hands. If my father had died, leaving me with all that responsibility at such a young age.

"You're staring," he interrupted.

I blushed and quickly looked away. "Sorry," I admitted. "I just have a hard time believing you really run an entire kingdom."

"What?" he asked. "Is that so hard to believe?"

"Yes," I responded. "You're barely older than me. What are you, twenty?"

"I will be in a couple of weeks," he said.

Saints. He was even younger than I thought.

"What about you?" he asked. "You have to be what, eighteen? Nineteen?"

"I'll be turning eighteen in a couple of days, actually," I replied. "Although I definitely feel much older than that."

"Being married so young can't help."

We both tread the water around us, relaxing in the cool stream of water.

"Trust me, I've lived through much worse than being married off."

"Really? Even to the fae prince?"

"He's not as bad as you think. He keeps me safe. That's more than I can say for any human back home."

"So, you plan on staying with him, then? You actually *like* being his wife?"

I couldn't ignore the tiny hint of disdain in his voice. The small amount of envy. "I don't know," I said. "I don't know what I'm doing anymore. I couldn't make it back home if I tried. Rewyth isn't my home, not so long as the King is alive."

"What about Fearford?" he asked. "Would Fearford ever be an option for you?"

His question caught me off guard. My mind went completely blank, but it didn't matter anyway because small hands wrapped around both of my ankles.

Isaiah was close, but not that close.

I kicked twice, but the grips on my ankles didn't move. "What is that?" I asked Isaiah. I splashed around frantically, trying but failing to see what had taken hold of me in the water. "Isaiah?"

"What? What is it?"

"I don't know, something's–"

I was pulled under before I could get the words out.

# CHAPTER 12
# *Jade*

My lungs tightened immediately as I was plunged deeper and deeper into the water. I kicked and thrashed, but the grip on my ankles only tightened.

Someone was trying to drown me. Someone or something.

I felt someone reaching for me, I desperately grabbed onto anything I could. Isaiah. Isaiah would help me.

The water wasn't that deep, I just had to reach the surface.

He was trying to pull me up, but whatever was holding me to the bottom of the river wasn't going to budge. The grip on me was so tight, sharp pain began shooting up my legs.

I was going to die here. If this thing didn't let go of me, I was going to drown.

I let go of Isaiah and reached down, trying to pry the grip off of myself. But it was no use.

I clawed and clawed and *clawed* at the hands, at the deadly grip that wouldn't let up.

There were many times in my life that I had accepted death. Saints, there were even times that I would have welcomed it.

But this was not one of those times.

Desperation controlled my movements. Isaiah's hands found mine once again, and he pulled so hard I thought my shoulders were going to pop.

People were yelling above me, but I could only hear the muffled noises from below the water.

My lungs screamed. I was three seconds away from inhaling a mouthful of water.

Two seconds.

One second.

The water around me stilled, and the grip on my legs let go. I didn't hesitate. I kicked toward the surface, Isaiah's hands pulling me toward the air.

The next few moments were a blur of coughing, choking up water, and being dragged out of the water by both Esther and Isaiah.

The others rushed toward us, but Malachi was the only one I saw as he dropped to his knees in front of me, peeling me away from Isaiah.

"What happened?" he yelled, possessive anger booming in his voice.

"I scared them off, but nobody's getting back in that damn water," Esther replied. "It was a kraken. It had to be."

"It was strong," Isaiah added. "If it weren't for Esther she would have drowned."

"Keep your hands off my wife," Malachi growled in his direction. "Jade," he whispered to me. "Jade, are you okay?"

I coughed one more time and pushed my wet hair out of my face. "Yeah, I'm fine," I answered.

I pulled myself into a sitting position, my wet clothes dragging me down. The group had backed up, giving Malachi and I some space as I recovered.

"I'm fine," I repeated, more for myself. "That thing was going to kill me," I said, shaking my head.

"I wouldn't have let that happen," Malachi replied.

"Wait a minute," Isaiah interrupted. "You're telling me that thing was a kraken? As in, the sea monster kraken?"

"Yes," Esther replied. "Don't be so quick to dismiss the stories of your elders, son."

"Let's give them some space," Adeline said. "Dinner isn't going to cook itself."

I gave her a half-hearted smile when she winked at me, and after a few minutes Mal and I sat alone on the riverbank.

His eyebrows were furrowed, and his jaw was clenched.

I knew that look.

"What?" I asked him. "What's wrong?"

He didn't look at me. Didn't respond. I followed his gaze to see what he was staring at in the distance with such a death glare.

Isaiah.

"Calm down," I said. "He's harmless!"

I even surprised myself with saying those words. Isaiah was harmless for now. Away from Fearford and the mess of politics that he was trying to put on a show for, he was just a regular guy.

Mal had nothing to fear.

"Still," Malachi responded. "Something's off."

I shook my head. "Whatever you say, Mal. He was trying to save me."

"The sun will be setting soon. Your clothes are wet," he said, changing the conversation.

"Great observation. Would you rather me have jumped in naked?"

"Isaiah would have preferred that, I'm sure."

"Come on!" I exclaimed. I stepped closer to Malachi and mimicked his body language, crossing my arms over my chest just inches from him. "All he did was pull me out of the water. Are you jealous, Malachi Weyland?"

He finally took his gaze off Isaiah and looked me in the eye. His stare was intense enough to send a chill down my spine.

"You don't want to see me jealous, princess."

"And why is that?"

He smirked for a moment before answering, "Because some people tell me I have quite the temper."

"Is that so?" I asked.

"Mhmm."

"Better keep my distance then," I teased, before turning around and walking back to the group of horses. Adeline appeared back in the clearing, followed by Serefin, carrying an armful of wood and sticks.

"For a fire?" I asked. "Isn't it a little hot for that?"

"It's going to get a lot cooler around here once the sun goes down," Adeline responded. "You'll be happy you took that jacket along with you."

We spent the next few hours eating some of the food we brought with us, feeding the horses, and trying not to rip each other's heads off.

Correction—the *brothers* tried not to rip each other's heads off.

It amazed me that they still bickered this much, that there was still so much tension between them all. The brothers had kidnapped me and put my life in danger, but it was all to protect me.

Allegedly.

I could see why Malachi wasn't so quick to accept their friendship. Adonis was really the only one who was trying, anyway. The others seemed like they couldn't care less.

Although I did catch them whispering amongst themselves and turning to look at Malachi on a number of occasions.

Something was up.

"Are they always like this?" Sadie whispered to me. The sun was starting to go down, and as the temperature dropped with it, we all had gravitated around the fire.

"For the short time that I've known them, yes," I answered. "It can get exhausting."

"Why does Malachi hate them so much?" she asked. "They're brothers, aren't they?"

"Half-brothers," Esther chimed in. "Malachi is my only son. The others are sons of the new Queen."

"Oh," Sadie stuttered. "I didn't realize. I'm sorry."

"Don't be," Esther continued. "The King doesn't discuss my time in Rewyth much at all. It's easier if everyone assumes Malachi is their true brother."

"That's why he's the heir to the throne?" Sadie asked. "Because he's your only son?"

Esther nodded. "My blood runs deep in Rewyth. I may not be there now, but Malachi will one day carry on my legacy. As soon as that bastard is off the throne."

"Wow," I chimed in. "You seem to have strong feelings about the King."

Esther gave me a knowing look. "Same as you, child. Same as you."

"What made you leave?" Sadie asked. I stiffened, knowing this answer would not be short and Sadie was brave to ask it in the first place.

Esther just smiled. "There were many things that led to my departure," she started. "But there are things that you two don't know yet. Things I'm sure your prince wouldn't appreciate me sharing."

I glanced at Malachi, who was too busy bickering with Eli and Fynn to pay any attention to us.

"Like what?"

Esther glanced at them, also, making sure there were no lingering ears on us.

"There has been talk of a new world. A world where fae and humans can get along in peace."

"What do you mean? Don't we get along just fine now?"

"With separation, yes," Esther continued. "I'm talking about together. In the same kingdom. No human kingdoms and fae kingdoms, just kingdoms."

"Really?" I asked, my interest piqued. "And I somehow have something to do with that?"

"As I said before, child, if everything we know is correct, you are the peacemaker. You are the key to everything."

Amazement, surprise, and curiosity all ran through me. "Those are just stories, though," Sadie said. "How can you be sure Jade is the one?"

Esther looked at me now, and with the reflection of the fire in her eyes, I saw genuine love. Genuine caring. She lifted a loose strand of my now partially-dried hair and placed it behind my ear. "I just know, child. I just know."

"That's why you saved my life," I said. "You had been waiting on me?"

Esther nodded.

I looked down at my boots. "It can't be me, though. I'm just a human. There's nothing special about me."

"And that, child, is where you are so painfully wrong."

I wanted to ask her a million questions. I wanted her to explain everything to me, about who she was and where she came from. I wanted to hear her talk about Malachi and what life was like before she left Rewyth. I wanted to know what she thought of the King and how she felt about leaving Malachi all this time.

What had she been doing? Why had she never tried to reach out to him? To protect him?

"What are we talking about over here?" Isaiah interrupted as he sat on the ground next to us. Esther stiffened but smiled at Isaiah.

"Just girl things," she lied. Interesting. Esther was keeping this hidden from Isaiah? I wondered if Sadie would do the same. "It would bore you."

"Anything is less boring than listening to them fight about nothing," he added. Sadie smiled at him, but still said nothing.

I decided to change the conversation. "So, Isaiah," I asked. "What are your plans for Fearford when we return?"

Isaiah nodded, clearly appreciating that some attention was now on him. "I have many plans for Fearford, Jade. As you know, humans have always lived in poverty. Humans have suffered for decades–if not centuries."

"Trust me, I know," I said.

"I want that to change. My father wanted that, too. But he never had the means to fulfill that."

"How could you possibly fulfill that?" I asked.

Isaiah held his hands out, gesturing to the fae on the other side of the fire and to us on this side of the fire. "We work together," he said.

Sadie laughed out loud.

"It sounds ridiculous, yes," he said. "But it's already starting. The fact that we're even taking this journey together is a step in the right direction."

I admired his thinking, I really did. But after living in Rewyth for a short amount of time, I knew it was a flawed plan. The fae were greedy. They loved their expensive things and their fancy parties.

They loved power.

They loved being powerful.

And they weren't going to give that up for a human. Not now, not ever. Isaiah was surely not the first person with a plan like this.

The King had thought of it, yes. But only to advance his own goal of getting the fae closer to enemy territory.

And that was clearly working so well.

But men like Isaiah, just like fae men, wanted power. The only difference was that Isaiah had none.

The fae held all the power.

"Let's get some sleep," Esther suggested. "It won't be long until we're on the road again."

We agreed, and everyone moved to get their sleeping bags from the back of the horses.

As soon as I stepped away from the fire, the cool of the night hit me. I wrapped my arms around myself but it was no help. My clothes were mostly dry, but not dry enough to hold onto any body heat.

Saints. It had to have dropped at least twenty degrees in the last half hour.

"Regretting that swim yet?" Malachi snuck up on me.

"Not at all," I lied. "Why do you ask?"

Malachi laughed and shook his head. "You know if you want to borrow my blanket, you can just ask."

"I'm fine," I responded back. I didn't need any favors from Malachi, not any more than he had already given me.

"If you say so, princess," he said. He reached around me, arms brushing my body on both sides as he grabbed his own blanket off the horse. "Don't say I didn't offer," he whispered in my ear.

My fists clenched. Malachi was infuriating. And now that he knew I was willing to kiss him in the middle of the crowd of humans during the bonfire, he was willing to tease me every second we were together in return.

It was torture.

I shook it off, grabbing my blanket and the extra jacket Adeline had made me pack, before walking back toward the fire.

"I'll take first watch," Adonis announced. "I'll wake you in two hours," he said to Malachi.

Malachi hesitated, but ultimately agreed. We positioned ourselves scattered around the fire, everyone making sure they could feel some heat.

I chose an empty spot and laid my blanket down on the dirt.

Malachi motioned to Serefin, who nodded and moved to settle in on my right. Malachi did the same on my left.

"Are you serious?" I whispered to him. "I don't need babysitters."

He eyed Serefin again, who didn't budge.

"It's not you I'm worried about, Jade," he said. Any teasing in his voice was gone now, replaced with a brutal seriousness. "Just go to sleep."

Normally, I would have argued. I would have spat back some sort of comment as to how he would just boss me around like that.

But this time...

This time I listened.

The cold night easily bit through my thin blanket. Even with my jacket wrapped tightly around my body, I was freezing.

How could it possibly be this cold?

It didn't take long until the whispering from the others subsided, everyone falling fast asleep.

Except for me.

And I didn't dare ask Malachi for warmth. Not when I had already objected so vocally.

I clenched my jaw, and focused on tightening every muscle in my body every few seconds to encourage some sort of blood movement.

I flipped from side to side, letting the heat from the fire warm one side of my body, and then the other.

"Warm enough, princess?" Mal whispered in the darkness. He had gotten closer since I last checked.

Much closer.

"Yes," I responded. "Very comfortable, thank you."

Mal chuckled lightly.

I didn't have to look at what he was doing. As soon as I heard the movement of fabric, I knew.

"Good," he responded. "I would hate for you to be cold. Wouldn't want you getting sick on the first night of our journey."

I clenched my jaw. Tightened my muscles. "Nope," I said through gritted teeth. "None of that happening here."

More movement.

Malachi's arm brushed against mine. He was moving closer. "Apologies," he whispered. "You don't mind if I sleep here, do you?" he asked. His body was very close to mine now. If I were to slide an inch to the left, we would be touching.

"You can do whatever you want to do," I answered.

Malachi made a noise of satisfaction and settled into his new spot on the ground.

I tried to remain still. I tried not to shiver. But Malachi was too close now, and I was far too cold to try and hide anything.

"Saints," he mumbled under his breath before rolling sideways, pressing his body close to mine. He extended his blanket so it covered me, as well, giving me an extra layer of warmth. "Don't even try to object," he insisted. "Or else neither of us will get any sleep."

I kept my mouth shut, and instead focused on the warmth of his body that was radiating through the thick blanket.

"Thank you," I mumbled after my body finally quit shivering.

Mal chuckled silently, but I felt the vibrations through the fabric. His arm was draped over my body, but he left it at that, giving me plenty of space yet plenty of warmth.

Somehow, he still held the ability to surprise me.

"Sleep, princess," he whispered. "I'll wake you in the morning."

With my body tucked tightly next to Malachi, and Serefin fast asleep on the other side of me, I let my heavy eyelids flicker closed.

*Thunder cracked across the sky, the ground in front of me illuminating with lightning for just a moment before disappearing into the darkness again.*

*I turned my head upward, only to be greeted by heavy raindrops slapping my skin.*

*Dread encapsulated me. In my bones, taking over my every waking sense.*

*I was paralyzed by fear, but I didn't know why. And where was I? How had I gotten here?*

*"Jade!" a voice yelled to me. "Jade, run!"*

*Run. I had to run. I had to move.*

*My legs were frozen, unable to get me away from something that I wasn't sure was after me...*

*It was so dark, so cold.*

*Another crack of thunder.*

*Another flash of light.*

*I took a deep breath of the thick, wet air and put all of my effort into picking up my foot. One step at a time. I had to get out. I had to escape.*

*From something, if not my mind.*

*One foot in front of the other, my bare feet sank into the mud.*

*"Run from what?" I yelled back after I mustered the nerve to yell back. At who? I couldn't tell.*

*Everything was blurry. So, so blurry.*

*"You won't make it!" it yelled back. But I knew that voice. I had heard that voice hundreds of times before.*

*Malachi.*

*I knew the name, but who was he to me? How did I know Malachi?*

*It didn't matter. What mattered was getting out. Getting away.*

*Running.*

*I ran as quickly as my feet could move, which wasn't quick at all.*

*Wasn't quick enough.*

*It was only a matter of time before whoever was chasing me caught me, and then I would be dead.*

*Death was always coming for me. Always.*

*"Malachi," I whispered. The name sounded foreign on my mouth, but familiar to my body. "Malachi!" I repeated a little lower. "Help me!" I yelled to him.*

*He was closer now, I could make out a dark figure in the distance, his face only lighting up when the lightning struck the sky.*

*"I can't help you," he yelled. His voice was somber in a way that made me stop in my tracks. "I can't help you, Jade. You have to get out."*

*I knew that was the end. I don't know how I knew, but I knew. I quit running. Quit fighting. And instead, I sank to my knees in the thick mud.*

*This was the end.*

## CHAPTER 13
# *Malachi*

Jade wasn't next to me when I woke up.

I sat up in a panic, making sure everyone else was still asleep, before I whispered her name in the darkness.

"Jade?" I whispered. "Are you out there?"

I looked to Adonis, who was supposed to wake me up after two hours. He was fast asleep on his log.

I kicked him in the leg, jolting him awake as I walked into the woods. "Where is she?" I asked Adonis. "Jade, where did she go?"

He stammered, giving his answer without having to say a word.

"Jade!" I whispered. No response.

But she was close. I could feel it.

I stepped into the darkness, the low embers of the fire barely helping as my eyes adjusted to the night.

Jade wouldn't be able to see a thing. She was human. This would be nothing but darkness to her.

I closed my eyes and took a deep breath, letting my senses stretch to the forest around me.

Jade was here. She was close. She was alive.

*Think, Malachi. Focus.*

My power flared around me, and I took another breath to reel it back in. I know I wouldn't hurt Jade, even if I did lose control.

But the others... I wasn't so sure.

I weaved through the trees, careful to be as silent as night as I drifted around the clearing.

I listened for her breath. Her heart beat.

And then I heard her.

"Please," she whimpered. "Please, don't."

I took five steps forward, and I saw her.

Her eyes were open, but they looked vacantly into the nothingness of the night.

"I've given enough," she whispered to nobody.

She had to be asleep. Sleep walking, as they called it.

I stepped forward, careful not to make a sound.

"No," she said, louder this time.

"Jade–" I spoke.

"No!"

"JADE!"

She dropped to her knees in the darkness, a sob of heartbreak leaving her body.

The sound alone froze me to my core.

It was the sound of deep, irrevocable suffering.

And Jade wasn't even awake.

"Wake up," I said, rushing to her side. "Wake up, Jade. You're dreaming."

Another sob wrecked her body. She collapsed entirely, losing all control of herself. I held her shoulders up.

"Wake up!" I yelled again.

She went completely limp then, her head rolling onto my shoulder.

"Jade," I pleaded, no longer hiding the desperation in my voice. "Wake up, please."

She blinked her eyes open and looked at me in the darkness.

Tears streamed down her face. "Malachi?" she breathed. Her voice cracked, which evoked an emotion within me I didn't even know I was capable of feeling.

"I'm right here," I whispered. "I'm right here, Jade."

Small hands wrapped around my waist. Jade's head crashed into my chest as she cried.

And cried.

I wasn't going to let go. I held onto her tightly, like she was the only thing holding me to this world.

"Breathe, Jade," I whispered. "You were sleeping. It was just a dream."

She sobbed again, but took one shaky deep breath.

"Breathe again, Jade."

She did.

"Again."

She took another breath and lifted her head, looking me in my eyes.

Jade opened her mouth to say something, likely to explain what had happened or what she was so afraid of, but no words came out.

"You don't have to explain anything to me," I whispered. "I know."

I knew my brothers were likely awake now. I knew they had probably found us in the woods and were lingering in the darkness.

I didn't care.

Jade's hand moved to my chest, where my heart was now pounding furiously. "You're here," she whispered to herself. "You're here."

"I'm here, Jade," I repeated. "We're okay."

Minute after minute, her breath became more even.

"Are you ready to go back?" I whispered after some time.

She nodded.

I moved to stand up, but Jade held tightly onto my arm. "Don't leave me," she said. She was awake now, but a soft haze of emotions I couldn't read shadowed her features.

"I'm not going anywhere," I responded. Her legs shook as she stood up, so I bent down and picked her up, carrying her back to camp in my arms.

Jade didn't object. She buried her face in my chest as I walked us back to the fire.

To my surprise, everyone was still fast asleep.

Besides Adonis, who stood at the edge of the camp with a look of concern.

"You're taking my watch now, too, dumb ass," I whispered as I walked by him.

I set Jade down on her own blanket. She settled in immediately, still barely conscious. I relaxed on the ground next to her, close enough to feel if she got up in the night.

We had a few hours left until daylight.

Jade wandering into the forest again while she slept was not an option.

"Go to sleep," I whispered in the darkness. The embers of the fire glowed softly.

Jade didn't respond. Didn't say another word. Simply shut her eyes and went back to sleep.

My heart was racing. Saints. Jade could have easily wandered deep enough into the woods that nobody would have found her. Or worse—where the deadlings found her. Or any other horrific beast dwelling in these parts.

Sleepwalking. That was new.

Nightmares, too.

I would have to keep a close eye on her for the rest of our journey.

A sick feeling sat in the depths of my stomach. I hated that she was afraid.

Did she have nightmares before she ever came to Rewyth? Did she dream about her family? About that bastard of a father beating her?

I stopped myself from clenching my fists as I stared into the dark abyss above.

I was going to make things right. I didn't know how, but I would. I would start by ending things with my father.

My brothers had a plan, but after talking with them earlier in the night, they were desperate for help. They needed someone with power. Someone with control.

They needed me.

The only problem was, as soon as Jade was somewhere safe and away from this mess, I was going to walk straight into Rewyth and kill him myself.

He had to know that. He had to know I was coming for him. Unless of course he still thought I was weak.

He had underestimated me many times before. That wasn't going to be happening again.

But I had other things to handle first. Trithen wasn't exactly going to welcome us with open arms, no matter what those messengers may have said. We would have trouble waiting.

Which meant Jade would still be in danger.

And Sadie and Isaiah...

Isaiah had crossed the line one too many times, like a child playing with a match. He was going to get himself hurt.

I stayed that way, laying in the darkness, listening to every minuscule noise that the forest made, until my eyelids drifted shut.

And I slept.

# CHAPTER 14
# *Jade*

I BLINKED MY EYES OPEN, ONLY TO FIND MYSELF PRACTICALLY DRAPED over Malachi.

Our legs were tangled under the blanket, and I had been using his chest as a pillow.

Saints.

I gently removed the arm that was draped around my body and began to stand. Everyone else was still asleep.

Except for Serefin, who appeared to be on watch.

"Morning," he greeted me as I walked by. "Did you sleep well?"

He must not have woken up during my little episode last night. That's what I was going to call it. An episode. Because there is no way I was going to sleep walk like an idiot into the forest ever again.

"Like a rock," I lied. He eyed me carefully, perhaps he knew I was lying. Serefin was one of the smart ones in the group.

He was also the type of person that would lie about it just to make me feel better.

The others began to stir awake.

Including Esther.

I couldn't even look at her. I couldn't think about her right now.

Not after that nightmare.

I only remembered small portions of it, but I remembered enough to know that she was there. And it wasn't good.

But she had just saved my life in the river. That was twice now that she had saved me. She wasn't going to hurt me.

"I'm going to wash up," I announced before walking toward the river.

I needed a clear mind. I had much of the trip left ahead, and I couldn't afford to crack.

There was too much at risk.

I walked over to the river and knelt down, dipping my hands into the cool morning stream. It was refreshing, and although the night had been cold and the morning was still brisk, I wanted more.

I cupped the water and splashed it into my face.

It was just a dream, I told myself. Esther was still fast asleep. She had slept around the fire like everyone else. They would have seen something.

It was crazy, anyway. To think that Esther had something to do with my nightmare.

Why wouldn't she just warn me of things in person? Sending a premonition in the form of a nightmare was not only cruel, it was useless.

I shook my head. I was thinking too much. I was thinking about everything too much.

I had no idea how long I had been sleepwalking last night, but I had the faintest memory of Mal finding me.

Thank the Saints it was him, too.

If I had wandered in the wrong direction in the middle of the night...

I didn't let my mind go there. I had been near death many times in my life. Last night was nothing special.

I splashed more water in my face.

"Long night?" Isaiah's voice made me jump. I wiped as much of the water off my skin before replying.

"Not long enough," I answered, keeping things casual. "Just ready to get moving."

"Me too," he responded. "Things are going to be different when we get to Trithen."

He walked forward and knelt next to me. A little too close, but perhaps I was just tense. "What do you mean?"

"You'll see," he answered. "But I think it's important to remember that we're on the same side, you and I. It wouldn't be so terrible if we worked together, would it?"

I shook my head. "You're a mysterious man, Isaiah. I wish you would just say what you mean instead of talking in riddles."

Isaiah dipped his own hands into the steam and brought them to his mouth, taking a short sip of the water.

"One day, maybe," he mumbled.

I sighed. "One day maybe what?" Frustration pulsed through my body, a hot wave that demanded answers. Esther. Isaiah. Sadie. Malachi. It was too much now. People were going to start answering me, whether they liked it or not.

I slapped the rest of the water out of Isaiah's hands. "Tell me right now," I insisted. "Forget this 'maybe' shit. Start talking."

Isaiah looked at me in surprise, then laughed.

He laughed.

"You're a smart girl, Jade. You know how to get what you want. That's a rare quality, believe it or not. Many people don't have the brains to think for themselves."

"Yet you do?"

"Yes," he replied quickly. "I do. And I think you could be very useful to me."

"Yes, you've implied that."

"And I can help you, too," he said.

"Yes, you implied that, as well. Very vaguely, I might add. More riddles."

"You want me to stop the riddles? Just tell you exactly what I'm thinking right now?"

A heart beat passed. "Yes," I answered.

"Fine," he breathed. "I think you're amazing, Jade. More than amazing. You're the one we've been waiting on for generations. I want you. I need you. I think we could be amazing together, and I curse every damn day that I didn't find you before him. Because I wish every day that you were mine instead."

I had to admit. Of all the things I was expecting him to say, that was not one of them.

My mind went blank.

I opened my mouth to respond, but words failed me. Isaiah waited expectantly, but Saints. What did he think I was going to say? This was absolute shit.

Sadie chose that moment to step into the clearing. "Isaiah," she said. "Esther is looking for you."

The odds of her not having heard everything we just said was low.

Very low.

Isaiah stared at me for a second longer before standing up and walking back to camp.

I stood up and prepared myself for Sadie's wrath. She might have denied any romance business between the two of them, but I was no idiot.

"Sadie, I–"

"Save it," she interrupted. "You don't have to say anything. I know."

"You know what?" She sighed, walking over to the river. "I know he's interested in you, Jade. He would be a fool not to be."

"What do you mean?" I asked.

"He's the leader of Fearford, Jade. You have something that can help him. You're not only favored, you're protected. That's not going to change. You're an asset to him."

I shook my head, hardly able to comprehend what I was hearing.

"Honestly, Sadie," I started, "I don't know how you put up with that. He makes me worried for the entire human race."

She smiled, but it didn't reach her eyes. "He has good intentions, Jade. I know you might not see it, but he does."

"Malachi won't like this."

"He doesn't have to know."

"He's my *husband*," I replied, shocked at how fierce I sounded with the word husband.

Sadie stared at me for a second, almost like she was surprised at my words. Did she think I wouldn't be loyal to Malachi? That I would ditch our marriage as soon as I was in the hands of humans who may want to protect me? Or was it the fact that they saw a weakness and they were willing to take it?

"Whatever," I mumbled to her. "We should go. They're waiting for us."

Sadie responded something as I brushed past her, but I didn't listen long enough to hear the words. Malachi was right. We couldn't trust them. They wanted something from us, and they would stop at nothing to get it.

I tried to neutralilze my face as I walked into the crowd of the Weyland brothers, accompanied now by Esther and Isaiah.

Saints save me.

"Everything okay?" Malachi whispered.

"Fine," I responded. Memories of his arms around me in the middle of the night flashed through my mind. "Everything's fine."

He eyed me, clearly not believing a word I said, but said nothing.

His dark eyes held promise that we would discuss this later.

"Alright," Adonis yelled to the group. "The sun's about up. Let's get moving! We have a ways to go before we arrive at Trithen, and we don't want to be late."

We nodded in agreement and resumed as we were, as if nothing had happened. As if everything was okay. As if everything was the same as it was yesterday.

But it wasn't the same. And everything was far from being okay.

# CHAPTER 15
## Malachi

"No. We were invited here. We'll walk in like the guests we are."

The others looked at me like I had just asked them to walk onto a battlefield. The only one who didn't was Jade.

Jade. Who may have been equally as suicidal as myself.

My heart was pounding in my ears. I ignored it. I also ignored the loud voice in my mind that told me this was a mistake.

That voice was lying.

I was Malachi Weyland, heir to the fae throne and the deadly Prince of Shadows. If these bastards demanded to speak with me, I would allow them the privilege.

But my friends and family had nothing to fear.

I took a deep breath and tapped into the rumbling power I now felt in my chest. It waited patiently for my command, just like it had done every day now for decades.

It had never once let me down. It wasn't going to start today.

"Can I talk to you for a second?" Jade asked me.

"Right now?" I asked.

"Yes. Right now."

The urgency in her voice forced me to listen. I nodded, and followed her into the safety of the treeline.

"What's wrong?" I asked as soon as we were out of ear shot. "Are you okay?"

"I'm fine," she answered quickly. "I'm okay, it's okay. I just..."

"What?"

"I just have a weird feeling about this, Mal. And I know we came all this way and the last thing you want is someone else questioning your decision to come here, but I just wanted to look you in the eyes and tell you myself. So that maybe you could look me in the eyes back and tell me that I was being crazy, that I had nothing to fear."

I smiled. I couldn't help it. "Well, you're right about one thing, princess. You are crazy."

She tried to smile back but stepped forward. She was close enough now I could still smell the slight scent of cinnamon lingering in her hair, even after our long journey.

It was intoxicating.

"If anything happens in there–"

"Stop," I interrupted. "Don't talk like that."

"And don't interrupt me."

I shut up.

"If anything happens in there, Malachi, I want you to know that this little arrangement has been more than a surprise to me. You've been pleasantly different than I imagined. And you've saved my life countless times, which you never had to do. And I don't know if I properly thanked you or not, but this might be my last chance. So, thank you."

It took me a second to find my words. "Wow," I responded. "Jade Farrow thanking me? Am I dead already?"

"It's not funny!" she said, but a real smile crept into her features. "Whatever they want, Malachi, just give it to them. I don't care what it is. We pretend like we're on their side, and as soon as we leave this place, we'll make a plan to deal with it. To deal with everything."

A wave of relief hit me. Relief that Jade didn't think I was a complete monster. That she cared about what was going to happen next. And that somewhere inside of her, she wanted to help me survive this thing, too.

"We can't trust the others," I said. "Whatever they want from us here, it won't be good. Isaiah, my mother. They have their own agendas. I can feel it. I just don't know what they are yet."

"The truth will come out."

"The truth will come out," I repeated.

Jade moved to walk away, saying, "We should probably get back."

I caged her against the tree with my arms, pressing my body lightly into hers. "Not yet," I whispered.

A flicker of satisfaction crossed her eyes.

It was the same look I had seen on her the first time I saw her in the forest of her home. Jade held a darkness inside of her that wanted her to survive, no matter how badly she wanted to believe otherwise at times. It was what made us so alike. I saw the darkest parts of myself in her.

I just hoped she wouldn't run away when she saw the same in me.

"Kiss me already," she whispered, her deep brown eyes blinking up at me.

I obeyed.

Her lips were gentle and soft against mine. The kiss wasn't a declaration of love or a desperate need for physical touch. It was simply a kiss. A promise that Jade was mine, and I was hers.

And for now, that would be enough.

"Let's go, lovebirds," Adeline's voice yelled from the trees. "We don't have all day!"

Jade smiled as I pulled away, silently cursing that we didn't have more time for this.

More time to just be Jade and Malachi. Husband and wife.

"We'll resume this later," Jade promised.

"I'm counting on it."

And then it was over. Back to business. Back to masks and charades and running around like pawns in a game.

And the game was only beginning.

We walked forward in unison. Jade and I led the pack with my brothers and Adeline behind us, followed by Esther, Sadie and Isaiah.

We walked for a few minutes before a familiar figure stepped into view.

"You came!" the leader of Trithen said as we approached the towering gates. His face brought back hundreds of memories of my time here.

Seth. The King of Trithen.

I only knew he was their leader because I had met him before.

And it hadn't been a friendly introduction.

Memories of war flashed through my mind, of hundreds, if not thousands, of fae dying on the battlefield over nothing but power.

Power that this man's family once wanted.

Power that the fae of Rewyth possessed.

"We did," I replied. My wings flared around my body, Jade standing partially behind my right wing. His eyes settled on them, as if he was just remembering exactly who he was dealing with.

The owner of the black wings. The wielder of the dark powers.

The Prince of Shadows.

"Although," I continued, "I must admit we were rather comfortable in Fearford with our new friends here. May I ask what business required us to travel all this way?"

"Not now," he replied. "Let's get your new friends here settled in, and then we'll discuss business."

I clenched my fists at my side. I could have sent him to his knees. I could have released a power so forceful that his heart eventually stopped from the pain.

But then where would we be?

"That's very generous of you," Esther spoke up from behind me. "We thank you for your hospitality. We'll talk about business later."

She sounded kind and light, but her last words were a threat.

"Please," he said, motioning to the group. "I've had the divine pleasure of meeting the Weyland gentleman, but I'm afraid the rest of you are strangers to me."

Isaiah stepped forward immediately, like a pet pouncing for a piece of meat. "I'm Isaiah. My father was Vincent, leader of Fearford."

The man looked Isaiah up and down before extending his hand.

It was a sure sign of respect. Fae didn't shake hands with humans lightly.

And for good reason.

"And this is my partner, Sadie. She helps me run things in Fearford."

Sadie shook his hand but said nothing.

When the others didn't speak up, I spoke up for them. "This is my mother, Esther. My sister, Adeline. And my wife, Jade."

They all nodded respectively but said nothing.

That didn't stop Seth's eyes from lingering on Jade, likely drinking in her human features.

"What I've been told holds true?" he started. "The others will be very intrigued by this... union."

"It's nothing that breaks any treaties," I defended.

"No?" he asked. "And how does the lovely bride feel about that?"

Jade stiffened behind me. I resisted the urge to grab her hand, but the last thing I needed to do was exhibit my weakness in new territory.

"She feels just fine about it, thank you for asking," I retorted before Jade spoke up. My brothers snickered behind me.

"Very well, then," Seth continued. He turned and led us through the gate. "There will be a Spring Festival this evening. I encourage you each to join us. After your long trip, it's the least we can do."

I nodded politely, the others did the same. Seth continued talking about the history of Trithen, explaining pointless facts that the others pretended to care about.

As soon as our business was over, I would unleash my power.

For Jade's sake, I had to hold it together.

Seth brought us inside the massive walls of Trithen. They were similar to Rewyth's, just like I remembered them to be. Of course, no height of walls could keep out a fae who was determined to enter.

But the walls were to keep out other things.

The fae had *some* enemies, after all.

"You can take the bed," I said to Jade after we were escorted to our rooms.

She laughed, but not a real Jade laugh. It was more of a nervous laugh, one I rarely heard from her.

"What's wrong?" I asked.

"You're my husband," she replied. "You don't have to sleep on the floor. I think we can both be adults here."

"Really?" I teased.

"Yes. Unless you disagree, then by all means sleep on the hard floor."

"Please," I teased. "I am much older than you, you know. If one of us is capable of acting like an adult, it's surely me."

She smiled half-heartedly, but her face grew dark just moments later.

"Something's wrong," I insisted. "Tell me what it is."

Jade turned her eyes to the ceiling, blinking away tears. "It's nothing," she said.

"It's clearly something," I pushed. "If something is bothering you, just tell me and I'll handle it."

She shook her head, a single tear dropping down her tan skin. "No, it's not like that. It's just..." She paused and looked at me with those deep, ocean eyes. "Today is my birthday. I'm officially eighteen."

My breath escaped me.

"And I'm sure Tessa is somewhere spending my birthday alone, thinking about all the possible ways I could have been killed by now. Or better yet, happily married to a monster."

Her words didn't hurt me. They were true. I saw the way Jade's sister had looked at her...like there was a stranger in Jade's own skin.

Tessa was the one person Jade had fought to survive for when she first came to Rewyth.

I didn't let another second go by. I crossed the room in two steps and wrapped my arms around her. She did the same in return, as if she were desperate for it. "Happy birthday, princess," I whispered. I was glad she couldn't see my face, the disgust that would be dripped all over it.

Not disgust at her, of course.

I felt disgusted with myself, that I had let my own wife's birthday pass and she could do nothing but sit by and watch.

"I'll make it up to you," I said to her. "I promise I will."

"I don't care about my birthday anyway," she responded. "It's never been more than disappointment and the depressing thought that I am yet another year closer to my death."

I couldn't respond.

"Things might be changing now that I married you and am still alive."

Still, I said nothing.

"You can talk, you know," she responded. "It's not like I blame you for any of this."

"No," I said eventually, "but that doesn't mean any of it is okay. You can be angry. Saints, you *should* be angry. With me or with the fae. You're allowed to be mad."

Jade shook her head. "If anything, I feel guilty."

"Guilty?"

She nodded. "It's almost as if, when I was home with my father and Tessa, I was waiting to die. But now, with you and the others, with people who actually care if I come home at night or if I'm stranded in the middle of the woods...I've never felt more *alive*."

I knew exactly how she felt. Like her family wasn't really her family. Like she was never really accepted before. But now...

"I get it," I whispered. "I do."

"I know you do."

We stayed like that for a while, I held her in my arms tightly to my chest until tears no longer threatened her eyes. "Okay," She started. "It's been a long day, and I'm sure we have a very long night ahead of us."

"That's an understatement," I responded. "There's probably a few things we should go over before we throw you into a fae party."

"Will it be like our wedding?" she asked.

"It will and it won't."

I wanted to tell her about the previous war with Trithen, about how these fae were vicious in ways that made the fae in Rewyth look like saints.

But Jade had no more reason to worry.

"Why don't you try to rest a bit before the festival?"

"And where are you going?"

"I have an errand to run. I won't be long. But don't go to that festival without me, Jade. I'll come back for you."

She stared at me like she knew I was lying. "Don't do anything stupid, Malachi. We don't want to start trouble."

I let my dark wings flare, just slightly, so she remembered they were there. "Don't forget, princess. You've married the Prince of Shadows. I was born starting trouble."

Jade rolled her eyes, but walked to the bathroom and shut the door behind her.

We had a few hours before the party officially started, which meant I had plenty of time to track down Seth and get the business over with before any fae tricks were involved.

And I had to do it before anyone got any ideas about messing with Jade.

I left our room, making sure the door was completely shut before walking across the hall and knocking. "Adeline, it's me," I announced.

"What do you want?" she responded. "Saints, I just laid down!"

"I need you to stay with Jade for a bit. Can you do that?"

She cursed under her breath, but I heard footsteps approaching the door.

She swung it open, clearly not satisfied about being interrupted. "Fine," she said. "Where are you going?"

"I have some business to take care of."

Adeline laughed, but grabbed my arm before I could turn and walk away. "Oh no you don't," she said. "We all got dragged here because of you, so you don't get to go off alone on some secret mission and not tell me what's going on," she said. "Spill it."

I shook my head. Adeline had always been this stubborn, so I wasn't sure why it surprised me now.

"Fine," I said. "I have old business with Seth. I just want to talk to him and make sure it won't cause any problems with whatever he wants from us now."

Adeline released my arm, only to smack me in the chest. "What was that for!"

"That was for you being an idiot, Mal! Are you kidding me?"

"What do you mean?"

She stepped forward and lowered her voice. "You'll start another war, and we both know it."

"Don't be ridiculous," I replied, knowing that her words did hold some truth. Any of us stepping out of line could start a war. Our political history with Trithen had been that patchy.

"I'm not being ridiculous, Mal. I'm being logical. You killed his father, for Saint's sake. That's not something that a man just forgets."

I rubbed a hand down my face, trying to hide my annoyance. "I'm aware, Adeline. Very aware."

"Fine," she responded after a few seconds. "But if you go and get us all killed, that's on you."

I rolled my eyes and backed away, beginning to walk back down the hallway. "Watch her closely, Adeline," I yelled without turning around. She mumbled something in response. I didn't wait to see if she would go to Jade's room, I knew she would. Not only was Adeline the only sibling capable of taking orders from me, but she genuinely cared about Jade's safety. And not because of some stupid blood oath, either. She actually cared about Jade.

I shoved her words out of my mind. I had no time for that. No time for fear. No time for reminiscing on the past.

"And where are you heading?" Serefin's voice echoed down the hall just as I was about to exit the building. "Storming into the heart of Trithen for a stroll, then?"

I cursed under my breath, but I was certain he heard it. "Not you, too, Ser. Not now."

Ser shook his head and marched toward me down the hall.

"No," he said. "I'm not letting my prince walk around Trithen alone. Whatever you have to do, I'm coming with you."

Saints. I suppose I should have expected Serefin of all people to be on my side, to not convince me to back down. "You don't have to do this," I replied.

Ser clasped a hand on my shoulder and squeezed. "Neither do you," was all he said.

"Saints, Ser. it's not like I'm going to storm out there and kill them all."

"I wouldn't put it above you, brother. Let's just go get it over with, okay? I'm with you."

*I'm with you.*

Words I had heard from Serefin a half a dozen times. Ser had followed me into war. More than once. He had killed for me. He had saved my life. He had put himself before me hundreds of times.

This was just another one of those times.

"Fine," I said. "Let's go."

We turned, and the two of us walked out of the castle and into the blazing sunset.

"Seth can't be trusted. Whatever business he wants to deal with, we can deal with it now," I whispered to Ser. We had to be careful, though. Too many fae ears surrounded us.

Trithen, like any fae city, shined with beauty. Similar to Rewyth, nature ran through every piece of architecture. Where Rewyth was dark and green, though, Trithen reminded me of spring. Red, pink and orange flowers twisted around endless vines, matching the glow of the sunset that reflected off the white, stone buildings.

It hadn't looked this clean during war. The white walls had been splattered with blood.

Most of it I had spilled. Some of it had been my army.

All of it had been deserved.

Images of Seth's father falling to his knees before me flashed through my brain. I had killed him, too. Simply another number to add to my total. Simply politics.

Trithen had a lesson to learn at the time.

I had hoped Seth remembered the consequences of his father.

Serefin must have remembered, too. Remembered this place shining red, but not from the sunset. He tensed as we walked past the center of the city, the same place we had forced everyone to bow before us, and the same place we had killed everyone who resisted.

Like I said. Politics.

Messy, messy politics.

"You know where you're going?" Ser whispered to me. We turned one last corner and approached a large building with a solid, stone door. Two guards stood on each side, all four of them immediately drawing their swords when we approached.

As if that could stop us.

"I'm pretty sure, yeah," I whispered back to Ser.

We approached the guards with caution.

"What do you want?" one of them asked. I saw the way their eyes all flickered to my black wings. And the way the grips on their weapons tightened.

I smiled.

"I would like to speak with Seth. He should be expecting me," I lied.

The guards didn't flinch. "Nobody is being expected," they said.

That was confirmation that Seth was in here.

"You're wrong," I said, clasping my hands behind my back and lifting my chin. "Seth has asked me to come here, and I'm a bit late. So, if you could just–"

"Turn around," he interrupted. "Nobody's getting past this door. Especially Rewyth scum."

I took a breath.

I counted to three.

The power that rumbled through my body begged for a release, it knew I wanted it, too.

So, this time, I let it go. I pictured each of the guards dropping to their knees in pain, screaming for mercy.

They did.

I pictured them scratching their own faces, wanting to dig into their own eyeballs to stop the pain in their brains.

They did.

I kept it going, too. Serefin whispered something behind me but I didn't stop. Had they forgotten who I was? The Prince of Shadows. Had they forgotten what I could do?

More pain. More misery. More power.

The stone door slammed open behind the guards.

"That's enough," Seth's voice boomed the area, echoing off the walls of buildings around us.

I let my power linger, a fraction longer of a second, before pulling it back in with a simple breath.

The guards moaned in pain, but would be fine. My power never caused real physical damage, it only made them think they were dying, burning from the inside out.

I assumed it was misery.

"Hello," I said to Seth. "I was just telling your guards here that I would like to speak with you."

"And this is how you treat your hosts?" he responded. Anger laced his words, but I saw his heart racing.

Fear.

Good. He should be afraid of me. Every bastard in this damned city should fear me.

I walked past the guards and approached Seth.

"You want to talk business?" I said quietly, inches from his face. "Let's talk, shall we?"

Seth was pissed. More than pissed. I had walked openly through his kingdom, dropped four of his guards to their knees with nothing more than a thought, and demanded to speak to him.

But he didn't have much of a choice.

"Fine," He agreed. He glanced at Serefin behind me, then turned for us to follow. "This way."

I glanced back at Ser, who only shook his head in disapproval. Except a small smile on his face told me something else.

"Perfect," I said, clapping my hands together as we followed. My large wings tucked tightly behind me as we maneuvered the hallway.

We arrived at what I assumed was Seth's library, Ser and I both taking a seat along a large wooden table.

Seth didn't sit. He only paced the room before us.

"So," I started when he never did. "You invited us here for a reason. To see if my marriage with Jade was legitimate. To see if we were breaking the treaties. Well we aren't, you've seen that. Yet we're still here."

Seth nodded. "And what would your father say about all of this? About living with the humans?"

"Don't speak to me about my father," I replied.

"The King of Rewyth, you mean?" Seth retorted.

Seth laughed quietly. "That is supposed to be your position soon, is it not? I can't help but wonder why you're parading around Fearford, a human kingdom. Shouldn't you be home, preparing to take the throne?"

"I prepare for the throne every day, Seth. Every single second is yet another second closer to becoming King."

"And where does that leave your human wife, Prince? Beside you on the throne?"

I merely nodded.

Seth shook his head again. "Your father will never allow it."

"How would you know what my father will and will not allow?"

"I am no idiot, despite what you may think. The King of Rewyth is many things, but a supporter of humans is not one of them. That's why he sent you to live with them in Fearford, isn't it? To destroy them all? To overpower them? Or maybe just to slaughter them all like you've done before."

Serefin stiffened beside me.

"I figured as much," Seth continued. "Humans and fae together, it will never last. You know this."

"And you brought us all the way here for what, exactly? A friendly warning?"

Seth eyed me, and moved to take a seat at the table across from us. "No," he said. "That's not all."

Serefin and I waited for more.

"We know about Jade."

My power rumbled. I didn't move a muscle.

"We know she's... special. That some believe she is to fulfill some sort of prophecy for the witches."

"The witches believe in many different prophecies, Seth," I stated, sounding as bored as I possibly could. "I can only imagine what else they think about Jade."

Seth shook his head. "If what they're saying is true..."

"What?" I pushed. "You'll keep her for yourself? Is that it?"

"No," He said. "No. If what they say is true, and Jade is the peacemaker, then we could work together."

Serefin snorted a laugh beside me. I hardly did the same.

"Work together?" I repeated. "And do what, exactly?"

Seth eyed me for a moment before saying, "You're a killer, Malachi. I, of all people, know that."

A silent pause filled the air.

"But I also know that you are much smarter than the King of Rewyth. And I know who gives the orders."

Still, I didn't respond.

"You better be very careful about what you're saying," Serefin warned.

Seth put his hands out on the table in front of us. "I didn't call you here for more fighting," he said. "I brought you here because I wanted to know if the whispers were true. If they are true, if Jade is the peacemaker and she is here to fulfill the prophecy, you'll want help protecting her. Every single kingdom on this planet will come for her, and you know it."

"Including Trithen."

"Not if we have what we want."

"Which is what, exactly?"

"Peace."

*That was unexpected.*

"You're a wealthy fae kingdom. You have peace," I replied slowly.

He nodded again. "Our enemies threaten us every single day. We're fighting for resources, mostly because Rewyth has cut most of our supply chains. These people may live in ignorance, Prince Malachi, but I won't be able to hide it for long. If we help to protect Jade from whatever is coming, if we work together, then when you become King of Rewyth, you will open all trading docks to Trithen again, how it once was."

I hated the thought, but Seth actually made some sense. Perhaps Trithen truly *did* need our help.

"This is all based on some story my mother is telling. How can you be sure that what they say in the prophecy is true?"

"We have very powerful witches working with us, Prince. We are not wrong, and neither is your mother."

I took a deep breath. I needed to talk to my mother. If the other kingdoms would came after Jade, having Trithen on our side wouldn't be the worst idea.

"We know you can't go back to Rewyth," Seth said. A hint of sympathy lined his words.

"That's not true," I replied. "I can go back any time."

"And Jade? My sources tell me your father was not her biggest fan the last time they interacted. How's Jade's back doing, by the way?"

I stood so fast my chair fell backwards behind me. "Do not speak of that," I growled. "Ever."

Serefin was at my side in an instant, grabbing my arm and holding me back.

As if that would stop my power if I dared to use it.

As if *anyone* could stop me.

"I apologize," Seth said. "I meant no offense. Just trying to verify some rumors, that's all."

*Rumors.* That was the last thing I wanted to deal with.

"If you kill your own father, Malachi, you will start a war. And you have no army. You have no backing. Work with us, and we will fight by your side. We will help you kill him. You will become the next King of Rewyth, you will sit on the most powerful fae throne. And Trithen and Rewyth can be at peace again. That is what I'm proposing. That is why I invited you here."

The tension in the air was palpable.

"Think about it," Seth said. "Talk to your mother. We have all evening to relax and enjoy yourselves. We'll discuss this again later."

Serefin and I turned to leave, but I couldn't quite make myself take my next step. I turned back around and looked at Seth.

"Why?" I asked. "Why would you help us? I killed your father."

Seth didn't blink. "I remember what you did," he said. "But I had a father and a king giving me orders once, too. Let's just say that I'm hoping things can be different."

# CHAPTER 16
## *Jade*

I LOOKED RIDICULOUS, BUT I EXPECTED NOTHING LESS.

My dress covered more skin than my wedding gown in Rewyth had, but it wasn't much of a difference.

Adeline gasped as I exited the bathroom, covering her mouth with her hand.

"Stunning," she responded. She then proceeded to squeal in excitement and clap her hands. "Just gorgeous, Jade! You'll be turning the heads of every male in this kingdom."

"Oh, fun," I mumbled. "I can't wait."

She turned me around to face a large mirror that leaned against the wall. "Look at you!" she whispered in awe. I took a look at my gown, covered in red and orange flowers, white lace, and not much else. I looked like spring threw up on me.

"This looks absurd," I responded. "Are you sure this is what we're supposed to wear tonight?"

Adeline had a similar dress on, covered in pink flowers that screamed spring. *That was Trithen*, she had explained to me.

And tonight's festival was to celebrate just that–spring.

"It's the Spring Festival," she replied. "I promise you, Jade, we'll be the least ridiculous looking people here. Besides, everyone will be too wasted to notice."

*Great.*

"Are you sure it's a good idea for me to go? The fae here can't be fans of humans either, I assume."

"Trust me, you'll be protected. I won't let you out of my sight. Malachi would kill me if I did."

My long hair fell down to my waist in loose curls, similar to Adeline's. Her face glowed with a hint of the sun from our journey.

My stomach erupted in butterflies.

Saints. Was I really nervous?

"You'll be fine," Adeline said, as if she could read my thoughts. "We'll show up, eat, drink, dance, and it'll be over before you know it. You might even be sad that it's over. Kingdoms all over the planet speak of Trithen Festivals, you know."

"Really?" I asked. "Why?"

Adeline grabbed both of my hands and pulled me toward the bedroom door. The sun had just set, and the call of sweet music flowed through the open window. "I guess we'll be finding out soon," she answered. "Let's go!"

I pulled back. "Malachi didn't want me to leave without him. I should wait."

Adeline rolled her eyes. "You're with me," she said. "You'll be fine, Jade. And if he gets all pissed off and protective, you can blame me. He's probably already down there, anyway!"

I hated that Adeline could convince me so easily, but she was right. I wasn't going to wait up in this room like some sort of helpless girl waiting for her savior.

I was going to the festival.

Adeline knew what I had decided as soon as I smiled.

And soon enough, we were headed out the door.

"This is amazing!" Adeline yelled in my ear. I could hardly hear her over the loud violins booming through the air around us. Saints, I didn't even know those instruments could play so loudly.

Adrenaline pulsed through my body. All around us, fae were covered in spring-colored jewels, dresses, and anything else they seemed to find. Silver and white wings covered the entire field, and fires around the perimeter allowed my human eyes to see in the darkness.

She was right. It was stunning.

Singing, dancing, laughing, eating. Hundreds of men and women littered the field. Nobody seemed to care that I was human, or that Adeline was from Rewyth. Nobody even glanced in our direction.

Perhaps this wouldn't be as bad as I thought it would be.

"Come on, Jade," Adeline said, pulling me toward a massive table of food and drinks.

She picked up a goblet of wine for herself, then handed one over to me.

"Is this okay for humans to drink?" I asked her, remembering the warnings I had been given about fae wine in Rewyth.

Adeline shook her head. "It's a festival, Jade. I won't tell if you don't."

I smiled. I loved this side of Adeline. She was nothing like her brothers. Her brothers were sneaky and stubborn. Adeline was wild, free, and alive.

I aspired to be like that. To be free.

To be alive.

I took the drink from her, and she cheered once more. Adeline's energy was contagious, there was no way I could say no to her.

We both took a small sip, and Adeline watched me carefully as I swallowed.

It didn't burn like I had expected it to. In fact, the drink was especially sweet. "Wow," I said, taking another sip. "This tastes surprisingly good!"

Adeline nodded and took another drink herself. "And the more you drink, the better it gets," she whispered.

We both laughed.

"Happy birthday, by the way," she whispered in my ear. "Malachi has a loud mouth."

I started to argue with her, but shut my mouth. It *was* my birthday. There was a time when I thought I would never live long enough to see this day. I deserved to enjoy myself tonight. "Thank you, Adeline," was all I said.

The cool breeze of night blew past us, blowing my hair off my shoulders.

I felt happy. I didn't want to admit that, and in many ways, it still felt so wrong, but it was true. I felt happy.

"Have you been to a party like this before?" I asked her.

Adeline nodded and hooked her arm through mine as we began walking the perimeter of the field. "I've been to many parties in my lifetime. I spent a decade or two lost in them. It can be exhilarating, yes, but at the end of the day, it's an escape. People like to party this way because they can forget about all their problems for a day. They can forget about war or famine or politics and they can just... be."

I nodded as she talked. Her words made a lot of sense. They were fae, and perhaps things were hundreds of times better in fae kingdoms than they were in human ones, but they still had their issues.

However dumb the humans thought those issues were, comparatively.

"And what were you escaping from?" I asked her.

Adeline smiled as she stared into the distance, but the smile didn't reach her eyes. "Many things," she replied quietly. "It's a miracle I ever came out of it, to be honest," she said.

"Issues with your father?" I pushed.

"Among many things. My father has been very controlling of all of us, not just Malachi. He lets the other boys off easier, yes, but he still wanted control every step of the way. And he wanted to prove his control."

"On you?" I asked. "It always seemed like he ignored you most of the time. He doesn't even include you in politics."

Adeline took a breath and finished the rest of her drink in one sip.

"The only daughter in the Weyland family sounds like a blessing, I know. But hear this, Jade. You and I are similar. We are women. These men will use us in their biddings for anything they please. That doesn't change for me just because I am fae. Nor does it change because I am part of the royal family."

Her voice cracked, and my heart nearly shattered. If I hadn't hated the King with every single ounce of my being before, I certainly did now.

I wanted to ask her what specifically he had made her do. Had he sold her as part of some deal like he had done to me? Traded her? Used her for seduction? Pawned her off like a fancy jewel?

Adeline was powerful and spontaneous. It shocked me that someone so vibrant could have suffered so much, but I saw it now in her eyes. A certain darkness lingered there.

"I'm sorry, Adeline. It's not right what they do."

Adeline rolled her shoulders back and lifted her chin. "No, it's not. But we're here. We're alive. And there's an entire evening ahead of us. We can escape for the night, Jade. We can be free for tonight. So drink that damn glass!"

I obeyed, swallowing the entire glass of liquid in three large sips.

She stared at me with wide eyes when I looked back up. "What?" I asked.

"Malachi's going to kill me," she mumbled, but she laughed.

I looked over my shoulders, making sure he wasn't approaching out of nowhere before answering, "Don't scare me like that!" I laughed.

Adeline shoved my shoulder lightly. "You love him," she said.

I scoffed. "No, I don't."

She rolled her eyes and brought us back to the table of drinks, grabbing another glass for herself. When I reached for one, she cut me off. "Maybe no more for the human, at least for the next hour or so."

"Why?" I asked. "I don't feel a thing."

"Oh, you will," she laughed. "I just hope Malachi shows up before you're passed out in the field."

"Adeline!" I yelled. "I'm going to pass out?"

She tossed her head back and laughed, her curls falling along her back.

Without answering me, she pulled me into the crowd.

This festival, even with the loud music and the group of dancing people, was nothing like the simple bonfire in Fearford. The fae never stopped. Never tired. And the way they danced...

I stared at a group of fae, two girls and a boy, dancing together on the dance floor. The way their bodies moved together, as if all three of them were *involved*.

I blushed and quickly looked away.

"Don't be embarrassed," Adeline said. "Humans are all prudes compared to the fae, remember? It's totally normal here."

I nodded and continued to follow her.

"Come on," she said once we got to the middle of the field. "We're dancing."

She grabbed both of my arms and began dancing slowly, moving to the rhythm of the music just like we had done in Fearford.

Our dresses blended with the massive, colorful crowd under the moon and stars. The sky was shockingly clear, allowing the twinkling of the sky to add to the essence of the festival.

Saints. Perhaps that drink was starting to kick in.

There was hardly space to move in the crowd. Bodies bumped against my back and shoulders, but Adeline didn't let go of me. She wrapped her arms across my shoulders, pulling me close to her as the two of us danced.

A slow warmth moved across my body, starting in my bare feet and working up my legs. It was more than just feeling intoxicated, it was life itself re-entering my body.

I had missed that feeling.

I tossed my head back and laughed. I couldn't help it. Pure euphoria spread slowly across every inch of me.

When I brought my head back up and looked at Adeline, I knew she felt the same way. Her eyes twinkled, reflecting the blanket of stars above us.

"Relax, Jade," she whispered into my ear. "Escape."

I knew exactly what she meant. I closed my eyes, same as her, and let the feeling of magic overtake my body, my motions. With Adeline's body touching mine, I swayed to the music. The violin called to me, like it was playing secretly for my soul and my soul only. Like it was mine alone to enjoy. I laughed and cheered, and nobody stopped to stare. Nobody cared, everyone was too busy living their own euphoria.

Escaping.

Adeline grabbed my hand and spun me in a circle where we stood.

We both laughed when I nearly fell over, large wings behind me bumping me and causing me to fall into her body.

We continued to dance like that, bumping everyone around us and laughing like idiots, until I truly thought my stomach would burst from laughter.

I wanted to tell her to stop, that I needed a break, but I couldn't find the words. It was addicting.

My legs were exhausted, yet they had never felt better. I grabbed Adeline's arm and was about to pull her toward me when strong hands grabbed me roughly from behind.

"Having fun?" Malachi whispered in my ear. He sounded... *not* euphoric.

An interruption in my ecstasy.

I spun around, but his hands didn't leave my body. "Yes," I said, not able to hide the laughter from my voice.

Malachi gave a death glare to Adeline, who only laughed even more. Which caused me to laugh again.

"I told you not to leave without me," he said.

"We're just dancing," Adeline defended. Malachi shot her another glare, as if to send a message.

"Fine," Adeline said. "I'll be dancing over there, come find me when your husband is done being a buzzkill, Jade," she said to me.

And then she was lost in the crowd, leaving Malachi and I clinging to each other in the night.

"How much did you drink?" he asked me.

I shook my head. "Only one cup. I am being very responsible, I swear."

"Adeline knows better. Even a sip is enough for you to trip all night."

I laughed again, then stood on my tippy toes in the grass to wrap my arms around Mal's neck. My feet nearly came off the ground.

"Who cares," I said. "Escape with me."

His hands wrapped around my body, holding me to him. A low growl rumbled in his chest, but he didn't object.

"Don't tell me you don't want to," I purred. "I know you do. Escape with me, Mal. Dance with me."

It was ludicrous. This was so different from Fearford, when we had been civil and I had been drinking *human* drinks.

This was a dream. Nothing felt real, and yet everything felt right.

With Malachi holding me to him, I tipped my head back and swayed. Laughter bubbled in my chest as the night air blew through my hair. When I lifted my head again, Malachi was staring at me with his lips parted.

"What?" I asked.

He shook his head. "You are breathtaking, Jade Farrow."

"Tell me what you're feeling," he whispered, lips brushing against my ear. A chill ran down my bare spine. "Tell me in detail, and don't leave a single thing out."

Where did I begin? "I feel...I feel alive," I stared, stating the obvious. "I feel weightless. My feet should be hurting but they're tingling with life, like the earth is feeding my soul and my body just wants more."

Malachi leaned in and brushed his lips against my neck, the kiss of a mere feather.

"I feel warm. Not hot, though, just warm. Like my blood is magic, pumping through each of my veins with every passing heartbeat."

"Mhmm," he hummed against my body.

"And I feel free," I said. I leaned back again, holding onto him while I stared up at the stars. They all blurred together now, but I knew they were there. I knew they were shining above us. "Like I could join them," I said.

"The stars?" Malachi asked.

"Yes," I said. "The stars. I want to be as free as the stars."

"Then I will rip this world apart until I can place you in the sky myself, princess."

Emotion overwhelmed me. Logically, I knew it was the fae drink. But I didn't care. Tears bubbled in my eyes before I could even blink them away.

"What?" Malachi asked me. "What's wrong?" I pressed my forehead against his. "Tell me what you're feeling."

"I..."

Saints. I felt confused. I wanted Malachi, I wanted him more than anything. And that scared me. Because I knew I could never have him, not really. Malachi was the fae Prince, and I was nothing but a mere human.

Even if he wanted to set me free, that would mean losing him.

And what world would that be? What type of life would I be living?

"I'll never be free," I admitted to him.

"Don't say that," he said. "You know it's not true."

I shook my head. "You don't understand."

I grabbed his body, pulling him closer and closer to me. As if that would save me. As if we could merge together and become one. "I want this," I whispered to him. "I want you."

Malachi's chest heaved. "Then you have me."

And then his lips crashed into mine.

Malachi was practically carrying me as we were swallowed deeply into the crowd. I wrapped a leg around his waist and he grabbed it, holding me to him.

His mouth was hot and heavy against mine. I was hungry, desperate for more of him. Each place he touched me left a scorching trail of passion, a fire that didn't burn out.

I clung to him, wrapping my arms around his neck and lifting myself up so I could guide him, kissing him with all the emotions I felt in my body. I wanted him. It was true.

And he was here. Kissing me.

Our mouths moving together was just another part of the dance, another part of the dream. Magic.

Malachi's black wings flared out for just an instant, eventually finding a way to surround our bodies. But it wasn't the privacy I wanted.

"Malachi," I whispered, trying to catch my breath between our kisses.

"Yes, princess?" he mumbled against my mouth.

"I want you to take me back to our room," I whispered. I scanned his face, searching for an inch of hesitation.

But all I got was a low purr of approval.

He kissed me again, deeply, before pulling away.

"I want nothing more than to take you upstairs and do what I've wanted to do since the moment I laid eyes on you, princess," he said.

My stomach swarmed in butterflies. Only for a moment, though, until Malachi's face hardened.

"What?" I asked, pulling away another inch. "What is it?"

"We can't, Jade. I mean...I can't."

I couldn't be hearing this correctly. "What do you mean, you can't?"

He mumbled under his breath before answering. "I don't want to complicate things," he said.

I would have backed up if it weren't for his strong hands holding me tight. "Complicate what, exactly?"

"We should have talked about this before, Jade. What this mess is between us. We've been acting like everything is fine. We've been acting like we can just go on living happily ever after after the politics are handled. But at the end of the day, you're a human. You're a human and I'm a fae."

"Where is this coming from?" I asked. "Why are you suddenly bringing this up?"

"Because we can't ignore it anymore, Jade. We don't have a future, and you need to understand that."

My ears were ringing, louder than the hundreds of thoughts running through my head. This was coming out of nowhere, a complete turn in directions.

Malachi wanted a future with me.

*Didn't he?*

"Let's just calm down and we can talk about this tomorrow," I said.

"What will change tomorrow?" he growled. "You'll still be a human, and I'll still be the big, bad fae that forced you into marriage."

"Stop!" I yelled. "You know I don't think of you that way."

"You should. This will never change, Jade. I'm the Prince of Shadows, remember? You'll be safer without me. You'll be safer with someone like Isaiah."

I couldn't believe I just heard him say that. I fought the strong urge I felt to slap him across the face.

"You don't mean that," I said, staggering backward. This time, he let me back away.

"I do," he said. His walls were back up. His eyes were darker than I had ever seen them. "I do mean that, Jade. And you need to listen to me."

Tears threatened my eyes, but I wasn't going to let him see me cry over him.

Not because of this.

I was the one that should be ending this stupid fling we had going on, not him. I was the one that had been ripped from my home and forced to live in Rewyth. I was the one who had suffered because of this union.

Not him. Not Malachi.

I ripped myself away and tore through the crowd. Malachi didn't follow me.

Adrenaline still pulsed through my veins. The way it mixed with the fae drinks had my entire body tingling in a way I couldn't put into words.

Bodies pushed and shoved me from every angle, but nobody stopped me as I continued to make my way through the crowd, back in the direction Adeline and I had come from.

I had to get out of here. I had to clear my mind. I just needed space to think.

Finally, the pool of bodies began to spread out. I saw the table where I had grabbed my drink from earlier, and the castle became visible in the distance. I was almost there.

*Almost.*

"You look like you're in a hurry," a male voice said from in front of me. My sight was blurred from unreleased tears.

"Leave me alone," I mumbled as I shoved passed him, keeping my head down.

He grabbed my arm and spun me around, forcing me to face him. He was a large fae, almost as tall as Malachi. He had blood-red hair and massive silver wings that tucked tightly behind his shoulders.

And he was looking at me like he had just found exactly what he had been looking for.

"That's no way to talk to a friend," he sneered.

"We aren't friends," I replied coldly.

He looked me up and down slowly, sending a chill down my spine. "Human," he stated. "Interesting. What are you doing out here with all of these fae?" he asked. "It's dangerous, you know."

"I was just leaving," I said. I lifted my chin and looked him straight in his eye.

"Great," he smiled. "Me, too."

Panic erupted through my body. The realization of exactly where I was and what I was doing began to set in. I was one of the three humans in this kingdom right now.

Nobody was coming to help me.

The man's grip on my arm tightened as he turned to begin walking toward the castle.

"Jade," a familiar voice said. *Lucien's voice.* "Everything okay?"

Relief and panic both swarmed me.

He walked up behind me and placed a protective hand on my shoulder. The other fae dropped his grip on my arm immediately.

I wanted to answer, I wanted to tell him to run, to help me. That I was far from okay.

But no words came out.

"We're just fine, thank you," the other fae said.

"She's with me," Lucien replied in a powerful voice. "I suggest you get lost."

It could have still been the effects from the fae drink, or perhaps the cool breeze of the night, but a chill ran down my spine.

The male in front of us eyed Lucien, likely noting his foreign appearance, and shook his head.

"Fine," he said. "But if you're looking for some real fun tonight," he said to me, "come find me."

I didn't exhale until he was out of sight.

Tears streamed down my face as I stood there, focusing on taking one breath after another.

"Saints, Jade. What was that? What are you doing?" Lucien asked. He moved to face me, but his demeanor changed entirely when he saw the tears.

"I'm fine," I insisted before he could ask any questions.

The words didn't even sound believable. I was the furthest thing from fine. I noted that I would not be drinking any fae drinks again for the entirety of my life. My emotions spiraled.

How could Malachi look at me that way? Like I was a stupid child he felt sorry for. Like he had been doing me a favor this entire time by pretending to be interested in me.

I shook my head.

How damn dumb I had been, believing that he wanted anything to do with me aside from his political aspirations.

I was simply a piece in a larger game. I had forgotten that.

I wouldn't forget again.

"You're not fine, Jade. What happened? Why was that man following you?"

Isaiah approached behind Lucien. "What's going on?" he asked.

Great. An audience.

"Why do you even care?" I asked Lucien. "You were the one ready to torture me not too long ago."

He drew his brows together. "Things have changed since then, Jade. If you want me to rip that guy's head off, I will. Or better yet, I'll tell Malachi what just happened."

"Don't!" I yelled. "Let's just drop this, please," I begged.

"Fine," Lucien said before turning to Isaiah. "Stay with her," he said. "It's not safe for her out here alone."

Isaiah nodded, and Lucien slipped away into the crowd.

"Why was that man talking to you? Was he following you?" Isaiah asked.

"Because I'm human!" I responded, likely a bit too harsh. "I'm a stupid, fragile human, same as you, Isaiah. If any male here wanted to do anything with me, there would be nothing I could do to stop it. So I don't know why he was following me, but I think I could guess."

Isaiah stiffened. "Is that why you're crying?" he asked. "Did he hurt you?"

I laughed. "No, he didn't touch me."

I didn't say any more. I didn't need to. Isaiah glanced back to the crowd, then back to me. "Fae take anything they want, Jade. They always have, and they always will. It's why we need to be smart about this."

"About what?"

"About business. About what they want from us."

How ridiculous. "They don't want anything from us," I replied. "That's the problem."

Isaiah stepped forward. "We have something that they want, Jade."

"Really?" I asked. "And what's that?"

He stared into my eyes, deeply enough that I thought I almost looked away. "We have you."

I took a step back. I don't know where I was heading, but my heart was pounding in my chest. So harshly that I thought it might jump out.

"He's right," Esther's cool, collected voice made me jump.

She approached us from the shadows. How long had she been listening? How long had she been at this festival?

"What does that even mean?" I asked.

"They know what you are now, Jade. And now that you're eighteen, more people will come looking for you."

They cornered me now, backing me up against the wall of the building.

"So what?" I spat. More tears came. My throat burned. "I'm just supposed to hide forever?"

"No, not hide, Jade. Let me teach you who you are. Let me show you what you can do."

"We can't run from them," I said. Esther had to know it. Isaiah had to know it. If the fae wanted to find me, they would.

"You won't have to. They know you as Malachi's wife right now, Jade. We just need time to develop your gifts. We just need something temporary."

My vision blurred.

"Come back to Fearford with us. You're safe there," Isaiah suggested.

"Malachi would never leave me," I spat. "He would never leave me alone."

Why was I defensive? Malachi didn't want me tonight, why would that change? If Esther was right...

"It's only temporary," Esther said. "Malachi will be on board with anything that keeps you safe."

"And living in Fearford is supposed to help? The King already knows I'm there. That's the first place he'll look."

"We won't have to worry about the King much longer," Isaiah chimed in.

My brain was spinning. Were they saying what I thought they were saying?

"I can't do this right now," I insisted. "I can't... I need..."

Malachi. I needed to talk to Malachi.

"Look," Esther said. "It's been a long night. You have a lot to think about. You're eighteen now, Jade. You're going to start changing very soon. Come find me in the morning, and we'll talk it over. There's no need to make rash decisions just yet."

I took a long, shaky breath. "I have to go," was all I could say.

"Jade, wait," Isaiah yelled at me.

I paused and looked over my shoulder.

"Is Sadie with you?" he asked.

The hair on my neck stood up. "No," I replied. "Why? Where is she?"

Isaiah's eyes widened.

And that's when we heard Sadie's blood-curdling scream.

# CHAPTER 17
# *Jade*

The three of us sprinted into the castle, following the sound of Sadie's voice.

"Sadie!" I yelled. "Sadie, where are you?"

"Jade!" she yelled back before her voice was cut off abruptly.

Isaiah's boots hit the ground running in the direction it came from, and he didn't even test to see if the door to the room was unlocked before he kicked it down.

Esther and I followed tightly behind him.

And then we saw him. The same fae that had cornered me just a few minutes ago.

He had Sadie pinned to the wall, looking absolutely terrified.

"What in the–" he started, turning toward us and letting go of Sadie.

His eyes scanned the three of us before ultimately falling onto me.

His bewildered look turned into a smile. "Ah," he said. "It looks like you took me up on my offer after all."

"Stop right there," Esther said behind me. "Or you will regret it. Leave us and get back to the party."

"And who are you, exactly?" he spat. "Another human? Tell me, what do you plan to do to stop me?"

Esther held out her hand and chanted something in a language I couldn't understand.

I could barely process what I was seeing.

The fae's eyes widened before he staggered backward. "What are you?" he whispered. He was already looking at the door, looking for a way out.

Esther didn't stop. She stepped forward, eyes darkening as she continued to chant.

The man didn't say another word.

Isaiah and I backed up enough so he could run out the door as he screamed in pain, and then it was over.

"Sadie," Isaiah said as he rushed to her side. "Sadie, are you okay?"

Sadie had tears streaming down her face. A knot formed in my stomach. Someone as strong as Sadie had to endure a lot to get to this point.

"Get her out of here," Esther ordered. "Take her to the infirmary where she'll be safe."

Isaiah didn't hesitate. He picked Sadie up and left, carrying her further into the castle.

My heart pounded in my ears.

"What the Saints was that?" I asked Esther. "What did you do to him?"

"Nothing you can't learn how to do, also."

I shook my head. "No, that was...that was magic, right?"

Esther nodded. "These fae see themselves as above us, Jade. You are the peacemaker. You are the one that will show them their rightful place."

My breath was shallow. "That fae...he would've..."

"But he didn't," she interrupted. "Because there are people like us to stop him. This is why they need us, Jade. This power imbalance is unjust. Do you understand me?" she asked.

"Yes," I gasped. "Yes, I understand."

"Good," she said. "Now get out of here and go straight to your room. Sadie is fine, everything is okay. Understand?"

I nodded one more time and turned toward my room.

Esther wanted me to be a protector. A *peacemaker*. But if tonight proved anything, it was that Malachi was right.

The fae and the humans were never going to be equals.

# CHAPTER 18
# Jade

The rest of the bed was empty when I woke up. The afternoon sun blazed through the open window, and *Saints.*

My head was pounding.

I groaned as I threw back the thick sheets, still in the dress I had worn the night before,

My eyes burned, likely from the tears I remembered running down my face for the majority of the night.

I had effectively embarrassed myself, that much was certain.

I silently hoped that everyone else would forget the entire thing.

And Malachi.

I shook my head, trying to forget the entire thing. He didn't matter. Anything I thought I had felt for him didn't matter.

Looking out the window, I saw the sun was nearly to the center of the sky.

I had to find Esther.

I rinsed off the evidence from the night before, tossing the flowered gown to the side and throwing on my comfortable trousers and tunic. I slipped on my leather boots and headed for the door, not even bothering to attempt fixing my hair.

Nobody waited for me outside my door. Nobody guarded me. Nobody was there to ask me where I was going.

At least I had *some* freedom.

I should be grateful for that, at least. Sadie and Isaiah were probably still hiding in the infirmary.

I turned to shut my door and saw there was a note attached to it.

*"Jade,"* it said. *"Come find me when you wake up. Down the hall and to the left."*

I shoved the note in my pocket and headed in that direction.

It had to have been from Esther.

She had been meaning to talk to me, and after what she told me last night, we had a lot to discuss.

Saints. Why hadn't I taken her more seriously? She talked on and on about this prophecy and about how I had to be protected, and I had never questioned it. I had never questioned her.

The truth was, if this prophecy was important enough to her that she would leave her only son in the hands of the monstrous king, it had to be important. It was worth something.

And if Esther was right, now that I was eighteen, things were going to be changing for me. And soon.

It was in my best interest to find out.

The instructions of the note brought me to a large, open room.

"Good," Esther greeted me. "You're here."

"You wanted to talk to me?" I asked.

Esther just nodded, looking me up and down as if she had never seen me before. My annoyance spiked.

"How are you feeling today?" she asked me.

"I feel fine," I lied. "Thank you for asking, Esther. That's very kind."

Esther eyed me and my sarcasm for a second longer and smirked.

It struck me then how similar she looked to Malachi. She really *was* his mother.

"Fae wine will do you no good in the future, child. If you were smart you would avoid it next time."

"I never claimed to be smart."

"And that's where I think you're lying," she said. "Follow me. I'm taking you somewhere."

She began walking before I could even follow.

I took double the amount of steps to keep up. "Where are we going?"

"To train you."

"Train me for what?"

"For the war that's coming," she said in a calmness that made my blood curdle.

"What war?"

She stopped walking long enough to turn and answer me. "The war we've all been waiting on, sweetheart. The war you're going to win for us."

"How am I going to help you win any war? I'm human, if you forgot."

"Trust me, I will never forget. But that may not be the case for long."

"What's that supposed to mean?"

Esther just continued walking. We walked out of the castle and down a small path that led to a large, open field away from the rest of Trithen. We walked and we walked, until we approached the massive wall that was keeping us separated from whatever evil creatures that lurked beyond.

And then I followed Esther as she led us through a tiny, hidden door in the stone wall.

"We aren't supposed to be out here, Esther. It's dangerous."

"Not for a witch, it's not."

I rolled my eyes. *Great.*

Trusting Esther was an uncertainty. She had saved our lives, but her intentions were still unclear. The prophecy was just that, a prophecy. I had yet to understand her part in all of this. What she wanted from all of us.

Vengeance, perhaps? Did she want the King to die just as badly as the rest of us?

Or perhaps she had made some sort of deal with the Saints.

*Time would tell.*

We walked into the tree line, far enough that the blazing sun was now covered by the towering trees.

"If we're attacked by a deadling and killed, Malachi won't be happy with you."

"That's a bit of an understatement, princess," Malachi's voice interrupted from behind a tree, causing me to jump.

"Saints! What are you doing here?" I asked.

"Training. Same as you," he answered with a smug look on his face.

I glanced at Esther, who only shrugged. "We had to get out of the castle," she said. "Too many prying ears."

"This can't be good," I mumbled, waiting for an explanation.

"If what my mother believes is correct, you'll begin forming certain... *gifts* now that you are eighteen."

I scoffed. "And nobody has thought about how ridiculous that sounds?"

"It's not ridiculous at all," Esther said. "In fact, the idea that you may not believe in your destiny is the most ridiculous part of all of this."

I shut my mouth.

I was absolutely certain that if I had some sort of magical powers, I would be aware of them. But I was also absolutely certain that Esther had no doubt as to who I was.

And after what happened last night, I owed it to Sadie to at least try and learn if I had any power.

I owed it to myself.

"Okay," I said after a while. "What do you want me to do?"

Esther stepped forward. "There are many forms of *gifts* in this world, child. There are the low-level mages, who are able to bend the elements. Air, fire, water, earth. They're common in the southern regions, and are more or less harmless.

"There are fae, of course, who are randomly gifted certain powers as the Saints allow it. Typically, they aren't as strong as Malachi's gifts. They have magic that can read minds, control air, things like that."

"Fae can read minds?" I interrupted.

"No," she laughed. "It's been decades since I've met another fae with a gift. They're becoming more and more rare, just like witches with natural power."

"Witches? Like you?"

Esther nodded. "Witches used to be the most powerful creatures that walked this earth. You heard what I said about witches needing sacrifices now, but it didn't used to be this way. Witches had free access to power, able to use as much as they needed to, whenever they wanted. That's changed now.

"Then there are the elites. Fae-born children who have been granted gifts much more than that."

"Like Malachi?" I asked, not looking at him.

Esther nodded. "Like Malachi. As you have no doubt seen with your own eyes, Malachi possesses an extraordinary gift. With a single thought, he can inflict crippling pain or even death on anyone he wishes."

From the corner of my eye, I saw Malachi's jaw tighten.

"Do other fae have his gift?"

"None that we have seen, although it wouldn't be impossible."

"And his wings? That's why they're black, isn't it? You're an elite?"

"Those are just titles," Malachi suggested. "It was purely a coincidence that I ended up with this gift. The black wings are a coincidence as well. A mistake by the creator."

"There are no coincidences," Esther spat. "And the creator makes no mistakes."

"What about you?" I asked her. "What type of magic do you possess?"

Esther smiled. "I've been practicing for decades, child. Long before you were ever born. My ancestors once wielded the most powerful magic known to any kingdom. That has long since passed, of course, but their blood still flows in mine."

I waited for her to answer.

"Over the last few decades, I have been known to perform each kind of magic."

*Impossible.*

"But unlike Malachi and others who were born with their gifts, I must pay a price. Magic does not come free to those who were not chosen for it."

"And you weren't chosen?"

Something flashed across Esther's face, but it quickly passed. "For some things, I was. Like delivering you for your purpose."

Now we were getting to the fun part. The part I had ignored for much too long. "And what, exactly, is my purpose in this war you say is coming?"

Malachi stepped forward, like he was ready to intercept at any second. "Esther," he warned. "Don't."

"No," I insisted. "I deserve to know. You have all been treating me like a child, talking in code and whispering to each other in the darkness. If I'm to be the tool for this grand plan of yours, I should know what my part is. I deserve at least that."

"She's right," Esther started. "She deserves to know."

Malachi took a long, pained breath. "Fine," he said. He then turned to face me, looking me in the eyes for the first time since last night. "But remember this is just a prophecy, Jade. We can take this one piece at a time."

I braced myself for the next words.

Esther grabbed both of my wrists in hers. Malachi stepped back, but stayed close. "You are the key to everything, Jade. Your mother knew it, too."

"My mother?"

She nodded. "Your mother and I were great friends. You remind me a lot of her, actually. She was stubborn and bratty just like you."

My breath hitched. "How? How did you know her?"

Esther smiled. "Your mother was a part of my clan, darling."

I fought to keep my reactions together. "You mean my mother was a witch?"

"If you want to stick to all these titles, yes. She was."

"Does that mean I..."

"No," she answered quickly. "Not exactly. You see, your mother was a practicing witch, but it was her blood that made you special. You're the one we've been waiting for. Not her."

"Why me? Why not her?"

"It wasn't time, child. Each generation of your family's blood has been waiting for this time in history."

"And what time is that?"

"The time when we needed you the most, Jade."

"I can't save anyone," I muttered. "I...I can't. I can barely keep myself alive, much less entire kingdoms of people. Of fae!"

"We have time, Jade," Esther said. "We have time to develop your magic into something deadly. Something powerful."

I shook my head and pulled my arms from Esther's grasp. "What magic?" I said.

"Come sit," Esther commanded.

I did as I was told, taking a seat on the cool ground of the outdoors. "Now I want you to lay back, all the way."

Again, I obeyed. Malachi stayed where he stood, arms crossed, watching my every movement with furrowed brows.

"Good," she continued. "Now close your eyes, and take three deep breaths."

"I don't see how this is helping anything," I said.

"Just do it."

I did. I closed my eyes and breathed deeply, letting the cool air of the trees refresh my lungs. I held my breath for a second or two before releasing, letting my entire body relax with it.

"Now picture your body connecting to something, like the stem of a flower, diving deep into the ground below you. Picture yourself as one with the earth. As one with the divine being of nature."

I followed her instructions, picturing my body connecting to the vastness of the ground below me. It was relaxing, I had to admit. I felt energized yet blissful at the same time, like I was right where I belonged.

"Now picture the air above you the same way. Imagine the air around you as an extension of your own being. Connected to you. Blessed by you."

I did.

"Feel that energy within you, Jade. Funnel it at your core, right where your heart lies. Make it part of you. Own it."

I tried to follow her instructions, but I still felt no magic. No powers of any sort.

"You aren't being patient," Esther spat. "You have to relax, Jade. Trust that your magic will come to you when you are ready."

"And who says I'm ready?"

"Your husband, for one."

I snapped my eyes open and propped myself on an elbow, glaring at Malachi, who was staring at me with an idiotic smirk on his face.

"Is this funny to you?" I asked. "Me humiliating myself on the ground?"

He didn't answer. Only smiled wider.

Holy Saints.

"Okay," Esther interrupted. "Perhaps we should try something else today. You clearly feel a lot of anger, and magic has a direct tie with emotions. So, let's try that."

"Try what?" I asked. "Being angry? Trust me, it hasn't given me any magical powers yet."

"But it will, Jade," Esther said. "You just have to focus your anger in the right direction."

"Great," Malachi mumbled. "Just what we need."

"Excuse me?"

"Let's start here," Esther interrupted. "Jade, tell us all the things that make you angry about Malachi. And focus on the feelings that come with them."

"You can't be serious," Malachi said.

"Oh, I'm very serious, son. I'll do anything to activate Jade's gifts, and you should feel the same way."

He huffed and crossed his arms again, leaning against the tree as if he couldn't care less what I thought of him.

I stood from the ground and brushed the dirt from my legs before I began.

"First off," I started. "I think he's arrogant. He walks around here like he's to be worshiped. He knows he can kill anyone here, and it goes straight to his head."

"Good," Esther said. "Keep going."

"He's stubborn. He won't listen to anything I tell him. He thinks he is the only one in an entire room full of people who can have a good idea, and it's absolutely absurd."

Malachi stared at me, amusement still twinkling in his eyes. "And he uses people. He used me. He made me think he actually cared about me, when the entire time I was just part of this greater plan of his. I knew it, too. I just let myself believe the other story. The better story."

"What else?" Esther pressed.

Malachi shifted uncomfortably. I had struck a nerve.

Good. He deserved it.

"He's selfish." He rolled his eyes again but returned his gaze to me. "He's the reason my family hates me. He took me from the only person I love. He's the reason the humans don't accept me. He's the reason I can't have a normal life with a normal man who will keep me safe."

A twig snapped in the distance.

The air shifted, and the hair on my neck stood up. Every part of me became alert, even a part of me deep down that seemed to want an awakening.

We weren't alone out here.

## CHAPTER 19
# Malachi

"Don't move," I whispered. "Stay quiet."

Jade stayed still, but her eyes widened enough to let me know that she heard it, too.

Someone else was out there. Someone or something.

Esther slowly picked up a foot and moved toward me, careful not to crack even the smallest twig.

She had been living comfortably in the forest. She would know how to help me protect Jade.

I reached for the sword strapped to my hip, but didn't unsheathe it.

The slightest sound would give away our location in a heartbeat.

Esther met my eyes and mouthed the word that made my blood run cold:

*Deadlings.*

I had dealt with deadlings many times in my life, and I had never left with so much as a scratch.

But that was never while I was with a human. Or a witch, for that matter.

I waved my hand to Jade, motioning for her to kneel down. She did, moving as slow as humanly possible.

Another grunt came from my left.

*Saints.*

There was a small group of them, at least four.

Killing them would be easy. As long as I got to them before any one of them got to Jade.

Esther held a small dagger tightly in her hand. If we made it out of here alive, I would be teaching Jade how to defend herself.

Successfully this time.

My power rumbled in my chest, but I knew it was no use. Because the deadlings were already, well, *dead*, my magic was no use on them. It was almost as if it passed straight through.

"What is it?" Jade whispered through the silence.

Not even one second later, a blood-curdling shriek split the air.

I couldn't move fast enough. A black figure, one of those disgusting deadlings, shot out of nowhere and tackled Jade. She screamed, and I lunged after her with my sword out.

They tumbled on the ground, Jade barely keeping her face away from its snapping jaws as it clawed its way toward her.

"Jade!" I yelled as I closed the gap between us. I held my sword out, but she was moving too much. One wrong move would be deadly. My heart stopped as she screamed again, the monster's claws digging into her skin.

I didn't hesitate this time. One swift motion, and the creature's head rolled to the ground with a thud.

I had no time to make sure she was okay. I spun on my heel, turning to where Esther fought off another deadling behind me.

They had each other by the shoulders, Esther backing up as the disgusting death overpowered her.

I grabbed the thing by the back of the head and threw. Hard. Its crunchy body smacked a tree a few feet away and fell to the ground.

Two more appeared from the trees. Coming directly at us.

Jade was still on the ground behind me.

"Protect her," I ordered Esther as I stepped in front of them both. Esther moved to guard Jade, dagger in hand. Esther may not have been strong enough to kill one with her bare hands, but she at least stood a chance.

I dropped the two other deadlings in an instant, my sword hitting true and slicing through the bodies with little effort.

"Saints," Jade breathed behind me.

I turned to see what she was talking about.

And blistering pain erupted in my shoulder.

I elbowed the creature that bit me, a sickening crack filling the air around us.

Adrenaline pulsed through my body, my power was begging to help me. But I knew it couldn't. With one arm, I raised my sword and cut the deadling in half.

Its body hit the ground with a thud.

And then...

Silence.

Our panting breaths were the only sounds in the forest.

We stayed there like that for a few minutes, trying to understand what had just happened. Processing it.

"Son," Esther said after a while. "Your arm."

I glanced down to where I had been bitten.

Red and black blood dripped down past my elbow. It stung like a bitch, I had to admit.

"Malachi," Jade whispered. She rushed past Esther and held her hands out like she was going to touch it, but changed her mind at the last second.

"It's fine," I whispered. "Nothing I can't handle."

"What will happen?" she asked. "What happens if you are bit by one of those things?"

"If I were a human?" I responded. "I would probably die."

Jade's eyes widened, just for a split second, before she rolled them at me. "I'm being serious, Malachi. You're not going to turn into one of those things are you?"

I nearly laughed at how concerned she was. "No, I won't. Although I have to admit that would be pretty fun."

"There will be more nearby," Esther interrupted. "They must have sensed we were here."

"Like they were hunting us?" Jade asked. "Do they have that ability?"

"Deadlings are killers. If they scent anything they can sink their teeth into, they'll stop at nothing until they get to it."

"Even fae?"

"Even fae."

Jade shook her head. "Then why in the Saints did we come out here? We could have done this in the cozy safety of those massive walls!"

Esther raised her hand. "Just because the leaders of Trithen have invited us here doesn't mean we are able to trust them fully. You are too trusting, child. You have to be more vigilant."

Jade put a hand on her hip and scoffed. "I'm the one that's too trusting? As if you two didn't just drag us out here into danger, with who knows how many other random creatures that want to eat us!"

I covered my mouth with my fist, but couldn't stop the laugh that erupted from my mouth.

"What?" she half-yelled at me. "Is something funny about us almost dying?"

"No, nothing at all," I responded.

"Good," she responded. "I'm glad you find amusement in all of this, Malachi. I think we've had enough training for one day." She turned toward the castle and started storming away.

"We'll have to train every day," Esther added. "Every day until your powers begin to develop."

"Whatever," Jade spat.

Esther gave me a knowing look. "Go," she mouthed.

I rolled my eyes and jogged to catch up to Jade.

"Jade," I said. "Wait."

"No thanks."

"Jade, I'm sorry," I said. I *was* sorry. Everything that I had said to her last night... she needed to hear it. It was going to keep her safe, especially while I plotted to kill my own father. But there would have been a better time and place to tell her those things.

And just because it was a terrible idea to be together didn't mean I didn't want it more than anything in the world.

Jade just laughed flatly and kept walking.

"Fine," I continued. "If you don't want to talk to me, you can at least listen. I'll oversee training you aside from magic work with Esther. Whatever drama is happening between us is going to have to wait until this is figured out."

Jade shook her head, her messy black hair bouncing with every step. At least she was listening to me.

"I don't want to train," she said. "Not with you."

The hatred in her voice made me inhale sharply, but it was my own fault. Her pain was because of me. I deserved that.

"I'll see you in the morning," I said anyway. "Meet me here at sunrise."

# CHAPTER 20
# *Jade*

It couldn't be more clear that Malachi didn't want me. I had been a mere tool to him this entire time.

I cursed at myself in the darkness of the empty bedroom. He wouldn't even sleep in the same room as me? I was his *wife.*

There had been a time when I thought I wouldn't be able to keep him out of my bedroom.

*Saints*, had I been wrong.

I rolled over and stared at the moonlight blaring into the window. I likely only had a few hours of darkness left, then I had to meet him for more training.

For more embarrassment.

But we had to work together. I had to stay alive, and if war was coming, Malachi *would* be my best teacher.

I wanted to learn how to fight. I needed to learn how to defend myself.

I stared at the ceiling, my body buzzed with adrenaline just thinking about fighting.

I had been able to defend myself against humans most of the time. I had enough practice with that back home, anyway. But taking on fae was an entirely different battle.

And now there was a target on my back.

I peeled back my silk sheets and crawled out of the bed. I was too antsy to sleep. Rest wasn't coming anytime soon.

I had to do something.

I slipped a robe over my thin nightgown and inched my door open slowly.

The library was nearby, maybe I would head there. Or head back outside for some extra practice on whatever magic tricks Esther was trying to teach me.

A woman's laughter caught my attention. I tiptoed closer in the direction it was coming from. Not because I cared, really. Moreso because my curiosity had gotten the best of me.

Who was awake at this hour, anyway?

Besides me, of course.

I wrapped my arms around my body in the chill of night as I peeked my head around the corner.

I had to squint my eyes to see in the darkness, but as soon as they adjusted, I regretted ever leaving my room.

Adeline was sitting in the middle of a large study, kicking her feet and laughing in the darkness.

Only she wasn't alone.

I could have spotted that dark hair anywhere. Serefin and her were together, with their arms wrapped around one another and their bodies tangled together in the darkness.

I pushed myself off the wall and back into the shadows as fast as possible.

I wasn't sure why I was the one who felt like I was doing something wrong. They were the ones *making out* in the middle of the night.

Saints. I wanted to laugh. I wanted to run and tell Tessa, the only person I knew besides Adeline who ever cared for stupid drama like that.

But instead, I covered my mouth with my own hand in the darkness until my breathing settled, and tried to make my way back to my room.

Only when I turned to head back the direction I had come, I tripped on the long skirt of my nightgown. I slapped my hand against the stone wall to catch myself, which was anything but silent.

"Did you hear that?" Serefin's protective voice boomed through the empty study.

Adeline just giggled again. "Hear what?" she cooed.

"Someone's out there."

"There's no one here," Adeline continued. "You're being paranoid."

I pressed my back into the wall, as if hiding against it would save me.

But footsteps came closer and closer. I couldn't move. I couldn't hide. There was nowhere to go.

Serefin rounded the corner like a man chasing something.

Yet he stopped dead in his tracks as soon as his eyes met mine.

"I– I was just..." I stuttered.

Serefin shook his head. "No, I mean I–"

We both stared at each other, completely blank.

Until Adeline rounded the corner. "Saints, Ser! You scared me! It's just Jade!"

She tossed her head back and took a deep breath.

"What are you two doing out here in the middle of the night?" I asked. Even though I already knew the answer.

Serefin batted his eyes. "Nothing," he answered in a heartbeat.

Adeline and I both just stared at him.

"Look," she stepped in. "We don't want Malachi to know. I'm his sister and Ser is his best friend. It would just be weird."

"What exactly are you hiding from him? Are you two..."

"We're just hanging out," she replied. "That's all."

"Right. That's what it looked like in there."

Adeline and Serefin looked at each other, then back at me. I spoke next. "Look, if you don't want me to tell Mal, I won't. Whatever this is, it's none of my business. It's not like he even talks to me anymore anyway."

"Oh, please," Adeline spat. "You two are head over heels for each other. It won't be long until we're re-doing the wedding just so he can declare his love for you."

I blushed in the darkness.

"I'll leave you two to it then," I whispered. I turned on my heel and started back down the hallway.

"Thank you, Jade!" she called after me. I held up a hand and waved back, not daring to turn back around.

I got back to my room and stayed there until the morning sun began peaking back through the glass window.

"Let's go," was all Malachi managed to say to me as he brushed past me in the garden, storming into the vast field of Trithen.

"Good morning to you, too."

"We don't have much time before the others meet us. I'll have to train you twice as hard to get caught up with the others. We have a few weeks before you need to be ready, but it took most of these soldiers decades to be able to fight off a trained fae."

"Great, lovely pep talk."

His eyes darkened. "This isn't a laughing matter, Jade. Your life is on the line."

"That is nothing new to me."

Malachi eyed me for a second, challenging me.

I didn't budge.

I had spent the last few hours of the night thinking of all the things I would say to him. I pictured how great it would feel to yell at him. To scream. To tell him how incredibly shitty it felt to be in my position right now, a mere human used as a pawn by the entire fae kingdom.

But nothing would do this justice. Nothing would be good enough.

I sauntered after him, walking deeper and deeper into the field until the only thing I could see around us was knee-high grasses.

"Okay," Malachi announced, surveying the surrounding area and nodding as if he had decided the spot was good enough for our training.

I stopped beside him.

"Now run back to the castle," he said.

Did he just say...

"Excuse me?" I asked. He did not just say that.

Malachi only nodded. "We'll start with endurance training. You aren't strong enough to fight a fae just yet, but you should damn well be able to run away from one if you need to. Get moving."

I clenched my jaw, but arguing would only satisfy him. I knew he was doing this to piss me off. He knew I wanted to train, wanted to learn to defend myself. He had known that since before we ever left Rewyth.

I guess today wasn't going to be the day for that.

So, I turned back toward the castle, which was now barely a blip in the distance, and I started to jog.

Jogging was nothing new to me. I used to run to the market and back at home, sometimes out of boredom.

It's not that I was particularly out of shape. I just hadn't moved much in the few weeks that I had been married off.

And there was a long way back to the castle.

"Tired already?" Malachi's taunting voice. "You'll have to be faster than that, princess."

I couldn't respond. My mouth was occupied by the heavy breaths as I panted with every step.

Saints. I was pathetic.

But I didn't stop. There was no way I was going to give him that satisfaction. There was no way he was going to get the better of me on our first day of training.

Sweat began to bead on my skin. The morning sun was fully visible now, blaring down on us with not a single cloud for shade.

I put one foot in front of the other again. And again. And again. Until Malachi's taunting wasn't even in my mind. Until the only thing I was focused on was that castle getting closer and closer and closer.

And we eventually made it.

"Not bad," he breathed behind me when we made it. He was hardly even out of breath, meanwhile I couldn't even waste enough breath to talk.

I nodded and knelt over, placing a hand on each knee while I caught my breath.

"Now do it again," he demanded. I didn't even have time to catch my breath before Malachi was insisting I move forward, running all the way back to the field.

But wasting my breath arguing wouldn't help me. I bit my tongue and started moving back to the field, even as my lungs screamed for me to stop.

We spent the next couple of hours doing the same thing. Malachi demanded. I obeyed every command. I didn't catch my breath once. Not one single time. Yet I continued doing everything Malachi demanded of me.

Sweat drenched my clothes. Even the linens I had worn were completely soaked, my top clinging to my damp skin.

"Take a break," he said to me. "The others should be joining us soon."

"The others?" I breathed.

"You thought you were the only one I was training?" he asked. "In case you forgot, sweetheart, I'm one of the most powerful fae in this kingdom. I've fought wars these men have only heard about in rumors. Seth asked me to train them, and I agreed."

I was exhausted, yes, but this still didn't make much sense. "What do you mean he asked you? Is that what we're doing here then? Training his men?"

Malachi nodded but wouldn't look me in the eye. "For the most part, yeah."

"And then what?"

"What do you mean?"

"You train his men, and then what? What are you training them for?"

Malachi exhaled and placed his hands on his hips, like he was finally tired.

A familiar sensation hit my stomach. "What?" I asked again. "Just tell me already."

"It's my father," he said.

"What about him?"

"Seth wants me to kill him."

# CHAPTER 21
## *Malachi*

"I really hope you were planning on telling me that sometime soon," Jade snapped.

"Why? It's not like it involves you," I retorted. I didn't care that I sounded harsh. I needed to keep her out of this.

"Are you kidding me? You really think that you being on a mission to kill your own father has nothing to do with me? The girl he wants dead?"

I sighed again. What did she want me to say? My brothers and I had already planned to kill him before Seth got involved. Now, we were just doing a small favor.

It was nothing. Simple politics. I needed an ally when shit went down.

This was the clear choice. *Wasn't it?*

Disbelief covered Jade's face. "I was going to tell you," I admitted after a few seconds. Saints. Her sweat had made her shirt nearly see-through.

"So, you're training Trithen, your previous enemies, on how to fight? Am I hearing that correctly?"

"Yes."

"Have you told Esther? Does Isaiah know? What about Adeline?"

"It's nobody else's business, Jade. This is between Seth and I, okay?"

She shook her head and backed up a step. I wanted to reach a hand out, but I stopped myself.

"Serefin knows. I'll tell the others."

"Your mother won't like it."

I laughed. "I don't really care what she thinks, Jade."

"You should. You're about to kill one parent. You might as well keep this one around."

"And why do you suddenly care? You didn't like Esther, remember? You didn't like any of them when we met."

I was yelling now, we both were.

"Yeah well, things change, Malachi!"

"They sure as shit do," I mumbled, turning my back to her. "The others will be here soon."

"Right," I said. "You'll be too busy teaching your enemies all your best fighting tactics to talk to me. Got it."

I spun around on my heel. My mind was spinning, Jade made me crazy. Absolutely nuts. "Why do you even care?" I asked. "Why do you care about what I'm doing, or what our business with Trithen is?"

Her face changed before she said, "You did not just ask me that."

All I did was shrug, even though I wanted to say more. My instincts begged me to say more.

Jade simply nodded, as if she were finally accepting who I was. Who the monster was that she had been forced to marry.

"If you even have to ask me that question, Malachi, then you clearly haven't been paying any attention over the last few weeks."

And with that, she turned toward the castle and stormed off.

"We aren't done with training!" I yelled after her. Saints, I was a dumb ass.

"I don't give a shit!" she yelled back.

Fair enough.

I let her walk away this time. Back to the castle. Back to another prison she was being held in.

Did she even want to stay? Did she want to help? Had she been interested in me because she thought it would help her get home sooner? Or was she starting to like her place at my side?

It didn't matter anymore, anyway. I had ruined it all. I had been a complete asshole to her. Jade didn't care about my reputation or the people I had killed. She cared about me. For whatever odd, insane reason, she actually cared about me.

And I had ruined it all.

"What's going on out here?" Serefin asked as he jogged up. "Jade looked pissed."

"Yeah," I mumbled. "That pretty much sums it up."

"You know, Mal, if you want to keep her safe, you should send her away. Get her out of here before this war goes down."

"We don't even know if there will be a war yet."

Serefin tilted his head and shrugged.

"Okay, fair," I admitted. "But she's safest here with me. I can keep an eye on her here. She has a target on her back now, and she's one of us from now on whether she likes it or not."

"Did you tell her that?" Ser asked.

"Why should I?"

Serefin took a long breath and laughed silently. "Look, Mal. I know you care about her. I knew that from the moment you first saved her life. But Jade doesn't just need you to protect her. Soon enough, if the rumors are true, she'll be able to do that on her own."

I waited for him to continue.

"Jade needs you to be there, idiot. I saw her walking around the castle at nearly three in the morning last night. Have you even tried spending time with her?"

"Why would I? I'll kill my father and she'll go back to her family. It's that simple."

"No," he said firmly. "It's not. Even if the King is dead, Jade will still be targeted. She'll have to fulfill the prophecy or she'll be hunted her whole life."

Shit. Ser was right about that. I hadn't bothered to think that far ahead.

"Pretending to be a real married couple won't help anyone," I said. "She was forced to marry me, remember? She doesn't want any of this."

"Did she tell you that, or is that what you've been telling yourself?"

I eyed Serefin. When did he become so smart? "You know I pay you to kill our enemies, not give me life advice, right?"

He just shrugged. "Consider this a free bonus then, brother," he said.

"And Ser?" I called. "What the Saints were you doing up at three in the morning?"

He smiled slyly and looked down at his feet. "Why don't you ask that wife of yours?"

The look on his face almost made me smile. Serefin wasn't one to smile frequently or laugh at himself. Something was up.

And Jade knew what it was.

"Fine," I admitted. "I'll talk to her."

"It's about damn time," he said back. "You can finally stop taking up the only extra spare room in the entire castle."

I rolled my eyes and shoved him in the arm. Other soldiers were approaching now, and they would expect warrior Malachi.

Killer Malachi.

Not *laughing-with-his-buddy* Malachi. That wasn't the person who won wars. Who ruled kingdoms.

Serefin knew this, too. We both rolled our shoulders back and crossed our arms behind our backs, waiting to greet our new soldiers.

The soldiers we had seen before.

On the other side of the battlefield.

"Gentleman," I greeted. "Welcome."

The crew in front of us looked like survivors, that much was certain. At this point in time, though, any fae over the age of twenty that lived here would have to be. Two decades ago, we had slaughtered nearly three quarters of their army in war.

Including their king.

The soldiers standing before me looked a lot like the soldiers back then. They were tall and mostly blonde. Compared to the people of Rewyth, they were lighter. Softer.

But their eyes were just as dark.

Some wore strips of armor, likely to train and practice for battle.

Others came shirtless, ready to fight with just their bodies.

The field before us filled and filled, soldiers trickling in from every direction.

"Alright," Serefin said, taking over for me. "Who here knows how to fight?"

Most of the men in front of us raised their hands.

Serefin nodded.

"Right, now who wants to tell me why you're all wrong?"

A few slurs were muttered in the crowd.

I knew these soldiers would hate us, especially if any of them recognized me.

And with my black wings, that wasn't going to be hard.

I tucked them a little tighter into my back.

"Traitors!" one of them yelled.

"Kill them!"

"King killer!"

"Who even let them into this kingdom?"

More insults were yelled and slurred from the crowd.

Serefin and I exchanged a glance.

"We came here to train you," I said. "Because, unlike some of you here, I have never fought a war and lost. Never. Can you say the same?"

This time, the crowd was silent.

"Good. Now we can stand here and bicker about the past, or we can get to work. What do you think?"

I thought they would finally listen, but in a flash, a dagger sliced through the air heading straight toward my head.

I dodged it effortlessly.

Gasps rang out around us, but nobody moved.

"I see some of us are not on board with training," I said, looking around the crowd. "So let me be clear. I have been asked by your king to train you for war. You can try to kill me, but you will fail. You can try to throw daggers at my head, but you will fail. Not a single one of you is capable of killing me. Do you know why that is, Serefin?" I asked.

Serefin shrugged dramatically and said, "No, please tell us."

I eyed the men in front of me. They looked smug. They looked defiant. They looked like they didn't listen to a single word I had just said.

That would get them killed. Their arrogance.

My power rumbled, like it already knew what I was thinking. I pictured my magic branching out and brushing everyone as it passed by, just a simple kiss on their skin.

And every single soldier on the field dropped to the ground in pain.

Serefin and I were the only ones left standing as I reeled my power back in, but the soldiers still moaned, some even yelling for the pain to stop even though it already had.

And someone else. Someone else stood in the back of the crowd, unaffected by my magic.

Jade.

My breath escaped me. "Saints," I mumbled. I stormed past the soldiers on the ground, needing to get to her.

Needing to see if I had hurt her.

But she didn't take her eyes off mine as I approached and grabbed her by the shoulders.

"What are you doing?!" I asked. "I could have killed you!"

"I'm here to train," was all she said. "Nice little trick, by the way."

I couldn't believe what I was seeing. My heart still pounded in my chest, adrenaline pulsing through me. "What do you mean?" I asked, looking her up and down and making sure she wasn't hurt. "You aren't hurt?"

"No, I'm fine," she said, sounding more annoyed than anything. "I'm fine, Malachi."

It was impossible. I had aimed my power at every single person standing in front of me in that field.

Every single person.

*Without* excluding my wife.

I turned around and looked at Serefin, who looked just as bewildered as I did.

But the other soldiers were starting to stand now, too. And they were not going to be happy. This would have to wait.

"Fine," I said. "But come to the front with me. You shouldn't be around all of these men anyway."

She didn't argue. Just rolled her eyes and followed me back to the front of the crowd.

"Alright men," I announced, shaking off any nerves that lingered. "Now you know who you're really up against. And trust me, that was only a taste."

Nobody replied this time. Nobody yelled anything toward us.

They were finally starting to learn.

"Serefin will lead you in a few combat warm-ups. Listen to him, or you'll get a taste of what this power can really do."

I grabbed Jade's arm and marched off, dragging her with me.

"Mal, stop!" she yelled. "I'm supposed to be training just like everyone else!"

When we were far enough away, I let her go. "Tell me what you did," I said. Her eyes widened, and I could scent the lingering fear in her emotions. The fear she was trying to hide. "Tell me what you did to block my magic. Did Esther teach you that?"

She only shook her head, eyes wide. "I don't know, Mal. I don't–"

"I need you to tell me, Jade. Because you should be dead right now. Saints..."

I paced, running my hands through my hair and trying to make sense of the situation. "Saints, Jade! If a human gets touched by my power...you blocked it somehow. That's the only thing that makes sense."

"I swear I didn't do anything. I was standing there just like everyone else when they all fell to the ground!"

Her teasing voice was gone now. She was dead serious.

"Shit," I said. I turned and headed to the castle. "Come with me."

"Where are we going?" I asked.

"To find Esther and ask her how it's possible that you're even alive right now."

## CHAPTER 22

# Jade

"It's not impossible that she can block your power," Esther whispered. Malachi had been desperate for answers, and had stormed us directly into Esther's bedroom. "I've heard of this before. An individual able to block the powers of others."

"Are you sure?" Malachi insisted.

"There's one way we can know for sure. Try it again," she said.

"Absolutely not. It's too dangerous."

I pushed myself off the wall and walked toward Mal. "It's not too dangerous," I insisted. "If you could hurt me, you would have done it. In that field. I know you can't hurt me Mal. It's like... it's like an instinct that I can feel. Just try it."

He stared at me, hesitating for a moment. "I don't like this."

"I know you don't."

Silence filled the air. Malachi had been a complete asshole to me recently, but the way he looked at me now made me rethink everything.

He was afraid of hurting me.

"Fine," he said after a few minutes. "I'll try it just this once, but if we're wrong..."

"We aren't," Esther and I said at the same time.

Malachi stepped forward and grabbed me by the shoulders. I pretended not to notice the feeling of warmth on my body where he touched me.

"If you feel anything, I'll stop," he whispered. His eyes darkened, and he looked at me now under those thick eyelashes of his.

"Okay," I tried to say, but it was more of a breath.

Malachi closed his eyes, as if he were focusing more than ever on the power within him.

I wasn't afraid, though. I knew what had happened. I knew that Malachi had sent his power out to hurt every single person in that field, and I was the only one who was unaffected.

It wasn't an accident. I felt it deep inside of me.

A few seconds passed, then Malachi let go of me. "It's true," he whispered to himself. His face had changed from one of doubt and worry to one of utter disbelief. "It's true, you aren't affected by my power."

The smile on his face was contagious. "Saints," I breathed. "What does this mean?"

Malachi ran a hand through his messy, disheveled hair. "I've never seen this before. In the decades that I've been using my magic, the only creatures my magic doesn't work on is the deadlings."

"That's a confidence boost," I said. My mind began to spin. "What are the deadlings, anyway? Are they born that way? Turned?"

Esther stepped forward to answer, her long, white dressing gown trailing the ground behind her. "They didn't use to be this way," she said. "Centuries ago, the deadlings were their own species. They hunted and killed, but it was purely for survival. Just like the rest of us at the time."

Malachi listened intently, too.

"Somewhere over the years, things changed. Some believe they were cursed by the Saints. That the Saints stopped protecting them."

"Does this mean I can block *any* fae powers?" I asked.

"Most likely, yes. If you can block the power from an elite, you can likely block them all."

"This is good news, right?"

Malachi nodded. "It's a relief, definitely."

Esther began talking again, going on and on about the history of magic blockers and what this could possibly mean for the prophecy, but I wasn't listening. I quit listening entirely. Malachi was staring directly at me, eyes burning into mine. It was like he was finally seeing me for the first time.

Actually seeing me. Not pitying me. Not worrying about me.

Like he really saw me.

I wanted to reach out to him. I wanted to throw my arms around him and not let go. I just wanted him.

Malachi broke eye contact before I did. "Okay," he said. "We better get back to training, then. And Esther, let's agree to keep this between us, yes?"

She nodded, and Malachi left the room. I followed behind.

"Back to training?" I repeated behind him. "You mean you're going to let me train with the rest of them?"

He nodded. "If you have these gifts now, more are surely on their way. You need to learn to protect yourself."

I agreed.

"But I won't go easy on you," he added. "If you want to train like a soldier, you'll be treated like one."

"Fine," I said. "I can do that."

He eyed me, his eyes dragging up and back down my body once, in a way that sent a shiver down my spine. But then he turned and walked outside, back to the field.

Back to training.

Serefin and Malachi led everyone through hours and hours of movements. They were basic, yet for my weak body, they took all the energy I had left. Saints. The day had already been so long.

The sun blazed hotter and hotter with every passing minute.

We watched Serefin and repeated his movements, one after another. Sometimes he would show us movements that involved a sword or a dagger, granted nobody had weapons just yet. We repeated the same motions again and again and again.

And we repeated it all the next day.

And the next day.

Before I knew it, two weeks had passed.

My body ached every single day, but I could tell I was getting stronger. Each motion became a sliver easier every day that I tried again. Serefin's nods of approval kept me going each day, although ridiculous slurs from the fae soldiers were also a decent motivator.

Every so often, I would glance at Malachi. He didn't speak to me. Didn't even give me instruction. But here and there I would look at him only to find him already looking at me.

He never looked away first, either. Just kept staring.

Outside of training, we didn't talk. I didn't see him. He would train me for endurance every single morning, and I was too busy catching my breath every single minute that striking up a useless conversation was not an option.

When it came time to train with the rest of the soldiers, Malachi quit talking to me entirely. His attention was on the crowd. He made a point to shut everyone up if anyone began yelling things toward me, but that was it.

He was all business.

This repeated every day. I thought I had been making progress with Malachi in the mornings, but he was harsher with me every single day. He pushed me further and further, until I thought I would break.

But I never did. Ever.

"Alright," Serefin said. "I think that's enough for the day." Soldiers grunted and nodded all over the field. "Get some sleep, we'll try more tomorrow."

I heard a few mumbling about how we weren't training real skills, not using real weapons, and I nearly laughed. Serefin and Malachi knew what they were doing.

Even I could see that.

The rest of the soldiers were wandering back to the castle, eager to eat dinner after another long day of training.

I lingered behind, though. A certain determination had been growing inside of me every day. I wanted to fight Malachi. I wanted to show him that I wasn't the same, useless human he had known weeks ago.

"Training is over," he mumbled when he noticed I had stayed back. "Go home."

I pulled my dagger from my belt, the one that he had gifted me lifetimes ago, and tossed it into the grass beside me.

It was an invitation for a spar. And he knew it.

He took a long, tired breath and disarmed himself before turning to face me. "Fine," he said. "Show me what you've got, wife."

Malachi did not wait another second. He threw his fist into my torso, but I was ready. I blocked it with my forearm, ignoring the satisfying sting that followed.

"You're stronger now," he admitted. I grunted in response.

"I better be."

I swung a leg out and tried to knock him off balance. He dodged it with ease.

Okay. I had to be smart about this. What had I learned in my training? The fae were fast, but they were predictable. After practicing the same movements time and time again for days on end, I should know his next move.

I stepped forward, acting like I was making a move toward his stomach, and when Malachi moved to advance on me I side-stepped, causing him to stagger forward.

We danced around each other.

He mimicked me, and I knew the wicked smile on my face matched his.

"You really are getting better, princess. I must say I'm impressed."

It was a compliment, but he still underestimated me.

I might have been human, but I wasn't completely useless.

Malachi's wings were tucked tightly behind his back. Wings were the most sensitive part of a fae. If I could get a solid hit...

My thoughts were interrupted when Malachi threw an arm around my waist and tossed me on the ground.

He laughed as I got myself up.

"Still not fast enough, though," he said.

I was angry now.

My face was hot, my muscles were ready. I sent a small fist flying toward his face.

He caught it and pulled my body toward him. "Gotta be better than that, princess."

With my free arm, I moved to elbow his side.

He blocked that, too, then shoved my body away from him.

I barely caught myself from falling to the ground.

He was taunting me.

"Again," he said. His voice boomed. It commanded.

I took two steps toward him and tried again.

And again.

He blocked me each time, and each time he had some sort of comment to add.

"I can't do it," I said after he had put me on my ass for probably the hundredth time. "I'm not strong enough."

"What did you just say?" he said. Something in his voice made me want to shut up, but I repeated myself anyway.

"I said I'm not strong enough."

Malachi tilted his head to the sky and took a deep breath before storming toward me and kneeling in the grass before me.

"Don't say that," he said. "The moment you admit it to yourself, it becomes true. And it's not true, so don't say that. You have to protect yourself, Jade. *You have to.* I won't always be around. And when this is all over and you end up going home..."

He didn't finish the sentence. I didn't say anything.

Malachi was close enough now that I could see the small freckles on his face that had formed in the weeks had spent training under the sun.

He looked good in the sun.

"Okay," I managed to breathe. "I understand."

"Good," he said as he stood up again. "Now try again. This time, don't try to overpower me. It will never work. Try something else. Remember your training."

I took a deep breath and tried to focus. He was right. Overpowering a fae wasn't going to be an option.

I had to be smarter than that. Smarter than him.

I stood up from the grass and got back into my fighting stance. Feet slightly parted, fists up to protect my face.

But that would never work. Not on him.

I dropped my fists and raised my hands over my head, pretending to stretch my sides. "Saints," I said. "I'm just so sore these days, you now? All that training, day after day..."

Malachi dropped his own defenses, and I watched as his gaze flickered down to the sliver of skin that was now exposed at my stomach.

His gaze lingered, and the air between us electrified.

With him distracted, I tried again. I swung a leg toward his shin, and to my surprise, actually landed a hit.

Malachi staggered backward, only a step. It took him a second to realize what the Saints had just happened.

And when he finally realized it, he looked pissed.

"What was that?" he growled.

"What was what?" I responded innocently. "Just fighting a little smarter, that's all."

Malachi growled and moved before I could even think, tackling me to the ground.

He pinned me there, holding my arms to the ground next to my head. "Do you think this is a joke?" he said.

I didn't back down. "I just did what you asked," I spat. "It's not my fault you were distracted."

Malachi laughed, but it wasn't out of joy. It was a laugh that nearly made me shiver in the heat of the sun.

He was still on top of me, his body directly on top of my torso. I tried to buck my hips, but it was no use.

Malachi bent forward, getting eerily close to my face. "Careful there, Jade. You don't want to give the wrong impression. Tell me, is this how you plan on taking down all of your enemies?"

Did he really just say that?

I frowned and tried to buck even harder. "Get off of me!" I yelled.

Malachi just smiled, and his gaze moved from my eyes down to my lips, then back again.

Was he going to kiss me? My stomach fluttered at the thought, but it left abruptly when he stood and stalked off, leaving me on the ground.

"What in the Saints is your problem?" I yelled after him. I was pissed off. Who did he think he was, toying me around and then nearly kissing me?

Malachi spun around. "What are you talking about?"

"You're a complete asshole to me for weeks and now this? Saints, Malachi. You're treating me like I'm a damn stranger!"

"No, I'm not," he said quietly.

"Oh really? Then where have you been? What have you been spending all your time doing? Because you sure as shit have not been spending it with me."

"I've been busy, Jade. You know that."

"Really? Ever since the festival?"

"That's what you're mad about? The festival?"

Malachi shook his head in disbelief.

"I'm not mad about the festival. I'm mad that my husband has been treating me like a damn burden on his shoulders!"

"Stop being dramatic," he mumbled. Tears stung my eyes. I fought to keep them back. I wasn't going to let him see me cry. Not now. Not after all this.

"I am your wife, Malachi," I admitted through gritted teeth, barely loud enough to hear.

"I know," he replied just as softly.

*"Your wife!"*

*"I know!"*

The silence that came after was more than enough to answer any lingering questions I had.

There was no hope. This was how it was going to be from now on. Malachi acting like he had better things to deal with, and me chasing after the dream that there had ever been anything more between us.

"Do you even want me here?" I asked. "Or is this all just part of the prophecy to you?"

Malachi snapped his attention to me, like he couldn't believe what I had just said. I waited for his response.

With two large steps, he closed the gap between us, grabbing my face with both hands. "No," he said firmly, almost yelling. "This is not just part of the prophecy, Jade. You are my wife, and I–"

*Love you.*

I wasn't sure why I expected those words, but when they didn't come, a familiar sick feeling sank in my chest.

And just as quickly as he had approached me, he dropped his hands and walked away.

I didn't stop him when he kept walking, leaving me alone in the field.

And I finally let the tears fall.

# CHAPTER 23
## Malachi

SAINTS, I WAS AN IDIOT.

I wanted to kiss Jade. I had come so damn close.

The fact that she still cared about me was a damned miracle to me. After the way I had been treating her, she should hate me. She earned the right to hate me.

But she didn't. That had to mean something, right?

Jade was going to turn into an extremely powerful woman. I could feel it in my bones. Esther could, too. She made that very clear a couple of weeks ago.

Jade being able to block my magic didn't change anything. She was still in incredible danger.

If anything, she was in even more danger now.

Being with me would put yet another target on her back.

"We need to talk," Seth approached me as I walked through the castle walls toward the dining room.

"About?"

"Your father is coming here. It's time."

Saints. Was everyone in this place losing their damn minds?

"My father is coming here?" I repeated. I had to make sure I heard him correctly before letting panic take hold.

Seth nodded. "He says he has a new business proposition."

"Could it be because he somehow figured out that we were here?"

Seth shook his head. "It's impossible. Trithen has no spies. I know every single person that comes in and out of these walls, and they're all to be trusted."

Just as ignorant as I thought he was, then.

I sighed and continued walking. "Did you hear me?" he called after me. "We need to prepare!"

"We are prepared," I said. "I'll keep my side of the deal, don't worry."

"You sure you'll be able to do it?" he asked.

My wings flared out by my sides. "What did you just ask me?"

"I just want to be sure."

"It'll get done," was all I could say back.

"Fine," he said. "He will be here tomorrow. You should prepare yourself."

I didn't look back as I stormed into the dining hall.

A few people looked my way as I walked into the room, but I kept my head down. If anyone approached me right now, I would have absolutely no problem punching them in the face.

I walked directly to the servant's table and grabbed food for myself.

A fight was coming, that much was certain.

My father was on his way here...

If he knew I was here, he would bring an entire army. Being here with the leader of Trithen was certainly treason in Rewyth. We had been enemies for too long.

There was too much at risk.

I had to find my brothers.

"And you think this will work?" Isaiah asked.

I looked at Lucien and Adonis, who sat across the large table. "It has to," Adonis answered. "This might be our only opportunity to kill him."

I nodded. "If anything happens..."

"It won't," Lucien spat. "We'll kill the bastard and it'll be done. Then we can all go home."

He was right. He had to be right.

The twins, Eli and Fynn, sat silently in the back of the room. I hadn't heard them this silent since... ever.

"Everything sound good to you two?" I asked them. They nodded in unison.

It had to be nerves. They had never been put into a fight like this. Had never gone to war.

Shit. They had likely never actually killed anyone.

"What about the soldiers you've been training?" Adonis asked. "Won't they want to know the plan?"

I clenched my jaw. "We can't trust them. I killed their king. I don't know what their game is here, but we can't assume they'll follow us blindly into this fight."

"And they shouldn't have to," Lucien said. "This is our business. This is our fight."

We all nodded in agreement.

For the first time since we had each been born, we were all on the same page.

# CHAPTER 24
# *Jade*

I HAD ALMOST FALLEN ASLEEP WHEN THREE QUICK KNOCKS ON MY DOOR pulled me awake.

"Who is it?" I asked, sitting up and flinging the covers off my legs.

"It's me. Let me in."

*Malachi.*

I glanced at myself in the mirror on the wall and brushed my frizzy black hair down with my hands before padding over to the door and flinging it open.

He didn't even wait for my invitation before pushing the door open the rest of the way and shoving himself inside.

"Great," I mumbled. "Come on in." I was wearing a thin nightgown that no-doubt would expose far too much if the sun was out, but the darkness protected me.

It always did.

Malachi didn't even greet me. He began pacing back and forth in the room, muttering to himself and dragging his hands down his face.

"What's going on?" I asked. "Did something happen?"

"No," he shook his head. "Not yet. But it's about to. Everything's going to change, Jade. Everything."

Panic began to creep into my senses. "What do you mean 'everything's going to change'? What's happening?"

I walked to the side of my bed and sat down, bracing myself on the tall bedpost. Malachi dropped his hands and paced over to me. I could see his face clearly now, his eyes were wild and his breathing was shallow.

I had rarely seen him like this.

"Tell me," I insisted.

My mind instantly spiraled to all the worst places. Was Adeline dead? Did Esther turn on us and run away? Was the King coming back to kill me?

Was it my family? My father? Tessa?

"They're coming," Malachi said. "Tomorrow."

"Who's coming?"

"My father and his soldiers. They're coming here tomorrow."

I stood from the bed and moved closer. "What?" I asked. "Why?"

"They've been invited by Seth to discuss business."

"Why would he invite him? He knows we're here and he knows we're not in the King's favor right now!"

"Because I'm supposed to kill him, Jade. Tomorrow. I have no doubt that Seth wants proof and wants it done on his lands."

I shook my head. "It's a setup. It has to be."

Malachi took a deep breath. "I thought the same thing at first."

"What are we going to do about it? Does everyone know?"

"Yes, the others know. My brothers and I have a plan. As long as Seth stays out of the way, we'll do what needs to be done and we'll get out of here by tomorrow night."

My heart was racing in my chest. I put a hand over it to feel the pounding.

The King of Rewyth will be here tomorrow. And Malachi will kill him.

"You'll become the King of Rewyth, then?" I asked, keeping my voice as soft as possible.

Malachi looked at me, a sea of emotions swarming those deep, beautiful eyes. "Yes. I'll become the King of Rewyth. Once we explain that something went terribly wrong during a business deal to Trithen."

"And they'll believe that?"

Malachi nodded. "My father has a lot of enemies. Not just us. I doubt anyone will have a problem with me becoming the King when they learn the news.

Malachi moved and grabbed me by my arms, forcing me to look at him. "You have to do every single thing I tell you to do, Jade. Everything. Can you do that?"

I nodded. "What do you want me to do?"

"I'll need you to stay here. Nobody will step foot inside this castle, but no matter what happens, you can't leave. I won't be able to focus if I think you might be in danger."

"You really think he believes we're in Fearford right now? What if he has spies that went looking for us?"

"If that were the case, they would be here right now. My father is too hot-headed to not act on information like that. If he thought we were here, we would know. There's no way he has any clue. Besides, I killed the King of Trithen. This is the last place he would expect us to go."

That made sense. The fact that Malachi and Seth were now working together was still a strange concept to me. Malachi's father would never expect that.

"Okay," I said. "I'll be hiding out of sight. Where will you be?"

"Killing my father, princess. That's where I'll be."

He had a straight face as he said the words, but I knew they had to hurt. Malachi hated his father. For probably decades, he had been harboring this hatred and hadn't been able to act on it.

He thought his father had been torturing his mother.

How wrong we had all been about that.

"And Esther is okay with this? What does she think about the plan?"

"She'll be okay with it. She hates him even more than the rest of us," he said. "If anything, she'll be angry that she wasn't able to do it herself."

"And your magic... it will keep you safe, right? I mean... isn't this risky?"

Malachi raised an eyebrow. "Worried about me, princess?"

I shrugged out of his grip and walked to the other side of the room. "You know what I mean," I said.

He chuckled once but eventually answered, "We'll be fine. For anyone else, yeah, it would be risky. But with my magic it won't even take more than a minute. Once the King and his men are close by, I'll drop them all with my power, and my brothers will help me finish him off."

I nodded again, taking it all in. The room felt lighter around me, and I suddenly fought the urge to vomit.

"Hey," Malachi said once I placed both my hands on the bedroom wall for support. "Hey, are you okay?"

I felt him come up behind me, close enough to touch me but not quite there.

Was I okay? *Saints, no.* I was far from being okay. Would he understand? He was the one killing his father tomorrow, after all. That had nothing to do with me.

And what was my job? To shut up and stay out of the way?

Malachi set his hands on my back. His warmth behind me was comforting in a way that made my knees weak.

"What happens next?" I asked. "What happens when it's done?"

"We go back to Rewyth," he said. "We go home."

I let a laugh escape me. *Home?* I didn't even know if I had a home anymore. It certainly wasn't here.

Would Rewyth be my home?

Malachi sighed heavily, and his breath on the back of my neck made me shiver. "What do you want?" He asked as if he were reading my thoughts.

*What did I want?*

My first thought was home. I wanted to go home and be with Tessa.

But did I really? Tessa may not even take me back after everything that happened between Malachi and my father.

That small, crumbling town didn't have anything for me. Did I want to go back there? Back to suffering every single day, selling my soul for a single piece of food?

Esther would likely never let me go back, anyway. If I was the piece to this grand puzzle like she thought I was, I wouldn't be safe there.

Rewyth may have been a prison to me in the past, but it just might be my haven now.

I turned around under Malachi's touch. He was so close, my chest was nearly touching his. "I don't know," I answered honestly. "If I go back home... there's nothing there for me. I'd be waiting to die every single day, just like I was before. But in Rewyth..."

"Rewyth is your home, Jade," he said. His voice was low and serious. "Rewyth will always be a home to you, even if you wish to leave."

I met his gaze. "You would let me leave?"

A sad smile played on his lips. "You're not my prisoner, Jade. My father forced us to marry. When he's dead..."

He didn't have to finish the sentence. I knew what he was thinking.

I shook my head and looked away so Malachi wouldn't see the tears welling up in my eyes. Saints. When had I turned into such a cry baby?

But Malachi grabbed my chin and forced me to look at him.

"You're my wife, Jade. *My wife.* That doesn't change for me. If you wish to go back home and live with your family, I won't stop you. But you are the Princess of Rewyth. If you wish to come with me to rule, I swear I'll make you the happiest woman in the Kingdom."

I couldn't believe he was saying this. My mind raced, running through everything he had said or done to me in the past few weeks.

"Why?" I asked. "I can't keep up, Mal. One second you barely talk to me, the next second you want me to come with you to Rewyth?"

Malachi leaned forward and touched his forehead against mine. My breath hitched.

"I've tried to ignore how I feel about you, Jade. It's safer for everyone if you aren't near me."

"But that's not true. If what Esther is saying is true, there's no place safer for me." He closed his eyes. "I know you didn't expect any of this, either. But I'm involved in all of this, whether we like it or not. I don't think running away is an option for me anymore."

"What are you going to do?"

I couldn't think. Malachi's breath tickled my cheek, invading my thoughts and taking over every emotion. I didn't care about the future. I didn't care. Saints, I never even planned on living this long.

Would it be completely crazy if I went back to Rewyth with Malachi? The Prince of Shadows?

My husband?

"Jade," he whispered, his voice holding the same longing that I was feeling. It wasn't just saying my name. He was begging me.

I pushed myself upward and pressed my lips against his, softly. He froze for a second, but his hands found themselves wrapping around my body, holding me to him.

I kissed Malachi, my husband, like we could forget everything in our crazy, messy lives. Like it was just him and I. His mouth was warm against mine. He kissed me slowly, his hands firm as he held me against him.

I pulled away, just for a second, and looked into his eyes. "I don't know what I want, Mal. I have no damned idea. But I do know that I want you. I want this."

He let out a long breath and said, "Thank the Saints for that, Jade, because I honestly don't know what I would do without you."

And he kissed me back, harder this time. My arms wrapped around his shoulders and he lifted me up against the wall so I could wrap my legs around his waist. Malachi kissed my lips, my neck, my chest. He kissed me until I was drunk on him, drunk on the thought of us together in this frenzy of the night.

His mouth didn't leave mine as he carried me to the massive bed, moving so he was positioned above me on top of the silk sheets.

My heart was pounding in my chest. This was everything that I wanted, everything that I needed. I needed Malachi with me. I had wanted this for longer than I had liked to admit.

Malachi was everything.

His breath was hot on my neck as his mouth moved lower, his hands moving to caress every inch of my body. I arched my back to get closer to him, not wanting a single inch of space between us.

I slid my hands under his loose shirt and up his back, running my fingers across the base of his strong black wings that hovered above us.

Malachi hissed against my neck.

"Careful, princess," he breathed.

Heat rushed to my face, but I didn't stop. I kissed him harshly, pulling his face closer to mine.

"I haven't... I mean I don't know..." I stammered between kisses.

Malachi pulled back, holding himself up above me. A wicked, untethered grin splattered across his face. "Don't worry, princess." He kissed me lightly on the lips. "I want this more than anything, but our first time is not going to be in an enemy kingdom where I am not king," he whispered.

Relief and regret both swarmed my head, and I realized how hard I had been breathing. "Okay," I whispered back, not sure of what else to say.

Malachi didn't move from above me. He brought his hand up to caress my cheek, running his thumb against my skin. "I love you, Jade Weyland. I would burn down any kingdom for you. I hope you know that. After everything, I am yours. I will always be yours."

My chest ached with emotion I didn't know I could ever feel. Yes, we were married. Yes, he had saved my life on more than one occasion.

But hearing those words from him changed everything.

A single tear slipped down my cheek. Malachi quickly wiped it away.

"I love you, too, Malachi."

# CHAPTER 25

# *Malachi*

I WOKE UP FEELING SOMETHING I HADN'T FELT IN DECADES.

*Fear.*

I wasn't even sure I was capable of fear anymore. Not for my own life, anyway.

Jade still slept next to me. Her features had grown softer since I had known her. She had changed so much since that first day I had seen her hunting in the forest, nearly throwing herself at a pack of wolves to feed her family.

The family that hadn't even wanted her.

Somewhere in the weeks that she had been with us, she had lost a sort of edge that used to consume her. Not in a bad way, no. It was in a way that made me want to protect her with my life.

And I would. I would do anything to protect her.

My father would be dead by the time the sun set. Jade wouldn't be safe until it was done.

And I had decades of pain that screamed for vengeance. Begged for it.

Today would be the day. Today would be the day my father paid for decades of pain. Of torture. Years and years of using me as his own personal weapon.

I had killed mothers. I had killed children. I had slaughtered innocent people time and time again, just because he had commanded it.

Granted, it took me decades to even realize what he was doing. He had been power-hungry as soon as he had learned about my gifts.

*"Be careful,"* he had told me once, the day after we learned of my power. *"People are going to try to exploit this power of yours. They'll try to use it for their own greedy intentions."*

How right he had been.

I didn't feel guilty. I had stopped feeling guilty for the way I felt about my father decades ago.

He deserved to die. His reign had come to an end.

My mind flashed back to the way his guards had thrown Jade to the ground and whipped her right in front of me.

No. I wouldn't have any problem killing my father with my bare hands.

The sun was rising slowly. I marched through the diamond streets of Trithen, making my way to the meeting spot that Seth and I agreed on.

Today would be the day. No mistakes. No errors. No hesitations.

"You're looking rather chipper this morning, brother," Adonis chirped as he swung into step beside me, Lucien following close by.

"Good morning to you, too," I spat. "Where are the twins?"

"We told them to hang back and keep an eye on Adeline, don't worry," he replied. "We execute the plan. We get the Saints out of here. That's it."

"We really think this army of brutes is going to help us with the ambush?" Lucien asked.

"We have to," I said. "And if they turn on us, they'll die."

"You sound confident. That's good," Adonis added. "You better have that same confidence as you push that blade of yours through our father's chest."

"You don't have to worry about me," I said. "Nothing is more important than our father dying today."

They fell into step behind me as we made our way out of the city, toward the front gates.

We didn't see another soul in the morning sun as we made our way to the meeting spot.

A small row of tents became visible at the edge of Trithen's land. A few hundred soldiers sat around, sharpening their weapons and warming up for the day.

My brothers and I ignored them all, walking straight to the largest tent. The tent where Seth would likely be *pretending* to have things under control.

"Seth," I said as I yanked back the flap to the tent. "Is everything in order?"

Seth straightened immediately. He was wearing a soldier's uniform, a far cry from his usual attire. His right hand rested on the handle of his sword, and his face was dripping in worry.

"Everything is in order," he replied. "Your father and his army should be here within the next couple of hours."

"You're sure about that?" Adonis asked from behind me.

Seth paused for a second before answering. "Are you questioning my intel?"

"Just verifying the facts," Adonis replied. "It's our lives on the line if this goes badly."

"It won't," Seth said. "I'll make sure of that. As long as we all stick to our plan, Malachi here will be the King of Rewyth before lunch is served."

The King of Rewyth.

The words made me stiff. This was the title I was born for. This was the title I had been seeking for decades, waiting for my turn on the throne.

Not for power. Not for popularity. I knew I could be a better leader than my father. I knew I could bring justice to our world in a way that he never had.

Rewyth deserved at least that much.

"Fine," I answered. "I'll find you when it's over." I turned and began exiting the tent, my brothers two paces behind me.

"Don't you want to stay and talk strategy with my advisors?" Seth yelled after me.

"We have a strategy," I yelled back. "And it involves murder, not staring at a useless map. Tell your soldiers to let us handle this, and it'll all be over soon."

Seth didn't follow us as we walked back into the makeshift camp. We recognized most of the soldiers before us, but they didn't speak to us as we walked by.

A few nodded, others looked in the opposite direction, but nobody would be approaching us today.

No, today would be a day of treason.

A day where I killed my own father, the King of Rewyth.

Nobody was going to mess with that.

My brothers and I found a quiet area near the edge of the camp.

"You're sure about this?" Lucien asked. "Feeling up to the task, brother?"

"There's not a doubt in my mind," I replied. It was the truth. I had no hesitation around the fact that killing my father would be as easy as breathing.

"Whatever happens today, brother," he said, "we're on your side. From here on out, we truly are. You haven't been able to trust us in the past, and we understand why. But things are different now. We're on the same team."

Lucien clenched his jaw, but tilted his chin in agreement.

I nodded to Adonis. "Thank you, brother," I replied.

We sat around for another hour, watching the soldiers around us prepare for a war they would have no part in fighting.

Not if everything went according to plan, that is.

Ambush the incoming crew, drop them with my power, and kill my father swiftly. That was the plan, and it was going to work.

It had to work.

My brothers and I didn't fidget. We didn't worry. We showed no signs of nerves. This was not our first war. It wasn't even our fifth war. We had lived through decades fighting battles for our father.

We knew how these things worked. Killing was embedded into our beings.

A horn blared in the distance.

My blood ran cold. I jumped to my feet, hand on my sword, as other soldiers moved into formation around our camp.

My father was nearby.

It was time for a fight.

# CHAPTER 26
# Malachi

"GET INTO POSITION!" SETH'S VOICE YELLED FROM BEHIND. LUCIEN, Adonis and I were already on the move, already rushing in the direction my father's men would be approaching from.

My sword was drawn. My power rumbled with every step I took.

I was power.

I was justice.

And today, I would be executioner.

Seth's men were instructed to stay out of sight unless something went wrong. My brothers and I would handle this on our own. Anyone else involved would be a liability.

My father had no idea that we would be waiting for him. He would be thrown entirely off guard, a perfect opportunity for our attack.

We marched forward, through the thick woods, until we heard the familiar vibrations of horse footsteps pounding the forest floor below us.

*They were here.*

"Stay out of sight until I give the signal," I whispered to my brothers. They dispersed on either side of me, following my orders without question.

My blood pumped rapidly through my veins. This was it. This was the moment that would change everything.

I deserved this.

Jade deserved this.

Saints, all of Rewyth deserved this.

The first horse came into view in the narrow path of the forest, the man riding it dodging the large tree branches that hovered. Relief flooded my body. A guard I had worked with dozens of times came fully into view.

"Malachi?" he questioned after he saw me. "Hold up!" he yelled to the party following behind him. My father was close. I could feel it. "What are you doing here? What's going on?"

"I need to speak to my father," I said sharply, loud enough that my father would hear me if he was part of this party.

*Show no weakness. Yield no mercy.*

"I'm afraid that's not happening right now," the guard responded warily. "Let us pass, and we can discuss whatever business you may have with the King back at Trithen."

He had always been an obedient slave.

They all had been.

But I couldn't blame them. They were just doing whatever it took to survive.

*And so was I.*

"Thank you, but I think I'll be speaking with my father right now," I said again. His black horse approached me, but I didn't budge. My black wings flared out on either side of me, blocking his path entirely.

The guard unsheathed his sword. "Don't do this, Malachi. Don't start trouble. Let us pass."

Another guard came into view behind him.

"What's going on?" My father's voice boomed from somewhere deeper in the forest.

Every single sense of mine was electrified. This was it. This was the moment I had been waiting on.

"It's your son," the second guard yelled back to my father. "Malachi Weyland."

"What?" My father yelled up. The surprise in his voice told me everything I needed to know. They had no idea we were going to ambush them. The plan was working. "What is he doing here?"

Silence filled the air as the guards waited for me to answer.

"I need to talk to you privately," I yelled.

Commotion from behind the guards told me it was working.

My father was coming forward.

The hair on my neck stood straight up.

"For Saint's sake, Malachi," my father mumbled. "We don't speak for weeks and you show up here? What do you want?"

He stepped into view, and I was no longer his son. I was a predator stalking his prey.

I felt nothing but numbness mixing with the increasing adrenaline in my blood.

As soon as I could see the sparkle of his wicked blue eyes, I unleashed my power. My brothers were standing behind me, so I aimed the deadly urge at every being before me.

And within a second, I had started a war.

My own power buzzed in my knees. There were six guards, the two in front and four more that had been hiding in the back.

I brought them all down in pain. They slid off their horses and hit the ground, moaning and clutching their chests.

It wouldn't be just pain in their chests, though. Each of their entire bodies would feel like they were nearly exploding by this point.

Including my father, who was on his knees before me, clawing at his own body.

A sight that brought a wicked grin to my face.

"Now, Malachi!" Adonis yelled from behind me.

I brought my sword up and stepped forward. "You have forced me to be a killer many times, father," I said to him, my final words to the man who had brought me so much suffering. "But this time, I choose to be the killer."

And just as I was about to bring the sword down on my cowering father's head, an arrow ripped through the air from somewhere deeper in the forest.

And pierced me in the shoulder.

I hissed in pain, quickly ripping the long weapon out of my flesh. It wasn't deep and I would heal quickly, but that meant there were more.

We weren't the only ones fighting this fight. The bastard had guards hidden in the forest.

Which meant he had been expecting an ambush.

"Lucien!" I yelled. He moved in an instant to send the signal to the other soldiers that we were in trouble.

Killing my father. That's what I needed to focus on. I didn't care about how many people were shooting at me.

I lifted my sword again, grunting against my pain.

My father looked up at me.

And began to stand.

Along with each of the soldiers.

No, no, no.

I dug deeper to find my power, desperate to belittle them again, to end them all for good.

But there was nothing there.

"Saints," I mumbled to myself. Panic inched its way into my veins.

It had to be that arrow. Laced with something that would block my power from being effective. I had heard stories of herb-laced weapons that would do such things, but I had never seen them myself.

Not until now, anyway.

"What's wrong, son?" my father sneered as he regained traction on his feet. "Plans to kill your own father not going as planned?"

The sarcastic note in his voice made me angrier than ever.

"I don't need magic to kill a bastard. I've done it hundreds of times before, remember?" I sneered.

I swung my sword down, but metal collided with metal.

And that's when absolute chaos erupted.

Seth's soldiers poured in from behind, but my father's men were ready. And they were trained in combat much more extensively than these men were.

"Malachi!" Adonis yelled from my right. "Malachi, watch out!"

A sharp pain sliced through my right arm. I spun around to see a young soldier with a knife impaled in my skin.

I cut him down quickly with my sword, no hesitation.

No hesitation in war. Hesitating meant dying.

I was not dying today.

I turned back to where my father was, and he simply stood with a nasty grin on his face.

"You're dead," I sneered. The words came out in a low growl.

Did he not believe me? Did he truly believe he could get out of this? He was outnumbered by hundreds.

One of Seth's men sliced his weapon through the one guard that had remained by my father.

And then there was a clear path to him.

There was nobody left to defend him. Nobody left to help him. Yet he was still the same, arrogant bastard that he always was.

He did not reach for his weapon. He did not try to run.

I took three steps between us and grabbed my father by the throat. "You deserve a worse death than this one," I sneered.

"Is that what your mother told you?" he managed to get out.

"Don't talk about her."

He laughed wickedly. "I knew she had something to do with this. Trust me, son. You don't want to listen to a word she says. There's a reason she left Rewyth."

"I'm well aware of the fact that she left you and your wicked ways," I said. "It's something I should have done long ago."

"She'll say anything to use your power," my father continued. His voice had changed from confident to desperate. "Believe me, son. Believe me! Was this her idea? This ambush?"

My blood was pounding in my ears. Yells of pain rang out around me, each of my fathers men dying.

Even the ones that had been hiding away in the trees. The ones with arrows.

They were all going to die. They were no match for an army.

And my father was no match for me.

"No," I said. "Killing you was my idea."

I let go of his throat and drew my sword.

Blood rushing through my veins hissed in my ears. The grip on my weapon was tight. I did not shake. I did not falter. This was something that had to be done. I had no doubt in my mind.

I was a killer. I had killed hundreds of people who didn't deserve it.

This was not going to be one of those times.

With the exhale of a breath, I brought the sword down. It crashed through my father's body with ease.

And his dead body fell to the ground with a thud.

I breathed in.

I breathed out.

It was over. I had done it.

"Malachi!" Serefin's voice pulled me from my trance.

There was still fighting going on around me.

"Enough!" Seth's voice boomed louder than mine, halting the fighting where it stood. "Surrender or die," he said to the rest of my father's men. "This fight is over."

The men dropped to their knees in surrender.

My breath became heavier and heavier.

*I had just killed my father.*

"Mal," Serefin said again, softer this time. I looked for him in the crowd of soldiers, and when my eyes finally landed on him, my stomach sank.

"Eli?" Lucien yelled, stepping forward.

*No, no, no.*

My feet moved without my permission, bringing me closer to where Eli knelt over another soldier.

No, not just another soldier.

His twin brother, Fynn.

Eli's head was now bowed, his body shaking in silent sobs.

"Fynn?" Adonis asked. All three of us now stood around them both.

"He was protecting me," Eli said after a few moments, his voice barely audible. "We came here to help, but everyone was already fighting when we got here. He tried...he tried–"

Adonis dropped to his knees beside Eli, checking Fynn's pulse. Blood smeared his neck, his chest. Too much blood.

When he couldn't find a pulse, he bowed his head in defeat.

It confirmed what the dread in the air was telling me. Fynn, our brother, was dead.

Lucien cursed beneath his breath. "You should have stayed out of this," he mumbled to Eli. Adonis shot him a warning glance, but Lucien didn't stop. "You two should have stayed behind like you were supposed to!"

Eli looked up at us and yelled, "Isaiah told us you needed help! He said you asked for us to come fight with you!"

Rage blurred my vision. *This was a set up.*

Seth approached me in the crowd, his soldiers parting way to make room.

"Well done, Malachi," he smiled. "I knew you would be able to complete the task. No motivation is stronger than revenge, right?" he asked.

Something in his voice was off, though.

And something in his eyes had changed.

I knew that look. I had seen it before.

*Betrayal.*

"How does it feel?" Seth asked. "Killing your own father? I planned on doing it myself, truly, just to show you what it felt like to have your own family murdered. But, well, it was so much easier having you do it yourself."

*No. This couldn't be happening.*

I lifted my sword again, holding it between Seth and myself.

"What did you do?" I asked Seth.

A few guards stepped forward to protect Seth. My brothers held up their own weapons.

"You sick bastard," Lucien sneered from beside me. "We were working with you as a courtesy. You did this. You killed Fynn!" He stepped forward again, sword raised.

"I wouldn't do that if I were you," Seth replied calmly.

"Yeah?" I responded. "Why not?"

"If anything happens to me, your brothers won't be the only one that gets hurt. Your precious bride will die, too."

My heart skipped a beat. "You're lying."

"Am I?" he asked. "Or is our friend Isaiah keeping her company right now, waiting to kill her at the very command?"

# CHAPTER 27
## *Jade*

POUNDING ON MY DOOR JOLTED ME FROM MY DEEP SLEEP, SOME OF THE only restful sleep I had gotten in weeks.

"What do you want?" I yelled at the door, scrambling out of bed and looking around for Malachi.

Who was nowhere to be seen.

"Jade, it's me," Isaiah said. "I need to talk to you."

"Right now?" I asked. I didn't try to hide the annoyance in my voice. I wrapped my arms around my body, hugging my thin nightgown, as I stomped to the door and cracked it open. "What could possibly be so important, Isaiah?"

"Can I come in?"

"Seriously?"

He didn't answer me, just stood there expectantly.

With a sigh, I let him in.

And instantly felt a shift in energy. "What's going on?" I asked. Isaiah paced back and forth in the room, not making eye contact with me. He even moved to bite the nails on one hand. In the days that I had known Isaiah, he struck me as a confident guy. Even too confident, at times.

This was a side of him I had never seen. "Isaiah," I said, approaching him slowly. "I need you to tell me what's wrong. Is it the King?"

He stopped pacing and faced me. "Get dressed," he said. His voice shook.

"For what?"

"Just get dressed, and I'll tell you when we're on the way."

I crossed my arms. "I'm not doing anything until you tell me why you're acting crazy."

"Fine," he spat. "You want to know why I'm freaking out? The King of Rewyth is on his way here right now and your husband is going to kill him. We're in a kingdom full of people who hate humans, and we're about to be in the middle of a war."

"You're being dramatic," I said. "Malachi will kill the King and this entire thing will be over."

"Seriously?" he said. "You're really that naive?"

I had considered the idea that something might go wrong today, but at the end of the day, Malachi was the most powerful fae in both of these kingdoms. Nobody would hurt him. The King didn't stand a chance, especially since he lost his one bargaining chip.

*Me.*

"Look, Jade," he said. "I know you're married to Malachi. I know you're loyal to that agreement, whatever that means. But we can get out of here right now, you and me. Say the word, and we'll go."

His eyes were frantically scanning me, searching for any inkling of hesitation. "I-" I stuttered. "I can't, Isaiah. I'm sorry, really. I know my life in the human world would be easier but I just can't leave everyone. Not after everything we've been through."

Isaiah took a deep, uneven breath. "Fine," he said. "I tried, Jade. I really did. I tried to warn you about the fae, I tried to offer you something better. But at the end of the day, you really love him, don't you?"

I shrugged. "What do you want me to say? He's my husband now, Isaiah. He'll always protect me. Always."

"We're counting on it," he said. Something in his face changed, darkened, and he turned his attention to my bedroom door. "Guards!" he yelled.

Two soldiers stormed into the room, coming straight for me.

"What the Saints is this?" I yelled at him. "What are you doing?"

The guards grabbed me by each of my arms, not giving me time to react.

"I'm sorry, Jade," Isaiah said. "It has to be this way."

One of the guards forced a small cloth over my nose and mouth, and the smell of something foul ripped through my lungs.

I wanted to scream. Malachi. Malachi would help me.

But before I could even yell, my world went black.

# CHAPTER 28
## *Malachi*

"Where is she?" I demanded. "If you even thought about touching her, you won't walk out of here alive."

Seth laughed, his white teeth gleaming off his blood-stained face. "And you think I'm just going to tell you?" he spat.

I was going to kill him. I was going to burn his entire damned kingdom to the ground and take everything for myself.

Seth had turned out to be a manipulative, sneaky bastard.

"Tell me where she is," I said carefully, "and you have a chance of getting out of here alive."

"Fine," he said after eyeing me. "But she'll be dead before you get to her."

But I had no choice. I would do anything for her. I would burn any kingdom to the ground if it meant she was safe.

Seth's guards approached, and I fought every instinct to slaughter each one of them.

"Happy now?" I questioned. "Happy that you can control me?"

"Yes," he answered quickly. "Very happy. Now you have two options. You can stay here and kill us all, or go save your wife. Which do you choose?"

He pointed to the large field.

"Serefin, stay here with Eli!" I yelled before taking off in a full sprint.

I didn't glance back at my brothers, but I knew they would be following my every move.

They had followed me to battle, they had helped me slaughter our father. We had all been betrayed, but for once in my life I was certain they were just as blind as I was.

I would kill Isaiah for this. If one of them didn't beat me to it.

I ran in the direction that Seth had indicated, stepping over the dozens of bodies that littered the field.

It wasn't my first time in a battle, if that's what you would even call this. It certainly wouldn't be my last.

Death was a weakness. Being sensitive to death was a weakness.

"None of you will survive this," I whispered to myself. "None of you."

My power was nearly recovered, I was seconds away from releasing it on anyone who dared to cross me, when Jade's voice entered the clearing.

"Someone get me out!" she screamed. I was certain the others couldn't hear it.

Only me. Because it was just for me.

"Where is she!" I yelled. My voice shook, I didn't care. I needed her. I needed her back. "I'm coming, Jade!" I yelled. I thought I heard her voice yell something back, but I couldn't be sure, I couldn't be certain that it was her.

My blood was pumping through my ears, Saints. I couldn't think clearly. Couldn't act clearly. One foot after another, one foot after another I ran to her.

"I'm coming, Jade!" I yelled again. "Just hang on, I'm coming!"

Seth's laughter in the distance was the only thing I heard as I turned the corner around the wall.

And saw Jade.

Trapped in a massive cage made of what appeared to be...*bones.*

"Jade," I breathed. "Jade, are you alright?"

I closed the distance between us in seconds. "Are you alright?" I repeated.

Although she was clearly not alright. Blood smeared the bones that held her inside, and tears streamed down her face, dripping from her chin.

"Jade," I mumbled.

"I'm fine, Malachi," she insisted. "I'm fine, but you're in danger. Isaiah, he set me up. This was all a trap, you have to run Mal. You have to run!"

Part of me, the primal part, wanted me to run for the hills. To ditch this place and never come back.

But the other part of me wanted to rip apart anyone who thought they could take Jade from me.

Perhaps that part of me was even more primal. These bastards touched my wife and they thought they could live.

It was certainly not an option.

But we would have to move fast.

Inside the cage, unconscious and lying on the ground, was a deadling.

# CHAPTER 29
# *Jade*

We were alone, but not for long. Commotion behind Malachi told me that others would be coming soon.

Every inch of my body stung with pain.

"We have to get you out of here," Malachi growled, pulling on the bones that held me inside. He was covered with blood, it dripped freely from his arm.

Something had gone terribly wrong.

"I already tried that," I yelled. "It won't budge!"

The deadling beside me began to twitch.

It was going to wake up and kill me.

I took a deep, shaking breath and tried to think.

Was this Seth's plan all along? To have Malachi watch me get ripped to shreds while Seth sat there and watched? Was this his sick form of revenge?

"Do something!" I screamed.

"Jade," Malachi said. "Jade, I need you to listen to me. I need you to use your magic."

"What?"

"Your magic, Jade! We don't have a choice!"

"No, no! I can't!"

"That thing will wake up, and then it will kill you, Jade. Do you understand? You will *die* if you do not use your magic to break out of this damned cage. You have to do it!"

"I..."

"You have to!"

The creature, just feet away from me, began to move more and more. A sickening growl escaped its jaws.

Saints. It was waking up.

I tried to control my breathing. I tried to dig deep into that grounding energy that Esther had tried to teach me, but all I found was panic.

I was panicking.

Malachi had no choice but to watch in horror.

The creature grunted and growled as it fully awoke, moving to stand on its feet.

And then it realized I was in there with him. Its black eyes locked on me.

"No," I whispered to myself. "No, I'm not dying this way."

"Dig deep, Jade," Malachi whispered in desperation between the cage bars next to me. "Dig deep, and you'll find what you need."

I squeezed my eyes shut and reopened them.

The ugly creature began moving toward me.

"I can't do it," I whispered.

"Yes, you can," he repeated. His voice held an emotion I had never heard before, an emotion that made me want to try.

Made me want to *live*.

Snapping jaws came closer and closer.

*Breathe, Jade. Focus.*

I was the peacemaker.

The key to the prophecy.

I was going to survive this.

I closed my eyes one last time, feeling warmth from Malachi's body behind me through the cage bars.

I felt the smallest inkling of power light up in my stomach. It was small, but I pulled on it, on the small fire that began lighting up inside of me.

I pulled and pulled and pulled.

Desperation kicked in, I would do *anything* to make this work. I would do *anything* to save myself.

"Saints, save us," Malachi whispered behind me.

Heat overtook me.

And everything erupted at once.

## CHAPTER 30

# *Malachi*

**Every bone in my body ached as I scrambled to my feet, desperate** to find Jade. The bone cage that had encapsulated her just seconds ago was now ash.

And the deadling had disintegrated with it.

"Holy Saints," I mumbled, taking in the scene around me. "Jade, are you okay?"

She sat on her knees, hugging herself around her waist. I ran to her side. "Jade, answer me. Are you okay?"

"Yes," she mumbled. My chest dropped to my stomach. "Yes, I'm okay."

Adonis and Lucien jogged up to the scene. "What happened?" they asked.

"Where's everyone else?" I asked.

"Eli won't leave Fynn. Serefin is protecting him. The other bastards already left, though."

"Is Seth dead?" I asked. "Please tell me one of you killed him."

My brothers looked at each other before looking back at me. "Not yet," Adonis answered.

"What are you still standing here for?" I asked. "Adonis, go find him and rip his head off. Lucien, I need you to bring Isaiah to me. I want to kill that traitor bastard myself."

Again, they didn't move.

"Are you two deaf?"

"We can't, brother."

"What do you mean you can't?"

Esther appeared out of nowhere, as if she had been there all along. "They mean they can't, son. Because I ordered them not to. I need Seth and Isaiah alive."

I stood, Jade rising slowly with me. "Excuse me?"

"I told them not to kill Seth and Isaiah, and they have no choice but to obey me."

If I had my power back, she would be on her knees.

They all would.

"And why would you do something like that?" I asked. "They betrayed me. They betrayed us, and they nearly killed Jade."

"I swear to you, Malachi, I didn't know they were going to hurt Jade. I didn't know they were going to threaten your brothers. Seth's past vendetta with you ran deeper than I had anticipated."

"You've been working with Seth, protecting him behind my back? For what? What is he doing for you?"

She didn't answer me. Didn't blink.

"Adonis? Lucien?"

More silence.

Esther, my mother, looked at them and nodded. Just once.

"We're sorry, brother," Adonis said, stepping forward. "I don't want to do this. You know I have no choice."

"Do what," I said as he took another step. Lucien followed. "Adonis, what are you doing?"

When I looked at Esther again, she looked down to her feet. "It's more complicated than us," she said. "This is more than just you and me, son. Sacrifices must be made. It will all be worth it in the end. Jade is the peacemaker, and we'll need her to do many things for us to fulfill the prophecy. She'll be the key to give the witches our power back. We'll be able to use our magic again without sacrifices. We'll be just as powerful as the fae once this is all over, son. But we can't have you getting in the way. I hope you understand."

"If I could stop it, I would," Lucien said. "We can't control it." Lucien unsheathed the blade at his hip.

*They were going to kill me.*

Under Esther's control, they would have no choice but to do it.

"No," I said, it came out in a whisper. I took a step back, Jade moving with me as she clung to my back. "Don't."

Adonis's brows furrowed, the only sign of regret. Of grief.

"Esther, stop this right now!"

She looked away.

"It's already been done, son."

My brothers both took another step forward.

"He told me not to trust you. His dying words to me were to stay away from you," I breathed to Esther.

No. Things weren't going to end like this. Not after everything. I had sacrificed too much. I had waited too long.

My heartbeat screamed at me to do something.

I couldn't think. I could only act.

There was one person here Esther would never risk losing.

With a roar of frustration, I stepped back once more and gripped Jade's arm, flinging her to the front of my body as she let out a scream.

"Trust me," I whispered to her. She would understand. She had to. She was a survivor, just like me.

I unsheathed my own knife, the small one I had kept at my hip. My brothers stopped where they stood.

Jade was frozen before me as I held her body to mine, confused and disoriented and barely there.

My hands shook for the first time all day.

I looked at Esther, my mother, who I believed was on my side this entire time.

"You kill me, your precious peacemaker dies, too."

And I pressed the blade to Jade's throat.

# CHAPTER 31
# Jade

*It wasn't real. It wasn't real. It wasn't real.*

That's what I was telling myself.

But the blade to my throat was *very* real.

And the man holding me tightly to his chest was just as real.

I didn't move. Didn't blink. My breath came out in shallow pants as I tried to decipher Mal's next move.

"You won't," Esther whispered, but her eyes were wider than I had ever seen them.

"I will," Malachi growled. The vibrations of his feral voice rumbled through my weak body.

If Malachi hadn't been holding me up, I would have been right back on the ground.

"You swore to protect her," Esther spat. "She is your *wife*. Jade is not a martyr, she is the peacemaker! She is the key to everything! She is the key to equality within our realm!"

Malachi shook me harshly. "I know what she is!" he yelled. I flinched with every word. "I will be protecting her from the plan you have to use her for your own good!"

Esther stepped forward, hands in front of her. Wild eyes landed on me, then back to Malachi who still held me tightly.

"Don't take another step," Malachi warned. He pressed the blade into my skin, just under my chin, until I felt the sharp sting.

*No.*

He was really cutting me.

"End the blood oath with my brothers, and everyone here can live. It doesn't have to be this way," Malachi said. I could hear his effort to regain control of his emotions, but the *sane* Malachi was gone. The Prince of Shadows stood in his place.

"You think I believe you won't kill me the second I free them?" Esther questioned.

Adonis and Lucien stood in limbo, half-ready to obey Esther's orders. Half-ready to end Malachi's life.

But also half-ready to kill Esther where she stood.

"Why?" I managed to say, although my voice came out as a low squeak. Malachi instantly stiffened behind me. "You helped us," I pleaded to Esther. "He's your son, and we were in this together. We were working together."

"Your husband is right," she replied reluctantly. "The prophecy requires more than I had let on before."

"Like what, specifically?" Malachi asked.

"When our power is returned to the witches, the peacemaker must fulfill one last piece."

"Which is?" Malachi pushed.

My stomach dropped as the realization of the situation washed over me. "I'll end up dead, anyway. And the witches will have control of all magic."

Malachi's grip on me tightened, and the blade he had barely loosened on my neck was sharp against me once again.

I yelped at the sting of pain.

"Is that true?" Malachi asked.

Esther's silence was the answer. She never expected me to live. I was merely here to fulfill her prophecy.

"Break it. Now," he demanded. "Break the blood oath."

Esther hesitated. "You need me alive," she said. "If you kill me right now, Jade is as good as dead."

"Isn't she already, anyway?" he asked.

"No," Esther replied. "There's another way. I swear it. But you'll need my help. I'm the only one who knows all the details on breaking the prophecy. Word has gotten out now, they'll be coming for her. You know they will."

"Who?"

"The witches of the Paragon. They'll come for her so they can control the magic."

An eerie silence stilled the air around us.

"Fine," Malachi spat after a few moments. "End the blood oath with my brothers, and you can live."

"You swear it?" Esther asked.

"By the Saints who dwell within us."

Esther stepped in front of Lucien and Adonis and chanted something quietly that I couldn't make out. The brothers glanced at each other once before they snapped, both physically being pushed away from Esther by a force we could not see.

"They're free," Esther said after the invisible force stopped. Malachi released a breath against my ear.

And all at once, as quickly as it had begun, it was over.

Malachi released his deadly grip on me, and I sank to my knees before him.

A sob shook my body.

*What had just happened?*

I was covered in blood now, some mine, some Malachi's.

My hands shook as I held them out in front of me.

"Jade," Malachi whispered as he knelt next to me. He reached a hand out gently.

"No! Don't–" I said, scrambling away from him on the ground. Who was this man? This wasn't the Prince of Shadows who would do anything to protect me, no. This was a stranger. A stranger who had *hurt* me.

My fingers moved to the cut on my throat, feeling the wet blood.

"Okay," he said, holding his hands up in surrender. "Jade, I'm sorry," he pleaded. His voice cracked as he crumbled entirely next to me. "I'm sorry, Jade. I was desperate, I had no other way out. They were going to kill us both! I would never hurt you, I wouldn't–"

"Stop," I breathed. "Stay away from me. I don't want you to touch me right now. I don't want any of this. I just want to go home."

Malachi's eyes were frantic, searching my face for any sign of forgiveness.

But I had none. I had nothing left to give.

A familiar numbness spread through my chest.

"I won't let them hurt you," Malachi whispered to me. The tears that streamed down his face matched the tears of my own.

They were tears of defeat. Tears of betrayal.

But it was too late. It didn't matter what Malachi said about protecting me. I knew he would, I knew he would lay down his own life for me. But at what cost? When did it end?

My entire body collapsed on the ground as voices around me blurred together.

Malachi wasn't going to let anyone else have me.

Dead or alive.

# CHAPTER 32
# *Jade*

"Good," Adeline's soft voice pierced the black pit of my consciousness. "You're awake. Jade, can you hear me?"

I blinked my eyes open, finding myself in a bedroom that looked familiar. "Adeline?" I asked.

"It's me," she replied. Her warm hands rubbed my stiff arm. "You're safe, Jade. You're home."

I lifted my head, but sharp pain shot through my head. *Home? Where was home?* "Where is everyone?" I managed to ask through the dryness in my throat.

"Malachi is safe. He's here. Everyone else is here, too. Esther, Isaiah, Sadie, Eli. They're all here. My brother is keeping the traitors in...*fair* conditions. He's just been worried about you, Jade. That's all."

I hated that I felt relief.

"He almost killed me," I croaked, recalling the events I could remember. I had never heard Malachi so...*monstrous.*

A chill ran down my spine just thinking about it.

"Look, Jade," Adeline said, lowering her voice. "A lot of things happened back in Trithen." She turned her gaze toward the ceiling and blinked back tears. "My brother died. Eli can barely get out of bed. Adonis and Lucien are going crazy thinking about avenging Fynn's death. And Malachi..."

"I don't want to hear about him," I interrupted. "I don't care."

Adeline grabbed each of my arms. "You say that, Jade, but you don't understand. You don't understand what he would do to protect you."

I sat up slightly in bed. "I do know. I know that he's the Prince of Shadows. He's deadly and dangerous and vengeful. And just when I thought he would do anything to protect me...just when I thought I could actually trust a fae...*he's* the one with a blade to my throat. *He's* the one who threatened my life."

Adeline bowed her head and took a deep breath. I knew she understood me. I knew she had her own life controlled by men before, she would understand this.

But Malachi was still her brother.

Tears stung my eyes as I looked at my friend. Adeline was beautiful and strong and compassionate. Yet she still wanted Malachi and I to be together.

"I thought I loved him," I started to say before my voice cracked. Adeline knew what I was trying to say, though. She always knew. "I thought I loved him, Adeline, and he turned on me."

She looked at me with fierce eyes. "He didn't, though. He didn't give up on you, Jade. Look, I've never seen my brother act this way. He's...he's a completely different person. He can barely live with himself for what he did to you. Just don't give up on him so quickly, okay? There's someone in there worth saving."

I let the tears fall from my eyes.

I had given Malachi a chance already. I wasn't sure how many more I had left to give him.

## CHAPTER 33
# *Malachi*

I STRAIGHTENED MY TUNIC AND LEANED BACK AT THE LARGE DINING room table.

My palms were sweaty as I rubbed them together. She should be here by now. She should have been here ten minutes ago. Saints, why was I nervous?

I glanced around the room one more time, making sure everything was perfect.

It *had* to be perfect. This might be my only chance I had at talking to Jade, at convincing her to forgive me.

She had needed space over the last few days, I understood that. I needed space, too, after everything that happened.

I also knew that if I even laid eyes on her while her neck wound was still healing, the wound that *I* had inflicted, I would have nothing left to live for.

I screwed up. I was willing to admit that. But she had to understand that I was doing what was best for us. I would protect her to any end, but I couldn't do that if I was dead. I couldn't let my brothers kill me.

The service door to the room creaked open. "She's here, Sir," one of the servants announced.

"Great," I replied, sitting up in my chair. "Send her in."

The air in the room buzzed with electricity as Jade entered.

Her black, silky hair was flowing freely around her shoulders. She wore a long, black dress that swooshed at her ankles as she walked forward and sat down at the end of the massive table, as far as possible from me.

I nodded a greeting. Jade didn't so much as look at me.

"Thank you for joining me," I said. "I know this probably isn't what you expected."

Still, nothing. I blinked once. Twice.

"And I'm sure you have a lot of questions about the future, about *your* future here in Rewyth."

"I want to go home," Jade said. It was the first thing she had said to me in days. Her voice was different. It was...empty.

"You can't," I said coldly. "You'll die there."

Her nostrils flaring was the only hint of a reaction.

"What about my family?" she asked. "What if they're already dead? What if the Paragon already came for them?"

I took a deep, calming breath. I knew she would come with these questions. And I knew how to answer them.

"We'll send someone for your family. We'll bring them here. They'll be safe, just like you."

"And the Paragon? They'll allow that?"

I took another deep breath and looked Jade in the eyes. "I didn't want to tell you this, Jade, but you need to prepare yourself. The Paragon knows you're the peacemaker. They'll use you to break the curse. You're being hunted every day, and others are coming for you."

She didn't respond for a long while. "I've been used as a tool many times before, as you know very well by now. This won't be the first time. I'm sure it won't even be the last."

Emotion I couldn't even explain rushed through my body. I clenched my jaw, desperate not to show it. Not to Jade. Not now.

"Do you think I liked hurting you, Jade?" I asked. I couldn't stop my voice from cracking. "Do you think I *liked* holding a blade to your throat? I did that so we could *live*, Jade."

"I was wrong to think you would protect me," Jade answered. "You're fae. You're selfish. You'll do whatever it takes to survive."

A growl escaped me. I *needed* her to understand.

"They can't have you, Jade. I'm not letting them take you and use you like some weapon. I'm *protecting* you, just like I always have been."

Jade stared at me, jaw clenched.

"Then what do we do?" she asked eventually. "You bring my family here and keep me locked up? You're the King of Rewyth now, so tell me. What are we going to do, Malachi?"

I took a deep, shaking breath. "If the price of winning is Paragon blood being shed, *princess,* then Paragon blood will be shed." I stated. "We will go to war against the Paragon."

# *War of Wrath and Ruin*

BOOK 3

# CHAPTER 1
## Malachi

Isaiah's blood-curdling screams ripped through the stone walls of the dungeons under the castle of Rewyth. He sat on the cold floor, chained to the damp wall behind him. His sun-yellow hair was hidden now, stained red along with most of his skin.

I lifted my arm and wiped the splattered blood off my face with my sleeve.

"You can scream all you want," I spat. He did. Isaiah screamed and screamed and screamed. After the weeks he had spent being tortured, I was surprised he still had a voice left. "Nobody will help you. Nobody is coming."

"You are a monster," he mumbled, although his words mostly blended together with his swollen lips and missing teeth.

I stepped forward with my small dagger. I had missed that dagger. Many warriors chose swords or large blades first, but there was something beautiful about the thin, sharp steel working its way through human skin inch by inch.

Much more painful, too.

I let the blade trail horizontally across the traitor's forehead as he thrashed against the chains. Blood fell into his eyes as he screamed once more and tried to flinch backward.

What a fool. Isaiah had nowhere to go.

*A monster.* I laughed quietly, pulling back and pacing the small cell. Being called a monster might have offended me once, lifetimes ago. Saints, I might have even started a fight over it. But now? A *monster*?

A wicked, feral piece of my soul flickered in delight. In recognition.

I was a monster, yes. Isaiah was *finally* seeing that. *Finally* understanding.

So many people *did not* understand.

So many people had *forgotten*.

They had forgotten who I was.

They forgot what I had done.

The fire of pain and chaos from my past ripped through my mind in the form of a distant memory. I saw all of it at once—all of the destruction. All of the evil.

The Prince of Shadows had been my identity for decades now, defining me before I even had a chance to speak in any room I entered.

Soldiers envied me. Children feared me. My father wielded me as his own personal weapon.

But I was no longer the Prince of Shadows.

*Good.*

I turned my back on Isaiah. What was left of him, at least.

*King of Shadows.*

Those who forgot what I would do to them would now remember. The King of Shadows walked the halls of this castle.

And he would not arrive quietly.

# CHAPTER 2
## *Jade*

"Don't," Sadie whispered as I entered her cell. "If they catch you in here, they'll punish you for this."

I knelt on the ground next to her and emptied my pockets. A loaf of bread was the only thing I managed to sneak away this time, but it would be enough for her.

"I don't care what they do to me," I answered. "It's not fair that you're suffering. You had nothing to do with any of this."

Sadie shook her head. "It doesn't matter. I was close enough to Isaiah that I should have seen something. I should have caught on."

I shut her up by tearing a piece of the loaf and placing it in her boney hands. "Eat," I demanded. "You need to stay strong."

She obeyed.

We both pretended like we couldn't hear Isaiah's torturous screams somewhere in the depths of the dungeon. Sadie had been listening to it every single day for weeks now. Even though he was a traitor, and even though I almost died because of him, I knew it hurt her.

She loved him.

And he betrayed her trust.

"Do you think things would have been different if Esther wasn't involved?" I asked her as she ate. "Do you think Isaiah still would have turned on me?"

Memories of my time with Isaiah flashed through my mind. He had been *kind* to me. He had saved me from the kraken in the river.

He asked me to leave Malachi for him. He swore I would be safe with him.

And then he conspired to kill me.

Sadie's eyes were focused on something that wasn't there. "I don't know," she whispered. "I don't think I know anything about him anymore. All this time I thought we were close, but it turns out he was a stranger."

A single tear left a watery trail in the dirt on her face.

"I'm going to get you out of here, Sadie. Just hang on a little longer."

She gave a half-smile, but her eyes never focused back on me. She had gone somewhere else. Somewhere deeper. Likely the same place she was forced to go to every day here in the dungeon to keep herself sane.

"I'll be back tomorrow if I can," I whispered as I stood up. "Just hang on."

My eyes had adjusted to the darkness of the dungeons. I had come down here as often as possible to check on Sadie, only bringing her food when I could spare some from the kitchen without being noticed.

Sadie didn't deserve this. I knew that.

But Malachi didn't see it that way. He saw them *all* as traitors. In his mind, Sadie was just as guilty as Isaiah.

I had to try talking sense into him.

My bare feet silently carried me through the dark tunnels of the underground. I had memorized the path by now. One long hallway and a left turn was all it took.

The temperature raised with every step I took toward the entrance of the dungeon.

I was close. Ten more seconds and I would–

"Enjoying the scenery, princess?" Malachi's voice echoed off the stone walls.

I froze, my bare feet halting to a stop.

"Yes," I responded without turning around. "The darkness can be quite beautiful."

A low growl rumbled the still air around me. "Sadie is down here for punishment. She doesn't deserve your company."

I spun around to face him, only to be greeted by a blood-soaked king.

That's who he was now, I supposed. *A blood-soaked king*.

Adrenaline pulsed through my veins.

"Sadie hardly deserves this. Torture Isaiah all you want, but Sadie did nothing to earn this fate."

Malachi clicked his tongue. "You know the rules, princess," he started. His voice had changed. It was colder now. Distant. "They almost got you killed. And you know just as well as anybody that I don't like people touching my things."

I stepped forward, now standing just inches from him in the darkness. "I'm alive, Malachi. And in case you have forgotten, Isaiah wasn't the only one who nearly killed me."

His breath hit my cheek as silence filled the tunnels around us.

I knew Malachi was in agony over what happened in Trithen. Not a day went by where I didn't think about it.

Malachi's blade to my throat haunted my dreams every night. I woke up screaming, drenched in sweat more nights than not.

He had made his choice then. He was protecting himself, I knew that. But I couldn't get myself to forget about the panic in my body. The hatred in his voice.

Malachi was a powerful fae creature, one of the most powerful fae in existence.

Only a fool would think otherwise. Even if that fool was his wife.

"Fine," I said eventually. "I'll leave Sadie alone." Malachi didn't say a word. "At least let me bring her a blanket or more water."

Malachi shook his head. His dark eyes reflected the tiny lantern light ahead of us. "You're too good, Jade Weyland. This world doesn't deserve you."

*Weyland.*

I didn't correct him, but hearing that name from his lips sent a chill down my spine.

"You don't like your name anymore?" he asked.

I shrugged. "I suppose I *am* still your wife, aren't I?"

Malachi stepped forward, a wicked grin spread across his face. "Until my dying breath, princess."

My stomach flipped, but I stepped back. "I should go," I muttered. "Adeline will be waiting for me."

"Wait," he said, grabbing my wrist. "Have dinner with me tonight."

My heart raced in my chest. I hadn't had dinner with him since the day after we had returned from Trithen, and even then, we barely spoke.

"Why?" I asked.

Malachi lifted a gentle finger and tucked a loose piece of hair behind my ear. His skin touched mine, just barely, and sent a spark of electricity through me. "Because I miss you," he whispered.

I would have ignored him…if it weren't for the way his voice cracked in hidden emotion.

I let a second pass between us before answering. "I'll think about it," I said to him.

His brows raised in surprise. "Okay," he stuttered. "Okay, great. I'll meet you in my dining room, then."

"And Mal?" I called to him as I walked toward the entrance of the dungeon. "Take a shower."

His soft laughter made me miss him, too. Even though I hated it.

I missed who Mal used to be. I couldn't deny that.

But that wasn't him. *This* was him. *This* was the new Mal, splattered in blood and torturing my old friends in the dungeons of his castle.

Yet he had touched me more than once and I hadn't flinched away.

Did he notice, too? Did he notice the way I allowed him to be close to me?

We hadn't had an exchange like that since before he held the knife to my throat in Trithen.

An exchange that didn't end in yelling or malice.

It was a start, I supposed.

*Did I want this?* I thought to myself. Did I *want* to rebuild my relationship with Malachi?

He was terrifying yet thrilling all at the same time. I couldn't keep my thoughts straight when he was near.

I did know one thing, though. No matter how much I said I didn't want to spend dinner with him…

I would be counting down the hours until I saw him again.

# CHAPTER 3
# Malachi

I SHOWERED THREE TIMES TO GET EVERY LAST DROP OF ISAIAH'S BLOOD off my skin.

Normally, I would feel some sort of guilt or sorrow while I washed blood off of myself.

This time, though, I felt *satisfied*.

Isaiah and Esther needed to be punished.

We had let them live, which showed more than enough mercy. I should have killed them both for what they did. I should have ripped their heads off for hurting Jade.

But they were alive. Esther wouldn't shut up about how we needed her to save Jade's life, although she resisted telling us why. It was a ridiculous thought, considering she was the one who had put Jade's life in danger.

With Isaiah's help, of course.

I shook my head as the hot water ran down my back. How could I have been so blind? I should have seen it coming. I should have known Esther had an ulterior motive to help us.

She wanted me dead. She was going to kill me so that she could have unlimited access to Jade without *me* getting in the way.

That wouldn't be happening again.

Jade hated me right now. I knew that. I cursed to myself silently as I remembered how it felt to hold the blade to her throat. To pierce her delicate skin with my weapon.

She was terrified, yes. But I had no other option.

Did she not see that? Did she not see how *desperate* I was to save us both?

I stepped out of the shower and got dressed in my usual black attire, making sure to strap my sword tightly on my hip.

These days, I wasn't going anywhere without my weapon.

Not after my own power had failed me.

The wound in my shoulder from the poison arrow had healed over the last few days, but the memory of being so helpless remained stained in my mind.

Never again would I feel that weak. Never again would I feel so helpless.

Serefin waited to greet me outside my bedroom door. "Everything is ready," he announced as I stepped into the hall. "Just as we planned it."

I smiled. "Good. This is good. Thank you, Serefin." He nodded, but worry lingered in his eyes. "What?" I asked. "What is it?"

"I just really hope this is a good idea, bringing them here."

If it were anyone else questioning my judgment, I would have snapped. But Serefin's concerns were genuine. "Me too," was all I said. "Either way, they're safer here than they were in that poor excuse of a house."

"Agreed," he nodded. "That much is certain. They weren't happy about leaving, though. Be ready for a fight."

I laughed. "They're Jade's relatives. I expect nothing less. Anything noteworthy?"

Serefin shrugged. "The father is just as drunk as I remembered."

# CHAPTER 4
# *Jade*

I HADN'T WORN A DRESS SINCE THE FAE FESTIVAL BACK IN TRITHEN. THE black silk gown was loose enough to be comfortable, yet tight enough to expose most features. The time I had spent training was beginning to give shape and muscle to my lean body.

I looked stronger now.

I *was* stronger.

My black hair matched the dress, both coming together to create a dark shield between me and the rest of the world.

*If only the shield were real.*

Malachi requested dinner. I would allow at least that. Ignoring him had been the easy way out over the last few days.

But we were ignoring the inevitable. We were denying the truth.

I lifted my chin, looking at myself in the golden mirror ahead of me. The reflection before me was a far cry from the girl who had stepped foot in Rewyth the first time around. That girl had been naive and weak, even though she wanted everyone around her to believe she was strong.

I clenched my jaw and tilted my head to the side, taking in every healing bruise that covered my skin.

It was nothing compared to the wounds that ran deep. The secrets. The betrayals.

A whisper of anger tickled my stomach. I had been living off that deeply hidden emotion. Fury. Pain. Resentment.

It was the only thing I had. If I didn't feel those things, I might not have felt anything at all.

I lifted the hem of my gown and opened my bedroom door, all while ignoring the increasing pounding in my chest.

"Ready to be escorted to dinner, Lady Weyland?" Serefin spoke as soon as he saw me.

My chest tightened at the name, but I pulled my shoulders back and rolled my eyes. "How long have you been waiting out here, Serefin?" I asked.

He smiled, a familiar kindness returning to his dark eyes. I nearly smiled, too. "Just a few minutes. Malachi is waiting for you."

I turned in the castle's hallway and began walking in the direction of Malachi's dining room. Serefin followed closely behind me. "I don't need a bodyguard, you know."

"I know," he replied. "But I couldn't pass up the chance to finally see you. It's been a while."

"It has," I answered. I was glad I couldn't see Serefin's face. I knew the coldness in my words would have stung him, even if he tried to hide it.

"Look, Jade," he started, grabbing my arm from behind me and forcing me to stop walking. I glanced down at his hand on me. This was out of character for him. "I'm on your side, okay? We all are. I know you think we are the enemy right now, but we aren't."

I searched his face for malice but found nothing other than genuine care. Could I really trust him, though? The fae were the reason I was in this situation to begin with. If I had learned anything, it was that the fae were *not* to be trusted.

But Isaiah wasn't fae. He was human. *He* betrayed me.

Esther wasn't fae. She was a witch. *She* betrayed me.

The list of people I trusted grew smaller and smaller.

I swallowed the emotion that now stung my throat and looked Serefin straight in the eye. "You might truly believe that, but at the end of the day, I am a mere human in the pits of fae. If I have learned anything, it's that I am nothing more than a tool to be used in war. That won't change, Serefin. If I am the peacemaker, it can *never* change."

He opened his mouth to respond, but closed it again and nodded gently. "I am truly sorry, Jade. You don't deserve this life."

I placed my hand atop his. "Thank you, Serefin. The amount of people I can still trust seems to be dwindling."

He gave me a small smile and we both continued walking down the stone hallway.

"I know you believe his behavior is uncalled for," Serefin said in a low voice. I didn't have to ask who his words were about.

"I was wrong to expect anything else."

"Prince Malachi does what he does because he cares so deeply. I hope you can forgive him enough to see that one day."

I considered his words as we approached the dining room.

"King," I corrected.

"Excuse me?"

"You said *Prince* Malachi. I believe you meant *King* Malachi."

He shook his head softly and looked at the ground as we walked. "Yes," he breathed with a slight laugh. "*King* Malachi."

We didn't speak again until we had arrived at Malachi's dining room doors. "Thank you for accompanying me, Serefin," I said.

He smiled again as he pulled the large door open. "It was my pleasure."

Butterflies erupted through my stomach as I took the last few steps into the small dining room. I met Malachi's eyes instantly, they practically forced my attention. "Thank you, Serefin. We're okay in here," he said.

And the large door boomed shut behind me.

I froze where I stood, taking in Malachi's massive black wings that hung lazily over the dining room chair he relaxed in.

His massive, terrifying wings.

"Please," he started. "Take a seat."

His deep voice echoed off the dark walls. I waited a second longer before taking a seat across from him at the table.

"You look much cleaner," I observed, noting the lack of blood-splatter on his skin.

He smirked, but his eyes were locked on mine. *Always* locked on mine.

"I'm flattered that you noticed," he teased.

"Don't be," I retorted. "You'll be drenched in blood again in no time."

"Don't tempt me, princess," he growled as he leaned forward an inch. "I tend to have too much fun when splattering blood is involved."

My breath hitched. This wasn't the Malachi I had grown to know. This wasn't the soft, protective man who hated killing.

"Don't call me princess."

"Why not?" he asked. "That is what you are, Jade. If not the–"

"Don't say it. I am not your queen. I never will be."

Malachi's brows furrowed as he stared at me. I would have given anything to know what was going through his mind. Did he want me to be his queen? Was he expecting that from me? I watched as his eyes glazed over, but he never broke eye contact.

Slowly, his emotionless mask reassembled.

He placed a hand over his chest. "You wound me."

I shook my head and gripped the armrests of my chair until my knuckles turned white. Malachi was trying to play me. "If you invited me here to antagonize me, then I should just go. There are better ways for me to spend my time, believe it or not."

He leaned back in his chair, finally cracking on the predator demeanor.

"Fine," he mumbled. "I invited you here for a nice meal. Let's eat."

I glanced around at the feast that had been prepared for us. Meats of all kinds, fruits I had never even seen before, and an assortment of fine wines littered the table.

My mouth watered just staring at it.

"This does not make me miss Fearford," I admitted.

Malachi huffed. "There's nothing to miss. We're home, and I don't plan on leaving anytime soon."

*Home*. I cringed internally at the word.

I may have considered Rewyth home. If it weren't for what had happened at Trithen...

"This isn't my home," I spat. "I'm only here to spare my own life from the Paragon. As soon as I can figure out how to survive this, I'll go back to my real home. Let's talk about that, shall we?"

I filled my plate with the tender meat as Malachi took a long breath. "Fine. Let's talk about it. Esther claims she knows something that will save your life, yet she reveals no further information. I've yet to decide if she can be trusted or not."

"She almost killed you."

"Yes."

"She would have used me as the peacemaker and left me to die as soon as she got what she wanted."

The crackling fire on the other side of the room grew louder. *Was it getting hotter in here?*

"Yes."

"What about you?" I asked.

Malachi's eyes met mine. I breathed slowly before he responded, "What about me?"

"Do you plan on killing me when you get what you want?"

He shook his head slowly, as if the thought alone was humorous to him.

"What I want?" he repeated, more to himself than to me. The fire crackled again, louder this time. "What I want is you, Jade. How do I make you see that? How do I make you understand that I would give up any of this to be with you?"

My chest tightened, as if my heart was using every single ounce of being to not believe his words, even though every other piece of me wanted to.

One of Malachi's servants entered the room and set a fresh jar of water on the table. The small click of her shoes against the wooden floor was the only sound in the room as she walked away, closing the door behind her once more.

Of course I wanted to believe him. Of course I wanted it to be true.

But that was a fairytale.

"Well," I coughed, changing the conversation. "We know I have magic now. I suppose I can't keep denying that I am the peacemaker."

"No," he agreed. "We can't. You used your power when you were desperate. We'll have to work on your control. It will grow stronger every day that we ignore it."

"And what exactly am I supposed to do with it? Just walk around and save the world?"

Malachi smiled wickedly. "Unfortunately for us, we're never that lucky."

*Luck.* Such bullshit.

"You're telling me you haven't talked to your mother since we've arrived back here? Too busy with Isaiah?"

"Isaiah deserves to die. Let's not get into this again, Jade. Esther will be handled when the time is right."

My name rolling off his lips evoked an emotion I had been burying deep down.

"Then kill him and be done with it," I spat. "He was looking out for himself and he chose the wrong side. Where does torturing him get you?"

Malachi leaned back, once again lazily draped over the chair. He picked up his porcelain cup and took a sip of liquid before setting it down again. The cup clinked against the saucer before he replied. "Let me ask you something, princess. What do you suppose the others think when they hear Isaiah's screams echoing through the dungeons? What do you suppose they would have thought if I had shown him mercy and killed him?"

I clenched my jaw and stayed silent. A bead of sweat began to form on the back of my neck.

"I am the new King of Rewyth. People will challenge me. People will try to undermine me. People will threaten my rule, Jade. They will threaten the people I care about. They will threaten you."

"So you torture Isaiah to send a message? A warning?"

"You almost died because of him. Why do you care? Why are you protecting him?" His mask cracked as his temper flared. I saw the wild emotion growing behind his eyes.

"He's a human being," I pleaded.

"He is a traitor! He is a snake!"

I bit my tongue. Isaiah wasn't the only snake.

"And what about the others?" I asked. "What of Sadie? Of Esther?"

"I don't know yet. But I do know one thing. Anyone who threatens you will die, Jade Weyland. They will die by my hand, and it will not be swift. If Isaiah must be the messenger for that, then so be it."

I set my fork down and leaned back, matching his body language. "I can fight my own battles, you know."

Enlightenment flickered across his features. "After what happened with your power back in Trithen, I think it's safe to say that you're going to become one terrifying woman."

"*Become* one?"

Malachi gave me a teasing wink. "All in due time."

I rolled my eyes again and continued eating. After a few minutes of silence in the room, Malachi leaned forward and placed both elbows on the table. "You disintegrated a cage made of bone, Jade. That deadling melted to ash. I should be lucky I wasn't roasted with it."

I shook my head. "It all happened so fast, I don't even know what I did to make that happen."

"You were desperate. Your power saved you."

"Is that what your power does?" I asked, genuinely curious. "Saves you when you're desperate?"

Malachi's gaze shifted into the space behind me as he thought. "It started off that way, yes," he answered. "But over the decades, the darkness has become a part of me. It's right here with me every second of the day. It acts on its own, but never without my permission. It's second nature."

I nodded, wanting him to continue.

"It took a long time to get to this point, though," he said. "There were times when I lost control. There were times when my power became a burden instead of a tool. It was destructive and brutal, but I was the one paying the price."

"What price?" I asked.

His eyes snapped back to mine. "Sanity."

Something dark within me stirred. "You think that will happen to me?" I asked in a whisper.

Malachi's jaw tightened. He rested his chin on his fist as he stared at me. "Never," he answered. "I won't let that happen."

My first instinct was to defend myself. I didn't need Mal watching over me. I could take care of my power on my own.

But I knew, deep down, that I needed him. I needed his help to control my power.

"Okay," was all I managed to say.

The doors to the dining room suddenly ripped open, causing me to jump in my seat.

Malachi tensed immediately. "What is it?" he asked the guard who entered.

"There's a problem in the castle's dining hall, King Malachi," he said. "Your presence is requested."

Malachi tossed his head back and exhaled a long, exhausted breath. I observed him closely, noticing the way he rubbed his hands across his face.

Malachi would make a great king. I never doubted that. But I also knew that deep down, the pressure would get to him.

"Fine," Malachi answered. "I'll be there in a moment. Leave us."

The guard nodded and left the room, leaving Mal and I alone once more.

"Duty calls," I mumbled.

"Not yet," he said. "I have something to show you."

He stood up and walked toward the rear entrance of the dining room. When I didn't follow, he stopped in his tracks. "Are you coming?" he asked.

"Why should I?"

"Trust me," he pushed. "You're going to want to see this."

I debated my options. I could sit there being stubborn, being difficult in any way possible and refusing to cooperate. Or, I could follow him, which would undoubtedly be seen as a win in his eyes.

I had to admit, though, I *was* curious.

"Fine," I said, standing from my chair. "But if this is a trick, I'm taking my power out on you next time."

Malachi laughed quietly. "I'd expect nothing less."

I followed him through the door into a dark hallway. "What is this?" I asked.

"These are the old servant quarters. We haven't used them in ages, but they're still here."

I instinctively reached forward to grab Malachi's hand in the darkness, but pulled back once I realized what I was doing.

"Dark, secret, abandoned tunnels in the fae castle. Sure. Not creepy at all," I mumbled.

"We're almost there," he ushered. "It's just right up...yes. In here." He twisted the doorknob on an old, wooden door and pushed it open. "After you."

I stepped forward and ducked through the dark doorway. The air was much warmer inside of the room, and my eyes quickly adjusted to a few lanterns of light.

"Jade?" a voice I recognized squeaked from the back of the room.

And then my eyes found Tessa.

"Saints," I whispered. "Tessa."

I wanted to run to her and crush her in my arms, but after our last interaction, I was hesitant.

Tessa had been terrified of Malachi. Terrified of *me*.

But now, that seemed like a lifetime ago. Things could change. Feelings could change.

Tessa didn't say anything, but her eyes darted between me and Malachi, who still stood behind me. That's when I noticed my father huddled in the corner of the room.

"You brought them here?" I asked Malachi without looking at him.

"They aren't safe at home. I figured you would–"

"Thank you," I interrupted. "Thank you for bringing them."

I couldn't see Malachi, but I felt his breath as he exhaled slowly, just inches behind me in the darkness. "I'll leave you all to get reacquainted, then," he said.

And then the door was shutting behind me. A cool breeze tickled my skin where he had just been standing.

"You're still alive," Tessa whispered. "I–I thought you might be dead."

I took a deep, calming breath and stepped forward, closer to my sister. "I'm still alive," I responded, trying to be as gentle as possible.

"Good," she replied. She folded her hands in front of her and glanced down at her feet. "I...I wouldn't want you to die."

I shouldn't have felt relieved by that statement, but I did. "That's good," was all I could manage to say. *Really, Jade?*

My father snored loudly from the corner. "He's been sleeping?"

"Pretty much since we arrived here. Although he spent the first few hours yelling about being kidnapped."

"Kidnapped?"

Tessa took a long breath and stepped forward, letting the dim light of the lantern hit her face. She looked older. Harsher.

Not the innocent, naive girl I had left back home.

"It was the middle of the night. They tried to tell us they were helping and that they were taking us to you, but he wouldn't listen."

I looked over at my father. The man had become a stranger to me. He looked much older now, even though we had only been apart for a short time. Deep wrinkles lined his forehead and his cheeks had sunken into his face, causing his cheekbones to jut out much sharper than they had before.

He looked much older than he was. He looked...*sad.*

I cleared my throat and turned my attention back to Tessa. "I can't say I'm surprised. He's never exactly been a great listener."

A long moment of silence passed between us. Tessa looked at me, drawing her eyes over each of my features. It was as if she were really seeing me for the first time.

"We missed you, you know," she said. "When you came to see us back home we... we were surprised. And the fae prince was..."

"I know," I interrupted, recalling the details of Malachi pinning our father to the ground outside our front door. "I didn't mean for anything like that to happen. I didn't mean to scare you."

Tessa broke our eye contact and glanced at the floor once more. "It was unexpected. That's all. We didn't even know if you were alive."

"I know," I said again, softer this time. I wanted to reach my hand out and grab hers, but I resisted. I'd been doing a lot of that lately, it seemed. "Malachi...he's not as bad as he seems. I promise you. He's kept me safe this whole time. He'll do the same to you."

Tessa nodded slowly. "You're different now," she stated. "You seem like you've changed."

The words pierced me like a dagger to the chest. "I *am* different," I whispered. I fought to keep my voice steady against the wave of emotions that rushed forward. I had changed. Not because I wanted to, though. No. I changed because I *had* to. Because I *had* to survive. I changed for *us*. For *Tessa*.

*For myself.*

"A lot has happened since I married Malachi," I said. I chose my words carefully. "I've come so close to death I should feel lucky for even standing here right now."

Tessa smiled gently, but it didn't reach her eyes. "Do you?" she asked.

"Do I what?"

"Do you feel lucky to be alive?"

The air rushed from my lungs. My life had been the furthest thing from *lucky*. I had been bartered away to the fae prince, who now tortured humans in the dungeons of his own castle. I had nearly been killed by assassins, a tiger, a kraken, multiple deadlings, and *my own husband*. The only reason I had for surviving at the beginning of all this was Tessa. I wanted to make sure she lived a long, happy life.

But Tessa grew up. She survived without me. She didn't need me anymore. She was no longer the ignorant girl I once viewed her as.

Without Tessa forcing me to keep fighting, to keep living, what did I have left?

*Malachi?*

Was I *supposed* to feel lucky? Was any of this supposed to make me feel lucky for not being dead?

I couldn't tell her that. I couldn't tell her any of it. She wouldn't understand what it was like to feel this endless pit of numbness. This welcoming emptiness.

"I think I do feel lucky," I lied. I lifted my chin and rolled my shoulders back. "Rewyth is a great home. I think soon enough, you'll be feeling pretty lucky, too."

Her expression changed entirely. "We're staying here?" she asked. I noted the small trace of panic that laced her words. "Forever?"

"It's not safe for you back home right now," I stated. "There are people who want me. They would find you and use you to get what they want."

"Who? The fae?"

My father began to stir in the corner. I wanted to explain, I really did. I wanted to tell Tessa everything that had happened so she would understand. So she would trust me again.

I saw the hesitation in her eyes. I saw the doubt.

But confronting my father right now was not in my best interest.

"I'll tell you everything," I said. "I'll come find you later and I'll explain it all." My father moved again and began mumbling words incoherently. "I just...I have to go."

I backed up, stepping closer and closer to the door I had entered from. "No," Tessa argued, stepping forward after me. "Don't leave."

"I promise I'll come for you, Tessa. I promise."

My father said something again, finally beginning to understand where he was and what was going on, as I slipped into the dark hallway and sealed the large door behind me.

I didn't look back.

# CHAPTER 5
# Malachi

"GET UP," I BARKED.

Eli draped himself over a bench in the gardens of the castle, passed out, with an empty bottle lying next to him.

When he didn't respond to my words, I kicked his foot. Not hard, just enough to wake him up.

His eyes blinked a few times before opening completely. And as soon as he saw who stood before him, he groaned and tossed his head back.

"I said get up," I repeated.

"What for?" he replied. "Are we at war so soon?"

I took a deep breath. I felt horribly for Eli, I did. He had lost his twin. His other half.

There were few memories I had of Eli that Fynn wasn't also involved in. And now, Fynn was dead. And Eli had nothing.

But I couldn't watch him sit around the castle and rot any longer. "Adonis and Lucien are on their way. We have to talk."

Eli laughed. Cold and bitter. "Apologies, brother. But I don't think I'm really in the mood to chat."

I looked to the sky, willing any sort of patience from the Saints to save me from biting his head off. "I know you're in pain, Eli," I said, "but you can't keep doing shit like this. We have a kingdom to run here, and I need your help."

This seemed to amuse Eli even further.

"Rise and shine, brother," Lucien's voice carried into the garden as he and Adonis approached. "The King is requesting your assistance."

Lucien bowed dramatically to make his point.

I rolled my eyes.

Adonis walked up slowly behind Lucien. "You look good, brother," Adonis said to me. I hadn't seen him since our return to Rewyth. I wasn't avoiding any of them, but I wasn't exactly going out of my way to speak with them, either.

Until today.

"We need to talk," I repeated to my other brothers. "Esther is rotting in that dungeon. If we don't make a plan soon..."

I didn't have to finish the sentence. Adonis and Lucien knew the seriousness of the situation. Esther was a powerful witch, but she was rotting away down there. If what she said was true, we needed her.

But how could we trust her?

"You want us to give you advice?" Lucien asked. "Aren't things supposed to be the other way around?"

"You were all there. You were sworn to her blood oath. You know more about her character than I do."

"What do you want us to say?" Adonis chimed in. "The woman is a witch. She's selfish and greedy. Jade is the peacemaker, and Esther wants to use her power for her own benefit."

I considered his words. He stated nothing but facts, but he still didn't offer a way out. "If we kill Esther," I started, distancing myself from the words as I spoke them, "we'll have no idea what's coming. She claims she knows a way to break this prophecy. Jade won't have to die."

"Have you spoken to her about it?" Adonis asked. "How can you know she's telling the truth? What if she's making this all up?"

I took a long breath. "I can't know," I said. "Which is why I haven't spoken to her since we left Trithen."

"You're kidding, right?" Eli chimed in from the garden bench. He sat up now, somewhat paying attention to the conversation happening around him. "She's the reason Fynn is dead. She deserves to die."

Silence filled the air.

He wasn't wrong. If Esther hadn't worked with Isaiah and Seth to try and kill me, Fynn would still be alive.

But that was the past. If I spent a single minute thinking about things like that, my entire world would collapse around me.

"We can't kill her if she's useful to us," I said, trying yet failing to soften my words. "She's valuable."

"For what?" Eli asked. "To save your human wife? No offense, brother, but I don't really give a shit if Jade lives or dies. Why should any of us care? What is she to us?"

A low whistle escaped Lucien, but my temper was already on fire. If Eli hadn't looked so pathetic already, I would have pummeled him to the ground. Instead, I lifted my chin and clasped my hands behind my back.

"I know you're going through a hard time right now, Eli, but if you say that type of shit again, you'll pay. Understand?"

Eli stared at me with wide eyes but said nothing.

I continued. "This prophecy is equally as important to us as it is to the witches. As it is to the Paragon. If Jade fulfills this prophecy and we are the ones to help her, the fae will be the ones to inherit the power. How would you like to have magic unmatched to any in the world, Eli?" I asked. "How would it feel to be so powerful, not a single enemy could take you down?"

Now I had their attention.

"If the Paragon comes for Jade, they will be the ones to fulfill the prophecy. They will be the ones to inherit the power. And then we will be nothing. We won't stand a chance against them."

"If they come for Jade," Lucien interrupted, "there's not much we can do to stop them."

I nodded. The Paragon was powerful. That much was no secret.

But so was I.

I tried to recall each of the special powers they possessed. If what I remembered was still true, they had a strong warlock who had no limit on controlling the elements. He did not tire. He did not pay any price.

I also remembered a man, a fae, who could freeze a person with just a stare. One look, and his opponent wasn't able to move a single muscle.

There were others, too. Fae and witches both with powers unheard of in other kingdoms.

Much like myself.

They would have strength in numbers, but nobody was certain they would even appear here in Rewyth. That was simply another piece of information Esther had given us, likely spun deeply in her unending web of lies.

"If they come for her, I'll kill them. Every single one of them."

"Can you do that?" Adonis asked. "The Paragon is smart. They won't come alone. They won't come unarmed. They'll have a plan."

"They will," I said. "But so will we."

"And what if they don't even know of Jade yet? What if Esther has made this entire thing up for her own benefit?"

"Then we'll kill her, too," I said. Agitation laced each word, but I couldn't bring myself to care. I was now the King of Rewyth, the most powerful fae kingdom in the lands. Nobody would question our power. If anyone tried to take what we owned, what I owned, they would pay with their lives.

The more I had to explain that to people, the more annoyed I became.

"Eli," I said, bringing my attention back to my drunk brother. "I need you to talk to her. Go befriend her. Find out what she knows."

This caught his attention. "Me?" he asked. "Why me? Why not Adonis?"

"She'll see Adonis or Lucien as a threat. She'll see you as someone who is hurting and wants answers."

Pain flashed through his features. I continued. "She's in the dungeons, but don't speak to anyone else. Especially Isaiah."

Lucien huffed.

"Something to say?" I asked him.

He shook his head. "Nothing," he started. "It's just that you keep torturing the human and you haven't laid a finger on the witch."

I knew this was coming. "It isn't her time yet," I said. "She'll get what she deserves."

"And will that be before or after we go to war with the Paragon?" he asked.

My power pulsed through my body, waving with each of my emotions that I seemed to be having less and less control over. "Enough of this," I barked. "I know we are brothers, but I am the King of Rewyth. My word is final, now. I got us into this mess, and I'll get us out. Nobody touches Esther without my say. Nobody interferes with Isaiah without my say. Understood?"

"And Seth?" Lucien asked. "We're going to let the King of Trithen live after what he's done?"

A wicked grin spread across my face. "His time will come, too. We have to be patient."

"Fine," he said. "But I do know one thing, brother. If others see us as weak, they will attack. The Paragon, Trithen, whomever else. Torturing the human in the dungeon does not show strength, brother. It shows hesitation. It shows weakness."

I didn't say a word.

"Just something to think about," he said as he walked past me, clapping me on the shoulder.

"Where are you going?" I asked after him.

Lucien didn't turn around as he answered, "I'm going to go live my life while I still can, brother," he said. "War is coming. I don't know when, but I can feel it. And I have a feeling Fynn was not the last of us to die."

Isaiah didn't react as I stepped into his cell. He had stopped reacting after the first few days—once he realized protesting wasn't going to help him.

Most of the blood on his body had dried. I stepped forward and unscrewed my flask of water.

"Open your mouth," I demanded. He twitched lightly, but didn't move any more.

I grabbed the back of his head and pulled his hair before drizzling the liquid over his face. If he didn't want to drink, that was fine by me.

After a few seconds, he began licking his lips. I drizzled a small amount more before letting go of his head and screwing the top of the flask back on. "Are you ready to talk?" I asked.

Isaiah only shook his head.

"Tell me what Esther really wants," I demanded. "Tell me why you turned on Jade."

The smallest hint of a smile betrayed him.

He opened his mouth to speak, making a couple of attempts to use his voice before finally saying, "She would have been safer with me."

A laugh escaped me. Isaiah must have been more delusional than I gave him credit for. "How, exactly? Considering you were the one who conspired to kill her, I have a hard time understanding how you could have kept her safe."

Isaiah tried to look at me, barely able to open his swollen eyes. "I asked her to leave you, you know. I begged her to leave you and come with me back to Fearford." Every muscle in my body stiffened. "She refused, of course. Jade surprised me—she really did. She wasn't the..." A coughing fit interrupted him. "She wasn't the helpless human girl enslaved to you. She wanted to be with you."

Anger flooded my senses. Dripping water in the distance was the only sound in the cell. Why was he telling me this? Why now?

"She knows I will protect her," I admitted. "Something you could have never done."

Isaiah's breath became labored as he slowly struggled against the heavy chains. "You will be the end of her. You will try to protect her, but you will fail."

"You know nothing," I hissed. "You are a traitor and a liar. Why should I trust anything you say?"

"I never wanted to hurt Jade. I only wanted her to see the truth." I clenched my jaw as I waited for him to say more. Isaiah's eyelids began drooping once again, "We can all see it," he whispered. His voice was barely audible in the dungeons as he continued, "We can all see that you will be Jade's downfall."

His bloodied head sagged against his chest.

I threw the flask into his lap and stormed out of the tunnels, ignoring the angry shadows that lapped at my dwindling consciousness.

# CHAPTER 6
# Malachi

SECONDS AFTER I DRESSED IN CLEAN CLOTHES, JADE MARCHED INTO MY bedroom without a single knock.

And she looked pissed.

"Were you going to tell me you practically kidnapped my family and dragged them here?"

"What?" I asked, sitting up in my tall bed. "I thought you would enjoy the surprise!"

"You can't make decisions about my family without me," she demanded. Fury swarmed her dark eyes. I loved the wildness in Jade. I always had. She was a strong, powerful woman and she was as complicated as anyone. "I should have had a say in the matter!"

"You're not happy about it?" I asked, tip-toeing with every word.

Jade shook her head, running her hands through her long, black hair. "No, I–It's fine. I just would have liked some sort of warning. I could have prepared, I could have–"

"Could have what? Come up with a huge lie as to what exactly has been going on?"

She stopped pacing and met my gaze. "I'm going to tell them the truth. Tessa deserves to know."

I admired her honesty, I really did. But telling her younger sister the truth about the prophecy wasn't going to help anything.

"Is she still frightened?" I asked, keeping my voice low.

Jade crossed her arms. "Of you? Yes."

I deserved that. "And what about you?"

I watched as Jade's chest rose and fell slowly with a long breath of air. "It's not me she's afraid of," Jade said. Her voice shook slightly, but she continued anyway. "It's... it's the things I've done."

I waited a few seconds before asking, "And what have you done that is so terrible?"

Jade looked at me as if I had said something ridiculous, but the fact that she thought she did anything wrong was ridiculous to me. Jade was a victim. She was dragged here and thrown into this world with no say. All she wanted to do was protect her sister.

And now she was the peacemaker with a massive target on her back.

Yet her only family made her feel *guilty* for surviving?

I wasn't going to sit around and listen to this.

"I've done so many terrible things," Jade said. Her eyes were wandering around my bedroom, but I knew she was lost in thought.

*Lost in the demons of memory.*

"You did what you had to do to survive," I reminded her. "You have nothing to be sorry for, Jade. You have nothing to apologize for. Especially not to your family. You did this for them."

"Tessa won't understand," she continued. "Humans and fae...I shouldn't have been...I mean..."

"She expects you to hate us all," I finished for her.

"Yes," Jade admitted. "She does."

I stood from my bed, very aware of the fact that the thin trousers were the only thing I wore. Jade's eyes didn't leave mine.

Although I noticed the way she stiffened when I stepped toward her.

"Are you saying you *don't* hate us all?" I pushed.

Jade swallowed once. "I didn't say that."

"No," I said, taking another step forward. I half-expected Jade to back up, but she didn't.

Stubborn girl.

"You said Tessa expected you to hate us all. And somehow that's a problem." It was risky, but I reached out and picked up a piece of her shiny hair, letting it slip through my fingers. "Because even though you want to, even though you try, you can't hate us. You can't hate me."

Anger flashed across her face, drawing her eyebrows together. "I never said I don't hate you," she spat.

"But you're not disagreeing with me," I pushed.

I knew I should have stopped. I should have given Jade space. That was what she needed. That was what she wanted.

But with every agonizing day that passed, I missed her more and more. Eventually, I wouldn't be able to stay away.

"I should hate you," she said. "I should hate you for what you did."

"Yes," I whispered, letting my fingers twirl around another strand of hair. "You *should* hate me. But you don't, do you?"

Jade's dark eyes were blazing into mine, sending a thrill of heat down my spine. Jade could lie and say she hated me. She could lie and say she didn't want to be with me.

But I knew her. There was something dark within her that I recognized. Some deep, wicked part of her called out to me. I knew she felt it, too.

"You can hate me, you know," I whispered to her, closing the distance between us slowly and letting my hand move from her hair to the nape of her neck. "If that makes it easier for you, you can hate me."

Jade's pulse moved under my thumb. Her breathing matched mine, shallow and heavy. Jade and I were different in ways I couldn't even count, but we were similar in so many, too. Being impulsive, for one. Being temperamental and wicked.

She didn't stop me as I brought my other hand to her neck, too, lifting her chin with my thumbs and bringing my lips dangerously close to hers. "Fine," she whispered back to me, letting my hands move as they pleased. "I hate you."

"You *lie*," I hissed, and then my mouth crashed into hers.

## CHAPTER 7
# *Jade*

My lips devoured his, drunk on his anger and fueled by my own emotions. I need him. I needed more.

*I hate you. I hate you. I hate you.*

I returned his kiss with an equally aggressive amount of passion, gripping his bare waist and pulling his body tight to mine.

It felt wrong. It felt so, so wrong.

But I couldn't stop. Malachi was everything that was wrong with me, everything that I hated.

And yet, here we were.

His hands were strong on my neck, moving my lips so he could kiss me however he liked. I wanted to be closer to him. I wanted more of him.

His hot mouth moved against mine with anger, longing, and something else.

My hands grazed the lean muscles across his back, narrowly avoiding the base of his wings.

I was dizzy, completely infatuated with Malachi.

The King of Shadows

*My* king.

I pushed against his chest, pulling myself away from the kiss. "Stop," I said, catching my breath. "We can't do this."

"No," he agreed, merely just to agree with me. "We can't."

But it didn't end there. I closed the distance between us this time, practically jumping into his arms and wrapping my legs around his waist. Malachi caught me with ease, resuming exactly where we had left off.

*I hate you, I hate you, I hate you.*

I kissed him again, our mouths becoming one as he carried me to his bed.

This was crazy. I needed to stop it.

*I hate you. I hate you.*

Malachi tried to lay me back, but I stopped him, flipping him over so he was the one lying on the bed, his black wings powerfully displayed on either side of him.

It was a sight that made my knees weak.

I crawled on top of him, straddling his waist and resuming our frenzy as if I had nothing to lose.

Did I have something to lose?

*Do you feel lucky to be alive?*

*I hate you, I hate you.*

*I love you.*

*I will rip this world apart until I can place you in the sky myself, princess.*

It had to stop. I had to stop this.

My mind raced through memories of him and my heart pounded just as wickedly. What in the Saints was I doing?

*Do you feel lucky to be alive?*

I didn't think. I couldn't. I could only act. I reached down to my thigh, where the same dagger that Malachi had gifted me on our wedding night was strapped, and pulled it out.

And I pressed it to his throat.

Malachi stilled beneath me, a sudden cool breeze slicing the heat between us.

"Jade," he said carefully. "What are you doing?"

I knew I couldn't kill him. We both knew.

But I needed to do something. Anything. He deserved it. He *deserved* to pay for what he had done to me.

*I hate you.*

"Jade," he said again when I didn't reply. His hands were out in surrender at his sides. "I know you are angry. I know I deserve this. I deserve worse than this, trust me."

I realized then that tears streamed down my face, dripping one by one onto his bare chest.

"No," I muttered through gritted teeth. "You deserve...you deserve..."

I couldn't finish the thought. What *did* he deserve? He had saved my life. He was my savior and yet he was also my captor.

I was lost. I was incredibly, irrevocably lost.

I dropped the dagger, letting it fall onto the bed next to us.

And I cried.

"Oh, Jade," Malachi said, bringing his hands to my face and wiping my tears.

He sat up, wrapping his arms around me and holding me to his chest.

I cried for Tessa, for the pain she had gone through. I cried for my father. I cried for Malachi, for everything he deserved and everything he didn't.

And I cried for myself.

*Do you feel lucky to be alive?*

The truth was, I didn't feel much of anything at all.

# CHAPTER 8
# *Malachi*

Two days.

Two days since I had kissed Jade, and two days since she had spoken to me.

I didn't care. I wasn't surprised, either. Jade told me she hated me and completely fell apart in my arms.

She needed space. *Real* space this time.

But I couldn't keep wondering if she was okay. I couldn't keep worrying about her day after day.

Two days.

I couldn't wait any longer.

"Looking for something?" Adeline chirped beside me. The dining hall in the castle was crowded, I avoided it as much as possible, keeping to my own personal dining room.

But Jade had to eat. She would show up sometime.

"No," I lied. "And I'm busy."

"Right," Adeline said, completely ignoring my *busy* warning. "Jade just left," she said.

My stomach dropped.

"I wasn't looking for her," I said. "I don't care where she is."

"You're a terrible liar," she said. "You should work on that if you're going to be a convincing king."

"Do you need something, Adeline?" I asked, stopping in my tracks to face her. If Jade wasn't here, there was no use for me to linger.

"Yes," she said, tossing her hands onto her hips. "I want to check in with my brother. You've been...you've been all over the place lately. I just want to make sure you're okay."

I took a long breath. "I'm fine," I lied. "I just have a lot going on."

"And you haven't made up with Jade?" she questioned.

Saints, this woman was going to drive me over the edge. "I would prefer not to talk about her, okay?"

Adeline opened her mouth to argue, but her attention was caught by something behind me.

"Mal," she said quietly, not taking her eyes off whatever it was she was staring at. Her features morphed, one by one, from my sassy sister to a terrified girl.

I spun around, looking for what she was staring at.

And I drew my sword.

"Stop it," Jade's voice hissed through the open room. "Just calm down!"

It wasn't Jade I was worried about, though. Her father stumbled around in front of her, barely standing.

How could he possibly have gotten drunk again?

"Who the Saints is that?" Adeline whispered to me.

I fought to keep my anger at bay. Jade wouldn't want me to step in. The last time I interfered, I nearly ruined everything. "That's Jade's father," I answered.

Adeline's sharp inhale told me she was not expecting that answer.

We both approached slowly, trying to stay out of view.

"I knew this would happen!" her father spat, although the words slurred together. "You spoiled little bitch!"

I took half a step forward, but Adeline put a hand out to stop me. "Let her handle this herself," she whispered.

She was right. I knew she was.

But watching that bastard speak to my wife that way made me want to kill anyone in sight.

"You can't do this, you can't demand I stay somewhere. Take me back! Take me home!" he yelled.

"This *is* home, now," Jade whispered. Something in her voice made my chest ache. "It's for your own safety. You know this, father."

"How is living with *them* safe? How is this better? They ruined everything, Jade. They ruined it *all*."

Jade stared at her father with wide eyes, oblivious to the room of people staring at her. "Just calm down, please. I'll explain it all to you once you calm down."

Her father stumbled forward, nearly knocking Jade over. He didn't lower his voice, though. "Calm down?" he repeated. "You want me to calm down? You drag me here, with these *monsters*, and you tell *me* to calm down? That everything will be fine? That we're safe? Tell me, daughter. Do you *feel* safe?"

"We are safe here," Jade repeated. I noted her clenched fists and her tight jaw. If it weren't for Adeline standing right next to me, I would have stepped in. "These fae will protect us."

"Like your husband? Is that what he was doing when he attacked me in my own home?"

Jade stiffened.

"You don't know anything," her father pushed. "You are a young, stupid girl. You think you can save us? You think you can protect us? You're wrong. And you're ignorant." Jade began speaking but her father continued. "You are nothing special, Jade," he said. She flinched away from the spit that flew off his tongue. "You are no different than all of the other idiots who think they are so high and mighty. You're certainly not *liked* here. You think these fae *like* you? You think they will protect you? You are *nothing*. You are *nobody*. Nobody cares about you. Saints. Your own sister can't even look you in the eye."

"That's not true," Jade interrupted. She was yelling now, her face flushed red.

"It is true," her father pushed. "Did you know she had nightmares for weeks? *Weeks.* She couldn't even sleep for three hours without waking up screaming! Dreaming about *him*. Dreaming about you and him together." He paused to shake his head in disgust. "It's pathetic. Running around with these fae as if you actually mean something to them."

"Can I rip his head off now?" I whispered to Adeline.

"No," she ushered. "Jade will stop him. If you step in, she'll look weak in front of everyone."

Saints, I hated that she was right.

"Are you forgetting that this is all your fault?" Jade retorted. "I'm in this mess because of you, father. You're the one with the problem. You're the one who's pathetic. You think I wanted to be here? You think I wanted to rely on the fae for my safety? I. had. No. Choice. Did you think I *enjoyed* scaring Tessa like that? I did everything for her. *Everything!* You're the one ruining everything. You'll ruin this, too. Like you always do."

"They'll kill you," her father mumbled, no longer looking at Jade. "They'll kill us all."

"That's not true."

He spun around, spit flying into Jade's face as he yelled, "We will all die!"

My heart raced, every inch of my power wanted me to send this man to his knees. But I waited.

Jade could defend herself.

"I am the peacemaker," Jade yelled right back in his face. "I am the key to everything! You're right, father. They might kill you. Because you're a useless drunk who's good for nothing but taking up space. But me? They'll protect me with their lives. Because *I* am the key to everything."

Her father froze, as if her words triggered some sort of memory.

"The peacemaker?" he asked, barely audible.

Jade didn't answer.

"We're dead," her father spat. "We're all dead. You, me, Tessa. We'll all die. All of us."

"No!"

"YES!"

"Please stop this, father. Stop this before you make it any worse for us."

"Any worse?" he yelled after her. His tired voice echoed off the stone walls of the castle. "How could this possibly get any worse?"

"That's enough," Jade demanded.

"My own daughter has secured my death. Saints! Thank you, daughter! Thank you for ending my life!"

I felt the power before I saw it. It was a small pulse in the air, a tiny tickle in the middle of my chest. It wasn't my power, but it caused my power to stir in excitement.

The familiarity made my entire body go still.

And then I saw the tiny tendrils of magic leaving her body, ready to defend her at the single thought.

She was going to kill her father.

I rushed forward, Adeline didn't stop me this time.

"Jade," I boomed, much louder than I expected. My power rumbled through my body, shaking the few stone tables around us as I grabbed her by both shoulders.

I wasn't afraid of her hurting me. My power would protect me.

I knew it would. I felt it.

"Jade," I said again, shaking her by the shoulders. Her eyes were black pits, ready to fight for justice at the single thought.

Heat practically sizzled between us as I shook her again.

She snapped out of her daze, finally, and looked at me with wide eyes. "Saints," her father whispered behind her. "You *are* a demon!"

I twirled around, no longer able to remain quiet. "Do you remember me, Sir Farrow?"

Recognition flickered across his features. He took one step backward, almost tripping over his own feet.

"Good," I continued. "Then you know what I will do to you if you speak to Jade like that again. I don't allow anyone to disrespect my wife, Sir Farrow. I don't give a shit if you're her father or not."

He gulped.

"You're here because Jade wishes to keep her family safe. I, however, wouldn't mind hanging you from a tree and feeding the hungry monsters that lurk in the woods. So the next time you find yourself over-indulging in liquor and starting a fight with someone, it better not be my wife."

I turned my attention to the crowd of fae that now gathered, everyone wanting a front-row seat to the spectacle. "Go," I demanded. "Get out."

They obeyed.

*Good.*

I turned back around to Jade, who had tears swelling in her eyes.

She wouldn't let them fall, though. No, she had cried over her father one too many times.

"I'm sorry," I said to her. "I wasn't going to interrupt, but..." I glanced around us, realizing there were way too many prying ears to say what I needed to say. "Follow me," I said, grabbing Jade's arm and dragging her after me into one of the old servant rooms of the castle.

These things were starting to come in handy.

We walked down another dim, empty hallway and I pulled her into a dark room.

"Your power was out of control, Jade. I felt it first, and then I saw it. You would have killed him. You would have killed your own father."

Her eyes were wild, darting around in the darkness. "I–I had no idea. I didn't know, I was just so angry. He wouldn't stop!"

"I know," I said. "I heard it all."

"It just felt like my temper at first, it really did. I had no idea it was my power."

"How did it feel?" I asked. "Describe it to me."

"It felt...*good*. At first. Powerful. I didn't feel any different, though. I just felt strong."

I nodded, knowing the feeling all too well. "It practically radiated from your entire body. A cast of light."

"Really?" she asked. "You could see it?"

"Yes," I said. "I could. And I'm sure others could too if they paid close enough attention. This is exactly what we don't need."

"You're angry with me?" she asked.

I took a long, calming breath. How could she possibly think that? Watching Jade defend herself to her father for once was one of the best things I had witnessed in my life. That man deserved much, much worse things than death.

Even in the hands of his own daughter.

I took a step closer to Jade, who was leaning against the wall. "Of course I'm not mad," I said. "I will never be mad at you for using your power. Even if you might kill a few deserving bastards in the process."

Jade smiled. It was nice to see her smiling again. "I guess it's safe to say my power is getting stronger. It was so easy. Like my power *wanted* me to use it."

"We need to begin training again right away."

"With Esther?"

*With Esther*. I knew this moment would come. We couldn't leave Esther rotting away down in the dungeon forever. At some point, we were going to need her again. "Yes," I answered. "With Esther."

Jade nodded in agreement. "And what exactly will I be training for?" she asked.

"You will soon possess some of the strongest power in history, Jade. We have to teach you how to control your power, and, if needed, how to use it as your weapon."

"Do you think I will need it to defend myself?" she asked.

"I think we will be very lucky people if we never get to that point."

My gaze moved from Jade's eyes to her perfect, soft lips. In the empty room, I could practically hear each beat of her heart in her chest.

I caught myself before I made any moves I might regret. "I have to go," I said. Jade mumbled something similar. "Meet me in the garden at dusk tomorrow. We'll begin training your magic again then."

Jade barely nodded before scurrying out of the room.

"Malachi?" She stopped and called back to me.

"Yes?"

"Thank you. For defending me."

I knew Jade couldn't see it in the dark, but a smile crept onto my face. "Anytime, princess."

# CHAPTER 9
## Jade

"Do you think if I ran away right now and started living with the deadlings in the woods that anyone would notice?" I asked Adeline.

She smiled as she walked next to me. "I think you have a better chance at becoming king."

I smiled back. "You have your sister back. That must at least be nice, right?" she asked.

I shrugged. "It's nice knowing she's not struggling for every meal like I used to do. But...there's a different type of worry with her being here. Malachi defends us, but most of the fae still hate humans. They don't want us here. I worry that she'll see something or change the way she sees me."

"You think she'll fear you?"

"I think she fears me already."

"Because of Malachi?"

The truth was, it was *so* much more than just Malachi that frightened Tessa. It was all of it. We came from a world where it was just us two. Us and our father, who didn't really count as a whole human being.

It was terrible and dreadful and difficult every single day. But it was constant. It was a painful type of comfort.

Tessa had grown to know a version of me that was defiant and scrappy. Before I was sold to marry Malachi, I would have laughed at anyone who tried to tell me what to do. Who tried to tell me who to be.

Tessa saw that. She was there every time, watching her big sister rip through this world with no regrets.

Who was I now? The human girl who walked on ice around the fae? They certainly didn't fear me. No, they *never* would.

I would *never* be their equal. Even with Adeline.

Adeline still waited for my reply. I wasn't going to lie to her. She had become a great friend to me over our time together. And I knew she would understand.

"Partly because of Malachi," I started. "But I think she will fear who I have become, too."

"The wife to the King of Shadows?" she asked.

A chill ran down my spine at her words, even in the warmth of the evening. King of Shadows. "No," I corrected. "She'll fear me because I am broken."

"Oh, Jade," she stared. "I think we're all a little broken. You, me, Malachi. Even Tessa. It's what makes us sane."

I smiled at her kind words. "You think we're all sane?"

"Well," she retorted. "To be honest, I think you and I may be the only ones."

I shook my head at her as we came to the clearing of the lagoon, the same lagoon where we had been attacked by a *tiger* of all things.

"It seems different here," I noticed. The large lagoon with the beautiful blue water seemed hardly larger than a pond now. The forest around the clearing looked half as threatening.

"That's because you're different, now," she said. "Saints, it feels like a lifetime ago when I brought you here the first time."

"Do you think Malachi will be just as pissed if he finds us here again?"

"Please," she said, tossing her long hair over her shoulder. "We can take care of ourselves."

Something stirred in my chest at her words. She was right. I had changed since I had been here last.

But so had she.

She wasn't the ditsy, naive girl I had taken her for when I first met her. Adeline was strong in ways I would never have to understand.

I silently thanked the Saints for that.

"Are you going for a swim?" she asked me.

"I think I'll pass this time," I replied. "I still have nightmares about those freaky kraken trying to drown me."

Adeline's face lit up, as if just now remembering the attack. "Saints, Jade! I'm so sorry! Oh my, I'm such an idiot for bringing you out here!"

"Adeline!" I said, grabbing her by her shoulders to calm her down. "It's okay. I have much worse things to be afraid of. Truly. Swimming just...I think I'll take a break from leisurely dips in the pond for a while."

She seemed to relax under my touch. "Fine," she said. "I can't believe I forgot about that."

"Don't worry," I said. "Lifetimes ago. Remember?"

She smiled softly. "So, have you spoken to Sadie at all?"

I snapped my attention to her, noting the directness of the question. "Why do you ask?"

She shrugged. "No reason. A little birdie just happened to tell me you like to lurk in the dungeons from time to time."

I rolled my eyes. "Malachi has such a big mouth."

"Oh, please," she spat. "I basically had to pry it out of him. He doesn't talk to me much at all these days."

"Yeah," I agreed. "That makes two of us."

Silence filled the air between us. I turned my attention to the nature that surrounded us. To my right, a bright red butterfly landed on a small yellow flower that bloomed from the wall of green shrubbery. Birds chirped lightly in the distance, just loud enough to add the ambiance of the flowing water. The sun glistened through the tall tree branches above.

"He misses you," she interrupted.

"What?"

"Malachi. He misses you. It's killing him that you two aren't together."

Heat rose to my cheeks. "Did he tell you that?" I asked, pretending to look around at the trees.

"He didn't have to. It's pretty obvious, Jade. But I know you know that, too."

I paused for a moment, considering her words. "I can't just forgive him, Adeline. He...he *betrayed* me."

"Look," she said, turning to face me. "I love you, so I'm going to be honest with you. Malachi didn't betray you. Not even close. He saved your life, just like he has done dozens of times before. And then he broke the treaty to go retrieve your family so that you might have a tiny chance at not hating him for once. He did not betray you, Jade. You just saw a different side of him than he had once shown you."

"I didn't like that side of him," I said, but something dark inside of me resisted the words. *Liar*. "He's dangerous."

"Yes, he is. And do you want to know the crazy part?"

"Sure," I sighed.

"When your power becomes stronger, which after what I saw in the dining hall tonight is already happening, you'll be just as dangerous."

Just as dangerous as the King of Shadows?

"That's not possible."

"It is possible, Jade. Malachi loves you. What would you do to protect the people you love? Where would you draw the line? I bet pretending to trade Malachi's life for your own doesn't even come close to the ends you would go to. What if it were Tessa?"

"But it wasn't Tessa. It was me."

"Yes, it was. You're strong, Jade. And you're his. You'll always be his, and he'll kill anyone who touches you. You know this is true."

I shrugged. "He still hasn't killed Isaiah, though, has he?"

"He will when the time is right," she said.

"You really defend him a lot, you know."

"Yes, I do. And it's not just because I love him. He's right. He is strong and gracious, yet terrifying and merciless. You can trust him, Jade. You can forgive him."

I finally looked Adeline in the eye. "If I forgive him, then what am I? How will Tessa look at me then? How will my father?"

Adeline huffed and propped her hands onto her hips. "I'm not going to pretend for one second that I give two shits about your father, Jade. But Tessa? She loves you, too. As long as you're okay, she'll find a way to forgive you for anything."

I spent the rest of the evening thinking about my time with Adeline. Saints, I hated how she was always right. Her and Malachi, both.

I needed to forgive him. If not for his sake, then for my own.

I laid in bed, staring at the dark ceiling above me. The castle was just as beautiful as I had remembered, I had to admit that much. Green vines looped in and out of the stones, creating a maze of nature that kept my mind at bay.

Until I heard a small knock on my door.

It wasn't Malachi. The knocking was too light.

I got out of bed and padded silently over to the door. Before I could say anything, my visitor knocked again.

More desperate this time.

"Who is it?" I asked.

"Jade!" Tessa's voice whispered through the night. "Jade, let me in!"

Saints.

I grabbed my door and flung it open. Tessa stumbled in, out of breath.

"What's going on?" I asked, scanning her body from head to toe in the darkness. "Are you hurt?"

"No, no," she ushered. "I'm fine. I came to see you."

"How did you find me here?"

"Please," she shrugged. "You have to give me some credit."

I huffed, placing my hands on my hips. "You can't be wandering around the fae castle at night, Tessa. It isn't safe."

"I wasn't going to stay locked up like a prisoner with him any more, Jade. I couldn't!"

She was talking about our father.

"What did you do to him?" she asked. "He was practically carried back to our room, completely disheveled."

I turned and walked to my open window. "You mean more than the usual?" I asked.

Tessa walked in and sat on my bed as if she lived there, too. "He's completely lost his mind, Jade. He's been mumbling on and on about mother."

My heart stopped. "Our mother?"

"Yes!"

I moved to sit next to her, fighting to keep any signs of alarm off my face.

"What's he been saying?"

Tessa shrugged. "Nothing I can understand. He's been rambling about you, saying something like 'he remembers'. When I ask what it is that he remembers, he shuts down."

Our father must have known something. I had been wondering this ever since Esther whispered about knowing my mother.

They had to have known. They had to have known that I was supposed to be special.

"We can't trust anything he says," I reminded her. "He's lost."

She looked at me with deep, glazed eyes. "I've never seen him like this before," she said. "It's like he's fighting himself."

Maybe he was fighting himself. Maybe he knew more than he had ever admitted. Maybe deep down, he had buried the truth in an ocean of liquor and never looked back.

Either way, it didn't matter now.

I crawled under my covers and patted the spot next to me, inviting Tessa to do the same. "He'll calm down soon," I said. "Being away from home has to be hard for him, too."

Tessa curled up next to me. "Do you remember her?" she asked after a few beats of silence.

I took a long breath, trying to recall any memories of my mother.

"No," I answered honestly. "Although sometimes I see a tall, beautiful woman in my dreams. I like pretending that's her."

Tessa giggled. "I think it might be."

I waited until her breathing slowed down, and I let my eyes shut.

Maybe I would see her again.

# CHAPTER 10
# Malachi

"I CAN'T JUST *SUMMON* IT LIKE YOU CAN," JADE SAID. "I DON'T KNOW how it happened. It was instinct."

"Exactly," I said. "Instinct. Your body knows what to do. Your power knows what to do. Listen to those things."

She huffed and closed her eyes again.

I had dragged her out of the castle into the safety of the forest. That way, she wouldn't accidentally burn the castle down if things went wrong.

But at the rate we were moving, the only thing burning down was my patience.

"Try harder," I demanded.

"You can't just bark at me to use magic and think that will work, Mal," she said. I had to admit, seeing her sass me again nearly put a smile on my face. It was a step up from her usual act of ignoring me.

"Fine," I said. "What do you want me to do?"

"Just...just *wait.*"

"I can wait," I said.

"Good. And be quiet."

I nodded, taking the hint, and backed up a few paces to give her some space.

"The two times I used my power I felt...I felt desperate. I felt helpless."

I continued to stay silent.

"But I don't want to feel desperate. I want to feel powerful."

Jade placed her hands on her stomach as if to center herself. As if to feel the power that lived there.

My own power tickled with excitement. I took a deep, calming breath to settle it.

It was an interesting thought—that my dark, murderous power recognized whatever power was blooming inside of Jade.

By the time I turned my attention back to Jade, she was looking at me with her hands on her hips. "It's not working."

I signed. "It never will work if you keep thinking that way."

"You know what we need to do," she said. "We need her."

*Esther.* "No, we don't."

"She can teach me how to use this."

"We can't trust her, Jade!"

"Maybe not. But if she needs me like she says she does, she has every interest to develop my magic as quickly as possible. You know it's true."

Saints. Yes, I did know it was true.

But I hadn't confronted Esther since Trithen. I didn't want to do it now.

Jade stepped forward, close enough that I thought she might reach out and touch me.

She didn't.

"I know you're afraid," she said.

"What?"

"You're afraid to confront your mother."

"That's not true," I said. *Why did I feel defensive?*

"She has no power here, Mal. She can't do anything to you. She can't hurt me, either. You won't let her."

I unclenched my tight fists and tried to relax. "It's not getting hurt that I'm worried about."

"Then what? What's keeping you from walking into that dungeon right now and demanding that Esther helps us?"

I turned and paced in the grassy garden. What was stopping me? If Esther so much as looked at Jade or myself the wrong way, I would end her.

So why was I resisting?

Jade walked up behind me, placing her delicate hands on my back. My wings flared in response, but Jade didn't back away. "Hey," she whispered, dangerously close. "I'll be with you the whole time."

Jade hadn't forgiven me. I knew that. This didn't change anything.

She wanted to learn her magic just as badly as we needed her to learn it.

Yet somehow, her touch on my bare skin sent a thrill of delight down my spine. "Fine," I said, clearing my throat.

"Fine?"

"If you want to speak with Esther so badly, we'll go."

Jade's face lit up. "Really? Right now?"

I nodded, and she practically jumped with joy.

"But I do the talking. And if she even tries to touch you, I'll kill her."

"I don't doubt that for a second."

And then we were on our way, marching through the grass to visit my mother in the dungeons of Rewyth.

# CHAPTER 11
# *Jade*

Malachi's body stiffened as we descended the stairs into the dungeon. Chills rose on my arms, and I knew it wasn't entirely from the sudden drop in temperature.

"You're sure about this?" I asked him as we continued to descend.

"It's better to get it over with now," he answered coldly.

I nodded. Fair enough.

I had come down to the dungeons a handful of times since we had been back to Rewyth, but never to see Esther. Or Isaiah, for that matter. I had cared about Sadie, and that was it.

No, I didn't care about Esther.

Esther was none of my business.

She tried to kill Malachi. The thought alone put a fire in my heart.

*Her own son.*

I was glad Malachi walked ahead of me. That way, he couldn't see the flash of anger that came over me.

I wanted to kill her. I wanted to be the reason that witch left this place for good.

Malachi deserved better. Even with all of the terrible things he had done, he deserved better.

Malachi led us through the maze of tunnels in the dark underearth. It continued to get darker and darker, with lanterns of fire spaced out more and more as we continued.

"How far back did you chain her up?" I asked, half-joking.

"She deserved worse," he said.

I followed him in silence until we walked to the near end of the dungeons. A guard perched just outside of a cell. Her cell, from what I assumed.

"King Malachi," the guard announced. He stood from his wooden stool so quickly that it nearly fell over behind him as he began brushing his uniform with his hands. "What a pleasure."

"Leave us," was all Malachi said.

The guard obeyed without another thought, scurrying into the darkness.

"You have a visitor," Malachi barked into the cell.

In the dim light, it was hard to make out anything far away. But I squinted my eyes, and within a few seconds, I could see a small figure huddled to the stone ground in the back of the cell.

*Esther.*

She lifted her head at the sound of Mal's voice.

"Malachi," she acknowledged. "Come to finish the job?"

Malachi huffed a laugh, but I could feel how tense he was standing right next to me.

"You won't get off that easily, *mother.*"

She attempted to move, but heavy chains held her down to the ground. They looked ridiculous on her tiny, boney body. But I knew, deep down, she was dangerous.

Too dangerous to be freed of her chains.

"I'm training my magic," I said, interrupting them before their feud could continue. Esther seemed to notice me standing there for the first time. Her hair was matted around her neck, and her linen clothes were covered in dirt. I pretended not to notice. "I figured you could be of use."

"Interesting," she nodded. "So you've come for my help finally?"

"We don't need your help," Malachi interrupted.

"Your bride says differently, son."

I stuck my hand out, cutting Malachi off before he continued. "We have no problem leaving you in here for the next decade, *witch,* but if you would like to offer your insight to training my powers to develop, we would accept it."

She opened her mouth to respond, but a coughing fit was the only thing that came out.

Saints. She wasn't going to last much longer down here. In the corner of my eye, I saw Malachi's jaw tighten.

"Will you unchain me?" she asked after a few seconds.

Malachi spoke up first, "Absolutely not."

"Mal," I hissed under my breath. If Esther was going to agree to work with us, we had to give her something. Otherwise, she had no benefit in this deal.

Malachi snapped his attention to me. I could see his furrowed brows in the darkness. "We're not letting her out of here."

"We don't have to," I whispered back. "Just unchain her. She won't get far, anyway. Look at her."

We both looked to where Esther still huddled on the stone.

She was decaying. She was half the woman she was in Trithen.

Did I feel bad? No, I didn't feel bad. A tiny, hidden part of myself actually delighted in her suffering.

That was the part that kept me alive.

That was the part of me that didn't feel sorry for those who had wronged me.

"Fine," Malachi sighed. He walked forward with the keys from the guard and knelt before Esther. I watched as he picked up each of her wrists that were buried in the heap of metal chains, and unlocked them.

After the chains rattled to the stone ground, he stood and backed away.

Esther moved to get up from her spot in the corner, but struggled to stand. I glanced at Malachi, who only tightened his jaw. I would have to do this myself. I took the few steps into the cell and grabbed ahold of her arm, lifting her to her feet.

"Thank you, child," she whispered. I knew Malachi would be mad that I helped her. That I touched her. But this woman was clearly nothing more than helpless.

"I almost lost control of my power earlier," I explained to her after I was a safe distance way. "But I haven't been able to summon it since then."

She nodded. "What were you doing when you almost lost control?"

"I was fighting with my father," I said.

Esther nodded, recognition flickering in her eyes. "Your family is here? In Rewyth?"

"Enough talking," Malachi interrupted. "Help her with her magic."

Esther signed, but eventually turned her attention back to me. "Show me."

I held my hands out in front of me, as if somehow envisioning power between my palms would actually make it appear.

We all waited for a few seconds. I tried to think about how angry I was when my father called me useless. How embarrassing it was for me to be humiliated in front of everyone.

I thought about Tessa, and about how terrified she would be to see this.

And I thought of Malachi. And how he was trying everything possible to keep me alive.

Yet still, I felt nothing. I felt no power.

I dropped my hands to my sides with a strong exhale. "Nothing," I explained. "I feel nothing."

Esther glanced between me and Malachi, suspicion in her eyes.

"What?" I asked.

"You didn't feel anything," she explained, "but he did."

Malachi uncrossed his arms from where he stood at the entrance of the cell. "What are you talking about?" he spat.

"I'm talking about the fact that you can feel her power. You can recognize it. Can't you?"

Malachi opened his mouth, and I half-expected him to curse at Esther for having such a ridiculous accusation.

But he said nothing and closed his mouth.

*Could he feel my power?*

I took a step closer to him, leaving Esther behind me. "Mal?" I asked. I called to my power, imagining what it would be like to wield it. To be powerful.

Malachi took a deep breath and closed his eyes.

My stomach dropped. "You can feel this," I whispered.

He opened his eyes, and his gaze blared into me with a heat that sent a fire down my spine.

"It's not *me* that feels it," he finally admitted. "It's my power."

"Like calls to like, darlings," Esther said from behind. "Your magic recognizes hers."

"How is that possible?" I asked her. "It's just power. How can it recognize anything?"

Esther shrugged. "I've heard of this happening. You two are so close, Malachi's mature magic has come to recognize when yours is close. His power either recognizes yours as a threat...or an ally."

I didn't dare look at Malachi, but I knew he was already staring at me.

Our powers were somehow connected.

But that wasn't going to help me learn to call it.

"How does this help me?" I said, cutting off the conversation. "Teach me how to call my power forward."

Esther took a long, shaking breath. "You were angry with your father when it came to you?"

"Yes."

"Good."

"Good?"

"Yes. You just need to get angry again."

"I've already tried that," I answered. "It didn't work."

"Well, you're in the depths of the dungeons of Rewyth," Esther replied. "Perhaps it will be different this time."

*Yeah, right.*

"Just try it," Malachi barked, still standing near the entrance.

"Fine," I mumbled. I closed my eyes and focused on anger.

The one emotion I had felt too much of lately.

*Anger.*

My father came to mind first, naturally. I did feel angry. I felt angry about the way he treated me.

But not angry enough.

Why was I *really* angry? Was it the things my father yelled at me? All of those nasty words?

He had called me trash. He had called me selfish and stupid. Did those things make me angry enough to call my power forward?

*I didn't think so.*

What else did he say? What else was he yelling at me in the dining hall?

The fae. He talked about the fae, about how they would never keep me safe.

That they would kill me the first chance they got.

My heart rate sped up.

He talked about how Malachi would never protect me.

I clenched my fists.

I didn't outright defend the fae. I wasn't one of them.

But...I had partially defended them, hadn't I? By not hating them, I was defending them.

In Fearford I defended them to the humans. In Trithen I defended them to the other fae.

Because they were...they were my family when my family was nothing.

A bead of sweat formed at the nape of my neck, even in the chill of the dungeons.

Is that what made me angry? The fact that I had fought so hard to defend these fae and my father just ran in here and slandered them all?

After all they had done for me?

My mind flipped.

After all they had done to me...

Yes, I defended them. But Malachi was the one that held my life at knifepoint.

Tessa's voice haunted my thoughts.

*Do you feel lucky to be alive?*

"Jade," Malachi's soft voice pierced through the voice in my head. "Jade, open your eyes."

I did what I was told, and my jaw dropped.

In front of me, between my hands and glowing bright red, was a ball of my power.

"Saints," I muttered. "Holy Saints."

"Good," Esther said. "Now more."

"More?" I breathed. "More what?"

"More power. Breathe into it. Release."

I took a deep breath, and to my surprise, the red ball in front of me grew.

Malachi stepped forward, finally entering back into the cell. "How dangerous is it?" he asked Esther.

"Why don't we find out," she answered.

Before I had time to process what was happening, Esther grabbed my wrist and pushed, flinging my ball of power directly toward Malachi.

My heart dropped. A scream echoed through the stone walls.

*My* scream.

"Malachi," I breathed, finally forcing myself to look at him, at the damage I had caused.

But when I opened my eyes, Malachi was standing just as he was before.

Totally fine.

"What happened?" I asked. "How are you not hurt?"

Malachi's mouth was slightly open, as if he was just as shocked by my power not hurting him.

"I didn't feel a thing," Malachi said. "I'm fine, Jade."

Esther laughed under her breath. "Jade can block your power," she said, "and you can block hers. What a sight."

"What? What does that mean?" I asked. An emotion I didn't even understand bubbled in my chest.

"I don't know," Esther breathed, "but whatever it is, you two should stick together. It can't be a bad thing that you are both immune to each other's power."

I was breathing heavily now, unable to slow down my heart rate. I still didn't understand my power, the damage it could cause.

It had completely disintegrated that cage of bones in Trithen, turning the entire thing, deadling with it, to ash.

Malachi's power was pain. Plain and simple. With a single thought, Malachi could drop an army of men to their knees.

I had seen it with my own eyes.

But my power was so *tangible*. It had been right there, sitting in my hands.

It was *different*.

Yet powerful. I felt the power now, calling to me. It was more familiar than it was the last time.

I knew my power could destroy that deadling, but what else could it do? Was there a limit to my power?

Was there a limit to anyone's?

Or was my power just as destructive as what it had done to that cage? Would my power disintegrate anyone it touched?

We ran through the exercise again and again. Malachi and Esther both watched as I drew that ball of power time and time again until exhaustion overtook my body.

I kept my eyes away from Malachi as much as possible, but I couldn't deny the increasing heat in my chest at the thought of his power recognizing mine.

*The King of Shadows, indeed.*

# CHAPTER 12
# *Jade*

I LET THE MAIDS FILL MY BATH WITH SCORCHING HOT WATER. AS HOT AS possible, I told them.

They only looked slightly concerned with my request.

"You may go," I demanded once the bath was full, steam radiating off the surface.

They both nodded and scurried away.

My towel fell to the floor. I walked to sit on the edge of the bath. My hand shook as I reached out, feeling the steaming surface.

And then I dipped it in.

The water felt hot, yes, but not in a painful way. The scorching water comforted me, warming the coldest parts of my soul.

I let my body sink fully into the water, my heart rate immediately slowing down in relaxation. I closed my eyes and leaned my head against the back of the bath.

Saints. Months ago, I was a normal girl. Now, I was a peacemaker with magic?

When would I finally wake up from the nightmare of my life?

The scorching water cooled with every passing second. My eyelids grew heavy, fighting to stay open.

After a few minutes, I let them close.

Until I heard footsteps approaching in the darkness.

Malachi's figure appeared in the doorway of the bathroom.

"Saints," I mumbled. "What are you doing here?"

"I had to see you."

"I'm kind of occupied right now, Malachi!"

"I'll be quick," he said, completely ignoring my objections and walking into the bathroom. "I promise."

I leaned back into the water, suddenly extremely grateful that the room was dimly lit.

"What's so important that you couldn't wait until I was *clothed*?"

Malachi crossed his arms and leaned against the bathroom wall. The shadows of the corner covered the expressions of his face, and his black wings were tucked tightly behind his shoulders. "Us," was all he said.

"What do you mean?"

Malachi lifted his eyes and stared at the ceiling, lost in thought.

"If you're talking about our magic, I don't think–"

"Not just our magic, Jade," he said, pushing himself from the wall and approaching the bathtub.

I tensed, but I didn't stop him.

He kneeled next to the tub but his eyes didn't leave mine. "I've known you were different from the moment I saw you, Jade. I could just...*feel* it. But not just me. I've felt something more than simply whatever this is between us, Jade. After today, it all makes sense."

My blood stilled. "What makes sense?"

"My power recognizes you, Jade. It calls for you. When you used your magic today, I could feel it electrifying my entire body."

"But why?" I asked. "Does that happen when you're around others with magic?"

"Never," he said. "I've spent years with the Paragon, each of them possessing a gift similar to ours. I've never felt anything like this."

I shook my head, trying to make sense of his words. "Well...what does that mean?"

"I don't know," he answered. "But as crazy as this sounds, I think we were meant to find each other in this life, Jade Farrow."

"Weyland," I corrected, shocked that I even said the word.

"What?"

"It's Jade Weyland."

An emotion I couldn't name flashed across his face in the dim room before he quickly covered it up, clenching his jaw and clearing his throat.

"Whatever you say, Jade Weyland," he added.

I didn't try to hide my own smile.

As much as I hated what had transpired between me and Mal, I *was* his wife. Sometime in the chaos of our lives together, I had accepted that.

There was no going back.

Even if I did pretend to hate him.

Malachi let his arm fall over the edge of the tub, his fingers barely touching the surface of the now-barely warm water.

I froze.

His fingers moved toward my shoulder, tracing the outline of my upper arm in the water.

"Beautiful," he muttered.

The sudden compliment nearly made my jaw drop. He turned his attention back to my eyes, and I saw the deep longing that swarmed beneath them.

My heart twisted.

"Malachi," I whispered. I wasn't sure what I was going to say next. I wasn't sure what I wanted. But I did know what I felt.

I felt pulled to Malachi in ways that were indescribable.

He must have known, too. He moved his hand up to my neck, cupping my chin.

"I know you hate me, Jade. I know I've ruined everything. I deserve this. I deserve you ignoring me. But..."

I found myself leaning into his touch. "But what?"

"I can't stay away from you, Jade. I can't. I tried to give you space. I tried to leave you alone. But all I can think about every second of every day is how amazing your lips taste, and how much I need you in my life."

Fire erupted in my stomach. I knew Malachi wanted me. That wasn't exactly a secret between us.

But saying it this way...

I was about to respond when a loud siren wailed through the air. Malachi stood up instantly, looking out the window.

Still naked in the bathtub, I froze, adrenaline already pounding through my body.

"What is that?" I asked.

Malachi's wings flared on either side of his body.

"Malachi," I repeated. "What is that sound?"

Malachi moved to the edge of the room and grabbed my towel, tossing it to me. "Get dressed," he demanded.

I obeyed immediately, standing from the tub and wrapping myself in the towel.

"Tell me," I yelled. "What's happening?"

Malachi spun around and closed the distance between us, grabbing hold of my shoulders tightly. "That's the warning siren," he said. "We're being attacked."

## CHAPTER 13
# Malachi

The castle of Rewyth had been attacked twice in my lifetime.

And twice, I had assisted in killing every single enemy that approached us.

Victory was not a question. Death for our attackers was not a question.

Still. That didn't stop my body from going into full-on *war* mode. Every single muscle tensed with adrenaline, ready to protect this kingdom at all costs.

Ready to protect Jade at all costs.

Jade finished getting dressed in the bathroom as I took a deep breath, trying to clear my thoughts.

It could have been a test, I told myself. It's entirely possible that this was just a test, or a mistake by whomever blew the siren.

Something inside of me knew that wasn't true, though.

The pit in my stomach told me that the siren rang true.

We were under attack.

Jade emerged from the bathroom wearing leather trousers and a tunic. It wasn't perfect battle attire, but it was better than a long skirt.

"Let's go," I demanded, sticking my hand out. She grabbed it without hesitating, and I pulled her into the halls of the castle.

Immediate chaos filled the halls. Guards were running in every direction, trying to figure out the best way to defend our castle.

They needed guidance from their king.

"To the gates!" I shouted. My voice echoed off the stone walls, and every single person in hearing range halted. "Defend the front gates!"

And then everyone began running. I pulled Jade tightly to my side and began running along with everyone else.

I needed to figure out what was threatening us. Once I found that out, I could decide how to protect Jade.

That's what mattered. Protect Jade. Protect the castle.

Jade stayed silent as we weaved through the castle walls. I pulled her through the front doors, ducking to the corner as everyone else continued to push forward to the front gates.

"Mal," Serefin's voice rang from behind me. I held Jade's hand tighter as I spun around.

"Serefin," I greeted. "Tell me what's happening."

"They came out of nowhere," he said, out of breath. "There are dozens, Mal. Dozens of them."

My stomach dropped. I knew exactly what Serefin was talking about.

Jade stepped even closer to my side. "What is it?" she asked.

"Deadlings," Serefin and I answered at the same time. I looked at Jade, who only showed the shock in the wideness of her eyes. "We're being attacked by deadlings."

Guards continued to rush toward the gates.

"We aren't surrounded yet," Serefin informed me. "But they keep coming out of the forest."

"What do they want?" Jade asked. "Why are they coming here?"

Serefin gave me a knowing look. "They're being controlled by something or someone," I answered Jade. "But they sure as shit won't make it past these walls. Serefin, take command of the gates. You know what to do. I'll get Jade somewhere safe and I'll be back."

Serefin nodded and was gone in the blink of an eye.

Now, it was time to get rid of Jade.

"Let's go," I said, turning to pull her back inside the castle.

"What?" she asked. "No! I can help!"

"Absolutely not," I barked. "You're going somewhere safe where I don't have to worry about you."

Jade resisted, but I pulled her hand even harder, causing her to stumble forward after me.

I didn't care. I would throw her over my shoulder kicking and screaming if I had to. She would not face this battle.

"Mal!" she yelled. "I'm not a helpless child! I can help!"

"I'm taking you to the dungeons," I demanded. The dungeons were deep enough in the castle, that even if a few deadlings breached our walls, they would never find Jade.

They would never make it that far.

"The dungeons?!" Jade yelled, panic arising in her voice. "You can't leave me down there, Mal!"

*This girl.*

I spun Jade around and pinned her to the wall. Others still rushed behind us, but I didn't care if anyone saw.

"I'm going to tell you this once, so you better listen up. I'm very aware that you can defend yourself. I'm very aware that you are not a child, Jade. But those deadlings will stop at nothing. They will kill and kill and kill until there is nothing left. You've seen a couple of deadlings in your life, but an army? This is entirely different. You won't last out there, Jade. And even if you could, I can't think of a single damned thing knowing you might be in danger. So shut up, and follow me. Because I need to defend my castle, and I can't do that if I have to look for you over my shoulder every damned second!"

Jade opened her mouth to reply, but quickly shut it. "Fine," was all she said.

"Good. Now let's go."

Within two minutes, we were at the entrance of the dungeon. The guards that normally guarded the tunnels were gone, all called to defend the walls of Rewyth.

"Stay hidden," I said to her. "Wait for me to come get you."

I didn't wait to see if she kept moving. I turned on my heels and ran as fast as I could to defend the walls of my castle.

# CHAPTER 14
# *Jade*

Malachi truly did not know me at all if he thought I was going to sit quietly in the dungeons while he fought to defend this castle.

As soon as he was out of sight, I ran in the direction of the servants' quarters, where I knew Tessa would be hiding.

At least I *hoped* she was still there.

I bursted through Malachi's personal dining room, remembering which door led to the secret hallway.

I had no problem finding it this time, fueled by adrenaline and a desperate need to find my sister.

"Tessa?" I yelled as I slowly pushed the door open. "Tessa, are you in here?"

"Jade!" she answered, slamming herself into my chest. I hugged her back, thanking the Saints that she was still here. "What's happening?" she asked. "We heard the siren, but I–"

"We're being attacked," I answered quickly.

"What?" she asked, eyes wild. "By who?"

"It's not exactly a *who*," I started explaining before I realized that Tessa would have no idea what a deadling was. People back home... they didn't know about those things. I had only recently found out what a deadling was.

And that was when I had been *attacked* by one.

"It doesn't matter," I quickly recovered. "I just want to know that you're safe. Is father here?"

Tessa stepped aside, motioning to our father who was still somehow passed out on the bed.

No surprise there.

I gripped Tessa's shoulders and bent down so that I was looking directly into her eyes. "I need you to stay here, Tessa. No matter what happens, I need you to stay in this room until I come get you. Do you understand?"

"Where are you going?"

"I have to take care of something," I answered. "I'll be safe. I just need to know you're safe, too. Do you promise you won't leave?"

Tessa nodded frantically.

"Good," I said. "It will be over soon." I kissed her forehead and was gone, the small wooden door closing behind me.

And then I was moving.

I had been trained for war personally by Malachi himself.

I could handle a few deadlings.

The knife I always wore was strapped tightly to my thigh, ready to be wielded. Adrenaline pulsed through my veins, but it was a calm rush. I knew what I needed to do.

I was focused. I was ready.

Most of the halls were empty now, allowing me to sneak back to the front doors of the castle without being noticed.

Serefin's voice commanding the front line became audible as I crept closer.

My power practically buzzed beneath the surface of my skin.

If these deadlings were attacking the castle, they likely had a target.

I wasn't going to sit back and wait for them to find me.

My feet bounced over the ground as I crept closer to the wall, closer to the fight.

I knew there was an opening at the–

"I'm more than certain Malachi didn't approve of this." Serefin's voice cut through my thoughts. *Shit.*

He stormed forward and grabbed me by the arm. "Let's go. You're getting out of here."

"I can help, Ser!"

"No! You can't! Now get back inside before you cause more trouble!" He spoke to me in a voice I had never heard of coming from him. It was stern enough to shut me up. Serefin had always been kind to me, but I wasn't in any position to get on his bad side.

His fae strength forced me away from the gate.

"Serefin!" Malachi whispered in the darkness, just around the corner. "Serefin, where did you–"

He was cut off by the sight of us.

"Jade?"

"Don't be mad!" I yelled. "I only want to help!"

"Serefin, go finish them off. The numbers are dwindling. Make sure there are no more hidden in the trees," Malachi demanded. Serefin nodded and ran into the darkness.

Mal grabbed my arm where Ser had just let go, dragging me in the same direction. "What were you thinking?"

"I was thinking I could blast some of those damn deadlings with my power, just like I did in Trithen!"

Malachi yanked my arm again. "And you didn't stop to realize how ridiculously stupid that plan was?"

"Wanting to help my *husband* in *war* is not stupid!"

He stopped walking to face me. "First of all, this is not war. This was an irresponsible attack sent to shake us up. Likely to see what power we had hiding behind these walls. If you were to walk out there and blast them all away with your magic, we would have given away our one secret to whichever one of our enemies is behind this."

*Shit.* I hadn't thought of that.

"I know you want to help," Malachi said.

"I do!"

"Then please do the kingdom a favor, and stay inside."

He pushed me toward the castle and stormed away, not bothering to look back.

Malachi had spoken to me like that dozens of times, but this time, his words stung more than usual.

He was my king. I knew that. But he was also my husband.

Did he not see that I was reaching out? That I was trying?

The sounds of the attacks from the deadlings dwindled with every second.

I snuck back inside and headed straight for my bedroom. Anywhere else would be no good.

Malachi didn't see me as his equal. He didn't see me as a strong partner that could help him rule this kingdom.

He saw me as a child he still had to protect.

I waited up until I couldn't hear a single clash of metal through my open window.

This fight was over.

But this was only the beginning of war.

I had just dozed off into sleep when Malachi knocked. I could tell it was him right away—he knocked like it pained him to do so.

I stood up and secured my robe around my waist before shuffling to let him in.

"Are you alright?" he asked as he shut the door behind him.

"Shouldn't I be asking you that question?" I examined him closely, running my eyes over all of the splattered blood that stained his skin. I grabbed his chin and tilted his face to the side, looking for any sign of injury.

"I'm okay," he said quietly. "The blood isn't mine."

A breath of air escaped me as I let my hands fall back to my sides. "Good."

I turned my back to him and walked further into my bedroom. My feet chilled against the cool, hard floor.

"You scared me half to death, you know," Malachi continued. "Seeing you out there wasn't exactly calming."

I tilted my head back and stared at the dark ceiling. "I was only trying to help," I admitted under my breath.

Malachi approached behind me. The shadow of his wings illuminated on the wall. "I know you were," he said just as lightly.

I spun to face him. "Then why not let me? Why not let me assist the people who are saving my life?"

"They were just fine without you," he said. He took another step closer.

"Well, that makes me feel very valuable. Thanks."

A bloodied hand came up to tug on the bottom of my hair. "There is nothing more precious to me in this entire kingdom, Jade. I'm sorry I lashed out at you, but..."

"But what?"

His eyes darkened. "I can't think straight knowing you are in danger. I can't... I can't–"

I interrupted him by placing both hands on his face. "I know," was all I said. He closed his eyes under my touch. I rubbed my thumbs lightly over his chiseled cheekbones before saying, "You're covered in blood. Let me help you."

Malachi let me pull him to the dimly lit bathroom in my room. Silence lingered between us as I dampened a cloth and returned to where he leaned against the doorframe.

When he reached for the cloth, I stopped him. "Let me do it," I whispered.

He nodded.

Malachi bowed his head under my touch. He let me clean the blood and dirt from his skin in silence until the sun began to rise.

When he suggested he needed to return to his own room, I didn't stop him.

But I couldn't shake the feeling that washed over me when I saw the pained look in his eyes as he went.

# CHAPTER 15
# Malachi

THE TITHE HAPPENED AT THE BEGINNING OF EVERY SEASON. MY FATHER used to say it was for the purpose of "receiving what was rightfully owed to the castle".

I had no idea what he meant by that, but the tithes continued, regardless. Year after year, members of Rewyth lined up, ready to offer anything they could as payment to the kingdom.

In return, the King would offer his good graces.

Sometimes the citizens would even hand over their firstborn children, they were so desperate to be seen as noble.

I tried not to actively grimace as I entered the throne room. This was never a room that I liked. It only reminded me of greed.

But that was my fathers reign. All of those terrible memories, all of those moments of brutality that took place on these very stone floors.

That reign was in the past.

I was here to create new memories. New reign. New power.

My heels clicked the shining floor as I walked up the stone stairs and took a seat on the throne that was now nearly overgrown with vines and greenery from the surrounding walls.

I tried to settle in, to relax. The tithe was beneficial to the kingdom, that much held true no matter who sat in this throne. But it also had benefits for the citizens. They had the opportunity to be seen. To have their problems and grievances heard.

Of course, those *problems* were rarely handled without bloodshed in this very room while my father reigned.

"Let us know when you're ready," Serefin said from the front doors of the room. A small nod of encouragement came soon after, small enough that only I would see.

I took a long breath. This was my first tithe as a king. This was my first opportunity to give everyone the impression of who I was and what I was made of.

It was time these people had peace here in Rewyth. *Real* peace.

But at the same time, I wasn't going to let anyone threaten my position as King of Rewyth.

The golden crown I wore felt heavier than it looked. It cut into my skin at my ears, not helping my irritated mood in the slightest.

"Let them in," I ordered Ser. He nodded and, with the help of another guard, pulled the massive doors open.

I held my breath and waited.

The first citizen to enter was a young fae, maybe a decade old.

His silver wings were still small, yet they flared around his body confidently. Likely to make himself appear stronger.

I should know. I had been there once.

"My king," he said as he approached the bottom of the steps. I watched him thoughtfully as he bowed, low and long, before looking me in the eye.

I nodded. A silent gesture of permission to continue speaking.

"My father has grown ill. We–we have no money to pay our tithe. I come here today to offer myself to your court."

My first instinct was to tell the poor boy to go home. But this was the first citizen of this tithe. The first example. So, instead, I looked the boy in the eye and asked, "And why would I want you in my court?"

The boy blinked once. It was his only sign of surprise. "I–I have special gifts, my king. I can fight in your army. I have been gifted with the power of air magic."

"Air magic?"

The boy nodded.

"Show me."

The boy's face lit up, as if he was waiting for this moment all his life. If it were true that he possessed air magic, then maybe he really had.

The boy held his hands out in front of him and closed his eyes for one second before a large gust of wind crossed through the room. Strong enough that I had to stop my crown from falling off my head.

The gust of wind ended just as quickly as it had begun. I instantly stood from my throne.

"How long have you had this magic?" I asked him, genuinely curious to see another fae with magic here in Rewyth.

"The last few months," he answered, keeping his eyes glued to the ground. He was nervous about his power, likely unsure how I would use him. Friend or weapon? Ally or enemy?

"Good," I answered. "We'll have plenty of time to strengthen your gift. You'll live here in the castle and we'll get you the training you need. What is your name, boy?"

The boy's eyes shot up, mouth agape. "Thank you! Thank you! My name is Kylar," he said. "You won't regret this, King Malachi. I promise you!"

I nodded to the guards, and the boy was escorted out of the throne room.

One down. The boy would be useful to us, no doubt.

But I was certain my luck would not continue.

"Bring the next one in," I ordered Ser.

He obeyed, and within a few seconds, I was looking at an older woman. Still fae, but by the looks of it, she was at least a few centuries old.

"I come with your tithe, dear king," she said, tossing a small bag of golden coins at the guard who stood at the bottom of the stairs.

"Your service will not be forgotten," I recited. "The kingdom thanks you."

The woman scoffed and rolled her bright green eyes. "Keep your thanks."

I didn't say another word as she was escorted out of the room.

"What was that about?" I asked the guards as soon as she was gone.

"It's expected to have some resistance to the new reign," one of my guards, Doromir, spoke up. He was an older guard, one that worked for my father for many years.

But he had also worked for me. I trusted him and his experience. "I can't imagine why someone would resist *my* reign," I muttered. "My father's death was the best thing to happen to this kingdom."

"It's not your reign they resist," he said. "It's change. Who knows what types of rumors have been circulating."

"Great. Let the next one in, then. Wouldn't want to disappoint."

Only it wasn't a citizen who entered the room next.

"What are you doing here?" I asked.

Jade strolled forward, a sleek black dress clinging to her curves as she moved. Her hair was pin-straight down her back, and a golden crown, one that matched my own, sat upon her head.

*Saints save me.*

"I was informed it was my duty to accompany you at your first tithe. Apologies for my lateness."

I looked for any signs of deception in her face, but found none.

Jade had actually come to run the tithe with me.

The guards watched in awe as she ascended the stone steps, approaching where I sat on the large throne.

"I am your wife, after all," she said when she got close enough.

My eyes flickered down her body, unable to stop themselves from appreciating the pure form of beauty that stood before me.

"Where did you get that crown?" I whispered. Jade watched the way my eyes dragged back up to meet hers, and she smiled.

"Borrowed it from Adeline."

Jade flipped a loose strand of hair over her shoulder and stepped forward, moving to sit on the armrest of the throne. I didn't pull my arm away as she leaned against me for support. What was she up to? Showing up to a royal event like this on her own free will wasn't something Jade would do.

"Are you sure you're up for this?" I asked her. *Give in now*, I thought. *Give in now, or accept your position as Queen of Rewyth.*

That's what they would see her as. Their queen.

But when Jade's eyes met mine, only inches away, I saw fierce determination.

"Bring it on."

Ignoring the way my stomach flipped, I motioned to Serefin to bring in the next citizen.

It was a fae I recognized. A middle-aged man who had fought in battle with me before. He stormed into the room with such strength that each guard placed their hands on their weapons.

Jade did not budge next to me.

"You kill our true king, yet you sit on his throne and demand I pay money to this wicked kingdom?"

"Careful how you speak to your king," Serefin warned from the back of the room.

The man only grimaced. "He is no king of mine."

From the corner of my eye, I saw Jade's jaw tightened.

"If you are unhappy here, you may leave," I said, choosing each word carefully and calmly.

The man only scoffed. "And go where, exactly?"

"Why should I care?" I replied, letting the coolness of my voice carry through the room. "If you do not wish to pay your tithe like every other citizen because of pure spite, you may leave. Or you will be forced to leave. Choose wisely."

"You would exile me for speaking my opinion regarding the throne?"

The man's presence here alone challenged me. *Clearly.* He was far older than me. He was seasoned. I, however, was not to be messed with. Not after everything I had done for this kingdom. After everything I had done to keep ignorant citizens like *him* safe.

I slowly stood from my throne, taking a step forward before crossing my wrists behind my back. "No," I spoke, much stronger than the last time. "I would exile you for treason. Now pay your tithe and shut your mouth, or gather your things and leave Rewyth for good."

The man shook his head, but after a few moments, he tossed his coin to the guards.

I nodded, not bothering to waste breath on thanking him.

Once the man had left, I returned to Jade at the throne. "See?" she whispered in my ear as I sat. "This is fun."

"I'm glad you're enjoying yourself," I whispered back, barely brushing her ear with my lips before pulling back and facing the doors once more.

I was starting to get bored of citizens entering, tossing coins, and leaving when another familiar face entered.

Another one of my father's men sauntered into the room. *Arthur.*

I stiffened as soon as I saw him. He walked slowly into the room, cocky as ever.

"Well, well, well," he started. "Looks like you got over your father's death quickly."

"Pay your tithe and leave," one of the guards barked.

I held a hand up to silence the guard. "My father's passing was unfortunate, but necessary," I stated.

"Unfortunate, yes," he said. "What's even worse than that tragedy is the *human scum* that sits on your throne."

My power rumbled, but I calmed it quickly. He was trying to get to me. "It was my father's wish to wed me to a human, Arthur. You should be happy to know his intent lives on."

Arthur drew his brows together before sliding his gaze to Jade. I half-expected

Jade to flinch away from the fae's attention, but she did no such thing. She didn't move an inch.

"It's a disgrace is what it is," Arthur spat without taking his eyes off Jade. "Tell me, human, why are you here?"

"Don't speak to her," I argued. "You speak to me."

"She is my queen, is she not?"

"It's okay, Mal," Jade whispered to me. "Arthur is free to ask me any question he wishes. To answer," she continued, "I'm here to rule Rewyth beside my husband."

Pride swelled in my chest.

"And what makes you think you are strong enough for that?"

"What makes you think I am not?"

"Any fae in this room could kill you right now," Arthur sneered.

Jade only smiled, calm as ever as she sat perched on the armrest of my throne. "Then do it."

Every guard in the room drew a sword.

Jade did not falter. When Arthur hesitated, she merely raised an eyebrow.

"You heard her," I added when he didn't move. "If you threaten my queen, you better plan on following through."

Jade's blank face flickered with an evil smile.

I fought the urge to reach out and touch her.

Arthur didn't move. He stood at the foot of the steps, clearly confused by Jade's orders.

"Something wrong?" Jade asked. "I'm sitting right here. If you think killing me will be so easy, go right ahead."

Every ounce of my body burned with desire.

Jade stood from her perched position on our throne and stepped toward Arthur. I stayed put, happy to watch as my wife pummeled this man with her power.

I felt it first—a low, magnetic pull of my power to Jade's. She summoned her own magic with a certain authority as she stood before Arthur and grew a large ball of power between her hands.

"Tell me, Arthur," she pushed. "Do you think you could kill me now?"

Arthur stammered in response, unable to form actual words.

Jade stepped forward, cascading down the few stairs that separated her from him.

Her ball of power grew larger. I glanced around the room, and found everyone's eyes glued to Jade in awe.

They felt it, too. The silent buzz of pure strength coming from her.

"What about now?" Jade pushed again. "I'm waiting, Arthur. Go ahead and kill me."

Jade pushed the ball of power forward, just a few paces, but enough to make Arthur stumble backward. He fell on the stone floor but didn't stop scrambling away from Jade's power.

I didn't even try to hide my smile.

Satisfied, Jade released the hold she had on her own magic, causing it to fizzle out.

When she turned to make her way back to me, I recognized the look on her face. It was a look I had rarely seen on her.

*Power.*

"If you're done insulting my wife now," I said, "you may leave."

But everyone in the room knew that wasn't true. Nobody threatened Jade and escaped with their lives.

Arthur struggled to get to his feet before turning toward the doors.

Although he didn't have time to make it that far.

In one swift motion, my wings lifted me from the throne and cascaded me to block him from exiting.

Horror dripped from every feature on his face when he realized the reality of the situation.

"You picked the wrong side," I growled. His neck snapped like a twig in my hands, and his body fell to the floor.

Nobody looked shocked. The guards in the room quickly got to work disposing of the body while I walked back to the throne.

"Took you long enough," Jade teased as I approached.

I wasn't sure what reaction I expected from her, but it certainly wasn't that. "You're not mad?"

Jade's head spun to me. "Mad?" she asked. "He threatened to kill me! I would have killed him myself if you didn't."

I sat on the throne and placed my hand on Jade's knee. She didn't pull away. "Well, that's good news," I said, "because if anyone else threatens you during this tithe, they'll suffer the same fate."

Jade's mouth tilted upward, only a centimeter, before she returned the cool mask of a queen. "Either by your hands, or by mine."

Her hand came to fall on my shoulder as we signaled for the next citizen to enter.

Perhaps ruling this kingdom wouldn't be as terrible as I had expected.

# CHAPTER 16
## Jade

I TUCKED MY HAIR INTO THE BACK OF MY JACKET. THE LESS identifiable traits I had, the better.

Pulling the fabric over my head only helped slightly. I hoped it would be dark enough in the dungeon to hide my features.

It had worked before.

If I was lucky, this would be the last time.

I placed a hand over my heart, feeling the pounding of every passing second.

The sun had been down for hours now. My feet were silent on the stone floor as I slipped from my bedroom and blended with the shadows in the castle. I became one with them, fluid and dark as I moved toward the dungeon in the path I had taken half a dozen times already.

This time was different, though.

I wasn't leaving alone this time.

I had waited until just after midnight, when the guards rotated positions. This guard in particular, though, had a habit of leaving early to meet with one of the maids in the servants' kitchen.

Terrible habit, that guard.

Goosebumps rose to my skin as I descended further and further into the underground of the castle.

"Sadie," I whispered once I reached her cell, grimacing at the way my voice bounced off the solid dungeon walls. "Where are you?"

"Jade?" her voice in the darkness made me jump. "Jade, what are you doing here?"

"Get up. We're leaving."

I navigated my way over to her, halting when I saw her huddled in the corner.

I closed the distance between us and dropped to my knees next to her. "Sadie, what's wrong? Are you hurt?"

"No," she answered, but her voice was barely a whisper. "No, Jade. I'm not hurt."

I placed my hands on her head. "Saints, Sadie. You're burning up. You're sick."

"I've been through worse."

"We're getting you out of here, Sadie. *Tonight.* You're sick and you can't stay here."

I tried to pull her up by her shoulders, but Sadie didn't budge. "I can't leave, Jade."

"Yes you can. The halls are clear, nobody will notice for days. I have a plan. Let's go."

Sadie took a few shaking breaths and finally met my eyes in the darkness of the dungeons.

"Okay," she said. "But I don't know if I can make it–"

"Put your arm around me," I demanded. "I'll help you walk. It's not far," I lied.

Her skinny arm found mine, and I pulled it over my shoulders.

Sadie was a tall girl, but she felt light as I picked her up from the ground. Too light.

"Ready?" I asked.

"As ready as I'll ever be," she whispered.

And then we were stumbling out of her open cell, down the long corridor of stone toward the entrance of the dungeon.

"I figured I'd find you here," Malachi's voice boomed off the stone.

I froze, Sadie along with me. "We were just–"

"Escaping?"

Even though Malachi was still several feet away, I felt his eyes piercing into me.

I weighed my options. I could try to lie, but Malachi would know it before it even left my mouth. If I told him the truth, I had a slim chance of him taking my side.

*He owed me.*

Malachi should have known that I stood with him. I showed him that I would defend this kingdom for him.

He needed to trust me on this.

"She's sick, Mal. She can't stay here. She doesn't even deserve to be here in the first place."

"Doesn't deserve to be here?" he repeated. His tone was cold and harsh. A chill ran down my spine.

"No," I said carefully. "She doesn't."

After what happened during the tithe earlier, I knew Malachi expected better from me. Better and worse.

He expected me to be stronger than this.

I had shown Malachi that I was strong. I had shown him I was on his side. How could I make him see that Sadie was innocent? She was not a threat to me. She never would be.

Malachi's laughter filled the dungeons. "Tell me, Jade. What would you have me do? Let her go free?"

"She had nothing to do with the attack."

"You're too trusting," Malachi spat. "You look at her as an ally because she's a human. If she were fae, would you even blink an eye? Would you care at all?"

I didn't say a word. After the tithe, I knew my behavior shocked Mal. He expected me to stand by his side after all of this. But Sadie was my *friend*. Her breath shallowed beside me.

"Nothing to say now, Jade? No bullshit excuse to why you're helping this human escape? Don't stop there. Why don't I unlock Isaiah's chains for you, too?"

Panic grew in my chest. "Malachi, I–"

"Now that I think about it, that's a great idea. Why don't we all go get your friend *Isaiah*. Let's see what he thinks about you saving his precious friend Sadie. Shall we?"

My blood ran cold.

Malachi pushed past us, barging deep into the dungeons. Leaving us no choice but to stumble after him.

"You need to calm down," I yelled to him. But he was walking much faster than I could carry Sadie. "I was just trying to get Sadie medical treatment. That's it."

"I think you'll need to get a lot more than medical treatment when you see this," he yelled.

Sadie tried to talk, but I quickly shushed her. "Stay quiet. I'll do the talking. He just needs to blow off steam."

"I can hear everything you say," he yelled back. By the time we rounded the last corner of the dungeon, Sadie nearly fell out of my arms.

Isaiah sat in chains, head hanging down onto his chest. His shirt was gone, and his skin was covered in blood. Some dry, some glistening against the dim lighting.

"Saints, Mal," I mumbled. "Is he–"

"Dead? Unfortunately for him, not yet. I didn't want to end all the fun too soon."

"Why are you doing this?" I asked. "What's the point, Mal? How does this possibly help you?"

"It doesn't help me, Jade. Don't you understand that? He tried to *hurt you*. He nearly got you killed. He nearly got me killed, too. This isn't for helping me, Jade. Isaiah is paying for what he's done."

"What about me?" I asked. My breathing came in short pants. "What about my revenge? What about my justice?" Malachi eyed me carefully. I lifted Sadie's arm off my shoulder and slowly lowered her to the ground before standing again and facing Mal. "What about *me*?"

"What about you, Jade?" he asked. "You want revenge?"

"Yes," I whispered, although it was mostly just a breath. Years of pain, betrayal, and hurt came rushing forward, acknowledging those words as he spoke them. "Yes, I want revenge."

Malachi held his hands out on either side of him. "Then take it," he said, words harsh and blunt. "If you want revenge so badly, Jade, go after it. It's yours."

"I can't," I said, feeling all of those emotions slip away, back to the depths where they belonged. "If I tried getting revenge on everyone who has hurt me, or on everyone who has *tried* to hurt me, I would have nobody left. Nobody."

"You would have me," he added.

"Would I?" My voice cracked, but I didn't care. He needed to hear this. I needed to say it more than anything. "Would I have you, Malachi? After everything we've been through. After everything you've *done*."

"Yes, Jade!" he barked. Any tenderness from his voice was gone, replaced by the brutal King of Shadows. "Yes, you would have me! Don't you see that? Everything I've done? Dammit, Jade!"

I flinched at his words, but I did not back away.

Not this time.

Not from him.

"*Every single thing* I have done has been for *you*. All of it!"

He stepped forward, close enough now that if I reached out, I would touch him. "And this?" I asked, waving a hand to Isaiah. "Is this also for me?"

"Yes," he responded without a second of hesitation. "It is for you. Because I know you want revenge just as badly as I do, Jade. I can see it in your eyes. Only you can't see it. You can't take Isaiah against his will and chain him up in a dungeon beneath your castle, but I can. *I can!* And I will, Jade. For you, I will."

Sadie whimpered on the ground.

I closed my eyes. Somewhere deep in my soul, into the darkest corners that I had spent years trying to bury, I wanted it. I *delighted* in seeing Isaiah, the man who sold me out, the man who betrayed me, bloody and beaten.

He *did* deserve this.

And I wanted my enemy to suffer.

But Sadie was my friend. Sadie had stood by my side, even if she also stood by Isaiah's.

I opened my eyes and found Sadie in the darkness, attempting to crawl to Isaiah. I walked over and knelt before her, grabbing her chin in my hand.

Something came over me, power I had never felt before. But not from magic.

"Did you know Isaiah was working with Esther to betray us?" I asked her, voice strong.

A single tear fell down her dirty face. "No, I swear it, Jade. I didn't know."

"She's lying," Malachi added from behind us.

Sadie snapped her eyes in his direction, then back at me. "No, Jade! I'm not lying! I'm telling you the truth. I had no idea! He never talked about that stuff with me. He never–"

"You lie!" Malachi yelled this time, his voice echoing off the walls and down the corridor of the underground.

Sadie was fully crying now, tears streaming down her face as she flinched away from Malachi.

And from me.

I stood and turned to Malachi. "She didn't know, Mal," I pushed, not even sure if I could believe the words I was saying.

Malachi shrugged, then closed the distance between himself and Isaiah. "If she didn't know, and if she's truly on our side, then she won't care if I kill her little friend here," he said.

Sadie immediately shot to her feet. "Don't!" she screamed, desperation dripping from her voice. I grabbed her shoulders to push her back, away from Mal and Isaiah. "Don't hurt him!"

"I think we're a little past that by now, don't you, Sadie?" he whispered. Something in his voice sent a chill down my spine.

I wasn't sure if I hated it or loved it.

"If you really cared about Jade," he continued, "you wouldn't care about a traitor. Would you?"

Malachi pulled a dagger from his belt and cut a thin line across Isaiah's bare chest. It was difficult to even see the cut with the blood already caked over him.

Sadie didn't need to see it, though. To her, it was all the same. She broke down, falling to her knees in the underground once more. "Don't!" she said. "Please don't kill him. He was just trying to protect himself! He didn't mean to get anyone in trouble!" Her words came out in a jumbled mess, drunk with emotion.

Malachi didn't care, though. I didn't expect him to.

Sadie took a long, shaking breath and looked Malachi directly in the face. "Please," she whispered. "Show him mercy."

"You want mercy?" he repeated. I stayed still where I stood, not daring to move an inch.

Not wanting to stop the scene before me.

Those dark shadows deep within me whispered for *more*.

"There is only one mercy for a man like Isaiah. For a traitor. For a man who tried to kill my *wife*."

My heart pounded in my chest. I knew what was coming.

Malachi was the King of Shadows.

Death would be a gift to Isaiah.

As if he read my thoughts, Malachi grabbed Isaiah's head with both hands and, in the blink of an eye, snapped his neck.

Sadie screamed.

Isaiah's chains kept him from falling sideways to the ground.

I stood there, not able to look away. A numbness I recognized all too well spread through my chest, across my entire body.

Isaiah was dead. Isaiah betrayed me, he betrayed Malachi, and now he was dead.

Malachi killed him.

I looked at Malachi, who was already staring at me.

Waiting for my reaction.

Did he want me to hate him? Did he want me to run away? Or did he think I would sink to the floor like Sadie, screaming my lungs out at the horror?

I did none of those things. I wasn't afraid of Malachi. I wasn't afraid of the things he did.

To be honest, I hated that I wasn't disgusted by him. No, I was the furthest thing from disgusted.

I saw something in him that I recognized deeply within myself. The horror. The shame. The guilt. The power.

*I wanted it all.*

"Let her go," I demanded. "She's gone through enough."

Malachi swallowed once. "Fine," he said. "Now she knows what will happen if she crosses us in the future. Run into the woods and find your way back to Fearford. You are not welcome back here, Sadie. Let this be a reminder to you of what will happen if you betray Jade."

My stomach twisted at the way Sadie scraped herself off the floor and stumbled to Isaiah, checking to make sure he was really dead.

He was.

"Go, Sadie," I said. I kept my eyes on Malachi. I couldn't look at her. Not now. Not after this. "Go before he changes his mind."

Sadie was sobbing hysterically, but she understood. She knew this was her only chance.

She pushed past Malachi and I, sobbing with every weak step, and she was gone.

"You didn't have to do that in front of her," I hissed. "She loved him."

Malachi shook his head. "She didn't love him," he muttered. "And she'll get over it."

"You're unbelievable," I said. "You drag us back here for what? This abusive show of power?"

Malachi stomped forward, inches from my face. "How do you think I felt, Jade, when I saw you escaping with her? You're supposed to be on my side. After the tithe, I thought we were on the same page. What was I supposed to do? Let you both go?"

"Nothing! You were supposed to do nothing! I was helping a friend. You would have done the same."

"No!" he yelled back. "No, I wouldn't have!" He stepped forward again, and this time, I took a step back, pressing my back to the cold stone behind me.

"You could have shown him mercy. For her sake."

Malachi placed his arm on the stone behind me, pinning me to the wall with his own body. "No, I couldn't have. You know that just as well as I do. He deserved to die. You know that."

"And you're the one that decides that?"

"I am the King."

"The King of Shadows," I repeated.

Malachi smiled, wicked and beautiful. "Yes, Jade," he whispered. His breath tickled my cheek. "I am the King of Shadows. My enemies will die merciless deaths at my hands. My allies will know no defeat when they fight by my side. You, of all people, should realize that."

"As your wife?" I asked.

He stared at me a second longer before answering, "As my queen."

# CHAPTER 17
# *Malachi*

"THIS IS REQUIRED?" I ASKED SEREFIN. HE WAS THE ONLY GUARD I allowed in my rooms these days. I trusted the others enough, but time would tell whether or not they were truly loyal to me.

The dinner of celebration to formally announce my new reign as King of Rewyth was set to take place tonight. It was more of a formality than anything, but Saints, it was going to be a pain in my ass.

"Unfortunately, yes. But you are the King. I suppose you can make your own rules now."

I shook my head and strapped my belt around my waist, making sure each weapon was secured tightly in its spot.

"Hours of bullshit conversations with people I don't even like."

"The court members were chosen by your father," Serefin reminded me. "But that doesn't mean they can't be replaced. Hear them out, but determine your own future."

I considered his words. The court members were going to fight every single thing I said tonight. I knew that. They had been loyal to my father, but their greed controlled them more than loyalty.

If I played my cards right, I would have no problem winning them over.

The court members were composed of fae that had been around much longer than I had. Some of them grew up with my father. Others were new. Each one held a great amount of land, money, or something else that had been deemed beneficial to Rewyth.

And because of that, each one of them thought they had a voice in this court. In the decisions made here.

*What a joke.*

"Jade will be there?" I asked Ser, keeping my voice calm.

He nodded. "Adeline is with her. They're getting ready as we speak."

"Good," I muttered. "Perhaps she'll distract everyone from stupid court politics."

Serefin laughed. "Careful what you wish for, brother. I'm sure half the kingdom has heard of the prophecy by now. Not to mention her special abilities."

*Saints.*

Jade could protect herself. There was no doubt that someone tonight was going to say something offensive to her. Someone would try to make a smart-ass comment about her place in this kingdom, her place as my wife.

Her place as queen.

And I had no doubt that if Jade didn't shut them up, I would.

Anyone who disrespected Jade disrespected *me,* in turn.

I had to admit, I was curious to see who would be bold enough to try.

But it was true. Jade *did* have a special ability. Certainly, rumors had spread by now, especially after her show of power at the tithe.

I was prepared to fight anyone who challenged her magic.

Was Jade?

I turned to the door and clapped Serefin on the arm. "I guess there is no better time than right now," I said. "Let's get this over with."

Serefin opened my bedroom door and stepped aside.

Only when I stepped into the hallway, I wasn't alone.

At the opposite end of the hall, Jade did the same.

Adeline had dressed her in a low-cut corset gown with a large skirt that moved with each step she took.

Even from far away, she looked stunning.

She would be the talk of the dinner tonight. No doubt about that.

"Good luck with that, brother," Serefin whispered to me. I walked down the hall, closing the distance between us, and held my arm out to Jade. After what happened in the dungeons last night, I wasn't sure she would accept.

I didn't regret it. Not for a second. Jade had to see who I really was. She needed to see, deep down, what I would sacrifice for her. *Who* I would sacrifice for her. Because nothing else mattered when she was around. Nothing else mattered, except that she was okay. Anyone who threatened that would pay.

Sadie had left—I made sure of it from a distance after Jade stormed away. What Jade didn't understand, though, was that I *had* shown mercy. I *had* shown Sadie mercy. I had sure as shit shown Isaiah mercy by killing him swiftly after dragging his poor life out for weeks in the dungeons.

He had given me everything I needed.

I was half tempted to rush to Jade and tell her that it wasn't personal, or that I wasn't myself. But neither of those things were true. It was personal on a deep, soul-aching level that I couldn't even understand myself. It was personal enough that I was willing to rip the head off any man who touched her. No matter what they were to me.

It was personal enough that I couldn't think straight around her. I could no longer see the big picture when she was near.

But the way I acted last night *was* myself. I hadn't felt that free in a long, long time. For weeks now, I had been restricting myself. Hiding myself. Trying to fit into the perfect version of me that Jade might actually understand.

Everything was clear to me, now. Jade did understand. I saw it in the sparkle of her eye last night, as she watched me snap Isaiah's neck without a single blink. When Sadie had dropped to the ground in screams, Jade stared at me.

Jade stared into me, deep into the dark corner that never saw light.

She saw it all.

And she did not look away.

"Are you ready?" I asked Jade as I held my arm out to her. She took it gently, delicately touching my bicep with her small palm.

"No," she answered, keeping her head straight ahead. Serefin and Adeline fell into step behind us. "I'm not. I'm not going to pretend like this kingdom appreciates a human as their queen, even if I do have special gifts."

My mouth twitched before I could control it.

"What?" she asked. "You think that's funny?"

"No," I said. "It's just nice to hear you calling yourself queen."

Jade's cheeks flushed red, and she snapped her attention back to the hallway ahead of us. "I don't see myself getting out of it easily."

"So you've decided to accept it?"

"I suppose I have," she said. "Because I'm being thrown into this world either way, right?"

Part of me wanted to open these doors and let her run far, far away from everything. The prophecy, my mother, her own family. She deserved better. She deserved a fresh start.

But that wasn't possible.

The other part of me knew that, and didn't want her out of my sight for a single second. Selfishly, I was glad she was here. I was glad she was in this castle. Every time I pictured this life without her, the vast void of loneliness staring me directly in the face became too much. Too heavy.

But with Jade, everything was...better.

"It will be over before you know it. I'll formally announce my new reign, we'll eat until we're sick, and then we'll be waltzing out of there like it never even happened."

Jade sighed as we turned a corner, the massive dining hall doors coming into view. I felt her tense up on my arm. "We're never that lucky, and you know it."

I wanted to tell her she was wrong, but I knew she wasn't. Luck didn't have a way of finding us.

But we made our own.

A guard near the door stepped forward and announced our arrival. I heard the scratching of chairs on the wooden floor as everyone stood from their seats, anticipating our arrival.

"Showtime, my queen," I whispered.

And we entered the dining hall.

Jade tried to pull away from my arm, but I quickly caught her hand and tugged lightly, letting her know she wasn't going anywhere. We were one unit now.

The truth was, we always had been.

"Thank you for coming," I said to the room. "Please, be seated."

I walked to the head of the table, taking Jade along with me, and we sat in the two open chairs. After Serefin and Adeline sat on either side of us, the table was filled.

The faces around me were mostly friendly. My brothers sat nearby, along with court members. Many were the same court members that watched as Jade was tormented under my father's reign. A few I didn't recognize sat near the end of the table.

And their faces weren't welcoming.

It was going to be a long night, indeed.

Jade sat in her seat, but I could practically feel the tension rising off her.

"Let me start this celebratory evening off by announcing that the deadlings who attacked us the other night were killed. Every single one. Not one of those beasts left alive."

A few nods of approval, but that was it.

I continued. "I also want to say that it was not a random attack. Based on what we know, we believe it was a warning."

Cue the muttering and whispering around the table.

"A warning?" Adonis spoke up. "A warning from who? For what?"

Wine. I definitely needed wine.

I picked up the cup in front of me and took a long gulp. "The Paragon has their eye on us. However, they aren't our only enemy. It's possible it could have come from elsewhere, but odds are, the Paragon sent those beasts our way to try and shake us up."

"Why would they do that? Why would they want that?"

I looked over to Jade, who was already staring at me, jaw set.

"Because Jade has the power that they want. They'll come after her. Sooner or later, they'll come."

"And what is she to us?" one of the strangers at the end of the table asked. "Why should we protect her?"

I had to remind myself that we were in public. Everyone at this table had their eyes glued on me.

*But didn't that make this a perfect time to put everyone in their place?*

Jade wasn't only my wife. She was now the *Queen of Rewyth*. It was time they treated her–and spoke about her–as such.

"Jade is the peacemaker, spoken of in hundreds of old prophecies. My mother recently told me that–"

"Your mother?" one of the men chimed in. "She's alive?"

I silently cursed to myself for not bringing this up earlier. A handful of people knew that my mother—the true Queen of Rewyth—still lived. Even fewer people knew that she had betrayed me.

And she was hiding away in the dungeons of our castle. That was something only Serefin, my brothers, and I knew.

"My mother is not the topic of this dinner," I yelled. My voice was strong enough that the delicate plates on the table rattled. "We're here to discuss my reign moving forward, and the challenges we'll be facing in the coming weeks. If anyone has a problem with that, you can leave now."

Nobody moved.

"And if anybody has a problem with our stance on protecting our queen—my wife, then speak up now."

Again, nobody moved.

But I doubted that would be the last I heard of it.

"Good. Now we can move on to discussing—" my attention stalled on a familiar fae at the end of the table.

*Kara.*

"What are you doing in here? This is for court members only," I stated. I felt Jade stiffen next to me.

She looked genuinely shocked. "Oh," she placed a dramatic hand on her chest. "You haven't heard? My father has chosen me to stand in his place in court."

"No," I barked. "That's not happening."

"But you can't–"

I slammed my hands on the wooden table and let my black wings flare out either side of me. "Please, Kara," I said, "continue arguing with your king."

My brothers choked on their laughter.

"She has a right to be here, King Malachi," one of the other court members chimed in. He was older, but I couldn't quite remember his name.

"Nobody has a right to be here," I half-yelled to the table. I reached over and clasped Jade's hand. "This is my kingdom now. I understand that things were run a certain way when my father sat in this chair, but he's gone. He was corrupt and vile and greedy. He was lost. And his reign will *not* continue. So when I say that a court member goes, he or she goes. Understand, Kara?"

I turned my attention back to her.

For once, she actually looked shocked.

Her eyes slid over to Jade, just for a second, before she stood from her seat and strutted out of the room.

"Good," I said again. "Let me remind you all that traitors are not welcome here. Anyone who questions me can leave. Anyone who questions Jade can leave. Understood?"

"With all due respect," the same man spoke, "your mother was the true queen. As your father's first wife, she holds certain rights here. If she is still alive and willing to accept the position, the throne is rightfully hers."

I was prepared for this topic to arise. Historically, it was rare for a woman to sit on the throne. Rewyth, however, held this unique tradition.

But it had been decades since my mother had been seen in Rewyth. Most of the kingdom will have forgotten about her presence here. And most of the kingdom would prefer a male on the throne, anyway.

My argument was strong.

I paused. "My mother is nothing. She is a traitor, she is a selfish witch, and she is no longer a free member of this kingdom."

"Why?"

Lucien leaned across the table and answered before I could. "Why?" he repeated. "You question your own king? Esther is nothing more than an old woman who wants to cheat her way out of consequences. Believe Malachi when he says she is a traitor."

The man clenched his jaw and leaned back in his chair. He had heard enough.

"Now about the prophecy," I started. "Jade's life is at risk every single day. The prophecy names her as the peacemaker. As you all know, the Paragon is in place to keep the power between witches and fae equal. Well, Jade's power will change all of that. Whichever side uses her power in the curse-breaking ritual will have access to her power. Will have control of all power. The Paragon is coming for her to use her power for themselves."

"And why is that so bad? They are fair, King Malachi. The Paragon will know what to do with her."

I wanted to yell into his face. No, they were not fair. These fae were only fed spoonfuls of information to make themselves believe as much.

"It is bad because they will kill Jade for it. And as Jade is my wife, I'm sure you can see how I'm not letting that happen."

The man glanced at Jade, then nodded.

Jade's hand tightened slightly in mine.

Serefin spoke next. "Have we heard back from the scouts? Any movement on the horizons?"

Adonis answered, "I haven't heard a single thing. It's silent out there."

"They're waiting until we drop our guard," I added. "They will hit us hard, and it will be soon."

Another man at the end of the table leaned in and asked, "Do we even have the resources to fight them? If they come for our queen, how will we defend her?"

*Our queen.* A wave of relief washed over me to hear those words from a court member.

And it was immediately ripped away when the man to his right began laughing.

I recognized him. He was one of the men who held me back while Jade was whipped.

My vision blurred. "Something funny?"

He stopped laughing long enough to answer, "You kill your father, you remove a court member, you hide our true queen, and you deplete the castle's resources in the name of a human. Yet you call *us* traitors?"

It took one second for my power to unleash upon him. He fell out of his chair, doubling over on the ground in pain.

Others gasped in surprise. I only narrowed my focus. More pain. More torture.

It only lasted ten seconds or so, but to him, it would feel like hours.

When I pulled my power back, he was nothing more than an empty threat on the ground.

"Yet another one of my father's men that cannot see our new way. Please, excuse yourself from this room."

He couldn't walk, though. Two guards from the door dragged him out.

I knew my father's remaining men would be the ones to threaten me.

I came ready to tear them all down.

Jade stood from her chair, the wooden pegs scratching the floor as she shoved it backward. "The Paragon will come," she repeated. Her voice was so strong, it echoed off the stone walls around us. "They want to use me for my power and kill me. You don't know me. You have no reason to believe in me. But I will tell you this..." She glanced at me before continuing, a sparkle of life twinkling in her eye. "If you stand by me—if you are willing to fight for me in the face of the Paragon—I will stop at nothing to make this the most powerful kingdom in history. How would you all feel to have a power like Malachi's? Like my own?"

The others said nothing, but I knew she had hit a soft spot. I saw the longing in their eyes.

They were men. Of course, they wanted power.

"Then it seems we are on the same page," I added. "Let's eat."

# CHAPTER 18
# *Jade*

I ATE UNTIL I WAS SURE THE STITCHING ON MY CORSET WOULD BURST open. After the initial discussion, nobody seemed to question what I was doing in court. For the most part, a few suspicious glances were the only sign of questioning coming from the other members.

Malachi explained the process of the sacrifice and the details of what the Paragon wanted to do with me. It took a while to convince everyone of the prophecy, but once Malachi had explained it fully, they didn't question it. I wasn't sure they were willing to jump in front of an arrow for me, but at least they were listening.

That was a start.

We stayed there for hours. Discussions of politics turned into old memories of battle and war. Bickering turned to friends reliving decades of life together.

Malachi leaned across the table, arguing to Eli about who could shoot an arrow further.

I took the moment to sneak away, out of the dwindling crowd of the ballroom and into the halls of the castle.

Somehow, the night had actually been enjoyable. Watching Malachi command the room as King of Rewyth warmed a place in my soul that I didn't know had chilled over.

I walked through the dark castle, turning the hall to my bedroom.

"Miss me?" a voice rang out in the darkness.

I spun around to find Kara walking toward me. "Not really, no. Although by the looks of you stalking me, it seems as though you certainly missed me."

"That's too bad," she spat. "Because I've been waiting to see you again. I wasn't so sure I ever would after you left the first time."

"You mean after you conspired with Esther to kill me?"

She only shrugged. I never found out how much she actually knew about Malachi's brothers working with Esther, but Kara meant nothing to me. She was an annoying fly that needed to get out of my way.

I turned to walk away from her, but she was in front of me in an instant. Even as a woman, her fae speed was shocking.

"What do you want, Kara?"

She smiled. "The peacemaker, huh?" she teased. "It must feel nice knowing you're not just a stupid little human anymore."

I tried to push past her. She blocked me.

"Trust me," I warned her. "You don't want to do this. And I'm not just a peacemaker, I'm your queen, in case you forgot."

A growl of anger escaped her, and before I knew what was happening, she had me pinned to the wall.

My power flared.

"Malachi might think you're special," she hissed, "but you will never be anything more than human scum."

My power flared again, and I didn't fight it this time. A burst of light flashed through the dark hallway.

Kara screamed.

When I opened my eyes, she was cowering away on the floor, crawling backward.

I knelt next to her. "Next time you threaten me," I whispered in her ear, "I'll kill you."

## CHAPTER 19
# Jade

"It's beautiful," Tessa whispered, staring in awe at the gorgeous greenery around us. I knew she would like it here. The lagoon had a certain presence of peace that instantly made us feel calm.

I still remembered the first time Adeline brought me here. I thought the exact same thing. Rewyth wasn't this nasty, criminal hole in the dirt like we all wanted it to be.

Rewyth was beautiful. Nature flowed in and out like breath. I looked around us, admiring all of the changes that had grown and bloomed since I had last been here.

One could spend days in this lagoon and still not appreciate its beauty in entirety.

"It is, isn't it?" I asked.

"You said you saw a...a..."

"Tiger," I finished for her. "And I didn't just see one. It attacked me while I was swimming right here in the lagoon."

Tessa stared at me, eyes wide, like I was the most interesting person alive. She used to look at me with that same look when we were younger. She used to look at me like I was...*special*. Like I meant something to her.

I missed that look.

"I was fine after Malachi stepped in," I added, "besides the nasty cut on my leg."

I lifted up my leg to show her the scar.

"Saints," she mumbled.

I smacked her arm lightly. "Hey! Who said you could start saying things like that?"

"Please," she added, turning back to look into the deep blue lagoon. "I spend my days with father. I hear more cursing than the insides of a tavern."

It was a joke; I knew it was. Yet still, something deep in my chest twisted.

Tessa was my baby sister. She wasn't supposed to experience this harshness.

I did that so she didn't have to. I took on all of that so she didn't have to.

Tessa sat on the ground, dangling her feet into the blue water of the lagoon. "So... I guess it's really not so bad here."

"No," I added, sitting next to her and dipping my own bare feet into the cool water. "I guess it's not."

"You seem happier," she said without looking at me.

What was I supposed to say to that? *Was* I happier? I was nothing when I lived at home. I was Tessa's provider, and I was the beating bag when my father came home drunk, but I had no future. No prospects. No life.

Here? I had a target on my back. I was married—against my will—to a king, which now made me a queen in a kingdom full of people who probably didn't give a shit if I was dead or alive.

But still. I found myself waking up every morning with a purpose. I found myself laughing, even when the dark parts of my soul told me I would never laugh again.

I found myself having hope. Which scared me more than any threat from the Paragon.

"It's...complicated," I explained.

"You can tell me, you know," she added. "I know you were the one taking care of me all those years at home, Jade. I never knew exactly how much you did for me, but I know now. I do. And I never actually thanked you for all you did."

"You don't need to thank me."

"I do, Jade. Because you didn't ask for this."

I suddenly felt the urge to throw up. No, I didn't ask for this. Not a damn thing. But I wasn't going to let Tessa take a beating from our father. I wasn't going to let her starve.

I wasn't going to let anyone who supported me get hurt.

Malachi, Adeline, Tessa. They were all my family now.

I may have gone through the deepest pits of darkness over the last few months, but I found myself with more to lose than ever before.

"I think...I think if things were different, I might actually be happy here," I admitted. *Shit. Did I really just say that to her?*

Tessa looked at me, eyes glazed over. "Me too," she added, which surprised me more than anything.

Footsteps crunched on the forest floor behind us. I tensed immediately, grabbing Tessa's arm. Adeline said this place was sacred, practically special just for her. Who else would be coming here?

"Look what we have here," a small group of fae, maybe five, approached from the brush. "Our queen and her baby sister. How sweet."

"Leave us alone," I demanded.

The fae in front, a young male by the looks of it, stopped dead in his tracks with a dramatic wave of his hands to stop the fae that walked behind him.

"Watch out," he teased. "Our queen is giving us an order. It wouldn't be polite to disobey."

Tessa tried to whisper something in my ear but I quickly shushed her.

"Stand up and get behind me," I whispered.

She did as I ordered, and the two of us stood up against the group of fae.

"What are you doing here?" I asked them, trying to make my voice as strong as possible. "What do you want?"

The leader of the group looked around and scanned the men behind him. Something about the way they looked at each other made the hair on the back of my neck stand up. "We hear you have power, human," he started. "We want to see it."

"What?" I instinctively reached back and gripped Tessa. I wasn't letting these bastards touch her.

The fae stepped forward. There were now just a few feet between us. "I said I want to see your power, human. Unless, of course, it's all fake."

"Fake? Why would I lie about having power? How would...that's ridiculous."

The fae took another step forward. I debated calling out for help, but there would be nobody around here. Everyone was inside the castle. "I don't care what it is," he said. "I just want to see it. Prove to us that you're special. You are our queen, after all."

"I don't have to prove anything to you. Alarms began shouting at me in my mind. This was bad. This was trouble.

Tessa tensed behind me. I couldn't back up anymore without pushing her into the lagoon.

"You're not *afraid*, are you?" the fae asked, taking yet another step forward.

Yes, I was afraid. Not for myself, but for Tessa.

She was brand new to this world, thrown in against her will just like I had been. She didn't need this trouble. She didn't ask for it.

"Back up," I barked, shocked at the boldness in my voice.

This only elicited a short burst of laughter from the fae and his posse.

"Malachi won't like hearing about this," I added. I hated that I had to resort to Malachi as a threat, but I'll be damned if I was going to let anyone mess with my sister. I would set my pride aside for this.

But the fae didn't even blink. "It doesn't look like your big, bad husband is anywhere in sight, now does it?" he asked.

Another step forward.

My blood was hot in my veins, beating loud in my ears.

I couldn't use my magic. Not now. Not with Tessa so close. If I hurt her...

And that was if I was even capable of wielding it right now with so much pressure.

If I lost control, I could kill us all.

"Do we have a problem here?" another voice asked from the tree line. I snapped my attention to the figure who stepped into the light.

*Adonis.*

I could have dropped to the ground with relief.

The fae in front of me backed up immediately, as did the few behind him.

"No problem," he lied. "We were just introducing ourselves to our queen. That's all."

Adonis eyed me, and I watched as his eyes flickered quickly to the tight grip I had on Tessa.

"Right," Adonis sneered, stepping forward. He seemed as calm as ever, arms lazily crossed behind his back and shoulders relaxed. "And I'm sure my brother won't appreciate hearing about this, either."

The fae mumbled a slur of words I couldn't understand.

Adonis took another step forward. "If you approach her again, it won't be me you answer to. Understand?"

"Bastard," one of the fae in the back of the group mumbled.

I tightened my grip on Tessa once more.

Adonis only laughed, low and cruel, before drawing the sword from his belt.

Tessa squealed behind me.

"Care to say that to my face?" Adonis asked.

"Five against one?" the fae in front started. "Your odds are low, Adonis. We meant no trouble."

Bullshit.

"I'll take those odds," Adonis sneered, pulling his sword into position between them.

My heart raced in my chest. I knew what I needed to do. I was the queen. I was the peacemaker. I was powerful.

I was no longer the helpless girl begging for her life.

No, I would never be that girl again.

I felt the rush of power in my body, the same way I had felt it in the dungeon with Esther. The same way I had felt it at the tithe.

I could do this. I could show them how powerful I was.

I slowly let go of Tessa, so slowly that nobody would notice, and I took a tiny step forward.

The group of fae now each had a weapon drawn, although it was clear that none of them had as extensive training as Adonis.

I stepped slowly to Adonis's side.

And I held my hands out in front of me.

"Jade," he warned, but I caught the slight hint of intrigue in his voice. He wanted me to do this, too.

I let my anger become tangible, focusing on that need for power that fueled me deep inside my soul.

I wanted them to pay. I wanted them all to pay. I could protect my own, now. I didn't need Adonis or anyone else coming to my rescue.

Before I could stop myself, my body became a rush of fire, anger, desperation, and power. A flash of light snapped before me, and I heard Tessa scream somewhere in the back of my mind.

It was a release, a release of the helplessness I was feeling, of the desperation, the embarrassment, the need for power.

I took a deep breath and opened my eyes.

The fae who had been antagonizing me was on the ground, unconscious.

I staggered backward, bumping into Adonis.

"Get out of here," he growled. "Take your sister and go."

He was lifeless, unmoving. A layer of burnt skin covered the majority of his front side. "Did I..."

"I don't know," Adonis snapped. "But you need to go. Find Malachi."

The power that I had felt seconds ago was replaced with something else, something much darker. My stomach dropped, my entire body shook with the question.

*Had I killed him?*

*Had I killed a fae?*

Tessa grabbed my hand and pulled me toward the direction of the brush, snapping me out of my trance. "We have to go, Jade," she whispered. "Come on."

I let her lead me away, but I didn't miss the desperate screams for help that came from the fae who stayed behind. And I didn't miss the way Adonis threatened them all to stay quiet about it.

He was dead. He had to be.

Nobody looked like that and survived. Not even a fae.

"Tessa, I–"

"Stop," she interrupted with a voice I had never heard her use before. "Stop whatever you're about to say. You could have just saved our lives back there, Jade."

"Is he dead?" I whispered, as if Tessa would know the answer.

She stopped walking and turned to face me, gripping me so tightly on the shoulders that pain shot down my arms. "Who cares if he's dead, Jade? He was going to hurt us!"

"I didn't mean to," I whispered. My voice cracked. "I didn't mean to hurt him, Tessa. I just wanted him to leave us alone."

"I know," she said. She let go of my arms and pulled me into a hug.

Saints, she was nearly as tall as I was. When did she get so tall?

When she pulled away, she had a small smile on her face.

"What?" I asked. What could she possibly be smiling about? Did she understand that I had just killed someone?

"You really are magic. I've heard the rumors, but I didn't believe them. I mean, our whole lives, and we didn't know!"

"I know," I responded, suddenly feeling a wave of guilt.

What I would give to go back to that naive version of us.

That version of us that only had to worry about finding food and staying away from our drunk father.

Now? The list of things to worry about never ended.

"Jade, wait up!" Adonis yelled as he caught up to us.

Tessa immediately stiffened again, taking a slight step to stand behind me.

"What do you want?" I asked.

"He's alive," Adonis said. "Barely."

I exhaled a deep breath, and my shoulders finally dropped from their tight position.

"Saints," I mumbled. "Are they pissed?"

"Don't worry about them. I let them know that was a merciful punishment for antagonizing their queen and her sister."

Okay. We were going to be okay.

"Thank you, Adonis. If you hadn't showed up..."

"You would have kicked all of their asses, I'm sure of it." I hadn't really noticed the bright green specks in Adonis's eyes before. He was nothing like Malachi, but in his own ways, he wasn't hideous. I supposed I had never really looked at him before. But now, standing before me after practically saving my life, I saw him.

"Tessa and I appreciate it," I added.

Tessa finally stepped out from behind me and looked at Adonis herself.

Adonis looked at her, too.

"Hello," he said, extending his hand. "It's nice to officially meet you, little Farrow."

Tessa took another step forward, and I watched the way her eyes flickered to his silver wings. "Hello," she said back to him, placing her tiny hand in his.

He shook it respectfully.

Saints, I must have been dreaming. Because I never would have imagined this type of interaction between either of them.

"Let's get you two back to the castle," Adonis said after dropping Tessa's hand. "I would suggest that we don't tell your husband about this, but..."

"He'll find out anyway," I finished for him. "I'll tell him. He'll take it better coming from me."

Adonis nodded in agreement, and we made our way back to the castle.

To find Malachi.

## CHAPTER 20
# Malachi

"You did *what?*"

Jade took a long, shaking breath, and began explaining once more. "I had no choice," she said, stammering and trying to breathe through her words. "I tried to control it, Mal, I swear I tried to keep it under control."

Saints, did she really think I was mad at her for using her power? Did she not understand how absolutely sexy that was?

"Jade," I said, stepping forward and grabbing her chin, forcing her to look me in the eye. "Take a deep breath."

Jade had come straight to my room to tell me. Adonis had left to walk Tessa back to her room, leaving Jade to explain the entire thing.

Jade took a long, shaking breath under my touch. "Good. Now take another one." She did. "I'm not angry," I said. "And you did nothing wrong."

She looked at me with glossy eyes. "I almost killed them, Mal. I could have killed them all!"

"But you didn't."

"But I could have!"

"Listen to me, Jade. If anyone so much as looks at you the wrong way, they should expect nothing less than death. Do you understand that?" Jade blinked, but didn't say another word. "And if I would have seen that, I would have killed them all myself. Not a single one of them would have survived for what they were about to do to you."

Jade shook her head, taking her chin out of my grip. "You don't even know what they were going to do."

"I don't care," I explained. "They wanted to see you weak. They disrespect you by challenging you, Jade, and in turn, they disrespect me. And I won't tolerate either of those things in this castle."

Jade walked over and sat on the edge of my bed. It had been so long since she had slept in this room with me, it stirred something deep inside me just seeing her sitting there.

"What if I never learn to control it?"

"You will."

"How do you know that?"

I walked over and sat next to her, keeping a safe distance between us. "Because I've been exactly where you are, Jade. I know exactly what you're feeling right now."

"Yeah, right," she scoffed. "You don't go around losing control often."

"Not anymore, but it took me decades to get here. I've lost sleep over the things I've done, Jade. I've killed hundreds of innocent people, and that wasn't all on purpose."

She finally looked at me with eyes wide. "Really?"

I nodded. "When I first discovered my power, I was a nightmare. My father practically locked me up so I would quit hurting people. It flared anytime I was angry, which, if you can imagine, was very often."

She smiled, but it didn't reach her eyes. "You don't seem to have that problem anymore," she noted.

"No. I don't."

"How many people will I kill before I learn?" she asked.

Her doe eyes were still watery, and I had to fight the urge to reach out and comfort her. "I don't know." It was an honest answer.

"I don't want to be a monster, Mal, but.."

"But?"

"But there was something about feeling that power that felt so...good. I felt powerful, Mal. They wanted to push me around and I..."

"And you stopped them."

"Yes. I stopped them. But if I would have killed him..."

"What?" I asked, pushing her even though I knew I should stop. "What would have been so bad about killing someone who wanted to hurt you?"

Jade shook her head and rubbed her hands down her face. "That's the thing, Mal. I don't know if I would have hated it...because as soon as I saw what I did, deep down, there was a small part of me somewhere that actually hoped he was dead."

I hid my smile. Jade was more like me than I had originally thought.

It's not that I wanted to kill people. Truly, I didn't. But there was something about possessing a power so strong, any enemy could be shoved to their knees before you.

It felt powerful, yes. But it felt *right*. It felt like it belonged to me. All those times where I was helpless, all those times where I could do nothing but stand and watch as my father did what he pleased.

Even though I was the King of Shadows.

No, I would never be that helpless again.

I had this power for a reason. The Saints had given it to me for a purpose, and I wasn't just going to stand by and watch injustice continue.

Yes, I killed people. Many people. Some good, some bad.

But at the end of the day, my enemies quit breathing. And that's what mattered. That's why my power rumbled in my blood.

I saw it in Jade's eyes, too. The need to right the wrongs. The need for justice. And in turn, the need for power.

"It's okay, Jade," I assured her. "There's nothing wrong with hoping your enemies are dead."

"But they were members of this kingdom. That does not make them *my* enemies."

"No?" I teased. "Because at one point, I think it sure did."

A flash of amusement flickered across her face. "I liked using my power," she said after some time. "And that scares me."

I ignored the voice in my head that screamed at me not to do this, and I slid my body closer to Jade's on the bed, grabbing hold of her arm so she looked me in the eye once more.

"Being powerful shouldn't scare you," I whispered. "It should excite you. You were made for this, Jade. I knew that the moment I saw you."

"I don't want to become like...like everyone else who put me down. Who abused their power. I don't want to be like them."

"Then don't," I said. "Become the advocate. Become the one that shows up when nobody else does. I don't know what you are, Jade, but as far as I'm concerned, you're still human. You can be *their* power. You can be *their* voice."

"The humans will never accept me again," she stated coldly. "Especially after everything that's happened."

"You don't know that," I said. "They'll love having you, Jade, because you're on their side."

"Am I?" she asked. She stood and began pacing again, this time lost in her own mind. "Am I really on their side?"

I asked her a simple question. "You're on my side, aren't you?"

Jade stopped pacing and looked at me. "I am."

I closed the distance between us, close enough that if she even took a deep breath, her chest would touch mine.

The space that lingered between us was a silent question.

"Are you with me in this, Jade?"

I could feel her emotional turmoil. Her power reacted to it, causing mine to do the same.

Jade tilted her head to meet my eyes. "I'm with you, Malachi."

"Be their queen," I pushed. "Be powerful and fearless and wild. And be *mine*."

Jade took the last step and pressed her body against mine. My power flared in reaction. Hers did, too. A small tendril of light surrounded her body.

I wasn't afraid of it, though.

Jade couldn't hurt me. I couldn't hurt her. We were made for each other.

She must have realized this, too, because her small hands found their way to my back, pulling me even closer.

"I am yours, Malachi Weyland."

# CHAPTER 21
# Jade

I HAD NEVER BEEN MORE SURE OF ANYTHING IN MY ENTIRE LIFE.

Malachi kissed me slowly, taking his time as he tasted my lips, my neck, my collarbone. His hands wandered my body and his skin created a trail of fire everywhere he touched.

Kissing him didn't feel like it had before. Malachi didn't feel like the evil fae prince who had to be gentle with this human wife. No, Malachi felt like my equal.

He *was* my equal.

I could feel my own magic rolling in excitement as I kissed him back, pushing against his body and guiding him to the bed. He let me lead him, giving me control and surrendering to my touch.

He was no longer in control of me. He was no longer the only powerful one.

Malachi was my equal in more ways than one. Our kisses grew fiercer, I grew hungrier and hungrier for more of him.

More of my match.

More of my husband.

Malachi leaned back onto the bed and pulled me on top of him. "I love you, Jade. I had no idea how much I needed you."

I kissed him again. "No more than I needed you," I replied.

*How true those words were.*

Malachi tucked his wings in and rolled us over, covering my body with his as he continued to devour my body with his hands.

I closed my eyes and let the euphoria of his touch spread over me.

I needed this for too long. I *wanted* this for too long.

Malachi's lips were hot against my neck as he pulled the shoulder of my top down, exposing more of the skin there.

It wasn't enough. I wanted to be closer to him. I wanted us to become one.

To finally be what I felt in my soul we should have been all along.

Malachi sensed this, too. His eyes locked to mine as he pulled back, just enough to slide his hands under my tunic. He paused, only for a moment, waiting for my approval.

Instead of answering with words, I pulled the rest of it up and over my head, tossing it onto the floor.

A growl of approval came from him.

Malachi was on me in an instant, covering the now exposed skin with his warm body.

He pressed against me in his large, silk bed. I could tell from his touches, his kisses that he wanted this just as badly as I did.

"I love you, Malachi," I whispered against his mouth.

Between our panting breaths and desperate touches, it wasn't long until there was nothing between us. Just our bodies together, blending in a way that lit up the darkest parts of my soul.

Malachi was mine.

I was his.

And that night, I surrendered to him fully.

# CHAPTER 22
# Malachi

"Malachi," Serefin's voice rang from outside the bedroom door, followed by a rapid knock. My eyelids shot open. "Malachi, are you in there?"

Jade stirred next to me, yanking the sheets up to her chin. My wings instinctively flared out, covering us both.

After last night, I never wanted her to leave this bed. I would never get enough of her laying next to me.

"Don't worry," I whispered. "It's just Ser." I then turned my attention to the door. It wasn't unlike him to be knocking this early. "Go away, Serefin!"

"Someone is here to see you," he persisted.

"Tell them to leave me alone," I said. I moved my hand to trace a long, delicate line down the side of Jade's perfect face. Her mouth twitched in a smile.

Serefin mumbled something I couldn't quite hear outside my door, then said, "It's the Paragon, Mal. Messengers from the Paragon are here and they're requesting to meet with you."

Jade's eyes shot back open. Any relaxation from her in that moment ripped away, like it was never there in the first place.

I couldn't deny that my heart rate sped up, too.

"Fine," I said after finding the words. "Keep them occupied. I'll be down in a moment."

I listened to his rushed footsteps as he walked away from the door, leaving Jade and I in the bedroom.

"What are they doing here?" Jade asked, sitting up in bed with a tight grip on the sheets. "What do they want? Why would they come all the way here?"

"Calm down," I said. "I'm sure it's nothing serious."

"Nothing serious?" she questioned. "How is the Paragon, our biggest enemy, by the way, showing up in our kingdom *not* serious?"

"If they wanted to cause us harm, half the kingdom would be dead by now. Trust me, Jade."

I rolled out of bed and began dressing myself, very aware of Jade's eyes watching my every move.

"Well?" I asked after a few seconds. "Are you coming?"

Her face flushed red, and she didn't say a word. She stayed put, holding the bed sheet tight to her chest. "I hate to break this to you, princess," I started, "but after last night, it's nothing I haven't seen before."

Jade rolled her eyes and threw one of the pillows at me, missing by a good foot. "Turn around," she said.

After fully dressing myself, I listened, turning around while Jade got out of my bed and got herself dressed.

I didn't stop my mind from wandering to the soft curves of her small body, and the way she felt in my arms last night. My chest warmed at the thought.

"Okay," she said, interrupting my thoughts after a few, agonizing minutes. "You can turn around now."

"Jade," I said as I turned around. "I know I said you have nothing to worry about, but I need you to listen to me."

"What's going on, Mal?"

I took a step toward her. How could I tell her, though? How could I get her to explain that I wasn't as calm as I appeared? The Paragon had haunted me for decades. If they were here, something was wrong.

Something was very wrong.

Panic threatened my senses.

What did they want? It was possible this had something to do with my new reign of Rewyth. Best case scenario, they wanted to express their condolences for my father. It was possible that they only meant to congratulate me on becoming king.

It was also possible they had heard that my human wife was actually not so ordinary, after all. Perhaps they had heard of her abilities. Did Seth turn her in? Did he go running to them about exactly what happened in Trithen?

Maybe they wanted to see her for themselves.

And that thought was the one that terrified me. The Paragon would not take Jade. They would not lay a single finger on her.

Because I knew, deep in my bones, that I would kill anyone who tried to take Jade away from me. Paragon or not.

"Tell me," she pushed. She closed the small distance between us and grabbed both of my wrists. "Tell me, Mal. What are you afraid of? What are we walking into?"

"Nothing," I lied. "It's going to be okay. I just need you to stay silent, and stay behind me. Okay? Don't trust them, whoever they are and whatever they want."

She nodded, as if she understood perfectly.

"I love you, Jade," I said, pressing a kiss on her forehead. "I'm not letting anyone hurt you."

"I know," she whispered back. "I know you won't."

I slid my hand into hers, and together, we began walking downstairs to meet our fate.

The castle looked different this early in the morning. It wasn't the same hustle of people that frequently filled these halls. No, the halls were practically empty, aside from a few servants who scurried in the shadows of the morning sun.

It was quiet. Saints, one might even say the castle was peaceful this early in the morning. That alone was an eerie thought, though, because I knew exactly how cruel this place really was. I didn't think any amount of quietness could make it truly peaceful.

Especially when I knew what awaited us.

Jade's hand was an anchor in mine, bringing me back to the moment. She had no idea what was awaiting her. Neither did I, though. Not really. It was possible that the Paragon had changed in the decades that I hadn't heard from them. Maybe they had changed their ways now. Maybe they ditched their methods of violence and blood for more peaceful methods.

I almost laughed at the thought. No, they most certainly hadn't changed for the better.

I pushed open the front doors to the castle, and my black wings immediately flared outward on instinct.

I tugged Jade's hand slightly, pulling her closer to my side.

Three black-hooded figures stood ahead of me, accompanied by Serefin, who was trying his best to distract them. Dozens of guards covered the surrounding area.

As if that would stop them.

"Ah," one of the figures acknowledged, stepping forward and pulling the hood from his head. "Here is our king."

He lowered his head just an inch. I knew that was the closest thing to a bow I was going to receive. I nodded in acknowledgement, and the figure returned to standing.

"I am told that you wish to speak with me," I stated. I didn't move from my position near the door.

The three guests looked at each other before the leader answered, "We have something we wish to discuss with you, yes. Is there somewhere more...private we can speak?"

I rolled my eyes. "If you have something to say to me, you can say it here. Everyone here can be trusted."

"Everyone?" he said. His dark eyes moved from me to Jade, who was now holding my arm.

My blood ran hot in my veins. "Yes," I barked.

"Fine," he said. "I suppose there is no harm in speaking of this here, then."

"Go on," I pushed.

"We heard word that you may have broken a treaty with the humans."

I waited for him to say more, but when nothing came, my jaw nearly dropped. That's what they came all this way for? "We broke no treaty."

"Well, we've heard otherwise. We've also heard whispers of something else happening over here in Rewyth."

There it was. The truth behind it all. "Really?" I asked, keeping my voice as flat as possible. "And what could that possibly be?"

*Say it.* I thought. *Say it right now, and let's get it over with.*

The other two visitors slowly removed the hoods from their own heads.

My power rumbled within my veins. I was ready for a fight.

Jade tensed at my side. I knew she was ready, too.

"Why don't you tell us?" the leader asked. "Something on your conscience, King?"

I watched as Serefin's hand moved to his sword.

Him and each of the other guards.

"Have you heard of the peacemaker?" the leader asked when I said nothing. I knew he saw the threat against him. Part of me wanted to test him, to see if he had any power that matched my own.

Or that matched Jade's.

Would the Paragon send ungifted messengers? Knowing that they were going to pose a threat to us?

Maybe they wanted to push us. Maybe they wanted to keep pushing and pushing until they saw what Jade was really made of.

"Peacemaker?" I repeated. "Hmm, I can't really say that I have."

"Interesting," the leader stepped forward, only half a step. "Because we have resources telling us that the peacemaker is alive, and that she looks terribly similar to your human wife."

My jaw tightened. "That's quite a statement."

"It is, indeed."

"Is that the reason you came all the way here?" I asked, "To inquire on the similarities between my wife and this said peacemaker?"

The leader smiled. "Not quite. You see, the Paragon, as you may know, is in charge of many things. One of these things is maintaining the power balance amongst fae, witches, and humans."

I could feel Jade's anger rising beside me.

The man continued, "If the rumors we have been hearing are true, your wife could greatly upset this balance."

"Weird," I chirped. "I wasn't aware that the mighty Paragon was in the business of listening to petty gossip."

"When that gossip involves the possible downfall of our system, we listen."

Their words lingered in the air, landing the final blow to the real reason they showed up.

I let go of Jade's hand and took one step forward. Everyone's eyes glued onto me. "Do we have a problem here, gentleman?"

The three of them stood there, staring at me. They knew the answer. I knew what they were going to say.

"We've had a problem since the day your wife was born, King Malachi."

Jade exhaled loudly behind me. "I would think very carefully about what you say next. This is my kingdom, and you're threatening my queen."

"We didn't come here to threaten anyone. We came here to see if the rumors were true."

My power ran hot in my body, ready to take these men down with a single thought. "How exactly do you plan on doing that?"

A single threatening word from them, and my power would wipe them out. Their bodies would never find their way back to the Paragon.

"We were hoping you would do us the small favor of exhibiting your wife's powers upon our request."

I laughed. I *actually laughed*. Were they serious?

"And why would I do that? So you could rip her away from here and take her back to your leader? Or is it for your own sick interests?"

"It's in your best interest."

"Really? How is that possibly in my best interest?"

"Mal," Jade warned from behind me. I ignored her. How dare these three march in here and demand to see Jade's power? Did they really think I would roll over and let them do whatever they wanted?

This was my kingdom. It was *my* job to keep the people of Rewyth safe.

Including Jade.

I found myself wishing Esther were here.

But I quickly shook it off.

"Look," the leader said as he lowered his voice. "I understand that you're trying to protect her. But we have very strict orders to discover if your human wife really possesses power or not. We can't leave here without seeing her gifts."

"And if we refuse to cooperate?"

"Then we won't be the ones coming down here next time. You'll be hearing from Silas."

The blood rushed from my face. *Silas.*

"What did you just say?" I asked. My fists clenched at my sides.

"If we don't deliver news about your wife, Silas will come here himself. And he won't be so peaceful."

"You call showing up here and threatening my wife *peaceful?*"

"We wish no harm on your wife, King Malachi. We only wish to discover the truth."

"The truth? You're looking for the truth of an ancient prophecy that could be complete bullshit, and you're hoping to find the truth from my wife?"

"Don't make this harder than it needs to be."

I looked at Serefin, who only clenched his jaw in response. *Get ready.* "This is *my* kingdom," I declared. "I will not say that again. I plan on making this very difficult for you. If you want something from me or my wife, you'll have to take it yourselves. I'm not giving you anything."

The three men looked at their surroundings, likely sizing us up to see how easily they could take us.

*Not happening.*

The man in front opened his black cloak and reached inside. I half expected a rush of magic to take us out. They were from the mighty Paragon, after all. But instead, he only pulled out a small dagger.

Every guard in the vicinity pulled weapons of their own. I backed up, reclaiming my spot next to Jade.

Although I was certain that not a single one of my guards would let these fools touch her.

"Really?" I asked. "You come here with nothing but a handheld weapon?"

"Like I said. I don't intend on making this harder than it needs to be."

The three of them spread out, just slightly. Enough to let me know that they were actually considering making a move.

"Jade, go inside," I demanded.

"Sending her inside isn't going to stop us."

"Is that another threat?"

"It's a warning, King Malachi. Silas gave us these orders. You know what that means."

I listened as Jade's footsteps grew quieter and quieter as she retreated into the castle behind me. I thanked the Saints that she listened this time. Being in the castle wouldn't make her safe, but she didn't need to be near this.

"Leave now," I warned. "That's a warning. And it's the only one you'll get."

"You know we can't do that."

"You know I'll kill you if you don't."

"I know you're a powerful man," he spoke, spinning his weapon in his hand. "I know you have a special gift, King Malachi. But you know that Silas won't allow us to return with nothing. So this battle is a chance I'm willing to put my wages on."

My heart began pounding in my chest. Not in a nervous way. I knew this would barely be a fight. These three would just be three more bodies on my list of casualties.

For Jade, I would gladly add them.

For Jade, I would do whatever it took.

Serefin and Doromir stepped around the back of the group. The three visitors were now surrounded.

There was no going back.

The leader turned to the other two and whispered, "Go find the girl."

And those four words were enough to start a war.

"Kill them all," I ordered.

My power flared in their direction. I allowed the tendrils of magic to drop all three of them to the ground. The ones that moved to follow Jade were now clutching and clawing at their insides, screeching in indescribable pain.

They deserved worse. They deserved much worse than pain.

"Serefin," I ordered, "end it."

Serefin's sword came down on the left one's neck, severing it with one motion.

One threat down.

The leader began groaning, clearly trying to speak. I pulled back my strong tendrils of power, just enough so I could hear his last words.

"They'll come for her," he said through gritted teeth, still in pieces on the ground. "They'll come for her and you know it. She'll never be safe."

"Why?" I demanded. "What will they do with her?"

He laughed, but pain laced every sound. "They'll do what they wanted to do with you. They'll use her power for themselves. The balance must be maintained."

Serefin's sword came down once more, and the leader flinched as his last shred of hope died along with his last companion.

"We'll kill anyone who tries to take her," I declared.

I didn't wait for Serefin to kill him. I pulled my own sword from my hip and brought it down, hard, on the last of our unwanted guests.

When I finally looked up, everyone was staring at me. Watching me. Waiting for our next move.

"Keep this to ourselves," I said to the guards. "Serefin, begin preparing our army. This is not the only time we'll be hearing from the Paragon."

"They'll come for her," Serefin replied. Something harsh crossed his features. That was rare for Serefin. "We need to protect Jade. It's too dangerous for her here."

I considered his words. "Jade's been running for a long time, Ser. This is her home now. Spread the word. If anyone approaches this kingdom with intent to harm my wife, they will be struck down on sight."

# CHAPTER 23
## Jade

Malachi stormed inside and, without looking at me, grabbed me from where I had been listening just within the castle doors and began pulling me along with him.

"Malachi," I said, careful with my words. He had just killed them. The messenger from the Paragon, he killed them all. Adrenaline buzzed through my body. "They're coming for me, aren't they?"

"Nobody's coming for you, Jade."

We passed dozens of guards in the halls, everyone now moving with a certain seriousness that I hadn't noticed before.

Would they stand for me? Would they protect me? Lay down their own lives for me?

"Mal, maybe I should–"

"No," I interrupted. The grip on his arm tightened as he pulled me into an emptier hallway. "Don't even say what I know you're about to say."

"It's just that if we–"

"Stop!" he argued. Malachi spun me in his grip, moving to press my back lightly against the stone wall of the hallway. "I'm going to say this once, Jade, so you better be listening. You're not going anywhere. I'm not letting anyone use you for this stupid prophecy, okay? Esther can't have you, the Paragon can't have you. Saints, *nobody* can have you. Is that clear?"

My stomach flipped in excitement. Malachi protecting me was nothing new, but it still shocked me that he was willing to give up everything for me. A *human*.

His wife. His queen. The peacemaker.

I stopped myself from thinking anything more. At the end of the day, I was still a human.

Malachi's eyes scanned my face, searching for any type of reaction.

So I answered in a way that words couldn't. I moved my hands to his face, gripping tightly and turning his head so his eyes were level with mine. "If you are willing to risk your kingdom, your reign, and your people for me," I paused, staring into those deep forests of eyes, "I won't stop you. But I don't think I'm worth saving, Mal. It's too much trouble–"

Malachi shut me up with a kiss.

His mouth moved against mine, the warmth from him moving across my entire body. His hands slipped around my waist, holding me tightly to him as he continued to kiss me.

Was this how it was going to be from now on? Desperate kisses in the shadows of the castle?

When he pulled away, his eyes were serious. "You are my queen, Jade Weyland. I will protect you with my life."

My heart erupted in a love I could not even fathom.

"Then I suppose we should talk about how in the Saints we plan on defeating the Paragon."

He grabbed my hand and gently began leading me down the hallway, in the direction of his bedroom.

Or was it our bedroom now?

"Before we do that," he started. "I think it's time I tell you a story."

"I'm not sure now is really the best time for st–"

"A story about my time with the Paragon."

In the peaceful hideaway of the bedroom, Malachi began from the beginning. He told me about when the Paragon came to him for the very first time, demanding that they were required to observe exactly how powerful each new gift was.

And Malachi's gift was particularly impressive.

Malachi was honored at first. Honored that such a powerful entity wanted to know him. Wanted to see what he could do.

He had no problem showing them what his power could do.

It was around that time, however, that his own father also began learning about just how powerful he really was. His father discovered that Malachi could become much more than a boy.

He was no longer just a son, no. With the expansion of his gift, and with years of training, Malachi became the most powerful weapon in all of Rewyth.

This attracted more and more attention to him, specifically from the Paragon. They tried building a genuine relationship at first. They explained that they would help Malachi, that they would take him away from his father who clearly didn't have his best interests in mind and they would harbor his talents like they do for other gifted individuals.

Malachi's eyes lit up as he explained all this. This was a side of him that I hadn't seen before. A side of him that I never even knew existed.

"I trusted them," he explained. "I was young and naive and I wanted a way out, so I trusted them."

Pain flashed across his features.

I reached across the short distance between us and grabbed his hand, holding tight. "And they betrayed you?" I asked.

"Not at first, no," he started. "At the beginning, they upheld every promise they had made. I packed my things and moved to the mountains, so deep that even my father could not find me if he sent an entire army after me. The mountains are a different place. They're secluded and hidden from all prying eyes."

The smile that flickered across his face was one of both joy and grief.

"But that didn't last," he explained. "Silas was the one who took me in. He nurtured me. I was so young, this was decades ago now."

My blood froze in my veins.

"Silas?" I repeated. "Why haven't you mentioned him before?"

Mal's eyes darkened. "He wasn't worth mentioning."

"And he's the leader?" I asked. "Of the Paragon?"

Malachi took a deep breath before answering, "Yes. He is. We were friends for a while, believe it or not. He guided me while I became powerful. He helped me realize who I could be in this world. But that was before I decided to leave. That was before I learned just how much they wanted from me."

I shook my head. "I have a hard time believing the Paragon, being as power hungry as they are, enjoyed the fact that you wanted to leave."

"They tried to convince me to stay. They offered me a home there, and a position in the Paragon. But I was the heir to Rewyth. I had duties back in the castle. After years, it was time for me to return home."

He stayed quiet for a few moments.

"Do you think Silas will try to kill me?" I asked, finally speaking the questions we had both been thinking.

Malachi looked me in the eyes when he answered, "If killing you will give him more power, I have no doubt he'll take the chance."

*Great.*

"We'll prepare for a full-on attack from the Paragon," he said. "I'll reach out to our allies and see who will come to our aid. We won't let them take you, Jade."

"Rewyth really has allies?" I asked. "I guess after what happened in Trithen I didn't think that was possible."

Malachi smiled. "My father had many enemies, but it's time I start cleaning up his mess. If it's true that you are the secret to this prophecy of power, they'll come to our aid."

"Thank you," I said. "For doing this. For caring."

Malachi reached up and tucked a stray piece of hair behind my ear. "You didn't ask for any of this, Jade," he stated. "To be honest, I'm not even sure how you're still standing."

"It's not without difficulty," I replied. Tessa's words rang loudly in my mind.

*Do you feel lucky to be alive?*

## CHAPTER 24
# *Malachi*

OVER THE NEXT THREE WEEKS, HUNDREDS OF FAE CAME TO OUR AID. I was surprised at first, I'll admit, that anyone was willing to come help us. It took days for our messengers to get back to me, and by then I was almost certain that everyone would decline our call for help.

But one by one, armies began showing up.

We filled every possible room in the castle, and the overflow of men camped out in the nearby fields.

We were a force to be reckoned with.

I stood on the tallest balcony of our castle, taking in the view of hundreds of allies when the door opened behind me.

I spun around, half-hoping it would be Jade.

*Eli.*

Eli had certainly kept his distance from me since Fynn's death. I didn't mind it. It only meant that I could keep pushing away these tough conversations.

"Brother," I greeted.

He came to stand next to me, looking out onto our kingdom. "You've had quite the turnout," he stated.

"I can't say I'm not surprised."

"New king. New rule. New hope," he said. Something in the way he said *hope* made me tense.

Did Eli still have hope? After Fynn's death, did he believe in a better world for us?

"How have you been, brother?" I asked.

Eli only shook his head. "I'm surviving. Trying to find the reason for all of this."

My heart twisted. "It will get better, Eli," I said. "I promise you it gets easier."

"How long did it take for you?" he asked. The words shocked me, but I knew he was coming from a place of genuine curiosity. "How long did it take for you to be okay after your previous wives died?"

I tried not to look shocked. It wasn't every day that my past wives were mentioned. Before Jade, I wasn't sure a single day would go by that I didn't think of them.

Now, though, they were only distant memories.

It's both relieving and heart-wrenching, that time can wipe away memories and emotions piece by piece.

Day by day.

"A while," I answered. "It took a long time."

I didn't dare compare my previous companions with the relationship that Eli had with his twin brother Fynn.

My wives had each been different in indescribable ways. Each of them human, each of them fragile, yet they all held a different place in my heart.

Especially when each of them were slaughtered while I stood by and watched.

I hadn't cared about any of them like I had cared about Jade.

Eli and Fynn had been inseparable since birth.

I could still hear Eli's scream that day when he found Fynn dead on the battlefield.

"We'll make them pay," I said, not able to find any other words. "We'll make them all pay for what they have taken from us."

Eli placed his hand on my shoulder. It was the closest thing to comfort that any of my brothers had ever shown me. "I believe in you, Malachi. I know you'll protect us. I know you'll make them suffer for what they have done."

"Thank you, Eli."

He turned to leave, but stopped before opening the door. "Someone is here to see you. They're waiting in your private dining room."

And then he was gone.

I waited for a few moments, taking in the view of the sun setting in the distance, casting a red glow on everything beneath me.

This was my kingdom. My responsibility.

Eli was right. Together, we would make them pay.

We would make them all pay.

When I arrived in the dining room, I was greeted with a large hug. "Carlyle," I breathed a sigh of relief that I was being greeted by a friend, not an enemy. "It's nice to see you."

Carlyle pulled away and clapped me on the shoulder. "It's been too long, friend. I only wish we were coming together in better circumstances."

I motioned to the table, and we both took a seat.

"When I heard you were being threatened by the Paragon..."

He didn't have to finish the sentence. He knew just how brutal the wrath of the Paragon could be.

"Thank you for coming," I said. "After everything my father did, I wasn't expecting much."

Carlyle nodded, words unsaid passed between us.

When I first met Carlyle, I was on strict orders from my father. My father wanted what he always wanted—power. It didn't take me more than a few minutes with Carlyle, though, to understand that he wasn't the monster my father had tried to convince me he was.

Carlyle was a kind man and a gracious leader. I didn't kill him that day, like my father ordered.

Instead, Carlyle and I became allies.

And it appeared as though he was returning the favor.

"I've brought my best men, but I hope for your wife's sake you have a plan on how you're going to take on the Paragon. They're the Paragon for a reason, and it's not because they are weak or easily defeated."

"Trust me, I know. But at the end of the day, everyone has a weakness. I just need to find theirs."

"The Paragon doesn't show weakness easily. You know this more than anyone."

"I'm desperate, Carlyle. If I can't find a way to stop them when they come, they'll take her."

Carlyle's eyes darkened. I didn't expect him to fully understand the situation I was in, but he was a caring person. Perhaps he would have an idea.

"You have an impressive amount of manpower here, Malachi, but is that enough? What happens when they come at you with power? It's been years since you've last seen them. They could be much stronger now..."

"Or weaker."

"I suppose that is a possibility."

We both took a long breath. I leaned back in my chair, running my hands across my face. *Think, Malachi.* There had to be an easier way out of this mess.

Carlyle set both of his hands on the table. "I don't mean to be presumptuous, Malachi, but I've heard whispers of your mother. And I've heard she's here in this kingdom."

"She's lucky she's still alive after what she did to me."

"Maybe. But instead of rotting away somewhere under our feet, you could use her."

I shook my head. I would be lying if the thought hadn't crossed my mind. But Esther couldn't be trusted. I felt no remorse about locking her in the dungeons. She deserved much worse. "It's too risky," I admitted. "She turned on me once, what's to say she won't do it again?"

"If the witch faces death," Carlyle said, dropping his voice to a low whisper, "she will have no choice but to comply."

"It's not that simple."

"Isn't it?" Carlyle pushed. "Right now, it's looking like you need all of the help you can get. You're a new king, that makes you weak enough. You have your power, and you have men that are willing to fight for you. But the Paragon will come with every ounce of magic they've got. It's in your best interest to do the same."

"She tried to kill me, Carlyle. Her own son."

"We've all done insane things to survive."

I let his words sink in, and I tried to fight the wave of anger that came from listening to them. Yes, we have all done insane things to survive. I couldn't even begin to count the number of times I had done something desperate to get out of dying. Holding a blade to my wife's throat being one of them.

But Esther wanted Jade's power. Esther was loyal to her bloodline of witches, even with them dead. She did not want us fae to fulfill this prophecy and become the most powerful with our magic.

She did not want magic returned to the fae.

But the only other option was the Paragon using the power. And they already had enough.

"I suppose it's worth a shot," I finally admitted through gritted teeth. "But she's been in the dungeon for weeks now. I can't imagine she's much stronger than a human at this point."

"A weak witch with some power is better than nothing."

Saints, he was right.

"You don't happen to know of any powerful witch bloodlines that would be willing to come to our aid, do you?" I asked, only half-joking.

Carlyle smiled, the wrinkles around his eyes multiplying. "If I did, we wouldn't hear the word Paragon ever again."

# CHAPTER 25
# Jade

"JUST SIT DOWN AND SHUT UP, OKAY?" I HISSED TO MY FATHER, motioning for him to sit at the large wooden table that stretched the length of the busy dining hall.

He nodded and stepped over the bench, Tessa sliding in next to him. It had been too long since the three of us had eaten together, and with everything going on, I wasn't sure I was going to get another chance.

Besides, after the last time my father and I encountered each other in this dining hall, I felt the need to redeem myself.

We could behave, couldn't we? For one meal, we could behave like a normal family for *one* meal.

*Normal family*. I almost laughed at the thought. I sat at the bench opposite of Tessa and my father, and began eating my meal in silence. My sister did the same. It was our father who sat there, hardly moving and staring at everyone around us.

"Are you going to eat?" I asked him after a few minutes of silence. "Your food will get cold."

"I find it hard to eat when we are surrounded by enemies," he mumbled, hardly audible.

"Father," Tessa warned in a low voice. I held my hand up to stop her.

After coming moments away from erupting into ash the last time my father and I fought, I was trying my best to keep my temper under control. He didn't need to fear me, and he certainly didn't need to fear the others.

"These aren't our enemies, father," I explained calmly, looking into his bloodshot eyes. "They're here to fight for me."

He shrugged uncomfortably. It was hard not to see my father as the weak and confused man he really was. Hidden beneath the decades of losing himself in ale, was a simple man who wanted to survive.

A man who had lived a terrible, difficult life.

A man who had lost his wife.

Who had nothing to live for anymore.

When he wasn't running around creating a list of enemies for himself, he was simply trying to live for the next day.

"For you?" he questioned. "They're fighting for you?"

"Yes, father," I said, taking another bite of my stew. "They tell me I am special, remember? I have a special power and people are trying to take it. So they are helping me. They're protecting me."

This was the sixth time I had to explain that to him. The second and the third time, I was annoyed. But not anymore.

He still looked confused at my words, but didn't push the conversation any more. "So," I started, desperate for any sort of conversation, "have you two been missing home?"

"Are you kidding?" Tessa replied with a sudden burst of energy. "You'll have to drag my dead body back there. I should have been living here all along!"

My father snorted in response.

"Wow," I started. "That's pretty much the exact opposite of the response I was expecting from you."

Tessa shoved her mouth with another bite of food, barely swallowing before adding, "I can't remember the last time I was hungry. Seriously, I think I've eaten more here in Rewyth than I have my entire life."

I smiled at my sister, but my stomach flipped. It was a joke, but it held a wicked truth.

Tessa was being taken care of here for maybe the first time in her entire life. "Yeah," I responded. "I know how you feel."

My father dropped his fork and shoved his tray away from him with a grunt.

I was all for keeping my temper cool, but he had no right to get angry over that.

He wasn't there for us. No matter what the reasons were, and no matter how messed up a man he had become, he didn't take care of us.

*I* did. *I* fed our family. *I* watched over Tessa. *I* put clothes on our backs. He wasn't allowed to get angry over that truth.

"Something to add, father?" I asked. I knew I was pushing him, but that dark shadow deep inside of me couldn't stop myself. "Because if you have something to say, you should just say it."

Tessa's eyes dropped to her food. She had always been the non-confrontational one of us.

"You two act like I am nothing in this family," my father whispered.

Normally, I would have snapped right back. But Tessa looked at me with a surprise in her eyes that set me back.

Because we both knew that was the most *real* sentence my father had said in years.

"We did a lot without you, I didn't think that was a secret," I said, barely a whisper.

"And you think I was off having a great time? I suffered just as much as you two, if not more so. I suffered every single day!"

Tessa and I didn't say a word.

My father placed both of his boney, frail hands on the table. They trembled.

"I am not a blind man. I know you two have not had a great life. But neither have I. I have–"

He paused to take a deep, long breath. I could have sworn he began blinking back tears.

Tessa's foot tapped against mine under the table.

"We love you, father," Tessa caved after a few seconds. She placed a hand on his shoulder and leaned in slightly. My father didn't back away from it. "We don't say it enough, but it's true."

My father smiled, but his eyes didn't meet mine.

I unclenched my jaw, realizing it had been clenched the entire time he was talking.

I wasn't going to repeat Tessa. I didn't need to. I can't remember my father ever saying he loved me. I can't remember ever saying it to him, either.

I wasn't about to start now.

"Well," he said, clearing his throat. "I'm exhausted. I should get to bed."

Without looking at either of us, our father stood from the table and walked away. Neither of us followed after him.

"That was weird," I mumbled to Tessa.

"He's been...different lately," she explained. "He hasn't been drinking. He's been talking more. Screaming less."

"That doesn't sound like him."

"No," she said. "It doesn't. Maybe he's realizing that this place is better for him than he originally thought."

Tessa looked at me with more hope than I had in my entire body. "Yeah," I agreed, knowing it was not likely that my father would ever change. "It's possible."

We returned to our meals, although after the conversation we just had, I wasn't hungry in the slightest.

"Who died?" Adeline's voice caused me to drop my fork. She slapped her tray down on the wooden table and slid into the bench beside me, sitting so close that her arm brushed up beside mine.

"What?" I asked.

"You two look like you're mourning a death. What's with the sad faces?"

"Nothing," Tessa and I said in unison.

"Well, fix those sad faces," she insisted. "Because we're going to have some fun."

"What are you talking about?" I asked.

"We're doing something for ourselves," she stated. "We're heading into town. Let's go now before I change my mind."

Tessa's face lit up in a mixture of excitement and fear that matched my own. "Town?" she questioned.

Adeline nodded with a mischievous twinkle in her eye. "Follow me."

I didn't hesitate for a second. Tessa and I practically jumped from the table and followed Adeline out of the castle.

She led us past the hidden lagoon in the woods and through a long and skinny dirt path, sometimes walking so quickly we had to jog to catch up. "Are you sure this is safe?" I questioned as we ventured further. "I mean, is it common to head into town whenever you want?"

Adeline flipped her long hair over her shoulder. "It's plenty safe," she answered, "but I wouldn't necessarily go telling Malachi about this little adventure. You know how he gets."

Tessa's eyes darted between Adeline and me, but she didn't say anything.

"And you go into town frequently? What if someone recognizes us?" Adeline didn't answer. Instead, she kept walking forward, further and further down the path. A few moments later, Adeline ducked off the path and into the tree line. "Adeline!" I hissed. "Adeline, where are you going?" I grabbed Tessa's arm and stayed with her on the path.

"Relax," she said as she stepped back into view a few seconds later. "We need these."

She passed us each a hooded cloak. "Seriously?" I asked. "You just hide these in the trees?"

"Where else am I going to hide them?" she questioned.

I helped Tessa adjust her cloak before covering my own head. After what happened with Kara in the hallway, I was fairly certain I could defend myself against a fae, but an entire town full of them? That would be a death wish.

We had to be cautious. With a target on my back, nowhere would be safe.

Adeline led us onward, through the trees and on the same narrow path, until the trees grew thinner and thinner.

Squinting ahead, I could make out the rough shape of small stone buildings. "Is that it?" I asked.

"It sure is!"

"It's smaller than I imagined."

Adeline laughed. "Trust me, it's much bigger once you're down there."

We continued walking with Tessa trailing silently behind us. I could feel the excitement buzzing off of her.

The stone buildings became bigger and bigger, and in just a few minutes, the streets of Rewyth became clear.

They were no longer smaller than I had imagined. The buildings themselves may not have been castle-like, but each fae we passed practically dripped in jewels and riches.

The town was magnificent.

I didn't let go of Tessa's hand, even as she gawked at each fancy new item we passed.

"Here we are," Adeline said, stepping into a doorway of one of the shops.

"Where are we?" I asked. "What is this place?"

The three of us walked inside, and the door closed behind us with the ring of a small bell.

A woman stepped forward with her gaze locked on Adeline. Her eyes held a certain warmth that instantly made me feel comfortable.

"This is Vespera. She's my favorite dressmaker in the kingdom. We're dressing up today ladies, my treat. The coronation ball is tomorrow and we'll be looking our very best!"

Tessa squealed in excitement as the realization hit her. I reminded myself to stay calm. "We're going to a ball? And you're buying us dresses?"

"No, silly," Vespera answered for her. She was a thin, pale fae with slender wings.

She had numerous piercings accenting her face, and her hand was thin as she stuck it out to me to shake. "We're making them from scratch."

Breath escaped me. I could have never dreamed of having my own dress back home, much less having one made for me.

Living in Rewyth, I had been given many dresses to wear. But none of them felt like mine. None of them felt like they were for me.

I knew Tessa felt the same way. Dresses meant much more to her than they meant to me. They always had. For her, this would be a dream.

This would be everything.

Adeline must have known that, too. This would be a lifelong memory for Tessa, even if she had to return back to the human lands once this was all over.

"Thank you, Adeline," I said, motioning to Tessa as she began running her hands over the different fabrics that lined the wall. "This is too kind."

Adeline only nodded. "What are friends for? Besides, I think your sister could use some distraction."

My heart tightened watching Tessa's entire spirit shine. She had never asked for much. I knew she always wanted more when we lived back home, but she knew. She knew I was doing everything I could. She also knew that new dresses, warm shoes, or a nice coat were out of the picture for us.

But this? I could give her this. I could let Adeline do this for her.

For us.

We spent hours in that shop. Tessa tried every single fabric combination, and Vespera eagerly debated which colors looked best with her light skin and caramel hair.

Adeline and I sat back and watched, laughing at each time Vespera stuck her with a sewing pin.

It wasn't too long until Tessa stood in front of us with a full, brand-new dress.

"You look beautiful, Tessa," I said as I gawked at her.

Tears welled in her eyes as she stared at her own reflection. She looked stunning. It was a shame what life could do to such raw magnificence.

She looked like royalty.

In another life, she would have been. I knew it.

"I can't believe I get to keep this," Tessa whispered. "I can't believe this is mine."

"You deserve it," Adeline spoke up. "That dress belongs on someone as beautiful as you. And now you'll have something to wear to the coronation ball!"

Tessa glowed.

We spent the next few hours running through the town, ignoring each of our problems. It felt nice, pretending to be three normal girls in Rewyth.

Tessa loved every minute of it.

But like all good things in my life, it had to end.

Later that night, after the three of us snuck back unnoticed, I crawled into my warm, comfortable bed. The memory of seeing Tessa smile at herself in that dress replayed in my mind until I drifted off to sleep.

*Cold, scrawny hands gripped my wrists. My eyes shot open in the darkness, and I found Esther kneeling before me.*

*"Esther?" I questioned. "What are you doing here?"*

*Her long white hair looked cleaner than the last time I saw her. She appeared healthier, too. "We need to talk."*

*I realized I was no longer lying in my bed. I wasn't in my bedroom at all, actually. I was in the dungeons, where Esther should have been chained up.*

*But she wasn't.*

*"Talk about what?" I asked, pushing myself up from the cold stone ground. How did I get down here?*

*"The Paragon is coming for you, child." Her voice grew tight with desperation.*

*"I know that. It's not exactly a secret."*

*"I told you I could help you get out of this. I can."*

*"Okay? Are you finally willing to share what you know?" She hesitated. "Why are you so afraid of telling me?" I pushed. She had been keeping information from Malachi and I ever since we left Trithen. It was time for her to start talking.*

*"I'm not afraid of you," she defended, "but Malachi won't like what I'm going to say."*

*I was officially interested. What was Esther so afraid of telling Malachi? What did she know?*

*"Whatever it is, he'll be happy if it saves my life. Just tell me, Esther."*

*"Fine," she sighed. She leaned in. "It's about a man named Silas. Has Malachi mentioned him?"*

*I fought through my brain fog to recall any mention of the name. Silas was the same man Malachi mentioned that practically raised him in the Paragon. Did Esther know? Did she know Malachi's history with Silas? I decided to play dumb. "No," I answered. "I haven't heard of him."*

*"Silas is the leader of the Paragon. He makes the rules. He calls the shots. If someone wants your power, it's him. If members from the Paragon are showing up at our kingdom, it's under his orders."*

*"And why are you telling me this?" I pushed. "Why should I care about a man I've never heard of?"*

*"Because," she started. "Silas and I grew up together."*

*I blinked. "What? You grew up with the Paragon?"*

*Malachi and Esther had ties to the Paragon? This was becoming too odd.*

*She shook her head. "It wasn't the Paragon back then. Silas was just a man. He wanted peace, and that's where it all began. That's where everything began, Jade."*

*"So you're friends with the leader of the Paragon? This could change everything, Esther. Why haven't you brought this up before? Why hide it?"*

*She leaned back slightly, looking away from me in the darkness. "I wouldn't exactly call us friends."*

*The ground beneath us shook.*

*"What is this, Esther? You're in my dream?"*

*"I can't stay long. Don't tell Malachi we spoke. When the Paragon comes for you, I'll talk with Silas. I'll make him understand."*

*I didn't have time to ask her any more questions. My vision faded to black, and everything went dark.*

## CHAPTER 26

# *Jade*

The coronation ball was more of a formality than anything. The castle wanted to celebrate Malachi becoming King of Rewyth, and any excuse for the fae of the castle to drink and party was seldom passed up.

I glanced at Tessa. Her bright blue gown practically illuminated against her skin. She had never been to a ball before, much less a fae coronation. Nerves tickled my stomach, but Tessa appeared to be calm. Calmer than usual, actually. She held her chin high and walked with promise as we approached the doors to the ballroom.

"Stay with me as long as you can," I whispered. "When the coronation ends, I'll come find you. Stay out of trouble, and find Serefin or Adeline if you need anything."

Tessa found my hand and gave it a quick squeeze. "I'll be okay," she replied. "You don't need to worry about me."

I would never stop worrying about Tessa, but she didn't need to hear that. Not before the party. Especially with Esther visiting my dreams, I had my guard up. There could never be a simple, boring event around Rewyth.

We approached the coronation, and the castle began stirring with life. Music flowed from the room, echoing off the stone walls and shaking my bones. The room already moved with fae dancing and celebrating, eager to participate in the event.

"Long live the King!" a few shouted as one song came to an end. The long strings of music easily flowed into another, and the dancers easily picked up where they left off.

I spotted Adeline and Malachi in the distance, both talking to fae I had never seen before. I couldn't help but notice how formal they both appeared—much different than the versions of them I had grown to know. "Over there," I whispered to Tessa.

She took the hint, and together we worked our way through the crowd.

Malachi's eyes lit up as soon as he saw us. "Jade," he nodded. He and Adeline dismissed their guests and turned to give us their full attention. "Tessa, you are both looking lovely this evening."

Tessa's face turned bright pink, but she mumbled a thanks and dropped her head in greeting.

"You're looking well yourself," I said to Mal. "And you're stunning as ever," I nodded to Adeline. "Serefin is a lucky man."

Adeline stepped forward and smacked my arm lightly. "I have no idea what you're talking about."

Malachi and Tessa both laughed. "What?" I asked, holding my hands out in surrender. "We all see the way you two look at each other! You're not as sneaky as you think you are."

Adeline rolled her eyes and grabbed ahold of Tessa's hand. "Tessa and I are going to enjoy the party. Find us after the coronation," she whispered. "And good luck."

I couldn't understand why we would need luck to get through the ceremony, but I watched as Mal nodded—signaling it was okay for them to leave us.

The hair on the back of my neck stood up. "Adeline will protect her," Mal whispered. His warm hand found my lower back. "There's no need to worry."

I watched them walk away until they were swallowed by the crowd of dancing silver wings.

"I don't like leaving her," I admitted. "She's too fragile. Any fae who messes with her could ruin her."

Malachi clicked his tongue. "Humans," he whispered close to my ear. "Fickle little things."

I elbowed him in the stomach lightly, but he only laughed harder. "Let's get this coronation over with," I whispered. "I'm growing tired of these ridiculous dresses."

When I turned to face Mal, his eyes were dark with hidden emotion. I watched as they flickered down to my dress—to the tight corset that exposed a good portion of my chest. "I don't think I'll ever grow tired of these *ridiculous* dresses." His hand tickled my shoulder as he traced the thin, sheer fabric there. "Care for a dance?"

I was shaking my head before I could even open my mouth. "No way," I declined. "Not in front of all these people."

"These are your people now," he pointed out. "And you didn't seem to have a problem dancing together at our wedding. Or at the festival in Trithen..." His voice grew thick as he took a tiny step closer.

I looked away from Mal and glanced around the room. Fae scattered throughout the room, but nobody seemed to be paying us special attention.

"One dance," I agreed after a few seconds. "But that's it."

A satisfied smile spread across his face. Malachi took my hand without a word and pulled me, walking backward, to the source of the music.

The melody was not slow by any means, but Malachi didn't seem to care. He held my hand and pulled my body gently to his, caressing my lower back as he began swaying.

"The King of Shadows dances much more than I would have expected," I teased.

Malachi's smile only grew as he spun me in a circle. "This is my official coronation," he replied. "I've been waiting to be officially recognized as the King for decades now. This should be one of the happiest days of my existence."

"It is well deserved," I replied. "The kingdom is in great hands."

His eyes searched mine as if they were looking for a lie in my words. But they found none.

I meant those words. Malachi was going to change the fate of the kingdom with his rule, I could feel that much deep in my bones. He was powerful, yet he held so much light inside of him. He had buried it in a place that was hard to find, but it was there. And I saw the light in him every time his eyes met mine.

The music continued to play, but I no longer listened to it. The fae around us seemed to disappear as I admired him. Malachi must have felt this, too. His hands tightened on my body. The small amount of space between us vanished.

And we danced.

It was more than one dance, but I didn't care. I let him guide me through the ballroom with ease, enjoying every second of our time together.

Minutes ticked by. I didn't think about Tessa, Esther, my magic, or anything else. I just let my husband hold me in the crowded room of our people.

It wasn't until the music stopped entirely that I noticed the fae around us.

Malachi stiffened as he, too, noticed it. The crowd around us stood in a semi-circle, watching us.

Blood rushed to my face. "Why is everyone staring at us?" I whispered to Mal. His hand never left mine. If he was in any way embarrassed, he didn't show it.

"Because I am the King of Rewyth," he said, only loud enough so I could hear. "They're waiting for us."

He cleared his throat and, without letting go of me, began walking to the throne. I followed. The silent crowd parted ways as we moved through it, and when we reached the bottom of the steps that led to the throne, Malachi paused.

Serefin and another guard stood next to the throne.

Another man, one I recognized from the court dinner, stepped forward onto the stage. "Fae of Rewyth," he announced. "Today we gather to commence the coronation of our new king, Malachi Weyland." Malachi bowed his head slightly as we waited for him to continue. "Malachi, please join me."

Malachi squeezed my hand once before letting go. I tried to ignore the wave of loneliness I felt as he stepped forward to stand before his throne and his kingdom.

He stood with his shoulders back and his chin high, like he deserved to be there all along.

"King Malachi," the guard announced. "Today we gather here to officially name you, Malachi Weyland, as the leader and king of this great fae kingdom, the Kingdom of Rewyth."

Cheers erupted in the crowd around us. Malachi stared straight ahead.

The guard held a large crown covered in bright red rubies before Malachi before continuing. "By accepting this crown, you promise to uphold the values of this kingdom. You promise to protect this kingdom by any means necessary, and you promise to lead the citizens of this kingdom to live peaceful and safe lives. You hereby recognize the sacrifices of our ancestors, and the lives they gave up to protect our people. You swear to maintain the utmost priority of defending this kingdom against any and all enemies. Do you accept this oath?"

Malachi's jaw tightened. "I accept this oath."

The guard lowered the crown onto Mal's head. Serefin stepped forward and secured the velvet red robe around him.

And when Malachi lifted his head again, he was officially the King of Rewyth.

"Long live the King!" Serefin cheered.

"Long live the King!" the crowd repeated. The cheers began once more, filling the room with their support.

Pride welled in my chest. Malachi had been a king since his father was killed, and maybe even before that. But this was the first time his kingdom officially saw him as one.

And by the sound of the crowd, they loved it.

Malachi stepped down the stairs and reached for my hand without looking at me. I slid my hand into his, not worrying about how the others would react.

"That was surprisingly simple," I whispered to him as he began walking me into the crowd.

"Yet the entire kingdom demands it happens," he replied with a wink.

Malachi led me through the crowd, and the fae around us congratulated him and bowed to him as we passed.

When we approached the edge of the ballroom, Eli and Lucien were waiting for us. "It's about time your arrogance is made official," Lucien teased before clapping Mal on the shoulder.

He laughed quietly. "Don't worry, brother. I'll refrain from abusing my power against you for the time being."

Adonis's loud voice in the distance caught our attention. "Back off," he growled.

I snapped my eyes in his direction, only to find him standing directly in front of Tessa with his hands in front of him.

Mal was pulling us in their direction before I could react.

"What's going on over here?" Malachi asked as we approached.

I let go of his hand and instantly rushed to Tessa, who was now cowering away from the fae.

Only when I looked at the others, my stomach dropped. Standing before Adonis were the same fae who had antagonized us in the gardens before.

The one I had nearly killed stood before them, only he was completely healed.

His eyes locked on mine, and a grin spread across his face. "Hello again, my queen."

Malachi stepped forward and placed a hand on the fae's chest, pushing him back a step. "Adonis," he said without looking away from the fae. "Tell me what's happening."

"They were messing with Tessa again," was all he said.

I wrapped my arms tighter around my sister and watched as Malachi smiled. "Is that so?" he asked. His black wings flared from beneath his robe. "Am I correct to hear that this is the second time you have disturbed Lady Farrow?"

The fae's jaw clenched.

"My wife dealt with you last time. If I see you talking to either Jade or Tessa again, I'll kill you myself."

Everyone froze, including the small crowd gathering around us. The fae shot me one last look before sliding his eyes over to Tessa. I could have sworn I heard Adonis growl.

"Get out of here," Malachi interrupted. "You're no longer welcome at this celebration."

As soon as they walked away, I grabbed Tessa's shoulders. "Are you alright?" I asked. "Did they hurt you?"

She shook her head. "No, I'm okay. They just wanted to start trouble."

I pulled her into a hug. "I'm sorry, Tessa. Nobody should be bothering you here."

Adonis stepped forward. "They won't bother her again," he hissed.

Tessa pulled away from my grasp and took a long breath. "Get back to your party," she said. "I'll be okay now."

"This is Malachi's party," I reminded her. "Not mine. If you want me to leave and–"

"No," she interrupted. "This is your party, too, Jade." A small smile tugged on her lips. "Let's at least try to have some fun."

And so we did. The air buzzed with joy and excitement of the new king. When the music started again, I pulled Tessa into the crowd and spun her around. At first, she tensed up. But after a few minutes, her and her beautiful blue dress were spinning through the night.

It wasn't until hours later that I noticed the crowd had nearly dwindled down to half. For a group of fae, leaving a party early was unheard of.

"What's going on?" I asked Serefin as I reached for a cup of water. "Where's everybody going?" Serefin paused for a moment and rolled his shoulders back, as if he were debating whether or not to tell me the truth. "Tell me," I demanded.

"It's the war," he whispered. "Citizens have been leaving all week. They're relocating to the outskirts, where they can stay hidden in case the castle is attacked."

I shook my head. "That's ridiculous. Who will protect them if they leave?"

It didn't make any sense. Citizens were leaving because of the war that approached? What if the outskirts were attacked first? There would be no army to protect them. No walls. No *king*.

"Malachi left the decision up to them," Ser explained. "If they want to leave so badly, they are free to."

A sense of dread built in my stomach. "It's because of me, isn't it? They know I'm the target."

Serefin's dark eyes met mine. "Who cares what they think, Jade? You're Malachi's wife, and you are their new queen. Malachi will protect you along with this kingdom, even if others don't see that."

My eyes found Malachi in the crowd, who was now in deep conversation with a few court members.

"He's giving up a lot for me," I whispered.

Serefin placed a warm hand on my shoulder. "Just as any of us would."

# CHAPTER 27
## Jade

DAYS PASSED QUICKER THAN I EVER IMAGINED THEY WOULD. ESTHER never visited my dreams again, and I never mentioned them. I tried to avoid thinking about her at all, and I stayed far away from the dungeons of the castle.

My life became a mixture of watching over Tessa, training for the upcoming war, and spending as much time as I could with Malachi.

But we could all sense change coming. We could sense the war moving closer and closer.

Our conversations grew quiet. Our training held a sense of desperation with every new movement. Tessa could sense it, too. She stayed hidden in her room more days than not.

Until one day, when life as I knew it ended.

Malachi and I were in his room. We had been spending most of our time there lately, locked away from the chaos of the castle.

A knock came from the door.

"Come in," Malachi ordered.

It was his brother who slowly creaked open the door.

I knew something was wrong the second I laid eyes on Lucien's face. He had *never* looked at me like that.

With such *pity*.

He looked over to Malachi, who stood behind me in the bedroom, and then back to me.

"What?" I asked. "What's wrong?"

Adonis stepped up behind Lucien, and then Eli behind him.

None of them looked me directly in the eye.

The hair on the back of my neck rose.

"Lucien," Malachi spoke. His voice was harsher than I had heard it in a long time. "Say something. What do you need? What's going on?"

"There was an accident," Adonis said. "In the garden. We ran to see what the commotion was, but it was too late."

"What. Happened."

*Something was wrong. Something was very, very wrong.*

"It's Jade's sister," Adonis said. He bowed his head and stared at the floor.

Panic took over my body. "Is she okay?" I asked as I stepped forward. "Where is she?"

Lucien was the one who stepped up, placing his body in front of me with his hands in front of him. "Jade..."

"Where is she?" I repeated. I couldn't hide the panic creeping into my voice. My mind screamed at me to *go find her. Go find your sister.*

*This wasn't happening.*

*This couldn't be happening.*

"Tell me!" I yelled again. The suffocating grip of an invisible hand tightened around my throat.

"She's dead, Jade," Lucien said.

A knife pierced my heart. *Dead.*

*No, no, no.* That couldn't be right.

"She's...she's dead?" I repeated. My own voice felt foreign. Those words were never supposed to leave my mouth. Not about her. Not about my baby sister.

"What in the Saints happened?" Malachi's voice boomed through the room. His hands came down on my arms, but I could hardly feel them. I didn't care about anyone else.

I needed to see her.

I needed to get to my sister.

"Where?" I asked. "Where is she?"

"There was a fight. We tried to stop it but we were too late, Mal. Tessa was...she was caught in the crossfire."

Malachi's voice thundered so loudly, the frames on the walls vibrated. "Who did it? If someone killed her, you better tell me right now!"

*No.* This wasn't real. *This wasn't real.*

My body was moving, walking past the brothers who simply slid out of my way as I approached. The gardens. It happened in the gardens.

I had to get to the gardens. I had to get to Tessa.

She wasn't dead. *No, it wasn't possible.*

Tessa was alive. I just had to find her and Malachi could get her to the infirmary and whatever happened, it would all be fine.

It would all be okay. Tessa was *fine.*

I felt Malachi's presence behind me. I walked and walked and walked. At some point, that walk turned into a run.

Before I could even fathom where I was heading, I turned the last corner into the garden.

People were everywhere. No, not people. *Fae.* Standing, mingling, whispering, and then looking at me.

Someone bumped my shoulder. There were too many. Too many faces, too many pairs of wings.

Too many *enemies.*

Malachi must have said something, because the fae in the garden began scattering. Away from the crowd. Away from...

*Tessa.*

My eyes glued to Tessa, laying in the middle of the walking path next to the bright red roses. I ran to her and dropped to my knees, grabbing ahold of her small shoulders. They felt so cold.

"Tessa?" I asked. I shook her lightly. She seemed so small, much smaller than I remembered. "Tessa, wake up!"

Malachi knelt on the other side of her, but he wasn't looking at Tessa. He watched me with wide eyes.

"Mal, do something!" I yelled. "She's okay, she's okay we just have to get her to–"

"Jade," he cut me off. His voice sounded soft, just like Lucien's. It sounded *sad.* "According to witnesses, it was the same fae who threatened you both in the gardens the other day...he snapped her neck. She's gone, Jade. Your sister is dead."

"No," I insisted. "No!" I looked at her neck. It was...it was twisted into a weird position, her head tilted off to the side. "She's...she's *safe* here. She's supposed to be *safe* here."

Malachi didn't say anything.

My vision blurred with tears. "She's not dead!"

"She's dead, Jade."

A sob ripped through my body. I hadn't felt this hopeless in a very, very long time. For as long as I could remember, Tessa was my anchor. She was the one thing I had to fight for. Even when I had nothing, even when I had no reason for continuing, I kept fighting. Because my sister needed me.

Tessa saved my life.

Malachi's hands found my face, wiping away the tears that were only replaced with more. How could I have let this happen?

I was her protector. I was the one who took care of her. I was the one who kept her safe.

*No, no, no.* This could not be real. Tessa couldn't really be dead.

I would wake up in the morning and this would all be one wicked, horrific dream. It was all a nightmare, *yes. That* made sense. That made *perfect* sense.

What didn't make any damned sense was my sister being dead!

I looked back down at her, tears dropping from my chin down to my chest. She was so pale. So lifeless.

I wanted to hug her. I wanted to pull her scrawny little body to mine and hold her until it was all okay, like I had done hundreds of times before. I wanted to go to sleep in our tiny little bed and give her my blanket, too, because hers was never enough to keep her warm in the winter.

I wanted to teach her how to tie a knot, even though she was completely helpless and wasn't getting anywhere with her hunting skills.

I wanted to look her in the eye and tell her I loved her, because Saints, I hadn't done that enough.

"Jade," Malachi's voice interrupted my thoughts. I finally looked at him, but he was staring at something behind me.

When I glanced over my shoulder to see who else was in the garden, another wave of debilitating sorrow hit me.

*Father.*

"Oh, Tessa," he moaned. He stumbled forward and fell to his knees beside me, grabbing her limp arm. "Tessa, Tessa, Tessa."

I couldn't say anything as I watched the horror. I had hated my father for years, probably more than half my life. I had watched him abandon her time and time again. And time and time again, *I* was the one that stepped in. That told him to sober up, or to get out of the house until he calmed down.

But he was our father. He was *her* father.

Tessa had never looked at him with the same hatred that I did. She was frightened of him at times, and certainly disappointed, but she never hated him.

And I think he knew that.

I wanted to reach out and console him, pat his shoulder as he knelt beside me. But I couldn't.

"What happened?" he said when he looked up. He glanced rapidly between me and Mal. "Tell me what in the Saints happened to my daughter!"

Numb. I felt numb nothingness as Malachi answered, "There was a fight. She was...she was killed."

A shaking sob wrecked through my father. I had only seen this side of him one other time.

*But not like this.*

My father bent down again, pressing his forehead against hers. Against his cold, dead daughter's skin.

He mumbled things that I couldn't understand, things that I didn't even want to try to understand.

When he looked up after quite some time, it wasn't sorrow that dripped over his features. It was anger.

"You swore to me that she would be safe. That we would be safe here!"

"I know," I breathed.

Shame washed over me. I deserved every bit of it.

"You SWORE to me! She was your sister! Your baby sister!"

"I know."

"She's dead, Jade!"

"I know that!"

The numbness and the adrenaline in my body was replaced in a wash of emotion, filled with anger and shame and despair. I didn't ask for this. I didn't ask for Tessa to die. To be killed by the very fae I risked my life to protect.

Did he not see that? Did he not see that my very reason for living had just been ripped away from me? That without Tessa, I had nothing?

Anger built inside of me, igniting a fire that used my despair to grow hotter and hotter. I should have seen this coming. I should have known she couldn't be protected here. Tessa was too fragile. Too *good*.

"Jade, calm down," Malachi whispered roughly. "You're losing control."

I didn't care. I didn't care if I lost control. I didn't care if this entire damned kingdom burned to the ground.

"Jade!"

Malachi's wings were around my body in two seconds, followed by the uncontrolled flare of my own power.

His massive black wings kept the sudden flash contained.

I wanted to stay there, wrapped away in the darkness.

But when the flash ended, Malachi slowly peeled them back.

And as soon as they parted, I saw the horror on my father's face.

I would have killed him, too. My power would have killed my own father if it weren't for Malachi.

And he knew it.

Hands were on my body, lifting me up and saying something I couldn't focus on. "Let's go. I'm taking you home."

# CHAPTER 28
# *Malachi*

"Talk to me, Jade."

It had been hours since we left the garden. I had to drag Jade away from Tessa's body, carrying her up to my bedroom.

And she hadn't said a single word since.

I didn't blame her. I had to hide my own shock when I saw Tessa laying there. She looked so small, so fragile.

So helpless.

Jade knew it, too. She knew that Tessa could have done nothing against a fae if a fae wanted her dead. It was a very similar position that Jade was in not too long ago.

Now, Jade had other problems.

"Just let me know that you'll be okay," I pushed. I sat next to her on the bed. She stared at the dark ceiling, although her eyes had been glazed over for the last hour. She wasn't in there. She was a hollow void, completely numb to any emotion.

I had felt similar at many times in my life. I knew Jade had, too.

Raw. Emotionless. Empty.

I brushed a piece of hair off her forehead. It wasn't until my skin made contact with hers that she blinked twice and her eyes met mine. "I can't do this," she admitted. "I can't do this, Mal. I can't be this person."

I caressed her cheek. "You can, Jade."

She shook her head, tears filling that emptiness in her eyes. "She was my reason for living, Mal. You don't understand. Without her, I have..."

I held her face gently. "You have everything, Jade. Do you hear me? You have Adeline. You have Serefin. You have entire kingdoms of people counting on you. You are needed, Jade. And you are loved. By a whole lot of people now, not just Tessa. The *world* needs you."

I knew my words were void. She wouldn't care. She wouldn't even have the capacity of caring about anything other than her dead sister right now.

But with war on the horizon, I had to try.

Jade needed to hang on. She needed to dig deep, into that small, hidden corner of perseverance that only came out in situations like this. In situations where you didn't want to continue. Didn't want to live.

But you had no choice.

Because someone counted on you. Someone would miss you.

*Saints.*

I had choked back those words for too long.

I leaned forward and displaced my forehead against Jade's. She needed to hear me when I said this. She needed to feel how I felt.

"I love you, Jade," I whispered. Jade's eyes closed. "I love you, and I know you are hurting. And I would trade places with you in a heartbeat, Jade, because it *kills* me to see you in pain. It kills me to see you like this. You are my everything, Jade. You *deserve* everything. And I know you don't care about what I have to say right now. I know you're empty and numb and contemplating how the *Saints* you'll continue, but you *have* to know this—I love you deeply, Jade. *Insatiably*. How I lived so many years without you, I have no clue. But you walked into my life when I had given up, and you pulled me back from the ledge when I only wanted to jump. So that's what I'm going to do to you now, Jade. I'm pulling you back from that ledge. Because I'm *selfish* and I *don't want* to go on without you. So I'll let you sleep this off, but come morning, I'll be here. And I'll be here the next day, and the next day. Because *I can't live* without you."

I stayed there for a moment, half-in awe at the words I had just spoken, before I moved to stand. If she wanted alone time, I would give it to her. No matter how badly I wanted to do just the opposite.

"Wait," her frail voice stopped me in my tracks. "Thank you, Malachi."

I turned around and grabbed her outstretched hand. The chill of her skin shocked me. "For what?"

Tears spilled down both of her cheeks. "You weren't the only one that needed to be pulled back from that ledge."

Later that night, while Jade was fast asleep next to me, I snuck out of the room.

I killed all five of the fae that were seen messing with Tessa.

And I strung each of their dead bodies from ropes in the dining hall.

# CHAPTER 29
# *Jade*

There were many times in my life that I wished my sister were dead. It would have been easier without her. Thinking that now sounded cruel, but it was true. At times, Tessa could be the most clueless human alive. Saints, all of those years watching me and I don't think she ever learned to hunt.

She had tried, of course. And failed. Many, many times. Part of me thought she was so bad at it on purpose, so that she would never have to be relied on like I was.

I smiled at the memory. If that were the case, she was smarter than I gave her credit for.

Malachi slept next to me. I listened to the sound of his deep, calming breaths.

I hadn't slept much at all. Every time I closed my eyes, I saw her. And then I saw her mangled, twisted neck laying on the pavement of the garden.

And I saw my father screaming over her dead body.

I tried not to care about him. I tried not to think about where he had gone after Malachi ripped me away. Saints, part of me wished he would just go get drunk. Anything to escape from the pain.

*Anything.*

Malachi's wings tucked around us on the bed. Somehow, I felt safer near him. My entire life had just been ripped away from me, but when I was near him...

I wasn't entirely lost.

He had gotten up just hours before, thinking I was asleep. I knew he was going to avenge Tessa's death. I knew he wouldn't let something so vile go on in his own kingdom.

And I also knew that the guilt was eating at him. The guilt that he didn't keep her safe.

Same as me.

Except he wasn't the one to blame. I was.

Malachi shifted awake next to me, slowly blinking his eyes open before he realized I was already awake.

He sat up instantly, half-jumping out of the bed.

"I'll get you something to eat."

"No. I'm coming with you," I insisted. "I'm not going to hide my face around here. I want everyone to see me. To see that I'm not just going to roll over."

"You can give it a day, Jade, you don't–"

"I'm coming, and that's final."

Malachi stared at me for a second longer before nodding. "Okay," he said. "But if you're uncomfortable for even a second, we're leaving. I have a private dining room for a reason, you know."

I didn't care. War approached us. I was not going to let my enemies within this castle think they had won.

For Tessa. I would do this for Tessa.

I quickly got dressed. My hair fell in loose waves, and I didn't even try to maintain the chaos of it. My arms were heavy, much heavier than they were yesterday. Everything was heavy.

"Let me," Mal said after he saw me struggling to braid it.

He came up behind me, his presence instantly electrifying my body. My eyes were raw, red, and glassy. I didn't care. Hiding it was pointless. This was how a grieving human looked.

"You know how to braid?" I asked.

Malachi pulled all of my hair behind my back, his fingers brushing the sides of my neck when he did. "How hard can it be?" he whispered.

I smiled. It felt wrong, but I let it happen. "You're awfully old to be a man who doesn't know how to braid."

He struggled to split my hair into three uneven sections. "I am a man of many talents, my dear wife," he started. His words sent a chill down my spine. "But braiding long, beautiful hair is not one of them. Yet."

I spent the next few minutes in silence, watching him in the mirror as he worked, with utter focus, on braiding my waist-length locks.

If I hadn't been in love with him before, I certainly would be now.

"Tessa was beginning to warm up to you, you know," I said.

Mal looked up in shock, either because of what I said or because he wasn't expecting me to be talking about her. "Really?"

I nodded. "I think Adonis actually made a good impression too, believe it or not."

Malachi smiled this time. "That's one that I'll believe when I see."

Our smiles both dropped then, because we would never see that. We would never see Tessa smile again. Would never hear her talk.

Malachi finished my braid and placed both of his hands on my shoulders. They felt no heavier than the weight that already lay there.

I leaned my head back onto his shoulder and closed my eyes.

Tears threatened my eyes. I let them come. If I tried to hold back every tear today, I wouldn't survive.

Malachi leaned his head on mine. A silent agreement, an unspoken promise. I wouldn't be going through this alone. I wouldn't have to carry this burden by myself.

"Your strength is inspiring, my queen," he whispered before pressing his lips to my temple. "We'll get through this together."

I didn't speak. I just took a few long breaths, taking in Malachi's presence behind me, before opening my eyes again and stepping toward the door. "It's now or never," I said, choking down the emotion that threatened to erupt. "Let's show those bastards they can't take me down that easily."

When Malachi didn't follow, I turned to look at him. The amount of utter pride in his expression was almost enough to drop me to my knees.

"I know you don't feel like you belong here all of the time," he spoke. "But you are the best queen these fae have ever known."

He grabbed my hand and we walked to the dining hall in silence.

Five minutes later, I was staring at five dead bodies.

Hanging from the ceiling of the dining hall.

The roaring conversations in the room around me seemed to halt. Blurs of wings and colors passed by as my vision locked in.

Nobody seemed to pay any attention to them. The entire dining hall was packed full of citizens, silently going about their business and eating their breakfast.

"I assume this was your doing?" I asked Mal.

His eyes darkened as he stared at the corpses. "This crime was not going to go unpunished."

There might have been a younger version of me that would have been mortified by the image in front of me. Blood continued to drip on the floor from each of their impaled bodies.

But today? A bright ball of satisfaction lit up in my stomach.

They had paid with their lives. By Malachi's hand.

And I knew more than anyone that Malachi was sending a message with this act.

I turned my attention away from the bodies and back to the room full of fae. "Everyone's staring at us," I whispered to Mal.

"Don't worry," he assured. "That's nothing new."

We walked to the head table of the dining hall, the one that was reserved for Malachi.

Even though he rarely ate here.

Servants greeted us as soon as we sat down, our backs to the wall with those corpses hanging in my direct line of sight.

"My queen," one servant asked me. "We have fresh fruit, picked just this morning from our fields. Absolutely divine." She set a massive bowl in front of me with an assortment of colorful fruits.

I nodded my thanks, but I didn't miss the sparkle of pity in her eye.

At least the servants cared.

Malachi's tension spread to me as we sat there, but his chin didn't drop an inch. He looked everyone in the eye as they stared at us.

Part of me wanted to look away. The other part of me welled with a familiar pride that reminded me of the way he had looked at me earlier.

My king.

I was completely thrown off guard when a body slammed into mine from the side, wrapping me in a tight hug.

Adeline.

"Saints, Jade. I'm so, so terribly sorry. I've been thinking about you nonstop and I wanted to come say hi but I didn't want to bug you and–"

"I'm okay, Adeline," I said, awkwardly trying to hug her back from where I sat

"Get off of her, Adeline," Mal warned from his chair beside me.

Adeline dragged a wooden chair next to me, so close that our legs were touching. "Tell me," she started. Her eyes filled with so much worry that I truly didn't know how to respond. "How are you?"

"I'm okay," I responded. The words were uncomfortably true.

She glanced at the hanging corpses, and I watched as her nostrils flared in disgust. "They deserve to rot for what they did," she muttered.

"They will," I whispered. A comforting wave of power fell over my senses. "I have a feeling everyone who has ever wronged me will get their turn very, very soon."

Adeline's eyes snapped to mine. Something dark lingered in her gaze. Something dark and...familiar. Something hungry. "I know you'll rip them to shreds, Jade," she said. Her hand came up to tug on my messy braid. "Just don't feel guilty about it," she said.

"About what?"

Adeline's eyes darkened. It was rare for me to see her in this spirit. "About taking over the world and ending anyone in your way," she said. "And liking it."

Before I could even process what she had just said, Adeline was leaving the table.

"Well," Mal cleared his throat. "I'm glad to know she hasn't completely lost her mind."

My heart warmed. Adeline was a cheerful, optimistic source of light in Rewyth. But ever since the festival in Trithen, I saw who she really was.

Adeline chose to be that bright light. She had overcome the impossible and survived a life around power hungry, abusive men. Adeline had risen from the ashes, and she was here to create her own destiny now. After so much of her own life had been stripped from her, she chose light.

I admired that about her. That she could have so much taken away and still choose to see the good.

I couldn't say I particularly felt the same.

"Jade?" Malachi's voice pulled me from my trance. "Did you hear me?"

"No," I stuttered. "Sorry. Can you say it again?"

Mal smiled, but it dripped in concern. "I said you better hurry up and eat before your food gets cold."

"Right," I agreed, hurrying to pick up my fork. "Sorry, I was just a little distracted."

"You have nothing to apologize for," he said.

I ate for a few minutes. Swallowing each bite was a nearly impossible task, but there were too many prying eyes watching me. Too many people looking for a weakness to exploit.

The flavor of the food, the same flavor that I had been disgustingly astonished with when I had first tasted it, was now nothing but bland mush.

It wasn't until Lucien and Adonis slid into the two seats in front of us that I really felt my senses light up.

"What are you doing?" Mal asked, slightly bored.

"You shouldn't be out here," Lucien started. "It's not safe."

"Not safe?" Mal laughed beside me. "And why is that?"

Adonis and Lucien exchanged a glance. "There are a few who aren't thrilled about their friends dripping blood on our breakfast plates."

The low murmurs of conversations around us halted. The only thing I cared about now was Malachi sitting next to me. He looked calm, but I could feel the thrill of power inside of me reacting to his.

Waiting.

"Tell me who," Mal shrugged. "Who's unhappy with the justice their king decides to bestow upon them?"

Lucien's eyes glanced over in my direction, only for a split second, before returning to Mal. "Many people, brother."

When Mal laughed this time, he didn't hold anything back.

"What's funny?" Adonis asked.

"What?" Mal asked. "You don't find this funny?"

"This is serious," Lucien hissed, leaning across the table and lowering his voice. "We're on the brink of war, brother. We can't have an uprising."

"Who?" It took me two seconds to realize that it was me who asked.

All eyes turned to mine. "What?" Mal questioned.

"Who was it that was concerned? You said many, so point to a few." *Shut up, shut up, shut up.*

I couldn't stop, though. It was like another force controlled me, controlled my words.

"There are too many to point to," Adonis answered.

"I'm sure you can point to one. Two, at the most. Don't be shy."

Adonis's forehead wrinkled. When I glanced at Mal, he just stared expectantly at his brothers. He, too, waited for an answer.

Time ticked by.

The utter void of emotionlessness inside of me churned, producing a low burn of anger and hatred and vile that crept–like fire–into the rest of my body. It started in my stomach, burning there slowly until it spread up my torso, into my chest. My breath got heavier. Thicker. More labored.

An emotion crept into that fire. More than one emotion, actually.

I couldn't tell. But I did know one thing—I wanted answers.

And I would not be denied.

I stood up from my chair and placed my hands on the wooden table in front of me. I wasn't angry at Adonis, no. Not even at Lucien, who had been the target of my anger on more than one occasion. My eyes scanned the room around me.

Some friends. Some foes. Mostly strangers.

Yet somehow, when my eyes met the ones that lingered upon me, powerlessness began to creep up my spine, biting and clawing its way back up.

That was what bothered me the most. I may have been broken. I may have been kicked and beaten and whipped into submission, both figuratively and literally. But I was still alive. Even when death welcomed me with open and cold arms, I had stepped forward.

And that made me far from powerless.

Mal's brothers stared at me with wide eyes, but I continued anyway.

"It's been brought to my attention that some of you may have a problem with the way my husband has chosen to punish our enemies," I spoke with strength. The chatter in the room halted, the air was all but sucked out.

Nothing. No answer. No admission.

*Interesting.*

Malachi stood next to me, either because he wanted to protect me or because he felt the pull of my power.

I felt it, too. That burning sensation in my chest grew and grew. "Nobody?" I asked.

A young male stepped forward. His silver wings tucked behind his shoulder blades. "They were our friends," he spoke. The words alone were innocent, but the malice that laced them sounded anything but.

"They killed my sister."

A male beside him laughed.

The power inside of me grew hotter.

Mal brushed his fingertips across my lower back. Enough for me to know he was there if I needed him, but light enough to tell me I had permission.

I lifted a palm from the wooden table, just in time, and a ball of white-hot power skidded through the dining hall, bursting just before the young fae's feet. He jumped in fear.

Others screamed.

"What?" I asked, lifting an eyebrow. "Something wrong?"

I stepped around the table and descended the few steps to the rest of the dining hall. Heading straight toward the fae who laughed.

Mal trailed my every step, but stayed silent.

"What-what are you doing?" he asked as I approached.

I held my hands out in front of me and let my power express itself again.

Others were staring now, half in horror and half in pure curiosity. I stared back, daring anyone to push me.

"They killed my sister," I said again. "And they paid with their lives. Now, lucky for you all, I only had one sister. But unlucky for you all, I'm feeling particularly fed up with being walked on in my own kingdom."

I dropped my hands and the power erupted around us. Everyone ducked to avoid the small blast—everyone but Malachi and me.

When everyone looked back up again, it was Malachi and I standing in the center of the dining hall.

"A move against my wife is a move against this kingdom," Malachi's voice boomed. "If anyone has a problem with the way that I punish traitors to the crown, it won't be me you answer to. It will be my wife."

"Let's get out of here," I said. I slid my hand into Malachi's and walked toward the dining room entrance.

I never wanted power. But in those moments where I would have given anything for it all to be over, I found myself wishing I had a single shred of strength.

Today, it was strength alone that pulled me out of bed. And strength alone forced me to continue.

# CHAPTER 30
# Malachi

JADE HAD NO IDEA WHAT TYPE OF MEN WOULD BE WAITING FOR HER outside of the castle. She had insisted that Ser and I take her out to the troops. It was only fair, considering they were fighting for *her* life.

Her black boots ground the dirt beneath us. Ser and I followed a few footsteps behind, but my eyes didn't leave her for a single second.

Ser and I had been coming out here daily, training these men and getting to know them. Not all of them were our friends, but right now, they were our allies. That mattered more than friendship.

But to Jade, it was all the same.

She was pushing herself. I could see it in her eyes. I would catch her staring into the distance, smiling to herself with her eyes glossed over. Each time, I wanted to ask her what she was thinking about. What memory was so precious that she was reliving it now.

But those were her memories, sacred between her and her sister. If she needed to escape into those memories, into those few moments of peace, then I would let her.

And I wouldn't interrupt.

Men greeted Ser and I as we entered the field of campsites. I noted the way they each either nodded their heads in Jade's direction or ignored her entirely.

Both were better than confronting her, in my eyes.

"These men are comfortable enough out here?" Jade asked without looking at me. She was too busy observing the makeshift housing.

"Comfortable enough," Ser answered. "We have given every possible resource to housing these men. They would much rather sleep under the stars than crammed into the old servants' quarters of the castle."

Jade smiled to herself again. "I can't blame them. The stars are beautiful."

My heart twisted. Jade admired the stars because they were free. That was something Jade had never experienced herself.

*Would she ever?*

Jade continued to walk through the masses, assessing every man who was preparing to give his life for our cause.

Until Carlyle approached. "Lady Weyland," he bent at the waist in greeting. "It's a pleasure seeing you again."

Jade bowed her own head in greeting. "You look well," she responded. I stepped to the side of her.

"Don't tell him that," I teased, placing a hand on her lower back. "It'll go straight to his head." Carlyle smiled, but the typical light in his eyes was gone. Replaced by something darker. "What's going on?"

Carlyle glanced around us and motioned to follow him back into the dining hall. Once inside, he leaned forward and whispered, "Our scouts have sent word. War is coming. Now."

"Now?" Jade asked. "As in, today?"

"Yes, my queen. We need to get everyone ready for an attack from the Paragon."

"How many of them?" I asked.

Carlyle took a deep breath before answering, "That depends on what you're asking. If you're asking how many deadlings, I'd say one to two hundred. If you're asking how many soldiers, it looks to be around a thousand men."

*Hundreds of deadlings. Thousands of men.* "Saints."

"What do we do?" Jade asked.

My body buzzed with adrenaline. This was it. Everything we had prepared for was happening. "Go find Adeline and tell her what's happening," I said. "I'm going to take Serefin and alert the troops."

"What about everyone else?" she asked, referencing the men around us. "What do we tell them?"

Carlyle stepped backward and spoke to the entire dining hall, "All able-bodied men—please make your way out to the front gates. Nothing to worry about, just a precaution." Would I ever be able to lie that easily to my own people? To tell them that everything was fine on the verge of war?

Jade tugged my hand. "What will you do?"

"Go," I urged, the room now slowly brewing chaos with Carlyle's announcement. "I'll come find you."

She hesitated, just for a second. Was she afraid? Was she regretting ever taking my side? She had to know that everyone in this kingdom was here to protect her by now.

But she was still a human...

After one more second, she let go of my hand and lost herself in the sea of fae.

She would be fine. She would find Adeline and Adeline would know what to do, Adeline would know to hide her away in the dungeons until I came for them both.

I hoped to the Saints that they actually listened to me.

# CHAPTER 31
# Jade

"Okay," Adeline said for the tenth time. "Okay, okay."

"Do you have a plan for this type of thing?" I asked.

"Yes, yes there's a plan. Malachi gave me strict instructions."

"What did he tell you?"

Adeline's mind went somewhere else, digging for the instructions that Mal had given her. Her eyes were wide with panic, but she fought to stay calm. "The dungeons!" she snapped back to the present time. In two seconds, she transformed from a frazzled girl to a fae on a mission. She grabbed my wrist and began pulling me to her bedroom door "Let's go."

I pulled against her, but her fae strength was no match for me. "What?"

"We have to stay in the dungeons until Malachi comes to get us"

"Are you kidding? We'll be sitting ducks down there!"

"It's the safest place for us," she argued. "The chances of anyone making it far enough to find us in there are slim."

My mind spun in circles. I wasn't helpless. I wasn't about to sit in the dungeon and wait for the Paragon to find me. I was to blame for this attack. I was to blame for the Paragon coming here.

I owed it to Mal to fight, even if he wanted me to hide.

But there was another person who could help us. Who could help me.

And in order to find her, I had to get to the dungeons.

"Fine," I said. "Let's go."

I let Adeline drag me under the castle. I had never seen the halls so busy, bustling with both fae men and women shuffling in opposite directions. The men rushed outside, and the women ran in a panic.

A wave of pity fell over me. They were fae, they were powerful. I had spent my entire life thinking they were indestructible. But at last, they too had something to fear. They too could be helpless against their opponents.

When we got to the entrance of the dungeons, the guards were waiting for us. "Malachi's orders," Adeline spoke. "The castle is being attacked. Today."

The guard's face didn't change as he stepped aside, letting us in. "Thank you," Adeline muttered, and then she was pulling me into the dark underground tunnels.

I followed silently behind her until we got to the fork in the long halls. Esther was to the right. But Adeline began pulling me left. "Stop," I halted. "Adeline, wait."

She stopped and spun to face me. "What?"

"Esther is this way," I pointed to the right. "We have to tell her what's going on. She can help us, Adeline."

"No way," she argued. "Mal will kill us if we even speak to her."

"Mal can't see past his anger. Esther is a witch, and we're being attacked by the Paragon. We can't just leave her chained down here Adeline, that makes no sense!"

Her nostrils flared as she debated the options. I knew she would see my side. Esther might be the only person in this entire kingdom with the knowledge to fight another witch, and if what I had heard about the Paragon so far was true, they would bring witches with them to fight.

Malachi was strong. But could he defeat them all?

"If we get caught," she started, "I'm blaming you."

"I'm totally fine with that." I turned on my heels and began rushing toward Esther's cell. It had been so long since I had been down here last. I hadn't realized just how long these halls really were.

We walked and walked and walked. "Are you sure it's this way?" Adeline asked me. "These tunnels really creep me out."

My senses tingled with every step. We were close. We had to be. "I think it's–"

"I knew you would be coming for me," Esther's voice muttered through the halls. Adeline and I followed that voice, rounding one last corner and finding Esther in her cell.

"You can see the future now?" I asked.

Esther was sitting in that same dark corner, yet she looked ten years older.

"Did you forget I am a witch, child?"

"Jade didn't forget anything," Adeline stepped in. "That's why we're here."

"Is that so?" Esther asked. She tried to shift herself on the ground, but a violent coughing fit stopped her. I looked away. "Need one more look before I finally die?"

"It's time," I said. "The Paragon will attack before nightfall. You told me you would help."

"Ah, so now you've finally decided you need me. Is that it?"

"You can either sit here and rot," I said, "or you can help your son win this war."

She was silent for a few moments. "Does he know you're here?"

"Does that make a difference?"

"It does," she said, "because I know my son will never want me to fight beside him again. If I show my face outside of these dungeons..."

"He wants your help," I interrupted. "He just doesn't know if he can trust you."

Esther smiled; her once perfectly white teeth were now beginning to rot. "I tried to kill him. I would have killed you, too. Although that would have been a mercy compared to what the Paragon will do with you."

"You really feel no remorse? You could have lived a long, happy life knowing that you murdered your own son?" Adeline spat.

Esther's face hardened. "I've lived a lot longer than the both of you combined. You have no idea what it takes to live a long, happy life."

"Don't speak down to me," Adeline said. "I know plenty. I am not a witch, but I know how to be happy. And turning on those who trust you is not going to help you. Especially since you failed in your efforts to take the power from the peacemaker."

I stayed silent. Hearing Adeline speak with so much passion was both inspiring and bone-chilling.

"Look," I interrupted. "You can fight this all you want. You can stay down here and rot and think that you're better than all of us because of it. Or you can get over your self-righteousness and try to make it up to Malachi. Fight beside him. Fight for him. Redeem yourself."

"Redeem myself," she mumbled. Her hands began rubbing at her chained wrists. "I'm afraid I lost that chance a long time ago."

"You won't even try?" I asked.

"I'm just one person. Even if I tried to help, I'm too weak now. I'll have no magic."

"You'll find a way," I argued. She had enough magic to enter my dream the other night. That meant something. "If it's important enough, you'll try."

Seconds felt like hours. Adeline and I stood at the entrance of the cell, waiting for her answer. Waiting for a sign of hope.

It was a dangerous thing, counting on someone else. I prayed to the Saints that this wasn't a massive mistake.

"Okay," she finally said. "If you let me out, I'll fight by my son's side. I'll do what I can, I'll talk to the Paragon. But I can't promise you anything."

I sighed in relief.

"We just have to get you out of these chains..."

"Please," Adeline shrugged, pulling a small pin from her long hair. "I've got this."

She approached Esther and knelt by her side, gently picking the cuffs on her wrists with the pin.

In a few seconds, the chains clattered to the ground. "Can you stand?"

"Of course, I can stand. I'm not dead yet." She attempted to move to her feet, but struggled with every movement.

Saints. Maybe she wouldn't be any help to us after all.

Adeline eventually grabbed her arm to help her up. "You just need to get out of these dungeons. You'll feel much better once you see the sun."

Esther stayed silent. Adeline didn't let go of her as she took one step. And then another.

"The next challenge will be getting past the guard."

"Well how did you two sneak in here?" Esther mumbled. "I assume if you got yourselves past them once, you can do it again."

"With a prisoner? Sure, sounds easy."

My blood was pounding in my ears. Even in the chill of the tunnels, a bead of sweat ran down my spine.

If this didn't work, I would be in trouble.

And Malachi would be pissed.

"Let me do the talking," Adeline said as we approached the entrance. "Stay back."

Adeline let go of Esther, and I had to grab ahold of Esther's arm to ensure she could still stand.

To my surprise, Esther didn't fight it.

We stayed back while Adeline trotted forward to speak with the guard.

I strained to hear what they were saying.

"I'm sorry about your sister," Esther whispered to me.

I snapped my attention to her. "What?"

"Your sister, Tessa. I'm sorry that she died."

If my heart hadn't already been pounding as fast as possible, I was sure it would have started. "How do you know about that?"

"I have many gifts, child," she spoke. "I sensed it as soon as it happened."

*Stay focused,* I thought. I couldn't get distracted. I couldn't let Tessa infiltrate my thoughts.

"At least those bastards got what they deserved," she said when I didn't speak.

"Yes," I agreed. My teeth were grinding so hard my jaw ached. "They did. And I intend on making anyone who lifts a finger against me pay."

Esther laughed quietly. "I have no doubt about that, child. You are only just beginning to learn how powerful you truly are."

I wanted to ask her more, but Adeline was trotting back in our direction. "What happened?" I asked.

Her face lit up. "He left. I told him Malachi would need his help, and that it was his duty to protect his king. Honestly, that was much easier than it should have been. We should restaff."

"Maybe the Saints are on our side," I stated. "Let's go."

"Where are we going?" Esther muttered. "What's the big plan?"

# CHAPTER 32
# Malachi

I FELT THEM BEFORE I HEARD THEM. HUNDREDS OF DEADLINGS tumbling over one another, catastrophically plummeting their dead, decaying bodies toward the kingdom.

Toward *my* kingdom.

My power wouldn't work against them, but I prepared myself for that. I didn't need my power to drop these monsters to the ground.

They would all die, just like they did the last time they came for us.

Every single one of them would die.

"You shouldn't be out here," Serefin spoke when he found me. "Go inside. You'll be the first target they aim for."

"There's no way I'm letting my own soldiers fight this battle without me."

"There is, brother," Serefin sheathed his sword and grabbed me by both of the shoulders. His eyes were frantic as they scanned my face. "I know you want to fight with us. I know that more than anything. But you're no longer a prince. You are our *king*. We need you alive more than we need you fighting beside us on this battlefield."

My first instinct was to shrug him away and tell him he was wrong. But that slightly desperate look in his eyes made me pause. I had only seen Serefin desperate like this a handful of other times.

I needed to stay alive, yes, but I also had no plans of dying. "I can't sit inside the castle while you all fight the war that I brought on, Serefin. I can help."

"Then help. But only when you can. You can't do anything against the deadlings that the hundreds of men you brought here to fight can't already do. We have the men. We have the weapons. Go inside and wait for the real fighting to begin."

"You want me to wait for the Paragon to arrive?"

Serefin nodded. "That's when we'll need you, Mal. And you sure as shit better still be alive."

I shook my head. "If you need me–"

"We won't need you, Mal. As much as I would love to fight by your side, we have more weapons and soldiers than anyone. We have traps set up in the forest and we have blocked the castle doors. Nobody's getting past that gate."

He was right. This was no surprise attack. We had spent weeks preparing the land around us, reinforcing every weak spot and creating as many obstacles as we could for potential attackers.

"Fine," I said. "But at the first sign of trouble, I'm coming to help."

He seemed to relax a little then, finally letting my words sink in. If it meant this much that I would stay out of sight for a while, I would oblige.

"Now go find your sister and Jade," Serefin suggested. "Because we both know there's no way they took your orders to stay put."

I laughed before turning away from the battlefield.

The soldiers I passed on my way inside did not look the least bit concerned.

Determined. Ready. Preparing their weapons and moving their bodies.

Those were the soldiers I trained. Those were the soldiers I could trust.

Jade could trust them, too. Trust them to protect her with their lives. Because that's exactly what we were all doing here today, laying down our lives to protect Jade's.

I walked through the front doors of the castle just before my men boarded them closed. Serefin was right. The odds of her and Adeline doing what they were told and staying hidden in the dungeons were low.

I made my way toward Adeline's bedroom. It was a start.

The heels of my boots clicked on the stone floor as I walked. The castle was now barren, emptied out and turned down as if nobody lived here at all. The servants would be hiding in the tunnels, along with the few women and children that lived here.

I hated that there was no better option. If anything were to go wrong, everyone would be sitting ducks in here.

Which only increased the pure desperation I felt to win this battle. To crush our enemies.

"King Malachi," a strange voice called after me. I spun around in the darkening hallway to find none other than Jade's father walking after me.

His clothes were worn and ripped. Saints, had the maids not given him enough changes of clothing? He walked slowly, but did not stumble. His usual blood-rimmed eyes seemed clear now. Focused.

*On me.*

"What are you doing out here?" I asked. "You should be hiding away. The castle is going to be attacked soon. You'll be safe in your rooms."

He held his hands up to stop me from talking. Not in a disrespectful way, though. I could practically feel the desperation of this man boiling off of him.

"I can't," he said.

"Can't what?"

"I can't hide while your enemies come for my daughter. Let me help you."

Both shock and disbelief washed over me. If only Jade could see this now. Would she laugh in his face? Or give the man a chance?

Surely, in a fight against a fae, this man would lose. Not only was he human, he was barely alive. A strong gust of wind would knock him off his feet.

If he stayed away from the liquor that long.

"I understand you want to help," I started with caution, "but I can guarantee you we have this covered."

I began turning back toward Adeline's bedroom when he closed the distance between us and grabbed ahold of my arm.

"Please," he begged. "I lost one daughter. I know I do not deserve this. I know you have no reason to trust me. But...I have to do something. Give me a sword and I'll fight. I'll protect the women and children. Anything."

I could have snapped his neck right there for laying a hand on his king.

Jade's father deserved no mercy. No kindness.

But if he wanted to lose his life fighting for his daughter, who was I to stop him?

"Okay," I admitted. "The front door has been nailed shut already. Follow this hall to the servant's entrance, and let them know I sent you. They'll give you a weapon there."

A flicker of something lit up his dark eyes. "Thank you," he said, bowing his head and holding his hands together. "Thank you, Malachi. You will not regret this."

"No, I won't," I said. "But you might."

I watched as Jade's father half-ran down the hallway, toward the servants' entrance of the castle and outside to face the battlefield.

Finding Jade was even more important after whatever just happened.

When I got to Adeline's bedroom, though, it was empty.

Every room in the entire hallway seemed to be empty.

My mind was spinning, heart pounding in my chest.

The dungeons. They must have actually listened to me and gone to the dungeons.

My feet carried me there until her pitch-black hair came into view. I stopped in my tracks.

"I hope this is some sort of twisted joke," I said. All three of them froze at the sound of my voice, including Adeline who let out a small scream.

"Malachi!" she stuttered. "We were just–"

"Save it. Whatever crazy plan you three thought up to get Esther out of here, it isn't going to happen."

"Esther can help us, Mal," Jade said. "You have to understand that."

"What I understand is the fact that you two thought letting a traitor free during a war was a good idea. But I suppose it was my fault for leaving you two unattended. My bad. It won't be happening again."

I stepped forward to grab ahold of Esther's arm, but Jade placed a hand on my chest to stop me. "Listen to me," she whispered, loud enough for only me to hear. "This war is happening because of me. *All* of this is because of me. This is a mess that I created, Mal. If I didn't do everything I could to prevent mass casualties in my own kingdom..."

Her voice cracked as she spoke. I placed a hand on top of hers, holding it to my chest.

"This is war, Jade," I explained. "Men have gone to war over *far* less. You don't need to feel bad for anything, and you certainly don't need to feel responsible. But I know what I'm doing. If I thought for even a second that Esther could help us win this battle, I would use her. But she can't."

"Why not?" she asked. Her deep, endless eyes searched mine. "She'll rot in that dungeon anyway, Mal. Give her a chance. If anything, let her prove herself to you."

Jade really didn't see it. She didn't see that my mother was just another wicked creature who would do and say anything necessary to achieve what they wanted. If Adeline and Jade were helping her out now, it wasn't so she could fight on my behalf in battle.

I would be surprised if the woman didn't try to kill me again.

But these two didn't see that. They saw an old woman on her deathbed. They saw a witch with no way out.

"Can you even stand on your own?" I asked over Jade's head. "How are you supposed to fight in battle?"

"I have other uses than fighting in battle, son. I know you don't trust me. Neither of you do. But this is the end of the road for me. I've lived my life. I've had my chance. I was wrong to betray you, son. I know that now. If you let me help your soldiers in battle with whatever magic I may still possess, you will not regret it."

"What I will regret is letting you free to betray my people again."

Something like pain crossed Esther's face. "The way I see it, you have nothing to lose."

Saints. She was certainly right about that. Esther had grown weak in the dungeons. She was not the witch she was before.

"Fine," I said after a few seconds. "But if you even think about betraying me, I won't capture you as a prisoner. I'll kill you right there. I don't care how useful you claim to be to Jade and I."

Esther nodded in gratitude. "Adeline, show Esther where to go. Then come back here immediately."

"You got it," she muttered. I waited until Adeline and Esther were far enough away before grabbing ahold of Jade's arm.

"Ow!" she yelped. "What are you doing?"

"What you should have been doing this entire time. Hiding you."

I began dragging her back toward the entrance of the dungeons. "Malachi, stop!" she yelled. She tried to dig her heels into the ground beneath her, but she wasn't strong enough to stop me from pulling her along with me.

"You're too valuable, Jade. Keeping you alive is the number one priority. Not only for me. For everyone on that damn battlefield right now."

"I'm not useless! My power can help them all!"

"It's too risky."

"You're not the one who decides that, Malachi!" she brought her free hand up and slapped me across the face.

*Hard.*

I let her go and she stumbled backward, hands covering her mouth. *Did she really just hit me?*

"Saints," she muttered. "Mal, I'm sorry. I wasn't thinking I just wanted you to–"

"It's fine," I said, unable to keep the amusement from my voice. "And you're right. I'm not the one who decides that, Jade."

I stepped forward and placed my hands on either side of her face, forcing her to look up at me. "I want you to be free. I want nothing more than for you to do whatever the Saints you want to do in this life. But you can't do that if you're dead, Jade. So please, if you have ever listened to me, I *need* you to do this. I need you to stay safe."

"They're your soldiers, Mal! If I can help them, even a few of them, by using my powers while also staying hidden, what's to stop us?"

I opened my mouth to reply, but was cut off by the booming sensation of a cannon hitting the grounds nearby.

Her eyes widened. "What was that?"

My blood ran cold. "They're here."

# CHAPTER 33
# *Jade*

"Where are we going now?" I asked. Something I said must have hit home with Malachi, because he was no longer dragging me into the depths of the dungeons to hide away for the entire battle.

We were heading somewhere else.

"You were right," he said. He pulled me down the hallways of the castle in a direction I had never been before. "These are my people, but they are also yours. We shouldn't just leave them undefended when we have power that can help them."

"Wow. Malachi Weyland admitting I'm right? Our kingdom might be falling, after all."

"Not the time for jokes, Jade," he sneered, but I saw the way he hid his smile.

Mal pulled me into a small wooden doorway that we both had to duck to get inside of. Once we were in, I could see a spiral staircase leading upward.

"We're going up?" I asked.

"To the roof," he answered. He led the way, taking step after step with his black wings tucked in tight so they would fit in the small corridor.

"Sounds much better than hiding in dungeons," I replied.

I tried to keep my voice calm, but the closer we got to the roof, the louder the shouts and screams from the battlefield became. "Deadlings?" I asked.

"They'll attack first with deadlings," Mal answered. Holding onto his hand was enough to keep me sane. He had done this before. Saints, he was practically a professional at battle.

I knew nothing.

"They'll try to weaken our armies. It won't work, though. Deadlings may have caught us off guard the last time, but we prepared for this."

"How are they even controlling them? I thought deadlings had a mind of their own?"

"It has to be the Paragon. Either a witch or a fae who has the power to control others. That's the only explanation."

He let go of my hand to pull himself through a small hole at the end of the staircase.

Once he was through, he reached down to help me up.

Saints. We really were on top of the castle.

The flat roof allowed us to maneuver easily, and a small ledge kept us hidden from the battlefield.

The smell of rotting flesh hit me instantly.

"You'll get used to it," Mal said, reading my thoughts. Together, we crawled on our stomachs to the edge of the roof, where we would be able to see at least some of the battlefield below.

I peeked my head over slowly, and instantly sucked in a breath.

Our soldiers were ready. Every movement of a fae's weapon brought down one deadling, if not two.

In comparison to the skilled fighters, the deadlings were slow and unorganized. I scanned the battlefield, looking for a single sign of a fallen fae.

When I saw none, I took a deep breath and returned to the safety behind the ledge.

"See?" Malachi breathed, doing the same. "There's nothing to worry about. Serefin and the others have this under control. They could defeat an entire army of deadlings in their sleep."

"Really?" I asked. "And what happens after the deadlings? An army of witches?"

I couldn't shake the feeling that this was too easy. We knew they were coming. We had prepared for weeks. We called out to the surrounding kingdoms, and nearly all of our allies had come to help.

*Luck never stayed by my side this much.*

Another boom of a cannon shook the castle beneath us. Closer this time.

"Tessa would be freaking out if she were here," I breathed. I felt Malachi's attention snap to me. "In a weird, terrible way, I'm glad she doesn't have to deal with this. I just hope she's found peace."

Pain shot through my chest, but I quickly brushed it aside. This wasn't the time for pain. This was the time for focus.

"This world is no place for the innocent," he said. His words were so quiet at first, I thought I had imagined them.

But when I looked over to meet his eyes, I saw a face of so much sorrow, I could nearly feel the grief.

We had both been hurt. We had both been betrayed. We had both fought to survive until our fists bled, our hearts ripped.

This world was not kind. This world would chew you up and swallow you whole.

The shouting from the battlefield increased. By the sounds of it, the deadlings were beginning to die out. Next would be whatever army the Paragon had pulled together.

And they would not be as easy to defeat.

I leaned my head against the stone ledge behind me and closed my eyes. *Breathe, Jade. Breathe.* Malachi was right. This army would have no problem defeating any enemy of ours. We were large and experienced. We had numbers. We had the advantage.

"Are you afraid?" Malachi asked, snapping me from my thoughts.

"Yes," I answered. "But…it's a good kind of fear."

"A good kind?"

"It's…it's the kind of fear that makes you want to survive. That makes you want to keep living. I don't want to die, Mal. Not anymore."

He reached over and grabbed my hand, squeezing tight. "Nothing scares me more than losing you," he whispered.

Malachi's free hand found my cheek, and he slowly leaned over to kiss me.

My heart swelled as his mouth moved against mine. I could practically feel the goodbye in his lips.

But I kissed him back, anyway. I kissed him on that roof, holding onto him like he was all I had left in this world.

Another cannon struck the castle wall.

And the screams of battle began.

# CHAPTER 34
## Malachi

Every instinct in my body told me to fly down to that battlefield and pick up my sword.

But holding Jade in my arms caused me to stay.

"We should help them," she said. "If we use our power from here, they'll never know."

"They'll know you're here," I replied. "It'll be a dead giveaway."

"How?" she asked. "They have no clue what type of power I have. And they won't be able to tell where it was coming from."

"They'll storm the castle to find you," I replied. "Using our power is a last resort, Jade. The less they know about our power and what we have, the better."

She nodded, drinking in every one of my words.

Jade was a fighter. She had rough edges. She had grit and determination and strength.

I knew all of this, yet I was still not ready to send her to war.

"This entire war is happening because they want you, Jade," I explained again. "And I'm not letting them take you."

Her soft hands found my face in the setting sun. "I know you won't."

We stayed there for what felt like hours, although it couldn't have been more than a few minutes. War had that effect.

Scream after scream, we sat on the roof of the castle, praying to the saints that the screams were from our enemies.

A few stray arrows landed on the roof ahead of us, but it was nothing to be concerned about. Nobody knew we were here. They certainly wouldn't expect us to be hiding on the roof.

"Do you think Esther is still alive?" Jade asked.

My fists instinctively tightened. Esther could die on that battlefield, I didn't care. It wasn't just that she had betrayed me. She was going to hurt Jade, too.

Jade might trust her again after what she did, but Esther wouldn't be receiving that same trust from me.

Never again.

"If she's on that battlefield," I answered, "I hope she's dead already."

Jade flipped over and began peeking her head over the wall, peering onto the battlefield. I didn't stop her from looking. Instead, I did the same.

Deadlings covered most of the ground. I couldn't even see the green grass anymore. Bodies and blood together covered the dark green that used to cover it.

But the deadlings were no longer the issue.

Carlyle had been right. Thousands of soldiers now clashed with our own, metal clashing metal as they pushed onward.

Our soldiers were standing strong. The walls of the castle still went untouched. Not a single enemy fighter got past our defenses.

But men spread out as far as my eyes could see. This battle was only beginning.

Jade saw it, too. She saw the forest around us infiltrated with enemy soldiers. Some fae. Some, by the lack of wings, appeared to be witches. But they all fought with weapons.

There was no sign of the Paragon yet. No sign of Silas.

Something deep in my bones told me there would be a sign soon. Very soon.

My eyes landed on Serefin, who was standing back-to-back with Eli. Together, they defended the front gates of the castle. My other brothers were close by doing the same.

Emotion stung my chest. Not long ago, I had thought of my brothers as heartless, idiot men who would rather sit around the castle doing nothing than fight for this kingdom.

Saints, was I wrong.

"I should go down there," I mumbled.

Jade's eyes snapped to mine. "What?" she hissed. "No!"

"I'm their king, Jade. I should be down there fighting side by side with them. Not hiding on the roof like a coward."

"And what about me? How is that any different from what you've asked me precisely not to do?"

I opened my mouth to reply, but shut it again. Jade was right. If I went down onto that battlefield, there was nothing stopping Jade from doing the exact same.

And something told me it wouldn't take her long.

"Even if you could control your power," I explained, "it would be too dangerous. You could easily take out one of our men."

"I'll be careful, Mal. You know I will."

"They'll overpower you. If someone came at you with a sword, you would be overtaken."

She shook her head. Saints, I hated how defiant she was. But at the same time, I loved her even more because of it.

"If you really want to help, you can do it from the safety of this roof. Do you understand?"

"But I–"

"I swear to the Saints, Jade Weyland, if I see you on that battlefield, I will lock you in the dungeons myself."

That seemed to shut her up.

"Fine," she said. "But be careful out there, Mal."

She threw her body at mine, pressing one last kiss onto my lips before pulling away.

I wanted more time with her. I wanted a lifetime of her mouth against mine.

This was the only way.

"Stay safe," I mumbled to her. I stood from the roof and dove to fight with my kingdom.

I landed fast and hard on the ground just inside the gate. The sun had fully set, giving me the cover of darkness as I prepared for battle. The ground shook beneath me and my power practically begged to be let loose. I unsheathed my sword and tucked my wings tightly behind my back.

There was no turning back now.

I leaped to the top of the wall, looking at the crowd of chaos below me. There were dozens of casualties, but I avoided looking at their faces.

We would mourn the dead later.

Now, we had to protect the living.

I spotted my brothers first. They were fully capable of taking care of themselves, but I leapt to the ground next to them anyway. Fae I didn't recognize fought against us, but they were no match.

Our steel cut deeper.

Our soldiers fought harder.

My brothers pushed forward on my left. I stepped right, slicing my sword through the torso of a young male.

My body buzzed with energy. The battlefield felt familiar in a way I could never explain. And I did not feel threatened.

My body moved without my permission. I sliced at anyone who came toward me, cutting down each enemy with ease. My power rumbled in my blood but I kept it at bay. Although my wings had been a dead giveaway as to who was fighting on this battlefield, my power would certainly put a target on my back.

I had enough to fight for.

Eli caught my attention. He looked ten years older now, wielding his sword with blood already splattered across the side of his face. He didn't look like a scared, inexperienced boy.

Eli fought like a warrior next to our brothers. With a battle cry, he grabbed his sword with both hands and brought it down–hard–against an approaching fae.

The body landed with a satisfied thud.

He didn't stop there. I watched as he ran forward, toward the forest, with a determination that others followed.

Back to reality.

I dodged a sword to my right, and my blade made contact with flesh as I swiped my weapon in front of my body. Another fae down.

Another body.

I stepped on top of the corpse and cut down another.

And another.

Saints. These soldiers must have been inexperienced in battle. I caught the look of a few terrified faces just before death greeted them.

This was no place for the weak.

"Malachi!" Ser's voice pulled my attention to the left. "Malachi, get out of here!"

"I'm not leaving, Ser!" I yelled as I sliced the head off another attacker. "This is my kingdom. I'm fighting!"

Serefin sliced his way toward me, cutting down two more fae and stepping over their bleeding bodies. "Then I'm not letting you leave my sight," he mumbled.

Together, we pushed forward, leading the army in battle as we pushed the troops further and further from the front gate of the castle.

## CHAPTER 35

# *Jade*

My legs shook as I ran, down and down that stupid spiral staircase. I wasn't planning on leaving the roof. I didn't plan on disobeying Malachi's direct orders. But watching him leap over that wall and into battle...

No. I wouldn't stand by and watch as my life was ripped from me again.

The front doors would still be bolted closed. There was no way I was getting out of there. I had to think.

How else could I make it out of this damned castle?

I ran down the hallway that Mal had led me through not even an hour before.

There was a servant's exit. I had heard him speak of it before, the servants would never use the front doors to the castle.

That would be my way out.

I ran, looking for any door that looked short or hidden. Those doors would be the ones to lead me outside.

And before I knew it, I was pushing a small wooden door open to the outside.

I was on the side of the castle now, not anywhere near the front.

But I could still feel the tension in the air. The smell of death was even stronger now. And it would only get stronger.

Darkness hid me in its comforting shadows as I kept one hand on the stone castle wall, letting it lead me to the front.

I heard the screams first. The towering wall stopped me from viewing any of the fighting, but from what I saw on the roof, I was close.

I just had to get over that damned wall.

I took a deep breath and bolted, closing the distance from the castle to the wall that now separated me from the battle.

Power pulled on my chest. I knew I could wield it if necessary. I only hoped I wouldn't have to.

The knife Malachi had given me ages ago fit firmly in my hand. My palm was sweating, but not from nerves.

No. I was prepared for battle.

Malachi might not have thought so, but I sure did.

A flicker of light caught my attention ahead of me.

There were other entrances to the kingdom. I knew there were.

I crept forward, careful to stay as silent as possible in the throes of screams and screeches of metal clashing.

It was an opening. A small, hidden opening in the massive stone walls.

Saints.

I knelt on all fours, my knees and palms pressing against the cool, damp night ground. When I caught a glimpse of what was waiting for me on the other side of that hole...

My blood froze in my veins.

The first thing I noticed was the pile of deadlings that accumulated near the wall.

And the smell that came with them.

The soldiers had pushed away from the wall, though. There wasn't a single soldier within fifty feet of the wall now. They were pushing back.

That was good.

*Right?*

I knelt through the small opening in the wall.

This was it. There was no going back now.

I squinted against the darkness, trying to identify anyone familiar. A mixture of wings and weapons clashed ahead of me, but everything was too dark. Too far.

I couldn't see a single damn thing.

"I've been waiting for you," a male voice made me jump. I tightened my grip on my weapon and stood from my crouching position.

A large, hooded male stood before me. I couldn't see his face under the black shadows.

"Jade Weyland," he spoke. "You're coming with me."

"Who are you?" I asked. I tried to slice my weapon toward him, but he easily caught my wrists.

A low, blood-curdling laugh escaped him. Accompanied with the screams of battle. "My name is Silas," he said. My legs shook beneath me. "And you have something I want."

I screamed as loudly as I could before Silas lifted me off the ground.

# CHAPTER 36
# *Malachi*

SERЕFIN AND I HEARD HER AT THE SAME TIME.

"Is that Jade?" he asked me in the midst of battle. Our enemies had thinned out in forces, but they were still coming.

Saints. I didn't even have to think about it. Yes, that was Jade.

I dropped another fae male to his knees before spinning around, looking for her in the darkness.

But chaos erupted around us, more with every second. I couldn't see past the spraying of blood and wings.

I couldn't hear past the battle cries of my men.

*Dammit, Jade.*

As our forces moved forward, pressing the enemy back, Ser and I moved toward the castle.

Toward Jade's scream.

She was okay. She had to be okay. I couldn't live with another possibility.

Ser and I trampled over dead bodies as we got closer and closer to the castle wall. She was nearby. I could feel it, I could feel my power deep inside recognizing hers.

A cool blade pressed against the back of my neck. "Kneel," a voice I recognized demanded.

Every one of my senses lit a fire. I could end them with a single thought.

But where would that leave Jade?

Would Serefin die, too?

"Just do it, Mal," Serefin demanded. He already knelt next to me, a similar blade on his own person.

So I knelt.

"The mighty Prince of Shadows," the voice said. I wanted to vomit when I recognized just who was speaking...

*Silas.*

"Or is it *King of Shadows* now?"

"Where's Jade?" I asked. When I tried to turn my head, the blade on my neck pressed harder into my skin.

"Your wife is safe," Silas answered. "For now. I must say, I'm a bit disappointed. After everything I heard about her..."

Jade whimpered in the distance. She was maybe fifteen feet behind me.

"Let go of me!" she growled. A breath of relief came from me. She was alive. She was alive and fighting.

My power rumbled. I could end them. I had to.

But so could Jade. *Why hadn't she used her power to get away?*

I closed my eyes and focused on my senses. Silas stood behind my left shoulder, just far enough that I couldn't see his face.

Serefin was a few feet to my right, kneeling beside me.

And Jade was directly behind me. I assumed she had a soldier on each arm keeping her stable.

Five against three. *I liked those odds.*

"I just want to chat," Silas said. His boots crunched the forest floor as he stepped forward into view.

Just as hideous as I remembered.

"I'd rather not," I spat back. I let my power flare in his direction.

Silas fell to his knees before he could even get a good look at me. I sent a rush of power toward Jade, too, toward the guards that held her.

We had one advantage. They didn't know that Jade blocked my power. They had no idea how special she was.

I couldn't see her, but I heard her. Jade cried out as the soldiers let go of her. Serefin was next, but he was already fighting. The guard behind him still had a grip on his sword.

So I sent my own into his chest.

Jade ran toward me, and I caught her in my arms.

"Stay by me," I whispered. "Do everything I say."

I turned my attention back toward Silas, who still knelt on the forest floor, and to Serefin, who now had his sword aimed directly at Silas.

"Give me the order," Ser barked. "Say the words and he's dead."

Battle littered the air around us. I couldn't think straight. Couldn't breathe. My heart pounded again and again in my chest, faster than I ever thought possible.

"It's no use," I muttered. "Let's get out of here while we can."

Serefin hesitated for a moment. I knew he was registering the shock of what I had just said.

But I couldn't explain now. I couldn't explain it all.

*Silas couldn't be killed.*

At least, not in any way that I knew how.

Jade's power was on the verge of losing control. I felt it in my own body, rumbling and begging for release.

I sent another wave of power toward Silas, keeping him on the ground moaning in pain as the three of us began running toward the castle.

Not before Jade's father jumped out of hiding and brought his sword down on Silas.

# CHAPTER 37
## *Jade*

My blood froze as my father's weapon pierced Silas's flesh.

"Father!" I yelled. I ripped myself from Mal's grasp and ran toward him. His sword was still sticking out of Silas's back, but he wasn't moving.

Neither of them were.

"Father, what are you doing? Come on!" I yelled. "We have to get out of here!"

"I'm not leaving," he said. I felt Malachi's power rumble through the ground, aimed at Silas to keep him down.

"There's no time for this. If you stay here you'll die."

"You are my daughter!" he screamed. The chaos of battle seemed to fade in the distance. "I will not run while there are monsters like him trying to kill you!"

My body trembled with emotion I couldn't even understand. *Why was he doing this? Why now?*

Malachi yelled my name behind me, but I ignored him as I grabbed my father's arm and began pulling him with us.

Serefin yelped in pain. When I turned to see what was happening, he and Malachi were both on the ground.

Three hooded figures approached.

I knew exactly who they were from the chilling in my bones.

*The Paragon.*

*They were here for me.*

Not a single soldier stayed behind. Rewyth's entire army had pressed forward, focused on keeping the attackers away from the castle.

Yet somehow, these enemies snuck through. Fear pricked my senses as I remembered what I had learned about the Paragon. They were each *gifted*.

"Jade Weyland," a hooded figure said. Silas stood behind me. My father grabbed me by the shoulders and began backing up slowly. "I hear you are the alleged peacemaker. Is this true?"

I opened my mouth to speak but I froze. Malachi was still on the ground. One of these hooded men kept him there, I was sure of it.

"Jade is my daughter," my father yelled. "You will not take her!"

Silas shook his head as he stepped into view. "Your daughter seems to have a secret. If you are the peacemaker, we need to know. My people have been waiting on her arrival for centuries now. It is in everyone's best interest if she comes with us."

"Bullshit!" my father yelled.

The hooded figures stepped forward. Malachi tried to stand but failed. "It's honorable," the hooded figure started, "that you protect your daughter this way. I am interested to know, though, were you protecting her when you sent her to marry the Prince of Shadows? When you sold her off to the fae lands?"

I couldn't see my father's face. At that moment, I was glad. My father had suffered plenty the last few weeks.

"I am not the peacemaker," I finally declared. "There's been some mistake. You have the wrong person. I am only a human, and I never wanted any part of this!"

Silas eyed me closely, but eventually turned his attention to Mal and Serefin. "Let them up." Whichever hooded figure that kept them pinned to the ground relaxed. Malachi was on his feet in a second.

Silas held out his hand and said, "Not so fast. We want to handle this peacefully. If everyone cooperates, perhaps we can."

"You call this peaceful?" Mal spat. "Infiltrating my kingdom? I assume you call the other messengers you sent *peaceful* as well?"

"You would have never given up the girl otherwise."

"She is not a tool for some prophecy. And she is not going anywhere. She is my *wife*. You will *not* take her."

His words were strong, but I knew deep down we were at the end of this road. Desperation crept through my body. *They shouldn't die for me. They had done enough.*

"What do you want from me?" I asked Silas, pleading for any way out of this situation. "If I truly *were* the peacemaker, why would you need me? To kill me in some ritual? Sacrifice me for the greater good?"

"It is custom that to prove you truly are the peacemaker, you must pass the Trials of Glory," he answered.

Malachi and Serefin seemed to freeze.

"No," Mal muttered.

"It is the only way to–"

"NO!"

"The Trials of Glory? What is that?" I asked.

Before Silas could answer, a flash of black and silver wings crossed my vision. Malachi tackled Silas effortlessly, and Serefin pulled his own sword on one of the hooded men. My power flared, and I didn't stop it this time.

Desperation and adrenaline mixed together to help me wield my deadly gift. I threw my hands in the direction of the Paragon members, and light exploded around us.

# CHAPTER 38
# Malachi

*Saints save us...*

Jade's magic erupted. I didn't have to look where she aimed it. I already knew. I felt exactly what her power wanted as if it were my own.

Silas stiffened beneath me. I jumped to my feet, releasing my grip on him and turned my attention toward Jade.

This was everything I had been trying to avoid. They had seen Jade's power with their own eyes.

*Even worse.*

One of the hooded figures now laid motionless on the ground. The smell of burnt flesh watered my eyes.

I stepped in front of Jade and her father, who was also staring at her in awe.

"Don't touch her," I demanded. "Let it go."

Silas stood up and approached the remaining two hooded men. "You know we don't have a choice, Malachi. The peacemaker comes with us."

"Mal," Jade whispered behind me. "You have to let me go."

*Did I just hear that right?*

"Nobody's going anywhere," I demanded.

"We've been waiting on her. She'll be safe with us until the trials," Silas announced.

"No! She's a human! The trials are not for her!"

"They are," Esther's voice interrupted. I turned to find her walking toward us, entirely unscathed.

"Esther," Silas announced. "What a surprise."

"How do you know my mother?" I asked him. He only smiled.

Anger stirred in my bones. Something wasn't right. Something–

Jade screamed.

I twisted to look at her, and found one of the surviving hooded fingers with a sword piercing her chest.

*No.*

A sound of pure terror escaped me. I snapped her attacker's neck before catching Jade's lifeless body.

"No!" I yelled. "You're okay, Jade. You're fine. Stay with me."

"Mal?" she whispered. Her voice already sounded weak. Too weak.

I looked at the amount of blood pouring from her chest. It was too much, too much blood.

Her father fell to his knees beside us.

"Help her!" I yelled. "Someone help!"

Jade's eyes flickered shut. I shook her shoulders, screaming her name. This wasn't it. This wasn't the end.

Jade would not die here.

"Malachi," Esther whispered.

"No! This is their fault! He did this!" I said, pointing to Silas.

"We meant her no harm, Malachi," he said in a gentle voice. "This is not what we intended."

"Did you know about this?" I asked Esther. "Did you know they would kill her?"

"I didn't know," Esther replied. "I swear it! I swear to the Saints! But they *will* let me save her life. If they want their peacemaker back, they'll let me do this."

Silas began speaking, but Esther cut him off.

"Jade is the peacemaker. I know you have your speculations still, but it's true. If Jade is dead, you will wait centuries more for the next. Help me save her life."

I could hardly breathe. Hardly think. The only thing I could do was hold Jade's body in my arms.

"You can save her?" I questioned.

Esther knelt beside me, grabbing hold of Jade's arm. "My time here is over, son. Let me do this one last thing."

Esther began chanting in a language I didn't recognize. Her eyes closed, but she didn't let go of Jade.

Jade's father screamed somewhere behind me.

The remaining Paragon members watched, entirely helpless, as Esther chanted and chanted.

"What are you doing?" I asked. But my questions fell void. Esther had gone somewhere else. Her eyes moved in wild motions beneath her eyelids as the chanting grew louder and louder.

When I thought she couldn't get any louder, she fell to the ground.

Unconscious.

"Esther!" I yelled. Serefin crawled over to her, shaking her shoulders.

"Wake up!" he yelled at her. "Wake up, Esther!"

Jade twitched in my arms.

*Jade.*

*Be okay. Be alive.*

"Saints," I muttered. Her body moved once more. "Jade! Can you hear me?"

I shook her lightly. Her wound still poured blood.

And then she coughed.

"She's alive!" I yelled. "She's moving! Serefin, help me over here!"

Serefin left Esther on the forest floor and knelt on the other side of Jade.

Silas spoke next. "I'll heal your wife right now if you agree to the trials."

Emotions flooded my body. I didn't want to fight anymore. I didn't want any of this.

Jade would not survive the trials. They were not created for humans.

But as her body twitched back to life, blood began pouring even faster from her wound.

She had minutes left.

"Let me come with her," I begged. "At the very least, let me help her. She will be the one completing the trials, but she will not be dragged into the mountains alone."

Silas considered my words. Jade moved again in my arms and my heart dropped as she began opening her eyes.

"You have yourself a deal, King of Shadows."

The last hooded figure approached Jade. I didn't stop him as he held a hand an inch above Jade's open wound.

I watched as tendrils of light escaped his hand.

And began closing Jade's open wound.

"Your wife will live," the healer announced with a cold tone.

I took a breath and leaned down, pressing my forehead to hers. She didn't deserve this. She didn't deserve any of this.

And she certainly did not deserve what would be coming.

"We will see you and your wife at the Trials of Glory."

# Trials Of Saints And Glory

BOOK 4

## CHAPTER 1

# Malachi

THE VIOLENT, ICY MOUNTAINS TAUNTED US ON THE HORIZON AHEAD. A challenge approached with each frozen step we took. My tired feet had well surpassed the point of pain. They were numb with the increasing amounts of ice we walked over.

I traveled through the mountains once before. *The monster mountains*, some had called them back then. It was decades ago now, yet I still remembered the path.

*Saints.* I had been so ignorant back then. If I knew then what I knew now, maybe I never would have left. Maybe I would have been living deep in these mountains all along.

But that time I spent in the bitter, biting cliffs had taught me how to turn them off; those pesky, vexatious emotions. Silas, the leader of the Paragon, had been my teacher. He taught me how to carry myself like a king. He taught me how to drop an entire army with my magic. I had loved him like a father at times, and yet he treated me like a wild animal.

*His* wild animal.

But he had taught me how to be dangerous. He had taught me how to be feared.

How to be a weapon.

I clenched my fists. *He was going to do the same thing to Jade if I didn't stop this.*

Silas was the most powerful fae alive. He possessed magic that terrified most, even the powerful witches could not compete with him. The Saints, for whatever reason, had gifted him with an outrageous amount of magic. He could freeze a grown man where he stood, could shield himself from anyone else's gift, including my own. He likely possessed magic that I hadn't seen yet.

Which is why it was impossible to kill him. Silas could see an attack coming from miles away. He had an uncanny ability to protect himself, and he would kill any attacker before they had a chance to protect themselves.

When I was younger, I thought he was a Saint himself. He sure acted like it at times.

But now...

My power flared under my skin, and it took everything in me to will it back down. The last two days had been a constant pattern of that; of controlling my temper. Of reminding myself that I would need to save my energy for later, for when we reached the temple.

I carried Jade through the path for hours until my arms ached. She insisted she could walk, but the life-ending wound on her torso still hadn't healed completely, even with Silas's healer working diligently to stitch her wound closed with magic. We were all exhausted, though, even the powerful healer. Healing her wound entirely would drain him during our travel.

Two days. Two days since the battle in Rewyth, and two days we had been traveling toward the Paragon's mountains.

Esther's waist-length, silver hair nearly blended with the white powder around us. She had come along with the group, even though she could hardly look at me. She, too, was weak. After bringing Jade back from death's wicked grasp, she had nothing left. Each step on the icy terrain seemed to drain her further.

I forced a surge of my power back down again. The memory of what had happened remained fresh in my mind, replaying like a torturous loop of consciousness that I couldn't escape from.

The blade slicing Jade's torso. Her slim, fighting body falling to the ground. Esther at my side, chanting something I couldn't understand.

*Jade coming back from the dead.*

And I knew from the moment Jade's eyes closed, cold and lifeless, that I was going to find a way to kill him.

If Silas really wanted Jade to compete in the Trials of Glory, I would end his life for it.

She was a human, for Saints' sake. She might have special abilities that we were just beginning to understand, but she wasn't a *fae*. The Trials of Glory were made for special circumstances, special powers. They were made to test and to break. Jade, as strongly as she fought and as stubborn as she was, was not *inhumanly* strong. She wouldn't survive a set of tests built to destroy the strongest fae and witches.

And even if she did, she would never be the same. The old Jade, the Jade that we all knew, would be gone forever.

Jade and I walked behind the rest of the group, far enough to attempt at least an ounce of privacy. At first, I worried that I might accidentally kill one of them out of pure spite if I got too close. For what they did back in Rewyth, they deserved it. Each and every one of them deserved to die by my hand, if not by Jade's.

"How are you feeling?" I whispered in Jade's direction.

She looked at me with tired, dull eyes. Dirt and blood smeared her face from the battle in Rewyth, and I could only imagine how much worse I looked.

"If you ask me that question one more time," she whispered back, "I'll have to move to the front of the group to get away from you."

I fought a smile. At least she still had her attitude.

"Fine, fine," I said, holding my hands up in surrender. "I'm just worried about you. I mean, you *died*, Jade. That blade cut deep. There's no way you're feeling up for a hike through the mountains."

She pressed her hands against her thighs as she walked, using more energy than necessary to shift her weight from one foot to the other. "The healer has been working hard. I feel fine, Mal. I mean that."

She lied, but I understood. Showing weakness in front of them wouldn't help us win this fight.

"I'm going to get you out of this," I whispered, quiet enough to ensure nobody else could hear. The howling wind around us helped disguise my voice. "I'll find a way to end this. You don't owe the Paragon anything, and you certainly don't deserve to go through those damned trials after everything else you've been through."

She stopped walking and faced me, her chest rising and falling with each labored breath.

"Don't I, though?" Her voice cracked. "That's the whole reason I'm here, isn't it? Maybe even the whole reason I was born. The Paragon keeps the peace between humans and fae. I am the peacemaker. If this is what I was born to do..."

"You were not born to be viciously slaughtered in the trials. They're out of their minds if they think you'll pass." A silent beat passed between us. My words came out cold and harsh, but it was only my worry for Jade's safety that put me on edge. She deserved better than this. Much, much better.

If she was insulted by my outburst, she didn't show it.

Another frigid breeze hit my face.

"You doubt me that much?" she asked as she turned and continued walking. "After everything we've been through, you don't think I would survive?"

"It's not you I doubt." Her limp was growing more severe with every minute that passed. I reminded myself not to stare, it would only set her off. "It's them. They have no honor, Jade. If they think for even a second you're a threat, they'll eliminate you."

She scoffed, clearly not as concerned about her own safety as I was. "Then I suppose I'll have to avoid appearing as a threat."

Something was going on in her mind. I had pried and pried around in her thoughts as much as possible over the last two days, but she was only just beginning to speak up more.

She had seen something when she died. Or gone somewhere. Either way, the subtle glimmer of light that used to glow in her deep eyes had disappeared.

The old Jade would have thrown a fit over the Trials of Glory, even when she didn't fully understand what they were. She would have blasted the entire world with her magic before going with the Paragon. She wouldn't have cared about being the peacemaker, about having this weight on her shoulders.

But then again, so would I. That was before *her*.

I would risk everything for her. I was willing to lose it all to save her life. But I couldn't tell her that. Because deep down, I knew she was willing to risk it all, too. But not for me.

She was willing to risk it all to save the world.

"You can't trust him," I whispered to Jade. She turned to look at Silas, who stopped near a half-frozen stream a few yards ahead. I watched as he knelt down to cup the water in his hands, pulling the liquid to his lips. Such a mundane task for a deadly, horrendous man. "He'd suck the power out of you and use it for himself if he could. He'd make every single kingdom bow to him again, he'd control every fae. Every witch."

Jade placed a hand on my arm, returning my gaze. "I'm growing tired of all the people we cannot trust." Her face flickered with sorrow, only for a second, before she was able to recover. "We're being alienated out here."

And she wasn't wrong. Esther, Silas, the entire Paragon. All I knew was that we couldn't trust them. Any of them. Jade and I only had each other.

"I won't leave your side," I admitted. "I don't care if I have to tear the mountains down myself to get to you. I'm not leaving."

"Until the trials?" she asked.

My jaw tightened. "Maybe even not then."

The smile that grew on her face was the warmest thing I had felt in days. I knew I would have to leave Jade at some point. I would have to let her show the Paragon just how powerful she was.

She didn't need my help for that. She never did. Jade had become more powerful than I had ever been. I would protect her with my life, yes, but I also knew she could protect herself from any threat, even if that threat was Silas.

"Get comfortable," Silas yelled from his crouched position near the stream, pulling my attention from Jade's face. "We'll camp here for the night, and we'll climb the mountain in the morning."

A chill betrayed me. Jade and I both adjusted our gazes to the towering mountains that now stood in front of us. There was nowhere else to go. We had made it to the base of the mountain, and all we had left to do was climb.

And then we would be stuck there, forced to live with the Paragon in the temple until Jade proved just how powerful she really was.

The frigid temperatures made flying dangerous, although not impossible. I could fly myself, but with Esther and Jade, we couldn't risk the extra weight. The cold weather and the thin air made flying an exhausting task even for one fae.

Jade and I, fresh from battle and with her still-healing wound, would have to hike through the monster mountains.

Esther, although not a Paragon member, practically kept herself glued to Silas's side. I watched the way she followed him, even going so far as to sleep next to him on the forest ground.

And the others...

Serefin's objections were endless when he couldn't join us on this journey, but I needed him in Rewyth more than I needed him here. If he were with us, he would be one more person I had to watch over, and I couldn't handle that right now. All of my attention needed to be focused on Jade.

Jade and those damned trials.

Our other companions were members of the Paragon, the same ones who were trying to kill my people just two evenings ago. We didn't speak. They didn't even look in our direction, although they knew who I was.

The King of Shadows was not to be challenged.

And neither was his wife.

Still far away from the group, I kicked a few sticks out of the brush beneath us and pulled off my cloak. "Here," I said, laying it down beside Jade. "You should get some rest."

Those big, brown eyes stared up at me. "You'll have to sleep at some point, Mal," she whispered. Her tired voice cracked again.

I had to look away. How could I tell Jade that I couldn't sleep? That I couldn't close my eyes? That I couldn't stop watching over her, not even for a single second?

Because those four minutes where she laid lifeless in my arms were the worst four minutes of my entire life.

And I never wanted to feel that pain again. I wasn't sure I would survive it if I had to. I didn't *want* to survive it.

Those few moments with Jade lying lifeless before me, I decided something. Something I knew from the moment I met her, but never fully realized. I would end the world before I lost Jade. I would overcome any obstacle, tear down any enemy. These trials? They were merely a stepping stone. An obstacle.

I wasn't going to let them touch her, Paragon or not.

Jade held her breath as she lowered herself onto my cloak, only exhaling when she reached the forest floor. She leaned back onto the cold ground, grimacing with every movement.

"Come here," she whispered once she settled in. "Come lay with me."

"I have to keep watch," I replied. My eyes flickered to the group ahead, arranging themselves in a small circle for warmth. There was no way I could sleep with our enemies so close.

"You've been keeping watch for two days and nights. You can lay with me for a few minutes. Please, Malachi, at least to keep me warm."

The forest around us *was* frigid. And I did crave being close to her, even if for a few moments, but the hair on the back of my neck stood up at a single movement in the forest around us.

This wasn't Rewyth. It wasn't Fearford, either, or Trithen. We were in new territory, and we faced very new enemies. Some of them camped beside us.

But Jade's eyes stared into mine with a need that included more than just keeping watch.

"Just for a few moments," I replied. I lowered myself next to her, keeping a few inches between us as I splayed my black wings around our bodies.

Jade only shifted her body closer, pressing herself against me as if I were the last thing she had in this world to cling to. Her head rested on my shoulder, her hands finding their way up my tunic and around my bare waist.

The slightest brush of her skin against mine sent my power into a feral spiral. I shuddered at her touch, and a small smile on her lips told me she knew exactly what type of effect she had on me.

"Careful," I growled.

"What?" she replied, faking her innocence. "I'm only warming myself up."

For the first time since we left Rewyth, I allowed it. I wrapped my arms around Jade and pulled her to my body, careful not to apply pressure on her healing wound. She exhaled deeply, taking in the warmth of my body just as I did to her.

My instincts flickered from the forest around us to the Paragon members that settled into sleep nearby. Certain that everyone was quickly falling asleep, I dragged my hand up to Jade's chin and tilted her head up to mine.

"I never wanted this for you, Jade," I whispered in the darkness. "If I could trade places with you, I would."

She exhaled slowly. "None of this is your fault. I don't blame you for any of it, Mal. I hope you know that."

*She should blame me, though.* I was the reason she got forced into this mess. My father forced me to marry her, yes, but I should have protected her more, shielded her away from the chaos of this world.

"I wish you would blame me," I admitted. "It would make me feel much better about dragging you through all of this."

Jade lightly hit my chest. "You're ridiculous," she replied. "We're in this together, okay? No blame, no hatred. We make it out of here alive and then we'll talk about hating one another again."

I couldn't stop the smile that formed on my face.

"You are my light, Jade Weyland," I whispered. "For so, so long, I was stuck in the darkness. Not anymore."

Jade smiled, warm and genuine, before settling her head back onto my chest. I ran my fingers through her black hair, soothing her in any way that I could. It wouldn't be enough. With the chaos that surrounded us, it would never be enough.

I listened to her heartbeat until it slowed. And just when I thought she had fallen asleep...

"I'm afraid, Mal," she whispered in her breath, barely loud enough for me to hear. "They want me to be strong, but I am not."

I let my body relax around her, giving her the comfort I knew she craved. "You are strong," I said. I pressed my forehead to hers and held her tightly in the privacy of my black wings and the lowering sun. "You are strong, capable, and resilient. You've died and come back from the darkness. You've lost so much and yet you're still standing, Jade. You are one of the strongest people I know. You can do anything, you can overcome anything."

A single tear slid down her face. I quickly brushed it away. "I don't want to be strong," she said. "I'm tired. I'm so tired."

Jade shifted against me, muffling sobs in my thick, ripped tunic. "We're almost to the end," I said. "I'll find a way out of this. I'll find a way."

# CHAPTER 2
# *Jade*

Sleep was nothing like dying. Sleep was sometimes terrifying, sometimes delightful. Sleep was healing and replenishing. It was necessary for daily functioning.

Death, on the other hand, was something else entirely.

To me, death had been the hands of a lover welcoming me to bed. It was so hard to say no, and saying yes seemed too easy.

So I said yes. And then the darkness followed.

Malachi explained that I was only gone for a few minutes before Esther brought me back, but that wasn't what it seemed like. That wasn't how it felt.

It felt never-ending. It felt like I had lived many, many lives in that darkness. It felt like I belonged there all along, but also like I had an eternity left to spend in the nothingness.

There was no fire. There was no punishment. There were no Saints.

Just...nothingness.

And then I re-awoke inside my own body, with Esther chanting over me and Malachi holding me in his arms.

And seconds later, I was here, being whisked away into the Trials of Glory that I couldn't win, to be someone I could not be.

But how did I tell them that? How did I tell them all that I would fail them?

How was I supposed to tell *him*?

There were no words to describe the pain on Malachi's face when Esther brought me back, in those few moments between life and death.

He thought he had lost me, and he was utterly, mercilessly broken.

And I never wanted to see that again. Not from him. He deserved better than me, he deserved better than someone who would die before they completed the Paragon's Trials of Glory.

I barely had magic. How was I supposed to complete the ancient trials from the Saints?

I reveled in the warmth of Malachi's body and tried to forget. I tried to forget the war. I tried to forget the darkness. My father. Serefin. Everyone we left behind. Tessa.

I tried to forget it all and focus on his arms around me. His wings keeping me safe. Sleep didn't come easily. I had dozed off a couple of times, but even though Malachi held me while I slept, I knew he would be wide awake. He wouldn't drift off for even a second.

His strong arms held me to him, close enough that I felt safe, but not hard enough to put pressure on my half-healed wound.

"I wish we could leave this place," I whispered, more to myself than to him. I gave up on sleep, but I didn't dare move from the warmth his arms provided. The forest was pitch-black now, and the nightlife created an array of noises around us, each one fueling the adrenaline in my veins.

His chest rumbled with a small laugh. "Trust me, Jade. I would carry you out of here and never come back if I could."

"Somewhere warm. With sunlight and plenty of nature."

"And no wars. No kingdoms."

"Can Adeline come?" I asked, tilting my face up so I met his gaze in the moonlight. "And Serefin?"

He moved forward and placed a warm kiss on my forehead. "You can bring anyone you want."

I tensed, and I knew Mal felt it. I couldn't stop my mind from wandering to my father. After everything, he had tried desperately to save me. Was he any match against a fae? No, not in the slightest.

But for once, he had fought. For once, he had tried to protect his family.

*What was left of it, anyway.*

"They'll all be okay," Mal whispered, brushing his fingers against the side of my face. "We'll be back home before anyone can cause any trouble. My brothers will keep things in line, and Serefin won't let a single thing happen."

"I know, I just... I hate to think of him in a kingdom of fae, all alone."

"He's not alone. And maybe it will be good for him."

A shaking breath escaped me. "I can't see how that's possible."

I ran my hands down Mal's sculpted chest. "I shouldn't care. If I cared about everyone's wellbeing, I would drive myself crazy."

His chest rose and fell. "You care because you love so much. And that's part of what makes you so marvelous."

His fingertips slowly grazed my body, settling on my lower back. I couldn't help but shiver. Being this close to him still made me feel this way, like it was my first day with him all over again.

"*Marvelous,*" I repeated. "That's an interesting word for it."

He moved his hand, inching his fingers under the loose fabric of my shirt so the rough, calloused skin touched my bare back. My breath hitched. "You should get some sleep," he whispered.

But I could hear the grin on his face as he said the words.

His index finger began moving in circles over that sensitive spot on my lower back, sending chills erupting through my body.

"Malachi," I grumbled.

"Yes, my queen?"

He then traced his finger along my spine, all the way up to my shoulder blades. He hovered lightly, kissing the skin with a delicate touch.

I shut my eyes, reveling in the sensation. "How am I supposed to sleep with you touching me like that?"

"Like what?"

He moved his hand to my bare side, caressing my ribs. Again, I shivered. "Like that." He then traced the curve of my hip, lingering on the waistband of my filthy trousers.

"Would you prefer it if I didn't touch you?"

I took a long, shaking breath. His hand lingered in a silent question. "No, *my king*," I answered. "I would very much *not* prefer that."

I pushed myself into him, gently pressing my lips to his. It had been days since he held me like this, since we kissed like this. A low growl rumbled in Mal's chest as he kissed me back. He moved slowly at first, gently maneuvering his mouth against mine. As if he were taking it all in. As if he were kissing me again for the first time.

His black wings blended with the night sky, shielding us from the outside world. Mal's hands were hot against my ribs, gripping my waist and holding my body tightly to his. I did the same, sliding my hands up his shirt and pulling him close to me.

I moved to slide my body on top of his when a piercing pain came from my abdomen. I hissed and pulled away.

"Are you okay?" Mal asked.

I pulled back and slid my tunic up, finding the bandages holding my wound together covered in dark red blood.

*Again.*

The healer had been working diligently to heal me every few hours, but the cut was deep, and he had to save most of his energy for our travels.

Malachi pushed himself up, immediately calling for the healer. "She's bleeding!" he yelled to the group that lay sleeping by the river bank, startling half of them with his booming voice. "Come help her!"

Mal knelt behind me, lifting my head and supporting my body as the healer woke up. He wasn't a pleasant man, and his hands were very, very cold. But I had to admit, a small amount of healing was better than none.

"You're moving too much," the man said as he approached. He had silver wings, but they were smaller than most. He clearly didn't do much flying, and I wondered if it had something to do with his old age. Fae were nearly immortal creatures, but this fae in particular was covered in history and wrinkles.

And whatever life he lived, it didn't teach him to be gentle.

His hands were cold as he peeled away my red bandages. The chilled air replaced the warmth of my own blood, causing my muscles to tense. The healer placed his hands on my torso, on either side of the wound.

I flinched.

"Careful," Mal hissed from behind me.

The healer only shot Mal an annoying glare with his blue eyes before closing them in focus.

I closed mine, too. Not because it hurt. It was a feeling that was hard to describe.

Warmth immediately radiated from his cold, lifeless hands, and the pain in my wound dulled as a tingling sensation took over my torso. This happened every time, and it was almost as if I could feel the tendrils of my flesh mending together once more.

Malachi's hands held on to me tightly. Saints, I much preferred Mal's hands over this old hag's.

A few more seconds went by, and the healer opened his eyes once more. "Lay still tonight," he warned. "We climb the mountains tomorrow, and I won't be able to heal you any more during the journey. We must wait until we reach the temple."

"Great," I mumbled. "Can't wait."

The healer stood up and returned back to his position with the others, who were now beginning to stir. In the shadows of darkness, I could see Silas staring at us.

I stared back at him. I wasn't sure what all went down between him and Malachi, but I didn't like it. Not one bit. Silas made Malachi stiffen when he was near. Mal treated him differently, looked at him differently.

What had happened between them in these mountains all those years ago? Who *was* Silas? And what was he going to do to me?

Mal explained very few details. Silas was a powerful fae, that much I knew. More powerful than Malachi. More powerful than anyone. That's why he was able to claim himself as leader of the Paragon. Nobody was ever able to kill him, nobody's power matched his.

I could tell Mal tried to hide the hatred in his voice when he spoke of Silas. For what? I still wasn't sure. I knew Silas was the one that trained Mal to kill, to use his own power. He was the reason Malachi became so powerful to begin with.

But what happened after that? Why would Silas attempt a war with one of his own friends, one of his own mentees?

Mal moved away, leaving me lying alone on his cloak. I immediately missed the warmth from his body. "Where are you going?" I asked.

"Get some sleep," he said. "You need to conserve your energy for tomorrow."

The heat I had been feeling in my body dissipated with his words. He didn't even look at me. His dark curls hung around his cheekbones as he sat on the cold ground next to me, ready to keep watch for the night and once again not getting any sleep.

I couldn't say I blamed him. I had died. I had left him, like each of his wives before me, I was lost.

I couldn't imagine how he felt now.

I settled into the darkness, enveloping myself in Mal's cloak. "Sleep well, my queen," he whispered.

But his voice was hollow.

I closed my eyes and drifted into an eerie, chilling sleep.

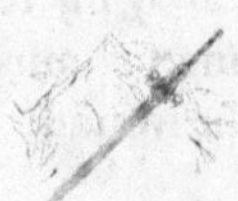

The sun woke me.

It began to rise in the distance, and the shreds of sunlight flickered in through the thin trees above us. I pushed myself up, feeling stiff from yet another night sleeping on the ground.

Today was the day. The day we climbed those damned mountains and arrived at the Paragon's temple.

"Are you feeling okay?" Malachi asked again, just like he had done hundreds of times yesterday. I nearly jumped at the sound of his voice, but he was leaning against a tree with his legs stretched before him.

"Good as new," I grunted. I glanced over to where the others were also waking up. "You up for this?" I asked.

His eyes were dark. "I don't think we really have a choice," he answered.

I waited for him to say more, but he sat there staring into the forest like I wasn't even there. I knew he was nervous. I knew he was afraid of his past, whatever that entailed.

But all we needed to focus on today was climbing the mountain.

Climb the mountain today, and deal with saving the world tomorrow.

*Easy enough, right?*

I left Mal and limped over to the stream to splash the freezing water on my face. I was no longer a fan of streams, not after almost being killed by the kraken. But these days, I had much worse enemies than those disgusting sea monsters. I had men wanting to put me through trials that were designed to break me. I had fae and witches trying to steal my power.

*Much* worse enemies than the kraken. At least I knew those creatures wanted me dead. The worst type of enemy were the ones you couldn't see coming, the ones that tried to protect you first before stabbing you in the back.

"The climb isn't so bad," Silas said. His deep voice made me jump. I stood from my kneeling position by the stream.

"It's not the climbing that keeps me up at night," I replied, rolling my shoulders back and lifted my chin. "It's what comes after."

He smiled and looked down at his feet. In his all-black cloak, he seemed small. Not terrifying. Not dangerous. Just...simple. He had to squint to make eye contact with me, which was amusing enough coming from the most powerful fae of our time.

"I think you'll find the temple to be quite welcoming. Just because we are the Paragon doesn't mean we don't enjoy the simple luxuries of life." He finished the sentence with a forced smile.

"I've heard otherwise," I spat. "And I'm not sure it's the luxuries of life that have earned you your reputation."

He considered my words. "What are you afraid of, Jade Weyland?"

"*Afraid* of?"

He took a step closer. His pale skin seemed iridescent, even in the morning sun. His eyes were sunken in against his cheekbones, and I could barely see the white hair growing against his shaved head.

"Yes, child. Tell me what you fear."

*Child.* I hated when Esther called me that, and now Silas?

"Why would I tell you such a thing? I don't know you."

"Not yet," he answered. "But you and I will be getting to know each other very well over the next few days."

I placed a hand on my hip. "And I can't tell you how excited I am for that." I couldn't keep the attitude out of my voice. Silas was trying to intimidate me, and it wasn't going to work.

He dropped his smile. "If you are who you claim to be, peacemaker, you'll have no problem completing the Trials of Glory."

"I don't see how that's true, considering I'm human."

He looked me up and down. His gaze was cold and eerie, but I didn't look away. I didn't step back.

"Humans don't possess magical gifts, Jade. Humans do not die and come back to life. Humans are not chosen to become the peacemakers of our world."

He turned on his heel and walked back to the group before I could ask what he was talking about, but my mind burned with his words like fire.

***Was I not human?***

# CHAPTER 3
# Malachi

I DESPISED HIM.

I despised that he was here, that he was still alive. I despised that he looked at Jade. That he talked to her. That he existed.

Even watching them converse near the stream put a fiery anger deep in my chest.

I had always been protective of Jade, but this was different. If he dug his claws into her, I was afraid she would never escape. And neither would I.

"What was that about?" I asked as Jade returned.

She was paler than usual, even with her face dripping in the cool water from the stream. "He doesn't seem to think I'm human," she answered.

I stood up from the tree base. "What?" I asked. "Why does he think that?"

Jade shrugged. "He said humans don't possess magic. And they can't come back from the dead."

*That bastard.* I had suspected whether or not Jade was truly human for quite some time, ever since we learned that our magic was connected. Why would the Saints give a human such a special gift, only to give her the life duration of a human?

But that wasn't Silas's place. He could keep his damned opinions to himself.

"I don't like it when he talks to you," I said. "He should leave you alone."

"You really hate him, don't you?" she asked. "What did he do to you, Mal?" She glanced at the crowd again before stepping closer to me and lowering her voice. "What are we about to walk into?"

I shut my eyes and shook my head. *That was the past,* I reminded myself. That was the old Silas, the old Malachi. That was decades ago now, and so much had changed. I changed. I was sure Silas had changed, too.

I had to tell myself that. If I let fear control me, I would become paralyzed. And that's not what Jade needed right now. She needed strength. She needed fearlessness.

"It's nothing," I answered.

But I could tell she wasn't buying it. "I'll find out at some point," she said. "And do you believe him? About me not being human?"

"I don't know," I said. "But I think we'll be finding out very soon."

"Everyone ready?" Silas yelled. Jade and I approached slowly, still lingering in the back of the crowd. "This will be a difficult journey. If we're lucky, we'll reach the temple before the sun falls. If we aren't lucky, we'll have a rough night of camping in the winter. Stay close and keep your wits about you. We don't know who's watching us out here."

Jade glanced up at me. "Should I be worried?"

"Stick with me and we'll be just fine," I answered.

For the first couple of hours, the climb was fairly simple. The cold forest ground turned to snow-covered rock, and then fluffy, freezing snow. For as far as we could see, snow.

I had given Jade my cloak to wear, but the sound of her teeth chattering still sent a feral anger down my spine.

"We need to move faster!" I called forward to Silas. "We're not making fast enough time."

"We're moving as fast as we can!" he yelled back, although his voice trailed off with the howl of the icy wind.

"Well, it's not fast enough." I caught up to Jade, who was only a few paces ahead of me. "Are you feeling okay?" I asked. I felt like I had asked her that every ten seconds for the last three days.

"I'm fine," she answered through gritted teeth. "Please tell me the path doesn't get worse than this."

I couldn't lie to her, so I stayed silent.

Two more hours passed like that, with the winds increasing and the snow growing deeper.

Until we reached the first passage.

"No way," Jade said before we even made it to the edge. "There's no way I can climb over that."

A rope bridge connected the two cliffs together, creating a pathway. One that I never wanted to cross again. And unlike Esther and Jade, I had wings.

"I'll be with you the entire time," I said. The group of us now congregated near the bridge while Silas brushed some of the ice from the first plank. "The others will go first, and you'll see it's not that bad. Right, everyone?"

The others prepared to cross, but I felt a pair of eyes lingering. I looked up to meet Esther's gaze. Her face was red with burns from the fierce wind, but her eyes were strong and angry.

Always strong and angry.

I waited for her to say something. Anything. These silent glances between us had been happening often, ever since she saved Jade's life. But we hadn't spoken. Not a single word.

What was I supposed to say? How could I possibly thank her for saving Jade's life when she was also the one who put it in danger?

"I'll cross first," Silas spoke. "Take your time following. The cliffs are too sharp for any of us to dive down after you."

Jade's jaw tightened.

"He's lying," I whispered, low enough for only her to hear. "I won't let you fall, Jade. Ever."

"I want to believe you," she hissed back, "but my hands are frozen and I'm not confident I can even grip the rope."

I grabbed her cold, stiff hands and cupped them together in front of my mouth. Her eyes widened as I exhaled on them, warming her with my breath.

But she didn't pull away.

"Better?" I asked.

"Not really," she replied. "Although I don't mind your mouth warming me up. I have a few other areas that are cold, you know."

I rubbed her hands between mine once more before letting go. "All in due time, my queen."

Ahead of us, Silas gripped the rope bridge. He put one foot on the first wooden plank, and we all watched in silence as it squeaked beneath his weight. A chunk of ice fell beneath him. He didn't move for what felt like a full minute.

But then he took the next step.

He slid his hands across the wooden rope, and a few steps later, he stood on the other side.

One had crossed. Six to go.

My faith in the bridge hardly existed, but at least the entire thing wasn't going to fall under the weight of a man.

And Jade was half the weight of Silas. She would be fine.

I would make sure she would be fine.

Silas's men went next, one after the other. With each step taken across the wooden planks, I found myself holding my breath. I angled my sharp ears in Jade's direction and found that she was doing the same.

Esther was next.

"Be careful," Jade said to her softly. I had to admit, I was surprised. That was the first time Jade had spoken to Esther.

But Esther just returned a grateful smile. "I'll be okay, child. There's nothing to fear."

Jade smiled, too, and then Esther turned to the bridge.

She gripped each rope with her small, frail hands. I wondered how stiff they were, if they were as cold as Jade's.

Silas watched intently from the other side, tracking her every move.

The bridge creaked as she stepped forward. It swayed in the wind, her weight not quite heavy enough to keep it from moving. But she held her head high and continued gripping that rope.

She took another step. Slid her hands forward. Took another step.

A few seconds later, she jumped onto the other cliff and into Silas's arms.

Jade and I were the only two left.

"You can do this," I said to her. "The bridge is strong, and you have me watching you every step of the way."

"Come with me," she pleaded. If she was hiding her fear earlier, she wasn't anymore.

I shook my head. "The bridge isn't strong enough to hold us both. You go first, and I'll be right behind you."

She stared at me for a second more before she turned back to the bridge. She stepped forward, and then she looked down.

"Don't look," I reminded her. "It'll only make you nervous, and you have no reason to be nervous. Look at the other side." She did. "Now take one step."

I held my breath, too, as Jade shifted her weight onto the wooden plank beneath her. Similar to Esther, she was too light to keep it from swaying.

But Esther had made it.

"Good," I said. "Now keep looking ahead of you."

She kept her head up, but I could see how tightly she gripped the rope. Saints, it felt like we were already in the Trials of Glory.

Jade was nearly across.

She had one more step to take when she slipped and lost her footing, her worn black boots sliding on the ice-covered planks. "Jade!" I yelled out, but I was stuck on my side of the bridge. The entire thing would collapse if it were holding both of us.

Esther launched herself forward and clamped a tight grip onto Jade's arm.

"I've got her!" she yelled.

Jade clung to that wooden plank for her life.

And Esther clung to her.

Silas and the others stepped in, pulling both Esther and Jade to safety on the cliff's edge.

As soon as they were away from the bridge, I crossed it without so much as holding the rope.

"Jade," I said again as I sank to my knees next to her. "Are you alright?"

Esther still held onto her, as if she were afraid of letting go all together. Jade nodded.

"I'm okay," she said. "But I never want to do that again."

"Deal," I replied. I helped her to her feet first, then I reached a hand out to Esther.

"That's twice now I've saved your wife's life. You could at least look me in the eye, son."

Jade began walking with the others. "I'm aware of how I am so indebted to you, mother," I replied.

"There is no debt," she corrected me. "You owe me nothing. I just wish you could see that I am on your side."

I stepped closer to her and dropped my voice. "*Are* you? Are you on my side? What about him?" I motioned to Silas. "Are you on *his* side? Because you can't be on both. Not with this. Not with what's about to happen to her."

"You don't need to worry about the trials," Esther whispered. "Jade can survive each one with ease. She's a fighter. You know she'll be okay."

A cruel laugh escaped me. "You really believe that blood-thirsty bastard is going to make this easy for her? He wants her dead. You're blind if you don't see that."

"If he wanted her dead, he would have killed her back in Rewyth."

"And I would have ripped his head off where he stood."

She held her hands up in front of her. "Enough with the scary alpha contest, okay? Silas isn't your enemy."

"You have no idea what Silas is to me. And why are you so sure you know his character? There's something you aren't telling me."

She took a long, shaking breath. In the distance, Jade called back to us, yelling for us to catch up.

"Tell me. Now," I demanded.

"I knew Silas very well, but that was decades ago. I hardly recognized his face when I saw him again. But I lived with him in the mountains for a very long time, long before you were born."

*No way.*

"You lived with Silas?"

She nodded, but glanced down at her feet. "I didn't want you to know. I know how you feel about him."

"How I *feel* about him? He turned me into a weapon!"

"Malachi!" Jade yelled, waiting for me a few paces ahead.

Anger burned inside of me. Esther had consistently been a lying, mischievous witch. I still didn't trust her, and I didn't care how many times she saved Jade's life.

"This discussion is not over," I hissed at her. I began stalking through the snow, back to Jade. Back to the one person in this entire group that I trusted.

"We're not your enemy, son!" Esther called from behind me. I didn't so much as turn my head.

"What was that all about?" Jade asked as I stepped closer.

"Esther being untrustworthy. Nothing new."

Jade gave me a sideways glance. "Untrustworthy? If my memory serves me correctly, she's the one who brought me back to life."

"She needs you. For what, I'm not sure yet. But she was using you before. I wouldn't be so sure that she's not doing it again."

# CHAPTER 4
# *Jade*

We climbed higher and higher through the mountains. The temperature dropped until I was positive that my nose was frozen on my face.

Sometime before the sun began to set, Silas stopped us. "We're here," he announced. I looked around us. There was no temple. No city. Not a single sign of life anywhere in the distance.

"Here?" I repeated. The pain from my abdomen slowly began to return, adding to the edge in my voice. After nearly falling off the bridge, my wound had all but ripped back open. My fingers were numb with ice, and I wanted nothing more than to be done with this horrid trip. "There's nothing here."

Silas turned and began walking into the side of the mountain, literally *into* the side of it.

A slight shimmer on the surface was the only thing I saw as Silas's body disappeared.

"Is that..."

"Glamour," Mal answered for me. "They use it to hide the entrance to the temple at all times. It's how the Paragon is able to stay hidden from the rest of us. Even if intruders managed to find their way through the mountain's paths, they would have no way of finding the temple."

"Isn't that exhausting?" I asked. "I mean, wouldn't it be tiring for someone to use their glamour all day long?"

Mal put an arm around my shoulder and squeezed. "This is the Paragon. The strongest fae in existence live here, and a handful of witches, too. For them, it's nothing. They could hold this glamour in their sleep."

The weight of those words hit me like a punch to the gut. "That's terrifying."

"You have nothing to fear," he said, but his voice wavered. I knew Mal was worried about what would happen here. He was right to worry. Still, I didn't argue with him. "You're the peacemaker. You are powerful beyond any gift these witches and fae might possess. They should leave you alone."

I couldn't help but scoff at the thought. *Peacemaker.* That still meant nothing to me. I didn't feel powerful. I didn't feel protected. "Until they see how *not* powerful I really am."

"Don't say that," Mal argued. "It isn't true."

"I have power, sure. But there has to be some other explanation. I mean, what *exact* type of power am I supposed to possess?"

Malachi shrugged. His calm, collected exterior didn't fool me. Not for a second. "I suppose that's what we're here to find out, my queen."

I watched the hidden passageway ahead of us. "What's on the other side, Mal?"

He gripped my hand tightly. Through the cold that infiltrated every ounce of my body, I could hardly feel it. "We'll walk through together. I'll be right by your side the whole time."

My teeth were still clenched together, but I could no longer tell if it was from the cold or from the nerves. We had finally arrived at the Paragon's temple.

It was now or never, and I didn't seem to have much of a choice. Surely Silas wouldn't drag us all the way up the mountain to ambush us.

Malachi matched my steps as I inched forward, closer to the glamour-covered entrance of the temple. Closer to the trials. Closer to answers and questions that I didn't even know to ask yet.

This was it.

I shut my eyes and stepped into what seemed to be the side of the cliff, and suddenly we were inside the temple.

Mal and I stood there, hand in hand. I squinted at first until my eyes adjusted to the dimly lit space. I was unable to move, completely encapsulated by what I saw.

We were... we were *inside* of the mountain.

"Holy Saints," I muttered. "It's...it's beautiful."

"The Paragon has had decades of hiding down here. It's impressive, isn't it?"

*Impressive* didn't even begin to describe the sight laid out before me. We stood at the apex of the room, which seemed to be the connecting point to dozens of underground tunnels that dispersed underneath the mountain. In the center, beautiful gold pieces of furniture and fire lanterns flickered through the dim lighting. Everything was elegant in a way that made me wonder how they got all of it here and under this damn mountain.

"Welcome to the temple," Silas announced, interrupting my thoughts. "We'll spend the week preparing you, answering any questions you may have about the trials. One week from today, you will start the first test."

"What's the first test?" I asked.

Silas stared at me with those large, vacant eyes. I noticed now that they had a hint of red in them. "You'll learn more about the trials tomorrow. Why don't you and your husband get some rest and warm up for the evening. It's been a long few days."

"I don't want to rest," I answered. I was unable to keep my annoyance out of my voice. I didn't feel tired anymore. I didn't feel like I needed to warm up. What I wanted was answers. I needed to know what I was walking into. "I want to know what the damned trials are."

Silas looked at Malachi for the first time since we had been talking. "I'm sure your husband can answer any questions you have. First, we need to finish healing your wound."

Silas waved toward the healer. "Do whatever it takes to finish closing the injury," he ordered. Now that our journey was over, I supposed the healer could afford to use more of his healing magic on me.

The healer only nodded, stepping toward me with his arm extended. My first instinct was to flinch away, but Malachi's hand on my lower back urged me forward.

"Come," the healer said. "Sit over here."

With Malachi following closely behind me, I did as I was told. My feet glided across the stone floor tiles as I approached one of the many gold-trimmed benches in the center of the room. A few Paragon members—all dressed in black cloaks—glanced my way, but quickly returned to their meals as I took my seat.

Saints, it felt good to sit.

The healer sat next to me, but not Malachi. He stood in front of us, wings flared and eyes vigilant. My stomach twisted at the sight of him on edge. I hated that he had a past here.

"Roll up your tunic, please," the healer ordered. I ignored the burning in my muscles long enough to reach down and lift the edge of my shirt that now dripped with blood, melting ice, and dirt. The healer didn't hesitate, pulling back my bloody bandages and revealing the half-healed wound.

"This won't take long," he said. His voice was stern, but I could have sworn I heard a hint of pity in his words as he leaned closer to the wound. "Sit still."

*Like I had a choice.*

The man's hand hovered over my torso, just like he had done before. Except this time, I could actually feel the warmth radiating from him. Warmth and...something else.

Magic.

When I looked at Malachi, he was staring at the man's hand, unblinking.

We sat like this for a few minutes until the healer gasped and pulled his hand away.

"What is it?" I asked. "What's wrong?"

The healer shook his head, eyes wide as he continued to stare at my wound. "Nothing, I–"

"What?" Malachi chimed in, stepping closer.

"I could have sworn I saw..." The man shook his head again, as if shaking the thought from his mind. "Never mind," he said. "It's been a long journey. I'm tired. Your wound should now be healed, peacemaker. If you experience any more pain, come find me."

Before we could ask any more questions, the man scurried away.

"Did you see anything?" I asked Mal, who had been watching the healer the entire time.

"Not a damn thing," he answered. We both surveyed my wound, which was now nothing but dried blood and smudged dirt. Whatever the healer had done worked entirely. Not even a slight cut remained on my skin.

"Well," Silas clapped, reminding us of his presence. I pushed myself from the bench to stand beside Mal. "Now that we've taken care of our peacemaker, you two should get some rest. Follow me, I'll show you to your rooms."

I kept my mouth shut as Silas began walking, his black robe trailing behind him as he moved, almost as if he were floating.

Malachi's hand on my lower back reminded me to move my feet.

"We aren't your prisoners? We're free to roam as we please?" I asked. Malachi remained suspiciously quiet next to me.

"For now, yes. Things will change once the trials begin."

"Isn't that a bit of a risk for you? What if you wake up one morning and we're gone?"

Silas stopped walking to answer me. "If you are foolish enough to think that you can evade the most powerful individuals of our time, you are not as smart as I believed you were, Jade Weyland. You can try to escape, but you will not be successful. Isn't that right, Malachi?"

Malachi stiffened. I could nearly feel the coldness from him on his light touch against my back.

*Had Malachi tried to escape from the Paragon before?*

"Just show us to our room," I interrupted. I hated the way Silas looked at Mal, as if he were a toy.

Silas nodded and began walking again. We walked through the tunnels until I thought there was no possible way they could continue, but then they did. We turned dozens of times, and I silently hoped Malachi had a great memory because there was no way I would remember the path. When I glanced up at him, though, his face held an unreadable expression.

We passed a few others in the tunnels, but each of them wore the same black cloak as the Paragon members we had already met, and not a single person looked at us. Not a single person met our gaze. I wondered if that was because of Silas, or if looking people in the eye was a rarity around this temple.

"Here you are," Silas said. He stopped in front of a small opening in the mountain edge. A door fit perfectly within the small curve of the stone. "Food is served in the main room at sunrise. We'll talk more then. Bathing is that way." He pointed down the tunnel. "Rest well."

And then he was gone, scurrying back down the tunnel the way he came, his black robe hiding him in the depths of the under-mountain shadows.

"Cozy," I said.

Malachi had to tuck his wings behind his back to duck through the doorway of our room. I followed closely behind him.

The room was small, but it was equally as elegant as the rest of the temple. A bed with solid-gold posts and white silk sheets sat in the center of the room, and a small table in the corner held a stack of clean clothes.

Not the black robes, to my surprise, but black trousers and tunics for both Mal and I.

Malachi still did not relax. His black wings expanded, but he looked smaller than I had ever seen him. He stared at the bed, and slowly shifted his focus to the moisture that dripped down the stone mountain wall. He wasn't really paying attention, though. He had gone somewhere else, somewhere distant.

I shut the heavy stone door behind me before I walked over to Mal. The echo of the tunnels disappeared, finally leaving Mal and I alone. "Hey," I whispered. I slid my hands up his back, narrowly avoiding the base of his wings. He flinched when I touched him. "Tell me what you're thinking."

His head dropped, hanging in a rare glimpse of defeat. "Being back here is more difficult than I thought it would be."

Malachi had mentioned that he had lived here with Silas. For how long? I wasn't sure. I also wasn't sure what exactly happened, or what Malachi endured. "This is temporary," I reminded him. "Once I complete the trials, we'll be out of here."

He turned to face me. "There's something you need to know about the trials," he said. "Something I haven't told you before."

An icy chill ran down my back, and it wasn't from the tundra we had just escaped from. "What is it?"

"Decades ago, before I became the Prince of Shadows, I completed them."

My breath hitched in my throat. "*You* completed the Trials of Glory? But that doesn't make any sense. Why? And how?"

He delicately placed both hands on my shoulders, over my cloak that was now damp from the melted ice. He picked at the loose strands of my hair that had escaped my messy braid. "I was young. Impressionable. Silas seemed like...he seemed like he wanted to take care of me. So I let him."

"And Silas made you do it?"

Mal met my eyes. I saw something deep, then, something animalistic. *Rage.*

"It was my only way of surviving. I was to complete the trials and then I would become the Prince of Shadows. The only non-Paragon member to ever attempt them and live. It was a death sentence."

I shook my head. "But you survived them? How, I mean? Why would Silas even want you to do that?"

"He saw how powerful I became. He knew I would never join him in the Paragon, not when my kingdom needed me. It was his way to eliminate the threat."

"Threat?" I repeated. "But he helped you. He saved you. He's the reason you stepped into your powers."

Malachi shook his head. "When Silas first approached me and offered me an escape from my father, I was more than happy to go with him. I had wanted nothing more than to get away from that foul bastard."

"What changed? What did Silas do?" I swallowed as I waited for an answer.

"He did exactly what he promised me he would do. He changed my life. Him and the rest of the Paragon taught me how to kill. How to harness my power in ways that I never knew possible. It took years before I could bring a man to his knees. Decades before I could use my power on my own will whenever I pleased. Silas was there the whole time, protecting me like I was his own son. Until he suggested the trials."

Malachi took a deep breath.

"He told me I could be just as strong as him. Just as powerful."

"If you passed the trials?"

"Yes. If I passed the trials."

"So you're telling me Silas passed the trials, too? And so did everyone else in the Paragon?"

Malachi turned around and pulled his own wet layers off. His skin was damp and sculpted underneath. I tried not to stare.

*Tried and failed.*

He sat on the edge of the bed. I dropped my wet cloak on the floor and did the same.

"The trials aren't the same for everybody," he explained. "Silas and the Paragon members passed them, yes, but they won't be the same trials you have to pass, nor were they the same trials I passed. They're mind games, Jade. They get into your thoughts and create a brand new reality."

I swallowed. I wanted to ask him to explain more. I wanted to ask him exactly what he had to do in his trials, exactly what was so traumatizing for him to be back here. But I didn't. I could see how difficult this conversation was for him already. He would tell me on his own time. When he was ready.

"Who decides that?" I asked. "Who decides what the trials are?"

"Silas. Silas decides."

The hair on my arms stood up. "Well," I stuttered. "That hardly seems fair."

"It's not fair at all. Each member passes three trials—one of the past, one of the present, and one of the future."

"Past, present and future? What's that supposed to mean?"

"It means something different for everyone. The trials are laced with magic from the ancient witches. Magic and power from hundreds of witches and fae that lived before us come together to create experiences that—" His voice cracked.

I gripped his bare arm. "You don't have to tell me now," I said. "We can rest, and you can tell me all about it this week."

His nostrils flared, but he wrapped his strong arms around me and pulled me onto his lap in one swift motion, burying his head into me. "We'll get through this," he whispered. "I promise you, we'll get through this. I won't let him hurt you."

I hugged him back. Malachi's arms had become my only home lately, after losing Tessa, after everything in Rewyth. "I know you won't," I said back.

We sat there for a while, holding each other. I silently thanked the Saints that Malachi had come with me on this journey. He had an entire kingdom at home, a kingdom that had just been through a battle, and here he was.

With me.

I wrapped my arms tighter around his broad shoulders. His hands slid up my back, keeping me sitting firmly on his lap. I could have stayed there for hours.

"Do you want to head to the baths before we sleep?" he eventually asked.

"As much as I would love bathing with you in the middle of this underground temple," I joked, "I think we both need as much sleep as we can get. Especially you. We'll worry about cleanliness tomorrow."

"Sleep," he repeated. "I don't deserve sleep. My men died in battle. I left them to take care of themselves after an attack."

"Shhhh," I whispered, pulling him with me to lie back on the clean bed. "Don't worry about any of that," I said. "Serefin and your brothers will deal with it all."

"I couldn't leave you," he said. "I couldn't let him take you. I couldn't live with myself if I didn't know what had happened, especially if—"

"I know," I interrupted. I rested my head on his chest, listening to his rapid heartbeat. "I know."

His hand fell onto the back of my head, as if ensuring I was really there. Mal hadn't slept in days. I had no idea how he was still functioning, but I *did* know he needed sleep. How this place of nightmares would grant him as much as an ounce of peace, I wasn't sure. But at least we were in the stone underground of the mountains and not on the exposed cliff side. Our enemies were known, and they were calling a ceasefire for now.

For now.

"Goodnight, my queen," he breathed. I listened to his heart rate until the beats slowed, until mine matched his, and until the warmth of his body pulled me into a deep, dreamless sleep.

# CHAPTER 5
# Malachi

I didn't want to wake her up. I wanted her to stay in her peaceful sleep, ignorant of the chaos she would endure while in the presence of the Paragon. The chaos we would both endure.

It was hard, explaining what had happened. How could I possibly make her understand? I couldn't tell her that Silas would discover her weaknesses, bit by bit, and expose them. Torture her with them.

The trials would be her own personal nightmare.

Yes, I was seen as a threat to Silas.

But in Silas's eyes, Jade was a threat to the whole world.

She stirred in my arms. "Rise and shine," I whispered. She mumbled something, still half-asleep, and nuzzled herself into my chest. I could have stayed right there forever, knowing Jade was safe in my arms.

Last night was the only night I had managed to get an ounce of sleep, although I couldn't stop my dreams from wandering to my past. To those trials. To Silas.

It was easy to brush the memories away when I was awake with Jade. *She* became my focus, not the past. Those things didn't matter. All that I cared about now was keeping her safe. And if I had to put my past behind me in order to do that, I would.

I could be civil with Silas.

*Even though he brought war to Rewyth.*

Even though he threatened Jade.

Who was I kidding? His very presence threatened Jade. He might have held a noble stance to anyone else, but to me? I could see right through it.

He was a scheming, vindictive, power-hungry monster.

But I was a monster, too. I wasn't the young boy he had trained all those decades ago. I was the King of Shadows.

He wasn't going to touch what was mine. Not again.

"We should eat something," I said.

"No," Jade grunted, tightening her arms around my bare waist. "We should stay here. Just like this. Forever."

I held her chin and tilted her face to meet mine. "You need your strength. You haven't eaten a solid meal in days." Whatever argument she was thinking of slowly dissipated in her deep brown eyes. "Just imagine a bowl of steaming hot stew waiting for you."

She moaned, and I had to fight the urge to shut her up with a kiss. "Fine," she said. "What are the odds that nobody else is awake, and we'll be the only people in this entire temple eating?"

"Hmmm." I ran a thumb across her cheek. "I'd say those odds are pretty low. But if you don't feel like talking to anyone, let me know. I'll be your personal bodyguard."

"Personal bodyguard?" She smiled, and for a split second of time I forgot where we were and what we were about to endure. "That sounds enticing."

"I think I've been your personal bodyguard since the day we got married."

"Before that, even."

I smiled. The memory of Jade, all that time ago, fighting off a pack of wolves with nothing but a knife played clearly in my mind. "Yes, even before that."

Jade pushed herself off of me and stepped out of the bed. "I do, however, believe you and I both smell. Badly."

I jumped from the bed behind her and wrapped my arms around her waist. "You smell of cinnamon, it's delicious and intoxicating and torturous as always."

Jade gripped my arms and pulled them tighter around her, pressing her back into the front of my bare chest. "Is that so?" she teased.

I pulled her black hair away from her neck and kissed the skin there, slowly dragging my mouth up to her jaw. She leaned further into my chest, and I couldn't help the possessive growl that came from me.

"Breakfast," I muttered. "Breakfast, or I'm afraid I'll throw you back into that bed and never let you leave."

"Don't tempt me," Jade replied.

I only released her from my arms when she reached for the clean black clothes on the table and began dressing herself. I did the same, swallowing the memories that came with the dark linens. A few moments later, Jade was fully dressed and stepping into the tunneled hallway. I followed.

The temple was almost exactly as I remembered it, only now, it buzzed with hundreds of residents.

I couldn't tell if they were all Paragon members, but I didn't doubt for a second that each person under this mountain held great power. Normal fae, witches, or human did not live here.

"I hope you know where we are," Jade whispered. Even with her voice lowered, her words created an eerie echo against the dewy walls. "This place is a maze."

But I had memorized these tunnels from the inside out. I knew every twist in the darkness, and could find my way back from the depths of the underground no matter where we were. "This way," I said.

We walked for a few seconds before a cloaked figure stepped into the tunnel ahead, staring directly at us.

I clenched my jaw and kept walking. There was no way I was going to let someone mess with Jade on her first day here. She at least deserved the *respect* of the Paragon members.

It wasn't until I got closer that I recognized the jutted hip and the long, sharp fingernails.

I remembered this woman from my time here decades ago. The way she casually leaned against the stone tunnel wall only confirmed my suspicions. *Cordelia.*

"What do you want?" I asked. I attempted to brush past her, but she side-stepped me and blocked our path.

She reached up and pulled back her hood, just as dramatic as she was back then. She looked at me and smiled, but it was more of an amused smile and less of a happy one. I didn't smile back, especially not as she slid her gaze over my shoulder to Jade, who still held tightly onto my hand.

I flared my wings, blocking Cordelia's view.

"Relax," Cordelia said, trailing out the end of the word to a low hum. Just like all those years ago, she had a voice that could slice flesh. "I only wanted to meet our special guest before all the fun began."

"Who is this?" Jade asked from behind me.

*Saints. We were actually doing this.*

I tucked my wings back behind my shoulders slowly, allowing Jade to look at Cordelia again. Cordelia wasn't stupid. She wouldn't try to hurt Jade right in front of me.

At least, I hoped not. But time in the Paragon was not kind. I may have known Cordelia back then, but I wasn't so sure anymore.

"I'm the one who will be training you this week," Cordelia said, reaching a hand out to Jade. Jade shook it with confidence, meeting the woman's sharp stare without a second of hesitation.

*Good girl.*

"If you don't mind," I interrupted, "we're in the middle of something here."

This time when I pushed past Cordelia, she let us through. I didn't miss the way her eyes scanned Jade as we passed, her dark eyebrow raised with intrigue.

There was no way I would be leaving Jade alone with her for training.

"You know her?" Jade whispered as soon as we were far enough away.

I grunted. "Something like that. We worked together for Silas when I lived here. She's powerful, I'll give her that. But keep your guard up around her until we know where her loyalties lie."

Jade nodded in agreement and didn't ask any more questions. I was grateful for that. In time, I would explain it all. The people, the trials. Jade deserved to know what had happened to me under this mountain.

But not now.

With her hand tight in mine, we walked to the dining room.

For being beneath a snow-covered mountain, the underground was uncomfortably warm. Even in my clean black trousers and linen tunic, my forehead grew damp with sweat.

Jade walked with an uncomfortable silence. She held her chin high, though. Not once dropping it. Not once looking away. Even as we weaved through the underground maze and eventually arrived at the dining hall.

And no, we were not the only ones there.

A dozen rectangular slabs of wood littered the room, glistening slightly under the golden chandeliers of low-burning fire.

Jade stalled, and I fought the urge to reach out and grab her hand. But she needed to show them she was strong. Independent. She didn't need me to protect her.

She could do that on her own.

"I hope you slept well," Silas stepped into view on our left, dressed in a brand new black robe that covered even the tips of his fingers.

"Good enough," I replied.

Silas held my stare for a second too long before sliding his snake eyes over to Jade. She stilled. "When do I find out what my trials are?" she asked.

The bastard had the audacity to laugh at her. My power became a caged animal inside my body, begging to be let out.

"You'll find out soon enough," he said.

"Why don't you stop with the riddles and tell her? She's here, isn't she? This is what you asked for."

"She's here because she is the peacemaker, Malachi. Not because I asked for her to come. The Saints require this."

The tiny, unsealed crack in his exterior began to shine with anger.

"She came here to complete the trials like you requested," I reminded him. "The sooner we get this over with, the sooner we can all go home."

Silas's smile fell. "Eat," he said. "I'll explain over breakfast."

Jade and I followed him through the room of lingering eyes and found ourselves at a table with Esther.

"You have a habit of showing up places," Jade said as she slid onto the stone bench next to Esther.

Esther smiled. "I'm always where I need to be, child. Always."

"If I'm completing the trials, don't you think it's time to stop calling me child?" Jade asked.

"Hundreds of years ago, I might have considered it," Esther replied.

Silas and I slid onto the bench on the opposite side of the stone table. "What's changed?" I asked. Esther's eyes widened when I talked, like she was surprised I was speaking to her at all. I didn't blame her, though. I was surprised by it myself.

"Life changed. Enemies happened. You two think you have problems now, but I've lived through worse."

"You've lived through worse than the peacemaker? Than your own son being threatened?" Jade asked.

"Yes," she answered without hesitating. "I have."

A woman dressed in the same black robe brought more food to our table, setting it in front of Jade and I. I waited for her to take a bite before I even glanced at my own. She was too skinny. Too weak. She needed her strength if she was going to have any chance at surviving the trials.

*A chance.* Flashing, violent memories of my own trials came crashing to the surface. They had been doing that, lately. Too often.

And I couldn't push them all away. Not anymore. Not when I was here, back in this dungeon. Back in this prison.

"One week," Silas started. "One week until your first trial. Today you'll be able to rest, explore the temple–"

"I don't want to explore the temple," Jade interrupted. I was the only one who noticed the way Silas's grip tightened on his fork. "I want to prepare for my trials. And that's awfully hard to do when I don't know what they are." Silas didn't reply. Jade pushed on. "Malachi tells me you design them."

Silas looked down at his food while he answered. "I don't design them," he said. "The Saints design them. I am a mere vessel of their wishes."

I could have laughed at those ridiculous words.

"A vessel? Are you trying to tell me the Saints speak to you?" Jade asked.

"Yes," Silas met her deadly stare from across the table. "That's exactly what I'm telling you."

It was just like him to come up with such an absurd lie, nobody would question it. But I knew the truth. The Saints did *not* speak to Silas. Saints were not that cruel.

Still, I bit my tongue and attempted to keep a straight face.

Jade scoffed. "And you cannot tell me what the Saints have planned for me one week from today?"

"That's what we'll be learning over the next week, Jade Weyland."

Jade picked at a piece of her food with the fork before setting it down and running her hands down her thighs. "I did not ask to be the peacemaker, Silas. Do you understand that?"

He cocked his head to the side, looking at her with curious eyes. "I understand just fine."

"Then you also understand that I have absolutely no idea what I'm doing here, or what completing these damn trials is going to prove."

"Well," Silas began, "the trials have been around for centuries. Designed by the Saints, they are a way to determine the gifted over the non-gifted or the average-gifted."

"Average-gifted?" Jade rolled her eyes. "You're kidding."

"I'm not kidding in the slightest."

"You mean it's up to you and the Saints—who speak to you—to determine who is powerful enough to survive the trials?"

"Like I said, Jade, the Saints speak to me. I am merely a vessel. They tell me what each opponent's weaknesses are, and what they must overcome to become closer to the Saints."

"Closer to the Saints?"

It was Silas's turn to set down his fork. "We have much to learn this week, Jade. You know very little about the Saints, about their origin and about where they come from. You must learn these things. Malachi can teach you some, I have tutors in the library that can teach you the rest."

"What will a history lesson do to help me survive?"

Silas leaned in over the table. I did the same, making sure he knew to keep his distance. He was already too close to her. "The Saints have gifted you, child. Just like they have gifted us all."

"Some gift," I muttered.

Silas retreated to his seat. "Your husband is a skeptic. He denies his connection to the Saints. It is a pure gift, you know. Even a gift that kills. Even one so deadly. It is pure, gifted from the most powerful. The most good."

I clenched my fists to stop from shifting in my seat. I wasn't going to show him any weakness, any discomfort.

Of course, I had heard this speech hundreds of times. The speech that I was special, that I was somehow chosen by the Saints.

It made no sense. I didn't believe it for a second. If I was so special, why did the Saints make me a killer?

I was not special. My black wings meant nothing. My wicked power meant nothing.

Jade, however, had a gift. She had something more than a deadly talent. She was a force so powerful, I had a feeling we were only beginning to see what she was truly capable of.

"Your power is magnificent," Esther interrupted, saying what I had been thinking. "You must learn to wield it properly if you are going to be the peacemaker."

"Not this again," Jade muttered.

"And what exactly are you doing here?" I asked Esther. "Or did you simply ride along to get a front row seat to what you've been trying to do all along—kill Jade?"

She tossed her head back and laughed. "If I wanted your precious wife dead, son, I wouldn't have brought her back from the depths of death. Or did you already forget that part?"

I didn't answer. I couldn't. I was beginning to miss the days when I thought Esther might be dead, when I believed my father had been holding her hostage. Life was easier back then; when I didn't have to decide on any new day whether or not I could trust my own mother.

Jade's leg brushed against mine under the table. It was enough to snap me out of my own spiraling thoughts.

When I looked at her, she wore a tiny grin. One that sliced through the growing hatred in my heart and actually made me want to smile back.

"Well," Jade announced to the table. "I can't say this breakfast has been enjoyable, but I smell. If you'll excuse us, I believe Malachi and I will go wash up."

"Meet me in the study this evening," Silas replied as Jade and I both stood. "We'll have your first round of trial preparations then."

"Where is the study?" Jade asked.

"Your husband can show you."

He turned back to his breakfast and resumed eating, obviously done with the conversation. Jade turned on her heel and began walking out. I followed tightly behind her.

Yes, I could show her where the study was. I could show her where anything in this damned temple was. She knew that. But Silas wanted to make sure I wouldn't forget my time here. He wanted me to suffer during these trials just as badly as Jade suffered.

"Has he always been such an arrogant asshole?" Jade whispered once we were out of the dining hall.

"Fae ears," I reminded her. "He can still hear you."

"Good. I hope he heard that. Is he even a real fae?" Our footsteps echoed again through the underground tunnels as we continued back the way we came.

"Unfortunately, yes, he is. All that shit about him being a vessel for the Saints, though, I'm not too sure about."

Jade scoffed. "I can't imagine the Saints choosing someone so arrogant to speak through. And I certainly can't imagine what the Saints want from me."

"Yeah," I agreed. "That seems to be the big mystery."

"And if the Saints really do speak through Silas, wouldn't they know what type of power they gave me? Why do I have to complete the trials to prove I am who they made me?"

The dull ache in my head began shooting pain down my temples. Jade was right to be suspicious. I had been thinking the same things now for decades. "I don't know."

"Whatever," Jade mumbled. "I guess there's not much we can do about it. I have to pass these trials to survive, whether Silas is full of shit or not."

We made it to our room before Jade turned around and met my eyes. "You're coming with me, right?"

"To where?"

"The baths. I don't want to be alone here. I don't trust any of them."

I reached out and tucked a piece of her black hair behind her ear. She leaned into my touch, just enough to make me want to push her back into the bedroom.

"Of course I'll come with you," I answered. "I'm not leaving your side."

"Good," she smiled.

I decided then that I would give anything to keep Jade safe. I would do whatever it took. Jade was my wife, and I loved her so fiercely, the thought of ever losing her again was something I could not bear to think about.

I followed Jade toward the baths, stalking behind her. I was her bodyguard, her husband, her protector. I didn't care who tried to hurt her.

I would save her at all costs.

# CHAPTER 6
# *Jade*

INSIDE THE PARAGON'S TEMPLE AND SURROUNDED BY MY ENEMIES, ALL of my senses locked on Malachi following behind me.

Following me to the baths.

Being intimate with Malachi hadn't exactly been on my radar. Though I knew the one night we spent together was special to us both, we never had time to discuss it. War loomed over our heads.

But here, in the underground tunnels of the mountains, I felt connected to him. I had felt connected to him throughout the long journey here, actually. I wasn't sure if it was because he was the only one I trusted, or because he had been the one holding me when I came back from that darkness. Either way, I felt much closer to him than ever before.

And it wasn't just my magic.

I hadn't told Malachi, but my magic felt different. It felt new, almost as if it had been refreshed. Before, I couldn't feel my power. Not in the slightest. It had been hard enough for me to use it when it was absolutely necessary.

But now, every ounce of my being was aware of that ball of power sitting inside my chest. I could feel the source like a ball of light summoning energy with every breath.

I wondered if Malachi could feel it. Our powers were connected, anyway. That's what Esther had told us.

Could he feel how strong I had become? How different I was now?

The young, innocent version of me had died when that sword pierced my body. I was new. Stronger. I didn't feel like a frail human, I didn't feel afraid.

I felt, for once in this entire life, like I had a chance.

At least, that's what I had to tell myself if I wanted to survive. There was no room for weakness. Not anymore.

"To the right," Malachi directed from behind me. His voice was low, barely over a whisper. I heard the same emotion that I was feeling, that heat-filled longing that we had both felt for days now.

"It's dark," I replied.

Malachi stepped forward and placed a hand on my lower back to guide me. I had been spending so much time with him, it was easy to forget how advanced his senses were. How advanced all of the fae senses were, actually.

"This way," he said. "They keep the baths dark, but your eyes will adjust after a few minutes."

"How do they even get water down here?" I asked.

"It's run-off water from the mountain. Originally, there was a natural stream that ran right through these parts. With a little manipulation, they were able to create dozens of natural bathing spots. Enough to give privacy, but it's completely natural."

"Everyone shares the same bath?"

"You won't be able to tell. This way."

Malachi didn't move the hand from my back as he led me through the shrinking underground tunnels. After another minute of walking, I began to hear the faint trickle of water running against rock.

And soon, the glistening surface of the water came into view. My eyes adjusted, just like Malachi said they would, and I could see at least a few feet in front of me.

"Are we the only ones here?"

Malachi nodded. "For now. There's a more secluded bay around that bend." I followed his instruction once more, leading us to a quiet pool of water that slowly spilled over the rocks below us.

As we got closer to the water, I could feel a tiny bit of steam rising from the surface. "How is this hot?" I asked. "Isn't the mountain water freezing?"

"Us fae and our magic," he teased.

If the Paragon was using their power to heat the water for baths, I wasn't going to complain.

I gripped the edge of my black tunic before I realized Mal watched me.

"Turn around," I said. I could hardly see Malachi's face, but I could feel his eyes on me all the same. Lingering, dripping in that same heat of an expression I had seen before.

"Whatever you say, my queen," he replied. *Always with the voice of a king.*

I waited until he was fully turned around before I peeled off my clothes.

Malachi wouldn't turn around. Not until I asked him to, anyway. And these days, it was getting harder and harder to keep my distance.

After I dropped all of my clothes into a pile, I stepped closer to the water. The bath was inviting, and somehow held the slightest scent of mint.

I dipped my toes in first, feeling for the smooth yet rocky surface below.

And then I sank my entire body in.

I couldn't help the sound of relief that came from me as I submerged my shoulders and relaxed into the heat.

"You better not continue to make sounds like that," Malachi growled. "Not while I'm standing over here."

"You can turn around now," I said, ignoring his comment and the hunger that laced each word.

He did as I said, and I watched the reflection of his eyes as he scanned the pile of my clothes and then slid his attention over to me.

He froze completely. I could see him taking heavy breaths, his chest rising and falling.

"I'll wait out here," Malachi said.

"Don't be ridiculous," I argued. "You're my husband. I think we can both bathe at the same time."

"You believe me to be stronger than I am," he replied, and the sound of his words sent a chill down my body.

"Get in here," I said with more finality in my voice.

He laughed quietly. "Yes, my wife." He replied with a wicked grin. Again, I couldn't see his face, but I could hear it in his voice.

I heard the sounds of him slipping his clothes off, dropping them on the ground.

And then I heard the sounds—torturous and slow—of Malachi dipping into the water next to me. Both of our breaths became audible then, as if we were back outside climbing that damned mountain.

I leaned my head back against the stone ledge. Malachi moved closer to me until his arm brushed against mine.

"Jade," he half-whispered, half-growled.

"Yes?" I replied, just as breathless.

His fingers came to my arm, brushing the skin beneath the water. He trailed his delicate touch from my wrist all the way to my shoulder, gently moving across my collarbone. I gripped his arm, splashing in the quiet stream.

"We should probably talk about the trials," he whispered. I pulled onto his arm, but that only resulted in me pulling myself closer to him. My thigh became flush against his.

"Probably," I replied.

"We should talk about a lot of things, actually," he said. His lips were close to mine, plump and firm.

"We really should."

The silence between us filled with our breath and the echo of the water. Mal's eyes scanned my face, lingering over each feature as if he were looking at me for the first time.

"Or," Mal said, "I could kiss you." My heart pounded against my chest. The heat that filled my stomach was a wicked, torturous mixture of my magic and my need for Malachi.

I swallowed. Malachi had a way of bringing this side out of me, the side that still lit up at his every word. He always had that effect on me.

"Kiss me," I demanded.

Malachi obeyed. In one swift motion, he hooked an arm around my waist and hauled me onto his lap. He held me tightly to him and his mouth found mine in the darkness of the baths.

I fit perfectly into his lap, and I tried not to think about how exposed I was; how naked we both were. Malachi kept his hands on my waist, though, until he wrapped them around my back and pressed me deeper against his chest.

"I've missed you," Malachi mumbled in between kisses.

"We've been together for days," I reminded him.

"I've missed touching you, kissing you. A woman like you deserves to be kissed."

He kissed me again. I didn't stop him. His hands moved back and forth from my back, my hair, my waist.

Malachi was my husband. He was my everything. At this point, he was all I had left.

"Someone could come in here," I said after I realized what we were doing.

Malachi replied by pulling my mouth back to his and running his tongue against my lower lip.

His wings splayed around us, adding to the darkness of the shadowed water. It was as if the entire place had vacated just for us, our secret hideout in the depths of this hidden temple.

Malachi kept kissing me, kept holding onto me like his lifeline. I did the same. My body was flush against his, but neither of us cared about hiding our bodies anymore. Not from each other.

Malachi was mine, and I was his.

"I want you," I whispered before I could process the words.

Malachi growled a low sound of approval, his sharp teeth moving to nibble on the delicate, exposed skin of my neck. Between the chilled mountain air and the steam of the hot water, my body erupted in sensations that sent goosebumps down every inch of my skin.

He seemed to notice this, too.

"I want to be the reason every inch of your skin raises in goosebumps," he muttered, "but I'm afraid we have company."

Just as he finished the words, footsteps echoed down the dark tunnels. I scrambled to climb off of Malachi's lap, although I wasn't sure why. He was my husband. I didn't care in the slightest what anyone in this damned temple thought of me.

And Mal's wings still splayed widely around him, also protecting me from any peering eyes. Although we were already hidden from view by sneaking around the corner of the bathing house.

I sank back into the warm water, somehow still feeling the chill of where Malachi's body had been.

"Don't worry," Malachi said. He was still sitting close enough that I could nearly feel the vibrations of his voice when he spoke. "Nobody will touch you. Nobody will even approach you, not when I'm here."

More questions began spiraling in my mind. Who was this man that I had married? I mean, I knew who he was. Deep down, Malachi had a kind heart and a protective soul. He had been hurt by more people than I could count. He had killed. Some deserved it. Some didn't. And above all, he was willing to risk every single person in this world to save me.

Did that make him a good guy?

I wasn't sure. But that did make him my...my something. My protector, my husband.

My king.

To everyone else, maybe he was bad. Maybe he was the killer, the enemy. From talking to Silas, he seemed to be the one that escaped the tight, sharp grasp of the Paragon.

But they didn't see him the same way I did. Malachi had reasons for hurting people. He had reasons for everything he did in his life.

"Tell me what you're thinking," he whispered. Splashing in the distance told me our visitor had just arrived to bathe themselves. They wouldn't be bothering us.

But I still couldn't resist glancing around at the tunnels every few seconds.

"I'm thinking I don't know that much about you," I half-lied.

Malachi smiled. "I prefer remaining a mystery."

"I'm serious," I said. "You know everything about me. You might even know more about me than I know about myself. But you? You have an entire past. You have lives that I've never even heard about. I mean, who were you when you lived here with Silas? Who is the Malachi that these fae know?"

His smile flickered before it disappeared entirely. It pained me to take away that gorgeous, tempting smile, but I needed to know the truth.

"I told you," he started. "I came to the temple as a lost boy looking for a way out. I left the temple a killer."

"But what does that mean?" I pushed. "Did Silas make you kill?"

An uneven breath escaped him. "Yes."

"Who?" I tried to keep my voice soft. "Who did you kill when you lived here?"

His brows drew together, and I could imagine his mind rebuilding the massive stone wall, piece by piece.

"Don't do that," I interrupted.

"Do what?"

I pushed myself over to him and placed both hands on the sides of his face. "Don't lock yourself away like that. Don't shut me out. I'm right here, Malachi, and I love you. We need to lean on each other if we're going to make it through this. Please, talk to me."

He stared at me unblinking for what felt like a century. "I had killed many people before Silas came for me," he said. The pain in his voice instantly weighed me down, holding me close to him.

"Because of your father?" I asked. I barely remembered the stories now, but I did remember Malachi telling me his father used him as a weapon. Time and time again, Malachi was the one killer for Rewyth.

"Not when I was younger," he explained. "When I was younger, it happened to be a consequence of my temperament. I was hot headed back then."

"Now that, I believe," I said. My poor attempt to lighten the mood only barely worked. Mal's smile was a quick one.

"My father had been quick to cover it up before. He always had some sort of looming excuse as to why another soldier was dead. He never blamed me. Not in front of the others, anyway. Silas was the one who made me face what I had done. He forced me to stare at myself in the mirror and see myself for what I truly was. A killer."

"You're not a killer, Mal."

"That's exactly what I am. Silas made sure of it. He taught me how to take down any enemy, any opponent. He trained me and created a weapon." Mal drew in a long, shaking breath before continuing. "He is the reason the Prince of Shadow was ever born."

# CHAPTER 7
# *Malachi*

I SCANNED THE STUDY, WHICH WAS JUST AS OLD AND RUSTIC AS I remembered it to be. Aisles and aisles of books lined the dark room, and barely enough light for Jade's non-fae eyes to see lit up the table before her as she read.

I stood behind Jade, lurking in the shadows and giving her the space she needed. We had been there for hours now, but there was no chance that I would leave her alone, especially not with Silas sitting across the table. I fought to keep my mouth shut every time he broke the silence, adding to something she read.

Jade, to my surprise, did not make any snarky remarks as Silas explained each of the Saints and what they were capable of. Jade knew of the Saints, but there was no way she knew that much.

Nobody outside the Paragon knew that much.

Silas spoke of the five forces that once guarded the magic of this world. They were strong—the strongest to ever walk amongst us. They were not fae or witches, but something else entirely. Something pure, even if not all of them used that purity for good.

Anastasia, the Saint of life, was the most loved of the five Saints. She was caring and wise, the first Saint to be recognized for her mighty gift. She was known as the healer, the one to save lives and bring dying children back from the darkness. In many ways, she brought balance to the world of witches and fae.

Erebus was the most hated. Not at first, of course. He began as all other Saints did, by having a special gift. His gift, though, was not pure and helpful like Anastasia's. His power was terrifying and brutal. He wiped out armies. He flattened kingdoms. With the gift of death, Erebus used the power of fear to subdue the witches and the fae who caused problems.

Phodulla, the Saint of air, could be temperamental at times, but she was nothing compared to the wrath of Erebus. Phodulla would conjure storms and winds that would shake any kingdom to their core. Where she walked, wind would follow. She was both a great asset and a mighty curse to her friends and enemies.

Detsyn was the Saint of love. Her compassion was one that balanced the power of the Saints. She was a guard in many ways, always making sure the other Saints used their power for good and not evil.

Rhesmus, the last of the five, was the Saint of war. Rhesmus did not crave chaos like Erebus, but he was just as fierce. Just as aggressive. Rhesmus would whisper into the minds of those on the verge of war, beckoning them for a fight. Beckoning them for blood. His mind-whispering abilities were ones that many of the other Saints envied.

Many of the humans only knew of the Saints as the world-saving individuals who protected them for so long. Being the most powerful creatures themselves, they were able to keep lands at peace. Fae, witches, humans. They lived together in harmony.

When the Saints decided to leave this world, after they began to lose control of the power of the world, they took most of the magic with them. It was the best for everyone at that time. To have magic running rampant would be detrimental to all species, not only humans. *It was for our own good.*

For decades, fae and witches had no magic.

Now, only a few gifted individuals could possess magic. Some say it was a gift from the Saints, a reminder of what once was. Either way, the Saints never returned.

Jade's eyes scanned page after page, drinking up this information until she slammed the book in front of her shut and cursed under her breath. "This isn't helping," Jade muttered.

Silas waited a few seconds before responding. "It's important that you know the history of the Saints."

"I know plenty about the Saints. What I need to know is how my power is supposed to make me the peacemaker. I need to know how to survive the trials, how I'll be tested. This is a waste of my time."

Again, Silas took a long breath. I was beginning to remember just how infuriating he could be, especially late nights in this library. Silas would push and push until Jade couldn't take it any more, until her eyes glazed over and she begged for sleep.

I clenched my fists. Being here brought back memories I wished to suppress forever.

Jade leaned back in her chair and crossed her arms.

"I told you, Jade," Silas started. "The Saints have chosen you for a reason. It is respectful, at the very least, to try and learn more about them. Learn about the ones who chose you for this destiny."

"Did Malachi? When he was here completing the trials, did he spend hours and hours memorizing useless information from books? Please enlighten me on how studying these pages made Malachi the Prince of Shadows."

I stiffened in the darkness.

"Malachi did as I instructed him," Silas barked. My power screamed under my skin, recognizing the threat in his words before they even reached my ears. I cursed under my breath as a small tendril of magic escaped my grasp.

"Careful, boy," Silas sneered, turning his attention to me in the back of the room. "We wouldn't want your bride getting hurt."

I scoffed. "Hurting Jade is not a concern for me."

Silas's eyes darkened and slid back over to Jade. "Is that so?"

Jade stared back at him, unanswering.

I quit caring entirely. We hadn't outright tried to keep it a secret, but Silas had been looking at Jade as if she were nothing but a useless human that happened to possess a singular ounce of magic. Magic he wasn't even helping her cultivate.

"My power doesn't hurt her," I said. "And hers doesn't hurt me, either."

"That's—" For the first time since I had ever known Silas, he looked genuinely surprised. His eyes widened as he looked at her again. "That's magnificent. Unheard of, actually. Malachi's power is so strong. How long have you known this, that you could not hurt each other?"

Silence filled the room. Water dripped somewhere in the distance.

Once.

Twice.

"I've suspected for a while, but we knew for sure a couple of weeks ago," I finally answered. "Esther helped us confirm it."

I recalled the way Esther practically threw our magic at each other, the way my heart stopped when I thought I had hurt her.

And the relief that flooded my entire damn body when I found out she couldn't be hurt. Not by me.

"You are immune to each other's powers." His eyes flickered frantically between Jade and I.

"Yes," I replied. "So, if you'd like to threaten Jade's safety, using my power against her will not work."

Jade stood from her chair. "I'm tired," she said. "If all you have in mind for me tonight is reading through ancient books, I can do that alone."

Silas didn't say anything. He continued staring at us in a way that made the hair on the back of my neck stand up. My wings flared out instinctively, but that only seemed to interest Silas more.

I turned to follow Jade out of the room when Silas added, "Do you know why your husband has black wings, peacemaker?"

Jade froze. So did I.

"He is the King of Shadows," she answered.

Silas laughed, dry and humorless. I stepped forward, inching closer to Jade.

"King of Shadows, yes. He is, indeed, that. But he had black wings before he was ever given the title of a king. Before he was ever given the title of a prince. He was born with these wings, with this mark. In a world full of silver-winged fae, his are black." Silas clicked his tongue.

The room grew so silent, I could hear Jade's rapid heartbeat. She was just as eager as I to hear what Silas had to say next, although I still couldn't trust a single thing that man said.

"Malachi Weyland, King of Shadows and ruler of Rewyth, has the blood of the Saints. One particular Saint was known for his black wings, a killer among fae and as ruthless as any of them. Can either of you tell me which Saint that is?"

"You're lying," I said. I moved my body to stand before Jade, blocking her from Silas's view. "My father was no Saint."

Silas laughed again. Each time he laughed, I grew more and more tempted to rip his vocal cords out of his throat. My power flared in my veins, wanting the violence just as badly as I.

"No, your father was no Saint. But you have the black wings of Erebus. You have a deadly gift, one that is unmatched amongst most fae." Silas shook his head. He stood from the wooden table slowly and walked closer to us, staring at me with wide, wondrous eyes.

My mind spun, sending my thoughts through tunnels of possibilities. Each one of them came up short. "It's not possible," I replied. "I would know if I were a descendent of a Saint, especially if that Saint were Erebus."

"Is it so absurd of a thought?" Silas asked. He looked at me now like he were seeing me for the first time. "To think that you might have the blood of a Saint pumping through your veins? It would explain so much, would it not? Your wings, your power. Your rare abilities."

"Erebus was not simply a Saint. He was a killer that nearly took over all humanity," I replied. I hated the way my voice shook. I hated that Silas had the ability to shake me.

"He was powerful," Silas explained. "He wielded a strong magic and he didn't care who got in his way. That sounds awfully familiar, doesn't it, peacemaker?"

I turned and looked at Jade, who just stared at me with wide eyes. I knew she was thinking it, too. If it were the truth, it would explain so much...

But my father had not a single ounce of magic. Esther was a witch. That was where my abilities came from. That was where my black wings came from.

Not from a Saint's blood.

Not from Erebus.

"If you're trying to distract us so that Jade is unsettled for the trials, it won't work," I stated.

"I'm not trying to distract anyone," he said. "I'm only piecing together what we have been seeing before our very eyes. Now you say that the peacemaker's power does not affect you. It makes sense."

"We don't have time for this," I argued. I grabbed Jade's hand and began pulling her out of the study. "When you want to be useful to Jade and help prepare her for the trials, come find us. We don't need you filling our minds with useless riddles."

Silas didn't stop us as we stormed out, although he was more than capable of doing so.

"What was that all about?" Jade whispered once we were alone in the tunnels.

"I have no clue," I answered honestly. "But I'm not going to sit around and pretend like I trust a single thing Silas says. I didn't trust him back then, and I don't trust him now. He's trying to get in our heads."

*And it worked.*

Jade tugged on my arm, forcing me to stop. Her eyes were rimmed with pink clouds and her face had grown pale with exhaustion. Even so, I was certain she looked much better than I did.

"Do you think it's possible?" she asked. "That you're a descendent of a Saint?"

With Silas out of sight, I could actually consider those words. *Was* it possible? I had been confused for so much of my childhood. I didn't understand why I was so different, why I was the one with the black wings.

Erebus had been famous for his black wings, of many things. But over the years of history, there had been many fae that wore the oddly-shaded wings. It was ridiculous to think each one of them were descendents of Erebus.

And my father's wings had been silver as day.

"Not entirely impossible," I answered. Jade's small hands lingered on my wrist. "It doesn't make any sense. Why would he bring this up now? I lived with that man for decades. He never mentioned the possibility of Erebus's bloodline."

Jade's brows drew together in concentration. "Maybe you're right," she replied. "Maybe this is all part of a distraction. To shake us up before the trials."

"Maybe. But why me? Why would he want to shake *me* up? You're the one going through the trials. He should be drilling you about your lineage if his goal is distraction."

She gave a weak smile, and it reminded me of our wedding day. She had been so brave then, too, standing alone in a kingdom of fae she didn't trust. She was just as brave now, with just as many people she did not trust.

"I think he was trying to bore me to death with those lessons," she whispered. The playful glint in her eye had returned, even if it only lingered for a few seconds. "It was about to work, honestly. He would not shut up about the Saints."

"Your magic is a gift from them," I said. "It wouldn't kill you to learn about who wants you to be so powerful."

She slid her arm around mine, tucking herself into my elbow. "Now you're sounding like Silas. We better get out of here before I really get bored to death. The Paragon wouldn't be happy if they didn't get their precious Trials of Glory."

I reveled in the warmth of her body next to mine. "I have a feeling the rest of the week will be anything but boring."

We made it back to the bedroom without running into any other Paragon members. I silently thanked the Saints for that. I couldn't handle pretending to be polite to anyone else.

I wanted to be alone. Truly alone. I wanted to grab Jade around the waist and fly her out of this temple, away from the Paragon and into the middle of an abandoned field where we could live without any threats.

Maybe one day I would.

"We need to get plenty of sleep," I said as soon as we were inside. "You'll train with the most powerful witches in the world tomorrow. You want to be ready."

I had turned to give Jade some privacy when her hands found themselves on my back. I flinched at first before relaxing into the warmth of her touch.

"I'll be ready," she breathed. Her breath tickled the back of my wings. Heat from her hands expanded, igniting every inch of my skin as she slid her hands under my tunic.

"Jade," I muttered. "We really should sleep."

Her hands slid around my bare waist, running over my torso as she stepped closer. "We should," she agreed.

I didn't stop her as she lifted her hands, taking my tunic along with it.

Leaving me shirtless in the darkness of our secluded, stone room.

I turned around to face my gorgeous, powerful wife. "There was a time when you were afraid to be in the same room with me," I reminded her.

A grin full of mischief flickered across her features. "I remember," she said. "You were deadly and intimidating and wickedly handsome."

"*Were*?" I repeated.

Her hands slid up my chest. I sucked in a breath of air. Her touch still had that effect on me, could still leave me breathless as if this were the first time she had ever laid eyes on me. She was that beautiful, that magnificent.

"I suppose I still find you wickedly handsome," she whispered. She leaned up on her toes and placed a hot kiss under my jaw.

"What about deadly and intimidating?"

Her finger slid up my chest to my collarbone, following the sharp line there.

"King of Shadows," she breathed, brushing her lips over where her finger had just lingered. "You are nothing if not deadly," she said. My stomach sank. "You bring each of our enemies to their knees," she breathed, kissing me again.

A predatory, feral instinct washed over me. In one second, I gripped Jade around the waist and flew us to the bed. She let out a surprised yelp, one that made the heat in my body grow hotter.

Jade was *mine*. She was my wife, my voice of reason. She was my lifeline. I was beginning to realize just how much of me belonged to her now, too. Just as she was mine, I was hers. I would do anything for her. Be anything for her. I would scour the ends of the world if it meant ensuring she was safe.

I wasn't losing her again. Ever.

"You could be the most powerful weapon any kingdom has ever seen," I said. My black wings splayed around us, creating a secret space where we could pretend we were alone. We could pretend we were anywhere else but these damned mountains.

"I'm no more powerful than you," she breathed.

"You are so much better than me, Jade. Your power is...it's something different. I can feel it. It belongs to you. It runs in your veins for you, as if it is loyal to you only."

The smile faded from her face as she searched my eyes with her own. Something sad lingered there, something dark and distant.

"What is it?" I asked.

"We could destroy them," she whispered. "We could destroy this entire mountain if we wanted to. We could end all of this."

I closed my eyes and rested my head against hers. "Our enemies will never stop," I reminded her. "They won't stop coming for you. They won't stop trying to take what runs inside your body."

Her brows drew together. "But why? Why me?"

"I don't know why it has to be you," I answered honestly. "But I'm glad it's you. I'm glad you're here with me, Jade."

Her hands found either side of my face and held me gently, forcing my eyes to meet hers. "I'm not going anywhere," she said. "We're in this together, now."

I knew that. I had known it for some time, now, that she would choose to stay with me. She was no longer entrapped. She was no longer forced to be my wife.

She stayed with me because somewhere deep inside of her, she wanted this, too.

She belonged with me.

I lowered my head and kissed her, slowly. Delicately. The blind lust that had pulsed through my body earlier was overtaken by love, by protectiveness. Jade was so much more than a weapon to me. She was so much more than the peacemaker.

She was mine. She had my heart.

And I didn't want it back.

I kissed her as long as she let me, until I forgot where we were. Until I forgot about Silas. Until I forgot about Erebus.

And I held her tightly in my arms as we both drifted to sleep.

*Memories of my past trials morphed my dreams into nightmares.*

*A scream woke me up.*

*I was no longer in my bed next to Jade, though. I was in the middle of a forest, a forest that was littered with red trees and black dirt.*

*Where was I?*

*Not a single sound rustled the air around me. The silence was so strong, I could hear my own heart beat growing louder and louder.*

*But I refused to give in to the panic. That was what panic always wanted; for me to give in.*

*I was the King of Shadows. I feared no one. I feared nothing.*

*"Who's out there?" I demanded.*

*No one replied.*

*I stood up, wearing nothing but my black trousers. The sun rose in the distance, and the red trees began to sparkle with something wet.*

*Something murderous.*

*It was blood, I realized, dripping from every tree in the forest. As if it had just been soaked in a fresh rain.*

*Blood covered every inch, every ounce of life.*

*My bare feet were stepping in it, too, as I took a few steps further into the forest.*

*And then I heard the scream again.*

*It was a boy's scream, one laced with pain and anguish.*

*I began running, filled with the need to find this person. They needed help. They needed my help.*

*I ran and ran, even as the bottoms of my feet were sliced open by the rocks on the floor of the forest.*

*I didn't stop. The boy screamed again, and again.*

*"Where are you?" I screamed.*

*"Help me, Malachi!" the boy yelled.*

*The voice morphed, turning from one voice of a boy to hundreds, echoing around the forest and into my brain like a storm of chaos.*

*I ran and I ran, and when I could not run any further, I took to the skies.*

*My wings beat against the stiff air. He was here. I was close. Someone needed my help.*

*Who was he? And why was I here? Why were we both here?*

*My eyes desperately scanned each of the treetops in the forest until I found a small opening, large enough that I could see a morphed figure lying below.*

*I tucked my wings and dove downward, only splaying my wings again right before I landed heavily on the forest floor.*

*One young boy stared up at me, tears in his eyes.*

*He had black, curly hair and his face was smeared with dirt. His clothes were ripped, his feet bare like mine.*

*And then, in the rising, glistening morning sun, I saw his wings. Those black, damned wings.*

*"Are you going to help me?" the boy asked.*

*I stared at him a second longer. "Who are you?"*

*The boy swallowed, but something inside of him seemed to change. He stood from his crouched position on the forest floor and he rolled his shoulders back.*

*"I," the boy stated, "am Malachi Weyland. Prince of Rewyth and heir to the fae throne."*

*My heart sank. No, this couldn't be happening. This couldn't be possible. Standing before me, with bloody hands and knees and wings black as night, was myself.*

*I staggered backward. There had to be some sort of explanation.*

*"What is it?" the boy—myself—asked. "Don't leave me," he pleaded. "I thought you were going to help me! Help me, please!"*

*"Why are you here?" I asked.*

*"I don't know," the boy cried. His shoulders sagged in utter defeat, sobs muffling his words. "I don't know why I'm here."*

*A sword appeared in my hand. I didn't remember carrying one.*

*"No," I said out loud, knowing what the world was trying to make me do. Nobody told me, but I felt it. I felt death approaching, urging me forward. I gripped the handle of the sword until my knuckles turned white. "I will not hurt him."*

*The sword grew heavier in my hand, along with the pressure to wield it. To act.*

*I would not hurt the boy. I would not—*

*My arms began to rise over my head, sword along with it. I wanted to scream. I wanted to tell the boy—myself—to run, to hide.*

*I was a danger to him. I was a danger to myself.*

*I couldn't stop my arms from lifting. I no longer controlled them.*

*At the very last second, the boy with big, dark eyes looked up at me.*

*We both screamed, the sound of it so cruel, so horrific, that all I could do was shut my eyes and give in to the darkness.*

# CHAPTER 8
## *Jade*

"Hey," I shook Malachi's shoulders, but he had drifted deep into unconsciousness. His face twisted in fear and he woke me up with a half-cry. "Malachi, wake up!"

His eyes shot open, and he immediately flipped me over in the bed, covering my body with his with a predatory hand on my throat.

"Malachi," I squeaked through gritted teeth. "Mal, it's me. You were having a nightmare."

His eyes frantically searched my face before he realized who I was. He pulled his hand back as if he were gripping fire itself. "Jade, Saints, Jade I'm so sorry."

He scrambled off of me and pressed his back to the stone wall. His chest rose and fell as he panted, his forehead glistening with sweat.

"It's okay," I reassured him. "Everything's fine, I'm fine."

We spent the next few seconds staring at each other, not knowing what to say.

"That seemed like some nightmare," I offered after a few moments.

"Yeah," he breathed. "It was."

"Have you been having them often? Nightmares?"

He relaxed a touch but kept his distance in the room. His shoulders hung heavily around his body. "No," he said. "I haven't had a nightmare in years."

I pulled my knees up to my chest. "Well, do you want to talk about it?"

"It was nothing," he answered. I watched as he ran his hands through his thick head of wild curls, something he usually did when he felt nervous. "It must be our time here that's bringing back old memories. It was just a stupid dream. Nothing to worry about. Go back to sleep."

I waited for him to say more. Instead, he said nothing.

"Are you sure?" I asked. My chest tightened at the way his jaw flexed. Malachi was many, many things. But fearful?

He finally stepped forward and slid back into bed, but he kept his distance. Even as he leaned in and pressed a cold kiss to my forehead. "I'm sure. Sleep."

I tried to fight it, but exhaustion overtook my body. Malachi was still awake when I drifted off into the darkness once more.

The next morning, we met with Esther for more magic training.

"Good to see you again," I said to Esther. Our encounters had been nothing but awkward since she managed to save my life in Rewyth. The few encounters we had consisted of hushed tones and hidden messages.

Malachi could barely look at her. Esther kept her distance. I didn't blame her. We all had too much on our minds. With the Paragon and the Trials of Glory, bigger issues were at stake.

"You as well, child," she said. Cordelia pushed herself off the stone wall behind Esther, finally acknowledging our presence in the training room.

"Jade," Cordelia said. She reached her hand out to shake mine. She had beautiful dark skin and braided black hair, and she stared at me with a rebellious, hungry tint in her eye. The same tint that Sadie used to have. "I'm Cordelia. It's a pleasure to formally meet you."

I accepted her hand again, similar to the last time we met. Her long, bright red fingernail claws scratched my skin as she shook it.

Many people had attempted to intimidate me in my life. My father, the fae king, Malachi's brothers. I wasn't sure exactly when, but somewhere over the last few months, I quit backing down so easily.

If Cordelia wanted me to be afraid of her, she would have to give a reason.

"We have a lot to get done today," Cordelia said. "We might as well get started."

"I'll be back in a few hours," Malachi said from behind me. We hadn't spoken since his nightmare last night, and he hardly looked into my eyes when we woke up in the morning.

I didn't push him. I could see the storm brewing behind Mal's eyes. If space was what he needed, I understood that. Even if it caused my chest to tighten.

"You're not going anywhere," Cordelia argued. "Esther tells me your magic is attached to Jade's. We need you here to learn the full abilities of her power."

"You're kidding," Malachi replied. I physically flinched at the harshness of his voice, even though I knew it wasn't directed at me.

"I'm very serious," Cordelia said. She stepped forward. She had a style that reminded me so much of Sadie; dark and different. Like she didn't care what anyone in the world thought of her. I instantly felt a wave of regret for my old friend.

And I prayed to the Saints that she was okay on her own out there.

"Let's just get this over with," I interrupted, refocusing my thoughts. I heard Malachi breathe behind me, but I didn't turn to look.

We had arrived in a small room of the underground tunnels near the baths. A stream ran through the ground on the other side of the room, filling the space with the echo of the trickling water.

"We can start with the basics," Cordelia stated. Esther followed behind her.

"Okay," I agreed. "What are the basics?"

Cordelia stopped and looked at me with a straight face. "Summon your power."

"You—" I glanced at Esther, but she stared back at me with a blank face. "You want me to summon it here?"

"Yes."

"And what if I lose control? What if I blow up this entire mountain?"

"Then you won't have to compete in the Trials of Glory, and it'll be your lucky day. Come on. Let's see what we're working with here, peacemaker."

I could feel Malachi behind me then, I could feel his temper. My power responded to his, as hidden as it might have been.

Yes, I was afraid to use my power. I had used it in Rewyth and it almost cost me everything.

"You have no reason to be afraid," Cordelia added. I snapped my attention to her. "What happened in Rewyth won't happen here. You're safe with us."

*Yeah right,* I thought. *Like she knew anything about what happened in Rewyth.*

"I know more than you think," Cordelia said. When I met her gaze, she stared at me with a grim smile.

"Are you reading my thoughts?" I hissed.

"I can infiltrate whatever I'd like," Cordelia replied. "You're in my temple now. I only read your thoughts so I can help you. When I know what you're afraid of, I can help you overcome it."

"Get out of my head!" I yelled.

Cordelia took a step forward. Even with her flat shoes, she towered over me. It was a power move, a step of dominance.

"Watch it." Malachi growled a warning at Cordelia from behind me.

"Stand down, boy. Show me your power, peacemaker."

Wild emotion and a small, cascading feeling of helplessness washed over me. It was enough to remind me that I hated feeling helpless. Feeling trapped.

And I didn't have to feel that way. Not anymore.

I held my hands out in front of me. "Come on, Jade," I whispered to myself. "You can do this."

Cordelia flashed before my eyes. She moved from standing across the stone room to standing directly in front of me. She gripped my biceps, her claw-like nails digging into my skin.

I screamed—half from the pain, and half from the surprise.

"I said show me," she demanded through gritted teeth.

I shoved her backward, but she hardly budged.

Malachi moved behind me. He descended on us in an instant, grabbing Cordelia by the back of the neck. "Let go of her," he growled.

She only smiled, flashing her perfect white teeth. "Very protective," she sneered. "That's cute."

Cordelia released her grip on me and used both hands to shove Malachi backward. I didn't think for a second that she would be strong enough to move him, but he stumbled back, catching himself on the wall.

"Enough of this fighting," Esther sneered. "We have actual work to do here. We're wasting precious time."

Cordelia flipped her black braids over her shoulder. "That's right," she announced. "Where were we...oh yes. Jade was just about to show us her lovely, peace-making power."

"What are you?" I whispered. I hadn't realized I said the words out loud until all three pairs of eyes glued to me. "I mean...are you a witch? How are you that strong? How are you reading my mind?"

Cordelia smiled, but it was not a smile of delight. It was one laced with malice, one laced with pity. "Oh, darling," she started. "I am half witch, yes. But I am also half fae."

"Witch and fae? But I thought Malachi was the only–"

"You've been told a lot of things, it seems," Cordelia interrupted.

I stood there, speechless, like a blindsided idiot. How was I supposed to know what was and was not the truth? Malachi had told me that his heritage—being half fae and half witch—was unheard of. Witches could rarely get pregnant, which meant they rarely had children—much less children with fae, who had spent decades being their enemies.

"I am not your enemy," Cordelia said, clearly reading my thoughts again. Saints, that was getting annoying. "But many of your enemies *are* here. Believe me, you are powerful. I can see it already. You have something great and strong running in your veins, just as your husband does. But you will never discover it if you are not pushed to the limits. If you are not forced beyond your breaking point. Although..." She stepped forward and reached her hand out.

I flinched away instinctively, and Malachi's power rumbled a warning once again.

Cordelia seemed to ignore all of this. She pushed forward again and gripped my chin tightly, forcing me to look into her eyes. "It seems as though you were already pushed pretty close. Your sister died." I tried to rip my chin from her grip, but it was no use. "And so did you."

"Let go of me," I sneered. "You don't know anything."

To my surprise, she did let go of me. She turned around and faced Esther. "You risked a lot by bringing her back." Her tone hinted at an accusation.

Esther lifted her chin, and I noticed the way she stole a glance at Malachi.

"What is she talking about?" Malachi asked. "What did Esther risk?"

"Nothing," Esther replied. "It's done, Cordelia."

Saints above, this was getting more and more interesting. "Esther brought me back to life," I said. "That was dangerous? How? What are the risks?"

Everyone spent the next few seconds staring at each other, like enemies waiting to see who would draw the first weapon.

"There is a delicate balance," Cordelia answered without looking away from Esther. "Life and death, there are two sides. Good and bad. Pure and evil. Pulling a soul from death and bringing them back to life is not natural."

"What does that mean?" Malachi asked. Only I could hear the hint of desperation in his voice. I wanted to reach out and comfort him, but I stopped myself. *Not here. Not now.*

"It means there will be consequences. You cannot bring one back from death and expect life to continue as normal."

"But she's been totally fine. There haven't been any changes at all. Right, Jade?"

All eyes shifted to me. What was I supposed to say? *Was I okay?* In all honesty, I was the furthest damned thing from okay. I had died, for Saints's sake. My sister had died. My father had nearly died. My mother was long dead, and who knew what type of secrets she had been keeping about me, about my identity.

I was not okay. But I wasn't sure how much of that had to do with dying, and how much of that had to do with living.

"Your past haunts you," Cordelia said.

"Are you going to crawl through my thoughts every time we're together?" I sneered.

"That depends," she replied. She stepped closer, raising one of her sharp eyebrows and pursing her lips before motioning to Malachi. "How much of your thoughts revolve around shadow-boy here being naked? I could hang around your thoughts for images of that all day long, peacemaker."

*That did it.*

I launched myself at her with full force, tackling her to the ground. I didn't realize I was screaming until we were both rolling across the cold, damp floor. Cordelia flipped me over and pinned both of my shoulders beneath her, holding me there with her weight.

Another yell of frustration escaped me as I thrashed beneath her.

"Good," she hissed. "Get angry. Show me how angry you are. Show me how powerful you can be."

I felt the power, the pure anger building inside of me.

And then I released it. At that moment, I didn't care if I hurt Cordelia. I *wanted* to hurt her, that bitch needed to learn her place with me, and there was no way she was going to get away with talking about Malachi like that.

My husband, my king.

She deserved it.

The light of my power flashed around us. I didn't flinch away, not this time. I didn't even squint as the blinding light erupted.

When it finally settled, Cordelia stood in front of Esther, a shield of what looked like glamour protecting them from my power.

Malachi stood on the other side of the room, completely able to protect himself.

"Good start," Cordelia said, still catching her breath. She turned to Esther with a grin. "You didn't tell me the girl had *life* magic."

"I wasn't sure," Esther replied. She looked at me in a way that made me want to cower. "I wasn't sure until now. It's been so long since–"

"Life magic?" Malachi repeated. "How is that… I mean, that isn't possible."

"What's *life* magic?" I asked.

"Life magic hasn't existed since the Saints walked these grounds," Cordelia explained. "It's extremely rare, and can be very dangerous."

I stood up, brushing the dirt off my trousers. "Why do they call it life magic if it's dangerous?"

"This explains a lot," Esther said. "It was easy to bring her back from the other side. If she didn't have life magic, it would have taken my entire essence to bring her back."

"What are you talking about?" Mal asked.

"Your wife possesses the magic that is so rare, only one of the Saints was known to possess it. Anastasia. This Saint was able to create life with nothing more than the touch of a finger, and when motivated the right way, she was able to take it away."

"Take away life?" I repeated. I certainly didn't remember any of her stories that involved taking life. "You mean kill. My power can give life and it can kill people."

"I didn't think that part was a surprise."

"It's not..." I struggled to find my words. *No,* it wasn't surprising that my magic could kill people. It was destructive and dangerous, yes, but to outright kill?

Nobody had said it that way before.

"Teach her how to use it," Malachi snapped. "That's why we're here, isn't it? So Jade can use her special magic?"

When I looked into Cordelia's bright green eyes, she was staring at me. No, not *at* me. *Into* me. Like she could see something deeper, something I couldn't even see myself.

I suddenly felt more exposed than ever.

"Are we doing this or not?" I pushed.

Esther also glanced between Cordelia and me with her eyebrows drawn together.

"Oh, we're doing this," Cordelia finally answered. "When I'm done with you, you'll be the most powerful creature alive."

With a scream of pain, Malachi fell to his knees beside me.

## CHAPTER 9
# *Malachi*

**Blinding, white agony ran through my veins, as if my blood** itself were rising into the sky through my skin.

"What are you doing to him?" I heard Jade scream, but it sounded distant. "Stop it!"

"That's enough, Cordelia," Esther snapped.

The pain lessened, but the force lingered. Cordelia had her claws in my mind. I had felt it before, with her.

Decades ago.

I forced myself to my feet, still recovering from the pain.

"What's your game, *witch*?" I asked through gritted teeth.

"I have no game. You are Jade's biggest weakness. If you hurt, she hurts. Am I the only one who sees how much of a problem this is?"

Cordelia reached her hand out in my direction again, and I braced myself for impact.

But I never felt the pain.

Jade took two steps to the right, positioning herself in front of me.

"You want to fight?" she asked Cordelia. "Let's fight. Malachi is not my weakness. He is my lifeline."

"Is that so?"

"He's the reason I'm still alive," Jade said with clenched fists. "He's the reason your boss didn't kill me the first time he laid eyes on me. You call that a weakness?"

Cordelia stepped forward. "Your power is connected," she stated.

"It is," Jade answered. My own magic flared within me in response, as if listening to her words.

"Show me."

Jade stalled. "Show you how?"

"Show me how your magic is connected."

"That's not how it works," I barked. I didn't know why Cordelia was trying to get under my skin. She had always been this way; a vindictive, bratty witch.

But she was strong. And she *was* powerful, as much as I hated to admit that. Esther was a powerful witch, but Cordelia's special blend of fae and witch blood created something dangerous.

*I would know.*

"It's not something I can simply show you on command. I can feel his power when he is near or when he is angry, and he can feel mine. It's like a tether."

"Well," Cordelia said. "Let's see how much of that is really true."

Cordelia closed the distance between herself and Jade, and before I could process what had just happened, her silver wings flashed and they both disappeared.

"Jade!" I yelled. It took one glance around the room to know that they had left. Vanished. Cordelia had taken them somewhere else, and I would be lucky if they were still under this mountain.

"She wants you to come for them," Esther said, almost sounding bored. "To see how strongly you two are connected."

"That crazy bitch," I snapped. "I should have never trusted her with Jade. I should have never trusted any of you!"

"She won't hurt Jade," Esther stated. "You know that, don't you? She's here to help her. To help you both. Cordelia can be trusted, Malachi."

"Is that what you'd call this?" I asked. "You'd call disappearing in the enemy's temple *helping*?"

"Find her," she said. "Relax, tap into your power, and find your wife. Follow that tether."

"I'm not the one doing the damn trials here." Irritation flooded my senses. I couldn't focus on that damned tether when I was this pissed off.

Esther stepped toward me with fierce, focused eyes. "You need to listen to me, son," she said. For what felt like the first time since I begged her to save Jade's life, she looked me in the eyes. "I pulled Jade back from death. She had passed that line, and she was never supposed to come back. She may seem like the same Jade, but she is not. Something is different. I can feel it, and I know you can feel it. Silas may not know it yet, but..." she glanced around the empty room before finishing, "she may not be a mere mortal anymore. You need to have your guard up. You both do."

My heart raced in my ears. None of this was surprising to me, but coming from Esther? "What do you mean she's not a mere mortal?"

Esther opened her mouth to reply, but quickly closed it, shoving away whatever thought first came to her mind. "I can't say too much. Not here. If Silas found out..."

"Found out what? What will he do to her? He already suspects she is not human. He told her so himself."

"There are things you don't know," she replied. Her voice came out as a hushed whisper. "Things I can't tell you. But once you complete the trials, you need to get as far from this temple as possible."

"Great idea," I mumbled as I ran a hand through my hair. "I was planning on sticking around for a few more decades."

"This is no joking matter. If Jade completes the trials without raising any red flags, it will be a miracle from the Saints."

She began stepping toward the entrance of the room. "Where are you going?" I hissed. "You drop that riddle on me and then leave?"

"Find your wife," she said. "And keep your distance from Cordelia. You two don't need to bicker any more than you already do. I have work to do. We'll talk more later."

And she was gone, her silver hair trailing behind her as she went.

My breathing echoed off the stone walls of the cave. *What in the Saints was going on here?* Cordelia had my wife somewhere in this damned temple, and my mother was, once again, speaking in mysterious riddles.

*I wasn't the one going through those damned trials.*

I didn't wait another second before I stormed out of the room. The temple was an underground maze, and Jade could be anywhere. It would take me days to scavenge the entire place, and that was assuming she stayed put.

I really hated Cordelia.

Our connected power was the only way. I closed my eyes and sank into that feeling, into that presence of hers that was always there. That was always inside of me. My anger slowly dissipated, clearing my body of those foggy emotions. I let my power flare—just a small amount—like a predator searching for its prey.

Jade was here somewhere.

It didn't take long before I felt it; that warm, calming presence. It was Jade, I knew it was. Her power, at least, which was now part of her.

She wasn't far.

"I'm going to kill that witch," I mumbled as I began walking through the tunnels again. My black wings tucked tightly behind me as I stormed through the halls. I passed a few Paragon members, none of whom I felt particularly excited to see or speak to.

I kept my head down, focusing on that small tether. Focusing on Jade.

Focusing on our connection.

I didn't feel any pain or panic through that tether, although I hadn't been able to focus that much on it before. I wondered if I could feel her pain, or if I could feel other things from her, too.

Maybe with time I could. Maybe with time, Jade and I would be able to communicate through our magic.

Life magic and death magic. *How great of a pair we were.*

"Where are you, Jade," I whispered to myself. I came to a fork in the tunnels when I began to feel a pull to the right. She had to be that way. She had to be searching for my magic, too.

So I followed it. I followed that slight, pulling feeling that guided me down the tunnel.

And that connection that I felt deep within my chest grew stronger and stronger.

I knew I was getting closer.

I followed the pull through the narrow stones and down a set of jagged stairs before I heard it; the faint, rapid flutter of Jade's heartbeat.

It was a sound I had grown fond of, and I was damn relieved to be hearing it now.

"Jade," I called out.

"Mal, I'm back here."

I made it to her in a flash, following her voice and my fae instincts in the darkness.

Jade was against the wall with a rope across her chest, shackled to the stone wall behind her, keeping her there.

"I'm going to kill her," I sneered. "I'm going to kill her for laying her hands on you."

My eyes quickly adjusted to the darkness to find Jade smiling at me. A wide, childish smile.

"What?" I asked.

"Nothing, it's just..." Her smile grew. "It worked."

"Of course it worked," I said. "I wasn't going to let you stay down here all day."

I ripped the rope away from her in one swift motion. "Now, tell me where that witch went. I need to talk to her."

"You're not killing Cordelia," Jade argued.

"Why not?"

"Look," she started, "I don't like her either, okay? But we *need* her. She's trying to help me."

I couldn't help but bark a laugh. "She keeps saying that, but I wouldn't be so sure. She's worked for Silas for decades now. We can't be certain where her loyalties lie."

Jade's hands found the tops of my shoulders in the darkness. She could barely see a thing, and my heart fluttered as I watched her eyes search blindly in the shadows.

"You hate her because she's powerful."

"I hate her because she's dangerous, and clearly has no respect for you. We can't trust her."

"I'm not saying she's my new best friend or anything," Jade said, "but she seems to know what she's talking about. I was able to pull you to me with my power. That's something, right?"

"That's something," I agreed. My hands found her waist as I pulled her to my chest.

Jade's arms wrapped around my shoulders. She drew in a long, calming breath. I did the same, feeling her chest rise and fall against me.

She pulled back just enough to ask, "What do you think she meant? About the balance between life and death?"

I debated telling her about my conversation with Esther, but it was still a mystery. Jade and I weren't lucky enough to get straight answers, especially in the depths of the Paragon. Everything either made no sense, needed more information, or turned out to be a flat out lie. I would have to dig to find the truth.

"I don't know," I answered truthfully. "I don't think we'll know for quite some time. Are you feeling okay? Are you feeling normal?"

Jade blinked and looked away. "I haven't noticed anything out of the ordinary, but considering how ridiculous my life has been lately, that's not saying much."

My hand on her back kept her pinned to me. "How long do you think we can hide down here without Cordelia finding us?"

Jade smiled again. "I think we have some time. She didn't seem to have much faith in your abilities to find me."

I leaned down and kissed her lips, leaning myself against the stone wall behind her. Jade wrapped her arms around my neck and pressed further against me, which only excited my power. Her mouth moved perfectly against mine, hot and needy in the darkness of the tunnel.

Heat tickled my stomach, and I was beginning to realize that as Jade's power flaring my own.

I needed more. So did my power.

I slid my hand under her shirt, feeling her flexing muscles underneath as she held herself against me.

She smiled against my mouth, and I pulled away just enough to ask, "What?"

"I can feel it," she said.

"Feel what?"

"Your power. I can feel your magic." She slid a hand down my chest. "Can you?"

"I've been feeling your magic since you blasted those damned deadlings in that cage made of bone."

And I kissed her again, hungrier this time. Like I needed her. Like she was meant just for me, here in the darkness. My tongue slid against her lower lip, and Saints, she tasted good.

She always tasted so damned good.

Footsteps approached behind us. I pulled away, barely, as they grew louder. Jade froze, too, her lips pausing mid-kiss.

It wasn't Cordelia. I could identify her footsteps from anywhere. It wasn't Silas, either. He never walked that fast. Someone was scurrying through these tunnels, and by the sounds of the random pauses at every turn, they were looking for someone.

Jade's eyes frantically searched mine, looking for guidance. Watching for my next move.

"What do you want?" I yelled into the tunnel, loud enough that my voice boomed off the stone walls and echoed through the caves.

The footsteps stopped.

"I'm looking for the peacemaker." A small, boyish voice echoed through the tunnel.

"What do you want with her?"

He waited a few seconds before answering, "I have a message."

I turned around and extended my wings, putting Jade behind me. By the sound of it, the young boy wouldn't be a threat, but I learned long ago to never underestimate any member of the Paragon. "We're in here."

The boy scurried closer to us, and I was surprised at how small he was when he entered.

"I need to speak with her," the boy said. He was young, maybe one decade old, with tattered clothing and dirty hands. His dark hair had been recently shaved, which made him look even younger.

"Speak," I demanded.

"Mal," Jade placed her hand on my back and stepped beside me. "It's okay. What's your message?"

He looked at us with wide eyes. Wide, terrified eyes.

"Is it from Silas?"

"No," he answered, shaking his head. "Silas can't know we spoke."

*Now I was interested.*

"What is it?" Jade asked again.

The hair rose on the back of my neck.

"Here," the boy said. He reached deep into his pocket and pulled out a letter. Not any letter, either. I recognized the deep blue seal on the envelope. The letter came from Rewyth.

I took the letter from the boy and immediately ripped it open. Serefin's handwriting scattered the page.

*"Our enemies lurk. Your throne is in jeopardy. Your brothers are fighting to keep Rewyth safe, but they are lost without their king. Come home as soon as you are able. Stay safe."*
*–S*

I read the letter twice before passing it to Jade so she could read it. "Where did you get this?" I asked the boy. "Why are you hiding it from Silas?"

"He can't know I gave this to you," the boy stuttered. "He doesn't want you receiving messages here."

*Of course he doesn't.* He wanted to keep us here as long as possible, and if that meant not running back to Rewyth when they needed me, he'd do whatever he could to intercept our messages.

"Why are you helping us?" Jade asked.

The boy shrugged. "My grandmother told me the peacemaker would come one day. I wanted to help the peacemaker. I saw you when you arrived."

Jade's posture instantly softened beside me.

"Thank you," I told the boy. "Now go."

He did without a second of hesitation, his small footsteps disappearing in the distance.

"Our enemies..." I thought aloud once the boy had left. "Saints, if only that narrowed it down."

"At least we know it isn't the Paragon," Jade sighed. "We can check one off the list."

"Who would threaten my throne? They know they will pay with their lives once I return."

Jade thought on this for a second, her brows furrowing in focus. "Maybe that's it," she said. "Maybe they don't think you'll return in time to stop them."

I was already shaking my head. "Don't think that way, Jade Weyland. I'm not leaving you here, and that's final."

She opened her mouth to argue, but I interrupted her with, "Final."

"Fine," she said. "But we need to figure out who's trying to steal your throne."

# CHAPTER 10 *Jade*

I STARED UP AT THE DARK, STONE CEILING WHILE MAL BREATHED heavily next to me on the bed. We had been there for hours, not moving. Just breathing.

"Each day is a day closer to the trials. Each day is one day closer to possibly dying. Again." I didn't look at Malachi when I said the words. I didn't think I would survive the look on his face.

We hadn't returned to training with Cordelia. Instead, we snuck away to our bedroom, where we had been silently staring into the darkness.

"You're not going to die," Malachi replied. "I won't let that happen."

My chest tightened. "I know you think that," I said, "but if Silas wants me dead in those trials, I think it will be hard for you to stop him."

"He won't kill you," Malachi stated. I finally looked at him, but his eyes had focused somewhere in the distance. "He needs you."

"Yeah," I agreed, "he needs me to disappear from this world. He needs me to stop being a threat. He needs all the power for himself."

Malachi let out a long breath. "As much as I hate to say this, I think we need to talk to Esther. She promised she could help us, and it's time she actually did that for once. She knows something."

I shifted in bed. "I think she's done plenty to help us already." I hated disagreeing with him, but Esther had saved my life. More than once. If it weren't for her, I would have been dead right now. Esther may have hid things from us, but she clearly had her own secrets under this mountain.

We had bigger problems to handle than Esther.

He scoffed. "Like what? Antagonizing her witch friends during your training?"

"Like bringing me back from the dead. Or are you still choosing to forget that part? She's part of the reason I'm still alive, Mal."

Malachi's dark eyes snapped to mine. "No, Jade. I will never forget that. You dying is the one thing that I can't seem to burn out of my memory. It's the one thing I see at night, and it's the one thing I can't get out of my head as I'm falling asleep."

His words were harsh, but I understood. I felt that same pain when I worried about Malachi. It was the reason I couldn't sit back and let him fight that war alone. It was the reason I had disobeyed him time and time again when he told me to stay put.

I couldn't lose him. I couldn't live with myself if I did.

"I'm sorry," I whispered. "I know you've been through a lot with her."

"Oh, Jade," he said, shifting his body closer and holding my face with his hands. "You have nothing to be sorry for."

I relaxed into his warmth and let him wrap his arms around me. My head always fit perfectly against his chest. "Do you think that *Erebus* thing is true?"

"What Erebus thing?" Mal asked nonchalantly, as if the fate of his heritage didn't linger in the air.

"Do you think you're his descendent?" I asked.

Malachi took another long breath. "I think I'll add that to the never-ending list of things my mother needs to answer."

My mind wandered to Esther. She *had* been acting different lately. Softer. Kinder. She defended me during the training, but I had to admit I was surprised. Esther was a powerful witch. Her coven was one of the most powerful that ever lived, yet Cordelia walked around like she owned the place.

Half witch, half fae. Just like Malachi.

But Cordelia's gifts were different. Malachi couldn't read minds.

At least, not that we knew of.

"This place is starting to creep me out," I admitted. Malachi laughed, and I rolled over to wrap my arms around his torso. "I mean it. The people, the black robes. I can't believe you lived here."

"In my defense," Malachi stated, "the robes were quite comfortable."

"Oh, shut up," I spat.

Malachi ran his hands up and down my back. "You're tense," he said.

"Not any more tense than you."

"Lay on your stomach," he demanded. He moved himself off the bed, giving me room to follow his orders.

I obeyed.

I couldn't help the nervous uptick in my racing heart.

"This is going to help you relax," Malachi said, lowering his voice to a sultry whisper. He peeled my tunic up and over my head, beginning to work his hands across the knotted muscles.

I hadn't realized how tense I actually was until each muscle started to relax beneath him.

"I hate this," he said after a few minutes. It took me a second to realize what he meant, but he was running his hands along the long, healed scars on my back. The ones his father's men gave me.

The ones he risked everything to avenge that day in Rewyth, standing up to his own father.

"I know," I whispered.

Malachi leaned down and placed a kiss on each scar, tracing the delicate skin of my back with his lips. I shuttered.

"I never wanted any of this for you," he said. His voice cracked.

"I know you didn't," I said. "You're too good, you're too kind. You shouldn't have gone through any of that, either."

He laughed, but it was humorless. "People like you don't deserve the things they go through. These things happened to you, and you're nothing but an innocent victim."

"And what about you? You're equally as innocent as I. You may have more blood on your hands, Malachi, but you did what you needed to do to survive. I would do the same."

When he didn't respond right away, I sat up in bed. I didn't care that my tunic was gone, or that Malachi could see me. I wanted him to see me. I wanted him to understand. I took his face in my hands and pulled him onto the bed.

"You are good, Malachi. You are kind and strong and vengeful. You are powerful, but you are also generous and caring. You are nothing like Erebus. Not even close. Do you understand me?"

He closed his eyes, but I only gripped his face harder. We were alone up here. It was him and me against the world. I needed him.

I needed him to not shut me out.

"You are *good*, Mal." I kissed his cheek, his forehead, his nose. "You are good. And even if you were not good, even if you were the worst fae to ever walk among this world, even if you killed and killed and took whatever you wanted whenever you wanted it, I would still love you the same. Because it's not what you *do* that makes me love you, Malachi. It's who you are. And if you have Erebus's blood in you that makes your wings black, well *good*. Because I like your black wings."

He cracked the tiniest hint of a smile. His wings spread, just an inch. "Really?" he teased. "These wings?"

"Yes," I answered. "Those wings. And don't push it." His wings spread out to their full capacity, almost touching each side of the small stone cave. "You're pushing it."

He laughed, and I laughed with him. It felt strange, laughing when we were in this terrible situation.

Malachi's arms fell around me, and he pulled me onto his lap in one swift motion. My arms settled on his shoulders as I relaxed against him.

"I love you, Jade," he said. "And you could also kill and kill and kill. I'd find that pretty attractive."

I punched him in the arm.

He laughed even harder. "What?" he asked. "It's true! Now I'm thinking of you dripping in the blood of our enemies. That's even sexier."

I punched him harder.

But my stomach fluttered. *Our enemies.*

Whatever we faced in the future, we would face it together. Descendants of Saints or not.

"Do you think Cordelia will be pissed that we never showed back up for training?"

"No," Malachi answered without a second of thinking. "I don't. And I don't care much about what she thinks, anyway."

"You really don't like her," I said.

"She's let her power go to her head. I never liked her, even when we were younger."

The way Malachi talked about Cordelia got me thinking about their past. He clearly had issues with her, and they must have gone through a lot while living here together. There weren't that many people under this mountain to begin with. To be trapped together for years, maybe even decades...

I couldn't stop myself from asking, "Did you ever...?"

Malachi shook his head "Saints, no. Never. Cordelia and I trained together, but we were never even friends. Sometimes, if we were too tired to fight, we were civil. But that's as close as things got between us."

I eyed him carefully. "Okay," I answered. "There's just so much tension between you two."

"Cordelia has a way of doing that. She's not exactly warm and welcoming."

"I hate to break it to you, King of Shadows, but neither are you. You two have a lot in common, you know."

I expected some sort of retort to my comment, but Malachi's eyes had gone into that far away place again. "Something is going on with her and Esther," Malachi said. "They're keeping a secret. I just don't know what it is."

I crawled off Malachi's lap—even though I instantly missed the warmth of him—and began looking for my tunic.

"Where are you going?" Mal asked.

I drew my black tunic over my head. "If you want to find out what they're hiding from us, we have to figure it out ourselves. They won't be serving it to us on a silver platter."

Malachi rolled his eyes. "We shouldn't be sneaking around the temple at night."

I rested my hand on my hip. "Now you're the noble one? What was that you were just saying to me about...oh yeah. *Dripping in my enemies' blood*?"

"Fine," he said after a second. He picked up his sword and strapped it to his waist. "But be quiet. Remember that the fae can hear and see much better than you can. Don't try to sneak up on anybody."

"You can't tell me you never snuck through these tunnels when you were younger. Not even once?"

Malachi remained silent, which was answer enough.

I pushed open the stone door to our room and stepped into the dark, shadowed hallway.

It had to be well past midnight. If we were lucky, most people would be avoiding the main areas.

I wasn't sure what we were looking for. A scroll with all of the plans for my trials would be nice. But I wasn't going to get my hopes up.

"This way," Malachi said. Instead of taking us back the way we usually came from, he turned and walked further into the tunnels. Malachi walked silently, and I cursed myself for not being as careful as him.

But he had been doing this much longer than I had, I reminded myself. He had decades of sneaking through castles and creeping down halls. I only had a few months.

"What's back here?" I whispered. Even with my quieted voice, I felt it echo.

The heat in the pit of my chest, the one that I now knew was connected to my power, flared. As if it wanted to protect me. As if it wanted me to know it could help.

Malachi instinctively reached back. I slid my hand in his.

The wet, stone wall on either side of us grew more and more narrow. "Are you sure there's something back here?" I asked. Malachi didn't respond, but he squeezed my hand.

The small amount of light that had been giving me the ability to see before was gone. We turned a tight corner, and to my surprise, the light disappeared entirely. I couldn't see a thing.

I squeezed Mal's hand even tighter. *He better not let go.*

A freezing cold breeze hit me out of nowhere. My breath was nearly taken away.

"Almost there," Mal said.

"Almost where?"

The wind grew stronger and stronger until I had to use my hand to catch myself on the stone wall next to me.

A couple more steps forward, and I could finally see again. But it wasn't a lantern that lit the path, nor a fire of any kind.

It was the moon. The sky.

The stars.

Glowing in a way that warmed my soul, that lit a fire of excitement in my chest.

"We're outside?" I asked. Goosebumps erupted over my skin, half from the chill of the air and half from the excitement of what we were doing. "How is this possible?"

"Let's say it's more of a secret spot. More secluded. We're safe up here."

"And how is this supposed to help us learn all of the secrets from our enemies?"

Malachi smiled. His white smile reflected the moonlight above. "It's not."

He stepped forward and wrapped his arms around me, encapsulating me in his warmth as I stared up at the night sky.

"I didn't notice the stars before," I admitted.

"They're beautiful, aren't they?" Esther's voice behind us made us both jump. Malachi slid away from me, drawing his weapon and pointing it in her direction.

Every sense of mine erupted with adrenaline.

"What are you doing here?" he asked.

"Likely the same thing you're doing here," Esther answered.

"I somehow doubt that."

Esther stepped forward, her pale face becoming illuminated by the moonlight. Malachi tensed with each step she took.

"We need to talk," Esther said.

Malachi finally lowered his sword. "Yes," he said. "We do. Did you follow us here to tell us that?"

"I didn't follow you," she said. "I've been waiting. Silas told me you enjoyed hiding away up here when you were younger. I don't blame you. It's beautiful."

I glanced between the two of them but stayed silent. "You and Silas are awfully close. Would you like to start by explaining what's going on with you two? Are you working together?"

Esther leaned against the stone mountain edge. "Silas isn't who you think he is," Esther answered.

A deep, unsettled feeling grew in my stomach. Were those Malachi's emotions? Was I feeling what he was feeling through the connection of our power?

"Are you telling me you know Silas better than I?" Mal asked.

I thought back to the conversation I had with Esther about Silas. She had known him. She had lived here with him, in fact, after Malachi had returned to Rewyth.

*Did Malachi know?*

Esther glanced down at her feet. It was unsettling enough that we were having this conversation, but it was even worse that she seemed so nervous about it. Esther, the most powerful witch bloodline to walk this world, was nervous to talk to Malachi.

Something was up.

She took a long, shaking breath before saying, "Silas is your birth father, Malachi."

# CHAPTER 11
# Malachi

"You lie," I demanded, but the words came out softer than I planned.

"I have no reason to lie to you."

Anger blinded my vision. "You have plenty of reasons to lie to me, I just have a difficult time discovering which of your motives is currently affecting our safety."

My mother stepped forward, a pleading look on her face. "Silas is your father. He has been this entire time. I let the King think he was your father because he would have killed me if he found out. He hated me enough already, Saints..."

No, that wasn't possible. *Silas?* My enslaver, my torturer? The leader of the Paragon?

"That's impossible." I backed up a step, but Jade was there, hands on my back.

"I'm only telling you this now because you need to understand what's at stake."

"Does he know?" I asked. "Does Silas know I'm his son?"

Esther took a long breath. "He does."

"All of that information he told me about Erebus...he told me I had the blood of that wicked Saint. Are you telling me that Silas is a descendent of Erebus, too?"

Another long breath. "I am."

*No,* none of this made any sense. Even the freezing mountain air couldn't clear my swarming thoughts. "But his wings, Silas has silver wings."

Esther looked away from me again. How cowardly, not able to face your own son with the truth. Jade whispered something behind me but I couldn't hear her through the pulsing anger in my veins.

"We've suspected that his Erebus blood mixed with my powerful witch bloodline is what brought out the black wings again. What he tells you is true, son. You are one of his descendants. And as a descendent of both a Saint and a powerful witch, you have more gifts than you can even understand."

I laughed, and I enjoyed the way Esther flinched at the sound. "You are a cruel, vindictive woman," I growled. "How is telling me this now going to help me? Why have you kept this a secret all this time?"

"He would kill me, Malachi. He would kill me if I told you the truth. He doesn't want you to know how powerful you really are."

"Is that why he brought us here? He doesn't care about Jade at all, does he? He just wants to exploit my power as his son." It all started to add up. The secrets, the attack on my kingdom, his interest in Jade.

Esther let out an exasperated sigh. "If Jade is truly chosen from the Saints, which we all know she is, she will have no problem passing the trials. I'll make sure of it."

"How? How can you make sure of it? Is Silas still blinded by you? Is he so in love with you that he'll do anything you suggest?" My questions were satire, but Esther's face made me reconsider. "You really have him wrapped around your witchling finger, don't you?"

Her face hardened. I didn't care if my words hurt her. Once again, she had blindsided me with a secret. "Silas has watched over you, Malachi."

My temper unraveled. Silas had done many things to me in my life, but *watch over* me? "He brought war to my kingdom!"

"And you walked away alive. Is that not a sign of good faith?"

"My people died. Innocent citizens lost fathers and husbands. The sense of safety in my kingdom shattered. The Paragon..." I took a shaking breath to gather my thoughts. "The Paragon is supposed to *protect* us. Silas's subordinates put a damn blade through my wife!" I reached back and grabbed Jade's hand. She squeezed tightly. "Was that *protecting* her? Was that protecting me?"

"His healer helped her after I brought her back from the depths, Malachi please!" Esther rushed forward with her hands before her. "Please, listen to me now. None of that matters. I'm here because of the trials."

"What does any of that have to do with Jade's trials? It seems as though they want to toy with us to make themselves feel more powerful. Is that not true?"

"They will push Jade to her limits to ensure that she is powerful enough to be the peacemaker. Silas will create these trials, but he needs witches to bring them to life. He needs us to string our magic into Jade's mind. That's why I'm here, Malachi. I'm here to help Jade."

The world around me spun. "Are you telling me you'll be helping Silas create Jade's trials?"

Esther took another long, shaking breath. Her eyes softened, and in another world I would have actually believed that she felt bad about all of this. "Yes, and I'm going to do everything I can to protect her from herself."

My fists pounded the training bag, stray feathers flying with every hit.

Another punch.

Another punch, harder.

Faster.

More painful.

I didn't remember leaving Jade and walking here to the training room, the only thing I could think of was Esther's voice.

She had betrayed us time and time again.

And every damn time I thought she might be on our side, she shifted.

I punched the bag again.

Again.

"Malachi," Jade's soft, angelic voice filled the room, echoing off the walls between my ragged breathing.

I ignored her. I didn't know what to say. My own mother was going to help Silas perform whatever messed up magical ceremony was necessary to turn his wicked plan into visions that would torture Jade's mind.

How could I face her? How could I look her in the eye after that?

"Malachi Weyland," Jade's voice echoed again, laced with an urgent sense of anger. "Don't you dare shut me out," she said.

I punched again, feeling the skin on my knuckles split.

I grabbed the training bag, stopping it from swinging on the rope it hung from as I rested my sweaty forehead against it.

Her footsteps approached.

Small, delicate hands slid onto my shoulders, just over the base of my wings. It took everything in me not to flinch away from the soft touch.

"Esther's not the one who designs the trials, Mal. You know this. You know she doesn't have much of a choice. We're all at the mercy of the mighty, undefeatable Paragon." The last words dripped with resentment.

I shook my head and pushed Jade's words away. "It doesn't matter," I said. "She's part of it. That's the reason she came here with us, isn't it? So she could help with the trials?"

A beat of silence passed between us. "She brought me back from death. You think she would throw me back at death's doorstep so quickly? She nearly died herself by bringing me back, Mal. It drained her. And you heard what Cordelia said. She disrupted the balance. She wouldn't have done all that just to kill me again when the trials came around."

It didn't make sense. It didn't make *any* damn sense. Why would Esther bring Jade back if she was willing to help Silas put her through the Trials of Glory?

"It's a trick," I thought aloud. "That's the only logical explanation."

Jade gripped my shoulder and spun me around. "Or," she started, "your mother is pretending to be on Silas's side for *our* sake, and plans on swaying his decisions in the trial so I have an easier time. Could that be a possibility?"

*Saints, when did Jade become the reasonable one?*

I repeated her words in my mind before answering, "It's highly unlikely, but I suppose it is possible."

Jade took another step toward me and picked up my bloody hands. "My wicked, violent husband," she said.

She leaned down and brushed a kiss over my red-stained knuckles.

I put a finger under her chin and lifted her face to mine. "You are too good for me, Jade. You are smart and trusting and true."

She leaned into my touch as I caressed her face. "I am nothing if not yours."

# CHAPTER 12
## *Jade*

Mal kissed me, not caring to be delicate. Not worrying if he would hurt me or not. And I kissed him back with an equal amount of aggression.

He gripped my waist and backed my body up until I leaned against the stone wall behind me. Our mouths moved together in a frenzy, giving me the release of emotion that I'd been needing for so much longer than I realized.

Malachi's hands ravaged my body, sliding down my back and up my torso as his hands splayed against my skin.

I lifted myself up to him, wrapping an arm around his neck to hold my body against his. One of his hands slid down my thigh, gripping my skin with need as he hauled my leg around his waist, pinning me to the wall.

"Someone could walk in," I noted as Malachi moved his mouth to my jawline, sending a hot, fiery trail of kisses down my neck and against my now-bare shoulder.

"Let them," he growled. His black wings beat around us, shadowing us even further in the dimly lit training room.

Malachi's mouth didn't leave my body. He kissed me everywhere he could, only pausing for a moment to pull my tunic up and over my head, tossing it to the floor with ease. I didn't remember pulling his shirt off, but soon enough it, too, was gone, our skin igniting with heat anywhere we touched.

"Is this your way of blowing off steam?" I asked, distracted by Malachi's hands as his fingers slipped under the hem of my trousers.

Malachi froze as if I had physically hit him. He pulled away from my body just enough so he could look into my eyes as he said, "Is that what you think this is, Jade Weyland?"

The intensity in his eyes took my breath away, not that I had much left after that type of kiss. "I don't know what this is," I answered honestly.

"Let me tell you exactly what this is, my queen. You," he trailed a finger down my face, pausing them on my now swollen lips, "are the most beautiful creature the Saints have blessed this world with. You are everything I have ever needed, and everything I will need forever. Everything else? The Paragon? Esther? None of that matters." He gripped my face with both hands now, although his body still pressed mine into the stone wall behind me. "I love you, Jade. That's all that's ever mattered to me, even before I truly knew what these feelings I have for you were. And this?" He motioned to the two of us together. "This is me showing you exactly how you deserve to be loved."

My head spun from the mixture of adrenaline and euphoria as I pulled Malachi's face down to mine so I could kiss him again. I didn't hold anything back. I pushed away all of the thoughts in my mind about the Paragon, the trials. I didn't care about any of that. What I cared about was how damn good it felt when Malachi lifted me up again, wrapping both of my legs around his waist this time. What I cared about was the fact that we were moving, his wings pumping for a split second before we landed on a padded mat meant for combat training.

"Malachi, wait," I said, pushing on his bare chest. My trousers were already untied, similar to his, and neither of us had to guess where this was headed. "Are you sure about this?"

A wicked grin spread on his face. "You never, ever have to ask me if I'm sure about you, my queen. The answer will always be yes. Every damn time."

"Well," I said, fighting the rush of emotion that came with his words, "that's good to know, then."

He laughed, and I closed my eyes as I felt the vibrations from his chest transfer to mine, our power linking together at our mere proximity. The magic in my veins pumped, too, harder than it ever had. With more power than it ever had.

I knew Malachi felt this. I could see it in his eyes, like a shining star in a black night.

There were no questions this time. No hesitations. No second-guesses. Malachi and I, made for one another in nearly every way possible, knew exactly what to do. Knew how each other's bodies would react before they did.

Skin on skin, intertwined breath and limbs. I pulled his body to me and held on like he was the last thing I would ever need in this world.

I didn't even realize my power was losing control until it was too late.

The stone room erupted.

A blast of power—not just mine, but Malachi's black, wicked shadows, too—blasted through the room, burning the training equipment, burning the mat under my back, burning it all.

Malachi's wings blasted out to protect me, as if I needed it. As if that would help.

We caused this. The eruption of power came from us.

"Holy Saints," I whispered.

Malachi stayed on top of me until our power settled. It wasn't until he pushed himself away from me that I saw how bad it really was.

We had...we had *burned* the entire damn room.

## CHAPTER 13
# Malachi

CORDELIA LAUGHED.

I couldn't bring myself to look at her until Jade finished telling the story. Jade tried to be as vague as possible as she told Cordelia what happened in that training room, for both of our sakes, but Cordelia only relished in that further, asking questions that I knew would turn Jade bright red in the face.

But it didn't matter. We needed answers.

"If we could go anywhere else to find the answers we're looking for, trust me, we would," I added. Jade exhaled, I could tell she was relieved I joined the conversation at all.

Saints, Cordelia would never let us forget this.

She laughed again. Jade and I waited patiently in her potion-covered bedroom as she finished entertaining herself with our situation.

"Okay, okay. I'm done. I'm sorry, I just..." She covered her mouth again to stifle another fit of laughter.

"If you can't help us," Jade interrupted, "We'll just leave. We don't need to stay here and listen to you laugh at us."

Cordelia cleared her throat and made a half-assed attempt at straightening her expression. "I can be serious," she said, more to herself than to us. "And I think I do know a little something about this."

"We're all ears," I added.

"You're telling me your magic connected? Combined? You both didn't simply lose control at the same time, did you?"

I squinted. "If by lose control you mean..."

"Of your powers, you imbecile! Jade's magic is fairly new, it's possible that you–"

"It wasn't that," Jade stated. "It was more like...more like Mal's power pulling mine from the source. And the same with him. We couldn't control it, I couldn't stop it once it began."

She considered these words. "But neither of you are hurt?"

"We're fine," I said. "But I can't say the same for the training room."

"The training room?" Cordelia asked. "You two couldn't take it back to the damn bedroom? Saints!"

Jade shifted uncomfortably, but I couldn't help the wave of satisfaction that came over me. I was a king, and Jade my queen. I would show her my love anywhere we damn well pleased. It wasn't our fault we happened to be cooped up under this mountain.

"Have you heard of this before?" I asked.

She paced in her bedroom, scanning over her small bookshelf filled with grimoires, spells, and decades of witch history. Cordelia may be sassy, stubborn, and a general stick in my ass, but she was knowledgeable. I had to give her that much.

"Not exactly," she started, "but I've heard of something similar. With your magic, both being so rare, I wonder if..."

She pulled a dusty, leather-bound book from her shelf and flipped through the pages.

"You wonder what?" I pushed.

She ignored me and continued scanning through the pages of her book until she stopped, finger on the page, and read aloud, "Anastasia and Erebus, the Saints of life and death, could not hurt each other. It was unheard of for such powerful beings to not cause damage to one another. But their love, as the prophecy goes, was strong enough to create a lasting protection around each other. Bound by forces beyond our understanding, they were meant for each other. Created for each other. The forces of lightness and darkness could not be separated, for the world knew that they belonged together. For eternity, they would belong together."

I waited for her to say more, but she only shut the book and turned to stare at us.

"What does that mean?" Jade asked, the smallest amount of panic lacing her words. "The Saints could not hurt each other either? Like us?"

"Life magic," Cordelia held a hand out to Jade, "and death magic." Her hand waved to me.

*Death magic.*

Jade's hand fell over mine.

"Are you saying we're supposed to be together?" I asked.

Cordelia only shrugged. "I can't say for sure, but you two are certainly not normal. Your magic isn't normal, being the peacemaker is definitely not normal. I think it's safe to assume you both possess the same magic as the Saints, and therefore are bonded the same way."

Bonded by the Saints.

It made sense. Before I met Jade, I had felt a deep, needy urge to protect her. My magic reacted to her presence, and I knew hers did the same. It was clear that Jade had been chosen by the Saints to be the peacemaker, so it did make sense that we...

"Bonded?" Jade repeated, interrupting my thoughts. "As in, our magic?"

"Magic," Cordelia answered, "souls, beings. You're already married, but yes. I'd assume you're bonded in all of those ways."

My heart pounded. Jade was not just my wife. Was not just the pacemaker. Was not just my queen.

Jade was a gift from the Saints, a light in my darkness. She was the balanced piece of me, everything I ever needed.

She was my other half.

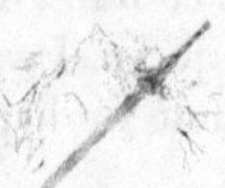

I was a damned idiot for being nervous.

Jade hadn't spoken since we left Cordelia's bedroom. She didn't speak as we walked down the hallway to our bedroom, either.

The things I would do for Cordelia's mind-reading gift...

"So," I started as we approached our bedroom door. "What do you think?"

Jade shrugged and took a deep breath, which didn't help my nerves. Would she be disappointed by the bond? Angry that she was tied to me? I tried to imagine how I would feel if I were in her shoes. She lost her freedom a long time ago. Marrying me was not part of her plan.

But was this? Was being bonded to me forever part of her plan?

Or was she secretly thinking of any possible way to get out of the situation?

I stepped to the side, letting her walk into our bedroom first. She opened her mouth as if she wanted to say something, but pushed the stone door open instead and headed inside.

I followed.

"It's—It's crazy. Right?" she stammered.

"What's crazy?" I asked, carefully choosing the tone of my voice. I turned to the wall and began unbuckling my weapon belt. *You don't care. You don't care.*

And then she laughed. It was a light laugh, one that bubbled from her chest until she couldn't hold it in any longer. I spun around to find her staring at me with bright eyes.

Damn, I loved those eyes.

"You're laughing," I noted.

She tried to open her mouth to speak, but fell into another fit of laughter. Her dark hair slid over her shoulders as she tossed her head back and continued laughing.

Her laughter spread like a fire, I had to admit.

I stepped forward and grabbed her shoulders, forcing her to look at me. "Please tell me what you're thinking," I said, "because I think I'll lose my mind if you stand here laughing for one more minute."

It took her a few tries, but she eventually straightened and withheld her laughter long enough to say, "It's crazy that we're only finding this out. We've known for a long time that we're meant for each other, Malachi Weyland."

*Thank the Saints for that.*

The sigh of relief that came from me was involuntary, as was the kiss I couldn't stop myself from planting on her lips.

"What?" she asked as I pulled away. "Did you think this would scare me off?"

I shrugged. "I think it would make a lot of sense if you didn't want to be my other half for the rest of your life, considering the circumstances."

I tried to turn back to the wall but Jade stopped me, pulling my arm until I stood even closer to her than before.

Not a single hint of laughter laced her features now, no humor at all as she said, "If I have to spend every waking day of my life with you, I will do it gladly. Saint or no Saint. Bond or no bond. You are mine, Malachi. And I am yours. Don't think for a second you can scare me off so easily."

When I kissed her this time, I didn't stop.

*Mine. Forever.*

## CHAPTER 14
# *Jade*

I COULDN'T HELP THE HINT OF NERVES AS I PREPARED FOR ANOTHER training session with Cordelia. The hint of burnt magic lingered in the air from my night here with Malachi, but Cordelia didn't seem to notice.

"Why do we need to do this?" I asked, ignoring the way Cordelia's muscles flexed as she rubbed her hands together in front of her body.

"You have no idea what you need to prepare for," she answered coldly. "If you're caught in a physical fight with your enemies in these trials, you'd be as good as dead. Physical combat is equally as important as your magic."

"I don't plan on letting anyone close enough to have to fight them physically," I replied.

"Really?" she teased. "And what happens when you lose your magic? What happens if Silas decides to restrict your power? What then?"

"Why would he do that?" I asked. "The whole point of the trials is to test my power."

She stepped closer to me, fists drawn.

Saints, I didn't want to fight Cordelia. I didn't want to get within three feet of her, actually. Her perfectly sculpted shoulders, her tall yet lean build. She could take me in a fight, I was sure of it.

Cordelia had likely been training for this. She had probably trained dozens of other trial contestants, and she'd likely been fighting for years.

"If you think that's all these trials are for, peacemaker, you have a harsh lesson coming your way."

I didn't have time to think of a reply. Cordelia closed the distance between us and threw a fist directly at my face.

I dodged her hit last second, stepping to the side and spinning around to face her. "What was that?" I yelled.

She didn't answer. Instead, she advanced again, trying to hit me.

This time, her fist flew so close to my face I could feel the breeze as I threw my body to the other side of the room.

Okay, she wasn't messing around.

I didn't love to fight, but I *would*. If my choice was between fighting or Cordelia landing that punch into my face?

I pulled my fists up and paid closer attention. Cordelia took her time crossing the room, moving slowly like a predator stalking its prey.

I wasn't going to let her get the satisfaction this time. I moved first, stepping quickly and punching toward her abdomen.

She dodged it with little effort, snickering as she moved aside.

"Nice try, peacemaker. You'll have to do a lot better than that."

*Saints above.*

Cordelia had a slim build and fast reflexes, but she was strong. She was quick on her feet. We weren't all that different in size and movements, I realized. She was just fifty times better at fighting than I.

Which meant she would be cocky. She would get too confident.

I took a long breath and focused. Cordelia shook her arms out before pulling her fists back up to her chest, ready to fight.

I moved again, attempting to throw her off guard with my left fist as I punched directly after with my right.

Which left me entirely unguarded.

Cordelia saw this opportunity and landed a hit to my cheekbone.

I hissed in pain, stumbling backwards.

"You bitch," I sneered.

"Get mad all you want," she replied. "We're doing this to help you, not hurt you."

"Right. Not hurting me at all."

I put my fingers to my cheekbone, feeling the nearly split skin there.

Cordelia wanted a fight? She would get a fight.

*Focus, Jade. You're plenty capable of doing this.*

I thought back to the time I spent training with Malachi. He was fierce, strong, and determined. He taught me how to be all those things, I had simply forgotten.

And Cordelia had underestimated me.

I used the anger that built in my chest and threw myself at Cordelia knocking her off guard and off balance. We both tumbled to the ground, a yell of frustration escaping me.

She hit the ground first, but quickly spun so we were barrel-rolling through the room. Her sharp fingernails dug into my arms, but I didn't let go. I didn't back down.

I widened my hips to stop us from rolling, pinning Cordelia to the ground beneath me. She was strong, yes, but not strong enough to throw my entire body off her.

Her claws eventually lost their grip on my arms as she switched her strategy, clawing at my neck, my face, my shoulders.

I still did not back away. I gripped her wrists and pinned them to the floor behind her head.

Hard.

A satisfied smile spread onto her face when she realized what had just happened. Her breath matched mine, coming out in harsh pants. "Very impressive, peacemaker. It seems you're not all looks after all."

"What is that supposed to mean?" I asked. I let go of her and moved away so she could sit up.

"You were forced to marry him, the deadliest fae in your kingdom. I should have known you'd be a fighter. I should have known they were wrong."

"*Who* was wrong?" I asked, trying not to sound too interested. After everything I had endured, I didn't quite care if strangers held negative opinions of me. They could think of me as weak, as afraid. They could think of me as the poor human girl who had to marry the evil prince.

They could think whatever they wanted. They had no idea what I had gone through, what my life was like.

"Everyone, peacemaker," Cordelia whispered, a twinkle of amusement in her eye. "You should really hear what the rest of the Paragon thinks of you. Saints, they might as well start a wager on how quickly you'll die in these trials."

I stood up and stormed out of the room. I didn't need this. I knew how much of a challenge winning would be. I didn't need it thrown in my face during my own training.

"Wait," she yelled before I reached the door. "You should take some pride in that, peacemaker."

"Why would I take pride in people thinking I am weak?"

"Because," she stood up and stepped toward me, her eyes flickering to the busted skin on my face. "Now, you can prove them all wrong."

# CHAPTER 15
## *Malachi*

Two days.

We had two days until Jade's trials began.

She seemed calm. Collected. During the day, she never showed an ounce of concern. She appeared confident and tough, ready for whatever training Cordelia seemed to throw her way. Even when Esther showed up to help, Jade did not falter.

She was ready.

I, though, could see the slight break in her scowl each time Cordelia landed a punch. Each time her magic flared beyond her control. The stress built day after day. I didn't blame her. Two days was not a lot of time to prepare for every possible scenario Silas might throw her way.

*The Saints chose her for this*, I reminded myself. She would not have been selected by the Saints if she wasn't ready. They would help her. She would get through this.

She had no other choice.

Jade had been training with Cordelia for hours now. They had the same routine down each day. Wake up, eat, study with Silas, train. Sometimes the training was physical. Sometimes mental.

I began to drop my guard around Cordelia. Not because I wanted to, but because I saw her. I could see how much she cared about Jade's training, how much she wanted Jade to succeed.

Why? I wasn't sure. Perhaps she believed in the prophecy of the peacemaker just as much as the rest of us.

Either way, I figured Cordelia could be trusted. For now.

I, on the other hand, should not have been left unsupervised. I snuck through the dark tunnels of the mountain, careful not to make a single sound as I turned the final corner to Cordelia's bedroom.

I needed that damn book.

Knowing that Jade and I were bonded was just the beginning. I needed to know more about Anastasia and Erebus.

I would have remembered a story like that before. The hours I spent in that library, the thousands of stories I heard about the five Saints.

Was there a reason Silas hid that piece of history? Was there a reason I hadn't heard about the bond of life and death magic?

My senses peaked as Cordelia's bedroom door came into view. It was a large stone door, just like any of the other doors in the tunnel. Still, it felt different. Darker. I ignored the slight uptick in my heart rate as my senses dialed in on the bedroom. I approached the door, placed both hands on the stone, and pushed.

And then I waited. I wasn't sure what exactly I waited for, an alarm? A trap? Some sort of magical force shoving me from the entryway of her bedroom?

But none of those things came. A small bead of sweat rolled down the back of my neck.

I took one step forward, leaving the door ajar as I walked through the threshold of Cordelia's bedroom.

It only took a few small strides to cross the bedroom and reach the bookshelf on the far wall. It wasn't difficult to find the book she had read from when Jade and I visited. The book was wrapped in a thick black leather and a golden string hung from the spine as a bookmark.

I stilled and quieted my breathing, waiting for any sounds coming from the hallway. My fae ears turned toward the open door. Still, I heard nothing.

So I pulled the book from the shelf.

I couldn't take the book with me. If Cordelia saw it missing when she returned, I would be the first one to blame. It was suspicious enough that I had left Jade and her alone to train while I stepped away to scavenge her bedroom.

Instead, I flipped through the pages, looking for any mention of Anastasia and Erebus. Immediately, I knew this was a book I had never read before. Pages and pages of history filled the thick paper, with handwritten notes scribbled into the margins outside of the text.

This book was older than Cordelia. And it wasn't part of Silas's library...

*Focus.* I didn't have much time.

I flipped through more and more pages, taking in as much information as I could. For the most part, the pages were filled with personal stories of the Saints. Stories of how they got their magic, how they struggled to come to power for so long.

Some of it felt so familiar to me, had been ingrained in my memory for so long. I knew the five Saints so well, I could recite some of the stories in this book.

But the other stories...

Stories of love, stories of loss. Stories of betrayal among the Saints, of uprisings and abused magic.

I had never read those stories before.

My eyes landed on a particular page that had been handwritten and scratched out.

*"It scares me, what I'm willing to do for him. He is everything I am not, yet he pulls me to him like I've belonged there all my life."*

I re-read it again and again, skimming the pages to follow and looking for any more handwritten notes in the same flowing style. I nearly gave up on the book when I found what Cordelia had read to us before.

The love story of Anastasia and Erebus.

Life and death, the perfect balance. The perfect match. My heart sank as I read the story, burning it into my memory.

The last sentence read, *"To love death is to become it."*

## CHAPTER 16

# *Jade*

I NEVER THOUGHT I WOULD MISS THE SCANDALOUS DRESSES IN REWYTH, but *Saints*. Looking down at myself in the long black cloak that the Paragon provided, I really, really, missed them.

The black fabric hid my frame entirely, dragging the ground beneath my feet as I took a step. The bruises from training with Cordelia had only multiplied, covering my skin with dashes of red and purple.

"You look amazing," Malachi said. His own black cloak somehow looked fitted and perfectly shaped to his lean, muscular body.

"You have to say that," I breathed. "You're my husband."

He moved closer, and my stomach erupted in heated butterflies as his eyes raked themselves down my body. "I most certainly do not have to," he replied, "but I'd be willing to tell you every day for the rest of our lives, if you're interested."

A teasing smile played on his lips.

"If you're trying to distract me," I said, closing the distance between us and sliding my hands up his chest, "it's working."

Malachi and I had been invited to a feast, thrown in my honor. What a joke, a feast to celebrate what might be my last day alive.

I wanted to laugh. How many times had I thought that? How many times had I thought that this day alive would be my last? I certainly thought that before my wedding, and look where that got me.

"What are you thinking right now, my queen?" Mal asked, pulling my hands from his chest and kissing each of my knuckles.

I watched his plump, perfect lips brush against my skin. "I'm thinking about how badly I don't want to do this. I don't want to eat with them. I don't want to look at Silas for one more second." The words were true, and I knew Malachi felt the same way. We couldn't exactly say *no* to the feast thrown in my honor.

"It's all part of their game," Mal said, lowering my hands to his sides. "They want to appear as your ally before they send you to the wolves."

"The wolves," I scoffed. "You mean the wolves that they create with their own messed up, magic concoction?"

He smiled, but it didn't reach his eyes. "Exactly," he breathed.

I eventually pulled my hands from his and began walking out of our room. "I suppose we should get this over with, then. The night can't last forever, right? We've attended plenty of dinners we wanted no part in. This will be nothing different."

Mal nodded.

We took our time walking to the dining room. I half-hoped that some sort of interruption would stop us from having to go, but it seemed as though we were the only two people walking through the underground tunnels.

Esther, Cordelia, Silas. They would all be there. They would all pretend like they had my best interests in mind, like they were on my side.

I threaded my fingers through Mal's. At least I could count on him. Of everyone that would be attending this feast, Mal would kill for me. He would kill them all. In fact, I wasn't entirely convinced that he wasn't thinking up some fool-proof plan to kill them all in their sleep before tomorrow's trial.

The dining room doors came into view, and even though they were shut, I could hear the cheerful sound of long, rich music coming from within. The loud voices carried out into the hall, voices I hadn't heard before. Voices of cheer and enthusiasm.

I stopped walking.

"Everything okay?" Mal asked.

"Fine, I just...I didn't expect music. The Paragon hasn't banned that luxury yet?"

His smile was real that time. "These wicked fae need something to keep them sane, right?"

With a light tug on my hand, we walked through the doors and into the dining room.

The entirety of the Paragon, over forty black-cloaked members by the looks of it, stood from the massive wood table and clapped at our arrival. Blood rushed to my cheeks from the wave of attention.

"Our guests of honor! Welcome, Jade and Malachi Weyland!" someone announced in the back of the room.

Silas approached from my left, arms extended in a welcoming gesture. "It's an honor, truly," he started.

Malachi stifled a laugh. "It's not as if we had other plans," he muttered. If he meant for only me to hear it, he wasn't nearly quiet enough.

Silas's eyes hardened for half a second before he returned his ignorantly large smile. "Either way, we're happy to host you. Please, both of you. Have a seat." He motioned to the head of the table, where two large, throne-like chairs awaited us.

"You want us to sit at the head of the table?" I asked. "Isn't that your position?"

Silas's smile remained plastered across his pale face. "Not tonight, peacemaker. Tonight, you two are to be celebrated!"

The entire room, Silas included, watched in anticipation as Malachi and I approached our seats. I could have sworn they even held their breath as they awaited for us to sit.

"Wow," I said as Mal and I sat on the cushioned thrones. "What an elegant way to send me to my death."

A few in the room chuckled, although I knew it was their attempt at being polite and not a real reaction to my comment. There was nothing funny about this situation. This was real, and this was happening.

Silas settled in on the other head of the massive table, feeling miles away yet still somehow much, much too close to us. "I would like to propose a toast!" Silas announced. The members in the room each raised their small, wine-filled glasses. Malachi and I, after hesitating for a few seconds, did the same. "To Jade Weyland, the peacemaker. The saver of worlds. The balancer of magic. The Paragon has been working for decades to ensure that the balance is not disrupted. Fae, witches, humans. We should all be able to live in peace without one species overtaking another with their *gifts*."

I waited for him to continue, my palms beginning to sweat.

"With Jade Weyland as our peacemaker, we will be able to complete the sacred ritual from the Saints to restore power as it once was. Magic will flow freely over the lands of the fae. Every fae will possess gifts, not only a few. Every witch will have access to ancestral magic, not just the powerful bloodlines."

The hair on the back of my neck stood up. I knew that fae and witches were not as powerful as they once were, aside from special instances like Malachi, Esther and Cordelia. Very few fae and witches possessed strong magic.

Humans, of course, had nothing. They would always have nothing.

"Once Jade completes these trials, we will know without a doubt in this world that she is the one. She has been chosen. She will be the one to break the lands of this curse." Silas's voice grew louder with every word until every pair of eyes, mine included, glued onto him in anticipation. "Raise your glasses, everyone. Tonight, we celebrate the peacemaker."

A roar of cheers filled the room, followed by clinking of glasses as the Paragon members saluted one another, all in celebration of me. Of future peace.

It was an interesting thought that more power would create peace. Why would the Saints need to limit the amount of power in this world in the first place? Were the fae and witches in power truly that greedy?

I thought about Malachi's power, how deadly it could be. In the wrong hands, magic like that could crumble kingdoms. Could overturn kings.

Malachi's warm hand on my lower back brought me back to the feast. "Still with us?" he whispered.

I replied with a reassuring smile, and we all took our seats. The sound of wooden chairs scratching against the stone floor pierced through the chilled air and added to the unsettled feeling that lingered in the room.

The Paragon members, all in the same black cloaks that Malachi and I now wore, didn't even look in our direction. They focused on their own hushed conversations around the dinner table, keeping their heads low and their voices even lower. Everyone, in fact, seemed to lower their heads. Except for Cordelia, naturally, who held her chin up as she glanced between myself and Silas.

She and Esther together found their seats in the middle of the table, equal distance from the two heads.

"So," Silas began, his words slicing like a sword through the low roar of voices, "I take it your training with dear Cordelia has been going well?"

A few Paragon members glanced in my direction. Their gazes didn't last.

"Define *well,*" I spat, staring directly at Silas's pale face. "It would be mighty helpful if I knew what I was training for. Right, Cordelia?"

She half-choked on the wine she drank before setting her glass down, re-focusing on the conversation. "Jade Weyland is very talented," she stuttered in Silas's direction. "I have nothing but confidence in her after our training sessions." She winked in my direction.

Silas gave a nod of approval. "Good," he started. "Cordelia here has prepared many of our Paragon members for the trails."

"How nice of her," I sneered. "She seems to be quite an asset to the Paragon."

With Malachi so close, I could feel his warning through that small thread of power. With it, though, came a low purr of satisfaction.

*My wicked, wicked husband.*

Silas chose to ignore the attitude that laced my words. "That, she is," he replied. "We're honored to host the few of those that still possess gifts in this world. I must say, it was a shame when your husband chose to leave us all those decades ago."

Malachi straightened in the corner of my eye.

"Yes," Malachi answered before I had the chance. "My kingdom needed me."

Silas shook his head, finally breaking eye contact and taking a bite of the food that sat in front of him. "A pity," he started, "that such power can go to waste."

A laugh escaped me at the same time Malachi's power stirred. I felt it in my blood, in my bones.

Yet he held onto it. I admired that about him. Malachi could be temperamental and reckless, but he never lost control of his power. Not even in front of the most deserving of enemies. He only made calculated, deliberate moves with his magic.

I, on the other hand, had not even a portion of control Malachi possessed.

I lifted my chin to the room. "I would not consider becoming King of Rewyth a waste," I chimed in. "Nor would I be ignorant enough to show the King of Shadows a single ounce of pity."

Malachi's hand found mine beneath the table, squeezing gently. Either a warning, or a thank you. Either way, Silas was really pissing me off.

"Well," Silas said, leaning back in his chair and placing both palms on the table beside his plate, "you don't know Malachi like I do."

I wasn't sure why, but I half-expected Malachi to lose control then. Launch across the table, throw the knife through the room, anything. But I waited and waited, and Malachi sat motionless beside me.

*I would have killed to know what he was thinking.*

Cordelia, who actually had the ability to know what thoughts rummaged around in Mal's mind, stifled a smile in the middle of the table.

"Out of curiosity," I began, "does Cordelia help you turn all of the gifted fae into weapons? Or was that just your son?"

Gasps filled the room. Silas's face morphed in anger. "Watch what you say to me, child."

Malachi's hand tightened around mine again, his free palm smacking down on the surface of the table, rattling the plates around us. "My wife will speak freely."

Another snarl came from Silas. "Such a powerful man succumbing to his own wife. What happened to you, Malachi? You used to be so powerful. Feared across nations. Now you let this girl control you?"

I felt him before I saw him move, the rush of power, feeling almost like a rush of adrenaline in my bloodstream, zipped through my body as Malachi rose to his feet and threw a violent, black-misted ball of deadly power in Silas's direction.

I had seen Malachi's power on a few different occasions. Each time, silence filled the room. Each time, a tiny prick of fear made the hair on the back of my neck stand up. Even though I knew Mal would never hurt me, there was something so feral about the way he wielded his dark power.

But this? Malachi was...Malachi was *furious*.

Although just when the rush of power nearly sliced into Silas's body, a shield of glamour protected him. Not as if he would need it, though. As Malachi explained, Silas could not be killed.

Fueled by adrenaline, anger, and the need to defend my husband at all costs, though, I couldn't help myself.

I, too, mustered my emotions into a hot ball of fury, pushing my hands out in front of me to throw my own power in Silas's direction.

Gasps filled the room again, mixed with a few shouts of fear. The Paragon members sat in limbo, unsure of what to do, as Silas's bubble of fae glamour protected him in an invisible fortress.

I pushed and pushed and pushed, wanting so desperately to crack that fortress, to rid us all of this pest that was the leader of the Paragon. Glass shattered in the distance.

I felt it, too. I could have cracked it. I could have put all of my energy into that attack and sliced through Silas's barriers to see exactly how unkillable he was.

If it weren't for the strong gust of wind that slammed into me, pushing me from my feet and slamming me against the wall behind us.

Malachi was at my side in an instant, helping me stand back on my feet as we turned to face the room.

"This is how you repay me?" Silas roared. "We throw a feast in your honor, and this is what I get in return?"

My breath came in heavy pants. I couldn't form any words. I knew that anything out of my mouth would only make the situation worse.

Esther whispered something to Cordelia. I could only guess what she said, because a second later, Cordelia walked toward us. "I believe this feast is over," she said in a low voice, more to us than to anyone else. I didn't dare look at Silas again. Neither did Malachi, although I could feel the anger radiating from him. "Come with me."

Nobody said another word. Our footsteps leaving the dining hall mixed with the sounds of ragged breathing as we exited. To my surprise, even Silas remained speechless. I avoided meeting his gaze as we left the room, the heavy doors shutting behind us.

"You two are idiots," Cordelia hissed as we made our way down the tunnel. "Did you know that?"

"That bastard is lucky he had his Paragon servants around to protect him," Mal muttered.

Cordelia scoffed. "Ha! As if he needs them. What was your goal there, anyway? To kill him? You know that's not possible. Unless your anger blinded you to that small fact, in which case you're even dumber than I thought."

"Come on, Mal," I said, gripping his hand and pulling him in the direction of our bedroom.

"Not so fast," Cordelia said. She turned to us with a mischievous smile on her face. "Tonight was supposed to be a celebration. You worked your ass off this week, peacemaker. You deserve at least some final send-off before the trials. You're coming with me."

"For what?" Mal asked.

Cordelia didn't answer. Her smile only widened as she turned on her heel and began walking in the opposite direction.

Mal and I exchanged a glance. "I suppose we don't have much else to lose tonight, do we?" I asked.

He exhaled loudly and wrapped his arm around my shoulders. "I suppose not, my queen."

# CHAPTER 17
# Malachi

Cordelia took a long, dramatic swig of the emerald glass bottle, her lips dripping with the red wine as she pulled it away and passed it in my direction.

"Is tonight a good night to be drinking?" Jade asked from the stone ground beside me. I glanced back to Cordelia, awaiting her answer.

She had taken us to a small stone cave, hidden in the depths of the temple. Condensation dripped from the cold walls around us, the sound of water constantly filling our silence.

"Trust me, honey," Cordelia answered. "There couldn't possibly be a better time."

I took the bottle from her and drank. The taste of wine had never been my favorite, but dulling my senses didn't sound like the worst thing in the world. Especially after that damned feast.

I passed the bottle to Jade. "Is this fae wine?" she asked. "Or human wine?"

"Drink it," Cordelia ordered. "Either way, it will make you feel better."

If it weren't for the light amount of pity and care that laced her words, I would have snapped at her for telling Jade what to do. But deep down, I started to understand that Cordelia had a soft heart. Even if it was hidden beneath layers and layers of Paragon skin.

Jade drank.

We stayed that way for a while, passing the bottle around and taking sips. The three of us were so different, but I knew that the same feeling of dread and anticipation hung in the air for all of us.

None of us wanted tomorrow to come, yet none of us could do anything to stop it.

"If you knew," Jade said after a while, breaking the calming blanket of silence, "if you knew what my trials would be, would you tell me?" She looked at Cordelia with a heart-wrenching amount of hope in her big, warm eyes.

Cordelia's jaw tightened. She took a long gulp of the bottle before setting it down on the stone ground before us. "Did Malachi ever tell you about my best friend, Tempesta?" Cordelia asked.

I felt Jade's eyes slide over to me, but I averted my eyes. I knew the story of Tempesta all too well, and the last thing I wanted to do was tell Jade about her.

"No," Jade answered softly.

"She was my sister. Not by blood, of course, but in spirit. She was my other half, my better half. She was kinder than me, smarter than me. I envied her for it, really, but nobody else saw her that way. She was a fae, born and raised. Her magic existed, but she struggled to wield it. She wasn't strong like Malachi and I. She was...she was innocent."

I kept my eyes glued to the floor. Jade remained silent, although I could hear her heartbeat picking up.

"She was raised here in the Paragon, and after only two decades in this world, Silas made her..." Her voice cracked. She cleared her throat before picking up the bottle once more. "Silas made her complete the Trials of Glory. We all saw it coming, of course. Silas is cruel and wicked in ways that don't even make sense."

"Why would he make her do that?" Jade asked, shaking her head. "Why couldn't she leave instead?"

I didn't look at Cordelia, but I heard the smile on her face as she replied, "Tempesta didn't want to leave," she explained. "She had family here. She had friends, she had... she had me."

I clenched my jaw to keep the rush of emotion back. Cordelia and Tempesta were more than friends. Though she would never admit it, Cordelia had looked at Tempesta in a way she never looked at anyone else. Cordelia could be cruel and brutal, but never to her. She never raised her voice, never lifted her sword.

Those weeks before Tempesta's trial caused more pain in Cordelia than I could imagine.

"So I trained her," she continued, pushing past whatever memories surfaced in her mind. "Like I did everyone, like I was told to do by Silas. I taught her to defend herself. I taught her to use whatever tendril of magic she had pulsing through her blood. I begged and begged Silas to tell me, to at least give me a hint. Saints, if he would have just..."

She didn't have to continue. We all knew what she was going to say.

If Silas had given her a single hint as to what Tempesta's trials would be, Cordelia could have saved her life. And maybe, just maybe, she wouldn't be lonely in this damned temple all these decades later.

"None of that matters now," she pushed on. "What I'm trying to say is that yes, Jade. If I knew what your trials would be, I would tell you."

A beat of silence passed between us as the effect of Cordelia's words settled.

"Thank you," Jade whispered. "For helping me, I mean."

Cordelia scoffed, her cold, emotionless mask reassembling on her face. "You don't need to thank me, Jade," she said. "In fact, after tomorrow, you'll probably hate me for not preparing you better."

Jade laughed, and the sound of it alone sent a warm thrill through the icy shield forming in my chest. "Trust me," she sighed. "If I survive these trials, you'll be my best friend on the other side."

Cordelia smiled, a genuine smile this time. Not her usual smile laced with malice and motive.

"Not *if*," I corrected her. "*When* you survive the trials."

Jade's eyes locked with mine. "Right," she replied. "*When*."

We drank until the bottle dried up, until the fear that connected us faded, until the emotions dulled. Only then could we at least attempt to get any sleep, the weight of tomorrow still looming over every single thought that crossed my mind.

# CHAPTER 18
## *Jade*

I STARED UP AT THE STONE CEILING, UNSURE IF I SLEPT FOR MORE THAN ten minutes. I couldn't quiet my mind long enough to doze off, I was too busy envisioning every possible way today could go wrong.

Malachi stirred next to me. Apparently he hadn't slept much, either.

I didn't blame him.

Today was the day. The first day in the Trials of Glory. It was the last day I would sleep in this bedroom. The last day I would lie next to my husband.

Possibly my last day alive.

*No, Jade.* I had to stop thinking like that. Saints, I was the peacemaker. I had magic and power that very few others possessed. Had I accessed all of it? No, not even close.

But doubting myself wasn't going to help me.

Trial number one. *The past.*

Part of me couldn't help but think back through my life, wondering which of my ghosts would haunt me during the trial. Malachi had warned me that everything would seem real. Sorting reality from magic visions would be nearly impossible.

My chest tightened as I thought of Tessa. Her perfect, pale face staring at me. Her bratty voice when she complained to me. Her soft, tiny hands as she clung to me when we were children.

I missed her. I missed her more than anything, and yet I rarely had time to grieve.

Maybe when this was all over I would grieve. I would have time to pity myself, to grieve the life I lost. And maybe, just maybe, I would see her again today during the trial.

Saints, I hoped so. I would do anything to see her face again. I would do anything to hear her say my name.

"You should be sleeping," Malachi mumbled. The grogginess in his voice made my chest ache. I silently prayed that I would be able to hear that voice again, would be able to wake up next to him again, even just once more.

"Can't sleep," I answered.

He rolled over and pulled me closer to him, using his arm to lock me into his chest, creating a fortress of warmth and love that I never wanted to escape. He had a way of doing that, of making me feel safe.

"I'll be there the whole time," he said, nuzzling himself into my neck and reassuring me with his lips. "You're not alone in this, Jade. Even if it might feel that way."

"That doesn't make me feel any better."

"Why's that?" He kissed my cheekbone, my temple.

I took a deep breath. "I don't want you to watch me get hurt. I don't want you to see that."

His hand trailed down the length of my body. "You're not going to get hurt, Jade. The challenges will be simple, and we'll be out of here before you even realize they've started."

"I get that you're trying to make me feel better," I said, "but I can't say it's working." I pushed myself out of his arms and crawled out of the bed. "I should get going. Better to get it over with, right?"

Malachi sat up onto his elbow, his black wings splayed beside him. I was going to miss this; Malachi's sculpted body, shirtless in our bed. His dazed smile and his lazy eyes as they flickered across my body like they so often did.

"I want you to take this," he said. He let go of me and crawled out of bed, reaching for his sword. "For the trials."

I shook my head when he handed it over. "No way," I said. "I can't take that."

"You can and you will. You need a weapon, and I want you to take mine."

"What if you need it?" I asked. "The enemies I'll be fighting are only in my mind. Yours are real, Malachi."

"It might look like they're in your mind from the outside, Jade," he said, "but to you they will be very, very real. And they'll be just as dangerous. Take it."

I held the sword in my hands, wondering how many lives he had taken with it. How many wars he had fought. I flipped the black sheath over in my palms, taking in every detail. "Thank you, Malachi," I said. "This means more than you know."

His features softened in a way that melted my entire heart. "You are everything to me, Jade Weyland. When I wield this sword, it is for you. Not for myself. There is nobody I want to have it more than you. Now, would you do me the utmost honor of accepting this gift, and wielding my own weapon in your Trials of Glory?"

Now I was sure my heart actually melted. "I would love nothing more," I breathed.

I took the sword from his hands. The weight of it shocked me, it was much heavier than the dagger I was used to. It might have been the strong metal used to carve the sharp weapon. Or, it might have been the hundreds of lives taken with one motion.

They held weight. I was beginning to feel it.

"If this doesn't work," I started to say before my voice wavered, my own body betraying me.

"Don't you dare say those words." Malachi pulled me to him with a hand on the back of my neck and wrapped his arms around me. Hard. I basked in the smell of him, the smokey danger that had lingered in his shadow since the moment I first saw him in that forest.

"I don't know how we got here," I said. "I don't know what I did wrong."

"You didn't do a damn thing wrong, Jade Weyland. You did everything right. Every single thing."

"Then how are we here? How did we get to this point?"

Heavy silence lingered. "People who do the right thing in this world don't have good things happen to them. They have the worst things happen, and every single person looks at them as if they deserve it."

I pulled away, choking back tears. I wasn't going to cry. Not today. Today, I had to be strong. I had to be someone else.

The peacemaker.

"How is this peaceful? I want to know who came up with that name," I said. "They should call me the chaos-bringer, or the death-flirter."

Malachi's mouth twitched at the corner. "I don't know, but now isn't the time to look for peace, either. You give them what they deserve, Jade. They've tried to take everything from you." He held my face and forced me to look into his torturous, dangerous eyes. "Now, it's your turn to take everything from them."

"How? They're in control here, Mal. I'm a stupid toy in whatever game they want me to play."

Malachi's jaw tightened. He knew it was true. He had been in this exact situation before.

Except he wasn't the peacemaker. Kingdoms weren't dependent on his survival.

"Show them how powerful you can be. Show them, and let them fear you the way they should. Bring them to their knees, my queen."

A new wave of heat filled me, but not one of anger or desire. One of confidence. One of eagerness.

I thought I wanted victory. I thought I wanted peace.

I realized now that was all wrong. I didn't want any of that. I wanted what Malachi had. I wanted heads to roll the second I walked into a room. I wanted the sound of my name to put a deep, ebbing fear in the hearts of my enemies.

I wanted people to fear me. I wanted people to think twice before they challenged me.

Malachi was right. Today, they would learn. Today, they would think twice.

"Okay," I said after what felt like hours. "Okay, I'm ready."

He kissed my forehead, fierce and harsh. "We should go," he said. "They'll all be waiting."

We both got dressed quickly, and Malachi helped me strap the sword onto my hip. It was bulky and heavy, but I liked it. I wanted a piece of him with me during the trials. Maybe, even in the midst of chaos and magic, I would recognize the gift from him and remember.

"What happens now?" I asked. "I mean, how much time do I have?"

Malachi stiffened, adjusting a black cloak around his shoulders before shoving the stone door to our bedroom open. He held his hand out for me. I took it.

"You'll have to stay in the arena. The arena isn't much, it's just a large stone room. But it won't feel like that when you're in it."

"Why not?"

He nodded. "They'll have the strongest witches and gifted fae working together to create a new reality for you. You won't know where you are, you won't know how long you've been there."

*Don't be afraid*, I told myself. This is all part of the process. Part of the facade. They want to scare you, they want to see you weak.

Don't give them that satisfaction.

Malachi didn't let go of my hand as we walked through the now-familiar tunnels of the mountain and approached the dining hall.

Silas stood in the middle of the room, clearly expecting us, with a group of hooded men and women behind him.

"Are you ready?" Silas asked. His eyes glared into me with an intensity that made the hair on my neck rise.

"Yes," I lied. Malachi squeezed my hand once and let it go.

Everything happened so fast. I felt as though just yesterday we were fighting against them at the castle of Rewyth.

I didn't want to die.

"Hey," Malachi whispered. "You can do this."

My walls were crumbling. They had been, I realized, for quite some time. But today would be the day the walls came cascading down, and I had nothing but my own magic to protect me. I wasn't sure that would be enough.

I didn't even realize I had stumbled until Malachi caught me in his arms and pulled me to his chest. I wrapped my arms around him, feeling like he was the only thing in this world I had left to fight for. "I'm scared," I whispered, not confident that I had even said the words aloud.

Malachi pulled back and smiled at me gently. "You would be insane if you weren't afraid," he admitted. "But fearful or not, this is the next step. Remember who you are, remember what you can do. And try to remember that it's all magic. None of it is real."

I nodded, drinking in every word; consuming everything he said, devouring the way he said it.

"Come with me," Silas said from behind me, ruining whatever peace I had left in my solitude with Malachi. I immediately stiffened away from Mal and rolled my shoulders back, lifting my chin.

This is how he would want me to act. Unafraid.

*Don't let them see your fear.*

"I'll see you when it's over," I said. Malachi nodded, and I held his gaze until the gentle smirk on his face faded away, replaced with a dark shadow of unreadable emotion.

I would do this for him. I would survive for him.

My feet moved, or more so glided, to where Silas stood in wait. He had a dumb smile on his face, staring at me as if I were his shiny new toy. "Let's get this over with," I said to him, although the words didn't come out as strongly as I meant them to.

Suddenly, my entire body grew numb. My heart beat, not any faster than it already was beating, but much, much harder. Silas said something to me, but a distant ringing in my ears grew louder and louder. His mouth moved, but I heard nothing.

And then we were moving. Silas put a cold hand on my arm and led me out of the dining hall, through a set of tunnels I had yet to venture down. I meant to look back at Malachi one more time, but my body stilled. Aside from my feet moving slowly, one foot in front of the other, I was frozen.

"Trust yourself, Jade," Silas said, but the words seemed to echo through the walls of my own mind.

*Trust yourself.* How was that even possible? How could I trust myself, when my entire life all I have done was destroy lives and torment the ones around me?

How?

Silas attempted to place a hand on my back for guidance, but I flinched away from him.

Cordelia stood before me now, and I realized we had entered a small cave in the tunnels. I wasn't sure how long we had been walking or how long we had been standing in the cave.

"Jade?" Cordelia asked. She shook my shoulders, and her hands were much warmer than Silas's. I didn't flinch away.

Time seemed to snap back to me. "What?"

"Were you listening to me?"

The ringing in my ears slowly dissipated, and I began to feel my own body again. "I'm sorry, can you say that again?"

Cordelia's expression hardened. "The trials typically only last a few days, but it will seem much longer to you. You'll have to fend for yourself, feed yourself, find shelter when needed. We cannot interfere with the trials in any way, including Malachi. So once you enter through those doors, you're on your own."

"What's out there?" I asked.

Cordelia ignored me and pulled the cork from a small vial of liquid. "Take this," she said.

"What's that?"

She gripped my jaw and forced my head back, pouring the sweet, purple substance into my mouth.

I swallowed it, not even trying to fight.

"This helps create the setting of the trials for you. To us, it will look like you're running around going crazy in the room. But your body will be affected by what you see in those trials, Jade. If you get stabbed in your trial, your body will bleed out as if you got stabbed here in this room. If you are stuck in the freezing mountains in your trial, your body will freeze to death inside this room. Understand?"

"Where did Silas go?" I asked once I realized we were now alone.

"I'm sure he's in the gallery by now. Nobody wants to miss the show."

My stomach sank. "Show? You mean people will be watching?" No, Malachi shouldn't watch me die. I didn't want him to see me struggle, to see me panic.

She stopped what she was doing and looked me in the eye. "We can sit around and pretend like the Paragon wants to prove you as the peacemaker, or we can look at this situation for what it really is, Jade."

My vision blurred. "And what's that?"

"Entertainment. Silas and the others, they only want a good show."

A show? Was she really suggesting that everything I was about to endure was for entertainment?

"Don't let Malachi watch," I blurted. "I don't want him to see me out there."

Cordelia snorted. "Honey, I don't think I could keep him away if I tried."

My vision swirled again. Cordelia pushed open the massive stone door ahead of me, which gave way to a large cave-like room.

I could hardly see what was in front of me, but I could feel Malachi. I knew he was near.

"Good luck, peacemaker," Cordelia said as I walked through the stone door. "The whole world is counting on you."

# CHAPTER 19
## Malachi

A FEW MINUTES LATER, I JOINED THE PARAGON MEMBERS ON THE STONE balcony that overlooked the underground arena. The room was not small by any means, but filled with the dozens of Paragon members gathered to watch, it felt miniscule.

I pictured myself in that stone arena below. How small I must have looked back then. How afraid. That was the last time I had truly been afraid. Until I met Jade, anyway. Now, with Jade at risk, it seemed as if everything frightened me. I did not fear for my own life, but for hers.

"It feels like yesterday that you were the one in this same arena," Silas said. "I remember it so clearly, how fiercely you fought."

Every single word out of his mouth pierced like a knife to my gut. I reminded myself to control my anger. He wanted to see me worried. He wanted to see me affected by Jade's pain.

I lifted my chin. "To me, it was lifetimes ago. I'm not the same person I was entering those trials."

Silas stepped closer to me. I fought the urge to throw him through the wall. "And you're a better man for it," he said.

I felt Jade before I saw her, her frightened presence struck like fire igniting in my spine. *Come on, Jade. You can do this.*

Cordelia approached from behind. I wanted to speak with her, but I couldn't tear my eyes away from the arena. Cordelia would tell me the truth. She would tell me how bad it was.

"The Saints have blessed this place," Silas announced. I had absolutely no idea who he was talking to. It's not like Jade could hear him. "This girl is full of power, full of this offering from the most gracious. Three trials will test her heart and spirit; trials confronting her past, her present, and her future. She will see herself for her raw potential, her pure spirit. And thus, the peacemaker will be born."

Paragon members cheered. It made me sick. How long had they been waiting for the trials, waiting to see Jade fail?

"Your nerves are palpable," Cordelia's voice over my shoulder made me tense.

I clenched my fists and tried to calm myself. Her slim body slid through the forming crowd that overlooked the arena and stopped at my side.

"I can't say I care, Cordelia," I replied.

"Your wife will be fine," she said. Her voice was barely a whisper.

*Is Jade nervous? How is she feeling? Is she afraid, confident? Saints, I hope she's confident.*

"Saints," she mumbled under her breath. "Your thoughts are louder than Silas's annoying voice."

Movement in the corner of my eye caused my heart to sink. Jade stumbled forward, confused and unaware. The effects of the serum finally kicking in.

The arena, as Silas so gallantly called it, was nothing but a stone pit under the mountain. Jade, however, would not see it that way. She would see whatever her mind forced her to see. For the first trial, it would be something of her past. Her father, maybe. Or Tessa. My chest physically hurt at the thought.

Jade was strong. But she had a breaking point. We all did.

Silas and the other Paragon members would be watching her, judging her. They would wait to see how she reacted to pain, to distress.

And based on how my wife reacted under the agony they inflicted, they would decide if she was worthy.

It made me want to vomit. They did not know Jade. They didn't know how strong she could be, how much pressure she could take. They knew absolutely nothing about her, and yet they thought of themselves as messengers from the Saints to test her spirit.

Jade had fallen to her knees on the stone ground, breathing heavily. It wouldn't be long now before the visions started.

"Come with me," Cordelia barked. "You need to get your shit together."

Her sharp fingernails dug into the flesh on my arm as she pulled me backward. I didn't fight her. I followed her out of the crowd, ripping my eyes away from Jade's struggling figure down below.

I didn't want to leave her, but something felt almost violating about watching.

Once Cordelia and I were alone in the tunneled hallway, she shoved me against the wall.

A warning growl was all she got. I had fought with Cordelia more times than I could count, and as much as I hated to admit it, she was a great sparring partner.

But I was angry. She wouldn't win a fight against my anger.

"You know just as well as I do that Silas is doing this to get to you."

*His own son.* How damned poetic.

Cordelia's face twisted in confusion before her features lightened. Nothing annoyed me more than having my thoughts invaded, but Cordelia wasn't my enemy right now.

"How long have you known that he's my father?" I asked. "I'm sure you've been having plenty of entertainment with this secret, you and Esther."

Her nostrils flared for a second before she smiled, cocking her head to the side.

"Actually, yes. Although I must say, I thought you would have figured it out by now. Not so smart these days, are you, king?"

I snapped, hauling myself forward and grabbing the witch by the throat. She hardly flinched, but that didn't stop me from slamming her backward.

"First," I spit back, "you can get out of my damned mind. Second, you can shut up about my mother and Silas unless you have actual useful information you'd like to share. But according to your reaction, you've known this since the beginning. Which doesn't make you my ally, Cordelia. In fact, that makes you pretty damn close to my enemy."

Her brows furrowed in anger. *Good,* she should be angry. "Silas took care of you. He favored you."

I tightened my grip on her scrawny neck. "He ruined me."

She gasped for air when I released her. "You really think so? You think Silas ruined you? He gave you a name, Prince of Shadows. Or is it King of Shadows now, I figure? He sent you back to the kingdom you were born to rule. He made you what you are, Malachi. He made you a *king*."

"He made me a killer."

"And that's any different from the rest of us?" I ignored the way her voice wavered. "Look at me, Malachi," she growled. I glanced up at her, finally looking at her tired, worn out face. "I am many things. Am I your friend? Saints, no. But I, of all the damned people under the mountain, am not your enemy. And *that* you can believe."

My power flared beneath my skin. Saints, I didn't know what to believe. Cordelia had never been my friend, at least she was honest enough about that. But what angle did she have? She was half witch, half fae. Just like me. How could she benefit from either side gaining the power of the peacemaker?

She smiled, and I could have cursed myself for even thinking the words. "I have no angle," she answered, letting herself wind through my thoughts. "I want nothing to do with your peacemaker."

"Then what is all this?" I asked. "Why are you..."

"Helping you?"

"I wouldn't call it that."

"I would." She lifted her chin. "Maybe I have my own motives, Malachi. And maybe they have nothing to do with you or your fragile, human wife."

"You dig through my mind all day long, witch. Tell me what you mean, I don't have time for riddles."

She glanced toward the arena door. "Not here," she said. I didn't flinch away when she stepped closer. "Trust Esther, and no one else. Not Silas. Not anyone. At this point, I'm not even sure I would trust a Saint himself standing before me."

As if I planned on trusting any of these Paragon members anytime soon. "Am I supposed to know what that means?"

"Your wife's trials are starting," Cordelia said. "Go."

*Shit,* she was right. I pulled my wings tight against my shoulder blades and turned to the gallery door when her hand fell on my wrist to stop me.

"If your wife dies during these trials, it would be a great mercy."

She was gone before I processed the words.

# CHAPTER 20
# *Jade*

I BECAME VAGUELY AWARE OF A SOLID SURFACE BENEATH MY KNEES, BUT when I tried to look around, my vision darkened. Clouds blurred my eyesight until I couldn't see anything.

Splitting pain in my head made it difficult to open my eyes. The blank, stone arena that I had seen before seemed to morph. It turned slowly from the open nothingness to a forest, one filled with tall, vibrant trees and I could even swear I saw the sunshine above.

*No,* it wasn't real. The trees, the sun. Malachi had warned me about this. This was all magic, I was in the empty stone arena.

A soft breeze caressed my skin, my loose black hair. Saints, when did my hair get that long? It fell nearly past my waist now.

"Jade?" a familiar voice asked.

When I looked up from my dark locks, I was standing in that forest. My thoughts grew foggy yet somehow clarified at the same time.

A girl I knew stood before me. Her choppy black hair and tall, lean figure would be identifiable anywhere.

"Sadie?"

Sadie smiled. Her short braids were just as I remembered them, yet she looked... healthier. Happier. "How–"

I stopped myself from asking. This wasn't real. None of it was real. Sadie left when I...when Malachi killed Isaiah.

*Right?*

I tried to recall who Isaiah was, but my mind lost the thought. I refocused my attention on the girl standing before me.

"I've missed you," she said. "I wasn't sure I would ever be able to see you again."

My chest tightened. "I'm sorry, Sadie. About everything. Did you make it out of the castle okay? Where did you go when you left?"

"Malachi made sure I was able to make it out. I scavenged the woods for a while before I found a small human camp, much like Fearford."

*Fearford.* It felt like decades ago that I had stumbled into Fearford, the human kingdom where Sadie had once lived.

"Good," I said. "I'm glad you're okay." Sadie stared back at me with a simple, clean smile on her face. "What are you doing here, Sadie?"

"I'm here to help you," she said.

"Help me with what?"

"I'm here to help you survive, Jade. Since that's what you did for me."

I snorted. "I wouldn't say that. If I never would have showed up to Fearford, you would still be there. You would still be happy."

She reached out and gripped my hand. Not a magical touch, not one of air, but a real human touch. Her skin was warm against mine as she held me. "You saved me, Jade. You made sure I was fed, and you forced your husband to show me mercy."

"I'm the reason Isaiah is dead," I admitted.

"You're the reason we aren't *both* dead. Isaiah betrayed you. I would never dream of doing the same."

Birds chirped in the distance, something I hadn't heard for a very long time. Or maybe I had heard it, but I was too busy living in chaos to notice. Sadie and I both looked up, scanning the tree line above before I closed my eyes and basked in the warmth of the sun.

The sun felt nice. Welcoming.

"Do you know where we are?" I asked after a few minutes.

"We're home," she answered. I opened my eyes again to find Sadie smiling at me. In all the time I knew her, I didn't know if I had ever seen her smile so much.

My chest ached. "Home? We're in Rewyth?"

She shook her head. "Your first home, Jade. Your *real* home."

A light flicker of panic threatened me, but I quickly shoved it away. I scanned the trees around us again.

The familiar patterns of the shrubs and trees sparked a memory of this place. We weren't standing in just any forest. We were standing in my forest, the same one I had hunted in dozens of times. The same one I had cried in, escaped to.

This *was* home.

"Follow me." I began walking through the forest, through the same path that I had walked hundreds of times. Everything came back to me like I had been there all along. The familiar path, the smell of the fresh air. It was different than the forest around Rewyth. The air smelled different, less crisp. More of flowers and less of spice.

But it was still home.

My heart fluttered at the thought of my old house, and who might be inside of it.

*Tessa.*

My feet moved faster, quickening in pace at the thought of her golden hair, her pale skin. She would be here, right?

Because she was home. If this was truly my home, Tessa would be here.

"Slow down!" Sadie yelled from behind me, but I didn't stop.

I did no such thing. My quick walking turned into a jog, and before I knew it, I was outright sprinting out of the woods and up the path to that first, worn-down house at the bottom of the hill.

My home, the place I had grown up in. The place that caused me so much pain and suffering for years on end, and yet here I was, running to it like a child.

I ripped the rotting front door open. "Tessa?" I yelled. "Tessa, are you here?" I scanned the kitchen and the small bathroom before shoving aside the ajar door to the bedroom we shared.

Empty. All of it empty, not a single sound echoed through the crumbling walls.

But the bed was unmade, something Tessa had a bad habit of doing. And a pair of her favorite shoes sat tossed in the corner.

My heart fluttered once more.

After ensuring she was nowhere in the house, I ran back outside. Sadie waited for me. "She's here," I said. "She's here somewhere."

"Where does she like to go? Where are her favorite spots?"

Sadie spoke as if Tessa was still around, as if she still lived and breathed. I stopped walking and spun around.

*Sadie didn't know*. She wasn't there when Tessa died, and she would have no way of knowing she was dead.

I thought about telling Sadie, but...what if Tessa *was* alive? What if she was here somewhere, living and breathing like the same girl she had been?

What if nothing had changed? What if this was all normal, and Tessa was simply in town shopping for food?

It was a possibility.

"Come on," I said to Sadie. And the two of us began the walk to town.

I waited for her to ask questions, like how we possibly lived in such houses when they were barely standing or why nobody even looked up when they passed us on the narrow dirt path.

But she didn't. She silently walked beside me, a silent presence of comfort. "The market is at the end of this path," I said after a while.

"Great."

"Tessa doesn't usually go to the market alone, but if I've been gone maybe she went there to find me. Or maybe she went there to get food."

"It's definitely possible," Sadie said. "I'm sure we'll find her there."

The path grew more and more crowded, each familiar face we passed stared down at the path or at their own feet as we scurried by. It wasn't unusual. People here weren't friendly. Being friendly wasn't part of survival, and that's all that happened in this town. Surviving.

The market came into view, and I recognized the meat seller at the first table. "Have you seen my sister?" I asked as we approached. "Has she been through here today?"

The man scoffed. He wasn't exactly friendly, either. "Move along, girl."

"Excuse me," I said, louder this time. "I asked you if you've seen my sister."

"I'm not a babysitter." The man didn't even look up from the table as he spoke. "If you've lost your sister, I suggest you go find her."

Sadie was already staring at me with a knowing look when I glanced her way. I didn't have to try much to summon my power. It was ready to go, ready for me to use it.

Light flashed around us, directed at the man's table. He screamed and slammed against the wood pile behind him. Burnt meat turned to ashes before us, completely ravished by my power.

"You crazy bitch!" he yelled. "What are you? A witch?" I pulsed another round of power in his direction, narrowly avoiding his body. He screamed again. "I told you I ain't seen your sister!"

A few others were screaming now, some running for the houses. *As if that would stop me.*

"Has anyone seen my sister?" I yelled as I turned around, surveying the scattering crowd. "Where is she?"

Slight panic turned into a forest fire of chaos. Screaming turned into non-stop cries of fear, and running turned into trampling. Everyone fled the market, running away from a danger they hardly knew existed.

To them, I was Jade. I was the poor girl with the drunken father at the bottom of the hill. They had no idea who I had become, they had no idea how powerful I had become.

"Tessa!" I screamed. Sadie followed tightly behind me as we walked against the sea of panic. "Tessa!"

She was here. She had to be here. *Right?* "We'll keep looking," Sadie shouted over the chaos. "I'll check the rest of the market."

Sadie pushed and shoved the pitiful crowd as she maneuvered herself around the rest of the market.

But I had my eyes locked on one place. One place that a small, heated tether inside of me pulled me to.

The tavern was the one place I hated, the one place I avoided at all costs. I knew what dwelled there, drunks and others who only wanted to escape the lives they had here in this pitiful town. My father dwelled there, often staying there for days at a time before stumbling back home.

I kicked the cracked door open with my dirty boot. And for the first time in my life, I stepped inside the tavern.

A few men turned from their spot at the bar to look at the intruder. "Jade?"

One filthy man in particular stood from a corner table and stepped closer to me. It took me a handful of seconds to recognize him as my father.

Of course he was here. "I'm looking for Tessa," I said. "Where is she?"

He stammered, looking at me as if he were staring at a ghost. "Jade, she's not here."

"What do you mean she's not here? She wasn't at the house, so where is she?"

"She was with you," he explained. "She left to find you."

My stomach twisted in a vile, desperate way that made me sick to my stomach. "When?"

He didn't answer right away. His mouth hung open, and I could feel the way he dug through all of the possible word choices, desperate to find the right one.

Tessa wasn't here.

"Forget it," I mumbled. "You're no help. You never are."

I spun on my heel and left the tavern.

The market had nearly emptied. Sadie stood in the center of it all, looking at me with pity. I hated that. Pity. As if people truly felt sorry for the situation I was in.

But I wasn't sorry. I deserved every ounce of the shit situations I had been put in.

"She's not here," I said.

"What?" Sadie yelled back.

I opened my mouth to say it again, but I didn't have the energy. I couldn't summon the strength to be heard, to repeat those words again. "She's not here," I breathed to myself.

My legs gave out beneath me. I crashed to the dirt pavement, not even feeling the pain that I expected. "She's not here," I breathed again. "She's not here, she's not here, she's not here."

Sadie was beside me, then, holding my shoulders and trying to lift me up. "She's not here, Sadie."

She needed to hear me. This was no use. Coming here was a waste of time. "Tessa's gone."

I tilted my head up to the sun that still warmed my skin. *Why?* Why would such a beautiful, healing light shine down on such a horrendous day?

I did not stop the tears that fell. Sadie spoke to me, but I couldn't make out the words. I opened my eyes and stared at the sun, not caring that it hurt. Not caring if it took my sight forever.

Exhaustion seeped out of my bones as if it had been hiding there, waiting for its time to creep into the rest of my body.

"Jade?" another voice asked, but this time it was not my father.

I looked away from the fire in the sky, and, when my eyes adjusted, saw Tessa standing before me.

# CHAPTER 21
## *Malachi*

**Her pain cascaded around me, filling the cracks in my exterior.** My eyes locked on her body in the arena. She saw something, something dreadful.

She paced around the stone room for a few minutes, talking in a voice too quiet for any of us to hear. Although, by the nasty look on Silas's face, the trial played out exactly as planned.

I hated this. I hated the pain she was feeling, I hated that I couldn't run down there and take it all from her.

But what I hated most was that I couldn't see what she was seeing. I couldn't see what hurt her.

She paced faster and faster before she stopped, stumbling backward with wide, surprised eyes.

"Tell me what's happening," I hissed at Cordelia. "What is she seeing?"

Cordelia rolled her eyes, but leaned toward me and whispered, "She's home. She's looking for her sister."

Dread ran through my body, drying my sweaty palms. "Is her sister alive?" I asked. "Saints, tell me she doesn't have to see her dead sister again." Cordelia's chest rose and fell. Twice. My patience dwindled with every heart-aching second. "Tell me!" I hissed.

My voice echoed, and I felt a dozen Paragon eyes slide in our direction from under their black hoods.

"You're causing a scene," she whispered. "Calm yourself, *king*."

"I don't care if I burn this entire damned mountain to the ground, *witch*. Tell me my wife is okay."

She took a long breath. "Her sister is alive," she answered.

At the same time, the crumbling suffering in my gut dissipated, turning into something much, much more dangerous. Especially in the trials.

*Hope.*

"I can't watch this," I mumbled. "You people sit around and watch an innocent girl torture herself with her own mind. It's sickening."

This time when I stormed from the room and into the tunnels, Cordelia did not follow.

Each step I took put distance between myself and Jade, and with each step, our connection weakened.

I had never felt so damned helpless in my entire life.

I remembered my first trial, how utterly confused I was. You could understand that this was all fake, that it was all part of the trial, yet still become completely blindsided by what happened down there in that arena.

Of course Jade would see Tessa in the first trial. She would be confused and hurt and lost. And I couldn't help her. Not in the slightest.

My wings tucked tightly behind my back as I walked, and I didn't even try to get out of the way when others passed me in the hallway.

They didn't care about her. They didn't care if she lived or if she died.

They wanted to exploit her power, humiliate her, and feel better about themselves during the process.

I needed a distraction. I couldn't sit around and watch this, feeling everything she felt through our magic bond.

I had to get my mind off those damn trials.

Rewyth. That would help me.

I ran my hands down my face, rubbing away the tension from the last hour.

Someone was trying to take my throne in Rewyth. Serefin needed me. Before I could register where I was headed, I found myself looking for the one person I had spent the last week avoiding.

Esther.

"No way," Esther said, shaking her head. "He won't allow it."

"My throne is being threatened, Esther, and he kept it from me. He doesn't want me to know about it. Saints, who knows what else he's been keeping from me? It was a damn miracle that little boy got us the first letter."

She stilled in thought. I had found her in her bedroom, alone in the darkness. It didn't surprise me that she didn't want to watch Jade's trials. She had saved Jade's life more than once, after all. It was an insult that her life was in jeopardy again.

I stepped forward, looking her in the eye, needing her to feel my urgency as I said, "I need to get a message to Serefin. Can you help me? Can you get it past Silas?"

She opened her mouth to reply, but shut it. At least she wasn't blatantly declining the idea.

"It's dangerous," she said. "If he catches us..."

"What?" I asked. "What exactly will Silas do to you, Esther? Tell me, is he still in love with you?"

She looked away from me and laughed quietly. "Love," she sneered. "What a damn waste."

"He's softer to you," I said, trying to quiet my voice. "He cares."

"He may have cared in the past, son, but the Silas I knew is long gone."

I shook my head. "People don't forget love that easily, Esther. If you ask him, he might say yes."

"Or," she pushed, "he'll get angry that we're trying to sidestep him and he'll retaliate. He'll take it out on Jade. Is that what you want, Malachi? Are you willing to risk that?"

Saints. No, I wasn't willing to risk that. But to think of Serefin and my brothers struggling back home, not knowing if we were still alive, not knowing if we were coming to their aid.

"I can't sit back and do nothing," I said honestly.

"I know you can't. Let me do some thinking. I'll find you when I have an answer."

## CHAPTER 22
# *Jade*

"Tell me this is real," I begged. "Tell me you're really here right now."

My sister—my frail, perfect baby sister—dropped to her knees in front of me. "I'm here," she repeated. "I'm here, Jade."

As soon as my hands felt her body, everything I thought was real and everything I knew was fake collided. I no longer knew what was tangible and what my mind was forcing me to believe, because what I *did* know was that Tessa—my dead baby sister—knelt right before me.

In the flesh.

And she was no longer deceased, no longer dead because I couldn't protect her. No, we were home, where we should have been all along. Where *she* should have been all along.

"I'm so sorry," I blurted out. "I'm so sorry I couldn't protect you."

"What are you talking about?" Tessa asked. "I'm fine, Jade. Look at me."

She lifted my chin with a finger and forced me to look at her. I dragged my eyes across her untouched face, across her neck that was perfectly *not* snapped.

She was okay. She was back to herself, how she should have been all along. "Where have you been?" she asked me. "I've been looking for you."

"We should get going," Sadie interrupted. I had almost forgotten she came here with me.

Another scream came from the market. I ignored it. "Go where?" I asked.

"Anywhere but here. Come on, Jade. Too many people have seen you."

"What do you mean?" I asked. "I live here, of course they've seen me."

Sadie shook her head, suddenly desperate to get me out of sight.

"What happened to you, Jade?" Tessa asked.

"I–" I held my hands out before me, examining them. I wasn't sure why, but I thought they might look different. "I don't know what happened."

Tessa and Sadie both stared at me then, side by side. They were so different.

Compared to Sadie, Tessa looked so pure. So perfect. Sadie, as beautiful as she was, had an edge to her. Her choppy, black hair had blunt edges and messy, stray pieces fell around her chiseled face. Not Tessa, though. Not a single strand of her hair fell out of place.

But they both stared at me like I was the crazy one, like I was the one that needed help. "What is it?" I asked.

They both held their mouths agape, as if they both desperately wanted to say something but couldn't. Then, their eyes shifted to somewhere behind me. Somewhere inside the tavern. I spun around and stood up, searching for what they stared at.

My stomach dropped.

Every single body from the tavern now hung from ropes. Dead.

Including my father. "Saints," I muttered. I didn't wait for Tessa and Sadie before running inside. "Stay back!" I yelled. They didn't need to see this, especially not Tessa. She was too young, too innocent.

I took a few steps forward and entered the threshold of the tavern, now eerily silent.

I should have been surprised or disturbed, but I had already seen this, hanging from the dining hall in Rewyth. The memory came back in flashes. I had seen plenty of death in my life, this shouldn't have phased me.

It wouldn't have, I was certain of it.

*If it weren't for my father.*

"Father?" I asked. He looked alive, no paler or no more still than usual. He looked entirely normal. But I knew, deep in my soul I knew that he was dead.

Tessa wailed a sob behind me. I ran to her, ran out of the tavern and shut the door behind me.

"Is he—is he—" She fought to get the words out, but I knew where she was going with it. Is he dead?

"Yes," I said, harsher than I meant to. "He's gone, Tessa. They're dead."

She didn't look confused, she didn't seem to even wonder what just happened inside that tavern. I was certainly wondering. I was just in there a few minutes ago, and everyone was alive.

Tessa looked me in the eyes. And then screamed.

She screamed and screamed and screamed, it was a sound that could not possibly have been human. I tried yelling her name, tried shaking her shoulders to get her to stop.

But the screaming continued, with more force than even possible.

When I could not possibly take the screaming anymore, I looked away from my sister and covered my own ears, trying to drown out the torturous sound.

But when I looked away, Sadie was on the ground. Unconscious.

Over Tessa's nonstop screaming, I dropped to the ground next to my old friend. "Sadie!" I shouted, but Tessa's screams only drowned them out. "Sadie! Wake up!" I placed a hand on her chest, feeling for any sort of heartbeat. Feeling for any movement that would wake me up from this nightmare.

But she wasn't moving. Her skin grew colder with every passing second.

Sadie was dead.

My scream matched Tessa's, and it was only then that her own screams stopped.

Tessa fell to the ground behind me. "Saints," I muttered, scrambling over Sadie's body to get to her. Tessa's eyes were still open, her mouth still agape as if she had stopped breathing mid-scream.

I touched her body, shook her shoulders.

Not again. This wasn't happening again.

Panic overtook me, seeping into each of my senses and constricting my chest like a fist tightening around my heart.

Not again.

"Tessa?" My voice cracked and broke, shattering like the world around me. I laid two hands on her body, feeling for anything. Feeling for hope.

But I knew what had happened.

My father was dead.

Sadie was dead.

Tessa...for the second time in my life, was dead.

I laid my forehead against hers.

And I cried.

Somehow, this hurt just as badly as it had hurt the first time. Even though some part of me, deep down, knew it was coming. Knew that it was too good to be true.

People like me didn't get happy endings. Tessa being alive was...it wasn't real.

Real. Somewhere in my mind, I knew what was real. But this pain was real. This grief that ate at my soul and devoured my heart was real.

My pain morphed into anger, anger that I had let this happen again. Anger that I was back here, back in this saints-forsaken village.

I lifted my head and surveyed the area around me. Everyone had scattered, leaving the place entirely abandoned except for the dead bodies that surrounded me.

Everyone left me. Nobody cared.

My power, the life power, flared within me. I did not have the energy to fight it, nor did I care to. I took a long, surrendering breath and released the power, letting a large flash of light surround me.

And I did not try to stop it.

Power flooded from my veins, pulsing into the air around me. I did not care much about Tessa's body, or Sadie's. Better they burn to ash by my power then rot in the dirt of this horrid place.

Tears streamed down my face, but the grief within me created a large, gaping hole of emotion. I relaxed into it, relaxed into the void of nothingness.

This was my destiny, I realized. To destroy everything and everyone around me. My power was not one of life. I knew, now, that it was one of death. And so was everything inside of me.

I belonged to the darkness.

I wasn't sure how much time passed. My power eventually fizzed down, reverting to the low void of emotion inside me. I was afraid to look at my sister. I knew I had burnt her body. I knew I had burnt the tavern behind me. The market was ash.

But I didn't quite care.

I didn't care about anything, actually. Not the fact that I was utterly alone. Not the fact that a few strangers had begun to creep around me, looking in horror at what I had done.

It was horrid, wasn't it? What I had done? Who I was?

I closed my eyes and imagined myself back home. Home. This was home, that's what Sadie had said.

But I knew, I knew deep in my bones that home wasn't here. Home wasn't this worn down, desperate, barely-surviving village of strangers. Rewyth was home. Malachi was home.

Malachi. I missed him. I missed him more than anything, yet my brain couldn't fathom the last memory I had of him. I missed his face. I missed his warmth. How long had it been? How long had it been since I last saw him?

Malachi, my husband. My everything.

Where was he? Wasn't he here? Why would he leave me here alone without–

Blood-curdling screams interrupted my thoughts. And they weren't screaming at me.

I turned my attention to the row of houses down the hill, or more so, the black-cloud of horror that followed.

Deadlings. Deadlings crawled over one another, clawing and destroying everything as they rushed forward up the hill, completely ripping apart everyone they came into contact with. The horrified screams were cut off by the gore of the deadly creatures.

For a second, I froze. Deadlings. The disgusting creatures had no right. It was then that I remembered something, something I must have known before. The deadlings were controlled by someone.

Someone or...something.

I stood, frozen in fear, watching the creatures attack and destroy as they made their way up the hill, closer to me. Closer to the destruction around me.

For a moment, I thought about letting them. I pictured their nasty, inhumane claws ripping my flesh to shreds, bleeding out on the ground until the jaws of the swarm tore out my heart.

But something deep within me resisted the thought, pushed it away. Something inside me wanted to live. For what? I wasn't sure. I didn't have an answer. But I knew that I had to keep going. I had to keep fighting.

The black creatures came closer. They didn't exactly have eyes, yet somehow I knew their attention had been locked onto me. As if they found their target.

I did not feel afraid. Not in the slightest. To be afraid of death, I would have to not welcome it. No, I was angry. Angry at whatever Saint had decided to take my sister away. Angry that my father hadn't died sooner, and angry that Sadie, who I thought I could protect, couldn't be saved, either.

And I was really pissed off that these disgusting creatures were creating even more of a damned mess.

Light burst around me, blocking the deadlings from my view. I found it amusing, how someone—although I couldn't remember who—had suggested my power was one of life. Clearly, my power was one of death. One of destruction, just like those deadlings.

Those deadlings were not as angry as I.

I pushed forward, screaming as I expanded my power. I pictured the deadlings burning to ash, just like I had done with my sister's dead body. I pictured the whole village burning to ash, actually, because I couldn't give any less shits about who lived or died in this damned place.

And when I opened my eyes again, when the screaming had stopped and the pain had turned from a burning passion of fire to a dull throb, I saw what was left.

I saw nothing. Nothing but burnt ash, not a single house and not a single tree left in the rubbish.

I had ruined it all. All of it, gone, just like everything else in my life. I had nothing left. I closed my eyes, dropped to my knees, and pictured the whole world turning to ash.

# CHAPTER 23
# Malachi

I WASN'T A FAN OF BEING IN THE LIBRARY ALONE. THE DARK SHADOWS that lingered in the corners never let me relax. I couldn't fathom how others actually enjoyed being in here, enjoyed studying of the Saints and history.

That didn't mean I didn't spend my fair share of hours and late nights in this exact room, bent over these books, trying to figure out why the Saints had done this to me.

This curse that disguised itself as power.

I headed for the study when Jade's screams had become too torturous for me to bear. I couldn't listen to them, knowing I was powerless. The Paragon did nothing but watch, nothing but nod along and act as if Jade was doing everything according to plan.

I hated them for it. I hated them for making her do this, for creating visions that only she and them could see.

Although part of me knew that I didn't need the visions to know what Jade was experiencing.

"I never thought I'd see you studying on your own free will," Silas entered the study. The energy in the air shifted, from one of frustration to one of anticipation. That's how it always felt when he was near. Like death was coming, and he would be the reaper. "What are you looking for?"

"Something I already know the answer to," I answered. Bile grew in my mouth. I quickly swallowed it. "And I enjoy the solitude. See yourself out."

I waited for his footsteps, my eyes returning to the words written on the script in front of me. But instead, I heard quiet, blood-freezing laughter.

"I'm glad this is humorous for you. It seems you're not getting enough entertainment with my wife in that damn arena."

His laughter subdued, followed by the sound of his approaching footsteps. He stood behind me, just a few feet back. "The Trials of Glory is not for my entertainment."

"Really? Could have fooled me."

I tried to bite my tongue, tried to fight back the anger that clawed at my spine and threatened to rip me apart from the inside, but now was not the time. There would be a time for revenge. Once all of this was done, once Jade was safe. I would give them all what they deserved.

Starting with Silas.

"You can be more than this, you know," Silas said. Each word hung heavy in the air between us.

"More than what? More than the King of Shadows? I thought this was what you wanted for me." I took a cooling breath. This was what he wanted from me; to shake me up. To get me angry. But it wasn't going to work. I had changed since my time here. He couldn't treat me like a confused child anymore.

I was a warrior. A king. A killer.

I became too distracted by my own thoughts to notice Silas reading over my shoulder. I slammed my hand over the scroll and stood up, turning to face him. "Why are you here?" I asked.

Silas's face flickered through a few emotions. I had become better at reading emotions since being with Jade. Her emotions, as much as she fought against it, displayed clear as day all over that perfect face of hers.

Silas's tedious smile faltered. "There's something I need to talk to you about."

"Why don't I spare us the formalities? You are my father, after all." Silas's face remained blank, but my own heart pounded like a wild animal in my chest. "Is that why you pulled us back here? Forced Jade into the trials? To get back at me? Was it all because I am your son?"

"Why would I want to get back at you?" he asked, ignoring the other questions.

"Because I left. You taught me everything I know. You taught me how to kill, how to sneak around, how to spy. You turned me into a weapon to use for your own good, and then I crawled back to my own life like a child."

"I trained you because that's what we do here. You needed to live up to your potential."

"And I've done that, right? I became the monster you wanted me to be."

"You're not a monster, and you know that. I took you in because that's what the Paragon does. We take the gifted and we make them great."

"I suppose that's what your excuse is for my wife, too? You think this will make her great?"

"Your wife..." he laughed again, muffling a cough. A vein on his forehead stuck out. "Your wife does not choose peace, Malachi. Although I'm sure you knew that already. Peacemaker?" He shook his head, as if shaking the very word that just fell off his lips. "The Trials of Glory have just begun. Your wife must face the present and the future before the Saints deem her worthy."

"They've already deemed her worthy!" My voice echoed off the walls. "Why can't you see that? You all sit up here with your black robes, high and mighty amongst everyone in this world, and you don't see it."

"See what?"

"Jade is better than me. Better than you. These trials will only prove that. She is more powerful than anyone who has ever walked here, and in a few days she will harness the power of all Saints, not just one."

Finally, something I said shocked him. His eyes widened for half a second before he stepped forward. After all this time, I think he grew even shorter. I stood a full head taller than him, I looked down at his thin, bald body. I wasn't sure why, all those years ago, this man made me feel so powerless.

I held the power now. And him, along with his power-hungry group of hooded figures, couldn't accept that.

For a fleeting second, I released the power that begged for his life. I unleashed the black threads, aiming them at Silas, and he crashed to his knees before me in pain. We had fought with magic many times before, until we were both bloodied and bruised. Until we both gave in, accepting defeat.

The truth was, Silas's power alone did not make him strong. It did not make him worthy of being a leader, and it damned sure did not make him the leader of the Paragon. No, his arrogance did that.

That was a hard lesson I learned.

"My wife," I barked, "will beat these trials. She will come out on the other side even stronger than she is now, with an even clearer picture of her gift. And when she does that, when she walks out of that arena after becoming exactly who you all thought she could never become, she will tear down this mountain with her bare hands."

His sounds of pain turned to gruntled laughter. Before I could fathom my next thought, pain slashed through my mind, a knife dissecting every inch of my flesh. I would have cried out in pain, would have screamed against my every will, but no sound would come out.

"You may think you are a king now," Silas said, "but make no mistake; I am the leader of the Paragon. I am the one the Saints speak through. I am the descendant of Erebus, same as you, and his strong, power-hungry blood runs in my veins, too."

I drew in a shuddered breath and clenched my fists.

"You may try to escape. By the glory of the Saints, your wife may just survive these trials. She may survive the depths of her own mind, but you will be the one picking up the pieces and putting them together. She is just a girl, Malachi. She is not your weapon. She is not stronger than you, and she most certainly is no stronger than me. Than what I have built here."

More pain exploded in my mind. I tried to send out those dark tethers of magic once more, tried to send him crashing back down to the ground where he belonged, but it was no use. I understood why Silas had been so undefeatable all these years. Impossible to kill. Stronger than anyone in the Paragon.

It was Erebus. This whole damn time, it was Erebus's power that Silas wielded.

It took every ounce of restraint in my body to back down from the fight.

"I should have known," I mumbled.

"Speak up," he demanded. "Kings do not mumble words beneath their breath."

Anger dulled my senses. I didn't care what Esther said before. Not anymore. "Did you know that my throne was being threatened?" I asked.

His face didn't change. Not a flicker of surprise, of denial.

"There's nothing you can do about that right now," Silas replied.

I couldn't believe this. I thought maybe—just maybe—Silas wouldn't know. Maybe he had been kept in the dark. Maybe it slipped through his communications, too, that someone was threatening Rewyth. "You want my kingdom to fall that badly?" I asked. "Why? So you can take it for yourself?"

"I don't wish to take your kingdom, son."

"Don't call me that," I argued. "We may share Erebus's blood, but you are not my father."

Silas attempted a smile, but his eyes remained dark. Emotionless. "If Rewyth needs you to return, be my guest. Leave. Your wife will be in great hands here," he spat.

"You know I won't leave her."

He shrugged matter-of-factly. "That's your choice, then. But don't blame me or the Paragon for whatever seems to be happening in your kingdom."

I turned around and ran my hands through my hair, trying to get a grip on the situation. He was never going to help me. He was never going to help my kingdom. Saints, he sure never helped me in the past. He might say he does not want my kingdom to fall, but I knew what he really wanted.

He wanted what he always fought for. Power.

"Fine," I said, turning around to face him. "I won't ask you to send aid to my kingdom, but at least allow me to send a letter to my men."

He considered this for quite some time before giving a silent nod of approval. "Our messengers are slow and I cannot promise anything, but if you wish to send a message to your kingdom, I will not stop you."

What bullshit. He had been trying to stop me ever since our arrival here. Nevertheless, I rushed to the desk behind Silas and found a piece of parchment.

*Ser,*
*Do what you need to do. I can't leave her yet.*
*-M*

I prayed to the Saints that Ser would know what that meant, would know what to do. I couldn't leave Jade. I couldn't leave her here with them, the ones who tortured her mind with every passing second.

Serefin wouldn't have asked me to come back unless it was absolutely necessary. I knew that. I knew that whatever threatened our kingdom likely moved closer and closer to my throne every day.

Still, knowing that my throne was threatened didn't begin to convince me to leave my wife. It wasn't a question.

I was staying.

"Here," I said, folding it and handing it to Silas.

He took it without breaking eye contact, a hint of something amused lingered in his gaze.

"What?" I asked.

He waited a few seconds, my letter hanging in his fingers, before answering, "You would risk your kingdom for this girl. You were right. You're not the same boy who won the trials all those years ago."

# CHAPTER 24
# *Jade*

When I woke up, I was back in the stone arena. Something told me I had been there before, but my thoughts were too foggy to focus, and even trying to recall where I had been the last few days put a piercing blade through my mind.

And then, all at once, as I laid there on my back looking up at darkness, I began to remember.

Sadie. Tessa. My father. Everything crashed back into my memory, along with all of the pain. All of the anger.

I had to watch her die. Again.

But Sadie had been there...and she wasn't really dead, was she? And my father wasn't dead, right?

I shook my head, trying to rid the thoughts that crumbled in my brain.

Something caught my eye in the upper corner of the stone arena. It was dark, and I had to rub my eyes to make sure I wasn't seeing things. I still didn't trust my own eyes.

What was that? A small glint of shimmer caught my eye, and it reminded me of the doorway into the Paragon.

That's where I was, wasn't it? The temple of the Paragon?

My chest ached as Malachi's chiseled face came to my mind. I missed him, and I hated myself for missing him. I knew this would be hard on me, these trials. Malachi had tried to prepare me, and he was probably somewhere watching me miss him.

I rubbed at that pain in my chest, trying to push it away. But nothing worked.

"Miss?" A yelp escaped me as I twisted around on the cold ground to see where the voice came from.

A small boy peaked his head through a hidden door in the stone. Wait, I recognized that boy. I had seen him before, he was the one who...who...

No. Maybe I hadn't. My memories faded as quickly as they arrived. The boy came through the same door I had walked through. How long ago was that? How long had I been here?

"Hello?" I asked. My voice croaked.

"I have food for you, miss." He crawled forward, glancing to that portion of the stone that shimmered as he brought a plate of food into the stone room. His feet were bare and dirty, and while he did wear black linens, they were not fashioned in the head-covering robe that others wore.

"How long have I been here?" I asked him. His eyes widened, as if he wasn't expecting me to speak to him.

"It's been two days, miss."

"Two days?" I shook my head. "No, that can't be right." Two days? Two days since I was forced to drink the elixir, and two days of the trials?

The boy began backing away when I reached out and gripped his arm. "The first trial. What did I do? What happened?"

The boy tilted his head, but didn't try to pull his arm away. "It was like fire," he started. "Everywhere, all over the stone and filling the whole room. We didn't think you would survive it, miss."

I let go of him and staggered back. He pointed in the distance, and I followed his finger to the empty arena behind me.

Burn marks, as if charred from a fire, lined the walls. I rubbed my eyes again. "Was that me?"

The boy nodded, and then gave me a look that caused my stomach to sink. "I have to go. Your second trial will be starting soon, miss. You ought to eat and try to rest."

He backed away and the stone slammed shut behind him.

And once again, I was alone.

I glanced at the plate of meat, but didn't feel the slightest bit hungry. Especially after what had just happened. Although when I tried to remember the specific events...

*Forget it,* I thought. *It doesn't matter.* If I had used my magic, I probably gave them a show. And that was probably exactly what he wanted.

Silas. Did he know I would see Tessa? Did he play that out specifically so I would have to relive that trauma?

Of course he did. He wanted this, he wanted to see me suffer. I took a quick scan of my body to make sure I hadn't been injured. Other than the low throb of my heartbeat that I could now feel in the temples of my head, I was fine.

I had survived, and that was enough for now.

Trial one, my past, was done. Two more to go.

# CHAPTER 25
# *Malachi*

Memory of my second trial came swiftly and violently in my sleep.

*Adonis, Lucien, Eli, and Fynn all sat around the dining table. Something felt strange about the situation, but I couldn't quite put my finger on it.*

*Adonis laughed, something about Eli's ability to hunt for the family. Or lack thereof, rather. He had never been a good hunter, but we didn't care. Apart from hurting his pride, he had nothing to worry about as long as he lived in Rewyth.*

*"What are you all going on about?" Adeline asked. She sauntered in the room as if the whole castle were built just for her. She did that frequently, and I was always surprised by the way she could entirely change the mood of any room.*

*"They're being idiots," Lucien groaned. So typical of him, the buzzkill of the group unless the group's activities involved getting into trouble.*

*"I can't say that surprises me," Adeline added, setting down a large plate of food. "Here," she said. "Father won't make it to dinner."*

*A dull emotion flared, right beneath my chest bone. I didn't care that my father hadn't attended dinner. He rarely had time for dinner, so why was I affected at all?*

*"Where is he?" I asked. My voice felt raw and distant.*

*"Politics, I'm sure. I don't tend to ask details when those are involved." She tossed her long hair over her shoulder and sat beside our brothers.*

*"Malachi?" Fynn asked, his voice as light and innocent as ever. "Are you alright, brother?"*

*I looked at him, at his sharp cheekbones and pointed ears. Something was different about him. Something was different about all of them, actually.*

*I didn't answer. Instead, I turned my attention to the room around us. The castle looked spotless. The green vines that threaded through the white stone of the walls looked extra green this time of year. It was my favorite, when the nature around the castle began to swallow it whole. I always loved that part about the castle. We didn't try to rid the nature around us completely. Instead, we became one with it. One with the land and the trees.*

*Everyone at the table stared at me as I finally quit daydreaming.*

*"What?" I asked, not remembering the question they were waiting for me to answer.*

*"I said, are you okay? You're acting strange."*

Was I acting strange?

*"I'm fine, Fynn."*

*"Here," Adeline insisted, shoving some food from the platter onto the smaller plate in front of me. "Eat this. You'll feel better."*

*I accepted the offer and shoved some of the meat into my mouth. How long had it been since I had last eaten? Saints, I didn't even remember what I had eaten for breakfast.*

*"Okay," Eli said, setting his own fork down. "We should likely discuss how we'll do it."*

*"Do what?" I insisted.*

*Eli scoffed. "How we'll kill you, of course."*

*I shot my eyes in his direction. Surely, I didn't hear him right. Everyone else continued eating as if Eli had said nothing.*

*"Kill me?"*

*"Yes," Eli replied. "We've already discussed this, Malachi. We have to kill you if we want the throne for ourselves."*

*I glanced at Adeline, who surely would tell Eli to shut up at any second. But she, too, continued casually eating her food.*

*"You can't kill me, Eli," I replied, still not sure if he was joking.*

*"Sure, we can," Lucien jumped in. "We've killed plenty of fae before. You'll be no different."*

*Were they serious?*

*"I must be exhausted," I said, "because I really can't tell if you're being stupid or not."*

*Adonis set his fork down and stared me directly in the eye. "It's nothing personal, brother. You've known we would try this for some time now. Just face it. You're not meant to be king. You're not meant to be heir to the fae throne."*

*Saints above. They were serious about getting rid of me.*

*My power flared in my blood, very aware of the threat we were openly discussing at the dinner table.*

*"Adeline?" I asked. "You're okay with this?"*

*She shrugged. "To be honest with you, brother, I try not to concern myself with the politics of the castle. Much too boring for me."*

*It was Fynn who picked up his knife, pointing it casually in my direction.*

*"Put your knife down, Fynn," I ordered. "Let's talk about this."*

*He didn't. Instead, he laughed. He laughed as if this entire situation were a game, and he had been waiting for the final blow all along.*

*"There's nothing to talk about," Lucien added. "In fact, it's better if we don't talk at all."*

*He, too, picked up his knife.*

*A few stabbings I could handle. But my entire family attacking me with one sole purpose to kill me? That would be a fight.*

*A fight I wasn't sure I could win.*

*My power sensed this, too. I let it come forward, engulfing my senses.*

*"Don't make me do this," I said. "I don't want to hurt any of you."*

*They all looked at each other, Adeline included, and laughed. As if it were a ridiculous thought that I could hurt them. As if I were weak. Powerless.*

*Fynn stood up, his wooden chair screeching against the floor as he did.*

*"We all knew this would happen eventually," he said. "We better get it over with now."*

*I lost it. My power blasted through the room, strong enough to wipe out any soldier if it needed to.*

*But there were no soldiers in the room. We were not at war.*

*My family—Adeline, Fynn, Eli, Adonis, Lucien—they all fell to the ground, screaming in pain.*

*It wasn't long until those screams stifled, the pain becoming too much to bear.*

*"I don't want to do this," I said again, more to myself than to them. "I don't want to hurt any of you."*

*I pulled back lightly, just enough to allow them a breath.*

*But Adonis, as strong-headed as he was, took this chance to reach for his dagger.*

*"Don't," I warned, but he ignored me. In one swift motion, he pulled the dagger from his sheath and threw it toward my chest.*

*I swatted it away effortlessly, but my power saw this as a threat on my life. I could hardly contain it as it pulsed through the room again—full force this time—and did not stop.*

*Did not stop as the pained groans silenced.*

*Did not stop as the breathing slowed.*

*Did not stop as each of their five heartbeats stilled.*

*Only then, when the room was calm, did my power relax.*

*A wave of nausea overcame me.*

*I had killed them all.*

# CHAPTER 26
# Jade

MALACHI SLEPT NEXT TO ME WHEN I WOKE UP, TWISTED TOGETHER with me in the silk bed sheets. I couldn't see his face, but I knew it was him. The familiarity, the intuitive comfort.

I rolled over and ran a hand up his bare arm. "Good morning," I whispered, squinting against the morning sun.

He mumbled a groggy response before turning around and wrapping me in his arms, brushing a hard kiss onto my forehead.

Birds sang somewhere on the other side of our open window. These were my favorite days—the days where the morning breeze pulled us from bed.

It felt like it had been so long.

His fingers ran across my cheek, sending a chill down my body. "You're trying to torture me," I insisted.

Malachi laughed, and I tried to soak in the way his vibrations spread across my own body as he pulled me tighter in the bed. "If by torture you mean with my mouth and hands, my queen, then I'll torture you all day long." His hot mouth moved to my cheek, my neck, my collarbone.

But then he pulled back. His features darkened as he looked down on me, holding himself up with his forearms. Concern dripped from his face as his eyes scanned me.

"What's wrong?"

Mal shook his head before answering. "Jade, you're..." he couldn't finish the thought.

"I'm what?" I repeated, sitting up in bed and pushing him back. "What is it, Mal?"

He picked up his hand and dragged a finger across my chest, right under my collarbone. He then turned his hand and showed me what was dripping from his finger.

Blood. Red, ruby blood.

My mouth fell open. I frantically began searching my body, looking for any indication that the blood was mine.

That wasn't the worst part, though. The worst part was the look on Mal's face.

Because he already knew. Deep down, he knew that blood wasn't mine. I knew it, too.

"I need to wash this off," I stammered. "Just...just hold on, okay? I'll go rinse it away and I'll be back."

Malachi didn't say anything. I staggered away from the bed—half naked—and stumbled into the bathroom where I shut the door strongly behind me.

My heart raced, too hard for this early in the morning.

But it stopped beating altogether when I glanced at myself in the jagged mirror before me.

Blood dripped from nearly every inch of my skin, some dried, some glistening with the reflection of the sunlight.

"Saints," I mumbled. My mind raced as I tried to think about where I went last night. Whose blood was this? And why hadn't I cleaned it away before crawling into bed with Malachi?

Pain pierced my temples, and I massaged them with my red hands to subdue the pain. I couldn't remember. Saints, I couldn't even remember whose blood was covering my own body.

I stepped into the stream of water that fell from the other side of the bathroom and tried not to think.

*It was an accident*, I told myself. An accident, or maybe it was self-defense. Either way, I wouldn't have killed someone if they hadn't deserved it.

I wasn't even sure I had killed someone. Maybe the blood was part of a ritual of some sort, where it was required that I dump blood over myself. Maybe that was it.

The water that ran off my skin ran red.

I knew that wasn't it, though. I had killed someone last night. And I was so much of a monster, I couldn't even remember who.

Malachi stood dressed when I exited the bathroom, free from a single drop of a stranger's blood. Maids had already begun stripping away the bed sheets, the ones that I had smeared the red substance across in my sleep.

"Busy day today?" I asked, leaning against the wall with my hair still dripping wet.

Mal barely met my eyes. "No more busy than usual."

I nodded and tried to smile, but Mal had no interest in being polite, it seemed. "Mal," I said, stepping forward. He flinched—actually flinched—away from me. "Mal," I said, more gentle. "Can we at least talk about this?"

"There's nothing to talk about," he replied with a king's voice. "You're covered in blood, and now it's my job to find out whose blood was spilt in my kingdom last night."

I reeled back, shocked that he would speak to me with that voice. He was always so gentle with me, so adoring.

Not anymore, it seemed. Something had changed. I wasn't that ignorant human that needed him to save me around every corner.

No, I was something else now. Something powerful. Something deadly. I felt it, deep in my bones I felt it.

And Malachi couldn't even look me in the eyes because of it.

"I should come with you," I said before he could storm off. "I should come so I can explain."

He looked at me with a sigh, his eyes like daggers piercing into mine, but at least he was looking at me. "Can you?" he asked. "Can you explain, Jade? You're covered in blood, and my guess is you have no clue what even happened. You could have slaughtered the entire kingdom while I slept." Exhaustion dripped from his words. Exhaustion and something else, something that hurt me as much as a punch.

Mal's jaw clenched as he shook his head, thinking something that I really had no interest in hearing. "Come on," he said after a few torturous moments. "At this point, I can't trust you enough to leave you here alone."

He didn't even wait to see if his words had hurt me. He stormed out of the bedroom, not slowing for me to catch up.

I slipped on my black boots and followed like an idiot after him.

His black leather wings tucked tightly behind his shoulder blades as we sauntered the halls of Rewyth.

I walked behind him, happy to be in his shadow. Happy to walk in his footsteps. I was never going to be his equal, I knew that. But times like this reminded me of how royal Mal was. How good.

His job as King was to get rid of threats. And I was becoming the biggest threat to this kingdom.

He stopped walking, and I almost ran into the back of him before I stopped myself, too. It took me a few seconds to realize that we were no longer in the castle. When had we walked outside? We were now standing in the tree-covered lagoon, one that I had been to a time or two before. Although now, I couldn't remember when, or with who.

But the lagoon still glittered with beauty.

Mal spun on his heel to face me, which forced me to rip my attention from the beautiful surroundings.

"Malachi?" I asked. He looked at me with something I had never seen from him before.

He looked at me with hatred.

The hair on the back of my neck stood straight up. "Mal, what's going on? Why did you bring me out here?"

His jaw tightened even further, and his nostrils flared in a predator's preparation. His pointed ears twitched out slightly from his mess of curly black hair, and I watched as he absentmindedly placed a hand on the hilt of his sword.

"You know why, Jade," he said through gritted teeth.

"Tell me," I insisted. I didn't even care that I sounded like a desperate child.

Every inch of my body told me to run. Malachi wouldn't hurt me. He would never lay a finger on me, I knew that.

Still, alarms blared in my mind. Something wasn't right here. Why would he want to get rid of me just because I had blood on my skin? He had blood on his too, right?

I took a slow step backward, away from the king before me. I tried to think of a time that Mal had killed someone, that Mal had been covered in blood.

But again, my mind fell blank.

He was perfect. He was golden and innocent and good, and I was the splatter of blood staining his perfect white kingdom.

"I don't want to hurt you," Mal said. His voice cracked, and in that moment I would have given anything to take away his pain, even if I were the one causing it.

Malachi deserved the world. I would give him anything.

*I'll do it myself*, I wanted to say, but I didn't get the chance.

I heard them before I saw them—sudden rustling in the trees around us. Too much, too many.

I spun around, searching the shadows of the tree line, only to find that we were completely surrounded.

By hundreds of silver wings.

"Mal," I pleaded. "What are they doing here?"

When I looked at him, his jaw was set, but a single tear slid down his tanned skin. "They're here to help you, Jade."

Weapons raised against me, but I knew they wouldn't need to use them. I was no match against a fae. I never was.

"You ordered them to get rid of me?" I asked. "Because you couldn't do it yourself?"

"Don't make this harder than it needs to be," he said. I didn't recognize him. Not anymore. Those chiseled cheekbones seemed dull. Those dark eyes fell distant.

This was not the same Malachi I fell in love with. This was not the strong, protective fae who pulled me back from the edge of darkness.

This was a coward.

One of the silver-winged fae to my left stepped forward. Out of nowhere and without my permission, a rush of anger flooded my senses.

"Don't do this," I pleaded to him. "It's not what you think. I can be better, Malachi! I can change!"

He didn't even look me in the eye. "You'll never change, Jade. You'll always be this helpless. This violent."

"No!" I argued, but the fae had already approached me, encircling Mal and I both in the tight circle of the lagoon—the one place I actually thought was peaceful.

I couldn't believe it, yet somehow I wasn't shocked at all. Malachi Weyland—the one fae who would once protect me with his life—was going to kill me.

# CHAPTER 27
# *Malachi*

I MINDLESSLY WANDERED THROUGH THE TUNNELS OF THE MOUNTAIN, not wanting to go to bed. Not strong enough to see Jade in that arena. Her second trial had started, I could feel it deep in my body. I could feel her emotions rolling like waves in the ocean.

*No,* I couldn't be near her.

Instead, I staggered through the underground, not caring where I ended up. Not caring if I got lost.

Saints, if I were lucky, I would find a way out of this place. Perhaps there would be a hidden entrance, one not monitored by glamour.

"Don't even think about it. You can't escape. You know that." Cordelia's voice pierced my thoughts.

"Get out of my head," I ordered. "Do you ever mind your own damn business?" I spun around to see her standing in the tunnel a few feet away.

"Usually," she purred. "But your thoughts are so entertaining. You really think you can escape with not only your life, but your precious wife's?"

"I've done it before," I replied. It was the truth. The last time I was here, I was able to leave without a single interruption.

"No," Cordelia corrected. "You left. You didn't escape. There's a difference."

My gut twisted again. I had been so sick just a few moments ago, I vomited three times. Something wasn't right. It was my magic—I knew it.

And I really hated it. Jade felt terrified and...*betrayed*. Her emotions came to me as clearly as if they were my own.

The second trial wasn't even over. Jade had to survive this, and then an entire third round of challenges before she was deemed worthy.

*Worthy.* What a pile of shit.

"You're sassier than I remember," Cordelia added, still clearly poking around in my mind.

"What are you doing here?" I hissed. I pushed past her and entered the hallway, facing the direction of Jade's trial.

She took a deep breath and followed after me. It was rare for her to watch what she was about to say. I had grown used to her blurting out whatever thought first crossed her mind. She glanced over her shoulder before answering, "I'll help you."

"Help me what?"

Her eyes narrowed before she answered, "I'll help you kill Silas."

I finished dragging her by the arm into the bath house where the running water at least attempted to cover our voices. "Please tell me you didn't just say that out loud."

"Trust me," she started. "They're occupied. Besides, if anyone were listening to us I would hear their thoughts. Now, do you want my help or not?"

"I don't...why would you want to help me? What's in it for you?" If I knew anything about the half-witch, I knew she always had an ulterior motive.

She shrugged and broke eye contact. "You're not the only one who's tired of his antics, you know."

"Explain."

She closed her eyes while she took a deep breath before she continued. "He's changed, Mal. He's power-hungry, even more so than he used to be. He gets...he gets these twisted thoughts, like he doesn't even care about the Paragon. He just wants to stay on top."

"He's the leader of the Paragon, by definition he's already on top."

"It's not just that. With Jade...he..."

My stomach dropped. "He what?"

"He sees her as a threat. Not as a tool. Not as the peacemaker, who has literally been in the prophecies of the witches for centuries now."

"Well that's not exactly groundbreaking news, Cordelia. He sees everyone as a threat these days."

"My point, exactly."

"So what? You want to kill him because he wants to kill Jade? I'm not buying that."

I moved to walk out of the bath house and back to the arena to check on Jade, but she caught my arm and forced me to stay. "Jade is no longer a human, Malachi." Her grip tightened on my arm. "Hear me when I say this, because I won't explain it again. Your wife is not human. Not anymore. What Esther did to save her life..."

This topic had a strange way of coming up at the worst times. Jade had died, we all knew that would have consequences. But to hear Cordelia say this with such urgency...

"What is she, then? A witch?" I asked.

Cordelia's nostrils flared. "It's complicated. But Silas knows."

Silas. He was the first one to whisper to Jade that she might not be human. Of course he knew.

"How? How could he possibly know what my wife is before I know myself? Is it another part of his gift?"

"Esther told him. She knew as soon as she brought Jade back from death."

Everything clicked into place, all my messy thoughts and rough intuitions finally piecing together.

Esther and Silas were working together. Jade wasn't human.

And I wanted to kill that bastard more than anything.

"We aren't so different, you and I," Cordelia said. "We want the same things."

I scoffed. "I doubt that, witch."

I ripped my arm from her grasp and turned around again. "Half-witch," she barked, her voice stronger than I had ever heard it. "And you forget how powerful I really am, *king*."

I turned to see her scowling at me, a fierce emotion in her eyes. Her silver wings flared on either side of her, as if she were trying to remind me that they were there. "Tell me what you really want with Silas and Jade."

My temper was beginning to tether out, but I didn't care enough to control it. She knew this about Jade and she was only now telling me. Even worse, she knew that Esther had kept a secret from me yet again.

"I want to see Jade rule by your side as leader of the fae," she started. "And I want Silas out of the picture so magic can finally flow freely. Witches have been in hiding for decades now. It's time we all live how we once did. How it should be."

I couldn't deny the chill that flickered down my spine. How it should be.

Jade deserved to rule. If what Cordelia was saying about her not being human were true...

She was born for great things. I had known that for some time now. The others were the ones who couldn't see. They refused to accept her for what she was—the peacemaker. The most powerful entity of our time.

Jade held the power of the Saints.

She could win these trials, and then we would be gone. We would leave this damn temple and never come back, never have to see Silas or any of the Paragon members again.

We could hold out until then.

"It's too risky," I said to Cordelia. "Jade will rule beside me, but we can't kill Silas. Not yet, anyway. She'll win these damn trials and we'll be gone before the week is over."

## CHAPTER 28
# *Jade*

"How?" I asked. "How can you live with yourself knowing you're killing your wife. We took vows, Malachi! You promised me!"

His face remained blank. Any amount of sadness he had been showing before now covered by the mask of emotionlessness.

"You're dangerous, Jade. If I don't handle the situation now, you'll be the end of us all."

The fae around us moved closer. With every step they took, with every inch of space around me that disappeared, I grew closer and closer to my own demise.

What I didn't expect, though, was my own power having a fighting instinct. Heat of power fueled my body, pumping through my veins. I stared directly at Malachi, straight into those dark, endless eyes, and held my palms on either side of my body.

"Don't fight this, Jade," he said, as if he could feel what I was about to do. "It's best for everyone if we get it over with now."

"You mean it's best for you!" I yelled. "Dammit, Malachi! Think about this for one second!" More power pulsed to the surface. It was ready to defend me, ready to save my life.

But the result? They would die. They would all die.

My power flashed around me, defending me from the one person I never imagined having to use my power against.

And as that light encapsulated us all, my heart cracked in two.

Screams of surprise came from the silver-winged fae. Not from Malachi, though. He wasn't surprised.

And he also wouldn't be affected by my magic.

I pushed my magic out with strength I didn't expect to have. It was fueled by something, though. Anger. Anger fueled my power, pulsing it through the screams of the fae until those screams turned silent.

Until those screams were drowned by my own thoughts, my thoughts that were directed at just one thing—Malachi.

"Is this what you wanted?" Mal screamed. I pulled back my power and saw the result of my actions—the hundreds of fae around us dead, their silver wings covering half their bodies as they lay on the floor of the lagoon. "Was this your plan all along?"

I stepped toward him. He stepped back. "No," I said, shaking my head. "You don't understand, Mal. I had to protect myself."

"Oh, I understand," he said. The way he looked at me...as if I were something disgusting. As if I were nothing but a pest in his kingdom. "You hate the fae, Jade. You hate what we stand for. You hate that we live in this castle, lavishing away at anything we want. You hate it. Have you been planning this all along? Have you been planning your revenge this entire time?"

Where was this coming from? This wasn't the Malachi I knew. This wasn't my husband. "Mal, I–"

"Don't call me that."

"I don't–"

"It's King Malachi," he corrected. "And you've just murdered nearly half of my royal guard!" Anger, feral and hot, flashed through his features. His pointed ears flickered in emotion, and his lips curled in a wicked snarl. "You are no longer welcome here, Jade," he said.

"Malachi, please!" I was crying now, although I couldn't remember when my anger had morphed into anything else. Nothing made sense. Not anymore. "Don't do this! We're supposed to protect each other, remember? We're supposed to look out for one another!"

"You're a stranger to me," he said, each word twisting that dagger he had already pierced through my heart. "Get out of my kingdom."

"So, that's it?" I begged. "You try to kill me, and when I retaliate, I'm banished?"

He said nothing. He turned on his heel and began walking deeper into the forest, away from the lagoon. I followed, stepping over the fae bodies in my way.

"You're a coward," I snapped. "If you want to get rid of me so badly, you'll have to kill me yourself." My voice shook, but my words held steady.

How did it get to this? How did we become these people? I couldn't remember a time before today that Malachi even looked at me with a single ounce of distaste, let alone the disgust that practically evaporated off him now. "Kill me, Malachi." I gripped his arm and spun him around.

He shrugged me off. "Get out of here."

"You're a coward!" I yelled. "A coward and a sad excuse for a king!" Part of me regretted the words as soon as I said them, but part of me didn't care at all. That part of me wanted to hurt him, wanted to inflict pain on him just like he was inflicting on me.

I wanted *him* to hurt.

"Kill me," I said again.

He shook his head.

"Kill me, you coward."

He stormed away again, mumbling something I couldn't understand.

His dagger through my chest would hurt far less than his words.

A wildfire of anger and sadness took control of my body, my thoughts. I couldn't hold it together. Not anymore. What was the point, anyway? I wasn't welcome here. I had nowhere else to go.

A scream ripped through the trees around us. It wasn't until my throat began to sting that I realized the scream was mine.

But Malachi didn't stop walking. He didn't care. I kept screaming as if that would make the pain go away. As if that would make any of this better.

I screamed until I ran out of breath.

Malachi stopped walking.

"Does this make you happy?" I yelled after him with a hoarse voice. "Does seeing me in pain bring you joy, King Malachi?"

He turned to face me and the blood in my veins ran cold.

Malachi—his dark eyes, his chiseled face—it was all gone. Malachi was morphing, right before my eyes, into a deadling.

"No," I breathed. "Mal, what's happening?"

He twitched and snarled, his fae wings disappearing and his sharp ears melting away. Until all that was left were black, disgusting claws and skinless features across his scrawny, boney body.

He—no, *it*—dropped its sword. The deadly creature took one step toward me.

Adrenaline like I had never felt before pulsed inside me, telling me to run, telling me to get out of there as fast as possible.

Malachi was deadly, yes, but a deadling? They had the one thing Malachi did not possess. They had a strong, unrelenting need for blood.

"Mal, please!" I yelled. It took another step toward me. I took another step back. I didn't want to run away. I didn't want to run from this thing as if my husband wasn't standing in its spot just seconds ago.

But this wasn't Mal. Not anymore.

*Which meant this deadling could also be affected by my magic. I could kill it right now. I could kill him.*

"No," I said to myself. "Malachi, I know you're in there," I whispered. "Please, don't make me do this. I don't think I'm strong enough."

Tears fell freely down my face now, dripping off my chin and down my chest. I froze, daring the creature to come closer.

*Please. Please don't make me do this.*

"I love you, Malachi!" I yelled. The words felt strange, almost as if they weren't real. "I love you!"

The creature didn't give any sign that it understood me. Power buzzed under my flesh. "Don't make me do this," I said again.

I decided then that I wasn't going to run. I wasn't going to let these creatures chase me through the Kingdom of Rewyth like I was a helpless animal.

I fell to my knees on the rough forest floor. I held my hands out to my sides.

"Is this what you want?" I asked. I knew the thing couldn't hear me, couldn't understand me. "Come on, then."

The creature stepped toward me slowly, as if confused as to why I wasn't running.

"Come on!" I screamed.

Two seconds passed. And then the nasty thing launched itself at me.

I didn't plan on fighting. My plan was to let this thing—this remnant of Malachi—destroy me. Kill me like he had planned to do all along.

But when the creature sank its teeth into my shoulder, when its long, deadly claws grazed my skin, I lost control.

Another snarled scream escaped me as my power exploded, disintegrating everything around me with its last attempt at self-preservation.

I shut my eyes tight, blocking out the scene around me. I didn't want to look. But when the sting of the teeth in my flesh disappeared, when I could no longer feel the weight of the creature leaning on my body, when my power pulled back an inch, letting me know I was safe once again, I opened my eyes.

I expected to see a deadling. The ashes of a deadling, actually. The trees around us were flattened, nothing but dust left where they used to stand. The sun of day warmed my skin, now that the thick green leaves were no longer shielding me.

And in front of me, lying on the ground with not even a scratch, was Malachi.

"Mal?" I asked. His eyes were closed, his face pale. "Malachi?" I reached out with a trembling hand and brushed his cheek.

And then yanked my hand back with a gasp. He was cold. Too cold.

"Mal!" I pleaded. My hands hovered over him, wanting to touch him but too afraid to. "Don't leave me, Mal. Don't do this to me."

I watched his chest, waiting for it to rise and fall like it always did. I loved the way his breathing was always steady, even when he was angry. Even when he was tired. His chest would rise with a breath, and then fall. Always.

But I watched and I waited. And when nothing moved, when he didn't take a breath for I don't even know how long, I crumbled completely.

"Come back to me," I sobbed, my words hardly audible. He couldn't hear me, though. He was gone, I had killed him.

*I killed Malachi.*

Another sob wrecked my chest, but the sound of the pain—the sound of the emotion and regret and hatred for myself crawling out of me—changed something inside me.

No, I couldn't do this. I couldn't be this person. I couldn't live without him, even if he did want me dead just a few moments ago.

He was everything to me. He saved my life. He deserved more than this.

I rested my head on his still chest. "Come back to me," I repeated. "I swear to the Saints I'll change. I'll be better. I'll do better."

My heart broke—shattered entirely into irreparable shards.

I was nothing without him, I realized. Nothing without the man who saved me, who resurrected me from a dying life.

Malachi was my life. I could not lose him.

I lifted my head and screamed to the Saints, screamed to the world for taking him from me. It was a scream that shook the trees around us, rippled the water of the lagoon.

I screamed and screamed and screamed. I screamed until my throat burned, my voice ran dry.

I screamed until Malachi...Malachi *moved*. Just slightly, small enough that I barely noticed it.

"Mal?" My voice was hoarse and raw. "Mal, wake up!"

His eyes moved under his closed eyelids. I placed my hands on his chest, willing him back. Willing him to return to me, to return to this world.

He blinked his eyes open—those deep, marvelous, pain-filled eyes—and looked at me.

"Jade?"

# CHAPTER 29
# Malachi

After my conversation with Cordelia ended, we both headed up to the gallery to watch Jade's trial. I didn't want to watch her suffer, but leaving her alone with those bastards watching her every move made me sick to my stomach.

So I watched. I watched as she fell to her knees and cried, shouting something we couldn't hear.

I couldn't even begin to imagine what she was seeing, but I could feel it. In that tether of magic, I could feel her pain. Her suffering. Whatever was happening, it hurt her. Badly.

*Come on, Jade. You're almost done.*

Suddenly, my vision blurred. I gripped onto the stone railing of the balcony to steady myself. Saints, something wasn't right. A few seconds later, my legs collapsed beneath me. I crashed to the floor, no breath in my lungs.

"Malachi?" Esther asked, rushing over to me. When did she get here? She must have decided to watch the trials, after all. "What's happening?"

I tried to inhale, tried to take a deep breath, but my lungs were paralyzed. Seconds passed, panic began to creep into my body.

*Jade.* My vision blurred, and I shook my head as an image of myself flashed through my mind. Me, but different. I lay dead on the forest floor of Rewyth.

No, I shook my head again, clawing at my chest. I couldn't breathe.

"Malachi!" Esther yelled. She knelt next to me and gripped my face in her hands. "It's her, isn't it?" she whispered. "It's Jade."

I couldn't bring myself to even nod. At the mention of her name, another vision flashed through me. It was me again, but I wasn't alone. Jade knelt above me, crying and chanting in a language I didn't understand, gazing up at the sky and pleading.

Pleading for...*my* life.

"Stop this!" Esther yelled to Silas. "Can't you see? Whatever torturous disaster you're putting that girl through is affecting him!"

Silas paid us no attention. His gaze was locked down in the arena, on something I couldn't see. But I knew what was happening.

Jade was pleading for my life in her trial.

Dark shadows swarmed the room around me. I needed air. I needed to breathe.

I willed my lungs to expand but...nothing. Not even a hint of relief came. My body began screaming, demanding air. Demanding that I live.

But there was nothing I could do.

Everything began to fade. Esther still knelt beside me, but I could not feel her hands on me.

Silas laughed in the distance, something dark and evil. It was the last thing I heard before I let the shadows take me.

*I stumbled through the forest, not entirely sure how I got there in the first place. I wasn't in the mountains of the Paragon, and I didn't recognize the forest around me as anywhere in Rewyth. The trees were different, the smell was different.*

*My third trial. It had to be.*

*The sun blazed overhead. It was hot out, so hot that even the breeze did not bring any relief. Sweat formed over every inch of my skin as I stumbled forward.*

*At least I still had my wings. They tucked strongly behind my shoulder blades, comforting me as I pushed forward. I had to find out where I was.*

*I found a small clearing in the thick woods, one where the sun shined into the forest floor in a large, circular form. I walked forward until I felt the heat of the sun above on my skin, and just as I was about to launch myself into the air, a woman appeared.*

*She had long dark hair that fell in loose curls to her waist. She looked young, maybe two decades old, but her eyes...*

*I stepped forward so I could get a better look.*

*Though she looked young, the woman's eyes appeared old and tired.*

*"Malachi?" she asked, cocking her head to the side.*

*How did she know my name?*

*"Who are you?" I asked.*

*The woman looked me up and down, taking in every inch of me as if remembering an old friend. Her eyes wandered from my black boots to my now-expanded wings.*

*"You don't know who I am?" she asked.*

*I was certain I had never seen her in my life. I would have remembered eyes so deep, beauty so radiant.*

*"No," I answered honestly.*

*"Come here," she said, holding her arm out. She smiled softly, and my body reacted to it without my permission. I stepped closer to her, allowing her to turn my body and face the forest around us. "Look there," she said.*

*I focused on the area she pointed at, surprised to see...her.*

*"What am I looking at?" I asked.*

*The clone of the woman—the one in the forest—held a knife out in front of her. She was hunting, by the looks of it, but she couldn't see the wolf that approached.*

*I wanted to scream. I wanted to tell her to turn around, to look.*

*"We have to help her," I said.*

*"You will," the woman beside me spoke. "Trust me, you will help her in ways you cannot yet comprehend."*

*I didn't know what the woman meant, but I quickly quit caring. I watched as...as myself appeared behind her in the woods.*

*"Is that me?" I asked.*

*"It is. Keep watching."*

*So I did. My heart raced, my blood pounded through my veins. More wolves appeared. The clone of myself relaxed, leaning against a tree and waiting for the right moment to help, to jump in.*

*I watched the encounter in awe. It wasn't a memory, no. I would have remembered. But it felt so...familiar.*

*The encounter between the two ended too quickly. I turned to the woman beside me, waiting for an explanation.*

*"Do not forget this moment, Malachi Weyland," the woman said. "You will see me again, and you'll help me save the world when you do. But you must be careful."*

*"Careful? Why?"*

*"Many people will have a target on my back. Many people will want to take my life. Some your enemies, some your friends."*

*My jaw tightened.*

*"Who are you?" I asked again.*

*The woman, shining with a light from somewhere within her and practically glistening against the sun with her beauty, only laughed. "I am your wife, Malachi. My name is Jade Weyland."*

"Wake up, dammit!" Cordelia's voice pulled me out of my memory.

She and Esther leaned over me as I woke up, they both breathed a sigh of relief when I opened my eyes.

"What's going on?" I pushed myself up to my elbows. We were still in the gallery of the arena. Still surrounded by Paragon members. Still with Silas. "What happened?"

The two witches looked at each other before returning their gazes to me. Shit. That couldn't be good.

Silas moved in the corner of my eye. He ran his hands across his head and shoved the black hood down, exposing his face. He was smiling.

Definitely not good.

"Is Jade alive?" I asked.

"Jade is fine," Esther answered. Cordelia sat back on her heels, jaw set. "The trials are going as planned." Esther sent a strange glare to Silas.

Going as planned? As in, Jade was being exploited for her magic?

"Explain," I mumbled.

"Maybe you should get some rest," Cordelia chimed in. "You're clearly being affected by these trials."

Affected by the trials? How would I be...

I remembered the darkness, the fighting to breathe.

Jade leaned over me, pleading with someone. It hurt to see her that way. I knew that feeling all too well. I wouldn't wish that upon her. Not ever.

"I died in Jade's trial," I guessed. The look on their faces confirmed.

Silas sauntered over to us, finally peeling his eyes from Jade down in the arena. I hated that he even looked at her. "Quite a turn of events, isn't it?" Silas sneered. "Jade is the one in the trials, yet somehow, you're being physically affected."

I jumped to my feet, ignoring the dizziness that followed. "You're behind this somehow," I argued. "What are you doing to her? What are you doing to me?"

He laughed, and I never wanted to punch him in the face more. "That's the intriguing part, really. I'm not doing anything." He stepped closer to me. "This is all on you."

I clenched my fists at my sides as my mind began to churn through the possibilities. I could feel what was happening in Jade's trial. The trials weren't real, they weren't physical challenges. Would Jade feel the physical effects? Yes. That's what made them so dangerous. But for others to feel it? For the mere figments of her imagination to feel the side effects?

Impossible.

That is, it should have been impossible. But clearly something terrible had just happened. I saw it in my vision, and Silas confirmed it now.

"What did she do?" I asked Silas.

Silas stared me straight in the eye while that wicked, arrogant smile grew on his face. He stared at me without talking until I was sure I was going to rip his head off.

But then he said, "The power of life, Malachi. Your wife brought you back."

# CHAPTER 30
# Jade

My face rested against a cold surface when I woke up. I didn't know how long I stayed like that—listening to the sound of my breath. Not opening my eyes.

I didn't want to know what reality looked like. That trial...it felt so real. So painful.

When I had the strength, I rolled onto my back. I cracked my eyes open to see nothing but darkness above. Darkness, and that small, shimmering corner of the arena.

My hand drifted to my heart and rested there, feeling my heartbeat. It was real. This was real, right?

The truth was, I wasn't sure. I wasn't sure what was real, if any of this was real. The more I tried to decipher the truth, the more pain I felt splitting through my head.

Warm blood trickled from my shoulder, reminding me of the deadling that bit me there. Pain began to radiate down my arm, sharp and fierce. His teeth had dug into me, and in the adrenaline of the moment, I barely noticed. Barely cared.

I looked down to see the row of disgusting, jagged teeth marks denting my skin, red with blood.

A single tear slid down my cheek.

I wanted to cry more, to heal that crack I felt in my chest. But my mouth grew dry as cotton, and I wasn't sure I had it in me to shed another tear.

What was the point? What was the point of any of this? Did they really think I was going to let Malachi kill me in that damned trial? Roll over and let the fae take my life?

Of course they did. They wanted to see me as weak, as defeatable.

Saints. If Silaș had a mission to make me look out of control with my power, I imagined it was working.

I could see it now. The black-hooded figures of the Paragon laughing and chatting about how I tried to kill them all...how I couldn't see the greater good.

If the greater good had to do with Malachi wanting me dead, I didn't want any part of it.

A fresh wave of grief washed over me.

It was all so terribly wrong. My thoughts mixed and swirled together, images of what I perceived as reality washed through my mind. Malachi would never hurt me. Never. He would cut down anyone who lifted a finger against me.

So why did I see *that*? Why would the Paragon want me to see Malachi against me?

Against me and dying in my arms.

I couldn't believe it. I begged for him to come back, and just when I thought I had lost him for good, he came back to me.

I wasn't sure which Saint had blessed us enough to help, but I was damn grateful for it.

*That was no Saint, girl,* a voice pierced through my mind, echoing within my skull. My hands immediately clamped on my temples.

"What?" I asked.

*You're the one who brought the King of Shadows back.*

*No. This isn't real. None of this is real.* I must still be in the trials. "Who are you?" I asked. "What do you mean *I* brought him back?"

Silence.

*Your power is one of life, child. You willed him to come back, and so he did.*

"No," I said out loud this time. "That's not true. If I could bring people back with mere will, my sister would not be dead!"

*You were human when your sister died. You've passed onto something else, something with more power.*

The female voice sounded steadfast and calm, even with my rising agitation.

"I...I couldn't have." I couldn't have. Right? "I cannot resurrect from the dead. That is impossible."

Although I couldn't hear it, I felt the presence of laughter and amusement somewhere in the echoes of my mind.

*The peacemaker, they call you. Do you want to know what we call you, Jade Weyland?*

"Who is *we*?" More amusement came from the space neither here nor there.

*We*, the voice continued, *are the five Saints that walked before you. We are the powerful beings that once ruled these lands. And we've been waiting for you, Jade Weyland.*

My mind spun, too much pain. Too much confusion. Too much fog.

*Vita Queen*

"What?"

*The queen of life. Vita Queen. That is who you are, Jade. That is who you will rise to become.*

I felt a strong, overwhelming need to protect myself. To get away from the voice, to end it all.

This had to be part of the...part of the trial? Right? That someone was testing me, someone wanted me to be tricked by the voice.

"Stop!" I yelled. I pushed myself up to my knees, peering into the darkness. "Just stop!"

My power came easily. Effortlessly. In fact, when the darkness around me became nothing but white, blinding power, I did not try to stop it. I did not try to pull back my power.

I blasted it until I had nothing left, had no voice left to scream. Had no energy left to fight. I blasted and blasted and blasted my power out around me until the source of it, deep in my soul and burning like fire, had depleted itself entirely.

And then I laid down, placing my head back down on the cold stone floor.

I couldn't stay awake any longer. I wanted it all to end, the pain, the torture.

I closed my eyes and filled my thoughts with images of Malachi until darkness silenced the voices echoing through my skull.

# CHAPTER 31
# Malachi

Silas and the others retired for the evening. They had enough of staring and laughing at Jade—helpless and alone—in that arena, I supposed.

But I stayed. I wanted to be closer to her. I wanted her to feel me there somehow, to know that she wasn't really alone. She would never be alone again.

I stared into the arena, not caring that my eyes were dry and burning from staring for so long. I wasn't quite sure how much time had passed, anyway.

It didn't matter.

Jade slept on her stomach with her arm propped under her, the sword I gifted her beside her. Someone had brought her food, but she didn't touch it. I didn't blame her for that. The trials weren't exactly an appetite churner.

She looked so small in the large stone arena. So...fragile. Although I knew she wasn't fragile, not really. Especially if she wasn't human anymore.

Saints.

I had to get to her. I had to talk to her, at least to let her know that I was still here, I wasn't going anywhere. I was okay. I just had to get down to that arena door, and I could sneak in for only a minute.

I would have killed to have someone visit me during my trials. To know that I wasn't really going crazy, to know that it was almost over. I remembered the way I lost track of time. I wasn't sure if it had been days, weeks, or months since I experienced something real. Visions morphed with dreams. I wasn't even sure I was out of the trials until weeks later when the fog began to lift.

No. Jade didn't have to feel that way. I slid out of the gallery and into the dark hallway.

Silas wasn't stupid. He would have guards at the very least, ensuring that I didn't try to break her out.

He wasn't stupid. But neither was I.

I crept through the dark tunnels, only passing a few Paragon members. Like always, they kept to themselves, their hooded faces not even budging as I walked past.

The tunnels grew more and more narrow. I knew I was getting close. I could feel it, I could feel her, her pain and her hunger and her confusion. I walked faster until I turned left in the darkness.

"I know you're not this idiotic," Cordelia said.

Saints. She pushed herself off the tunnel wall ahead. "Why are you always lurking in the shadows, witch?" I asked.

"To save your ass from dooming us all!" she hissed. "What's your plan here, Malachi? Swoop in and carry your bride off into the sunset? I hate to break it to you, but the sun has already set."

"I'm not trying to escape with her," I explained. "I only want to talk to her."

She scoffed. "Like anyone will believe that."

"Well, aside from you, nobody else knows. And nobody else will know. It's harmless."

She took a long breath, her curious eyes blaring into mine. "You're asking her about your resurrection, aren't you?" she asked.

There was no point in lying. She could read my thoughts. It wasn't my goal to ask Jade about what happened during her last trial, but I couldn't deny that I was interested. Silas was interested, too, which put her in even more danger.

"I'm going to see my wife," I growled. I shoved past her and continued walking down the tunnel. Cordelia's hair-pulling footsteps lingered behind me.

"If you want to know what she's been thinking," she whispered as we turned down yet another tunnel, "you can ask me, you know."

*Ask her.* I didn't want her poking and prodding through Jade's thoughts. I didn't want her anywhere near Jade, actually. I didn't want anyone near Jade when she was like this, hurt and confused.

"I have no intentions to hurt the peacemaker," Cordelia said.

"Saints, you can be damn annoying. Did you know that?" I kept looking forward, but I imagined her shrugging and rolling her eyes behind me.

We reached the end of the tunnel. We were close, I could sense it. If I focused enough, I could even hear Jade's heartbeat, slow and steady and peaceful, even if it were just for a few moments.

"If you don't want my help, fine," she complained behind me. "But you will soon. And I'll be right here to laugh at you when you realize how big of a mess you've got on your hands. This way," she said. She switched directions, leading me through a tunnel I did not even know existed. The dark stone pathway became darker and darker until I saw a small crack in the stone. It had to be the opening.

"Go," Cordelia said, nodding toward the crack. I rushed forward and pushed it open. And the stone opened into the arena.

"Stay here," I ordered Cordelia. "I'll be right back." I didn't wait for her response before stepping into the arena and closing the door behind me.

"Jade," I whispered. She twitched lightly in response but didn't open her eyes. "Jade, it's me."

Again, she didn't move.

I moved to her side and knelt next to her. She looked so pale and skinny, as if she had been in this arena for weeks. Saints, I hated it. I hated all of it.

I reached out and tucked a piece of her black hair behind her ear. Only when my skin brushed hers did her eyes flutter open. She looked at me for a few seconds with absolutely no reaction, no recognition, nothing.

And those few seconds were enough to terrify me. "It's me, Jade."

Jade flinched and scrambled away from me, shrieking quietly with wide eyes. "Get away from me," she hissed.

I held my hands out in surrender, trying to hide the crack of emotion that pierced my chest. "It's me," I said again. "It's Malachi."

She shook her head violently, squeezing her eyes shut and pushing her palms against her temples. "This isn't real," she said, rocking back and forth on the stone ground. "This isn't real, this isn't real."

It took every ounce of control I possessed to stop myself from carrying her off that mountain. Whatever happened in that last trial had hurt her. Badly. Blood soaked he shoulder of her tunic, already drying against her skin.

"Look at me," I said softly. "Open your eyes and look at me."

We sat that way for a few minutes, Jade slowly pulling her hands away from her face as her breathing settled. It broke my heart to see her in so much pain.

"Do you remember me?" I asked.

"Malachi."

"Yes," I replied. "I'm your husband and I'm here to see you."

She pushed herself to a sitting position. Her brows drew together as she stared at me. "What are you doing here?" she asked. Saints, her *voice* even sounded weak.

"I came to check on you," I answered. "I came to make sure you were okay. You've been doing a great job, Jade. It's almost over."

Her attention shifted to the arena around us as she took it in. I watched a storm of emotions cross her eyes. "Is this real?" she asked.

I held her cold hands in mine. "This is real."

Without looking back at me, Jade began to laugh. It was a quiet laugh, a tired laugh, but a laugh nonetheless.

"Jade?"

She continued to laugh, but the sound of it only pained me. It wasn't a laughter of happiness. Not in the slightest. "You have one trial left, okay? One trial and this is all over."

"One trial left?" she asked.

"Yes."

She shook her head again, trying to hide from my words. "I've done them all," she replied. "I've done all the trials."

"You have one left. It will start tomorrow. Just hang on a bit longer, Jade, and when this is all over, we go back home."

Her eyes slid to mine. "Rewyth?"

"Yes, we can go back to Rewyth?" She smiled and shook her head. "What is it?" I asked.

"Sorry," she stammered. "Something someone else said. Not you."

"Someone else—what are you talking about, Jade? Who else have you been talking to?"

Her brows drew together again, and I watched as she took a breath and crumbled as she exhaled. "So many people. I can't tell if they're real."

Ah, the trials. "That's normal," I explained. "You'll be confused for a bit, and that's okay. When this is all over, I'll help you understand. I'll help you decipher what's real and what's not real. Okay?"

She tightened her grip on my hand. "I want to go home, Mal."

"I know you do."

"I don't want to do it again. I don't want you...I killed you, Mal. I killed you and you were dead."

The strain in her voice told me she was seconds from falling apart. And she couldn't afford to fall apart, not yet. Not when we were this close.

"Look at me," I said. I slid forward and gripped her small shoulders. "I am right here. I am alive and warm and with you. You cannot kill me. You'll never be able to kill me, Jade. Even if you could, I wouldn't let you. You and I are together now. Forever. Do you understand?"

Her eyes strained. "Yes, I understand."

"Good."

Jade attempted a smile, but damn. She looked so tired. I leaned forward and placed a gentle kiss on her forehead.

"The Saints don't need me to finish these trials," she whispered so quietly I barely heard her.

Time froze. "Why would you say that?" My heart pounded, every tendril in my chest tightening as soon as those words left her mouth.

"They told me," she replied. "The Saints told me this is just a show, and I must keep moving forward. But Mal, I don't know if I can do it again. It's all too much."

She began rocking again, her eyes focusing on something that didn't exist. She was confused. That was the only explanation for this. She couldn't decipher reality from visions.

"We're almost done with the trials, Jade," I said. "You have one left, and then we're out of here."

"One more trial," she repeated. "The Saints do not care for the trials."

A knock came from the stone door, causing her to jump. "Who is that?" Jade asked.

"That's Cordelia. It's time for me to go. Just hang in there, okay? I'm not going to let you die here, Jade. I swear it."

Jade nodded. I brushed a quick kiss onto her dry lips before I stood and left her, alone and exhausted, in the Paragon's arena.

Cordelia waited on the other side of the door, a knowing look on her face. "Don't say it," I growled before she could open her mouth.

She only smirked. "I don't have to. You already know I was right. And someone's coming."

Damn. Even with my fae ears, I could only pick up so much. Cordelia, though, could hear thoughts from a mile away if she wanted to. I suppose she had some useful qualities, although keeping her mouth shut wasn't one of them.

"Let's go," I said. I gripped her arm and dragged her through the tunnels into the darkness. We walked in silence until we reached the study.

"She loves you," Cordelia said. "I could feel it."

I scoffed, ignoring the first part of her statement. "Feel it?" I questioned. "Or did you peer into her mind again and dig around as you pleased?"

"Does it matter? She loves you, Malachi, and that trial nearly killed her."

I slammed my hands down on the wooden table. "What do you expect me to do about it, Cordelia? I can't escape with her, you said so yourself. I don't see a choice here!"

She stepped forward, unfazed by my outburst. "Answer me honestly, Malachi. Do you think she'll survive another trial? After what happened to her in the last one? After what happened to you?"

No, I wanted to say. Jade was losing her grip on reality. She wouldn't survive a third trial. I could tell simply by looking at her.

Jade was losing her mind.

"Get to your point," I barked.

"You know what I'm thinking. There's one person in this entire temple who benefits from this."

*Silas.* And what if what Jade said was true? What if the Saints did not actually need her to complete the trials? What if this entire charade existed for Silas's wicked games?

Cordelia tilted her head. "My offer still stands. We can kill him and get Jade off this mountain before he can cause any more damage. He's killing her, Malachi." She turned to leave the library. A desperate, clawing feeling gnawed at my chest as I watched her walk away.

This was my chance. I had wanted to kill Silas for decades now. If Cordelia truly had a way to do it...

Her eyes met mine, determined and angry.

I had to save Jade's life.

"What's your plan?"

# CHAPTER 32
# *Jade*

My third trial would start soon. That's what Mal had said, right? That I had already completed two. I just had...I just had one left.

*That was real, right? Mal was really here?*

I brushed my fingers across my lips. The kiss felt real. His hands on my face felt real.

Then again, him dying before me felt real, too. And it wasn't. At least...I didn't think it was...

That stone door opened, and the young boy from earlier walked inside. "I'm not hungry," I said before he entered.

He walked in anyway, carrying the same small plate in his hands. He shut the stone door behind him before moving to set it down next to me.

"I have to bring you the food anyway, miss. It's my job."

"Really?" I asked. My voice was dry, and I realized then how thirsty I had been. "You have quite a peculiar job, don't you think?"

The young boy shrugged. His dark hair had been shaved recently, I caught myself wondering what it looked like before. "I don't mind," he said. "I'm usually bored."

"Huh," I sighed. I couldn't bring myself to say anything else.

The boy stared at me with pure curiosity. "Are you a fae?" he asked.

I laughed, it felt like the first time I had laughed in ages. "No," I answered. "I'm not fae."

"Then what are you doing here?" he asked.

What was I doing here? Saints, I wished I had an answer for that. "Someone wants to see how much power I possess," I said.

"Oh, so you're a witch?"

I shook my head. "I don't think so, kid."

He stared at me for a few more seconds, rocking back and forth on his feet. "I should go," he said. "I'm not really supposed to be talking to you."

"What's your name, kid?" I asked. I shouldn't have. I instantly regretted it. The second I knew this kid's name, I would actually care. And caring about anyone but Malachi in this damned temple was a death wish.

But the boy's eyes lit up, as if nobody had ever asked him that before. "Dragon," he answered.

My eyes widened. "Dragon? That's an interesting name."

He nodded while the grin on his face grew.

"Well," I said. "I'm not going to eat this." I pushed the small plate of bread toward him. His eyes instantly widened. "Would you like to help me with it?"

Dragon couldn't help the smile that lit up his face. I couldn't help but wonder how long it had been since he ate a proper meal. Was anyone looking out for him here?

He slowly picked up a piece of bread, as if confirming that I really wanted him to have it. I nodded at him, and he scarfed the entire piece down in less than two seconds.

I smiled so wide, my lips cracked. "It was very nice to officially meet you, Dragon. I hope we can talk again when I get out of here."

He turned on his heel and walked toward the door, swallowing his food. It wasn't until he had one hand on the stone that he turned to face me, eyes bright and hopeful. "I can help you, you know," he said. "I know a way out of here."

"I—what did you just say?"

"If you want to, I mean. I don't think it's very nice that you have to stay down here. You're dirty, and you kind of stink."

The weight of his words bubbled in my chest. "You can get me out of here? Without anyone knowing?"

The boy nodded. It was ridiculous, trusting a child. But then again, this entire situation was ridiculous. Thinking I could survive another trial was even more ridiculous.

I could get out of here. I could find Mal and get off this damned mountain.

And I didn't see another option.

I squeezed my eyes shut and tried to focus. This wasn't another trial, was it? This was real?

"Okay," I said to the boy. "But the man I came here with? My husband? We have to find him first."

The boy thoughtfully considered my words, his gaze falling to his feet, before he asked, "Do you know where he is, miss?"

*Yes,* I wanted to say. I knew where Malachi was. He would be somewhere in this temple waiting for me, waiting for the next trial, or maybe planning our escape.

But the truth was, I didn't really know where Malachi went. This temple was massive with endless amounts of winding tunnels and turns. I would get lost in a heartbeat.

"No," I answered. "No, I don't know where he is. He's somewhere under this mountain."

"I'll find him," the boy said. "Wait here in case they come to check on you. I'll find your husband with the black wings and I'll bring him with us."

Joy bubbled in my chest, joy and something else, something cruel and delightful. Hope.

"Okay," I nodded, not able to contain my smile. "Okay, Dragon. That sounds like a great plan."

I turned around and walked back to the arena, no longer terrified that I wouldn't survive. No longer fearful of what I could not see.

*Vita Queen.*

I ignored the female voice that echoed through my mind again as the boy closed the stone arena door behind himself.

*Vita Queen,* it said again.

"What?" I hissed. "What do you want from me?"

*I want you to stop running away from who you are, child. Leaving this place will not solve your problems.*

"Do not take offense to this, but I hardly think you'd know what will and will not solve my problems."

I waited for an argument, but the calm, steady voice said nothing.

# CHAPTER 33
# Malachi

THERE WERE TWO TIMES IN MY LIFE WHERE I HAD ATTEMPTED TO KILL Silas. The first was ages ago, the first week he had brought me to the temple.

I did not plan on killing him. But the younger me had a bad temper, even worse than the temper I had now. And Silas, as self-righteous and all-knowing as he was, pissed me off like no other.

We had been training, and I was just beginning to understand the potential of what my power could do. I had brought down a few grown men at that point, and I knew I could take Silas. He wasn't the height of most grown men, anyway. He was so scrawny, so old.

So, one day, while we were sparring after dinner, I threw all my magic at him. I mustered up every ounce of strength I possibly could, determined to kill that man. Determined to bring him to his knees and more.

But of course, it was useless.

I didn't know it at the time, but Silas could not be killed. *Why?* I still wasn't entirely sure. I had built up my theories over the years, of course, but they were just that. Theories. Cursed by the Saints, I thought. Perhaps he made a deal and sold his soul. That option made plenty of sense. Or, maybe it was his magic. Maybe his magic had created an impenetrable force, saving his life every time a fae like me tried to take it.

It didn't make sense.

The second time I tried to kill Silas was one week before I left the mountain. I had seen what he was doing. He wanted power more than anything, and everything about him was so fake. He kept the peace, he would claim. He creates equality between fae and witches, balancing the power.

I knew how much bullshit that was the first time I heard it. I just had no idea it would all come down to this—to my wife risking her life to prove that she was the most powerful one here. Not him.

Jade would change the world. Not him.

Jade was blessed by the Saints.

Not him.

"You're sure this will work?" I asked. Esther stared at me with a blank face. When Cordelia first insisted that we needed her to move forward, I shut the idea down.

But even though Esther had lied to me, she did know Silas more than anyone here. Including me.

Her eyes focused on something that wasn't there. "It will work," she replied, her voice barely a whisper.

"If this goes wrong, it's all of our lives on the line. Including Jade's," I said.

Cordelia scoffed from the back of the room. "I think your wife is perfectly safe, Malachi. Silas's power will be no match for hers."

"I'm not particularly excited to find that out," I replied. It was possible. In fact, somewhere inside myself I knew Jade would become stronger than Silas. But did Jade know that? Did Jade believe in herself enough to stand up against him alone?

"And you're sure you're up for this?" Cordelia asked Esther. "This can't be undone, Esther. Once we begin the ritual..."

"I'm sure," Esther said. She took a long, shaking breath. Her eyes had dark shadows under them, and her face had sunken in slightly, her cheekbones jutting out. "He wasn't always this way, you know," she said. "In the beginning, he truly wanted peace."

"I find that hard to believe," I scoffed.

"It wasn't until he got a taste of power that he wanted more. When I found out I was pregnant with you..." She trailed off, a ghost of a smile flickering onto her face. "When I knew you were on the way, I knew I had to get out of there. You were going to be a powerful fae, I could feel it in my bones. But he had already been showing signs of hunger for power. One night, when Silas had left the mountain on some sort of mission, I wrapped you in my arms and left. And I did not see him again until he came for you all those years later in Rewyth."

*Saints.* Part of me already knew this story, had pieced together the parts that made sense. I clenched my fists and shook the memories away. The past wasn't going to help me today.

I pushed myself up from the table, tearing my gaze away from Esther's sea-filled eyes. "Stick to the plan. We all must be fully committed in order for this to work. This could be our only chance at getting rid of him for good. Let's get this over with."

The others were silent as I walked out of the room and into the tunnels, aiming for one thing.

*My wife.*

Our bond grew stronger with every step I took. She was close, so close that I had to remind my power that we would save her. We would protect her.

"I'm coming for you, Jade," I whispered to myself, hoping that somehow she would know. Somehow she could sense me.

Cordelia followed tightly on my footsteps. This was the first portion of the plan, to get Jade. This was also the most important part, and frankly, it was the only part I cared about.

When we came to the stone door of the arena, I didn't hesitate. I had so much adrenaline pumping through my body that it took only a single shove to open, and we were inside.

My fae eyes quickly adjusted to the darkness. "Jade?" I asked. She flinched—painful and soul-aching—away from my voice.

Those damn trials.

"You're okay now," I said softly, taking a step in her direction. She looked at me as if she were staring at her enemy.

"Get away from me," she whispered.

I dropped to my knees next to her. I wanted to give her time. I wanted to explain that I was real, the trials were fake. I wanted to be gentle.

But we were running out of time. We had a small window to escape, and that window closed with every passing second.

"Jade, look at me." Her glazed eyes scanned the room frantically, not settling on any one thing. I grabbed her head with my hands and forced her to look into my eyes. "You're safe, Jade. We're getting you out of here."

"No," she repeated. "This isn't real. It's not real."

"It is real. We're going to kill Silas. We need to get out of here before the other Paragon members realize what's happening."

She pulled out of my grasp and began shaking her head. "She said this would happen."

"Who?"

"That Saint. She told me I would be tested and that I, and that I had to remain true. *Straight ahead*, she said."

Saints, I had no clue what she was talking about. She shook with a nervousness I had never seen before. "When did you talk to a Saint?"

A harsh laugh escaped her. "More like the Saint talking at me. She's not a great listener."

I gripped her face again. "Listen to me, Jade. Whoever you've been talking to doesn't understand what's happening right now. You and I are going back to Rewyth. We're going home."

Her brows drew together. "Rewyth?"

"Yes, Jade. Come with me now or I'll have to throw you over my shoulder and carry you out."

Her hands came up to hold my wrists. "You're dead," she whispered. "I killed you."

"No," I said. "That was part of your trial. It wasn't real, Jade. It was all in your head."

"I...I can't tell. I can't tell what's real, Malachi. I don't even know if this is real."

I brought my lips to hers and kissed her, fierce and quick. She seemed confused at first, but quickly began moving her mouth against mine.

"I'm real. I'm here, and I'll never leave you. This is happening. Do you trust me?"

Her lip quivered. "I trust you."

I picked up the sword I had given her and secured it at my hip. "Good. Now let's go."

"Wait!"

*Saints.* "What's wrong?"

"There's a little boy, he told me he could help us. He told me he knew a way out of here."

"A way off the mountain?"

"Yes. We can't leave without him, Mal. He's lonely and he doesn't deserve to stay here with these people. He said he could help us get out of here."

"Where is this boy?"

Her eyes unfocused. "I don't know."

I ran my hands through my hair in an attempt to straighten my thoughts. "We can't wait, Jade. If we see him on our way out we can take him with us, but it's too risky. I won't put you in danger again."

Her eyes held mine for a few moments, and I could almost feel the turmoil inside of her. If this boy even existed, Jade wouldn't be able to leave him.

I grabbed her hand and intertwined our fingers. "Let's go, my queen. Cordelia is waiting."

This time, when I pulled her hand to follow me, she didn't object. One obstacle down. Dozens to go.

The tunnels remained quiet, our labored breaths were the only sounds echoing off the mountain stone walls. That, and our constant footsteps, one after the other, over and over again.

"Where is everyone?" Jade whispered. "Shouldn't there be guards or something?"

*Yes. This was all too easy.* Finding Jade, the silence, the lack of Paragon members in the halls.

Something was off.

"Stay behind me," I ordered.

Without the boy that Jade said somehow knew a way out of here, there was only one other survivable way off this mountain. And it was the same way we had entered it, in the middle of the dining room with a wide open view.

If anyone was there to stop us, it would be nearly impossible to escape without a fight.

But I was ready for a fight. Saints, I had been ready for a fight for decades now.

My grip on Jade tightened, unfaltering. My black wings tucked as tight as possible behind my shoulders.

Something waited for us. I could feel it, like a tether of adrenaline and anticipation, but not from me. Not from Jade, either. Her emotions felt sweeter in my body. This was the anticipation of the Paragon, of our enemies.

As if on cue, Esther jumped into view. I nearly ran directly into her in the confines of the tunnels.

"What in the Saints is—" Silas stepped into the tunnel after her. His body practically buzzed with anger as he realized what we were doing. The air stilled around us.

Jade tensed behind me. I would be damned if I let him hurt her again.

"We're leaving," I said, loud enough that my voice echoed through the stone walls.

Confusion, anger, and resentment morphed together in flashes on Silas's face. Enough to where I was already drawing my sword, already summoning my magic.

I saw Cordelia duck out of the way from the corner of my eye.

*Saints save us, we were really doing this.*

I needed to distract him. Esther and Cordelia would do their ritual to bring him as close to death as possible. All I needed to do was distract him long enough.

"Get back, Jade," I ordered.

I widened my wingspan, filling the tunnel from wall to wall to shield her.

But Silas clearly did not care. His magic, dark and sinful, pulsed through the tunnels. Not directed at me. Not directed at Cordelia.

Directed at Jade standing behind me.

A scream of pain escaped her, and I didn't have to turn around to know she had fallen to her knees.

I roared, angry, desperate, and sick of this bastard ruining my life. Sword out, I charged him.

Silas, though, wielding the power of Erebus, only held out one palm. One motion with his hand, and I froze in time.

I couldn't move an inch. I could hardly breathe.

Jade stopped screaming, though. Silas apparently could not focus on us both.

"You thought this would work?" Silas growled. Esther moved behind him. I didn't look away from his empty, evil eyes. "You cannot kill me!"

I tried to thrash against his invisible grip, but I didn't budge an inch.

"You deserve worse than death," I managed to get out.

Esther and Cordelia began to chant.

It was a blood-chilling, repetitive, demonic chant. One I did not even wish to understand. Cordelia and Esther had only discussed it vaguely before, and I was the furthest thing from interested in whatever sacrifice they were about to make.

Silas's grip on me disappeared.

I stepped back, putting space between Silas and myself and getting as close as possible to Jade behind me.

"What are you–" Silas was interrupted by his own scream as the chanting increased, echoing off the stone walls and creating a chamber of magic.

Of witch magic.

It only lasted a few seconds, but it felt like hours. Days. The chanting was endless. I barely noticed Esther pulling out a dagger, the dagger that would entrap Silas, the dagger that would remove his immortal ability.

Would it outright kill him? No.

But he would be very close to dead with no magic, no power. And we would never see him again.

Jade mumbled something behind me.

"What?" I asked, turning to see what she was talking about.

She only shook her head, and we both turned in time to see Esther slam the dagger down into Silas's heart.

The chanting stopped.

Esther, who I expected to show some signs of remorse, only stared at him with clenched fists and dark eyes.

Silas's body fell to the ground, eyes wide. I wondered what was going through his mind in that moment, what he was thinking. *Did he regret it? Underestimating us?*

Thinking Cordelia and Esther would defend him?

Thinking I wouldn't try to end him? To save my wife?

I hoped so.

His eyes glossed over, his head hit the stone.

He could not talk. He could barely breathe.

Small footsteps approached, quickly enough to tell me someone ran in our direction.

I pulled Jade's body closer to me just in time for the small boy that delivered my message from Serefin to step into the tunnels.

"This way!" he yelled in a hushed whisper. "We have to go! Now!"

Esther and Cordelia glanced at each other, not moving. I didn't move, either. Did this boy realize what just happened?

Jade let go of my hand and pushed herself in front of me. "Dragon!" she yelled. She knelt before him and held his hands in hers. He smiled at her, warm and genuine. "Are you sure you know the way out of here?" Jade asked him.

His eyes glanced to the three of us who now stood behind Jade, waiting. He stared at us all for a few seconds before nodding.

"Good," Jade said, giving him a reassuring smile. She stood and turned to us, still holding his hand. "This is Dragon," she announced. "He's coming with us, and he knows the way off this mountain."

"Thank the Saints for that," Cordelia mumbled.

"Come on," Esther said. "Let's leave him here to rot before he can cause any more damage for us."

# CHAPTER 34

## *Jade*

**Malachi, Dragon, Cordelia, Esther, and I huddled together** around our dwindling fire, attempting to shield ourselves from the wicked weather of the blizzard-filled mountain. We had managed to climb far enough down the mountain that the assortment of trees now partially hid us, creating cover while we rested up for the remainder of our journey.

"We should have dragged one of those wind-wielding Paragon members with us. Would have really come in handy right about now," Cordelia said.

"You're the witch," I replied. "Can't you and Esther pull your magic together and do something?"

"After what we did to Silas back there?" Cordelia replied. "Not likely."

"We have to save our strength," Malachi chimed in. "This fire is warm enough. In two days, we'll be warm in our beds at Rewyth."

*Rewyth.* The sound of the name on Malachi's tongue was enough to warm me from the inside. I leaned over and rested my head on his shoulder, holding my bare hands out to the flames in front of me.

"This feels like a fever dream," I said. "I can't believe we made it out. I can't believe Silas is dead."

"Dead enough," Esther said. It was the first time she had spoken since we left the temple.

"As far as we're concerned, he isn't our problem anymore," Mal said.

The howling wind overtook the conversation, which was a relief. I didn't want to talk about Silas. I didn't want to talk about how we practically killed the man who could not be killed.

And I certainly did not want to talk about the damn trials.

Malachi's wings curled around us, blocking our bodies from the cold. His presence at my side was the thing I needed more than warmth, more than the fire, more than hope itself.

"We should all get some sleep," Cordelia said after a while. "I'll keep first watch. We'll need our energy if the Paragon decides to come after us."

"The Paragon is nothing without Silas," Mal said. "We'll be safe. But you're right, we need to rest."

Dragon had already half-drifted to sleep closest to the fire, nuzzled against Esther as if his life depended on it.

Esther didn't seem to mind, though. She rested her head against his, eyes watching the flames as if she expected to get some answers from them.

"You need sleep," Malachi said, low enough that only I could hear.

"I don't think sleep is coming to me any time soon," I replied. "My mind won't rest."

His hand ran up the length of my arm, a delicate, loving touch. "This is all real," he answered. "This is all happening. I'll remind you of that every minute of every day if I have to."

I exhaled a long breath, letting his words sink in. After what happened to him during my trial, I wanted to soak in every single moment like this. I never wanted to forget how it felt with his arm around my body, with his sweet words meant just for me lingering in my ears.

"I understand now," I breathed.

"Understand what?"

"I understand how scary it was for you. When I died that night in Rewyth. When you held me as the life faded from my veins, wondering if there was anything you could possibly do to get me back. I get it now."

His calming hand on my shoulder stilled. "You brought me back in your trial," he said. It wasn't a question.

"Yes."

"When that happened, when I died in your visions, I felt it," he said. "I could feel the pain, physically in my body. I couldn't breathe. I couldn't think."

My heart stopped beating. "You could feel what was happening to you? I thought you weren't supposed to be affected, nobody but me was supposed to feel those things."

He shook his head. "I wasn't. But I did. It's our magic, Jade. Life and death, connected for eternity. I can feel you, you can feel me. When you brought me back to life during your trial that day, *Saints.*" His voice trailed off as he dragged his free hand down his face. I twisted in his arms, looking up at him with intense eyes.

The light from the fire reflected off his now-pale skin. I watched as his nostrils flared, his eyes searching in the darkness for answers that weren't there. But I knew the answers. I knew what Mal was about to say.

"I brought you back, too," I finished.

His eyes snapped to mine. "You did," he confirmed.

I breathed deeply. "How? How is this possible?"

"It must have been some awakening when Esther brought you back from death. You're different now, Jade. They say you're not human anymore. This could change everything for you."

A quiet laugh escaped me. "I can't even say I'm surprised," I admitted. "With everything that's happened to us, it wouldn't even surprise me if I grew wings out of my back tomorrow."

Mal's black wings flickered in response. "That would be a sight," he growled in my ear.

He placed a delicate kiss on my cheek, warming the skin there. I gripped the front of his shirt with my hands, pulling him closer, taking him in.

*Wings would suit you,* the voice dormant in my mind said. I jumped at the sound of it, almost forgetting that someone or something had been speaking to my mind.

"How long did it take you?" I asked Mal, "When you completed the trials, how long did it take you to know what was real?"

He shrugged. "Some days I still have to remind myself."

Great, so I would have to listen to this insane voice for the rest of my days?

"Have you ever..." I started. I wanted to ask him about the voice, about the Saint who claimed to be speaking to me. I wanted to ask him if he had ever spoken to a Saint, had ever known someone who had. Because I needed some sort of validation that I was not, in fact, crazy. That I wasn't actually losing my mind. But what would he think? What if I really was just going crazy? He would worry, even more than he already did—which was saying a lot. "Never mind," I said instead.

He only pulled me further into his chest, letting me rest my head against his warm body. "Sleep," he insisted. "Your worries will still be here in the morning, too."

Nothing had ever been more true. I took one last glance at Esther and Dragon, both fast asleep, and one last glance at Cordelia, who sharpened her dagger with her back to the fire, before closing my eyes.

Your worries will still be here in the morning.

"Thank you, Mal," I whispered with my eyes closed.

"Why are you thanking me?"

"For not leaving me. For dragging yourself to that temple with me when you didn't have to. For backing me up always, even when I'm not right."

I felt him smile. "Always," he said.

Sleep came swiftly.

R*un.*

*Get up.*

*Run.*

My eyes shot open. We were still in the dark forest, the sun was just beginning to rise in the distance. "What?" I asked aloud.

Malachi was already staring at me, worry in his eyes. "I didn't say anything," he said. "Bad dream?"

*Run. Get out of here.*

That calming female voice now practically yelled against my skull. "Wake up!" I yelled to everyone. "Wake up, we have to go! Now!"

Everyone woke up slowly, but nobody moved. Nobody ran. "Jade, what are you talking about?" Malachi asked.

I jumped to my feet and pulled him after me. I didn't know which direction to run, I wasn't even sure what I was running from. But I could feel that thread of fear pulling me to move, to act. "She told me to run, Mal, we have to–"

The next words escaped me. Every inch of my body pricked with adrenaline as a few snow-covered twigs snapped in the distance.

Someone—or something—was coming.

"Run!" I hissed, and they actually listened this time. Everyone sprang to their feet, desperate as I was to get away from whatever approached in the distance.

"Let's go!" Malachi ordered in a hushed whisper. "Head down the mountain, go!" We waited until the others were in front of us, Dragon holding tightly to Esther's hand, before we followed suit.

"What is that?" I whispered over my shoulder to Mal. "Did someone follow us here?"

"I don't know," Mal replied. "But I'm not sure I want to find out."

We half-ran, half-stumbled down the mountain. It wasn't until Esther and Dragon stopped dead in their tracks that we halted, too.

"What's wrong?" I yelled to them.

Esther held a hand out in waiting.

One painful second passed.

Two seconds.

I was about to urge them all to keep moving forward when that same voice echoed in my mind, *Now you fight.*

And then chaos.

Cordelia yelled first—a battle cry filled with anger and frustration.

And then deadlings came into view, one at a time. They weren't moving quickly, but they were certainly targeting us.

Cordelia cut one down with her sword.

Then another, slicing its head clean from its body.

Esther pulled her dagger out and shoved Dragon behind, pushing him safely in the center of our circle.

Mal and I both spun around.

We were surrounded.

Deadlings came at us from every direction, slowly clawing and barring their razor-sharp teeth as they moved after one thing—our flesh.

Mal drew his sword next to me.

"Shit," he said. "I've had enough of these damned creatures." He stepped forward and sliced down, cutting through two bodies and watching them fall into the snow.

"Damn Silas!" Cordelia yelled as she killed another. "He couldn't have taken these rancid things with him when he died?"

"What are you talking about?" I asked. My power prepared itself within me, ready to take out all of them if I had to. As long as I knew the others were safe...

"Silas is the one controlling these damn things! His disgusting little pets," Cordelia answered.

I replayed those words in my mind, ensuring I heard them correctly. Silas was the one controlling them?

"What do you mean, *Silas controls them*?" Mal sliced down another.

Cordelia did the same. "I mean, he controls them! His wicked magic blood or something. He's the one that makes them attack in numbers."

Anger washed over me—hot and feral—as I realized exactly what she was saying. All those times the deadlings came to Rewyth, all those times they attacked, all those times they randomly showed up in mass numbers.

It was no mere accident.

Malachi had told me once that something must control them, something must tell them to attack as if they were a controlled army.

Now it all made sense. This was his last attack, his last piece of damage in our lives.

"His dying wish was to make these creatures kill us all?" Malachi growled. He must have felt the anger, too, because with one swing of his sword he cut through four deadling bodies.

"He can damn well try," I mumbled. "Cover them, Mal! Now!"

I didn't have to explain further. He knew exactly what was about to happen. I gave Mal a few seconds to duck behind me and flare his wings out, covering the three with his large wingspan.

And then I took a long, calming breath, fueling that anger and frustration into one place. Into one overwhelmingly hot, fiery place deep in my soul. My power responded with a flicker of delight, ready to act however I willed it too.

I didn't even realize I was screaming, not until my magic poured from me like blood, lighting up the icy forest around us. I held it there, letting it pull from that place of anger and betrayal and hatred, until I finally felt like myself again.

And then I pulled it all back.

"Saints," Cordelia muttered from behind me.

I turned around to find them unharmed, each with open mouths as they surveyed the area around us.

All except Malachi, who stared at me with an adoration that made my toes curl in my boots.

"Amazing," he said, his dark eyes filled with a primal heat under his thick lashes. "Absolutely stunning."

And for the first time in a long time, I actually felt that way. I looked around us, at the piles of ash that were left in the place of the deadlings. It had been so easy to kill them all, so easy to tear down our enemy.

I lifted my chin. It hadn't been that long ago that I was the helpless, poor girl who could do nothing but scream in the face of danger.

Not anymore. My enemies would turn to ash before me. My challengers would meet the Saints before they ever drew my blood.

Malachi knew this, too. He rose and stood beside me, placing a hand on my shoulder.

*Vita Queen,* the voice whispered, so quietly I almost didn't hear it.

Malachi's breath tickled my ear as he whispered, "You'll bring entire kingdoms to their knees, my queen."

The warm kiss on my temple was enough to send a thrill of fire through my body. That, and the unsettling truth of his words.

Entire kingdoms on their knees.

For Mal, I would deliver any kingdom. If power was what he wanted...

I would be the one to give it to him.

# CHAPTER 35
# Malachi

Silas controlled them. It made so much sense, I grew more and more angry with each passing minute that I hadn't figured it out sooner.

Of course, Silas controlled those creatures. They were spiteful and disgusting, just like him. Hopefully with him dying, the deadlings would no longer be a problem. If we were lucky, he would already be dead.

Jade walked in front of me, not the slightest bit weary from using her power. It was unheard of to have an ability like that, to turn an entire army of deadlings to ash.

It wouldn't be just deadlings, either. She could kill anyone she wanted to, anything that rose against her.

My chest swelled with pride. She was much more powerful than I was, that much was clear to anyone who paid a single second of attention.

She felt it, too. She felt power. I could feel the tiny bead of emotion deep in my core, my lifeline to her that was growing stronger and stronger with each day we spent together. It was almost as if I could read her thoughts, could sense what she was going to do before she did it.

And when she used her power without holding back, without fear of what might happen, Saints, she was marvelous.

"We have to be getting close," Esther sighed. "Rewyth isn't more than a two day's walk from the temple."

"You would know," I sneered. "Tell me, how long have you been traveling back and forth from these woods to meet with him? How long have you been spying on us for his benefit?"

She stopped dead in her tracks, and the others continued as I nearly tripped over her. For the first time that I could remember, anger lit up her eyes. "Have I not proved my loyalty to you?" she hissed in a whisper. "I helped you kill him. I..."

"You what? You loved him? Is that what you're going to say? Because considering your ability to betray him so easily, I'm not too sure about that."

"Easily?" She scoffed. "You think the choice I made came easily, son?" She shook her head and broke our eye contact, smiling at something imaginary. "You know nothing about the choices I've had to make."

"I think I know enough to know that I would never betray Jade. Not if it cost me everything."

"And what if it cost you your child?" she asked. The words were unexpected, they hit me with a force like a punch. "What if you had to choose between the one you loved lifetimes ago, and the one you love now?"

Shit. My mother had done plenty to prove her loyalty to myself and Jade, yet each time I began to trust her, something else happened. Some new information turned up.

Like the fact that Silas was my father, Erebus's blood ran through my veins.

I brushed past her and began walking after the group, slow enough that Esther could catch up. "He was evil and twisted," I muttered. "We're all better off now that he's gone. Including you." It was the closest thing to sympathy I could muster for her.

Esther stepped into stride beside me, feet crushing against the icy forest floor. "There's a reason I did what I did, son. I meant what I said about Jade being the peacemaker. She's going to change everything for us."

"If you know anything else about my wife, I suggest you tell me now."

Esther paused in a way that made my stomach drop. "You already know."

"Know what, exactly?"

I couldn't help but stare at Jade as I waited for Esther's response. My wife. Human. Magic. The peacemaker. Something else entirely. Esther once told me that Jade would save us all.

Maybe it was time for that. Maybe Jade really would save us all.

I had no doubt that she could do it.

"Jade has made it out of the trials, but there's still a great sacrifice that must be made," Esther replied. "The stories of what the peacemaker can do aren't stories with happy endings."

"You told me we could avoid this. You told me you would help us save Jade's life, that there was another way."

I couldn't even look at her. I was certain if I did, my world would erupt in anger. Esther was only alive, had only lasted this long because she held a promise. She would protect Jade from her fate. She would make it so Jade, as the peacemaker, would not have to sacrifice herself.

But now this?

"There is another way," Esther replied. "But that doesn't mean she will not suffer greatly."

I was about to lose my temper, was about to scream and demand that Esther tell me exactly what Jade needed to do, when Jade's voice interrupted my thoughts.

She still walked on ahead of us, and probably had forgotten that I could hear her low muttering with my fae ears.

"I can't do that," Jade whispered to herself. "I'll never be strong enough to restore the balance of power. They don't respect me. A year ago, I was nothing more than a useless human living in poverty."

Esther must have sensed this too, her magic allowing her to hear much further than a human.

"No, no," Jade argued with nobody. "They won't believe that. This is all insane, all part of my trial. Saints, get out of my head!"

My blood froze over, an eerie chill raising the hair on the back of my neck. Jade thought we were still in the trials?

"Stop here," I yelled loud enough for everyone to hear. "The sun is setting. Let's get some rest and finish the final journey to Rewyth tomorrow morning."

Saints. I hated that we were stopping for one more night, but I didn't hate it as much as what I had just heard coming from Jade's mouth.

Esther gave me a knowing look before walking away to talk to Dragon.

A bitter feeling grew in my chest watching them together. I was happy that Dragon was out of the temple. I was happy that he was being taken care of, and that Jade cared enough to try and save him.

But watching my mother take care of him when she did nothing but abandon me? I didn't expect it to upset me, but it did.

"What's going on?" Jade asked as she walked up. "If we walk through the night, we'll be there by sunrise."

The sun was beginning to drop below the horizon, nothing but a red glow in the distance giving us light.

"We need our rest," I said. "We don't know what we're coming home to, and I don't want to push you any harder than I already have."

The harshness in her face slipped away with each second that passed, replaced by heavy, tired features.

"Fine," she said. "Just for a few hours, though."

"Whatever you say, my queen."

She flashed me a mocking smile and turned to find a large tree trunk to lean against. It hurt me to see her grimace in pain, barely making it to the ground without releasing a grunt. She stuck her legs out, using her hands to help lift each one, before finally resting her head on the tree bark behind her.

"Come on," I said to the others. "Let's start a fire."

Nobody spoke as we collected wood, brushing off the dirt and throwing it into the pile. Even Cordelia kept her mouth shut, which could only mean she was far too exhausted for any snide remarks at this hour.

I didn't mind it, though. After everything we endured, a moment of silence was necessary. To gather my thoughts, to react from the chaos.

Even as we all found our place around the fire an hour later, we were silent. Nobody complained about the cold. Nobody complained about the hunger. We all sat still, staring into the fire.

I eventually looked up from the fire to see Jade staring at me from across the flames.

"Tell him," Cordelia said. She stared at Jade with her brows drawn. Jade ripped away from my gaze and shook her head.

"Stay out of my head," Jade mumbled, but her voice trailed off.

"Tell me what?" I pushed. Whatever Cordelia found by sniffing around in Jade's mind, it had to be important.

Cordelia only rolled her eyes and stood from her spot around the fire. "Come on," she said to Dragon and Esther. "These two lovebirds need to discuss something in private."

Esther and Dragon stood up silently, following Cordelia into the woods. Which was entirely pointless, by the way, because I knew they would be eavesdropping.

"What's going on?" I asked Jade. I moved to sit closer to her. "What do you need to tell me?"

"Cordelia's gift can be very annoying," Jade mumbled. "I didn't want to bring this up right now."

"It's okay," I reassured her. "We don't have to discuss anything you don't feel comfortable–"

Her hand fell onto my thigh. "No," she said. "It's okay." I waited in silence for her to continue. "During those trials, you were right. It all felt so real." Her voice cracked. I waited for her as she took a shaking breath and continued, "After I killed you, something changed. Something...something hardened inside of me. And that bond that connects us? The bond of life and death, or whatever you want to call it. It's stronger now. I can feel it so much more, even though you didn't really die."

I gripped her hand. "You were amazing in there, Jade. You brought me back. You saved me. I could feel your terror as if it were my own. I would trade places with you in a heartbeat if I could. You should never have to go through something like that."

She turned her body to me as her eyes searched my face. "You actually died?" she asked. "I really killed you?"

I placed my hands on the sides of her face and forced her to keep looking at me as I explained, "You could never hurt me, Jade Weyland. You are a miraculous, astonishing woman. You brought me back from death, Jade. You can resurrect lives." I let the words sink in, urging her to hear me. "You do not need to worry about hurting me. Ever."

I still wasn't convinced that she knew how much I meant those words, but I let go of her face anyway.

"Is that what you wanted to talk to me about?" I asked her.

An unreadable expression crossed her features. She opened her mouth, but shut it again. Turmoil swarmed her eyes. I wasn't going to push her, though. Not after everything she went through.

"Yes," she answered. "I just...I just can't lose you, Mal."

I put my arm around her and pulled her closer to me. "You'll never lose me, Jade. I swear it. I'll be by your side until the end, until Erebus himself pulls you from my cold, dead hands."

She leaned her head on my shoulder. "Saints, save us," she whispered, barely audible.

"Saints, save us."

## CHAPTER 36

# *Jade*

**The castle of Rewyth was bigger than I remembered.**

The footsteps from my damp, filthy boots echoed against the stone walls. And white—so much white—sharply contrasted with the greenery that somehow still grew throughout the estate, even though winter chilled my bones.

Yet each time I found myself returning to this place, it felt more like home.

Disguised in the darkness of night, Malachi had snuck us all in through one of the many hidden entrances in Rewyth, which I became very grateful for. He had shown Dragon, Esther and Cordelia to the servants' rooms down the hall before leading me back to our bedroom.

My entire body sagged in relief. I wanted to do nothing more than drop onto that massive, beautiful bed and stay there for weeks.

But Malachi's hand fell onto my lower back. "I hate this," he whispered. He tugged the edge of my sleeve, causing it to expose my bare shoulder. When I looked, I saw the bite from the deadling in my trial.

"It's not as bad as it looks," I said, but the words weren't true. The bite itself might not have been that terrible, but the memories...

"You're safe now," Malachi replied. "He can't hurt you anymore."

His body behind me became a wall of support as I leaned into him. "I'm so tired," I admitted, barely hearing my own words out loud.

"I know you are, my queen. We're home now. You can rest."

I closed my eyes and replayed those words over and over again in my mind. Malachi helped me peel my shirt from my dirty, bruised body. He pulled my boots from my swollen feet. He guided me into the bath in the other room, filling it with steaming water.

We didn't have to talk. He had experienced the trials, too. He knew what I had gone through. For over an hour, he sat there with me in the bathroom, not asking a single question. Not demanding any information.

I almost told him about the Saint who spoke to me, but my body grew too tired to form words.

Once the hot water had turned cold and my skin had finally been rubbed clean, Mal helped me out of the bath and into our bed.

"Tonight, we rest," he said, pulling the sheets around my body. "Tomorrow, we fight for what's ours."

*Yes, we will.*

The next day, after a full night of rest and a massive breakfast, Malachi gathered Esther and Cordelia for a court meeting.

They walked behind us as we descended the halls of the castle. I held Malachi's hand so tightly, I couldn't tell if it was his hand sweating or mine. I held his hand until the force of someone's body hitting mine nearly knocked me off my feet.

Gentle yet urgent arms wrapped around my neck.

It was Adeline, nearly suffocating me and half-squealing as she embraced me. I hugged her back, not realizing how desperately I had missed her, how desperately I had needed my friend.

"Thank the Saints you're okay," she whispered as she held me. "I've been worried sick about you!"

She pulled away to smile at me for only a second before throwing herself at Malachi, hugging him equally as fierce.

Malachi chuckled with a warmth I hadn't heard in quite some time. "We missed you too, sister," he muttered.

I fought back a surprising wave of tears, not wanting any of them to see me cry. Not anymore. Not after everything. Adeline pulled back before surveying Cordelia and Esther behind me.

"It looks like you've all made it back in one piece."

Cordelia scoffed but said nothing, which only resulted in a raised eyebrow from Adeline.

"We have a lot to discuss with you," Malachi said from beside me. His king voice was now turned on, back in these halls where we had real responsibilities and people relying on us every day. "Where are my brothers?"

Adeline turned on her heel and began sauntering down the hall. "They've been waiting for you. We have a lot to discuss, too."

She left us scurrying after her, a sinking feeling weighing me down with each step.

Malachi tensed the second he heard the name.

*Seth of Trithen.*

The man who should be dead, the man who threatened us all, the man who killed Fynn, Malachi's brother.

"And you're telling me he's still alive?" Malachi asked, fury radiating from every word.

"He's not alone," Serefin explained. "He came with an army of *gifted* fae."

"Gifted?" I asked.

"They have magic," Lucien chimed in from the table. "They've been camped right outside the kingdom for a few days now. We couldn't risk a war, not knowing what type of power they brought with them."

I scoffed. Seth was bluffing. Gifted fae were rare, and *exceptionally* gifted fae were nearly nonexistent these days.

For now, anyway. Until I reclaimed magic to how it once was.

"Besides," Serefin chimed in. "The last thing we want is Silas and the rest of the Paragon on our asses for killing the King of Trithen."

Malachi and I shared a glance. Cordelia laughed quietly somewhere in the back of the room.

"He won't be a problem for us anymore," Malachi explained. I glanced down at my worn, dirty shoes, not wanting to look anyone in the eye.

"And why is that, brother?" Adonis asked.

"We may have killed him. Or put him in an eternal death-sleep. However you'd prefer to view it," Mal explained.

"You did *what*?" Adonis paced back and forth in the empty dining hall as Malachi replayed the events of the last week.

The trials, Malachi nearly dying, my magic through our strange power bond somehow bringing him back to life.

And yes, *Silas.*

"It needed to be done," Cordelia said. Surprisingly enough, she had been the one with enough presence to make Adonis back down during his outburst. "Who knows what he would have done after Jade completed the trials, and who knows what he would have done to her. To her power."

I watched in amusement as Adonis's nostrils flared. He paced the dining hall once more, his hand rubbing his chin.

The other brothers, Eli and Lucien, sat down at our table, silently taking in all of this information.

A strange feeling washed over me as I watched them sit together. They were still brothers, of course, but it was different now. They weren't really related, not in blood.

The one thing holding them together was the old king's blood, the blood that we now knew did not run in Malachi's veins.

It explained a lot, honestly. Like the fact that Malachi had black wings. Like the fact that he held such a strong magical gift when the others did not.

Adonis stopped pacing long enough to calmly place both his palms on the large wooden table. "None of you thought that this might end badly for us? That the fae would turn against you for what you did? I mean, Saints, Malachi. That's treason!"

"Treason to whom?" Cordelia once again spoke up before Malachi even opened his mouth.

I needed a damn drink.

"I think my brother is capable of answering for himself, *witch*," Adonis spat.

Saints, things really had changed in the weeks I had been gone. Adonis had always been the even-tempered one, the calm one.

Cordelia smiled and put a hand on her hip in a way that reminded me of Adeline, who sat silently at the table next to me.

"*Half*-witch," Cordelia corrected. Her decadent silver wings flared on either side of her, reminding us all they were there. "And you'd be wise to remember that, *prince*."

"Enough," Mal barked. "None of us have the energy for this. We did the right thing by killing him, he would have ruined us otherwise."

"You mean ruined her!" Adonis's finger pointed directly at me, I didn't need to look at him to feel the attention.

A low growl came from Malachi. "Watch what you say, brother. We've been down this path too many times before."

"Because you continue to choose her over your kingdom!"

Malachi erupted, his chair falling behind him from the force of jumping to his feet as he replied, "We have no kingdom without her! Do you not understand that? Can all of us please get on the same page here and understand that Jade is our future?"

Now, I really felt the attention.

Every single pair of eyes in the room slid to me, and if it weren't for Adeline's hand that slid softly into mine, I would have bolted for the door.

"He's not wrong," Esther spoke up. "The time is coming. Jade will have to perform the sacrifice and fulfill her duties as peacemaker."

"And what duties are those, exactly?" Adeline asked. "Since you seem to know so much."

I could have sworn I heard Cordelia chuckle at that one.

Esther took a long breath as we all waited for her response. I glanced at Malachi, whose night wings were tucked tightly behind his shoulders and whose brows were pulled together with concern.

Perhaps I should have been feeling more concern for myself, for what Esther was about to say.

Somehow, though, I didn't. Because I knew my reality, I knew that whatever my fate was, I would be wanting to change it not for my own sake, but for his. Because I knew how much pain it would cause if I left him, and I couldn't do that to him. Not again. Not after experiencing it myself.

For him, I would fight.

When I finally turned my attention back to Esther, she was already staring at me. Her eyes held something that looked like pity, although with her, I never knew.

*She doesn't know about us,* the voice said. *She doesn't know I speak to you.*

Great. Now was not the time for an imaginary Saint to be speaking to me. My mind spun, a mixture of dreams and reality flashed as images in my memory.

Cordelia turned to face me, her eyes locked on me.

*Shit.* I had forgotten about her gift to hear thoughts.

She raised an eyebrow, as if listening to that, too. "Who is that?" Cordelia asked me.

Everyone, including Esther and Malachi, continued to stare.

"Who?" I asked.

"Don't play dumb," she said. "How long have the Saints been speaking to you in your mind?"

Pain burst through my temples. I wasn't sure if it was really happening. I wasn't sure if it was real, or how long they had been talking to me. It was part of the trials, wasn't it? It was part of my mind, part of the visions.

Like Mal dying. Like Sadie dying. Like Tessa...

I dropped my head into my hands and tried to focus.

*This is real,* the Saint spoke. *The sooner you accept that, the sooner we can move on.*

"Jade?" Mal asked.

My eyes slid over to his, dark and concerned, before I nodded my head. "I–"

"She couldn't tell if it was real or not," Cordelia answered for me. Normally, I would have felt invaded with a half-witch poking around in my mind. Today, though, I was grateful. "The trials have botched her mind, Malachi. She didn't know."

Shame crept up my neck, red-hot with digging claws.

"Saints," Mal whispered. "What do they say? What do they want with you?"

"They want her to fulfill her destiny!" Esther finally said.

"She hasn't told me what she wants," I answered.

"*She*?" Malachi asked, his features dripping with concern.

I shrugged. "The voice is female, I'm assuming it's one of the female Saints."

The room erupted, a chaotic mess of arguing over what to do next, what the Saints could possibly want, and what I had been hiding.

I barely heard any of it. I focused on my own thoughts, on that angelic voice that only came so often. I waited for her to chime in, but she didn't.

"Enough!" Malachi yelled after the fighting went on for a few minutes. "This conversation is beyond inappropriate to be having. Jade is sitting right here! We can discuss the Saints with her later. Right now, we have bigger issues."

I looked at everyone in the room. They once hated me. I remembered it so clearly. Most of them, besides Adeline and Serefin, had at one point wanted me dead. Would they still sacrifice me so quickly? Or would they think twice, knowing I had life magic?

"This has gone on too far," I said. "Esther, tell us exactly what is expected of me as the peacemaker. You said before I had to give my life. What's changed?"

"Nothing has changed," Esther said. "Nothing has changed, except for the fact that you are no longer human. You can no longer die a mortal death."

My ears rang.

"To fulfill your duties as the peacemaker, you must perform a ritual. A ritual that, under normal circumstances, would require your life. But your life is no longer mortal, child. You will perform the ritual, and you will restore magic in this world."

"To the fae or to the witches?" I asked.

"You are the peacemaker," Esther explained. "Only you can decide who is worthy of the magic."

"This is ridiculous," Malachi mumbled. "Serefin, stay here with Adeline and the witches. The rest of you are coming with me." He turned toward the door and began walking out of the room.

"Where are you going?" I asked.

"I'm going to get rid of our current problem."

## CHAPTER 37
# Malachi

"Slow down!" Jade yelled from behind us. Adonis, Lucien, and Eli marched me in the direction of Seth and his men near the back wall of Rewyth. "Not all of us have fae legs and height!"

"Go ahead," I ordered my brothers, stifling my laughter. "I'll catch up."

"We count on it," Adonis remarked before the three of them walked ahead.

"Saints," Jade breathed, finally slowing herself down to a normal-paced walk. "If only I could have gotten some of your fae speed when I came back from death."

Only Jade could make jokes in this type of situation.

"Trust me, Jade," I said. "We are in no rush."

I wrapped my arm around her shoulders and began walking, my brothers in view ahead.

"How are you feeling?" Jade asked. "About seeing him again, I mean."

I shrugged. I didn't want to tell her that every ounce of my body burned with anger and hatred when I heard his name again, but I'm sure Jade had already felt it through our connected power.

"It will be a miracle if I don't kill him on sight," I said.

"After what he did to you and your family, I don't blame him. I'm surprised your brothers haven't taken care of him already."

"If it weren't for the damn gifted fae, I'm sure they would have." I knew they would have. Either that, or they respected me enough to leave the kill for me. Either way, they wanted that bastard dead. I wasn't about to let him walk out of this kingdom without paying for what he did to Fynn.

"What type of gifts do you think they have?" Jade asked me. If she was nervous about my answer, she hid it well. Genuine curiosity was the only thing I heard beneath her words.

I shook my head. "Nothing I would worry about, and certainly not something you need to worry about, Jade. Do I need to remind you of who you are?"

She smiled and shrugged my arm from her shoulder. "You're arrogant," she mumbled. "Did you know that?"

I put a thoughtful finger to my chin, pretending to consider her words. "You know, I believe someone has told me that before. But she was ruthless and fierce, so I didn't pay her much mind."

She spun to me, preparing to counter my banter, but the beginning of Seth's men came into view ahead of us.

Maybe one hundred men, camped out and settled in right here on the outskirts of Rewyth.

Wow, Seth really had some guts.

Did he expect us to let this happen? To not retaliate?

My pace picked up the closer we got, but Jade easily kept up this time. I knew she was eager, too. Eager to confront him. Maybe as eager as I was to kill him.

My brothers unsheathed their swords ahead.

It was only when we reached their side that I saw Seth, standing behind a wall of men that I only assumed to be his 'gifted' fae.

His eyes widened when he saw us approaching. Clearly, he didn't expect me to come home any time soon.

"I can't say it's a pleasure to see you again," I spat.

"Our presence here is nothing personal," Seth shouted from behind his protectors. "We were told that the King of Rewyth no longer resided in his kingdom. A shame, really, that nobody was left to lead your people."

He had always been such a damn coward. At least that hadn't changed.

"We should have killed you when we had the chance," I barked, remembering the short period of time we spent in Trithen. I had never trusted him. I ignored my instinct when my heart told me he was a snake. A traitor.

And look where that had gotten us.

Seth, King of Trithen, deserved to die.

"Did you bring these gifted fae here to protect you?" I asked, waving a hand to the men that stood before him. I recognized some. Had spent days training them in Trithen with my own sword, my own skill set.

"I am no fool," Seth replied. I laughed along with my brothers behind me. "I knew your people would be angry. It is only wise that I bring my own protection."

"Well," I said. "You are here now. My men tell me that you've made your intentions very clear. You plan to take my throne." My power rumbled like thunder in my veins. "*My. Throne.*"

Seth opened his mouth to speak, but I cut him off. "Not only did you march all the way here to attempt an impossible task," I pushed, "but you brought these fae, these gifted fae, along with you. Did you think they would be stronger than myself? Than my wife?"

A few of the fae standing before us shifted uncomfortably. One of them, in particular, even flared his silver wings.

If they were smart, they would stand down. They knew what my power could do. Unmatched and derived from Erebus himself, they could not—*would* not—defeat me.

It was animalistic, the instinct they would have to bow to me. To not turn against me.

I let a small amount of my power flare, not enough to hurt anyone, just enough for the deadly black tendrils to expand around my body for a few seconds.

Their eyes widened as they stared at me.

"Everyone standing before us today," I announced to the crowd, "I do not hold you to the crimes that your leader has committed. Join me. Join us. Claim me as your king, and my wife as your queen, and live. But those of you who do not join me..."

I sent my dark, seeking power of death in Seth's direction. Beyond the fae wall that protected him, he collapsed in pain, withering on the ground.

"Those of you who do not join me will die here, today, with your leader."

A low murmur spread through the crowd of men around us. I was about to send the blast of death through my tendrils of power when Jade's hand fell onto my arm.

"Let me do it," she whispered to me. "Let me end this."

Never in my life had I given up death so easily.

# CHAPTER 38
## Jade

"MOVE ASIDE," I ORDERED THE SILVER-WINGED FAE BEFORE ME. THEY hesitated, glancing at each other to see who would move first.

Cowards. They were all waiting for the first one to falter. For the first one to give in.

They needed a push.

Mal's power was on the verge of exploding, I felt it as truly as I could feel my own body. He held back, for whatever reason, he held back.

He felt bad for these fae. I knew he did. He had been in that same position many times before, standing up for the wrong man because that's what he had been told to do.

Me? I did not have the same challenge. I did not have that same conflict.

I held my hands out before me and summoned a small ball of light energy, life power. "Life magic," I said aloud, "I'm told is as rare as the Saints." The fae around me jolted with surprise. "I'm told it can resurrect life as well as take it. Men," I addressed the men protecting Seth, "you each have special gifts, I am told. That's also rare. You should be proud. Now, which of you would like to test your gift against mine?"

I grew the ball of pure life wider, brighter, until it illuminated against their faces. One of them would test me. The hair standing up on the back of my neck warned me of it.

Malachi stood tall and strong at my side. He was not afraid of my magic. He could not be harmed by it. But everyone else...

Even Malachi's brothers backed up, giving me space. Not out of fear, but out of respect.

Just when I thought I had proved my strength to them all, a gust of wind shot at me, strong and fierce. Air magic was a rare gift, yes, but it was no match for mine.

Or Malachi's.

Malachi rushed to my side, keeping me upright. It took me half a second to identify where the gust of magic had come from, and even less time to aim my power in the fae's direction.

He disintegrated while the fae beside him screamed.

My breath came out in pants. Power fueled me, inflamed me. "Anyone else?" I asked. "Or are we done pretending you all have a fighting chance?"

"Do not back down!" Seth ordered. "That's what she wants!"

I stared into their eyes, into the souls of the men before me. I did not necessarily want to kill them, but I would. For Malachi, I would.

The men directly in front of Seth stepped aside, heads lowered.

I could not stop my own smile.

I stepped forward, Malachi at my side, until I stood only a few feet away from Seth. Malachi would make sure the fae did not change their minds, but I had a strong amount of confidence in them.

If they wanted to live, they would stand down.

Power seeped from every pore in my body. I let myself get angry, remembering everything that happened those days in Trithen. Remembering what Malachi had to do to save my life, what we all had to do to survive.

"Did you think I wouldn't react?" I asked Seth, half-yelling. "When you had Isaiah lock me in a cage with a deadling, did you think I would let that go?"

Power pulsed from my body, like red-hot fire that could not be controlled.

Seth stumbled backward.

"Or did you think, like most of my enemies, it seems, that I would back down? That I would submit to you?"

Malachi's sword touched the back of his neck—just barely—reminding him he was still there. Seth could not run. He could not hide.

"You, King of Trithen, have threatened me too many times to still be standing. What's worse, even, is that you threatened my husband."

More power erupted, a small ball of it even grazing the side of Seth's face. He squealed in horror, his skin burning to ash anywhere my power touched him.

Good. I wanted him to be afraid. I wanted him on his knees, begging for my mercy.

I'm sure he thought I would give it to him. I was nothing but the stupid, weak human girl who played directly into his hands.

"Well?" I asked him, demanding an answer.

Seth's eyes slid over my shoulder, to Malachi's brothers that stood behind me.

"Don't look at them," I barked. "They won't help you. Look at me." His eyes met mine, wide with terror.

"Please," he stammered. "Please, Jade–"

"Queen," Malachi corrected from behind him.

"Queen!" Seth yelled. "Please, Queen Weyland! I made a mistake!"

"You did," I agreed. "And unfortunately for you, I am not one to easily forget."

My power blasted forward, eagerly and effortlessly seeking its target. The tenseness I felt in my body slowly dissipated as I let Seth's body burn and burn with my light, ridding the world of his evilness.

And when it was done, when nothing remained but ash, I took a long, relaxed breath and withdrew my power.

"Saints," Lucien muttered behind me.

I turned my attention to Malachi, who stared at me with nothing but adoration and pride.

I lifted my chin, turning to face the others. "Anyone who betrays us dies. Anyone who threatens my husband dies. Anyone who hurts my kingdom," I pointed to the castle behind us, Adonis, Lucien, and Eli standing close by, "dies."

# CHAPTER 39
## Malachi

Days later, the entire kingdom stood before us. I recognized each and every one of them, even the ones I had only seen once or twice in passing.

Each one of them stared up and me with wide, expecting eyes. Before, I would have worried that they hated me. Hated my reign. Hated the fact that I killed my own father—who I thought was my father.

But I stood before them now with pride. With certainty.

And Jade stood next to me.

Beautiful and terrifying, she looked out at my people. Our people.

No longer human, no longer fickle or weak. She was powerful, stronger than even me.

And our people knew it. They could feel it, not in the same way I could, but in the same way that we could sense when a storm brewed nearby.

Even my brothers—Adonis, Eli, and Lucien—stared upon her with awe.

The past two days blurred together. Seth's men retreated to Trithen after swearing loyalty to their new king and queen. We would have repercussions, I was sure of it. We would have resistance from other kingdoms claiming what we did was wrong.

But I knew the truth. Killing Seth was justice.

Now, we stood before our kingdom, overlooking each loyal member from the stone balcony we stood on, to announce what we all had known for some time now to be the truth.

"Fae of Rewyth," I declared, "we have all struggled over the last few months. We lost our king, we lost a prince, we lost countless soldiers in battle, and most importantly, we lost the sense of peace and freedom that used to dwell in these lands." Jade's hand fell onto mine. "But I can say to you right now, as your king, that nobody will ever be a threat to us again."

The crowd roared, erupting in a sea of applause and shouts of agreement.

"I stand before you with my wife, Jade Weyland, Queen of Rewyth. The same queen whom many of you doubted just weeks ago, and the same queen who has sacrificed her life for this kingdom. Jade stands before you now with the magic of Saints, more powerful than any fae or witch who walks among us."

Again, the crowd roared.

"Together, we will protect this land. Together, we will put out any threat to our kingdom. And together," I lifted Jade's hand in the air, intertwining her fingers with my own, "we will rule the fae!"

# CHAPTER 40
# *Jade*

I THOUGHT I WOULD FEEL OUT OF PLACE STANDING BEFORE THE kingdom of fae. It was never my place, although Malachi had said dozens of times that it was.

It never felt right.

Until today. Until every single one of them stood before me, paying us their respects. Adeline, Adonis, Lucien, Eli, my father. I scanned these faces with a knowing certainty that they would support me for who I was. For who I could be.

And the power I used to kill the King of Trithen, the power that sent every fae before me bowing on their knees, still pulsed through my veins.

Malachi felt this, too. His satisfaction lit up the inside of my chest as if it were my own happiness.

*You should be careful with him,* the voice in my head interrupted. My fingers, still interlocked with Mal's, tightened.

*Why?* I thought back. The crowd before us continued to roar with applause at Malachi's words.

*He has the power of Erebus running through his veins,* the voice said. *You should know better than anyone why that could be detrimental.*

*He is my other half*, I thought back.

An amused sensation washed over me. *He is your downfall, just as Erebus was mine.*

My chest tightened. I didn't need to know the name of the Saint who spoke in my mind, because the clues were easy enough to put together. Anastasia, Saint of life.

I nearly laughed. From the stories I had read, I knew I was nothing like her. I was no Saint.

I held Malachi's hand tighter and listened for the voice of Anastasia that spoke in my mind, but she was silent. *Good.*

There was only me and my wicked, glorious husband.

His hand tightened around my own in a silent promise. Nobody would defeat us. Nobody would stand against us.

With Silas gone, we would be the future. We would be the decision-makers.

A dark shadow tickled my mind, delighting in my thoughts.

*We would be the end.*

It wasn't until the crowds dwindled and the cheers subsided that the voice came back with a fierce sense of urgency.

*He is your downfall. He is your downfall. He is your downfall.*

# Queen of Fae and Fortune

BOOK 5

# The Time Of The Saints

The Saint of love awoke tired. She had been tired, she realized, for some time. Not the typical kind of tired, not physically dreary or simply worn out from a busy day. Tired? No, she felt exhaustion in every ounce of her body, in every bit of her being.

The Saint of love was quite done.

Gone were the days where Anastasia would walk the gardens in the morning, admiring the blooming white roses or the warm sunrise. Gone were those peaceful songs the birds sang, that light breeze from the mountain wind.

Now, Anastasia woke with a familiar feeling of dread in her heart. She sat up, looking around her pristine bedroom.

"Go back to sleep," Erebus, the Saint of death, whispered from his silk pillow.

She had to admit, they were an odd match. The Saint of life and the Saint of death. But they were equals, in many ways. In more ways than they were opposites, she supposed. She had seen that familiar light in him that he tried so desperately to hide, and he had seen that darkness in her.

Many did not understand their relationship. *She should hate him,* they would say. *And he should despise her*. But that could not have been further from the truth.

"I can't sleep," she replied, turning her attention to him. He would have slept all day, if she had let him. He was always so relaxed, so confident. Even if their world was ending today. "I'm worried. How can you be so sure that we are doing the right thing?" Anastasia picked at the lace hem of her nightgown.

Erebus groaned, but eventually sat up, propping himself beside her.

Anastasia's stomach flipped, like it always did, at the sight of him and his dark, unruly hair in the morning.

"Right or wrong," he started with his scratchy voice, "it has to be done. Magic is not what it used to be, Anastasia. If we let things continue as they are, we will have nothing here. This world is a corrupt one, and even I can see that."

Anastasia leaned her head on his shoulder. “You’re right,” she admitted. “They can’t control themselves anymore.”

“We must end it now until the peacemaker is born,” Erebus said. He leaned back in the bed, closing his eyes and covering them with a lazy arm.

They had agreed on these terms months ago, along with the other Saints. They would peacefully pull most of the magic from the lands, leaving just enough for only a few fae and witches to wield. Once that was done, the Saints would retire from the lands, pulling away completely to let the world heal from the aftermath.

And eventually, when the peacemaker was born—someone strong enough to avoid the temptations of the darkness, someone pure enough to not abuse such power—they would allow the magic to come back.

Anastasia liked this plan, she did. But they were putting a lot of faith into someone who did not even exist yet. This person would be expected to sacrifice everything for the greater good, and Anastasia knew how hard that could be.

“Right,” Anastasia said after a few moments. “We will wait for the peacemaker.”

Hours later, after Erebus and Anastasia had crawled out of bed to meet with the other Saints, Anastasia found herself picking the ends of her golden hair.

“Is everyone ready?” Phodulla, the Saint of air, asked.

Anastasia nodded, feeling Erebus’s hand fall onto her shoulder. She had to be ready. She had no other choice.

The others nodded, too. *Ready or not, this was ending today.*

“Good,” Phodulla continued. “Erebus, you may begin.”

Erebus stepped forward, entering into the small circle they stood around. As the Saint of death himself, Erebus would be the one to pull them all from the world, taking most of their magic with them.

Anastasia was not afraid of this next step in her life. She knew that whatever happened, she would be with him. That was enough for her.

But the rest of the world? The fae, humans, and witches they were leaving behind?

She worried for them. She worried deeply.

Erebus closed his eyes and held his hands out before him. The shadows of death leaped and skipped from his palms, infiltrating the air around them.

The lanterns flickered out.

A small thrill of excitement stirred within Anastasia. She always felt this when Erebus drew on his magic, it was their deep soul connection that allowed her to sense these emotions of his.

“On this day, we sacrifice ourselves so that this world we now inhabit may know peace. Our magic has brought joy, greatness, and influence to those who have needed it for many years, but those days are over. Where our magic brought light, it now brings darkness. Where our magic brought peace, it now wages wars."

Silence fell upon the Saints at the weight of his words.

"With these items, we extract the magic from this world until the one who may wield it all arrives."

Erebus opened his eyes and signaled to the other Saints.

Anastasia pointed at Erebus's feet, starting a small fire before him. This was the part of the ceremony where the magic would be trapped within these items, stored until the Saints themselves allowed it to be released.

They had each chosen something special. Anastasia had chosen a small pendant, one with a carving of a small flower to remind her how delicate life could be. Erebus brought a dagger, Phodulla a pipe, Detsyn a ring, and Rhesmus a horn.

One by one, they brought these items to the fire.

Anastasia was surprised that nobody objected, nobody even seemed to raise a brow as each item sat in the fire.

Erebus backed up, regaining his position in the circle.

Rhesmus was the one to speak next. "Join hands," he demanded. They obeyed, joining the circle around the sacred items. "Repeat after me. Together we rise, together we fall. Until the peaceful one arrives, the power shall be no more."

*Together we rise, together we fall.*

Anastasia repeated those words, squeezing Erebus's hand a little tighter.

They repeated the words over and over again, until the flames leaped through the shadows Erebus had sent into the room, until the items on the floor began to rattle with magic, until the entire room began to overflow with the influx.

This was the power of the world returning home.

Her vision darkened, her ears rang. This would be their last time walking on these lands, living in this world.

She shut her eyes tightly, waiting for the transition. Waiting for the end.

It would be thousands of years later when she would see those objects again, see the world again, feel that power again.

For when the peacemaker was born, the magic could return.

# CHAPTER 1
## *Jade*

MY FATHER ATE WITHOUT SPEAKING. EVERY MEAL WITH HIM FOR THE last two weeks had been that way—silent. I wasn't sure why it surprised me. He had never been a talkative person, and even when he did speak, it was usually nothing I wanted to hear.

Until now, anyway. Now, I wanted nothing more than to talk to him, than to hear what he was thinking. Every few moments, when he wasn't busy pushing his food around his plate, he would steal a glance at me, probably hoping I wouldn't notice. I figured one of these times he would build the strength to say what he was thinking, to get his feelings off his chest.

But it had been two weeks in Rewyth, and my patience grew thinner with every passing day.

My curiosity could no longer be contained.

"I must say," I started, attempting to strengthen my shaking voice, "I didn't expect you to protect me when the Paragon brought war to Rewyth. That was a shocking turn of events, to see you on that battlefield." *Saints*. In the silence of the room, my voice nearly echoed off the stone walls.

His shaking leg froze beneath the long wooden table, but his eyes remained glued to the food in front of him. "You are my daughter," he replied matter-of-factly. "Of course I protected you."

The silence filled the room again, although I was sure he could hear my heart racing in my chest. I hated that after all these years, I reacted to him this way. I cared.

I had been replaying those moments over and over again in my mind. Weeks ago, when the Paragon had been fighting us in our own kingdom, my father saved my life. He had jumped from nowhere to attack one of the Paragon members that nearly killed me, and I still had no clue how he managed to escape with his own life.

For me. He did it all for me.

It had been years since my father cared about my life. In fact, I was convinced he wouldn't care at all if I had died back home, all those years yelling at me and fighting me.

"Well," I said as I cleared my throat, "you could have died."

He dropped his fork, metal clacking. "I do not care if I could have died," he said. His voice came out in a rushed whisper. "We are family, Jade. They were going to–" He pressed a closed fist against his mouth before continuing. "They were going to *kill* you. And I couldn't lose you, too. Not after everything."

*Family.* The word hit me like a punch. There were many people I considered to be my family, now. Once, it had only been Tessa. She was my only family for as long as I could remember, even when we lived in the same house as our father. He was never there. Was never protecting us. Was never looking out for us. That was the purpose of family, wasn't it? To protect one another against any enemy? To help each other get by?

Now, I had Adeline. She was just as much of a sister to me as Tessa was. She had even managed to fill that dark, endless pit of sorrow that sometimes became much too heavy to bear alone. Serefin, too, who also lingered around, constantly uplifting the mood of any room. He had started in my life as Malachi's most trusted guard, and I now saw him as my brother.

Then there was Cordelia, half-witch, half-fae who was prickly and sharp and temperamental, but she would defend me in an instant. She had defended me, too, over the weeks. Anytime I needed her, she was there. She had my back.

There were others that I now considered part of my family. Malachi's brothers had their moments, but I no longer needed to watch my back when they were in the room. Over the weeks, we had even begun to enjoy each other's company. Eli had a great sense of humor, and even made Adonis and Lucien laugh once or twice in the last few days. They were all always there, one step behind me, protecting me.

And then there was Malachi, who had become so much more than family to me. He was my other half, my sanity. I needed him like I needed air, and I was quite sure I would be buried in the ground somewhere if it weren't for him.

*That* was my family.

Sitting across from my father, though, watching him swallow down emotion that he had likely been carrying alone for weeks in this kingdom filled with people he once saw as his enemies, I paused. *Did he fit into that group of family?* His furrowed brow was permanent now, almost as if his face froze in worry. His hair was more gray than anything else, and even though he ate more than he ever had at home, his arms grew thinner with each passing day.

"Adeline told me you wanted to come with us to the Paragon's temple when we left," I said.

His jaw tightened as he picked up his fork once more. "Yes," he said. "It all happened so quickly, I tried to follow you but they...they..." His foot tapped under the table again, shaking the floor slightly with each nerve-igniting movement. "They would not let me follow you. I tried, Jade. I didn't want you to go without me."

*My father actually wanted to go with me to the Paragon?*

"I'm sorry," I blurted out. "I'm sorry I left you here, father. You're in a kingdom that is not your own, surrounded by strangers. That could not have been enjoyable for you while I was away."

He huffed. "I don't care about the kingdom or the fae," he said. "None of that matters. Not anymore. What I cared about was your safety, Jade. I could not help you from here. I did not know what they were doing to you. Adeline explained that they tested you? That they made you complete some trials?"

His eyes searched my face. He had never looked at me like that before, like he cared. Like he would be sad if he lost me.

He had never looked at me like a father.

"They did," I said. I brought both hands to my lap and clasped them together as I searched for my next words. "They made me pass trials in my mind. They wanted to see how strong I was."

He cursed beneath his breath, shaking his head. "Those ignorant bastards. They have no idea who they're dealing with. They don't know how strong you really are."

I watched in awe as my father began eating again. This was not the drunken, idiotic man who cared about nothing but himself. This was not the fool that stumbled home just minutes before the sun rose, nor was it the same fool who bartered away any extra coins Tessa and I managed to collect for food.

My father sat before me today with dignity. With purpose.

In a wicked, dangerous way, it gave me hope. Hope that he could grow, that he could actually become part of this messed up family. Hope that I wouldn't lose the last piece of home I had left.

I looked into my father's tired eyes. "You really think I'm strong?" I asked before I could stop myself.

His foot stopped tapping. "I do."

"Why?" I asked. "What's changed? You never saw me as strong before. You never saw me as powerful."

He shook his head again, his eyes flickering to the room behind me. "I was too selfish," he said. Saints, even his voice had changed. "I did not see you for the woman you truly were, Jade. I saw you as her daughter, and it broke my heart every time I looked at you."

*My mother.*

"She had to have been pretty strong, too," I said, treading each word like new territory. "Did she know? Did she know I would become this person?"

Esther had told me once that she knew my mother. She knew my mother would give birth to the peacemaker, the changer of worlds and the breaker of curses.

"My memory of her had been tainted for so long. Sometimes I can't even remember her face. Some memories are clear, but others I can't even trust are real."

I swallowed. "Like what?"

My father smiled softly, his mind going somewhere far, far from that dining hall. I let him sit in silence, reveling in whatever memory had come to his mind. I couldn't remember the last time I saw him smile that way.

"She was always speaking of the Saints. Always wanting them to approve of her. Their history fascinated her. She would do whatever it took to learn more about them, to hear more of their stories."

*She spoke of the Saints?* "Did she ever speak to you about the prophecy? Did you know that she was friends with Esther?"

His eyes darkened. "Your mother...she was brilliant. She was always smarter than me. She always knew what to say, what to do next. When she found out she was having you, she was so happy. I had never seen her happier. But she had a dark side, too. She had secrets. She sometimes snuck away into the night and would not return for days." My father's smile faded until it disappeared entirely.

"You never asked where she went?" I asked. My heart sped up in my chest. "You never followed her?"

He only shrugged. "She had her dark side, Jade, and I had mine. That's what made us such a great match. Without her, I..." He tore his gaze away again, only looking back at me to say, "I know you want answers from me. I want answers, too. But the truth is, your mother was very good at hiding. She hid secrets. She hid another life. It's possible that she knew of your destiny from before you were even born."

We ate the rest of our meal in silence. That was the most he had ever talked about her. That also might have been the longest conversation we had without either of us growing angry or storming off.

It was progress. And progress was good enough for now.

## CHAPTER 2

# Malachi

I SMELLED HER BEFORE I SAW HER. CINNAMON—SWEET AND ALLURING—filled my senses as the bedroom door creaked open. I remained facing the window, looking out upon the rising sun that filled the fae kingdom with a cascading sheet of gold light.

"Enjoy breakfast with your father?" I asked, not bothering to turn around. Her footsteps approached, followed by the warm sensation of her hands sliding up my bare back, gently grazing the base of my wings.

"Always," she replied with a long sigh. I admired her for wanting to spend time with her father. She was certainly kinder than I could ever dream of becoming. It was her idea to eat with him every morning. I didn't question her. Her father had attempted to save her life, after all. No matter how much of a drunk he had been, no matter how bad the things he had said to her were, he was still her father.

At least he tried.

"You amaze me with your kindness, you know," I whispered. Her forehead came to rest on my shoulder as she wrapped her arms around my waist from behind. I immediately felt stronger with her near. I always did.

"I'm not sure sitting in near silence for an hour every morning constitutes kindness," she replied. "Although he did talk about my mother today."

"Really? Anything specific?"

She hummed in thought. "Nothing much. He doesn't remember anything useful, other than the fact that she had secrets. That much I could have guessed on my own."

It didn't surprise me that her father couldn't remember much. He had drank his life away for the last fifteen years. That would damage anyone's memory, much less a human's.

Grief would do that to a person.

Jade's father now faced the nearly impossible task of digging himself out of that hole, of repairing this relationship he had ruined.

"With time, he might remember more," I suggested. "I'm surprised he talked about her at all."

"Yeah," Jade replied with a long exhale. "Me too."

We stayed that way for a few minutes, watching the sun rise together over the kingdom. *Our* kingdom. This had become a habit for us. Jade would return from breakfast, and the two of us would take a few minutes each morning to simply *be*. Together. Just us. Before we had to resume the role of King and Queen of Rewyth, before we had to deal with politics and war. Before we had to speak of Saints and secrets and prophecies, we could simply be us.

Jade and Malachi.

It quickly became my favorite part of each day.

But no amount of time with her would be enough. No number of sunsets or sunrises would be enough. Each day, the dream would come to an end. Jade would step away from me, leaving a cold breeze to replace where her body had just been standing, and we would have to put on those crowns.

"Come with me to town today," I blurted out, grabbing her hands and pulling her tighter around my waist.

"Town? What for?" she asked.

"For nothing, for fun. To escape for the day."

She laughed quietly, the vibrations of her rumbling through my back. A feral heat washed over me.

"Is that a good idea?" she asked. "What if we get caught?"

"We'll conceal our faces," I said. "Besides, we are the rulers of this kingdom. It should be nothing but a mundane task for us to wander through the towns of Rewyth."

Even as she grew silent in thought, I knew her answer would be yes. That was one of the parts I loved most about Jade. She had always been rebellious; she had always been willing to take risks. I knew that from the first time I saw her, fighting those wolves in the forest of her home.

Jade had a dark side, and it lit up even the coldest parts of my soul.

"We have to be careful," she said after a while. I spun around in her arms, pressing my lips to hers in a long, delicate kiss.

"We will be the two most careful people in this world," I said after I pulled away. "I need one day with you away from this damn castle or I might not make it to one more court dinner."

She smiled, the familiar light flickering in her eyes. "Come on," she sighed. "Those dinners aren't so bad. Serefin and Adonis fighting, Lucien telling Cordelia to shut up. They've been entertaining, at least."

"You are the only thing that makes them bearable," I said. "Discussing politics all day was exactly what I dreaded taking over the throne for."

"Well," she replied, her body pressing flush against mine as she closed the small distance between us, "it is your kingdom. If you don't like the court dinners, you can always change them."

I growled quietly, holding her body to my chest. "Tempting, but I don't know if having an uprising so soon after becoming King will help our efforts."

"They could try to rise against us," she said, "but they would fail."

Her words hung in the air between us. They were true words, of course. Nobody could rise against Jade. She had become the most powerful person in existence. Stronger than Silas, stronger than me.

Stronger than anyone.

She had no need to prove herself over the last two weeks. After her show of power to the Trithen army, she earned everyone's respect. Nobody doubted her. Nobody questioned why I had protected her for so long.

Jade had wanted to be one of us for some time. Even now, though, she wasn't. Not really. Other fae looked away as she walked through the halls of the castle. They dropped their heads as she spoke to them.

Each time I saw it, my chest warmed.

To Jade, though, I knew it was different. Jade wanted this to be her home. She wanted power, too, but not any more than she wanted to belong.

"Grab your cloak," I suggested. "If we sneak out now, perhaps nobody will notice us leaving."

"Escaping your own castle," she replied. "I like this mischievous Malachi."

"Mischievous," I repeated, catching her wrist as she tried to pull away. "I like the way you say that word."

She let me pull her body back to mine. "I am the King of Shadows, you know," I said, brushing my lips softly against hers as I spoke. "There's plenty more mischief where that came from. You just have to stick around long enough," I said.

"I like the idea of that," she mumbled back to me.

"The idea of what?"

"Of sticking around."

She pushed herself up onto her toes and kissed me, the warmth of her sending a thrill of adrenaline down my spine. I kissed her back, wanting more of her. Always wanting more of her.

She was smiling when she finally pulled away. "We better get going. Cordelia is always wandering the castle in the morning, and I don't care to have her digging around in our minds while we're sneaking off into town to avoid our problems."

"After you, my queen."

# CHAPTER 3

# *Jade*

After running into Serefin in the hallway and convincing him we would be back before the day was over, Malachi decided flying us to town would be faster than walking. I didn't argue with him on that, and I wasn't about to decline a chance to fly through the morning sky in his arms.

It still amazed me—how strong his wings were. How powerful his muscles were as he shot us into the sky, the wind brushing through my hair. I instinctively tightened my arms around his neck. A low laugh from him told me he felt it, too. He was never going to let me fall, though. Never.

The stone white castle disappeared below us, replaced by the thick forest that surrounded the kingdom. Even with the chilled air of the cold season, the greenery thrived below us.

"It never gets less beautiful," Malachi said. His warm breath against my neck created a deep contrast with the cold air around us as we flew. "At least we'll always have that."

Malachi—the deadly, feared fae with the power to kill anyone he wanted—admired the beauty of the castle in a way that made my stomach drop. I always loved that about him. He was terrifying to most, but not to me. I saw through that tough exterior. He could be frightening when he wanted to be, yes, but he always had my best interest at heart.

And he would always, always protect me.

We flew like that for a few minutes before Mal brought us to the ground, just behind the tree line of the forest.

"We'll walk from here," he said, setting my feet on the ground. He reached toward my head and pulled my hood around my features. "Keep this up. With any luck, nobody will know who we are."

*His hope was admirable.*

"And what if they do recognize us?" I asked.

The corner of his mouth twitched upward. "Then we'll hope they're fans of ours. Or else things might get ugly."

I smiled back at him, ignoring the warning I felt in the pit of my stomach.

Malachi took my hand in his and walked us toward the bustling town below. I had been here before, the most recent time being with Adeline and Tessa. I remembered it so clearly, how happy Tessa was that Adeline had bought her a dress.

Her face lit up like a thousand suns. It was the smile that came to mind every time I thought of my sister.

I remembered Adeline's face, too. She was equally as happy to be the one providing for Tessa.

Saints. There were so many times in my life that I hated the fae. Before I met any of them, all I knew were the dozens of stories I had heard about how terrible they were. How dangerous they were, how predatory. I heard stories about how they would kill any human they came into contact with just for fun. Some even thought they would disguise themselves as humans and crawl over the wall that separated the human kingdoms just to torture them.

How ridiculous all those stories were. I knew that now, these fae wouldn't do that.

Most of them wouldn't, anyway.

Adeline wouldn't. She was even kinder than most of the humans I knew. Her intentions were pure, I could tell just by looking in her eyes.

"Hey," Malachi said, pulling my attention back to him. "Are you with me?"

"I'm with you," I replied. "I was just remembering the last time I came here."

He nodded, eyes widening as he suddenly remembered. "We can go back to the castle if you don't feel comfortable being here," he said. "I completely understand."

"No," I interrupted. "These are our people. It shouldn't be a problem for me to walk through this town. It's...it's a happy memory, anyway. One of the last times I saw Tessa smiling before she died."

Malachi smiled softly, but it didn't reach his eyes.

He knew what it was like to lose a sibling. Close to it, anyway. Fynn hadn't been blood-related to Malachi at all. That became clear to us when we learned that Silas was actually Malachi's father. But still, they had grown up together. They weren't nearly as close as Tessa and I had been, but they were family.

I guess we had both lost family.

"She would be proud of you," Mal said in a hushed voice. We were entirely out of the cover of the trees now, and the sun beat through the chilled air to warm the small amounts of exposed skin on my face. "Tessa would adore the woman you've become, Jade. I know it."

I shook my head. "Maybe," I said. "Or she would be terrified. If she knew that the Saints communicated with me, I think she might never speak to me again."

"People fear what they do not know," Mal replied. "Tessa may have feared you once because she did not understand. Once she truly understood you, though, and once she truly understood your power, she would be nothing but awestruck. Just like the rest of us."

I gave him a reassuring smile and squeezed his hand, suddenly grateful that he was holding on so tightly. Tessa and I hadn't always seen eye to eye. Saints, there were times over the years when it felt like we were never going to get along.

Right before she died, though, things changed. *Tessa* changed.

The memory of her brought forward the memory of the trial, too. My mind couldn't separate the two; couldn't keep reality away from those twisted tests from the Paragon. The sound of her heart-shattering scream was always there, lurking in my thoughts. I could no longer think of my sister's perfect, shining hair without that ugly sound ruining it all.

Sometimes I wondered if I would ever remember her the same.

The narrow dirt path turned to scarce cobblestone. I kept my chin tucked, not daring to make eye contact with anyone who passed us on the path. Malachi did the same, although I knew he used small amounts of glamour to keep us hidden, too.

Over the last two weeks, I started to notice how his magic felt. Through our bond, I could feel him using even the slightest amount of glamour. His death magic felt like a strong force of nature in my soul, like he demanded it from the world. But small amounts of glamour were much, much harder to detect. Whenever he used it, it felt as though a jolt of light tickled my heart, right below my chest.

It was still such a bizarre thing, to be connected to him this way.

"In here," Mal whispered. He tugged my hand, and we ducked through a small wooden door that led to what appeared to be a tavern. We were the only ones inside, other than a young fae who busied himself with drying ale mugs across the room.

His eyes lit up when he saw us, but the pull on my chest told me Malachi had just increased the glamour he was using to keep us disguised.

"Two mugs of ale, please," Mal ordered. We took a seat at a table near the far wall, one that was half-hidden in the shadows of the morning sun.

"Of course," the man replied. Mal sat directly next to me, blocking me from anyone who might walk in through the front door.

I pulled my cloak a little tighter around my shoulders. "Isn't it a little early for drinking?" I asked him.

Mal shrugged. "I think we make our own rules today," he said. "Besides, who knows how long we'll have until we're needed back at the castle? We might as well take advantage of it."

The fae brought the two mugs to our table, taking the coins from Mal, before he bowed his head and walked away.

I held the overflowing mug in my hands. "Please tell me this isn't laced with more fae magic," I said.

Malachi just smiled at me as he brought his own mug to his lips, taking a long drink without breaking eye contact.

"Great answer," I replied.

"Even if it did," he said, "I'm not sure you would feel it the same."

"Why's that?"

"Remember the wine we drank with Cordelia at the Paragon's temple? The night before your trials began?"

*Of course I remembered.* The three of us drank the wine while we all pretended we weren't living for Silas's twisted entertainment. "The human wine, right?"

He smiled again. "Except it wasn't human wine, Jade. You just never felt the full effects."

My mind raced. I wasn't a mere human anymore, that much was clear. I had powers that nobody else could explain, and the Saints spoke into my mind. "You're telling me that was fae wine? And I didn't start hallucinating?"

He nodded. "And I must say, you acted much differently from the last time you drank fae wine."

I recalled the festival in Trithen, when Adeline and I had drank until we had nothing left to do but dance our hearts out in the crowd of fae.

My problems had been much simpler back then.

"I don't recall you having a problem with the way I drank the fae wine back then," I said, bringing my voice to a hushed whisper. "In fact, I remember you quite liked the way we danced."

Something dark crossed his expression. He took another drink of the ale. "I'd much prefer you dancing for me that way in the privacy of our bedroom."

His words held a joking tone, but the heat that pulsed through my body was very serious. Just like his magic, I had begun to sense his emotions within my own body, too.

The heat that I felt wasn't entirely mine, but a wickedly tempting mixture of both mine and Malachi's emotions.

And damn, it made me want him that much more, knowing he wanted me just as badly.

I gained the courage to break eye contact with him, finally bringing my own mug of ale to my lips and taking a long sip.

And I nearly spit it out.

Malachi laughed as he watched me struggle to swallow the liquid. "Not your favorite?" he asked.

"Saints," I muttered. "Why does anyone drink this? I much, much preferred the wine."

Malachi reached across the table and brought a thumb up to the corner of my lip, wiping the foam that lingered there. "You'll get used to it," he replied. "And once you drink that whole mug, it'll start tasting a lot better."

"That, I don't doubt," I said.

I took another drink of the liquid, holding my breath this time as I swallowed the bitter ale.

Malachi and I fell into the comfortable silence together as we turned our attention to the sounds of the bustling town outside. The citizens were just beginning to awaken. Footsteps, hushed voices, and carriage wheels all began to fill the air.

It reminded me of home. Although back home, most humans kept to themselves. Nobody even bothered saying hello to their neighbor, or partaking in any sort of conversation. We were simply focused on surviving, one day after another.

Here? The fae actually seemed to be enjoying themselves. They were...pleasant.

"Do you ever miss it?" Malachi asked, breaking through my thoughts.

"Miss what?"

"Your home. Your house. Your human town."

I shrugged, but stopped myself to really consider his words. "I miss some things,"

I answered honestly. "I miss Tessa, mostly. She was what made most days bearable. Although half the time, she really made my life more difficult." I couldn't help the smile that spread across my face. "I miss having to hunt in the forest every day. Well, I suppose that isn't entirely true. I miss being in nature all the time. I miss the dirt under my bare feet as I washed up in the stream. I miss the morning air, before anyone else in the town had awoken."

I looked up at Malachi to find him staring at me with intense eyes across the table.

"What?" I asked.

"I've been thinking," he said. "About the humans. About how unfairly they've been living."

"You don't need to worry about that," I said. "You have enough to worry about as it is. We both do."

He leaned in, propping both elbows on the wooden table. "I know you think about it, too, Jade. About how things could be different for them. Things could be easier."

I shrugged. The truth was, I hardly let myself think about it. Humans had lived in poverty for centuries. Compared to the witches and the fae, humans didn't deserve luxuries. They were the scum, the pests that had to scavenge to survive.

For a long time, I fell into that role. I hated the fae, just like all humans, because they didn't care about us. They didn't care if we had enough food to eat, or if our land produced enough crops. They didn't care if the animals had migrated away right before a rough winter, or if a bad storm had taken most of our houses from us.

The fae lived in their own prosperous lands. They took the best resources for themselves. They always would.

I didn't see life any other way.

"Things will never be easier for humans," I whispered back. "They'll never be as powerful as the fae. They'll never be able to defend themselves."

Mal's eyes grew wild. "But what if they didn't have to defend themselves, Jade? What if *we* could protect them?"

I scoffed. "There are treaties that protect the humans," I said. "Even those are no use. I'm not sure what else we could do."

We both leaned back in our chairs, taking another long drink of the ale. My head was already beginning to feel lighter.

"What if they lived here, with us?" he asked. His voice had grown so quiet, I barely heard him.

"You mean, bring humans to the fae kingdom?"

He shrugged again without looking at me. "It could work."

"Or, it could end in disaster. You saw what happened to my sister, Mal! The power divide is too great! Humans like her don't stand a chance against the fae."

"But that was before you, Jade. You've changed everything for us! For them!"

"It won't work," I said. "I'm not a human anymore. To them, I am just as dangerous as the fae."

"But you *are* a human, Jade. In here," he pointed to my chest, "you're just as human as any of them. You'd fight for them. You'd protect them. You'd stand up for what's right."

"And what is right?" I asked. "What's the end goal here?"

He swallowed, and my eyes trailed his throat before meeting his dark eyes. "Peace," he said. "Peace is the end goal. It always has been. It always will be."

*That's what we've always wanted,* that smooth, feminine voice in my head said. Anastasia, Saint of love, had been speaking to me more and more often. It seemed as though I couldn't get away from her, could never quiet her when she decided to show up.

I picked up the mug of ale and swallowed as much as I could.

Malachi's eyes widened as he watched me.

"You okay?" he asked.

I nodded. "Everything's fine," I replied. "*Peace.* That sounds almost too good to be true."

Concern hardened his features, but it quickly passed. He hadn't asked me about the Saints that spoke to me, although I could tell he wanted to.

That was a conversation for another time.

Today, we were pretending those problems didn't exist. We weren't talking about Saints today, not here.

I took one more drink of the ale, starting to get used to the taste of the bitter liquid as it fell down my throat and into my stomach, creating a warm knot there.

"This will all be over soon, right?" I asked, more to myself than to Malachi. "Once I fulfill my destiny as the peacemaker, we can put this all behind us."

He leaned in and placed a hand on my knee. "I'll make sure of it," he said.

# CHAPTER 4
## *Malachi*

JADE HANDLED THE ALE MUCH BETTER THAN I EXPECTED. TWO FULL mugs gone, and she only began to slur her words slightly. I loved seeing her this way, this relaxed. Not worried about being the peacemaker, not worried about the weight she held on her shoulders. It had been ages since we'd been able to strip ourselves of the responsibilities of the castle.

Even if that's what seemed to trace each of our conversations. Even if this freedom from our duties was only temporary.

I was about to ask the barkeep for another round of ales when the front door of the tavern burst open. The wooden planks smacked against the wall behind us, causing Jade to practically jump out of her seat.

Whatever peaceful getaway we had been experiencing was about to come to an end.

I had been using glamour to disguise my black wings. To any other fae, they would look silver. Normal. I even pushed my magic further and gave Jade a matching set of silver wings, although she couldn't see them.

Over my shoulder, I could see two fae entering. Not casually entering, either. No, they sauntered into the tavern like they owned it. Like they belonged there. Like they ran the place, and they were astonished that anyone else had dared to enter.

"What's goin' on here?" one of the men asked. He wasn't talking to us. He barely gave us a glance before turning his attention to the barkeep, who appeared equally as surprised as we were.

"Nothing," the barkeep said after finally finding his ability to speak. "Nothing's going on."

"Really?" the fae asked. He had dark hair that he pulled into a knot right above his neck, and he wore a long, clean cloak. Clearly, he thought he was important enough to upkeep his appearance. In this part of town, that was a rarity.

Just as much of a rarity as a clean cloak.

"Is there a problem?" I asked casually from my seat at the bar.

The two men slid their attention back to us, as if they were surprised that I would speak up at all. "No problem," one of them said. "This barkeep owes me, that's all. He can't serve customers here without paying me my share."

I expected some sort of argument from the barkeep, but he only dropped his shoulders and glanced down at his feet.

"And why's that?" I pushed. "Isn't this his bar?"

The two fae looked at each other and began to laugh. The one with the clean cloak—who I now began to realize was the one in charge here—stepped forward. "I don't think that's any of your business," he said. His eyes scanned my body quickly before his attention slid to Jade.

That was the first mistake he made.

I pushed my bar stool back and placed my body between him and Jade, blocking his gaze. "I'm asking, which makes it my business," I demanded. "Now answer my question. Why are you taking his money?"

This fae's nostrils flared. His hand fell to his hip, reaching for a weapon.

That was the second mistake he made.

My power unleashed on him in an instant, just enough to send him to the ground screaming in pain. I let his companion watch in horror as he slowly backed away from the scene unfolding.

"I said, answer me."

"Who are you?" the fae on the ground asked. "What do you want?"

Jade's hand fell onto my shoulder. "I believe he told you he wants an answer," she said, her voice slicing the air like a sword.

All eyes in the room fell to her. She commanded that, she demanded that respect.

It was like we could all feel what she was capable of, primal and powerful.

The fae on the ground tried to scramble to his feet. Another pulse of my power sent him back down. His clean cloak now dusted the dirty floor of the tavern.

"We have an arrangement," his companion managed to spit out. "The barkeep pays us a portion of sales, and in return, he receives our protection."

"Protection from who?" Jade asked. "Why would the barkeep need to be protected in his own town?"

Silence fell over the room. With the two cowards stuttering for words, I turned my gaze to the barkeep.

His wide eyes and messy hair made him appear even younger amidst the chaos. "Who are they protecting you from?" I asked. He did not look away from me. Instead, his jaw tightened. I noticed the way his fists balled at his sides.

*Nobody.* This barkeep didn't need protection from anyone besides these two bastards.

"Great," I said, not needing the barkeep to confirm anything else. "You're telling me that you walk into this young fae's establishment, bully him into giving you money, and you have the nerve to tell me that you're *protecting* him?"

The fae on the ground squirmed again. "It's not like that!" he yelled.

I always hated that—how men would lose all sense of pride when they faced death. He could at least pretend to have strength. To have dignity.

But they were all cowards. I had known plenty of men just like him in my life;

men who preyed on the weak. Men who took whatever they wanted from those who didn't have anyone to help them.

Men like my father. Men like Silas. It made me sick.

They would never stop. They would take and take and take, and the evilness would never end. Why should it? Nobody stopped them. Nobody put them in their place.

Until now, anyway. *Until us.*

I pulled the sword from my hip, the weapon they didn't realize I carried until I moved my cloak aside. Cowards were always ignorant, too. Unprepared.

It made them fools.

The fae on the ground began to stammer, began to beg for mercy.

"Please, don't do this! You'll never see me here again! I'll never enter this tavern again!"

"No," I said, holding the sword in front of me. "You won't."

I did not hesitate to kill him. With a steady hand, I pierced the sword directly through his heart. His friend's scream was the only sound accompanying the thud of his body falling back onto the floor.

"What about you?" Jade asked the companion. He sauntered backward, glancing between us and the barkeep. "Do you still think this man owes you anything? Or perhaps you'd like to ask the barkeep for it yourself instead of letting this fae handle your dirty work?"

Jade took a step forward, narrowly missing the pool of blood that now formed around the dead body, the heels of her black boots clicking the wooden floor as she moved toward him.

The man backed up until he could not back up any further, his eyes in a frenzy as he glanced between Jade and myself. As if I would help him. As if I would stop her. The wooden wall of the tavern kept him there, ready to meet his fate. "Please, Miss," he begged as Jade stopped before him. "Please don't do this. Have mercy!"

*Show no weakness. Yield no mercy.*

Jade lifted her hand, palm facing the sky, as torturously slow tendrils of her magic escaped her, dancing in the air until they landed on their target.

The man's face contorted in pain, but only for a moment. Seconds later, he was on the ground next to his friend.

Also dead.

"Saints," the barkeep muttered. Jade turned to look at him, but I kept my eyes on her, unable to look away from her beauty.

From her power.

I could feel it inside of me, how much more she was capable of. The fact that she now controlled her power so well was merely a sign of how strong she was getting with every passing day.

Did she realize what she just did? Did she realize what just happened? Without a sword, without a weapon, without hesitation, she had killed him.

The power of life, taking what was rightfully owed to her.

The peacemaker, the judge.

Without so much as a drop of blood on her hands, she stepped away. Although I knew as well as anyone that the blood still stained that perfect skin of hers. It wasn't visible to the eye, but it was there.

And that was just as dangerous as being drenched from head to toe.

"Who are you people?" the barkeep stuttered. He was fearful, his eyes wide with caution, but he did not back away. We had just solved the biggest problem he had.

Jade looked at me and held my gaze as she answered, "We are Jade and Malachi Weyland, King and Queen of Rewyth."

I dipped my chin to her, giving her the respect she deserved.

The barkeep sucked in a sharp breath before falling to his knees. "Please, forgive me," he stammered. "I had no idea." He began digging in his apron for the coin I had paid for our ale. "Here," he said, holding it out as he bowed his head. "You need not pay for anything in this tavern."

"Keep it," I said, stepping forward and grabbing Jade's hand. "And if you have any other problems in this place, send word for us. Nobody takes your money. Nobody unwanted steps through those doors. This is our kingdom, and we're here to keep it safe. Is that clear?"

He lifted his head to look me in the eye, his mouth hanging open. "Thank you, King Weyland. Thank you."

I tugged on Jade's hand lightly, pulling her in the direction of the door. "We'll send men to dispose of the bodies," I added as we stepped over them.

A few seconds later, we were out of the tavern and back in the bustling streets of the town.

"Saints," Jade mumbled. "That was insane, wasn't it? I mean, how dare they act that way! That poor barkeep was trying to run a business."

I reached up and pulled her black cloak further around her head, covering her face. "They're cruel," I said. "But they won't be a problem anymore, and that's what matters."

She looked away and her jaw tightened. "They deserved to die," she whispered.

Was she trying to convince *herself* of that?

"Yes," I replied. "They would have kept stealing from him, and who knows how many others they were doing the same to? We did the right thing, Jade. This kingdom is a better place without them."

"Right," she breathed.

I squeezed both of her shoulders before placing a finger on her chin and forcing her to meet my eyes. "These weaker fae cannot protect themselves," I reminded her. "We're the ones who must do it. We're the ones who keep the balance. Things will only get worse after the peacemaker ritual is completed tomorrow. What if a fae like him gets power? What if the balance is disrupted even more than it already is? They need us, Jade."

I ran my thumb across her lower lip. She closed her eyes, leaning into my touch.

"You're right," she said after a few seconds. "Thank you, Mal. It just felt so..."

"Wrong?"

"No," she said, shaking her head. "It didn't feel wrong at all. It felt good, actually." She blinked a few more times, her throat bobbing as she swallowed. "And that's what scares me."

I pulled her body into me and wrapped my arms around her, using my wings to block us from anyone who passed. "You have nothing to fear," I whispered. "We're in this together, Jade Weyland. You and me. Do you know how many times I thought I had lost myself to the darkness? That's what this power does, Jade. It makes you think that it's taking over, but it's not. It never will. Do you know why?"

She pulled away just enough to look into my eyes. *Damn, she was beautiful.* "Why?"

"Because you're here. And I care about you, and I know you love me. And that keeps me here. That keeps me sane. When I think I've lost it all to the darkness, you're right here, fighting for me. And you always will be."

She smiled.

"I don't know," she started. "I'm half-tempted to believe that you'd be just as willing to dive into the darkness."

I smiled back. "If darkness swallows you whole, I won't hesitate to dive in after you. But I'll pull you back, Jade. I'll always pull you back."

We stayed there for a moment, reveling in each other's arms, before sneaking out of the town and back to our kingdom. Back to our duties. Back to being royal. Back to politics and war and enemies.

But we had each other, and that made it all worth it.

# CHAPTER 5
# Jade

THE NEXT MORNING, BACK IN THE CONFINES OF OUR ROYAL CASTLE, Cordelia's fists pounded on the door, barely louder than my heart beating in my ears.

Today was the day I performed the peacemaker ritual. Esther had been preparing everything, gathering witches to help her in whatever needed to be done.

It was finally time.

"Are you sure about this?" Malachi asked. He rolled his shoulders back and took a deep breath. Saints, he looked so noble. Each time he put on his formal court clothes with black leather strapped across his chest and his dominant wings tucked behind his shoulders, I couldn't take my eyes off him.

He looked as if he were born for this.

I, on the other hand, felt too small in the grand ball gown I wore. The neckline covered my right shoulder but my entire left arm was bare. The thick, black pleats fell in waves down to the floor, making each step more difficult than it needed to be. It wasn't much exposed skin compared to what I had worn in Rewyth before, but *Saints*.

It felt much, much too vulnerable.

I nodded anyway, letting Mal know I was ready. I knew he could see the lie, knew he could see right through my barriers, right through the walls I had in place after spending so much time with the fae.

He could see how terrified I was. I could see the fear in his eyes, too. Dark yet barely there, mixed with dozens of other emotions I didn't have the time to name.

"Good," he sighed. "Let's get this over with, peacemaker."

The weight I had felt for this moment seemed to dissipate. Days of waiting, days of wondering. Ever since the first whisper of *peacemaker*, I had been longing for this day. Somewhere in the back of my mind, I always knew it would come. I would have to face this, face my duty.

I tensed at the thought. *Duty.* How ridiculous, that after all this time it was my *duty* to fulfill this prophecy. It was my *duty* to restore power to the fae.

Malachi's hand fell onto my back, warm and confident. "You were born for this, Jade Weyland. You have nothing to fear. If anything, it's everyone else in this damn kingdom that should be afraid. But not you. Never you."

I smiled, a real smile this time. Not a fake smile full of pleasantries and lies. Malachi's words...they felt real. They felt like they were true, like everyone in the kingdom really should be afraid of me.

The last couple of weeks had certainly proved some of that. Between court meetings, training with Cordelia—which I really didn't think was still necessary, but I kept my mouth shut about that—and all of my other duties as Queen of Rewyth, I felt as if I finally had a place here. I had a purpose.

The fae of Rewyth did not dismiss me. They did not roll their eyes as I walked by. No, they nodded with respect in my direction anytime I passed. They even bowed to me on occasion when I entered the dining hall or when I exited the room after a court meeting. It felt odd at first, but day after day, I grew into the new position in court.

By Malachi's side, it felt so natural.

Malachi was more than accommodating. I had been the Queen of Rewyth in *his* eyes for some time now, but not to me. Not to everyone else. He was just as surprised as I was to see the overwhelming change of attitude from our people.

Even my father, surprisingly enough. The fae began to respect him more, too. Although I wondered how much of that had to do with his lack of drinking and how much of it had to do with the fact that his daughter was now Queen of Rewyth.

I didn't mind, though. Malachi came with me to most of my training sessions. Cordelia began to test his magic, too. After learning that he was a descendant of a Saint, we figured he had boundaries to push. Unlimited power could live somewhere inside of him, he only needed to let it out.

And my power...

To say that my power had grown stronger would be a disrespect to it entirely. No, *strong* wasn't the word. *Unstoppable,* maybe. *Undeniable.* I wielded my power easily; it took little to no effort to blast an entire stone wall or turn any object—big or small —to ash.

And late at night, after Malachi had drifted into an endless sleep beside me, I often thought about how powerful it would feel to turn bone to ash. To burn flesh away as if it never existed.

And that voice...

*You have the power of life,* the voice said in my mind. *Give it. Take it. Do as you must. Your wishes are divine, Vita Queen. Whatever you want is yours.*

I stopped being annoyed by the voice that visited my mind. I stopped being annoyed because I liked the things this Saint said. I liked the confidence she had in me, in my power. Always in my mind, always telling me to want more. To burn more.

But none of that mattered. Not really. Because I had a duty to uphold.

"I am not afraid," I answered Malachi. It was an honest answer now, one that rolled off my tongue with ease.

"Good," he replied, opening the door to Cordelia. "Because no matter how much power is restored to the fae, you are our queen. You are our light, Jade."

Cordelia looked between us, hand cocked on her hip with her thin eyebrows raised, as if she had been waiting on us for hours.

I liked that she never lost her attitude. It was beginning to grow on me.

"You two finally ready?" she asked. "I was starting to think you ditched us and were halfway to the sea by now."

I pushed past her, brushing her shoulder with my own. "You wish you could be so lucky," I teased.

Cordelia and her power to read minds, though, knew the truth, knew I secretly liked the small friendship developing between us, no matter how much of it had been hidden in punches to the face and sneak-attacks with my magic.

The half-witch was actually not so terrible.

The three of us walked the hall in silence, our footsteps synchronizing as we grew closer and closer to the ballroom.

Esther would be waiting for us there.

The energy shifted as we walked through the large, wooden doors. I had been in this room many times now. My wedding was the first. Countless dinners. I remembered the way those bodies hung from ropes when Malachi strung them not so long ago.

Although it felt like a lifetime ago. We were so, so different now. I was not weak. I was not afraid.

For once in my entire damn life, I felt peace.

Of course, the peace did not always last. All it took was that one voice—the voice I liked to pretend didn't exist—to talk in my mind. To tell me something big was coming. To tell me I had to be ready to fight.

*Vita Queen,* she would call me.

Queen of life. What a joke. Apparently, the Saint hadn't realized just how much I craved death and destruction these days.

"Welcome," Esther said as we walked in. "We've been waiting for you."

I quickly scanned the room, taking in the witches that Esther had been working with to prepare the ceremony. They weren't from her bloodline, but they did have some magic running through their blood. Esther was able to send messages out to old friends, and I was surprised by how many people wanted to help.

But I was the peacemaker, after all.

The three women, Esther included, stood with their hands crossed in front of them. Waiting. They wore white dresses, simple and pure. I wasn't sure if it was part of the ceremony or not, but the sight of it made the hair on my arms stick up.

The rest of the dining hall remained empty. We wouldn't have an audience for this. Wouldn't need one.

I approached Esther and began to kneel before her, next to a small fire that burned inside a golden bowl. Malachi grabbed my arm, pulling me to him.

"You don't have to do this," he hissed in my ear. "Do it or don't, but let it be your decision. This is your life, Jade. You choose your destiny."

*Saints,* I wanted to believe him. I really, really wanted to believe him. But we both knew I couldn't walk away from this.

*Vita Queen,* that voice said again, as if warning me. As if pushing me. *You're about to learn how powerful you really are.*

No, running wasn't an option. I placed my hand above Mal's hand and squeezed gently. "I'm ready for this," I said, feeling more truth in the words this time. "I'll be okay."

He held my gaze under those heart-wrenching thick lashes before nodding and letting me go.

I knelt. Both knees hit the stone floor beneath my thick dress. My hands shook—barely enough to be noticeable. I wasn't sure why I was nervous, though. Esther had walked me through it dozens of times.

First, the witches would draw upon the power of the Saints. This required relics, relics that they had apparently been hiding all these years. Gifts from the Saints. One necklace, belonging to Anastasia. One dagger from Erebus. A beautiful air pipe from Phodulla. A small, stone ring from Detsyn, and finally a horn from Rhesmus. These were not any relics. They were special relics, ones that held the remaining power of the Saints before they left this world.

Secondly, I would have to swear my oath. I didn't ask too many questions when Esther explained this. I think she understood, too. I would swear the oath, no matter what I had to swear to. I wasn't backing out. We both knew that.

Lastly, a sacrifice was required. A sacrifice of my life. Since I had already died, though, Esther explained that the Saints would accept my blood.

I silently prayed that she was right.

"Peacemaker," Esther began. She held the five relics in her now open palms as she stood over me. I could have sworn the fire to my right flickered with a flare of life. "We are here today to fulfill your duties as the chosen one. Chosen—not by us, but by the greater powers. The Saints that used to walk these lands. They have chosen you, blessed you, and tested you. You, child, are the one to fulfill the prophecy that they began many centuries ago."

Malachi sucked in a breath behind me. His nerves became a ball of fire in my own stomach, mixing with my emotions and fueling the power that ran hot in my veins.

"What now?" I whispered, although my voice practically echoed across the room.

"Give me your hand," Esther ordered. I held my hand out before me. She lowered the relics and knelt on the other side of the small altar, holding my hand in hers with my palm facing upward.

"This may hurt," she said. I nodded anyway, giving her the permission to do what she needed.

She picked up a small blade, no bigger than my hand, and sliced the skin on the center of my palm.

I instinctively flinched away, but she gripped my hand tighter, holding me there.

Malachi's presence became a comforting force behind me, although I knew he couldn't touch me. I had to do this entirely on my own.

Blood began dripping off my palm, smacking against the silver bowl beneath it. Esther flipped my hand over, squeezing until blood had covered the bottom of the bowl.

"Close your eyes," Esther demanded.

I obeyed, letting my head fall back as I shut my eyes, blocking out the room.

"I'm going to call the Saints forward," she explained. "Accept any messages you receive, Jade. Open your heart, open your soul. They will come forward with what they need from you."

Unable to speak, I nodded.

"Let's begin," Esther said. The witches began to chant, repeating words in a language I did not understand. I kept my eyes shut and tried to focus on what I was feeling, searching for any signs from the Saints.

*Come on, Anastasia. Don't be shy now. Come forward. Tell me what to do.*

The chanting grew louder and louder until I could no longer hear my own heartbeat, could no longer feel Malachi's presence behind me. The words became all-encompassing, caressing my body as if I were part of the air myself.

The voices of the witches, some of the strongest to exist, echoed through my mind, through my bones, through every inch of my body.

And then, all at once, it stopped.

My eyes shot open, searching to see what had happened to Esther and the witches.

The room was nothing but darkness.

"Esther?" I whispered. Instead of echoing off the walls as it did before, my voice carried endlessly into the dark void.

"Esther isn't here," a voice responded. Anastasia's voice, smooth and calming.

"Anastasia?" I asked. "What's happening?"

Then, in the midst of the darkness, a woman appeared. She wore a white lace dress that rippled in the air around her. A light illuminated her body, but I didn't know where it came from.

She was the only thing in the darkness, the only thing that mattered at all. My attention pulled to her like an instinct, I had no choice but to stare at her with wide eyes as she stepped forward.

"Jade," she said, smiling. Her white teeth glistened as she tilted her head and scanned me with her golden eyes. "I'm so happy you are here."

"Where am I?"

"You're with the Saints, my dear. The witches have sent you to us just as they were instructed to do."

Panic crept into my chest, morphing my senses and igniting my power, until Anastasia's small, pale hand landed on my shoulder. Warmth immediately radiated from her touch, covering all those feelings of fear and panic, and replacing them with something else.

Something pure.

"You do not need to fear," Anastasia said. "You will be back in your kingdom soon enough. First, however, we must discuss something with you."

"Who is *we*?" I asked, scanning the darkness around Anastasia's golden light. "Are the other Saints here?"

A silent beat passed. "They are."

I blinked once, and when I opened my eyes again, Anastasia was not the only figure standing before me. No, four more now joined her.

The five Saints, all standing before me in a vision I could hardly look at straight on.

Pure beauty, pure excellence, pure power.

I instinctively dropped my head, bowing before them. "Apologies," I said. "I did not know I would be meeting you all personally."

"Rise, child. We have business to take care of."

I stood up from my bowed position and finally, one by one, looked them all in the eyes. It felt wrong to stare at such power directly. I wanted so badly to look away, but I forced myself not to.

"You all have chosen me to be your peacemaker," I said, trying to steady my voice. "Can I ask why?"

The five figures before me glanced at each other, smiling.

"You question our decision?" The one Saint with black wings stepped forward. I knew immediately who this Saint was, and the chill that crossed my body only confirmed it.

Erebus, Saint of death.

"No," I said, holding his wicked stare. "I'm only curious."

Anastasia stepped beside him. "We knew for decades who you would be when you were born, Jade. We knew before your mother even grew you that you would be the one."

"But why? What makes me special?"

A small smile grew on her face. "The fact that you think you are not."

Her wings, silver with gold flecks, spanned multiple feet on each side of her body. Her skin even seemed to glisten in the light that shone down on the group of them. Pure, lean muscle sculpted her body, the body of a warrior. The body of a fighter. Yet she held an enormous amount of grace. Even her words brought me comfort.

"I have the power of life," I said. "Same as you."

Anastasia nodded. "Yes, dear. You do."

"And Malachi," I stole a glance at Erebus, "the gift of death." I could have sworn I saw him smile, but it was quickly replaced with the cold, emotionless surface.

"I was wondering when you might mention him," Anastasia said with a soft voice.

"I'll be your peacemaker," I said, unable to swallow the sudden wave of desperation that clawed at my chest. "I'll do whatever you need me to do, but I won't hurt him. I'll protect Malachi to whatever end."

Anastasia stepped forward, caressing a warm hand across my face. "Oh, I know you will," she said. "You and I have a lot in common, you know. It's part of the reason this decision was so easy."

I bowed my head. "I'm ready."

"Good," Anastasia said. "You must swear an oath to us, an oath of protection. An oath of peace and of power. If you break this oath, Jade Weyland, your life is ours. Your soul is ours, to live in our realm alone for the rest of eternity. Do you understand this?"

I blinked. "Yes."

"Then let it be done. Phodulla, please continue."

The Saint of air stepped forward, chin high and shoulders back. She contrasted Anastasia greatly, with pale skin and midnight black hair. Her bright green eyes held a promise in them, a promise of power. A promise of vengeance. She held a mightiness that at first seemed similar to Erebus's, but in a more subtle way.

*I did not want to be on her bad side.*

"Peacemaker, born Jade Farrow, married to Malachi Weyland, and chosen by the

Saints. You will fulfill your duties as the peacemaker to us, you will uphold our values and our truths, you will keep peace among fae, humans, and witches. You will not let any one entity overpower the others, and you will be fair in all your ways. You, Jade Weyland, will be the most powerful individual walking in this realm. You will carry yourself as such, never taking advantage of those weaker than you. You will feel a strong pull to this power, as all of us have, but you must not give in. You must not let this power break you, peacemaker. If you do, you will have failed your destiny as our peacemaker, and power will become uncontrollable across the lands. The weak will die. The powerful will reign. You must succeed, Jade Weyland. Accept this oath and become who you were born to be."

The words hit me with the force of a punch, creating an entire new reality right before me.

I had no option. Failure was not a choice. Succeed or die.

Succeed, or sacrifice my soul to the Saints.

"I accept this oath," I said. Delight flashed through Phodulla's features.

"You already have Anastasia's gift, the gift of life. Life magic. You will now receive the gifts of the rest of us, so that you may control the power that flows across the lands."

I nodded, trying to calm my rapid heart.

*This was really happening.*

I stood, frozen, as each Saint approached me.

Phodulla came first. The Saint of air. She stepped forward and blew, releasing her breath and something much, much stronger into my face, blowing my hair back over my shoulders and nearly knocking me off my feet. Her power buzzed through my body. And then it was over. The wind stopped, she stepped back.

Detsyn, the Saint of love, was next. She grabbed both of my hands, interlocking our fingers and leaning forward to place a kiss on my cheek. I did not flinch away, even as a welcoming, overjoyous warmth washed over me and did not leave.

Rhesmus transferred his power to me by gripping my shoulder. Tightly. It was not as delicate as the others, but the power of war suddenly filled my awareness, settling like a heavy weight at the bottom of my stomach. With a nod, he released me and stepped back.

Anastasia came next. She smiled at me like she always did, radiating a light from her hands and placing it directly onto my chest. I had known this power, had felt it in my body before, but never so forcefully. A new stream of magic ignited within me; Anastasia's full powers awakened in my body.

Erebus was the last Saint to give me power. I expected something harsh and painful, as he was the Saint of death. But he stepped forward and tilted my chin up with a finger under my chin. His eyes were dark, his brows drawn together as he lowered his head and pressed his forehead against mine. It was not pain that came next, nor was it a coldness. Instead, a familiar warmth washed over me, very similar to the way Anastasia's power had. It settled in my chest, right next to her power, and pulled on each of my senses.

All five Saints, all five sources of power.

Now, it was all mine.

Phodulla cleared her throat, regaining my attention. "It was our plan for you,

Jade Weyland, to die. The peacemaker must die and be renewed as a stronger, unstoppable force. However," the Saint looked back at the other four. "We witnessed your death once. The witch called to us, and we answered."

My heart raced uncontrollably in my chest. "What does that mean? I don't have to die again?"

"You are strong, peacemaker. Stronger now than you were before, are you not?"

I nodded.

Erebus stepped forward in the corner of my eye. I tried not to look at him, tried and tried until he stood directly in front of me, gently pushing Phodulla aside.

"Death," Erebus started, his voice as thick as stone, "is very fickle. Death is what forced us to remove magic from the free lands. But you know that already, don't you?" He stepped forward again, coming uncomfortably close as his breath tickled my cheek. He towered over me, his powerful body blocking my view of the other Saints. "You have been close to death many times," he said. "You have witnessed it. You have given in. You have craved it."

My blood turned to ice.

"Yes," I breathed.

"Good," he said. I jumped at the boom of his voice. "Then you know the consequences. We did not expect the human that would eventually fulfill the peacemaker's destiny to be so familiar, so we have decided to make an exception."

I finally dared a glance at his eyes, black as night. I said nothing.

The Saint of death continued. "We will accept this previous death of yours as your sacrifice to us." He reached down and grabbed my hand, pulling it into the space between us. His touch was cold and warm all at once, filling my body with a strange sense of both belonging and danger.

"I've already died," I said, though I wasn't sure why I said it.

A smile grew on his face, one that put a chilled knot in the pit of my stomach. "Yes, child," he said. "Your blood is not the blood of a mere mortal any longer. You are now something different. Something stronger, stronger than even a fae."

He used the edge of his fingernail—though I didn't notice it being that sharp or long—to slice the skin on my wrist. Blood dripped down, wrapping across my palm and slipping off the edge of my fingers.

It didn't hurt. It didn't sting. It just fell, drop after drop, as a dark numbness spread up my arm.

Instead of letting me go, Erebus tugged tightly on my arm. I stumbled forward, but he caught me with a hand on each side of my face. He pulled me up quickly, and for a quick, torturous second, I thought he was going to kiss me.

But he didn't. Instead, he blew a breath of air into my face.

Except it wasn't air. Not entirely, anyway. What came out of his mouth felt like air, but it danced with black shadows that spread across my vision and around my body.

"What is this?" I stuttered.

"This is what is owed to you by death," Erebus half-growled into my ear. I heard a gasp from one of the other Saints, I assumed it to be Anastasia, but I couldn't quite tell.

He finally let go of me, letting me stumble backward as I wrapped my mind around what had just happened.

"That wasn't part of the plan," one of the Saints said to him.

"She was to get all of our power by fulfilling this. She is strong. She can handle a hint of death, as well."

"She's had plenty of death already, Erebus," Anastasia argued.

"The boy does not count," Erebus replied.

"He is your descendant, mind you!" she hissed.

"He is, and he is powerful. But now they can share this gift, be one with it." Erebus argued as if he had just given me something great, but the look on the other Saints' faces told me otherwise.

"What was that?" I asked again.

Phodulla stepped forward. "Erebus has given you a touch of death, child. Seeing as you have already died, this shouldn't affect you much."

"I can handle it," I said confidently.

"Yes, you can," Erebus growled.

"The last step is for you to decide, peacemaker. You have seen the witches. You have seen the fae. It is up to you to decide which species is to be gifted the free flow of power. Which is the most deserving?"

I shook my head. I knew this was coming, but I didn't think the decision would be so hard. Witches were born for magic, they thrived on it. They had been able to survive since the Saints had taken their power, but barely.

And the fae...the fae were powerful and fierce, but I had seen so many abuse their power. The entire Paragon, for instance.

But did that mean Malachi did not deserve his power? Did that mean the rest of the fae who possessed gifts did not deserve them?

"I don't know," I said. "I can't decide."

"It is your destiny to decide, child."

I didn't dare look at the Saints. Any of them. I didn't want to see any sign of regret lingering on their faces.

"They all deserve to have magic back," I said under my breath. "I cannot choose one species over another, because they are equally deserving." I finally lifted my gaze. "The truth is, when you took most of the power from these lands, you stripped them of who they were, of who they could be."

"What are you saying?" Anastasia stepped forward.

"I'm saying I cannot choose if just the witches or the fae gain their power back. They both deserve power. If you are going to revive magic in the lands, give it back to everyone, and let it be done."

The Saints all looked at each other again. I was really starting to feel like the outsider here, like they all had some sort of hidden communication between them.

"That is it, child," Anastasia announced. "You now carry the power of the Saints. All the Saints." She tossed Erebus a sideways glance. "It is now your duty to keep the balance on earth, to stay true and right and pure no matter what the circumstances. We're trusting you, peacemaker."

A flash of light, so bright that it encompassed everything I thought I knew and everything I thought I was, spread throughout the room. And then there was nothing.

Malachi knelt over me when I woke, panic and desperation flashing through those dark eyes of his. "Jade?" he breathed. His fingers dug into the skin on my shoulders, as if he had been shaking me to wake up for some time now.

"I'm okay," I breathed. I thought I might have been confused or somewhat disoriented from my visit with the Saints, but I wasn't. Not in the slightest. I saw very clearly what had just happened to me, and I knew deeply what I had to do. What I had to carry.

"It is done," Esther announced from the other side of the dwindling fire. "If all has gone accordingly, your wife now carries the power of the Saints. They have sworn her in as the peacemaker, and she has agreed to fulfill her destiny to them."

Malachi didn't take his eyes off me. "Jade? Is that true?"

I let him pull me into a sitting position. "Yes," I breathed. "They asked me to pick, Mal, and I couldn't."

His eyes searched mine for an answer I didn't have. "What are you saying?"

"I chose both. Magic will be returned to witches and fae, both."

"Well," Cordelia chimed in from behind me, not sounding the least bit surprised. "What happens now?"

Esther stopped what she was doing and looked at me. Not at Malachi, not at Cordelia, at me. She stared into me with a fierceness I had never seen before, a fierceness that held the strength of an entire coven, a fierceness that reminded me of who she really was and where she came from. "We wait for the magic," she said. "And we pray to the Saints that Jade is strong enough to control it all."

## CHAPTER 6
# *Jade*

"You're sure you did it right?" Adonis asked. "Because I don't feel any different."

"I'm pretty sure, Adonis," I replied. Lucien and Eli joined him, lingering in the back of the study as Adonis questioned me. Serefin and Adeline remained relaxed, observing the interrogation from the other side of the large wooden table.

"How do you know?" he asked, taking a few desperate steps forward. I couldn't help but stare at the dark circles under his eyes. He hadn't slept much either, it seemed.

"Stop questioning her," Malachi barked beside me. "If she said it's done, it's done."

We had been at this for over an hour, sitting in this room waiting for...well, I wasn't sure what we were waiting for. A magic bolt of lightning to hit the room? The Saints themselves to arrive and grant everyone their magic gifts?

"Wouldn't that be nice," Cordelia said as she entered the room, reading my thoughts like she always did. Although I was starting to get used to it. Dragon followed tightly behind her as the study doors closed. "And I'm not a babysitter."

Dragon stepped out from behind her. He looked much different now, even a bit younger without his ripped clothing and dirty face. I hated that I barely talked to him since we left the Paragon's temple, but I trusted that Cordelia and Esther were watching over him.

Which I now realized might have been a mistake.

"We're a little busy, Cordelia," I said, trying to keep my voice level as I gave Dragon a smile. He seemed ignorant of the tension in the room, though, as he walked forward and helped himself to a seat at the large dining table next to Adeline and Serefin.

"I can see that," Cordelia replied. "And thank you for the invitation to this little meeting, by the way," she added. "It's been absolutely riveting listening to your thoughts from halfway across the castle."

"Seriously?" Adonis asked. "How are you allowed anywhere near us with that gift of yours? I'm surprised they let witches like you live."

"I'd like to see anyone try and kill me, prince boy," Cordelia replied.

I tried to hide my smile. And failed.

Adonis accepted his defeat and eventually retreated, joining his brothers at the back wall of the study.

"Dragon," I said, willing to do anything to change the subject, "how have you been enjoying your time here in Rewyth?"

His eyes lit up with so much excitement, I nearly felt it myself. "I like the trees," he explained. "And the food."

Adeline laughed beside him. "Good," she added. "You need some more food in you. It will help you grow big and strong."

An emotion I began to recognize as Malachi's twisted in my chest. It was...it was guilt, so sour that I nearly doubled over.

"They treated him like he was nothing," Malachi whispered in my ear. "I can't believe they would starve a child like that."

"He's out of there now," I reassured him. "And that's all that matters. He'll have a better life here."

"Because of you," Malachi said, running a finger up the inside of my forearm as he turned his back to the rest of the room. "You fought for him to get out of that wretched place. You never cease to amaze me, my queen."

His eyes flickered down to my lips, and in that moment, I didn't care if the entire room saw. I wanted him to kiss me. I wanted to feel those lips on mine, and so did the power that burned in my center.

"Peacemaker," Dragon's young voice cut the air, breaking any tension that lingered between Malachi and I.

Mal smiled, which was more like a promise, before backing away.

I took a few steps toward Dragon, who now attempted to braid Adeline's hair in a way that reminded me so much of Tessa.

"Yes?"

"I knew you could do it," Dragon replied, not taking his attention off Adeline's perfect cherry hair. "They always knew it, too. Even if they did not want to tell you."

"Who?" Malachi interrupted. "Who didn't want to tell her?"

Dragon finally looked at us. "Everyone at the temple. I heard them whispering about her when they thought I wasn't around."

"I find it hard to believe that anyone in that temple believed in what I could do," I said. "Especially Silas."

Malachi flinched before quickly covering it up with a blink. I instantly regretted bringing him up.

That was the second father Malachi had to kill. It had to be done, I was the first person to understand that. Still, Malachi's hands were covered in so much blood, I sometimes wondered how he didn't drown in it all.

"Did Silas ever speak to you?" Adeline asked. She had a gentleness about her that felt so comforting, even for me. I was glad she was here, I was glad Dragon had her, too.

Dragon shrugged. "Sometimes. He told me not to talk to anyone else, though."

*Now he had all of our attention.*

I glanced at Cordelia, who would no doubt be reading his thoughts and digging around in his memories, but she just stared at him with a raised brow.

"What?" Lucien asked. "What's so surprising about that?"

"Silas wanted to keep him a secret?" Serefin questioned. "Why?"

Malachi stepped closer, looking at Dragon as if he were looking at him for the first time. "I don't know yet," Malachi replied. "But I'm starting to question what exactly was going on in that mountain. Cordelia?"

Attention in the room slid to her. "Don't look at me," she said with her hands raised. "Like I said, I'm not a babysitter."

"Can you search his mind? Find out what was so special?" I didn't care if it sounded like an invasion. If something interested Silas, we needed to know. Especially since we had practically kidnapped him to raise in our own kingdom.

She cleared her throat and dropped the hand that propped against her hip, focusing all of her attention on Dragon. To my surprise, he didn't even squirm. Just looked at her with his head tilted in curiosity.

And for the first time since I had known her, Cordelia looked truly clueless. "No," she said, hardly over a whisper.

"No what?" Mal asked.

"No, I can't read his mind."

"It's been hours," I announced. "Surely it's safe for us all to go to sleep."

Most of our company had left us, leaving only myself, Malachi, Serefin, and Adeline in the room waiting for magic to manifest. I enjoyed their company, I really did, but exhaustion was beginning to take over.

Malachi insisted that we stayed awake until the magic began to show, but I was starting to doubt, well, everything.

"I agree," Adeline added. "If we start to get magical powers, we'll come find you!"

Malachi shook his head. "It's dangerous," he added. "What if our people begin to manifest gifts and lose control? What if we need to maintain the peace?"

"We will," I added. "But I can't maintain anything if I'm half-asleep."

Serefin quit pacing. I could see the tenseness that lingered in his shoulders. "I agree with Malachi."

"Of course you do," Adeline retorted. "He's your king."

"I'm your king, too," Mal added.

Adeline gave him a soft smile. "You were my brother, first."

"Well, I'm not anymore. We know that much for sure."

Hurt flashed across Adeline's face, and I reached out to grab her hand. She quickly covered it with a smile of pity.

They were raised like family, but they were never blood related. That became very clear now that we knew who Malachi's real father was.

And Adeline was nothing like the Saint of death.

"We never got to talk about what happened under that mountain," Adeline said softly. "Just between the four of us."

"There's not much to talk about," I said, knowing Adeline would see right through the words. "Malachi saved my ass before the Paragon could kill me."

"I still can't believe they would do that to you," Serefin added. "After everything you've been through. You were chosen from the Saints, and they doubted you even then."

"Yeah, well I don't think they doubt me anymore."

Adeline squeezed my hand. "What happened to you in there, Jade? We were worried sick every single day that you were gone. Saints, I wanted to storm into those mountains and kill them all myself for taking you."

*They knew.* Of course, they would know what Malachi went through under that mountain, but I doubted anyone else knew. Maybe his brothers, but that was it.

I looked at Mal, who gave me a reassuring nod. We could trust them.

"The trials were rough," I started. "Malachi warned me what they would be like, but..." I was grateful for Adeline still holding my hand, because I was sure they would be shaking. "It felt so real."

"You don't have to tell us if you don't want to," Serefin chimed in. "You don't need to relive it."

"No," I said. "It's okay. It wasn't real, right? I can't bury those images in my mind. I need to get them out." Serefin nodded, his jaw set. I continued. "I saw Tessa, I saw my father. I saw...I saw a lot of deadlings. Nobody survived, though. There was so much death..." I remembered what Erebus had said to me during the ceremony. Surrounded by so much death. He was right about that. "I had to kill him," I added.

I didn't need to explain who I was talking about. Adeline sucked in a sharp breath. "Oh, Jade," she whispered.

"That's not the worst part. Because of our magic connection, he was affected by what happened in my mind. When I killed him in the trial..."

"Saints," Ser mumbled.

"And my power somehow brought him back to life."

Adeline snapped her head in my direction. "You're joking."

"She's not joking in the slightest," Mal said, placing a warm hand on my shoulder. I instantly felt reassured, safer. He was here. He was alive.

*That was all in your mind.*

"Jade has the power of life," Malachi added. I waited for some sort of reaction from the two, but they stared at me with wide eyes, waiting for more.

"Just as Malachi has the power of death."

And then slowly, in a way that put a fire in my stomach, they both smiled. "What a damn pair you two are," Serefin said.

"Yeah," Malachi said, giving my shoulder another squeeze. "What a damn pair."

We sat like that in silence, letting another half hour tick by as we waited for something. Anything. The castle was silent at this hour, right before dawn. It came to my attention that we had been there all night, waiting for something we weren't sure was coming.

*Can you at least give me a hint?* I silently thought to the Saints. *When exactly is magic going to be restored?*

A beat passed with no response. It's not like I was expecting a response, anyway. They hadn't said anything to me since I saw them in the ceremony, and I was half-convinced that they were done speaking to me altogether. I knew what I needed to do. There was nothing else for them to say.

*Patience, peacemaker,* a voice spoke back to me. But it wasn't Anastasia this time. The voice was low and fiery, and I recognized it immediately. It was Erebus who spoke.

*Where is Anastasia?* I asked.

*We're all here,* Anastasia spoke back. *You can channel all of us now, if you wish. We are all here to help you, if you need us.*

*Can anyone else speak to you?* I asked, making eye contact with Malachi, who stared back with a raised brow.

*Not yet,* Erebus replied.

*Yet?* I asked. *What does that mean?*

Apparently, they were done with our social hour. Nobody spoke back to me. Nobody explained. Nobody answered my questions.

"You okay?" Mal whispered, leaning over the wooden table and dropping his voice.

I nodded. "Just trying to get some answers."

"And?"

*"Patience, peacemaker,"* I repeated, imitating Erebus's deep voice.

Mal's eyes widened, realizing what that meant. "That wasn't Anastasia speaking to you that time, was it?"

I waited for a second, half-tempted to lie so he wouldn't worry about me. But it was no use. Malachi would know if I was lying, would know any emotion I felt now because of our bonded magic.

"No," I answered bluntly. "It wasn't."

A flicker of something swam in his deep eyes before he blinked it away. Even though I could feel his concern as deeply as I would feel my own, I knew he wouldn't show it. Not if it meant suggesting something was wrong. Not if it meant suggesting I wasn't strong enough to handle the Saints speaking to me.

And Malachi knew I could handle it. Deep down, he knew.

"Alright," Adeline said from the large stack of books she had attempted to busy herself with. "I'm exhausted, and I love you both dearly, but I need sleep."

I stood, unable to fight the exhaustion any longer. "Me too."

"Go with her," Malachi ordered Adeline. "I don't want her to be alone."

"I don't need a babysitter," I snapped. "I'm fine, Mal."

He stood and walked around the table, placing both hands on my shoulder. "I know you're fine," he said, brushing a soft kiss onto my forehead. "Do this for me, please? So I can at least attempt to not worry about you every second we are apart?"

My chest tightened. I let myself melt into him for a second, leaning into the pine and warmth and smoke that was so incredibly *him*.

And then I pulled myself away. "Okay," I said. "But just for one night." *Even though it was practically already morning.*

"Come on," Adeline said, reluctantly throwing her arm around my shoulders as we turned our backs on the two of them. "I've been dying to have a slumber party."

"You two be careful," Serefin yelled from the far side of the study.

"Always are," Adeline teased.

I let myself think of Malachi until we made it to Adeline's room.

"Promise me if you start melting the castle with some crazy fire magic, you'll wake me up," I said to Adeline. My voice had grown groggy and tired.

"Only if you promise me that you'll put the fire out with whatever magic the Saints have given you."

"Deal," I said.

We fell onto her white, silk sheets, and slipped into a deep, deep sleep.

## CHAPTER 7
# *Malachi*

VITA QUEEN.

Four entire days passed with nothing peculiar happening. We met with our court, we discussed politics of the kingdom and of neighboring kingdoms, we ate, and we slept.

There were no odd instances of magic. There were no Saints showing up among us. There were no rebellions of magic and newly gifted power breaching the walls of our kingdom.

None of that.

The only change I noticed among any of us, was the change I saw in Jade.

"You're getting slower," she teased. The wind snapped her hair around her face and blew the trees in the distance. We had been outside all day, the warmth of the sun beginning to heat the frigid air.

She swung forward with her fists once more, and I barely dodged in time to miss her punch.

"You're getting faster," I rebutted.

"Please tell me you're not going easy on me because I'm a woman," Jade hissed.

*Saints.* I wished that was the case. The reality was that Jade was strong. Our normal sparring sessions that typically left her breathless were leaving me sore and gasping for air. Each punch she threw hit a little harder. Each maneuver I dodged took a little more effort.

Focusing on her stance, I anticipated the next kick. When she swung her foot toward my upper leg, I caught it, pulling her body forward so she had no choice but to fall against me.

I caught her with one arm while using the other arm to pull her leg around my waist. Her face came inches from mine, breathless and wild.

"That's a dirty move," she whispered. Her arms came to rest atop my shoulders as she relaxed against me. Sweat glistened across her forehead and dripped down her neck.

"Trust me, my queen," I replied, letting my gaze fall to her plump, inviting lips as she continued to pant for air. "You haven't seen *dirty*."

I closed the short distance between our mouths and kissed her, rough and needy. We hadn't taken much to delicacies lately, but rather stole these kisses in the passing moments of our busy days.

Jade kissed me back, tightening the leg around my waist and lifting herself up so both legs secured around my body, just below the base of my wings.

*Made for me. Mine. Forever.*

My power flared in response, and I couldn't control the short tendrils of my power that lapped around us, momentarily shading us from the sun as I fought to keep control.

"Careful, killer," Jade mumbled into my lips. "Don't want to hurt anyone."

The tickle of delight I felt in my chest was her power, flaring equally as wild as mine. Though she could hide hers a bit better, I still felt it. I felt nearly every emotion she felt now, and it had only gotten stronger since the peacemaker ritual had been completed.

But with that slight, delightful flicker of Jade's life magic came a darker sensation of lust, a feeling that was never there before the ritual.

It felt familiar, yet so unlike her.

Whatever it was, though, whatever had changed deep inside of her whenever she agreed to fulfill the peacemaker's destiny, my power was pulled to it like it belonged there all along. Like it deserved to be there, like it was made to be together.

Like we were made to be together.

"Your power is growing," I said. Jade continued kissing me, running her lips along my neck. I gripped her hips harder, holding her to me. "Do you feel it?"

"Mhm," she hummed against me, not pausing her mouth for even a moment. Her hands wound through my hair, lightly pulling and holding my head up.

"I'm serious."

"So am I. I'm serious about this," she said, kissing my jawline. "And this," she mumbled against my neck, my earlobe.

*Damn it all. This conversation could wait.*

My mouth found hers in the daylight of the field, kissing her like I had wanted to for days. My fingers tightened around her, but she only moaned against my mouth in response.

I half-walked, half-flew us to the nearest tree, pinning her body against it for support as I pulled myself toward her, getting as close as possible to my wife. Nothing but forest surrounded us to my right, and to my left, the castle was nearly out of view.

Still, I pulled my wings out, spanning them against the sun that beat down through the trees.

"Mal," Jade murmured against my mouth. "Mal, Mal, Mal."

*Shit.* The way she said my name sent my power into an unstoppable frenzy, and I was suddenly grateful that nobody was near us to be injured.

Jade did that to me. Against everything, even my wild temper, Jade was the only thing that made me lose control. And I loved every bit of it.

I pulled her tunic down past her shoulder, exposing the skin of her neck so I could kiss her there. She tilted her head back with a gasp, easily giving me access to everything I wanted.

"I love you, Jade," I found myself muttering. "I've loved you since before I even knew you, and I'll love you forever. Long after I'm gone."

"Don't talk like that," Jade said, pulling her face down to meet mine. "You're not leaving me. Not now, not ever."

All I could do was nod in agreement, and her lips found mine again, dancing together in the same wildness that I felt inside of me. That my power felt within.

"I love you, too," Jade said after a while, long enough that I had forgotten I even said it at all. "I love you more every day, so much that I'm not sure I'll be able to handle it sometimes."

I knew that feeling. I knew it very, very well.

Every damn second I spent with Jade gave me more of that feeling I never thought I could get enough of.

Jade clawed at my clothes now, needing to be closer to me. Each slight scrape of her fingernails ignited more of a fire within me, pain mixing with pleasure in a way that only Jade could satisfy.

"I hate to break up the party," Cordelia's voice split through the air, freezing any heat that may have still lingered. "We're waiting for you two."

"Really?" Jade sneered, still partially on top of me. "You choose *now* to interrupt us?"

I didn't have to look at Cordelia to know the way she stood, glaring at us with her hand cocked on her hip. "Why?" Cordelia replied. "Something important happening over here?"

"Saints," I mumbled, reluctantly pulling away from my wife. "You have no idea where you aren't wanted, do you?"

"Oh, I have plenty of ideas," Cordelia sneered. "Would you like me to tell them to you?"

"No!" Jade and I yelled in unison.

Cordelia stared at us for a moment longer before turning on her heel and walking back through the field toward the castle.

"That was short-lived," I whispered, giving Jade one more quick kiss.

"But worth it," she whispered back.

She slid her hand into mine, and with our hearts still beating like wild animals, we followed Cordelia back through the field.

Today was not just any other normal day in Rewyth.

Today was our last morning here. We were leaving for...well, everywhere.

# CHAPTER 8
# *Jade*

An hour later, we were ready to set off on our tour of the surrounding kingdoms. I couldn't deny that it was necessary. I would be the peacemaker, the one responsible for maintaining the power of these lands. The least I could do was show my face, to let them know I wasn't their enemy.

"I'm not sure who decided that you could join us," I hissed to Cordelia. "Don't you have enough torturing to do here in the kingdom? Or have you exhausted all your new toys in Rewyth?"

She laughed dramatically, kicking her somehow *always* clean boots onto the wooden ledge of the carriage. "I'm always up for an adventure, peacemaker," she replied, looking aimlessly out the small window of the carriage door. "Besides, all the interesting people are coming with you. I'd be bored here all alone."

She was right about that. Malachi and I weren't traveling the kingdoms alone. Along with plenty of his guards to travel with us, we were accompanied by his brothers—Eli, Lucien, and Adonis—along with his sister, Adeline, and his most trusted guard and companion, Serefin.

Some of the other court members wanted to come along, too, but Malachi insisted we keep the group small.

*If that's what you'd call this.*

Adeline piled into the carriage next, giving Cordelia a dirty look before sliding onto the carriage bench beside me. "I see you're riding in the carriage with us *royals,*" Adeline sneered, emphasizing the last word. Cordelia would not care, though. She cared very little about making friends here, especially with Adeline, and that was made clear from the second we arrived back in Rewyth.

Adeline didn't seem to care that much about Cordelia, either.

I didn't blame her. They were complete opposites. Adeline was always so gentle and kind, and Cordelia, while she was kind in her own ways, was anything *but* gentle.

*Maybe this trip would help them bond.*

"Ready in here?" Malachi asked, peeking his head into the carriage. He had insisted on riding one of the horses, along with the rest of the men accompanying us on the trip. He wore his royal uniform, one made of black fabric and gold emblems, fitting snugly across his sculpted muscles. His black wings never ceased to amaze me, either. They drew attention to him everywhere we went, always a reminder of the death that came with him.

And damn, it was sexy.

"We're ready," I said back. He stared at me for a second longer, scanning his eyes down my body before shutting the door to the carriage, leaving me inside with the other women.

"Wow," Cordelia said, pursing her lips. "He might as well undress you right now. He practically already did with his eyes."

Adeline gasped in surprise. She wasn't as used to Cordelia's *fun little comments.*

But I was.

"I'd be careful with your suggestions," I snapped back. "Would hate to make you ride a horse all the way to Paseocan while Mal and I occupy the carriage."

Cordelia squinted at me.

Adeline rested her forehead against the carriage wall and exhaled. "This is going to be fun," she mumbled under her breath.

Cordelia turned her head to Adeline. "Don't even get me started with you and the handsome guard," she teased. "Am I the only one here without someone keeping me warm at night?"

Adeline's cheeks flushed red in the corner of my eye. I tried not to smile. Her relationship with Serefin was certainly not public knowledge, though Mal and I had known about it for quite some time. Mal didn't mind. If anything, it brought him comfort that Adeline was being watched over. But that was Adeline's secret to tell, not Cordelia's.

"Don't worry," I said before Adeline could muster a response. "I'm sure you'll draw in plenty of willing suitors with your warm attitude and kindness. It's a very attractive quality."

Adeline snorted beside me.

The carriage jolted into motion, and we were on our way.

The entire day passed before the horses needed to stop for a break. Adeline and Cordelia were both already asleep on the wooden carriage bench, slumped on either side of the walls. At least they weren't up bickering, which took the majority of the afternoon.

*The silence had been welcomed, to say the least.*

"We'll stop here for the night," Malachi announced. "There's an inn through that path. It's small, but it is discreet and safe. It will do just fine while our horses rest."

I pushed the carriage door open and jumped out, my stiff muscles practically screaming at me from the long trip.

Malachi made his way in my direction. "Enjoying the journey so far?" he asked, placing a hand on my lower back and guiding me toward the path.

"Oh yes." My voice dripped with sarcasm. "My favorite part has been Adeline and Cordelia arguing about which of your guards is the tallest. It's riveting."

Malachi laughed. "Once we're in familiar territory, you can ride one of the horses."

"I'm not sure why we need to wait," I pushed. "It's not like I'm any safer inside the carriage."

"A stray arrow can't hit you inside the carriage. Assassins can't jump from trees and take you out. You're not even with us, as far as anyone else knows. You're hidden, and that's not a bad thing."

His arm fell around my shoulders. "Everyone in this inn is about to discover that I'm here."

I watched as glamour fell over him, turning his black wings silver to hide any identifiable traits. Even so, he looked tall and strong. He held himself like a king would, and anyone could see that.

"We'll see about that," he whispered, lips brushing my ear.

We approached the inn, which was no more than a worn down, wooden building. A few lanterns lit up the windows on the second level, but other than that, it was silent.

Eerily silent.

"It's okay," Malachi whispered. Surely, he could feel how nervous this place made me. "I know the owner."

That wasn't entirely enough to ease my nerves, but I trusted him. Malachi wouldn't put me in danger.

*Knowingly.*

A couple of his guards walked in first, another holding the door open for us to enter. They bowed their heads as we passed through.

And before I could think about how the hair on the back of my neck stood up, we walked inside.

The building inside was just as bland as the outside, with planks of wood propped up to create tables and a bar on the far end. An older woman sat near a lantern next to the door.

"What do we have here?" the woman asked, standing from her stool behind the rickety table. "Tell me that's not–" she walked toward us a few paces before she stopped in her tracks. "Saints, it is you!" Her face lit up as she took in Malachi.

"We're on a low profile here," Malachi interrupted before she could say anything else. "I don't want anyone to know who we are."

The woman looked past me and peered out the door we had just walked through. "With all these men?" she asked. "And all those horses? You might as well have announced your arrival, boy."

*Boy?* They must have known each other well if she was comfortable enough to call the King of Rewyth *boy*.

"If anyone asks about them, tell them it's one of my brothers."

"Will do," the woman replied. Her eyes finally slid to me, raking me up and down. "And this must be..."

"Yes," Malachi said, cutting her off again before she could say my name. "It is. Do you have rooms available for us tonight? We'll be out of your hair by sunrise."

The woman stared at me for a beat longer, and I almost thought she wasn't going to look away at all. I wanted to squirm under her attention, but Malachi's warm hand on my back kept me standing tall.

*I didn't have to prove anything to this woman.*

She eventually broke her stare, scurrying back behind the table. "Oh, don't be silly," she said, waving her hand. "You are welcome to stay as long as you need. A few of the rooms are occupied, but I'm sure we can make this work."

She and Malachi went back and forth for a few moments before he dropped a small bag of coins on her table.

"Ready?" Malachi whispered against my ear. I nodded, and he led me through the nearly empty bar and up the wooden stairs in the back of the room.

To my surprise, the few bodies at the bar remained focused on whatever conversations they were already having. Nobody even glanced in our direction.

Maybe Malachi's glamour worked better than I thought.

"Don't worry about them," Malachi said as we reached the top of the stairs. "Nobody here cares enough to acknowledge who we are."

*They don't care?* "Don't you find that a little odd?" I asked as Mal pushed the key into one of the doors at the end of the hall. "That they don't care?"

Malachi just shrugged. "For tonight, I think it's our best-case scenario."

*Okay, he had a point there.* Being in and out of this place was better than drawing any sort of attention to us, good or bad.

After wiggling the key in the lock for what felt like an entire minute, the knob finally twisted open. I stepped inside, taking in the room. It wasn't much, which was to be expected. A bed, one I'm sure Malachi wouldn't even fit on, sat in the corner of the room. A dresser pushed against the wall with a small, dusty mirror resting atop it. The room did, to my surprise, have its own washroom, which was a blessing of its own.

I silently sent a thank you up to the Saints.

*Don't thank us just yet,* Erebus hissed back in my mind. *Stay close to him.*

*Like I was going to leave him and wander around a strange inn by myself anytime soon.*

"Do the others get rooms?" I asked as I made my way to the window that overlooked our horses and carriage.

"I secured a room for Adeline and Cordelia, but the rest can fend for themselves with whatever's left."

"Wow," I sighed, "that's awfully generous of you."

Malachi came up behind me, pulling me back to him with his hands on my hips. "That's what they say about me, you know," he said. "Generous, deadly, and incredibly sexy."

"Oh really?" I asked, spinning in his arms. "Who, exactly, says that about you?"

The raw pull of attraction in his eyes was the same I felt deep in my stomach every time he and I were alone together. "You, for starters," he mumbled, bringing his lips down to my jaw and kissing me there, hot and slow.

"Well, I suppose that's not entirely a lie," I mumbled back, my voice giving way to the rush of emotion that filled my veins.

But all of that emotion, all of that heat and need I felt for Mal, faded quickly when my stomach rumbled. Loudly. Loud enough for Mal's pointed ears to flicker.

He froze mid-kiss, pulling away to look into my eyes. "You need to eat."

I pulled on his neck, attempting to bring him back into the moment. "I will later," I said. But my stomach rumbled again, louder this time.

*Saints, I really was hungry.*

"Stay here," he said. "I'll get you something from downstairs."

*Go with him,* Erebus's voice boomed in my head, more demanding than before and forceful enough to make me jump.

I didn't argue. "Let me come with you," I said to Mal.

"No way," he said. "I don't want anyone down there to recognize you. It could cause more trouble than we need tonight, and I'm too exhausted to kill everyone who touches you."

*No, he's not,* Erebus said.

"Then I'll kill them all if they even give us a second glance," I said. It was mostly a gesture, but *damn*, the words felt good leaving my mouth. Because for once in my life, I was confident that was actually true. And a small flicker of my power told me I was more than capable of protecting myself.

We would be just fine.

He eyed me for a second, squinting slightly, before turning to the door. "Don't talk to anyone," he whispered. "Don't even look at anyone."

"Got it," I replied. I followed him down the hallway, now littered with Mal's men fighting over who would get which room, and descended the stairs.

Glamour still hid his black wings, but there was no hiding the sheer height of him. The sheer power that turned heads to him like a beacon.

I followed closely behind him as we approached the bar on the far side of the room. "Dinner for two, please," Malachi ordered in a low voice to the middle-aged man who worked behind the counter. Mal glanced sideways at the others who sat at the bar before adding, "Quickly."

"Coming right up," the barkeep replied.

Before Malachi could even pay the man, he was pouring two large mugs of ale and setting them down on the bar.

Mal turned slightly, shielding me from the few men that sat at the far end of the bar, while he raised a brow in question.

I answered by reaching across him and picking up one of the mugs. *Saints,* we would need more than a mug of ale to get us through this trip.

*Careful,* Anastasia spoke in my mind. *You need your senses to be on guard at all times.*

*Really?* I thought back. *Now you decide to speak to me? After all this time?*

Only I didn't say the words silently. Malachi's eyes snapped to mine. He grabbed his own mug of ale before ushering us to a small table in the corner of the room, hidden in the shadows. "They're speaking to you? Right now?"

I glanced over his shoulder, making sure nobody was eavesdropping, before I nodded. "Nothing important, though."

"What are they saying?" His eyes searched mine desperately. I knew what he really wanted to ask. I could feel it. *What did Erebus say?*

"He told me not to leave your side tonight."

"What? Why? Does he think something will happen?"

I shrugged. "Not that I know of," I said, taking a sip of the golden liquid. "Although they're very picky about what they do and do not choose to tell me."

"This place is safe," Malachi said, although I wasn't sure who he was trying to convince. "I've been here multiple times before, decades ago. We can trust these people."

"Everyone here is fae," I guessed, looking at the wings around the room. Malachi wasn't using glamour to give me wings like he did last time, just using enough to hide his own. "Won't someone notice that I don't have wings or pointed ears?"

Mal shrugged. "Like I said, everyone here is too busy caring about themselves to pay us any attention. For all they know, you're a witch and I'm your human escort."

I nearly spit out my drink. "Wouldn't that be a sight," I added.

A wicked smile spread across his face. "Perhaps Erebus knows that, too."

I shook my head. I had my own reasonings for why Erebus might want us to stick together. Either he thought I was helpless and needed my husband to protect me—which was a ridiculous thought considering he had literally blown the essence of his magic into me—or he thought Malachi, his descendent, could use some of my protection.

Which also seemed strange, considering I had no idea how to use any of the powers they had given me.

I could feel it, though. When I needed to use them, they would be there, ready for me to wield. I had worked for this, trained for this.

And I would protect Malachi at all costs. The Saints knew that more than anyone.

"Could it be that Erebus wants to protect his bloodline?" I asked in a whisper. "Maybe he cares about *you*, Malachi. He knows I'll do anything to protect you."

Malachi shook his head, shaking the thought from his own mind. "Not possible," he replied. "He didn't seem to give a damn about Silas. I'm sure he has hundreds of other descendants around here that he doesn't even know of."

I tilted my head. "Hundreds?"

He took another sip of his ale. I watched as his throat bobbed, swallowing the liquid in one big gulp.

"Let's talk about literally anything other than how many possibly related fae may be running around here."

I fought a smile. "Fine."

We sat there in a comforting silence until Cordelia came into view, pulling up a chair and plopping herself down at the table. "There you are," she said. "I've been looking everywhere for you two."

"Everywhere?" I asked. "Because we're not exactly hidden."

She grabbed the ale out of my hands and took a long drink. And then another.

"Everything okay?" Malachi asked.

She finished a couple more gulps before wiping her mouth with the back of her hand. "How could everything not be okay?" she asked, leaning forward with her palms on the table. "We're in a strange inn with strange people in the middle of nowhere. I've been kicked out of my own room by your bodyguard and his little girlfriend, and I'm starving."

The barkeep decided that was a good time to bring our plates of food to our table, a large serving of meat that was still steaming.

Cordelia moaned.

"Here," I said, pushing my plate between us. "Share mine."

"Serefin and Adeline kicked you out?" Malachi asked.

Cordelia shrugged. "Well, they didn't exactly force me out the door," she started, "but I'm not really into observing."

Mal and I both rolled our eyes.

"You shouldn't be alone here tonight," I said. "You can't share a room with one of the other guards?"

She scoffed. "I'd rather take my chances, but thanks."

The three of us sat there, sharing our dinner with Cordelia, while the rest of the inn buzzed around us. Adonis and Lucien were nowhere in sight, and a few of the other guards Malachi had brought with us lingered casually around the bar.

An hour later, after three mugs of ale and as much food as we could possibly eat, I was ready for bed.

"Be careful, Cordelia," I warned.

"You're cute when you worry," Cordelia teased. "But I'm a powerful witch, remember? You're the one who needs to watch your back."

*At least I tried to be nice.*

"Come find me if you need anything," Malachi added, although I couldn't tell if it was a serious offer or not. Either way, Cordelia would never take him up on it. They had been cordial over the weeks we had spent together, but never even *close* to friendly.

I think that was as good as it was going to get.

Mal followed tightly behind me as we left the bar and wandered back to our room. The warmth of his body radiated through the thickness of our clothes. He reached around my body to unlock the door in front of me before pushing it open and following me inside.

And then, finally, we were alone.

The slight buzz of the ale and the exhaustion from the trip washed over me, like my body was waiting for this moment to finally let its guard down.

Mal did the same, shoulders sagging in exhaustion in a way I was sure only I would notice.

Sleep. Sleep was exactly what I needed.

Arms groped down on my body, pinning me backward. The familiar feel of metal on my throat made me freeze.

"Scream and you die."

# CHAPTER 9

# Malachi

My sword was in my hand before I could even blink, spinning to Jade while every single one of my senses focused on the body behind her. Silver wings, but none that I recognized.

Fae, but not from Rewyth.

"Let her go," I growled.

His blade pressed against her throat, but if he wanted her dead, he wouldn't be hesitating.

"I just want to talk," the attacker said. Sharp features reflected the lantern light, giving me small glimpses of his face.

"This isn't a great conversation starter," Jade mumbled. Any fear or shock she had been feeling was replaced by anger; each of her features now held a promise I knew she would be keeping.

She didn't let the intruder say another word. I watched—every one of my senses on guard and ready to act—as Jade sent a sharp elbow into her attacker's ribs. Hard.

He grunted and doubled over, immediately losing his grip on her. Jade quickly stepped toward me until I pulled her the rest of the way behind me.

Safe at my side, Jade drew her own weapon. Her anger burned with mine, mixing together in my chest in a way that made it difficult to control my power.

"What do you think you're doing?" Jade asked, her voice bewildered.

The man dropped his dagger and held his hands up in surrender, still catching his breath from Jade's hit.

*Good girl.* She really *was* getting stronger.

"I came here to see you," he managed to choke out.

"Obviously," Jade snapped. "Would you like to inform me why you thought holding your weapon to my neck was a good idea? Or should I kill you now and get it over with?"

Cordelia burst into the room, using her black boots to kick the door open. "What's going on here?"

"Saints," I mumbled. She stormed in, eyes frantically searching Jade and I with our weapons out. She didn't need to ask, though. She had probably heard our thoughts from her table downstairs.

"That's exactly what we're trying to figure out," Jade answered.

A dark, amused smile contorted Cordelia's sharp face. "Well," she said, clasping her hands in front of her. "Isn't this exciting? These two don't like company, buddy. I've already tried."

"There's going to be an attack!" he blurted. "I came to warn you!"

"Warn us?" I replied. "Is that what you call that?" I took a step in front of Jade.

"There's few that don't like what's happening. They don't want their magic to be controlled."

"What's that supposed to mean?" Jade asked. "They're planning on killing me so they can use magic? Do they think I'm forbidding the use of magic?"

The man shrugged.

This was a mess. If anyone was actually planning an attack on Jade, we needed to know about it. But there was absolutely *no way* I was going to trust this stranger, when just seconds ago, he had his hands on my wife.

"Sit down," I ordered him.

His eyes snapped to me, and I recognized that familiar shine of fear lingering.

*Good. He should be afraid.*

He did as I ordered, sliding his feet over to the worn-down, wooden chair in the corner of the room and taking a seat.

"Assuming you *are* telling the truth," I started, "why would you warn her? Why would you want to help us?"

He shrugged. "She is the peacemaker," he said. "There have been many times in my life that I have wanted power, but now is not one of them. These fae...they'll take over. They'll create unease and they'll destroy everything to get what they want. Please, you have to believe me!"

He began leaning toward Jade with his hands out, pleading.

"That's enough," I barked. I turned my attention to Cordelia. "Is he telling the truth?"

She cocked her head sideways, like he was about to be her new form of entertainment. "From what I can tell, yes," she said. "Although he's leaving something out." She took a few steps forward, passing Jade, and knelt before the man. He looked terrified now, shaking where he sat with eyes wider than ever.

But why would someone so afraid be willing to put their hands on the peacemaker?

"Who's planning the attack?" Cordelia asked. "And how do you know about this?"

He answered without hesitating. "A group of rebels. I overheard them when I passed them on the road. I saw one of the royal crests on your horses and I knew it had to be you. Please, I would never do anything to hurt the peacemaker. I only wanted to warn you!"

I glanced at Jade, who now looked annoyed at the entire situation. "How are we supposed to know you aren't lying to us?" she asked. "How are we supposed to know you won't run directly to them and tell them the peacemaker is here at this inn?"

"I won't!" he stammered. "I swear to you, I won't!"

Cordelia glanced up at us. "Your call," she said.

*To kill him.* Jade was right, we could let him go and risk the fact that he might be lying, or we could kill him and eliminate the threat.

I looked at Jade. She was the one who was at risk here. It would be her decision to make.

She nodded, understanding what I was thinking.

"Well," she said, taking a step forward and kneeling next to Cordelia. The man glanced between Jade, Cordelia, and me as if one of us would show him mercy. As if one of us were good.

As if one of us would hesitate to kill him.

*Stupid, stupid man.*

"I'm not a fan of strangers putting their hands on me," Jade started, whispering into the man's face. "And neither is my husband here."

I lifted my chin.

"Unfortunately for you, you've got things wrong," she continued. "You think of me as weak. You think you can put your blade to my throat and survive." Jade laughed, harsh and bitter. "You were wrong."

Cordelia stepped back, just an inch, but I saw it. Right before the magic inside of me lit up with anticipation, recognizing the power inside of Jade rumbling to life. Life force, with the ability to kill.

And Jade was done with him, done with threats, done with feeling weak. I wasn't surprised when the tendrils of her magic escaped her outstretched hand, wrapping around the stranger like warm rays of sunshine, before he stilled entirely—mid scream—and slumped back in the chair.

*Dead.*

"You made the right choice," Cordelia said. "Although I have to say that was entertaining."

"Go find Serefin," I ordered. "And keep this to yourself." She waited a second more, glancing at Jade one more time, before nodding and leaving the room.

Following orders for her was rare. She knew how serious this was.

"Are you okay?" I asked as soon as Cordelia was out of earshot. Jade stood, still not taking her eyes off the man before us who grew paler with every passing second.

"I'm fine," she whispered. "More than fine, actually."

I stepped forward, sliding my hand into hers, shocked at the cold I found there. "He deserved to die," I said. "He should have never entered this room."

She blinked, holding her eyes closed for a few seconds before opening them again. "I know," she replied. "Do you think any of that was true?"

"We can't expect everyone to be happy about you being the peacemaker."

She laughed under her breath. "Even though I'm the one who allows them to have their power restored. I'm really feeling the love there."

I tugged gently on her hand, pulling her from the dead fae. "That's why we're doing this," I reminded her. "To show everyone who we really are. To show them that they don't have to be afraid of you."

Her eyes snapped to mine. "You think they're afraid of me?" she asked. Suddenly, we were back in those woods, fighting off a pack of wolves that wanted Jade's meat.

"Yes," I answered honestly. "I do."

I expected Jade to feel bad, to feel embarrassed. I wasn't sure why, though. Jade had spent so much of her life afraid of the fae, it served them right to be afraid of her now. Even if she wasn't human anymore. Even if she could kill them with the simple command of her power.

*Damn.* I should definitely not have found that sexy, but I did. *I really, really did.*

What was even sexier was the smile that flickered across Jade's face. "Good," she said. "They should be afraid of me. Of us, I mean. The wicked will fall, Malachi. Finally, the wicked will fall."

Serefin helped a few of the guards get rid of the fae's body. After ordering a couple of my men to stand guard outside my door to stop any more unwelcome visitors, Jade fell fast asleep in my arms.

Her voice repeated in my mind until I, too, fell asleep with the rising moon.

*The wicked will fall.*

# CHAPTER 10
# *Jade*

**THE NEXT DAY HAD ME WISHING SOMEONE *WOULD* ATTEMPT AN ATTACK** on our carriage. At least that would be interesting.

The low hum of the carriage wheels on the dirt road only added to my exhaustion, and based on the way Adeline and Cordelia slumped on the bench across from me, I assumed it added to theirs, too.

I couldn't stop my mind from wandering off, thinking about the fae who snuck into our room last night. Why would he sneak all the way through the inn just to get himself killed? Why risk it?

*Unless he knew something we didn't...unless he was holding onto more secrets than he let on...*

I barely had to try to kill him. Death came easily, easier than I ever thought it would. It was no longer difficult for me to summon my power. It hadn't been, I realized, for some time.

*Because it belongs to you,* Erebus's voice echoed in my mind.

I jumped in my seat.

Erebus was nothing like Anastasia. I could feel the calmness in Anastasia when she spoke in my mind, like a warm bath or a cool breeze. Nothing harsh, just smooth words softly echoing in my own mind.

The Saint of death did not come and go with that same grace. He held a rigidness that made the hair on my arms stand up whenever he spoke to me. Anastasia sounded powerful, too, in a way that I could feel deep in my bones whenever she made herself known, but Erebus could command me without even speaking. His presence in my mind simply put a small, life-altering amount of fear inside of me.

The closest way I could describe it was a *thrill.*

*Any hints on when everyone else will get their magic back?* I thought back.

*When they are ready,* he said.

*Great. That's very helpful, thank you.*

*You can sass me all you want, child, but that won't make the magic manifest any sooner. Why are you in a rush, anyway? You're the one who didn't want any of this to happen.*

I stared at Adeline and Cordelia, both ignorant to the conversation I was having in my own mind. It's not that I cared, but some small part of me somewhere was concerned, just slightly, for how our little group would change.

How the world would change around us.

Adonis, Lucien, Eli. How would they change when they got magic? Would they grow power-hungry? Try to throw Malachi off his throne?

*No,* Erebus's voice boomed. *They will not remove the death-fae from the throne.*

I snorted. *You sound so certain.*

Silence. The sickening sound of the carriage wheels over the terrain re-captured my mind.

Until...

*Did you know Malachi was your descendent?* I thought when he didn't reply. I pictured Mal's harsh features, his black wings. He even looked a little like Erebus, with the same distinct features and curled hair.

Surely, one of the most powerful creatures to exist knew who his descendants were.

*That's none of your concern!* Erebus replied, sharper this time.

*It is when his life may be at risk. How can you be sure another descendant isn't planning on taking over his title? He may not be your only heir, which we learned very quickly with Silas.*

Dark laughter filled the space in my mind.

*What's humorous about that?*

*Do you see any other fae walking around with black wings, child? Have we allowed any other fae to carry around the death-gift? Did we allow Silas that same courtesy?*

*Shit.* I hadn't thought of that. The Saints had... had *let* Malachi have his black wings?

*But why? Why would you want him to stand out?* I asked.

*Because,* Erebus replied. *You are the peacemaker, and you are fated to him. Light and dark, just as you have been told. We knew this for longer than you have been alive. We have known his fate for some time now, child.*

*So what? So you gave him black wings?*

*We gave him the ability to protect you, and you to protect him.*

My heart sank. Erebus, the Saint of death, gave Malachi his power of death, gave him those midnight-black wings and cursed him in his world, so he could protect me? So he could be with me?

I pounded my fist on the carriage door. "I need a break!" I shouted. "Stop the carriage!"

A few shouted orders from Malachi, and we were rolling to a stop. Erebus said nothing as I tried to control my racing heart, tried to calm myself from the truth he just imparted on me.

*Thank the Saints.*

I needed to stretch my legs, I needed water, I needed...I needed...

Serefin opened the carriage door, allowing sunlight to flood into the space. I threw a hand up to cover my eyes as I slid toward him on the wooden bench.

"Everything alright?" he asked, holding his hand out for me to step out of the carriage. His eyes, though he always tried so carefully to hide it, dripped in concern. He relaxed only slightly at the sight of Adeline sleeping next to Cordelia.

"Everything's fine," I muttered, stepping out of the carriage and onto the dirt path. "I need some air."

Malachi brought his large white horse to a stop beside us. He swung his leg over the saddle and landed on both feet beside me. "I suppose now is just as good of a time as any to take a break," he said. "Let's eat something and let the horses rest. We'll be in Paseocan within the day."

"Can't wait," I mumbled.

He gave me a knowing look before handing the reins of the horse to Serefin, who guided it toward the trees around us.

"Come with me," Mal said. "You look like you could use a walk."

A breath of air escaped me. "You have no idea."

With his hand in mine, he pulled me from the small crowd of our crew and into the trees around us. The smell of the forest air brought back so many memories, memories of my home before I ever met Malachi and memories of the two of us together, catapulted into this new life.

I thought of the first week I was with him in Rewyth, when the tiger attacked me in the lagoon. When he brought me through the forest back to the human lands. And all the times he had killed those deadlings for me, protecting me...

Maybe Erebus was right. Maybe he was here to protect me.

It sure felt like it at times, but that didn't make any sense. Anastasia had said something quite opposite of that before...

*He will be your downfall...*

"What's on your mind?" Mal asked. We paused near a large tree. I let go of his hand and leaned my back against the rough bark, looking up at the leaves above.

"That's a dangerous question," I muttered.

He laughed quietly. "I'm willing to risk it."

*Could I tell him?* Could I tell him that Erebus had been talking to me, had been telling me these things about him?

My fingernails bit into the palms of my hands.

He was Malachi, my husband. My other half. He deserved to know.

"Erebus has been speaking in my mind more often than Anastasia," I stated.

Malachi's face didn't show a single sign of shock or distaste. In fact, he stared at me unblinking for what felt like minutes, staring into me with those soul-seeking eyes of his. "And this bothers you?" he asked.

I shook my head. "It doesn't bother me that he speaks to me, it's what he says."

Mal shifted on his feet. "And what is it that he says?"

Another beat passed between us. Birds chirped in the distance, mixing with the subtle wave of wind and nature that nearly fooled everyone into thinking this forest was safe, was peaceful. I knew better than that, though. Something so beautiful always held a darker side, a deadlier side.

It was the beauty that drew you in. That got you killed.

"He claims you are my protector, that you were gifted with your magic and your wings so you could protect me when our fates collided."

Malachi considered this. He considered this for some time, actually, until I was certain I was going to have to scream to get him to say something in response. To say anything, to tell me that he wasn't angry. That he was okay with this curse if it meant he could protect me when the time came.

Slowly, his sharp features morphed into an amused smile.

"What?" I asked. "You're not upset?"

He stepped forward, nearly closing the distance between us as I rested on the tree behind me. "You think I would be upset about protecting you?" he asked, eyes seeking my face in a way they so often did.

"No," I replied, "but I know you've been alive a lot longer than I have. You've had to live with this... this *gift* for a long time before you met me, Mal. Your magic hasn't exactly made life easy for you, and neither have your black wings."

His smile grew. "It's all been worth it," he whispered. "Every kill, every war, every torturous mission from my father. The Paragon. The Trials of Glory. I would gladly go through it all again if it meant I could protect you, Jade."

My stomach blossomed in a warm wave of love so deep, so pure, I would never be able to put it into words. "Do you mean that?" I asked. "Because if you want out of this, if you want to change your fate, I wouldn't blame you for it."

His left hand came up to brace himself on the tree trunk behind me. He brought his face so close to mine that if I moved forward an inch, we would be touching. "You are a damned fool, Jade Weyland, if you think for even a second that I would *ever* leave you in this world. That I could ever spend even a single day away from you, not knowing where you were. Not knowing when I would see you next."

I couldn't help but smile, reaching out and sliding my hands up the sides of his torso, pulling him that last inch closer to me. "My dark savior," I whispered, pushing myself up on my toes to brush a soft kiss against his lips.

He let out a slow breath. "My saving light."

That shadow of Malachi's power inside of me sparked to life, fueling my body with adrenaline and magic and desire. Desire for Malachi, desire for...for more. Of what? It was hard to tell. Being close to Malachi like this always stirred up these feelings. At first, I had quickly brushed them off as my longing for my husband, my need for more of him. But now?

Malachi kissed me back, his lips slowly moving against mine in a gentle yet claiming way. His black wings whipped outward, shielding us from the sun that filtered through the branches over our heads. My protector. My husband.

*My downfall.* No matter how hard I tried to push it down, Anastasia's voice came screaming back into my mind.

I pushed Mal's chest, sending him a step backward and breaking our kiss. He stared at me in confusion.

"What's wrong?" he asked.

My fingers brushed against my lips, feeling for the ghost of our kiss. How was something so perfect for me supposed to be my downfall? Erebus had said it himself; Malachi was made for me. The darkness to my light, the death to my life. He was my equal in nearly every way.

*So what was Anastasia talking about?*

"Nothing," I lied. "I'm sorry, I just thought I heard something."

My power flared again, roaring deep in my stomach.

"You can tell me, Jade. I don't want you to go through this alone." *Damn him.* He was right. Of course, he was right. Malachi always had a calm, sensible way about him, the way that made me not want to lie to him anymore.

I exhaled, giving up all the secrets I had been hiding. I was so, so tired of keeping secrets. Of telling lies.

I rubbed my aching eyes with the palms of my hands and finally let my shoulders hang. Malachi was next to me in an instant, holding me up much more than the tree behind me. "You can tell me anything. Let me carry some of this for you."

*Some of this.* I knew what he meant, even if he didn't say the words. Some of the darkness. Some of the power. Some of the burden.

If Erebus was right, perhaps this was our burden to share. Perhaps we were supposed to share the weight of this.

But if Anastasia was right...

I shook my head and looked at Mal, blurting the words out before I could stop myself again. "*You are my downfall,*" I said. "Anastasia keeps telling me that, but I don't know what she means. It can't be true, right? I mean, you're here to protect me, so that can't be right."

Mal's mask of strong emotionlessness vanished for just a moment, long enough for me to see his nostrils flare, his eyes swarm with shadows. His soft hands went rigid on my shoulders, but only for a flash, before he recovered back to himself.

So sneaky, my husband. But I knew him too well.

"You believe her?" I whispered, not caring that my voice cracked. Not caring that my knees weakened.

Mal was already shaking his head, urging me to look at him. "No, not for a second," Mal whispered. "That could never be possible, Jade. I'm here for you. I'm always here for you."

He stepped back, running his hands through his unruly black hair, the same thing he always did when he was stressed out. I could feel it, too. Deep in my soul, I could feel the dark flush of power, fiery and hot, as unsettled in me as it was in him.

"Then why would she say that?" I asked. "Why would she keep saying that, reminding me of it every time I might forget it? It's driving me mad, Mal, I–"

I rubbed my eyes again, trying to get rid of the chaos, the uncertainty.

*Calm yourself, child*, Anastasia said. *I did not tell you of this so you could lose control.*

"Then why did you tell me?" I asked, only realizing I said the words out loud after they had left my lips.

Malachi let that shield drop once more as he searched my face, showing me the pain and love and regret.

*You forget, child. I was tied to a fate very similar to yours, many, many moons ago. You are not alone in this. You mustn't worry.*

Tears fell down my face. Not necessarily tears of sadness, but more of exhaustion. *I was so damn tired.*

"Make it stop," I said to Mal, barely over a whisper. "Make the voices stop, Mal. I can't do it anymore. I can't keep hearing all these riddles."

He wrapped his arms around me, pulling me to his chest. "You're going to be okay, Jade. You're strong. You were made for this."

I nuzzled myself into him, wanting to escape into his arms. Maybe he could shield me from the voices, hide me from this fate.

*He will be your downfall.*

Anastasia wasn't going to explain herself. She wasn't going to make it any more clear. My life had been out of my hands for longer than I could remember. I rarely made my own choices, rarely designed my own future. But this? *This* I would control. Malachi was not going to be my downfall. He was my strength, my better half.

He may have wielded death, but he gave me nothing less than life itself.

I wasn't sure how long we stayed that way, wrapped in each other's arms and hiding from the world around us. I would have stayed there forever, too, if it weren't for Adeline's scream ripping through the forest, scattering the birds that surrounded us.

I jumped from Mal's arms, and the two of us were running before we even knew what had happened.

It took ten seconds to reach the carriage, and less than one to see the entire thing in flames.

# CHAPTER 11
# Malachi

ADRENALINE HAD ALWAYS BEEN A WEAPON, PERHAPS JUST AS LETHAL AS a sword. Just as powerful as a fist. There were many times in battle when that extra burst in my veins saved my life, or helped me save others.

And hearing Adeline scream? I was going to kill whoever laid their damn hands on her.

Jade rushed beside me as we halted in the clearing. The carriage—or what had once been the carriage—was now nothing but a ball of flames, heat radiating into the sky and crackling into a fiery mist.

"Adeline!" I yelled. Many of my men were picking themselves up from the ground, also trying to get a hint of what had just happened here.

"Adeline!" Jade repeated. "Cordelia!"

If they were still in that carriage...

Jade stepped forward, closer to the burning mess in front of us. She thought the same thing I did, that there was a chance they didn't...

Another scream rippled through the air. Adeline's scream.

I exhaled. She wasn't in the carriage.

Jade and I both jogged around to the other side of the fire, where Adeline stood in absolute horror.

Serefin watched a few feet away, his hands out in front of him as he slowly approached her.

"What's going on?" I asked, drawing my sword. Cordelia, Lucien, Adonis, and Eli all waited nearby, similar looks on their faces as Serefin.

"Adeline?" Jade asked, her voice dropping to a soft whisper. Adeline snapped her eyes in our direction.

"She can't control it!" Cordelia called out.

"Can't control what?" I asked.

A second later, we saw what terrified them. Flames—literal burning flames—

leaped from Adeline's hands. She screamed as they grew, only stopping when they sputtered out a few moments later.

Adeline was wielding fire magic.

"Holy Saints," Jade mumbled.

Adeline had magic. Adeline, my sister, who had never wielded a single type of power in her life, had magic.

And it was a damn powerful one.

"Holy Saints!" Jade said again, this time with a bubbled laughter that she could hardly contain. I smiled, too. I couldn't help it. Everyone else might have been terrified by this, afraid that she would burn them all into ashes, but not me.

*My sister finally had some damn magic.*

I relaxed, lowering the sword I didn't remember drawing. Serefin stood up, his wild eyes snapping between me and my sister as he tried to figure out what to do.

"Finally," I said aloud. "I was starting to think Jade's entire sacrifice was going to be for nothing."

Jade walked—or ran, rather—up to Adeline and threw herself into her arms, not caring if she was going to burst into flames. Not caring that Adeline had burned the tall grass around her, not caring that the rest of the crew clearly kept their distance.

And if it were in any way possible for me to love her more in that moment, I would have.

Adeline wrapped her arms around Jade, too, letting herself cry.

"It's okay, Adeline," Jade whispered, patting her back as she continued to hug her. "You have magic, now! This is supposed to be a good thing!"

"How is that possibly a good thing?" Adonis yelled. "We don't have a carriage anymore!"

I sauntered over to him, clasping him on the shoulder. "Oh, come on, brother," I teased. "Are you jealous that our dear sister got her power before you did?"

His eyes darkened. "Careful, brother," he joked. "You might be the King, but I could still kick your ass."

Lucien cleared his throat next to us. "Adonis is right." Unlike Adonis, his voice held no hint of joking. No cues of amusement. "How will we complete this journey without a carriage? It's too far to fly, and the two of them don't even have wings."

"Sharing is caring, brother," I said to him. "You can ride with Cordelia. Trust me, she's very kind and generous."

Cordelia half-growled at the words, giving Lucien a death-glare that only he could return with such hatred. "If you even think about touching me," she started, "I'll gut you."

For the first time in a very, very long time, I saw Lucien smile.

"Good luck," I whispered to them before walking over to Serefin. "At least nobody got hurt," I said once I was close enough.

He looked at me with a worry that I understood all too well. "This time," he said. "It all happened so fast. First, she was arguing with Cordelia about Saints knows what, and the next thing we knew the carriage exploded."

"Jade will help her," I said. "And if she can't, I will. We're all in this together, Ser. We'll get her through this."

He nodded, but he didn't look convinced. "She scared the shit out of me," he mumbled.

I threw my head back and laughed. Serefin had always been so reasonable, but this? Falling for my wild, arrogant, stuck-up sister? It was a challenge for him. It didn't fit into his perfectly planned, thought-out life.

"You have quite an uphill battle on your hands here, Ser," I said. "You better pray to the Saints that you get some sort of water magic, because trust me," I nodded to Adeline, "you're going to need it."

Jade had stepped back from Adeline now, but talked to her in a hushed whisper as she wiped the tears from her face with her thumbs. I didn't have to eavesdrop to guess what she was saying to her.

*Breathe in, breathe out. Feel the power in your body, but do not give in to it. Command it. Lead it. Control it.*

Adeline would be the first of many to regain the magic that once flowed through these lands.

But she would not be the last.

Jade's hips settled between my thighs as our horse fell into line near the back of the group. I had grown used to this, used to the flush of her body against mine. What I wasn't used to, though, was the fire inside of me at the connection of our magic.

I could feel her power reacting to me, reacting to our closeness. And when she leaned her head back against me...

"You're taunting me," I whispered, low enough so only she could hear. Each slow, torturous step that the horse took caused Jade's hips to roll back against me. I remind myself not to moan aloud at the blatant pleasure of it. "And you know it."

I felt the vibrations of her laugh through her shoulders nuzzled against my chest, but she didn't move away from me. "I am not," she replied, "but I delight in it all the same."

Jade immediately stiffened away from me as the horse in front of us reared, nearly sending Cordelia and Lucien both flying in our direction.

"Will you stop moving?" Lucien shouted. "You're going to kill us both!"

"I wouldn't have to move if you kept your damned hands to yourself!" Cordelia growled back at him.

I coughed on my own laughter. "How are things going up there?" I yelled.

"Don't you dare say a single word, brother," Lucien shouted over his shoulder. "If I end up dead before we reach Paseocan, blame this witch."

"Half-witch! And don't give me any ideas, *prince*. I'd do just about anything to not have to share this horse with you for a second longer."

I pulled back, giving them space as they eventually calmed their horse.

I had to admit, watching Cordelia with my brother was at least entertaining. If anyone could put her in her place, it was going to be him, just as wicked and brutal as she.

"You're loving every moment of this, aren't you?" Jade whispered to me, turning in the saddle so I could see the smile on her face.

"Perhaps slightly," I replied. "We only have an hour or two before we reach Paseocan. We could use all the entertainment we can get before then."

The smile on her face slowly faded. "Do you think they'll be happy to see us?" she asked.

Of all the kingdoms on our tour, Paseocan was not one I worried about. They had been our rival at times, but they were nothing like Trithen. And Carlyle may have been enemies with my father, but he was my ally. He was more than that, even. He was my friend.

"You have nothing to worry about," I assured her. "Once they discover that they'll be getting magic very soon, they'll be thrilled."

"I hope you're right," she said. "The last thing I want is to start any more wars. We're here to protect them. We just need to make them see that."

A wave of caution in my veins reminded me that was not all we were doing here. That was one of the goals, yes, but there was also another, more important reason we were visiting each of the surrounding kingdoms.

A chill washed over my body as the realization hit me once again. We would be forcing each kingdom we visited to submit.

Take a knee to the peacemaker, or forfeit your life.

# CHAPTER 12
## *Jade*

I FELT THE PRESENCE OF PASEOCAN BEFORE I SAW THE GATES. THERE was a quietness that surrounded the kingdom, one that could almost be confused for a calmness.

But I felt the sharp, tricking edge that warned me to stay alert. Perhaps that was part of my new power, to feel these things much more intensely than before.

"Carlyle knows we are coming," Mal whispered against my ear. "You have nothing to fear."

I wanted to believe him. Saints, I wanted to. The times I had talked to Carlyle were pleasant, and I didn't think of him as a specifically violent man. Still, he was the leader of his own kingdom. And in anyone's eyes, we were outsiders. We were a threat.

Malachi may have been a threat before, but now? With me?

We were unstoppable.

Nobody talked as we made the final leg of the journey. Even Cordelia and Lucien had shut up, falling into the quietness of the group as the horses clicking on the dirt pavement became the only audible sounds around.

The front gates to Paseocan came into view.

Massive, black iron gates surrounded the entire kingdom. They were tall, tall enough that the fae would need to use their wings to fly over the sharp spears that lined the apex of each iron segment.

I ripped my eyes away, focusing on what lay within the iron gates. From what I could see, a large stone castle hid far behind those royal boundaries. Far enough that they would be alerted to any attacker, but not too far so they could not respond in time.

*Interesting tactic.*

The iron gates shook and creaked as we approached, and before Serefin and Adeline's horse at the front of the group even came close, the gate was swinging open.

It was now or never.

Nerves tickled my body, putting every sense of mine on alert. I felt the nerves that laced Malachi's power, too, although his also had a tone of confidence and control. His arms, which held onto the horse's reins in front of me, fell a little tighter around my body.

*Always my protector.*

"Bring the horses toward the castle," Mal announced to the group. "They should be waiting for us beyond the stone wall."

Of course he would know. This wasn't his first time here in this kingdom. My chest ached as I remembered Mal's past life, the life he had come so far from. The life he had been forced to live, the man he had been forced to become.

A killer. A weapon.

That's who he had been the last time he entered this kingdom.

"I can feel what you are thinking, my queen," he whispered, his lips brushing the space directly behind my ear. "And I love you for caring about me, but you do not need to worry. All I'm concerned about now is you and your safety."

I brushed him off. "That doesn't mean I can't be concerned for your feelings," I said. "Are you honestly not the least bit worried about returning here?"

He sighed against the back of my neck. "Without you, maybe I would be worried about my past reputation, but not anymore. We come with good news, not bad news. We're bringing them word of magic, not of war."

His voice hardened at the end of his sentence. He knew just as well as I did that entry to new land could easily be seen as an act of war, especially since he was a new king.

But we had made it this far, and this kingdom would be the first stop of many. We had no other choice than to trust that Carlyle saw our intentions for what they were —pure.

We stayed silent as those large iron gates closed behind us. The horses even seemed to tense up at the new territory. We did not see a single soul as we approached the large stone castle, but I knew they saw us. They likely had hundreds of eyes on us at any given moment, anticipating our arrival.

Watching our every move.

Every one of the guards now rode their horses with straight backs and solid shoulders. Nobody joked now. Nobody got distracted.

Once we were close enough to the castle, we could see a small, tunnel-like structure built into the wall.

"Through there," Malachi said, although his voice seemed to echo. One by one, we rode through that arched opening. One by one, we officially entered the threshold to Paseocan.

The tunnel was dark, dark enough that I could barely see the white horse beneath me. As soon as we reached the other side, though, I had to squint to keep the sunlight out of my eyes.

"Welcome!" Carlyle's voice chirped. "Come in, come in! We've been waiting for you all, you must be exhausted!"

I scanned the small crowd of armed men, all dressed in black military uniforms, and found Carlyle. He wore a cloak, too, shielding himself from the chilled temperatures. His hair had grown longer over the months, but the smile he wore was as genuine as ever. His look was even finished with a golden crown sitting atop his head, the clear signal that he was the king here.

Not Mal.

Still, when Carlyle outstretched his hand to me, I took it. "King and Queen Weyland, it is truly a pleasure to have you and your men in our home today. Please, let me help you!"

Mal's hands slid off my hips as I let Carlyle assist me off the saddle. Once I landed on the ground, Mal swung off the horse and placed a protective hand on my shoulder. "Carlyle," he replied with a wide smile. "It's been some time. You've been more than generous with us, it's time we came to visit you in your kingdom for once."

Carlyle dipped his chin in gratitude. Of all the kings we had met so far, of all the royals, even, Carlyle was my favorite. He had a certain grace about him that became comforting over our few interactions. He was loyal; he was intelligent. I trusted him, and that mattered more than anything around here.

"I believe you two have quite the story to tell me," Carlyle started. "You must tell me everything over dinner this evening. My men will bring you to your rooms to rest before then."

"We sure do," Mal said. I followed his lead as he turned with Carlyle and began walking across the stone courtyard. "Thank you, Carlyle. For everything."

Another nod of the head, and Carlyle was off greeting the rest of our men. He even scooped Serefin into a large, bear-like hug.

"This way," one of the guards announced. "We have a special wing cleared out for you."

*An entire wing?* I glanced at Mal, who only raised his eyebrow at me. Carlyle really was generous. That, or he wanted to get on our good side. Either way, my body now ached from riding on the horse for so long, even if I had Mal to support me the entire time.

I jogged forward, catching up with Adeline. "Hey," I started. "Are you feeling okay?"

She let out a shaking breath but shook her head. "As good as I can. Although fearing that I might blow up this entire castle doesn't exactly put me at ease."

I smiled at her. "I used to fear that all the time," I said honestly. "My magic would come out when it was the least convenient, and when I really needed it, it was nowhere to be found. But you're fae, you were made for magic. I'm sure you'll have perfect control in no time."

She gave me an attempt at a smile. "Where's Esther when we really need her?" she joked.

"You have Cordelia if you need her," I added. Adeline rolled her eyes. "I'm serious," I hissed. "She could be a great asset in helping you control this. She'll be needing to help a lot more than just you here shortly, anyway."

"Still," Adeline retorted, glancing over her shoulder to where Cordelia followed in the crowd. "She's not exactly inviting."

"I can hear you two!" Cordelia yelled from our backs.

I hooked my arm through Adeline's as we laughed, continuing to follow the guard into the massive stone structure.

For a royal castle, it was very comfortable. Fabrics and linens covered most of the stone walls, creating a relaxing and inviting feeling throughout. We walked into a large hall with red velvet armchairs lining the walls, accompanied with massive works of art and candles to keep the place well-lit, even though the sun still filtered through beautiful large windows every few feet.

"Here you are," the guard announced. "There should be plenty of rooms for everyone. Each room is stocked with clean clothes and anything else you all may need, but if you are in need of anything else, please send word. The King has prepared a feast in your honor this evening, we will send a guard here to lead you to the dining hall when it is time."

He bowed at the waist, and then he was gone.

We spent the next few minutes sauntering through the halls, in awe of how large it really was. When the guard said Carlyle reserved an entire wing of the castle for us, he wasn't lying. Bedroom after bedroom lined the structure, perfectly decorated and truly filled with anything we might need. Fruit baskets, bathing chambers, dresses.

Carlyle had thought of it all.

"Is this what it's like to travel as a royal?" I asked Mal, who said nothing as I took in the beauty around us. Most of the group had settled into their chosen bed chambers by now, leaving Mal and I alone in the hallway.

Mal laughed quietly. "In the decades that I have known Carlyle, I have never had this much royal treatment from him. Trust me, Jade, you make quite the impression. I'm sure each kingdom on our tour will be more than happy to accommodate the peacemaker, even if that means clearing an entire wing of their castles."

*Damn.*

"Here," Mal said as we reached the end of the hall. With a hand still solid on my lower back, he guided me into the last bedroom. Which also happened to be the largest bedroom. A large bed on massive iron posts stood in the center of the room, so large it did not even touch a single wall.

To think that Tessa and I used to share a tiny bed shoved into the corner of our father's house...

"Wow," I managed to say. "Carlyle has truly outdone himself here."

Mal shut the door behind me as I sauntered in, taking in the beauty of the room.

"He has quite a talent for flare," Mal said, but something else laced his words. I turned to face him.

"You've known Carlyle for a long time," I stated. "You trust him, right? I mean, he would never try anything stupid."

Mal shrugged, his eyes leaving me to scan the room around us. "Carlyle is a good man," he said. "But nobody has seen anyone as powerful as you, Jade. We can't know how he'll react to you. And if their powers start to develop like Adeline's, we need to be on alert. I don't anticipate Carlyle trying anything, but that doesn't mean his men will grant us the same courtesy."

I nodded. With powers coming to light around us, we needed to be on alert. Always.

"The good news is that if anyone tries anything, Adeline will be there to burn them to ash," I added. This joke only earned me a small, tired smile from Malachi. I walked over to him and placed both hands on the sides of his face. "Hey," I said. "I am with you on this, Mal. You are not alone in this kingdom. The burden of our safety is not on your shoulders alone."

His hands came up to cup mine. "I know," he replied. "But I can't stop myself from thinking of every possible way our enemies might challenge us."

Even now, his eyes swam with something fierce and powerful. The King of Shadows, the most powerful fae in existence.

He had nothing to fear.

"Sleep," I ordered him. "I'll wake you when it's time for dinner."

He held my stare for a moment longer before pressing his lips to my forehead in a soft kiss. We both needed to rest before dinner, but Malachi needed it much more than I.

Exhaustion seeped into every ounce of my being as we walked to the dining hall. This was why we were here, this was what we came all this way for.

Tonight, we would feast with Carlyle's people and declare that we had finished the peacemaker ritual. If they hadn't already, they would start to see fae appearing with magic gifts. This would change everything.

Malachi dressed himself in clean black clothes, similar to the rest of the men in our group. I had been given a conservative silver dress to wear, one that contrasted greatly with my black hair, which I tied back into a braid.

"You are the peacemaker, Jade Weyland," Mal whispered in my ear as we walked into the room. "Don't back down from anyone, even for a second."

It was strange that he was saying such things when we were so safe in this kingdom, but I nodded anyway. I didn't need Mal to worry about me, especially not tonight. Still, my senses told me to be alert. To be strong.

It seemed the entire dining hall was already full by the time we arrived. The second Mal and I walked through the door, everyone stood up, silencing all conversations they had been having seconds before.

"Right this way," one of the guards whispered. He held his hand out, waving us to a long table that faced the rest of the room. There had to be hundreds of Paseocan fae sitting in the massive hall. Sparkling stone chandeliers hung from the ceiling, and the firelight flickered throughout, reflecting off the beautiful tapestries on the walls.

Carlyle already sat in the middle of the long, elevated table. His eyes widened when he saw us. "Friends!" he started. "Come, sit!" That same, warm smile spread across his features.

We obliged, Mal leading me to the seats next to Carlyle. I sat beside him, Mal sitting next to me. The rest of the men arranged themselves around us, all of us facing out to the rest of Paseocan. The nervous tickle in my stomach grew as I looked at their faces, scanning for any signs of distaste or distrust. To my surprise, all I saw was interest.

Interest and something else—hope.

Carlyle held up his glass of wine. "Let me be the first to congratulate Malachi, my old friend, and Jade, the peacemaker, on their accomplishments over the last few months. They have managed to change the world as we know it, and in time, magic will flow through our lands like it did when the Saints walked among us."

The crowd cheered. Mal inched closer to me, his comforting heat radiating off his body as we continued to listen to Carlyle.

"I can honestly say no two people are more deserving of their rule. They have provided a stronghold in Rewyth after the death of the previous king." Silence thickened as Carlyle paused. "However, they have managed to come back even stronger than before. Even more powerful. And with the help of this one," Carlyle held his hand out. I placed my palm on his, and he raised our clasped hands to the air. Mal's hand fell onto my back, reminding me that he was there just in case I needed him. Always. "These two will rule the fae!"

Another chilling pause filled the air, one I thought would never end, before someone in the back of the room began to cheer. And then the entire room erupted.

"Thank you," I said to Carlyle. "You and your people have been too generous."

"After the sacrifices you've made," he said quietly, "you deserve not a single ounce less than greatness."

Malachi lifted his glass next. "Thank you, Carlyle, and the rest of Paseocan, for being so welcoming to us. When Jade and I married not long ago, we had no idea she was destined for this life. We had no idea she was to become the peacemaker, chosen by the Saints to save us all from our own demise."

I glanced across the room to see everyone staring at Malachi in admiration.

"Today, we are here to announce that we have completed the peacemaker ritual. The Saints have spoken to Jade, have guided her to this moment, have given her the same power that they themselves once wielded. The Saints have released the hold they had on our powers, and we have proof that fae powers will be restored once more. No longer are the days when only a handful of fae and witches possess gifts. Now, every fae will possess some amount of magic."

Everyone in the room—including me—clapped for this. I fought back tears as my throat burned, a pride I had never felt before washed over me as I stared at Mal, his chin high and his shoulders back. In a room full of silver-winged fae, my husband held the power.

"Let us eat and celebrate!" Carlyle announced over the applause.

And that we did.

No longer affected so fiercely by the fae wine, I drank. Some of the best food I had ever tasted was provided to us, and we all ate until we couldn't possibly eat any more. Malachi and I filled Carlyle in on everything that had happened under the mountain, including the trials. His empathy and warmth radiated from him as we told him of our losses and our struggles. He asked as many questions as he could, including how we possibly managed to escape the grasp of Silas, and we did our best to answer them.

I allowed Malachi to do the talking when it came to the Paragon and Silas, but he had no issues explaining every detail to Carlyle. Clearly, he did not feel the need to hold back.

And when we told him of the peacemaker ritual, when we told him of the Saints that spoke to me and of Adeline's magic, he could hardly contain his smile.

I didn't blame him. Adeline, and everyone else who would soon turn out similar to Adeline, created something great. They created a sense of hope, a sense that great things were coming to us.

"It seems that this tour of yours to visit the kingdoms is also one to see the magic that has breached the surface of our lands so far, is it not?" Carlyle asked.

I nodded. "That is part of our tour, yes. We are interested in seeing the fae's gifts and helping them control their magic in any way we can while we are here."

"Well," Carlyle said, wiping his mouth with his dinner cloth and pushing himself into a standing position. "It seems it is my turn to present you all with a gift."

"A gift?" I repeated.

"Trust me," Carlyle said, sending me a small wink, "this is a gift you will like very much." He waved his hand, signaling something to the guards.

I took this moment to glance down both sides of the table, ensuring the rest of our crew was enjoying the feast as much as we were. Everyone seemed perfectly content, even Cordelia, who finished laughing at something Lucien had said.

Malachi's hand fell onto my thigh below the table, squeezing gently.

We watched as seven fae entered the room, lining up in front of our long table. They turned to face us, standing equal distance apart from each other.

"What's this?" Malachi asked.

"This," Carlyle announced, "is what you have come all this way to see. This is what you've done for us, Jade Weyland. This is magic being returned to our world, one by one."

The seven fae still looked at us, waiting.

"These fae have gifts now?" I guessed.

Carlyle nodded. "Would you like to show the King and Queen of Rewyth your new powers, ladies and gentlemen?"

The entire room was silent. My heart began to beat in my chest, loud enough that I was certain Malachi could hear it. His grip on my thigh tightened.

The fae on the far left, an older man with smaller silver wings, took one step forward. He finally looked up from the floor and met my gaze.

A lightness flickered there; one I knew all too well.

He held his hands out before him, and the entire room waited to see what type of power this man could wield, what type of gift he was blessed with from the Saints.

I nearly yelped in surprise when all of the wine in the room—including the wine in our glasses at our table—raised into the air. The man held it there, too, controlling the liquid with a big, knowing smile on his face, before he let the wine drop back into the glasses with an astonishing amount of control.

My jaw could have hit the floor.

Cheers and applause ripped through the room. The look of joy on the older man's face was worth the entire journey over here.

This was what we did this for—so fae who were otherwise normal could possess something special, something curated to them in a way that would create value we could not even comprehend yet. Who knows how many ways this man's power could be used? Who knows how many people could be helped with this gift, as minuscule as it might seem to some?

This would change lives forever. This would change...it would change *everything.*

Five more gifts were displayed to us, each one as unique and special as the last. Air magic, more water magic, and even the ability to move at shockingly quick speeds around the room.

But the best part was seeing the look on each of their faces. These were not power-hungry fae. These were not fae that held malice in their hearts, these were not fae who would use this new gift for evil. No, each of these fae would cherish these gifts with everything they possibly could. They would use these gifts for nothing but good, and the world would be a better place because of it.

I believed this with every ounce of my being.

Until the last fae stepped forward.

I felt the difference, like a storm rolling through the air around us. Even the look in this woman's eye glinted with something different, not the same sparkle of lightness that had been seen in the other fae's faces. A recognizable darkness lingered there, one of power and one of need.

I recognized it all too well.

Carlyle stiffened beside me. I only noticed it because we sat so close. Nobody else would have been able to tell how he tightly held onto his wine glass, much tighter than before.

"Nari," Carlyle started. "Please demonstrate your magnificent power to the leaders of Rewyth, the leaders who have given you the opportunity to possess such a gift."

Malachi stiffened next to me. Carlyle hadn't given an introduction like that to the other fae.

This one was different.

I sat up a little straighter in my seat. My own magic, that lightness and darkness that mixed together with the sense of Malachi's power, seemed to be on edge, too. It buzzed in my veins, creating the heat of anticipation that would have anyone reaching for their weapon.

We waited.

Even Cordelia leaned across the table, placing her elbows on the wooden surface as she focused intently on what we were about to witness.

The fae—with fierce, dark eyes and silver rings decorating her fingers—held her hands out. The fae beside her began to move, parallel to her own actions. It took me a second to realize truly what was happening.

She flicked her hand, and the fae standing beside her stumbled forward, unable to stop. She raised her hand and he jumped, she lowered her hand and he dropped to the ground.

My breath nearly stopped. This was dangerous. It was wrong.

Nari's magic controlled his body entirely.

# CHAPTER 13
## *Jade*

I didn't hear Eli until he had already taken a seat on the chair across from me. He exhaled deeply as he sank into the fabric, his face lighting up by the lanterns scattering the room of the hall.

"You should be asleep," he said. "Everyone else sure is."

"Not you, though," I stated. I took a sip of my wine. After the events of the evening, I had snuck out of the room and found myself here, filling my own glass and doing anything to numb my thoughts. They were becoming too much to bear, too much to keep.

"No," Eli laughed. "Not me. I figured I would come talk to you while you were alone. You've been busy."

"Yes, I have. Is everything okay with you?"

Eli nodded, his eyes flickering across each of my features. It had been ages since I had spoken to Eli. Saints, I knew fae aged slowly, but Eli seemed to have grown by twenty years in the last few months. Those immature, boyish features were replaced with harsh lines of worry and strength.

And he looked exhausted, likely a mirror of myself.

"It's not me I'm worried about," Eli replied. "It's you."

I nearly spit out my wine, coughing once before I recovered from the shock. "I have to say, hearing Malachi's brothers worry about me still surprises me. It wasn't too long ago that I thought you all wanted to kill me."

Eli smiled softly and shook his head. "Yeah, we were all pretty ignorant back then. Especially Adonis and Lucien. They care, too, you know."

"I'll take your word for it," I replied. "I think what they really care about is my power. I'm sure you're all just waiting to see what powers you might possess yourselves."

"Yes," Eli responded, "but that doesn't make us care about your safety any less."

I met his eyes, only to find him staring intently back at me. "What makes you say this, Eli? What's changed?"

"Things have been different for a while now," Eli said. "When you two left to go with Silas to the Paragon's temple..." He paused, shaking his head. "We didn't know if you two would ever come back. That said a lot about Malachi's love for you, but it said even more about what you were willing to do for us. I mean, we weren't exactly *welcoming* when you first arrived in Rewyth."

I smiled as I remembered the first few interactions I had with them. Malachi's brothers had been fierce and intimidating and deadly, but now? They weren't my best friends, but they were there, always having my back. Ever since we returned to Rewyth from the temple, ever since Malachi and I had forced Seth's men to bow.

Before then, even. When we rushed into battle together.

Malachi's brothers had certainly had a change of heart.

"Well," I started. "After what you've been through, I think you deserve someone to fight for you, too."

Eli flinched, and my chest tightened. I had been so worried about myself and Malachi, it was easy to forget what everyone else in this kingdom had been through, too. Especially the rest of Malachi's family.

They had lost a father, too. They had lost a brother. They had, in many ways, lost Malachi at times.

And they were still here. Still standing. Still fighting. Even if that fight was fueled by anger, even if it was fueled by hatred at times, or by retribution, they fought.

And that meant something, even to me. Family wasn't supposed to be perfect. I knew more than anyone how cruel family could be at times.

This family was no different.

"Our powers will come soon," Eli said softly. "And when they do, I want you to know we're on your side. All of us. Even Lucien."

"Thank you," I replied. I took another sip of the wine. "Sometimes I feel like I've lost myself in the darkness somehow, like I've gone way too far to ever find myself again."

"Impossible," Eli said. "We've seen darkness, Jade. We've seen Malachi's darkness, we've seen the darkness in others, as well. You don't even come close."

I wanted to believe him, but he didn't know that dark voice in my mind. He didn't hear the dark thoughts I had, especially when I got the taste of power.

Sometimes I didn't recognize myself, didn't recognize my actions.

"You're doing it again," Eli interrupted my thoughts.

"Doing what again?"

"Getting lost in whatever world you've created in here," Eli said, tapping his temple with his finger. "You'll get lost in there if you keep doing that. Be here, Jade. With us."

"It's harder than it sounds."

"I know exactly how easy it is to allow yourself to fade off into those thoughts," Eli said. His voice hardened, laced with pain and grief. "But you can't. People need you, Jade. People need you now more than they ever have, and I'm not just talking about Malachi."

I stared at him, breathless. "That's a lot of pressure," I said honestly.

"It is," Eli stated. "And if anyone can handle it all, it's you, peacekeeper."

I took another drink of my wine, gulping the sweet liquid and letting it calm my nerves once again. Eli did the same with his own glass, and we sat like that for some time, reveling in the silence.

Those thoughts came back, dark and desperate, but I listened to Eli's advice and pushed them away. I didn't have time to wallow. I didn't have time to pity myself, to get lost in that darkness.

"When did you get so wise?" I said after a while.

Eli smiled half-heartedly. "I was a child before I lost Fynn, I can see that now. But that pain changed me, that grief made me realize what was really important in life."

"Yeah," I said. "I know the feeling."

Eli and Fynn were much closer than any of the other brothers. They were nearly as close as Tessa and me.

I knew what he felt more than anyone else here.

"I'm sorry, Jade," Eli said.

I snapped my eyes to him. "For what?"

"For not being able to protect your sister. We should have been there for her; we should have had her back when you weren't around." His voice cracked in hidden emotion.

I had to swallow back my own tears, feeling a new wave of grief that I had never expected to feel. Not for Tessa, though. For...for Malachi. For his family. For my fae friends who had also lost something that day Tessa died.

"I'm sorry, too," I replied. "For your brother. His death—" I stopped to clear my throat before continuing, "His death was not necessary, but it was courageous all the same."

Eli smiled, tears glistening in his eyes. "Thank you," he said. "I don't know how in the Saints you've managed to remain kind when you have lost so much, but thank you."

That was the final straw.

I let the tears I had been holding back fall freely, tumbling past my emotional barriers and down my face. I stood from my sofa and crossed the room to Eli, sitting next to him and throwing my arms around him. He stiffened at first, clearly surprised by my affection, but eventually returned the hug.

"We're family, now," I said as I tightened my arms around him. "It's time we start acting more like it."

He laughed against me and didn't let go. We stayed like that for a few minutes, until both of our tears and dried up, our grief fading to a low dull and morphing into something much deeper that connected us beyond words.

"Go get some sleep," Eli said, finally pulling out of my embrace. "Malachi will kill me if he thinks I kept you up all evening."

"Fine," I said. "But you know where to find me if you need me. I mean it, Eli."

"I know," he said with a smile.

I stood up and walked out of the common area, heading to the hallway where Malachi would be fast asleep, like everyone else.

But as I approached in the darkness, something made me pause. I still had my human vision, even if the rest of my senses seemed to be getting stronger. And something didn't feel right...

A hand shot out from the darkness and gripped my bicep, pulling me against the wall. I would have screamed if it weren't for a large, warm hand clamping over my mouth.

"Shhh," someone cooed. "It's just me, Adonis."

He removed his hand from my mouth.

"What are you doing?" I hissed. "Are you trying to scare the shit out of me?"

A silent beat passed.

"I heard what you said back there," Adonis whispered.

"Eavesdrop much?"

I thrashed my arm from his grip, and he easily let me go.

"I just wanted to say thank you," Adonis whispered. The words were kind, but his tone still held the fae harshness that he always carried with him. "For saying that to him. He's been hurting since we lost our brother, and...and the rest of us aren't as gentle as you are. So, thank you."

*Wow.* Was everyone losing their minds today? Or were the Weyland brothers simply learning to trust me after all this time?

I nodded. "You're welcome," I whispered. "He knows I'm here for him."

My eyes adjusted to the darkness of the hallway, just enough so I could see his jaw tightened as he stared at me, eyes like daggers piercing into my chest.

I glared back at him, not for a single second thinking about backing down. I began to move away from the wall in the direction of my bedroom when he stopped me again.

"He was telling the truth, you know. About us being on your side."

I kept moving, away from him and Eli and away from the darkness of the hallway, but I stopped for a second to turn over my shoulder. "I know he was."

# CHAPTER 14
# *Malachi*

**Jade and Cordelia met with Adeline the next day to help teach** her control over her fire magic. I was grateful for it, because it gave me a moment to speak with Carlyle alone.

The two of us walked along the outside of the castle, listening to the morning birds and the rest of the world beginning to wake up with the rising sun.

It was peaceful. It reminded me of Rewyth, of home.

"You weren't expecting that type of power to be shown yesterday," Carlyle started. It wasn't a question.

"No," I replied, clasping my hands behind my back as we continued to walk. "I wasn't. I can't say any of us were."

We took a few more steps in silence. Carlyle had always been a kind, gentle man, but he had his moments. Moments where he was hard to read, moments where I didn't quite know what he wanted from me.

"Carlyle," I started again after some time, "I trust that if there is something on your mind for either myself or my wife, you'll come to me with it. We've known each other for far too long to dance around the truth."

He laughed quietly. "That, I agree with."

"If there is something you worry about with her, or with magic returning to these lands..."

"It's not your wife that I worry about, my friend. I know that she is just as fierce as she is powerful, and her love for you and the fae has grown impeccably since my first introduction to her. I have no doubt that she acts with the best interests of us all in mind."

"Then what is your concern?" I asked. At least Jade was not the cause of his worry. That much alone allowed me to breathe a little deeper.

"My concern comes from the unknown. You and Jade are here now, your power is practically radiating off of you both. But what happens when you leave? What happens when my magic is not as powerful as the magic of my people? Will they overtake the throne? Will they use their power for evil?"

The stress in his words became audible. I knew that feeling well, the feeling of not knowing. Of having to hope that others are as pure as heart as you've thought them to be all this time.

When you give angry people power, they rise up. The trick is to ensure they are not angry. Never angry.

We stopped walking. I turned to face Carlyle, this man who I have known for so long. He was my longest ally, even if my father once disagreed.

Carlyle had done his best to help me, even when I did not deserve it. And he was standing before me now, needing my help.

I placed a hand on his shoulder so he would truly hear my words when I said, "We are here for you, Carlyle. You are the King of Paseocan for a reason. You did not become king because you were weak or powerless. Even if your magic never manifests, you will still be the rightful king. That throne is yours, Carlyle. You lead with grace and with truth, and that means more to the people than any gift of magic ever will."

He smiled. "Your words are kind, Malachi, but I can't say they are all true. These people have been waiting on magic for many, many decades. The hope they have now that they may possess some powerful gift..."

"It is good for them to hope."

"Yes, it is." He took a long breath, looking behind me into the sky for what seemed like many minutes. "I only wonder if too much hope will unsettle the balance."

"What balance?"

His green eyes met mine. "The people here who are poor and powerless will manifest magic of some sort. It may not be today, it may not be tomorrow, but it will happen. What happens when they decide they are tired of being poor? Of being stepped over?"

"That's what we are here to do," I assured him. "Jade and I are here to ensure they understand the consequences. Jade is the peacemaker, Carlyle. This is what she was born for."

"Well, it might take a little more than–" Carlyle's words were cut off by a loud, wailing siren that ripped through the air.

"What is that?"

Carlyle's eyes widened, he was already turning toward the direction of the front gates, pulling the sword sheathed at his hip. "That's the war siren," he explained. "We're being attacked."

# CHAPTER 15
## Malachi

"ATTACKED?" I YELLED, RUNNING CLOSE AFTER HIM. "WHO WOULD possibly be attacking you right now, Carlyle? Does Paseocan have enemies close by?"

He didn't slow down, not for a second. Other fae began to run toward the front gates, too, but we all stopped when we heard a few screams coming from inside the castle.

All of our attention slid from the gate of the kingdom to within. *Were our attackers already inside?*

*Jade.* I had to get to Jade.

I didn't wait for Carlyle. I sprinted ahead, shoving through the other men and women running inside and following that tether of magic in my soul, the one that tied me to her.

I had to get to her. She had to be okay.

My feet pulsed against the dirt pathway until it turned into the stone floor of the massive building, guiding me to her. She had to be inside somewhere, she would be with Adeline and Cordelia. They would protect her.

*Who was I kidding?* Jade didn't need anyone to protect her anymore. She was more than capable of eliminating anyone standing in her way.

Still, my heart ached to be near her, to know for sure that she was okay.

"What's going on?" Carlyle yelled behind me, following close on my heel. His voice was no longer the kind, gentle fae I had grown to know. He spoke with the commanding, chill-igniting voice of a king.

"They're in there!" someone yelled.

I snapped my attention around the room but saw nothing. "Where?" I yelled.

Another scream. Female. *Was it Adeline? Cordelia?*

My magic hissed with anticipation, waiting for me to command the movements. Waiting for me to make the first move.

And I would. Saints, I would end anyone who hurt them. *Any* of them.

Serefin ran into the room, almost knocking me over entirely. "Have you found them?" he yelled.

"No," I said, pushing forward. "This way, I can feel it."

Along with Carlyle, Serefin and I barged into the secondary dining hall of Carlyle's castle. Unlike the dining hall in Rewyth, this hall was dimly lit, separated by partially-built stone walls that looked as if they could fall at any minute.

And in the back of the room...

"Malachi," Jade called out, her voice low and smokey. I felt her, too, as she said those words. My power reacted to her like a wild animal on a leash, lapping at any signal we were getting from that magic connection.

"Jade, is everything okay?"

"Stay back, everyone!" Carlyle called out. "Leave the dining hall until I command otherwise!"

The lingering fae obeyed his order, bowing their heads as they ran past us and out of the room.

I didn't pay them any attention. My eyes were glued onto Jade. She faced me at the far end of the room, but one of the stone walls blocked my view from what she stared at. I could tell by the darkness in her eyes and the flare of her nostrils that it wasn't good. Not good at all.

I rounded the corner, finally meeting them where they stood, and stopped dead in my tracks.

"Jade," I said again, lower this time. "What's going on here?"

Carlyle froze beside me, and Serefin moved to wrap Adeline in his arms. It was then that I noticed Cordelia brushing herself off on the other side of Jade, clearly shaken up by something. That was very, very unlike her.

*What happened here?*

"Nari," Jade said, "would you like to explain this? Or shall I?"

The promise of death laced each word. And *damn,* it was sexy.

Nari stood with three other fae, all of them with their backs to the stone wall, rebellious defiance in their faces.

I knew that look. That was the look of a fighter, of a rule-breaker. Whatever they had done, it really seemed to piss Jade off.

"It isn't fair," Nari started. "We have all this magic now. We don't have to take orders from anyone, especially not this human."

Jade's power flared, not noticeable to anyone but me.

"Watch what you say," I warned. "That is the Queen."

"Not my queen," Nari replied.

"Think again," Jade replied before I could say anything, stepping forward with her hand out before her, ready to summon any power she could possibly need. "The four of you think you are smarter than this? The four of you think you can defy your king here? Rise up?"

"What do you care?" the fae next to Nari spat. He hadn't been one to show us his magic earlier, but now I wondered if there weren't more fae than we thought developing powers. "You aren't even part of this kingdom. You're not my leader."

Carlyle stiffened. "It doesn't matter who she is to this kingdom," Carlyle interrupted, anger and sharp emotion cutting the air. "She was chosen by the Saints, you fool. Hand-picked from every soul that walks among us now. Do you understand that?"

Jade stared at the fae, jaw set. He stared back.

"The four of them attacked Cordelia," she explained.

I snapped my attention from Jade to glance at the half-witch.

"I'm fine," Cordelia replied. "I wasn't expecting it, that's all."

*Those bastards.*

"Do you know why the Saints chose me?" Jade said, taking another step forward. She was dangerously close to them, now. Close enough that if one of them wanted to attack her, they easily could.

I took a half-step closer.

Did these idiots really think they could attack Cordelia? Part of me was shocked that they managed to catch her off-guard, but the other part of me was royally pissed off that they would even try.

If they were willing to attempt such a thing when we were in the kingdom, what would they try when we left?

Jade gave me a knowing look. "I'm sorry, Carlyle," Jade started. "But I was given very clear instructions from the Saints."

Carlyle's mouth opened. "What are you saying?" he said. "These are my people, Jade. They will not try such foolishness again!"

Jade clenched her jaw, fighting with herself. I knew the choice she had to make.

*Let them live and risk more of an uprising, or eliminate the threat.*

She closed her eyes and took a breath. I came to recognize that was what she did when the Saints were speaking to her mind. She was focusing on them, talking to the Saints we could not see.

They would be the ones making the choice. Not her. At least, I prayed that would be the case. Bloody hands came with a price.

One I never wanted her to pay.

"Malachi," Jade pleaded. I stepped forward with a hand on her lower back, letting her know I was there. "They hurt her," she whispered. "This has to happen."

"I know it does," I replied. The four rebels on the wall began to squirm, began to realize what they were facing. They were looking death in the eyes.

They had been all along. Their flaw was underestimating her.

*A human girl*, I'm sure they thought. *What would she possibly do to stop them?*

"Do it," I pushed.

Carlyle moved behind us, but Serefin stopped him with a drawn sword. "Don't move," Serefin ordered. "You know this is right. Let her do what needs to be done."

Jade brought her other hand out, spreading her attention across all four.

"No," Nari begged. "No, this is all a mistake. We didn't mean to attack the witch, we swear! We were simply testing our–" Her words were cut off with a painful scream.

The four of them screeched in pain, pressing themselves as deep as possible into that stone wall behind them.

"The peace must remain," Jade said slowly, her voice void of all emotions. "Above all, the peace must remain."

The light that radiated from her was not one of tranquility, but one of viscous poison. The tendrils did not flow freely into the air like I had seen them do before, but rather pierced so fiercely around the room, I almost flinched away before I saw them encapsulate the four screaming fae.

Carlyle yelled something behind us, but I could not make it out. I was too busy focusing on my wife. My powerful, justice-seeking wife.

When the light disappeared, Jade dropped her arms.

The four fae slumped to the ground. All dead.

My own power twisted in delight within me, clearly pleased with the outcome. Clearly rooting for this death.

Jade breathed heavily beside me. "It had to be done," she said.

"Yes," I said, rubbing my hand up her back. "It did."

"If you wouldn't have done it, I sure as shit would have," Cordelia said, stepping forward.

Carlyle stood there, staring at the four bodies. I took half a step in front of Jade as we all turned to face him, waiting for his reaction. Surely, he would understand. Surely, he would take her side.

It was the Saints will, after all. Not hers.

"I'm sorry for the mess," Jade said.

A flash of an emotion crossed Carlyle's features, his hands tightening in fists for half of a second, before he retained his calm demeanor. "No need to apologize," Carlyle said. "If you say it had to be done, then it had to be done."

Jade nodded, though I could see the tenseness still lingering in her body.

"That is quite a power you have," Carlyle stated through gritted teeth. "You really have been gifted."

I could tell he wanted to say more, but he refrained.

"Yes," Jade replied, so quietly we could barely hear her. She turned to give the bodies one more look as she said, "It is quite a gift, indeed."

"Come on," I started. "We should get out of here. I'm sure Carlyle needs to address his people and explain this little...situation."

I began to guide Jade out of the dining hall, away from the death she had just brought on. Away from Carlyle and from anyone else who might judge her, who might not understand her.

"I had to do it," Jade said again, only to me. Her voice sounded strong, strong enough that I wondered if she was trying to convince herself that she had to.

Only when we exited the dining hall and entered into the stone courtyard of the castle, we froze. A large crowd of fae had gathered, at least a hundred of them, all looking at us expectantly. Some looked in fear. Some looked in anger. Most looked in confusion.

"Is everything okay?" one of the fae asked. "We heard screaming."

There was no use lying to them, they would find out soon enough. I took a deep breath, preparing for the chaos that would surely follow the truth.

Only Jade beat me to it.

"Your friends are dead," she shouted. Gasps rang through the air, murmurs began in the back of the crowd.

*Shit.*

Jade lifted her chin and looked out amongst the fae of Paseocan.

"I suppose I should introduce myself to you all personally," she started. She took half a step forward, placing herself in front of me. "My name is Jade Weyland, wife to Malachi Weyland and Queen of Rewyth. I was chosen by the Saints to be the peacemaker. For a long time, I wasn't quite sure what that meant. I was confused and angry by this fate, especially considering I was not fae. I was simply a human."

Fae stared at her in awe. Me included. The others stepped out of the dining hall, too, but halted when they saw Jade speaking.

A dark, electrifying feeling washed over me, from the bottoms of my feet up through the back of my neck.

"Kneel," Jade ordered to the fae around us. The crowd did not kneel. They took the next few seconds to look around, watching for who would first submit. And not submitting was a damn mistake. "Kneel or die!" Jade said again, her voice a roar of thunder through Paseocan.

Denying her was death.

Every feral part of my existence begged me to submit, to obey. So I did. My knees hit the ground as I bowed before my queen.

As did every other fae in the courtyard, Carlyle included.

Jade stepped around, surveying the group of fae before her. Her feet clicking against the stone of the courtyard became the only sound. No more murmuring. No more second-guessing her rule.

"I do not wish to command you in your own kingdom," Jade announced, her voice softer but still laced with a deadly force, "but make no mistake, I will eliminate any threat. The Saints command my hand, and if they see you as a threat, you will die. If you stand against me, if you stand against my husband," she reached down and pulled me up from my kneeling position. Even my instincts fought against it, but I stood beside my wife as she added, "you will die."

And damn, every single fae in Paseocan felt that truth.

# CHAPTER 16
# *Jade*

"You kicked ass back there!" Eli cheered, bringing his black stallion back to ride beside Mal and me. After the incident in Paseocan, we said goodbye to Carlyle and took our leave, deciding we had done more than enough damage.

I gave Eli a soft smile. "Thanks, but I don't think the entire kingdom of Paseocan would agree with you."

Eli shook off my words. "I disagree. Do you know how safe you probably made them feel? They know you'll end anyone who tries to step out of place, Jade. There won't be any bullies, any power-hungry bastards trying to take over. You saved them."

*That was one way of looking at it.*

I didn't object when Malachi packed our bags and insisted we leave right away. If anything, I felt uneasy.

But it wasn't because I had just killed four fae. And that scared me—the fact that I wasn't even slightly shaken by it. Rather, it gave me such a rush of power, I wasn't sure I would be able to pull back. Malachi's hand on me was the one thing that reminded me of where I was, of who I was supposed to be.

*The peacemaker.* Not a killer. Not seeking revenge, but seeking justice.

*Your thoughts are loud,* Erebus spoke in my mind.

I stiffened immediately, hoping Malachi didn't notice.

*So are yours,* I thought back.

*You did nothing wrong,* Erebus replied. *The boy is right. Death suited them. You're worrying your king.*

*Why do you care about my king?* I mentally snapped back. *Besides, he always worries.*

A dark wave of emotion washed over my body, coming from the origin of that voice.

Damn Erebus.

Eli's horse trotted ahead with the others, leaving Malachi and I, once again, in the back of the group. I noted the way Mal pulled back on the reins, slightly enough where the others wouldn't notice, but enough to where we could have our own privacy.

"You're worried about me," I stated when we were far enough behind the others.

"You're my wife," Mal replied, his voice steady. "I think I have a right to worry."

"Maybe, but you shouldn't. I swear to you, I'm fine."

Mal took a long breath; I felt his chest rise and fall behind me in the saddle. "I know death, Jade. You may not remember, but they called me the Prince of Shadows for a reason. You don't need to hide from me."

I did, though, because how was I supposed to tell him that I was a monster? That I was no longer the innocent human he met who wanted nothing to do with death?

Erebus's laughter echoed in my mind.

"It should have scared me," I said eventually, giving him half a truth. Half was better than none. Half was a step in the right direction, a step to truth. "It should have terrified me, even. I should have been vomiting from the adrenaline and running for the hills."

Mal's hand slid up my arm. "Death should not frighten you," he whispered. "Especially when it is so deserved."

I shook my head. "That's easy for you to say," I replied. "You had hundreds of years to discover who you really are. You're good, Mal. I see it every day. But me? I don't know who the Saints want me to be. On one hand, Anastasia seems to really believe in peace. But then Erebus says things entirely different, and I feel like I'm losing my mind."

"I can tell you one thing," Mal replied. "Watching them bow to you was nothing less than chilling. You commanded everyone, including me, with such force, Jade. I've never seen anything like it."

I brushed him off. "Yeah, well that's hardly saving anyone."

"I think my brother was right. You saved a lot more people than you killed back there, Jade. They will never forget what you did. Carlyle included."

I couldn't keep my laughter back. Carlyle had been terrified as we walked out of his kingdom. He might not have said it, but I could see it in the way he looked at me. That warm smile had a wall built before it. Those eyes had a hint of wariness. It was natural, like a self-preserving instinct that you couldn't deny.

But I saw it in Carlyle, just like I saw it in every damn fae we passed as we left his kingdom.

Two days and two nights passed. I spent my time riding on Malachi's horse, nested safely between his legs, as the crew pushed forward to the next kingdom. The Saints did not speak to me during our travels, although half the time, I craved a little entertainment from their familiar voices.

The nights were cold. Without another inn or a castle to sleep in, we only had each other and a small fire to keep us warm.

Thankfully, we didn't need to fear the deadlings in the thick of the forest. Ever since we had eliminated Silas, the deadlings hadn't been a problem. Cordelia must have been right; Silas was the one controlling them. Without them, they would have no need to attack. No reason to cause chaos.

Hopefully, as time went on, they would grow extinct altogether. *We could only hope.*

On the third day, I was damn exhausted. Exhausted enough that when my instincts told me something wasn't right, I ignored them.

We were just beginning to re-pack our horses from the night, the sun just beginning to filter over the horizon as the world began to wake.

"Did you hear that?" Lucien asked, looking up from the dried meat he ripped apart with his teeth.

"Hear what?" I replied. Granted, I should have been more alert. After the vague warning about rebels at the inn, we all should have been.

But nobody seemed to pay any attention. Nobody cared at all, really, as Lucien brought up his concerns.

He stared off into the forest around us. "I don't know," he said. "I thought I heard something."

"You're paranoid, brother," Adonis said, walking up and clapping Lucien on the shoulder. "We're all exhausted. You're probably hearing things."

"Yeah," Lucien said, though he didn't sound convinced. "You're right."

I brushed it off, too, walking over to Malachi who was stroking his white stallion. He had been nothing but supportive and affectionate over the last few days, and damn if I didn't want to get him alone as quickly as possible. I snuck up behind him and slid my hands up his back, narrowly avoiding the base of his black, leathery wings.

He hissed in surprise, but immediately relaxed.

"Aren't your terrifying fae senses supposed to alert you when an attacker comes up from behind?" I teased, kissing his shoulder.

"Mmmm," he hummed. "Maybe they did. Maybe they knew you were there all along." He twisted in my arms to face me.

"I don't know," I replied. "What was that you said about having sensitive wings?" I ran my hands across his back again, closer this time.

He stiffened, shuddering lightly at my touch. "Careful," he purred. "I don't think you want to do that again when so many people are watching."

His voice dripped in heat, and I felt it deep in my body. We hadn't had alone time since Paseocan, and we had been so exhausted then, it hardly mattered.

We were still exhausted.

"Get ready to go," Cordelia yelled. "If I have to spend a single extra second in this forest with you all, I might not make it to Trithen alive."

We rolled our eyes and ignored her.

"Ladies first," Malachi said, motioning to the horse. I gave him a tight nod and took his assistance, lifting myself up and onto the saddle.

He followed soon after, and we fell into that familiar habit that now fit us so perfectly. Malachi held the reins, I rested against him, and together, we were ready to make the final leg of the trip.

At least, I *thought* we were ready.

What I didn't know, though, was the fact that we were being watched.

The wind around us picked up, swirling together and picking up the loose leaves, blowing the trees and the branches until the silent air around us roared to life.

At first, we didn't think anything of it. But our horse began to rear, and it took Malachi half-flying us into the air to stay in the saddle.

"What is that?" Adonis yelled over the roar. I barely heard him. "Who's out there?"

"I knew I heard something!" Lucien yelled.

The ones that weren't on horses ducked, shielding their faces from the spiraling wind.

Adrenaline cut through my exhaustion, especially when that voice in my mind said, *You have a visitor.*

The wind continued, pulsing and pushing until not even Malachi's expanded wings could keep us shielded from the flying debris. Our horse panicked beneath us, and within the next few moments, we were thrown off its back entirely. Malachi's wings saved us from hitting the ground too hard, but we still remained helpless in the dirt, waiting for the windstorm to pass.

And when I thought we were going to be entirely blown away along with the trees surrounding us, it all stopped.

One second, we were being pulled into a tornado of wind, and the next second, nothing.

Not even a light breeze.

"Everyone okay?" Malachi asked, tucking his wings back into his shoulders.

A few grunted a response, but nobody spoke. Everyone felt what I felt—the pricking feeling of being watched.

"Who's out there?" I yelled to the forest. "Show yourself."

My hand fell onto my hip where my dagger was strapped. Not that I would need it.

"Relax," a young woman's voice purred. Slight rustling to my right, just behind the tree line, caught my attention. "There's no need for weapons. Don't you agree, peacemaker?"

I squinted until the woman stepped forward. She was maybe my height, and looked to be no older than myself. She wore tight black clothing and thick charcoal lined her piercing green eyes.

And what surprised me the most was the fact that she didn't have wings.

A witch.

"I would agree with you, but it seems you've already deployed your own weapon." I motioned to the settled wind around us. "Who are you?" I asked. "What do you want?"

The woman stepped out further, but immediately stopped when her eyes slid over to Cordelia.

"Lenova?" Cordelia asked. "Is that you?"

"Saints," the witch—Lenova—whispered. "Cordelia?"

A few other rustling sounds in the forest behind Lenova had me reaching for my dagger once again. Malachi did the same beside me, even moving slightly so his body shielded mine. More witches—from what I guessed—stepped out onto the path.

An entire group of them.

"What's going on?" I asked again, ignoring the fact that they somehow knew Cordelia.

Cordelia didn't move, though. Not until the entire group was visible, sizing us up like they had been stalking us all along. I didn't like it.

I didn't like it one bit.

Malachi's power rolled in my body, alerting me to his same level of unease. Witches would be even more powerful now if magic had been unleashed. Esther and Cordelia had some levels of magic, yes, but as Esther had explained to me long ago, it was harder and harder for witches to conjure their powers. Many were too weak since the Saints took the magic of the world with them.

But not all.

"Jade," Cordelia spoke first, not taking her eyes off the witches that now half-surrounded us. "These are Sisters of Starfall."

"You know each other?" Malachi asked.

Cordelia's jaw tightened. "We all lived together for some time," she explained. "This was my old coven."

Out of the corner of my eye, I saw Lucien inch closer. He had been doing that lately, finding himself closer to her when danger was near. I noticed it in Paseocan, and ever since Cordelia had been attacked by those fae and their new magic, he had barely left her side.

Cordelia was powerful, one of the strongest witches in existence according to Esther.

But her old coven?

Dozens of questions began circulating in my mind.

"Well," I started. "Any ideas on why your coven has us surrounded right now, mysteriously coming out of the forest unannounced after invoking a massive windstorm?"

"*Old* coven," Lenova corrected. "We haven't seen Cordelia in years. Saints, we thought you were dead."

"Aw, come on," Cordelia replied, her regular, snarky attitude coming back to life. "You can't get rid of me that easily. Although I'm sure you would all throw a party over my death, anyway."

One of the witches standing behind Lenova sauntered forward, brushing her shoulder as she approached Cordelia. "And it would have been a damn good party."

All of my senses lit up as she stepped out of the forest and threw her arms around Cordelia, surprising me and everyone else in our group as she pulled Cordelia into a tight hug.

*Cordelia hugging someone?* This was all much, much too strange.

"If we would have known a witch was traveling with the peacemaker, we would have found you all a long time ago. At least we know someone's around to keep them safe, right?"

The witch pulled away from Cordelia. They all laughed, and I finally found myself relaxing. Maybe they weren't going to attempt to kill us all on the spot.

Not Cordelia, at least.

"Want to tell us what you're all doing out here? If you wanted to see us, you could have made the trip to Rewyth," Cordelia replied.

"We heard the fae had been picking up a few stray witches. Didn't take you as the type to follow someone else's orders, though, I have to admit."

Cordliea laughed again, sending me half a glance over her shoulder.

"Okay," Mal said, his king-voice on full volume. "Someone can tell me what's going on here before I start to get pissed off."

"Calm down, king," Lenova said. "We're here for your wife, not you."

Mal stiffened. "As if that makes a difference to me, *witch*."

"Everyone can relax," Cordelia interrupted. "This coven travels through the forest frequently, like nomads. Isn't that right?"

A few of the witches nodded. "We can't say running into you all was truly an accident, though," Lenova explained. "Especially since you opened the gates of magic back to our lands."

"So?" I asked, hating how defensive I sounded. "What do you want from me, then?"

"It's not what we want from you," she replied. "It's what we want to give you."

"Really?" Malachi responded, sarcasm dripping from his voice. "And what might that be?"

Each one of the witches stood a little taller. I noticed the way a few of them even lifted their chins as Lenova replied, "Our loyalty."

"Are we supposed to believe that?" Malachi hissed. We had congregated without the witches, far enough away to get a small ounce of privacy. "Because I can't say I've grown very trusting of witches lately. And they're clearly powerful."

"What's not to trust?" Lucien replied. "If they wanted your wife dead, they would have killed her already."

"I'd like to see them try," I replied.

Adeline linked her arm through mine. "Why did Cordelia leave the coven, anyway? Aren't witches tight about bonds like that? There's got to be some big reason."

We all glanced to where the witches gathered, now talking in hushed voices with Cordelia.

"I don't see any harm in it for now," I said. "If they want to join us and follow us back to Rewyth, we might as well let them."

"You're too trusting," Adonis spoke up. "You always have been, Jade. No offense. Jade is the most powerful person in our realm." He turned to the others. "We can't risk it."

Everyone thought on these words. "Adeline?" I asked.

She squinted in thought. "I can't say I'm a big fan of Cordelia," she answered honestly, "but she's protected you before. If she trusts these witches, I think it's safe. As much as I hate to say it."

She was right. If these witches wanted to become loyal to me and join us on our journey, we shouldn't get in their way. This was the new world, anyway. The new age. We were supposed to be combining forces and making peace with our enemies all across the world.

Perhaps this was a start.

"Alright," I announced, breaking away from our group and walking over to the witches. "You're welcome to join us. But I have one condition."

The witches waited.

"No violence. No more rivalry with the fae. If your coven wants to join us, that's fine. But we become one. We do this together, and we do this as a team. Everyone. Is that clear?"

Lenova stepped forward, holding her hand out to me. "Our coven is yours, peacemaker." She wore a small smirk on her lips, but the words were genuine. A small tickle of my power in my stomach confirmed she was telling the truth.

"Well then," I said, holding out my hand. "We better get moving. We've got a busy day ahead of us."

Lenova clasped her arm around mine, grabbing hold of my forearm. Her smirk spread to a smile. "Yes, we do."

# CHAPTER 17
# Malachi

THE DAY PASSED QUICKER THAN THE OTHERS, LIKELY BECAUSE WE finally had some new entertainment. The sun fell quickly, and before we knew it, we were gathered around the fire.

Rewyth's crew on one side, the witches' coven on the other.

Jade sat across from me, speaking to Adeline about something I could hardly hear.

"We can help you, you know," a new voice made me jump. It was Lenova, the leader of this new coven. She hadn't said so, but I could tell based on how she spoke to the others. They respected her. They looked up to her.

"Help me with what?" I said. I kept my gaze straight ahead into the fire, but I could feel her looking at me from the corner of my eye as she laughed quietly.

"Look," she started, settling into the log beside me. She matched my posture, resting her forearms on her knees as she, too, turned her attention to the fire. "Cordelia tells me you're the descendent of Erebus, the Saint of death. It's no secret that you have a dark power," she pushed, dropping her voice so low that only I could hear. "But I think we both know you have a lot of untapped potential."

*Was she kidding?*

"You know nothing about me," I retorted. "What makes you say that?"

"You may be a very powerful fae, but you haven't studied the power of the Saints like we have."

"You have no idea what I've studied, *witch*. I learned with the very best from the Paragon. Are you telling me you know more about the Saints than the Paragon?"

"I'm not saying anything," the witch replied. Her calmness only agitated me further. "But if you want to become as strong as you possibly can, I think you might want our help."

"And what could you possibly help me with?"

"You have the power of death," Lenova replied. "Just like your wife now has, thanks to the Saints. Don't you want to explore your magic connection? Push the limits?"

"I've had no problem with limitations on my magic in the past," I spat. "I don't think it will be an issue now."

"Maybe not," she whispered. "But if I were you, I'd be doing everything in my power to make sure nobody could ever hurt the people I love. You were connected for a reason, you know. You were practically born to protect her. Do you feel confident that you could do that? What if another coven of witches decides to harm her? Could you stop an entire coven?"

Yeah, this witch pissed me off.

"Are you suggesting I cannot protect my own wife?"

"I'm suggesting the fact that you are one of the strongest fae in existence, King of Shadows. That is all. If you don't want my help, that's fine. I was simply offering."

"Fine, then," I spat.

"Fine," Lenova replied.

We stayed that way for a while, listening to the low buzz of the conversations around us mixing with the crackling of the fire ahead.

I knew I was powerful. I wielded *death.* I was, after all, Erebus's descendent. I didn't need any help protecting Jade.

Right?

On the other hand, if this witch was offering me something, I should accept it. She was just as annoying as Cordelia, but at least she couldn't read my thoughts. Not yet, anyway. I wasn't sure what would happen when the new wave of magic reached the coven.

No. We had everything figured out. We didn't need her help. I shouldn't even be trusting her, anyway. We barely knew her, and we barely knew what this coven wanted from us.

"A world full of magic," she said to herself. "Do you wonder what it will look like when it's restored to its full capacity?"

I settled my attention on my sister, who now conjured a small ball of fire in her palms while Jade cheered her on.

Something in my chest lit up at the sight. Adeline was a pure example of what this magic could do for people. Adeline had been powerless at times. My father—who I thought was my father—had used her time and time again, simply in different ways than he had used me.

Adeline was a sweet, caring sister on the surface. But below the surface? She had been hurt just as much as any of us.

This gave her the chance to fight back.

"If it's done right," I replied, "it will be the best thing to ever happen to us."

"And if it's done wrong?" the witch asked.

I slid my gaze over to Jade, whose smile practically lit up her entire face as she laughed with Adeline. "Then I fear we'll have nothing left to save."

Our trip to Trithen was swift. Good, because any unrest in that horrific kingdom would have put us all over the edge, especially Eli.

None of us enjoyed going back there.

Some of the fae we recognized from that day in Rewyth, the same day we killed Seth. The same day Jade declared herself the strongest person in the entire kingdom, in *any* kingdom. The day our enemies, these fae of Trithen, decided to bow.

But not everyone saw her that day in Rewyth. Most of Trithen, in fact, had been living in ignorance since Seth had been killed. His court had heard the news, I made sure of it, along with clear instructions on what to do now that Trithen was under Rewyth's rule.

*Our* rule.

Still, a quick appearance in their kingdom and a small display of Jade's powers was enough to put them all in their place.

I silently thanked the Saints for that, too, because I was absolutely exhausted. We had a handful of kingdoms left, but the dreaded part of our journey was over.

"That went surprisingly well," Jade said. It had been hours since we left Trithen, and the terrain of the thick forest was finally beginning to thin out.

"Don't sound too surprised," I replied. "You're only the most terrifying person in the world."

She leaned into me more, resting her hands on the tops of my thighs as I held the reins of the horse.

"That's a lot coming from you," she said. "I think everyone in that damn kingdom avoided you the minute they saw your wings."

I flared my black wings to the side for emphasis. "These black wings?" I teased, tickling her neck with my breath from behind.

She smiled. "Those would be them."

"Next time you talk to Erebus, tell him he could make these a little bigger. That way I would be strong enough to transport us anywhere I wanted to without these damn horses."

"Right," Jade laughed. "Because the Saint of death is very open to suggestions."

We rode in silence for a few more minutes until she said, "I talked to Lenova."

"I'm sure that was delightful," I joked. "Almost as delightful as talking to Cordelia, I'm sure."

"She told me you have more power than you realize. And that she told you this and offered to help you."

*Damn, I really hated witches.*

"Is that so?"

Jade nodded. "She also said you declined this offer with little to no explanation as to why."

"Hmmm."

"Care to explain to me why you wouldn't want to strengthen your power? Your death power, I might add?"

I let out a long breath. "I'm not sure how much more my power can strengthen. It already kills when I need it to. Is that not enough?" The words even felt false coming out of my mouth. Yes, my power could kill. Yes, my power was strong. It gave me an edge. It forced me to be feared, forced me to become a deadly force on the battlefield time and time again.

But deep down, I could feel it. I could feel the untapped potential. I could feel the extra surge of death that wanted to escape so often.

And these days, especially being around Jade, the need for death seemed to keep growing.

"You're holding back," she said, interrupting my thoughts. "That's not very King of Shadows of you. The Malachi I married wouldn't dare to hold back."

"If it meant protecting people, he might."

"How do you know it's protecting anyone?" she asked. "If you never try, you'll never know."

I shook my head. My power had done more bad than good in the world. It had killed and killed and killed. At the time, of course, I thought that was the right thing. During war, when my father would use me as his own weapon, I relished the way my power could take out hundreds on the battlefield.

It felt damn good at the time. The power. The control. I loved it all. It's what made me a king.

But now? With Jade? I became more and more aware of every kill. I had blood on my hands, yes, but I was trying to stop the blood from transferring to hers. Our magic connection now could not be denied. We were tied together for eternity, and Jade was not a killer.

If I had untapped potential, it wasn't going to be used for good.

I had to control myself. I had to control the death, the killing, the darkness. I had to shove it away, somewhere deep, deep down, so Jade couldn't see it. Couldn't sense it.

But damn. When Jade had her moments of darkness, it took everything in me not to fall to my knees and worship her. She was not the same kind of darkness I was. She was...she was a force. She wielded power like she had done it all her life, a stark contrast to the Jade I knew before.

She was a goddess, wielding death like it belonged to her, like she was the reaper.

Jade ran a hand up my arm, pulling me from my thoughts. Her eyebrows furrowed in question.

"Fine," I said. "If it'll make you feel better, I'll try to wield more of my magic. But if I end up killing more people, I stop."

Her eyes lit up. "Deal," she said. "And you won't kill anyone. I'll make sure of it."

The next few hours became a blur of traveling like every day before. Only, the promise of death grew thicker with every minute, and each of my primal senses buzzed with the thick anticipation of darkness.

# CHAPTER 18
# Jade

Three days later, screaming pulled me out of my sleep and had me reaching for my dagger before the sun had risen.

Malachi moved before me—jumping to his feet and scanning the camp around us.

We found the source of the scream within seconds, and my heart sank as soon as I saw it.

It was Eli, Malachi's youngest brother.

We all jumped into action, running to where he slept on the forest floor. "Eli!" Malachi yelled. Adonis and Lucien met him there, the three brothers crashing to their knees beside him.

"Nightmare?" I asked Adeline as she ran to my side.

Her breathing came heavy. "I don't know, that's got to be some nightmare."

Cordelia walked up to the other side of us but said nothing. Eli thrashed and thrashed on the ground, even as his brothers tried to pin him down. He was screaming something, but it was hardly audible.

"No!" Eli yelled, evidently in his sleep. "No!"

"Wake up, Eli!" Adonis yelled, trying to hold his head still. "You're having a bad dream!"

"Don't do this!" Eli yelled again.

I wrapped my arm through Adeline's. Her body grew stiff and rigid as she stared at her brother. We were all thinking the same thing: *Eli was probably dreaming of Fynn.*

His dead brother.

Cordelia stepped forward and knelt with the brothers, staring down at Eli who still thrashed against their grasps with his eyes closed.

"Get away from him!" Adonis yelled.

"Let her help," Lucien growled in response.

Cordelia ignored all of them, leaning over Eli and gripping his chin with her hand. She said nothing, but Eli stilled immediately.

Cordelia's eyes grew wide. I even thought I heard her inhale sharply.

Eli's eyes shot open.

"Eli?" Malachi asked. I felt his worry inside of my own chest, thick and desperate as it so often was. He cared so deeply for his brothers, especially Eli. Over the last few months, their bond had grown more than I ever thought possible.

Even if it was hard to understand at times.

But I felt his pain now, his fear for his brother.

Eli gasped for air as he stared at Cordelia, their eyes locked in a hidden communication.

"What's going on?" Adeline asked from beside me.

A beat of silence passed.

Two beats.

Three.

Cordelia answered without looking away from Eli's wild gaze. "Eli's power has awoken. The Saints are showing him our future."

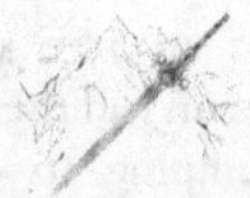

We sat around the fire as Lucien skinned a rabbit for us to eat. Eli had taken a while to gather his thoughts, but still said nothing about what had made him scream. Even as Malachi and his brothers pushed for answers. Even as Cordelia refused to give us any information.

She had seen whatever was going on in his mind. That much we knew. Whatever she saw, it was bad enough to make her shut up for once.

We all stared at Eli as he cleared his throat. He glanced to Cordelia for confirmation, who sat silently next to Lucien on the other side of the fire. She nodded.

"I thought it was a nightmare at first," Eli started, his voice hoarse and raw from screaming. My chest tightened.

Malachi slid his hand into mine.

"But it felt so real, and it looked...it looked just like this," he continued, holding his hands out and signaling to the forest around us.

"What did you see?" Adeline asked.

He met her gaze. "Death. A lot of it. Fighting. Magic everywhere, some good and some bad."

I tried not to show my shock.

"You saw us fighting?" Adonis asked.

"Yes." Eli took a shaking breath. "But I only recognized us. The others were strangers."

"Could it be the rebels?" Malachi asked. "Would the Saints want to warn you of a rebel attack?"

Eli shrugged. "It's possible. It all happened so quickly, like a sky-view of everything happening in fast-motion. I only saw…" He stopped himself before he finished.

"Saw what?" Mal asked. The sinking feeling in my stomach told me he already knew what he saw.

Eli's eyes slid to mine, and I saw nearly every emotion written in his face. He saw *me*. He saw me fighting. He saw me surrounded by death.

"It's okay, Eli," I assured him, trying to keep my voice steady. "You can tell us."

Cordelia cut in from the other side of the fire. "I think that's enough for now," she interrupted. "We should let Eli rest. Who knows when he'll get another vision?"

She wasn't meeting my gaze, either.

Strange. Even for her.

"Right," Malachi said. "We'll pass the human kingdoms in the next day, and we'll be back in Rewyth before we know it. We can deal with all of this then."

Eli nodded, glancing once more at Cordelia. They knew something else. They had seen something else in Eli's mind, in the vision from the Saints. Whatever it was, they didn't want us to know. The pit in my stomach told me it was *me* they wanted to hide it from.

But pushing them wasn't going to help, either.

I decided to change the subject.

"We're stopping by the human kingdoms?" I asked. The sound of *human kingdoms* alone sounded foreign falling off my tongue. Kingdom was not the right word for where the humans lived. Granted, I had only ever been to my own home and the small, makeshift town of Fearford. But those two places had been proof enough—the humans all lived in poverty. Against the fae, they had nothing.

"We'll make our appearance, and we'll leave. We won't stay long. I doubt the humans have gotten any magic from the Saints, so we'll announce our reign and we'll be on our way."

"Doesn't that break the treaty? Humans and fae are not supposed to cross into each other's lands."

Malachi shrugged. "Silas and the Paragon were the ones who made those rules. We won't do any harm, I can promise you that."

I nodded, suddenly feeling sick. Malachi would never want to harm the humans, but after Eli's vision…

"Okay," I said. "As long as we're home soon."

The others began to stand from the fire. Malachi slid his arm over my shoulder, tucking me to his side. "I'll never get tired of you calling our kingdom your home."

I took a long breath. "It's funny," I started. "I dreaded going there when I first married you. Now I can't wait to get back."

He pressed a gentle kiss onto my forehead. "We'll be home soon enough, my queen. This will all be over and we can finally relax."

*Over.* My stomach flipped at the thought. All the fighting, all the death. It would all come to an end soon.

I closed my eyes, taking in the smoky pine scent that was so, uniquely Malachi. *He* was my home. *He* was my peace.

As long as I didn't let darkness take over, this would all be over soon. I felt it deep in my bones, that the end was coming.

Although the warning from the Saints played repeatedly in my mind as I tried to imagine a peaceful future with Mal.

*He will be your downfall.*

# CHAPTER 19
# Malachi

OF ALL THE FAE KINGDOMS WE HAD VISITED, I WAS MORE NERVOUS about the humans. *What a joke.*

It's not that I feared their power. We outnumbered any witch they may have been harboring. They wouldn't have the speed or the strength of the fae. Any fight they started against us would result in their death, I knew that. I was confident in that.

But my heart sank every time I thought of Jade visiting the humans. She wasn't exactly human anymore, although she wasn't a fae, either. She was something else, something in between yet more powerful than any of us.

She didn't belong to them anymore, but they wouldn't see her that way.

"I can feel your worry," Jade whispered. "And while I appreciate the sentiment, it's not necessary."

I stiffened behind her. "They won't like us entering their land," I reminded her. "They might try to fight."

"They won't fight," she said. "Not unless they're truly stupid. They know we'll kill any one of them who tries."

Fearford was now only half an hour away, we would be there before the sun fell. Memories would hit us like punches as soon as we arrived.

Memories of my mother. Of Isaiah. Of Sadie.

*Saints.*

The crueler version of me had done those things, had killed Isaiah. Had banished Sadie. But I would do it all again if it meant keeping my wife safe.

"You don't need to worry about me going back there," Jade said. "I'm not the same person I was the last time we were in Fearford."

"No," I agreed. "You most certainly are not."

"And I'm no longer the ignorant fool who will trust any human who shows them kindness." Harshness laced her words. She spoke of Isaiah.

"You're trusting. That's not always a flaw, you know. It's one of the things I admire most about you."

"That's a shame," she said with a sigh, "because I'm trying to be less trusting."

We rode in silence for a few minutes.

"Do you think she made it back here?" Jade asked.

*Sadie.*

Her friend, one of the few humans from Fearford she had built a friendship with. The same Sadie who tried to save her life, but also the same Sadie who defended Isaiah.

And Isaiah had turned on her, had betrayed her. Had gotten Fynn killed.

"I don't know," I answered honestly. I had been so damn close to killing Sadie the same time I had killed Isaiah. For hurting her. For tricking her.

She would be dead, too, if it weren't for Jade. Jade was the one who forced me to show her mercy. Who forced me to let Sadie escape.

Would Jade do it again? Let someone who betrayed her get away? Or would her new gift cut them down before they even had a clue as to what happened?

I prayed we wouldn't find out. Jade's dark side was growing, and killing Sadie would push her to a place I wasn't sure she would return from.

The ragged, makeshift gates of Fearford came into view.

"That's it?" Cordelia asked. "That's the gate that's supposed to protect them?"

"They do their best," Jade snapped. "They know they are the prey. You don't need to rub it in as soon as we get inside."

"Fine," Cordelia said, rolling his eyes. Apparently, she hadn't been to the human kingdoms before. She was in for a rude awakening.

The horses clicking their hooves against the dry, cleared path became the only sound as we inched closer. I guided my white stallion to the front of the group. It would be better for them if they saw familiar faces, not a random crew of fae breaking into their kingdom.

Only, nobody manned the gates. Nobody stood by. We couldn't see a single person within.

I turned my fae ears to the kingdom, listening for any whisper of hiding humans. Aside from a few animals scurrying in the distance and a few tents flapping in the wind, I heard nothing.

"Hello?" Jade called out. "Is anyone here?"

When we got closer, we noticed the front gate was not even closed. It was cracked open, allowing anyone and anything that wished to simply push inside.

Jade turned in the saddle and gave me a wary look. "This isn't right," she whispered.

"I know. Let's go."

We moved through the gate, the rest of the group falling silently behind us as we pushed onward.

The first thing I noticed was the crumpled buildings. When we had been in Fearford not that long ago, the buildings were barely standing at best. But none of them were downright ripped apart. The buildings now looked like they had been destroyed completely.

Random piles of wood and tent materials lay in piles, not a single human in sight.

"Do you think they left?" Adeline asked. "Perhaps after Isaiah was killed, they decided not to stay?"

"But where would they go?" Jade asked. "They're humans, they can't survive for long in the fae lands. If the deadlings didn't kill them, traveling fae surely would have."

"Not necessarily," I chimed in. "It's possible that they moved somewhere safe, somewhere we didn't know existed."

Jade tensed in front of me. "Maybe."

I turned to my brothers. "Spread out," I ordered. "If you see anything, shout. Make sure this place is really empty before we move on. Maybe there are clues hidden."

They nodded and got moving, beginning to scan the abandoned kingdom for any hints as to what happened.

The hair on the back of my neck stood straight up. Something wasn't right. I just didn't know what.

The others felt it, too. Felt the hesitation and doubt lingering in the air.

"Someone could have wiped them out," Cordelia said. "Forced them to leave."

"The only people who knew this kingdom even existed were us and Esther."

She considered this. "That doesn't mean someone else couldn't have stumbled on it by accident. We aren't that far from Rewyth. Anyone traveling this way could have stumbled across the gates."

She had a point. These humans weren't living on the other side of the wall. Any fae traveling through here could have wiped them out before they had any clue what hit them.

Or, they could have left on their own. Either way, the humans were gone.

Jade slid off the saddle. "What are you doing?" I asked.

"If something happened to them, I need to know for sure." She gave me a reassuring nod before sauntering into one of the nearby buildings, one of the few that was still partially standing.

*Saints.* I climbed off the horse after her and followed her inside.

I remembered that building. The dark steel walls, the cramped indoors. This was what Isaiah had used as his office. If there were any clues, they would be in this building.

Jade knew this, too. She was already rummaging through random papers that lay on the desk.

"Maybe they left to find other humans," Jade suggested. "Or moved on to a safer area."

"It's possible," I said, taking careful note of the way her voice had tightened. "I'm sure whatever happened, it was for the best. Living here wasn't much of a life, anyway."

She froze from the papers on the desk and looked at me, her eyes fierce with determination and another hidden emotion I couldn't quite place. "This was all they had. This was their home, Malachi. No matter how disgusting it might be to the fae."

*So that's what this was really about.*

"Hey," I said, approaching her slowly while my boots brushed over the dust-covered ground. "I am not my father, Jade. I'm not here to destroy the humans. If there's anything we can do to help them, we'll do it."

She dropped her head and took a long, shaking breath. "I know you aren't your father. Either of them," she said. "But you're still fae. You always have been. You have no idea what they've been through. And if they've been forced out of their home, out of the only place they've known..."

"We'll find them," I said. "We'll find them and we'll protect them. That's what we do now, right? We protect people."

"Even people who are afraid of fae?" She looked at me with glossy eyes. "I mean, is this what we do now? Are we supposed to protect everyone?"

"If it was fae that drove them out of their homes, then yes. We make it right. We equal out the power." I walked up behind her and ran my hands up her arms. She instantly relaxed into me.

"And what if it wasn't fae?" she asked. "What if something terrible happened to them? Or what if it was the rebels?"

"Why would the rebels kill the humans?" I asked. "If anything, they would be recruiting."

"Humans aren't great allies," she reminded me. "They're weak and fickle. They're no match against the fae."

"Some, maybe," I agreed. "But I happen to know a few humans who could kick a fae's ass."

She turned in my arms and smiled. It was exhausted and weak, but it was still a smile. "Oh, really?" she asked. "Because that's not how I remember it. I remember you threatening to kill me on many, many occasions after we first married."

"Well, I'm relieved I didn't follow through. Life would be awfully boring if I did."

"It sure would," she mumbled.

We were interrupted by that steel door bursting open, sending a flood of light in with it. "Sorry to interrupt, lovebirds," Cordelia sneered. "Adonis found something. You'll want to see this."

*Shit.*

# CHAPTER 20
# Jade

"This could mean anything," I said, staring at the dead body. "We shouldn't jump to conclusions."

"Jade's right," Malachi said behind me. "We don't know who did this."

"Well, he didn't do it to himself," Lucien replied.

"I wouldn't be so sure," Adonis sneered. "The humans didn't exactly thrive here."

I shot him a sharp look before returning my attention to the body. It was a man I didn't recognize, but the lack of wings and pointed ears confirmed that he was, in fact, human. Likely a resident here.

*Was* a resident.

A dagger pierced his rotting chest. The attacker didn't even bother to hide their tracks.

The smell hit me next. I backed up, using my arm to cover my nose.

"How long do you think he has been here?" I mumbled without breathing.

"I'd say two weeks at least. If they didn't even try to bury the body, I'd assume everyone else left around then, too," Adonis replied.

"Two weeks? Where could they possibly have gone?" Adeline paced around the room, looking anywhere except the decaying body before us.

Serefin walked into the makeshift tent and pulled out a box of matches, lighting it immediately.

"What are you doing?" I asked.

He paused for a second and met my gaze with dark eyes. It was rare to see Ser so serious. "Burning the body. He deserves at least that."

And then it was done. Adeline helped, some, with her magic, and we all walked out of the room while the entire tent went up in flames.

"I don't like this," Lenova said once we were outside. "I don't like this at all."

"Maybe it was someone from Fearford?" I suggested. "We can't immediately assume it was an outside force."

"No," Malachi chimed in, "but it's a good start."

"Okay," I said, starting to process the information. "So someone came here, attacked the humans, killed only one, and left the body? Why does that make any sense?"

"It doesn't," Lucien stated. "It doesn't make any sense at all.

"It has to be the rebels," Serefin added. "They probably came here and forced the humans to show their support. It's likely this man was a martyr."

I shook my head. "Who are these rebels?" I turned to Lenova. "Have you heard anything about this? About rebels who want us dead?"

Lenova shook her head. "I heard rumors, but that's it. I didn't think anyone would actually be dumb enough to try and kill the peacemaker. Most of us know what a death sentence that would be."

Her features remained harsh, her eyes locked in mine. She had to be telling the truth. She had no reason to lie to me.

But Malachi was right, I had been too trusting in the past. I had to be careful around this coven of witches. Around everyone, really.

"We haven't seen any signs of them yet," Serefin chimed in. "From the looks of it, they've likely hit this human kingdom and headed east. We may run into them on our way over the human wall."

*The human wall.* The towering stone wall that was meant to protect my human kingdom from the fae. What it really did, though, was stop humans from wandering into the fae lands to get themselves killed.

And considering Fearford laid beyond that wall...

"Would humans be able to cross the wall alone?" I asked. "Without fae, I mean?"

I remembered back to the time I crossed the wall with Malachi and Serefin to visit my family. Saints, that seemed like ages ago. But it was difficult, even for me. The climb alone was nearly impossible, and Malachi had flown us the rest of the way up and over the wall before bringing us safely down.

Surely, humans would have issues crossing without magic.

"It's possible they've been able to find another way here," Malachi chimed in. "But even that would be difficult. Especially for humans."

Normally, I would get defensive at a statement like that, but in this case, I knew the truth. "We should move on," I said. "The longer we linger here, the longer we're targets."

"Please," Cordelia chimed in. "You have nothing to fear, peacemaker. One blast of power and any rebel who gets within ten feet of you is dead."

I looked away, turning to the direction of our horses. "It's not me I'm worried about. It's everyone else who would be caught in the crossfire."

Malachi's hand fell on my shoulder. "We're going to figure this out," he said. "We'll find whoever did this and we'll deal with them. We'll find where everyone who lived here went, too. I'm sure they're not far."

The sinking feeling in my stomach told me otherwise, but still. We mounted our horses and pushed forward.

"More," Lenova ordered. Her and Malachi had been training for hours now. The sun was beginning to fall behind the horizon.

From the looks of it, they weren't getting far.

Malachi's hands pushed a little further, summoning a large black shadow of his death magic.

"I can't," Malachi replied.

Lenova rolled her eyes. "You can, and you will. You're afraid you're going to hurt one of us, but you won't."

Mal's jaw tightened. "You can't know that for sure, witch."

I leaned back against the tree trunk, stretching my legs out before me. "She's right," I shouted. "You don't need to worry about controlling it so much, Mal."

He dropped his hands and ran them through his messy hair, dissipating the magic he held in front of him. "That's easy for you two to say," he said. "You're not the ones holding literal death in your hands."

I shot him a glare. "You're the descendent of Erebus. You have an incredible power, Malachi. Don't do this to yourself. Don't lock yourself in this cage."

*Death is the opposite of a cage,* Erebus spoke in my mind. *Death is freedom.*

*Not when you're stuck with the guilt for eternity.*

I expected a snarky response from the Saint of death, but my attention became occupied by a snapping stick in the distance.

Someone was out there.

"Wait," I said, turning my attention to the woods around us. "Did anyone hear that?"

"Hear what?" Lenova asked, breathless, as she paused her training.

I didn't answer. Instead, I stood from the ground and took a step closer to the trees, closer to where I could have sworn I heard—

"Jade, look out!" Adonis yelled from somewhere behind me.

"Kill the peacemaker!" a voice shouted from the trees.

What was–

My thoughts were interrupted by five individuals sprinting out of the woods, heading directly toward us.

Black cloths covered their faces, leaving just enough room for their eyes as they ran forward, weapons in hand.

I staggered backward, Mal instantly finding me as he pushed himself in front, holding his own sword out to defend us.

The attackers instantly halted.

"Who are you?" Mal growled. "What do you want with the peacemaker?"

"Magic is soon to be free," one of them replied. His voice sounded young, too young to lose his life by charging at us like imbeciles. "The peacemaker must die so he can rise."

"Who?" Mal growled. I placed a hand on his back between his wings, reminding him of my presence.

The five didn't answer, though. They simply looked at each other and nodded.

Saints, I nearly laughed out loud. They really thought they could walk in here and kill us? I didn't even have to turn around to know that the others—fae and witches both—were banding together behind me.

Together, we were an unbeatable force.

If they wanted to kill me, they would have to go through them.

Still, one of the five, the smaller one on the right, stepped forward. A girl, I realized, as her long blonde braid fell over her shoulder.

"You're not as powerful as you believe you are," she yelled. "We have power too, you know. You underestimate us!"

I stepped sideways, out of Mal's protective shield. "It would be impossible to underestimate you," I explained, "because we don't think anything about you at all. You're clearly part of whatever little rebellion has formed around here, and that's cute, but you should leave before you are killed."

None of them moved. None of them backed down.

*They must really be looking forward to dying, then.*

A dark flare of adrenaline ran up my spine. It was Erebus's power, fiery and fierce, alerting me of its presence, ready to protect me.

Part of it felt so familiar, I had felt it through my bond with Malachi many times. But in my own body, on my own will...

Death belonged to me.

"This is your last chance," I yelled. "Back down now and we'll consider sparing your life."

Instead of backing down, the girl on the right leapt forward, hands in front of her. Malachi's presence behind me let me know he was ready to interfere.

And then the wind picked up.

Air magic, swirling around us and blowing my hair across my face.

*Is that really all they had? Did they really think that would beat us?*

Malachi laughed behind me. The wind died down, and when I brushed my hair from my face, I saw the girl charging at us with her knife held high.

*Seriously?*

I didn't lift a finger. Malachi's magic dropped them all to their knees before us, including the brave one.

The weapon fell to the side of her as she yelled out in pain, clutching her torso.

Malachi stepped out in front of me. "You five thought you could kill her?" More screams echoed through the forest. "You thought you could get past us, defeat us? With what, this air magic?"

More screams. More pain. I watched in satisfaction as one of them began to roll in the dirt, desperate to get rid of his agony.

It wouldn't stop, though. Not until Mal wanted it to.

I smiled until Mal withdrew his power, ending the fun and leaving the five gasping on the ground.

"If you have any sense at all, you'll return to whoever sent you and tell them to think again. Rebels will die. My wife has strict orders from the Saints to maintain power, anyone who defies her will feel her wrath." His voice boomed through the trees, shaking the leaves and rattling my bones.

Even Lucien and Cordelia stood a little taller.

"Understood?" Mal asked.

The five scrambled to their feet, nodding their heads in fear.

"Not so fast," I said, stepping forward to survey the five. They had come here, likely tracked us, and attacked us. They announced that they wanted to kill me, and they made an attempt on my life. A poor attempt, yes, but it was an effort nonetheless.

A dark, primal feeling fell over me.

Now they would escape with their lives?

No, nobody who threatened me would escape. Nobody would raise a weapon against me—against my kingdom—and live.

I did not hesitate.

Where Mal's magic had just been, mine followed, attacking each of the five as they were about to turn and run.

*What a shame,* I thought. *They could never run fast enough to escape me.*

"Jade," Mal started from beside me.

I shot him a warning glance. I knew what I was doing. The rebels, whomever they were, clearly did not understand the first message.

Maybe this one would be more clear.

I pushed more of my power out, wanting them to pay with their lives.

And so they did.

With not even a few screams later, all five bodies dropped to the ground. Silent this time, not screaming and withering in pain. Not moving at all, actually.

All five of the rebels were dead.

Nobody spoke behind me.

"Jade," Mal said again.

"What?" I hissed. "They tried to kill me, Mal. Nobody rises against us and lives, you said so yourself."

He gave me a look I hadn't seen before, one of pity and sympathy all at once. His boots dug into the forest floor beneath us as he walked to the bodies, starting with the girl, and removed the black mask.

Any satisfaction, any darkness, any will for death vanished immediately.

The girl was maybe sixteen, clearly still a child.

My stomach dropped.

*I had killed her.* She wasn't any older than Tessa had been, and now she was dead.

By my hands.

I didn't realize I had moved until I was kneeling next to the girl, looking at her sun-kissed, freckled skin. So young. So innocent.

Mal moved beside me, revealing the faces of the others. They were older than her, full adults who should have known better.

Why would they let her come with them? Why would they put someone so young in danger like this? Not a single one of them tried to stop her when she attacked.

Did they really think she would succeed? Did they really think this girl was their best chance at power?

I dropped my head.

*No.* I wouldn't be this person. I wouldn't succumb to this darkness, wouldn't allow death to come so easily.

I could bring her back. I had the power of life, too. I could bring this girl back from this horrible fate.

I laid a hand on her torso and closed my eyes. Please, I thought. Please, bring her back.

*She tried to kill you,* Erebus's voice spoke in my mind.

*Nearly everyone here has wanted me dead at some point. This girl is young. Too young for this fate.*

Erebus did not respond. Instead, Anastasia's warm presence washed over me.

*Please,* I begged her. *Please allow me this. Take this back.*

*This gift is not one to use lightly, child,* she said to me.

*I know that. Allow me to bring her back this one time. I'll control myself in the future, I swear it. I didn't know she was only a girl.*

*You let darkness overcome you,* Anastasia replied. *Erebus's power is not one to be underestimated.*

*I know that. I made a mistake.*

*One you will not make again,* she said. The finality in her words shook me, sending a thrill of fear through my body.

She had to bring her back. She had to listen to me.

I shut my eyes even harder, willing all of Anastasia's power to come forward, to resurrect.

*Bring her back. Bring her back. Bring her back. Bring her back.*

The girl moved under my touch.

My eyes shot open. Someone behind me gasped.

I held my breath as the girl's eyes fluttered open. "What–" Fear filled her eyes as she looked around, seeing the other four still dead beside us.

"It was a mistake to come here," I told her. "Your friends are dead. Go home. Tell everyone that an attack on the peacemaker will result in the same fates as them."

My words were harsh, but I didn't care. Exhaustion ebbed in the corner of my mind, my body feeling the toll of all that power.

The girl sat up with a grunt, slowly moving her body as she pushed herself away from me, away from Mal, away from the dead bodies.

She got to her feet slowly, her hands out beside her, as if waiting for one of us to attack.

"Go!" I yelled again, emotion leaking into my voice.

This time, she didn't wait.

She ran until we could not hear her panicked breathing fleeing through the forest around us.

"Saints," Adeline breathed behind me. I turned to find everyone, including Mal, staring at me with wide eyes. "You are a force to be reckoned with, Jade Weyland."

# CHAPTER 21
# Malachi

I didn't need to say anything to Jade. I didn't have to. I could feel the turmoil of her emotions as clearly as if they were my own.

She gave into that wicked flare of darkness, and she regretted it deeply.

I should know. I had been there dozens of times before, wallowing in the inevitable guilt that followed after realizing what I had done with that death magic.

Only, Jade could bring them back.

The sun fell over the horizon, casting a golden light over everything we could see.

Jade leaned over, resting her head against my shoulder as she took a long breath. "She was no older than Tessa," she whispered.

"She had no business trying to attack you," I replied. "They were foolish to bring her along, and even more foolish to believe they would be successful."

I meant those words. I was just as shocked as Jade when I pulled off the girl's mask. Fae or not, she was merely a teenager at best, likely brainwashed by the very men who brought her to attack us.

I had felt the darkness in Jade just seconds before she killed them. I knew the feeling very well, had lived in that dark void for years of my life.

But frankly, I would be lying if I said that what I saw back there didn't terrify me. That look in her eyes, that void of emotion, that thrill of the kill. Jade had given into that darkness without even a second of hesitation.

"It was so easy," she said after a few minutes. "I barely had to try."

"Erebus's power is strong. It takes more control not to kill them."

She lifted her head and looked at me, her deep eyes holding so many unsaid words. "I don't want to be this person. I don't want to be the killer. I mean–"

"Jade," I said, interrupting her thoughts. I moved to hold her face in my hands so she could see me, so she could truly understand me. "You are the peacemaker. Just because you kill does not mean you have to be a killer. Life and death, there is a balance. You know this more than anyone."

She shook her head, but I still did not let her go. "How am I supposed to fight this? What happens when I kill again and Anastasia does not let me bring them back?"

I took a long breath. I wanted to comfort her, to tell her that it wouldn't happen again, that she could control it next time.

But that would be a lie. The power of death was addicting, was all-consuming. Jade would have to fight the pull of the darkness every day if she wanted to get away from it.

"You once told me that I was good," I reminded her. "You told me that I could kill and kill and kill, and I would still be good. Do you remember that?"

She smiled softly at the memory, nodding against my hands. "You are good," she said. "They fear you because of what you can do, but they also respect you."

"Well, it took years before even one person respected me. You already have that. You are their queen, you are chosen by the Saints."

She wouldn't believe my words, but it didn't matter. I leaned down to rest my forehead against hers.

"You have to say that," she muttered. "You're my husband."

I pulled away so she could see me as I said, "I love you, Jade. There is nothing you could ever do to make me stop loving you. You could end the entire world if you wished, and I would stand right behind you. I'll remind you of this every day if I have to, I'll pull you from the darkness myself every single time you slip into it."

A tear fell down her cheek. I quickly wiped it away. "Thank you for standing by me," she whispered.

We turned, watching the sun as it descended past the land beyond, encompassing the orange glow in darkness.

"Always," I reminded her. "I will always stand by you."

# CHAPTER 22
# *Jade*

"YOU'RE NERVOUS," MALACHI WHISPERED IN MY EAR. WE WERE ON FOOT now, walking the last portion of the trip to my hometown.

I exhaled a shaking breath. "Maybe," I said. I rubbed my dirt-covered hands together in front of me, trying to rub away the nerves. "The last time I saw this place was in the Trials of Glory. It wasn't pretty."

He nodded. If anyone would understand what I was going through, it would be him. He knew what it was like to go through those trials and have to face reality on the other side. "If this becomes too much, you say the word and I'll fly you out of here. You don't have to do this alone, Jade."

"No," I agreed, "but I do have to do this. They need to see me. They need to know I'll protect them."

The forest became familiar almost immediately. Just like the trials, I was back home. I belonged here for so, so long. Many years I had spent hunting in these woods, surviving off barely enough food for myself before giving Tessa the rest.

But this wasn't my home anymore. I had nothing here except the old, broken memories of what life I used to live.

Cordelia pushed her way up to the front of the crowd, falling into step next to me. "So this is where the mighty peacemaker was born?" she waved her hand to the edge of the forest, where the barely standing slabs of wood just became visible. "I have to say, I'm impressed."

I shoved her lightly. "Don't be rude."

"No, I mean it," she nodded. "It reminds me a lot of my own hometown, actually. You've risen from the ashes, peacemaker." She placed a hand on my shoulder. I somehow managed to not flinch away from her. "You should be proud."

I saw nothing but genuine emotion in her eyes and gave her a slight nod.

Cordelia was right. This place was nothing. It was worse than nothing. Fighting to survive every single day gave me the edge I needed to live in the fae kingdoms. Without this, I wouldn't have made it.

Of course, I wouldn't have been forced to marry Malachi if it weren't for my drunken father. I would have never fought so hard to survive for Tessa's sake if I weren't the only one she relied on.

But that was my reality. This was my life. I quit feeling sorry for this life of mine when I burned it all down in those trials.

"This way," I said. "I want to see my home first."

The others fell into line behind me as the forest turned into an open, dirt field with a small row of spaced-out houses. Mine was first, closest to the forest.

I hated that I was nervous, but I needed this. I needed to see what this old life looked like now. Tessa was dead. My father lived in Rewyth.

This house didn't belong to us anymore. It belonged to the old me. The *dead* me.

A few of the others began to whisper behind me as we approached the old, wooden building that used to be my home. The door had fallen from the hinges, now leaning against the hole-filled wall on the outside of the home.

"Wait here," I whispered to Malachi as I stepped forward. "I'll only be a minute."

Malachi's eyes darkened, but he nodded anyway. I could feel his worry within myself, intertwining with my own nerves and creating a sinking feeling in the pit of my stomach.

Memories from the trials flashed through my mind, as real as any other memory I had here. Deadlings everywhere. Burning the place to the ground. Tessa, dead.

I blinked and pushed them away. That wasn't real. *This* was real. The wooden doorframe cracked as I stepped through.

*This was real.*

It smelled the same. Somehow, after all the time, the light scent of ale and cinnamon still remained. I ran my hand across the dirty kitchen table, now scattered with broken glasses and spiderwebs. How many times had I fought with my father here, begging him to stop drinking? Begging him to return to his family?

I turned to the bedroom. I wasn't sure I would be able to walk inside. Not at first, anyway. Tessa was everywhere in that damn room, every single inch of it reminded me of her.

But somehow, the pain of Tessa's memory didn't sting quite as badly as it did before.

"You okay in there?" Malachi yelled from the doorway.

"Yeah," I called back. "Just a second!"

I took the final step forward and entered my old bedroom. The bed was unmade, as if Tessa had just slept in it. The quilt that my mother had made for us when we were children lay crumpled on the bed.

Tears threatened my eyes. Not at the pain of the memories, but at all the *change*. I walked to the bed and picked up the quilt, holding it to my nose.

It smelled just like her—Tessa. I used to hate the way she would pull the entire thing over herself at night, but after some time, I quit fighting for it back. I would allow her to cocoon herself in the entire thing during those winter nights.

I didn't mind. Even after the fighting and the bickering, I wanted her to be warm more than I wanted it myself.

The rest of our few belongings were covered in dirt, rummaged through, likely by the animals of the forest.

Malachi's footsteps pulled my attention to the doorway. He stopped at the opening, leaning against it with his hands in the pockets of his now-dirty trousers. "I remember the first day I came here with you," he started, glancing around the room. "I hated seeing this at first."

"Yeah," I sighed, setting the quilt back on the bed. "I can't say I loved it too much, either."

His mouth twitched into a small smile. "Your father didn't get much of a great first impression when I showed up here."

I thought back to the way Malachi had almost killed my father, his power unleashing in a way I had never seen before. "You were very territorial," I said, matching his smile.

*"Were?"* he asked, stepping forward and away from the doorframe. "Rest assured, my queen, I will still rip this entire world apart for you." He came to stand before me, tilting my chin upward with his finger. "You are mine. I will kill for you any day."

The emotions hit me hard.

The past version of me had no idea what type of love and security waited for her on the other side of that risk, on the other side of that fae wall.

Saints, Malachi was supposed to *kill* me. That's what I thought when I lived here, cooped up in this small wooden shack with nothing but the rumors of humans to keep me occupied.

What I didn't know back then was that Malachi would actually be my savior.

We stayed in that room for a while, taking in the surroundings silently.

It wasn't until Mal and I walked back outside that I noticed something was wrong. Nobody, not even a random stranger in the distance, was to be seen.

"Serefin?" I asked. He crept forward ahead of the group, step by step, up that small dirt path. He held his hand up, signaling all of us to stay put.

Malachi stepped in front of me, protective as always. I didn't need anyone else to tell me that something was wrong, I felt it now, radiating through my body like a blaring alarm telling me to run.

Once again, the memories of the trials came rushing back to me, all too much.

"I'm sure everything's fine," Adonis said as he approached from my side. "I wouldn't worry." His hand fell to the sword on his hip, his silver wings flaring outward.

"You look worried," I muttered. "Besides, I've never heard this town so quiet. There's always something going on here, even if it's nothing good."

I ignored Serefin's warning and followed him up the hill, past the few empty houses that neighbored my own. Malachi and the others followed tightly behind me.

"We should wait for Ser," Mal whispered in my ear. Even so, he didn't try to stop me. He knew just as well as I that something was going on here.

"If something's happened to these people, we need to figure out what."

"I agree," Mal pushed, "but it could be dangerous. If the rebels..."

"If the rebels what?" I asked, spinning to face him. The others walked around us, continuing to follow Ser up that hill.

Malachi bit his tongue, eyes fierce and jaw tight.

"If the rebels come after us, we'll wipe them out. It's that simple, Mal. This is what we're supposed to do. This is our job."

"Did the Saints tell you that? That you have to put yourself in danger anytime there might be a risk?" His words dripped with sarcasm.

My teeth clenched, my fists tightened. "If you doubt my abilities as the peacemaker, you should come out and say it. You know just as well as I do that I can protect these people."

"Sure," Mal continued, "your power matches anyone's. But you aren't invincible, Jade. If there's a planned attack on you, this could be the perfect distraction. In your old home, in the human lands. You're smarter than this, Jade. You know this."

A dozen rebuttals came to mind, but I took a long breath and pushed them all away. Malachi had a point. I also had to acknowledge how much he had changed recently, too. The old Malachi would have thrown me over his shoulder and kept me far away from danger. The old Malachi wouldn't have let me tour these kingdoms with my power, constantly putting myself at risk.

I was a walking target here. Out in the open, with dozens of structures crumbling to the ground creating a perfect hiding spot for the rebels.

"Wait!" I yelled, calling after Serefin and the others. "This could be a—" *Trap. Trap. Trap.*

Only I didn't get the chance to finish. A loud, ground-shattering boom split through the air around us, and smoke filling my air, lungs, being was the last thing I remembered.

# CHAPTER 23

# Malachi

It happened too fast.

The strike, the rebels running out, Jade screaming and falling out of my grasp.

No—being *pulled* out of my grasp. First there was nothing, then, everything happened all at once. White, blinding pain came splitting in my mind, overwhelming every one of my senses until all I knew was that pain, that white-hot agony.

I tried to scream for her, tried to scream to the others to help her, to get to her.

*Jade. Jade. Jade.*

She was all that mattered, all that would ever matter. Not just to me, either, but to all of us.

I dropped to my knees and reached my hands out, unable to see, even with my fae eyes. Unable to see anything but the blinding pain.

"Jade!" I yelled. "Jade, where are you?" The agony lifted, just for a moment. Long enough where my vision cleared and my eyes opened.

"Malachi!" she screamed back to me, but she was no longer right here. No longer next to me, no longer near us at all.

And the rebels...

I pulled at my power, but felt nothing. Didn't feel that flare of heat, of magic, that always rested in the base of my chest. Panic began to take over.

*No, no, no.* This was not happening. It couldn't be happening.

Every one of my dulled senses focused on Jade, on where she could possibly be.

Those bastards had touched her, had taken her. Had tricked all of us into walking straight into their damn hands.

More screams filled the air, not just Jade but the others, too, all feeling the same crippling pain that I felt.

If I could just get a single ounce of my power, I could flatten these rebels before...

"Malachi, they're taking her!" Serefin's voice roared through the crowd, cutting through all the noise. All the screaming.

In that moment, I didn't care how much pain I felt. I didn't care how crippling it was, or how blinding. I didn't care about anything at all, just getting to her.

Everyone was on the ground, cowering in pain. Adeline doubled over, arms wrapped around her stomach. Lucien lay next to Cordelia, both with their fists to their temples as if they could stop the pain.

And then I saw her.

Everything stopped. I knew nothing else but her—Jade, my wife—halfway down the hill with men flanking her, half-carrying her thrashing body into the forest.

*Blast them,* I thought. *Blast them as hard and as deeply as you possibly can, until their skin melts from their bodies and their bones burn to piles of ash.*

Then it hit me. Jade couldn't blast them. Not even close. Whatever these attackers were doing suppressed all of our magic.

Another wave of pain threatened my body, and it took every ounce of strength I had to remain standing. Yelling from behind told me the rebels—whoever they were—were trying to get me back down.

I searched for any trace of my power, anything that might still connect me to her.

But I felt nothing. "Jade!" I yelled again. She still screamed, still fought as hard as she could even though I knew, I knew she was in pain.

I was searching, begging my body for something, anything that might be able to stop this, when Jade glanced over her shoulder and locked eyes with me.

In the flash of pain, I saw something there, something that hurt much worse than any pain those damn rebels could inflict. With eyes wide and brows drawn together, I saw the small glimpse of sorrow.

Jade had given up. She was going with them. She knew they would continue hurting us until they got what they wanted—her.

Someone behind Jade pushed her, breaking our eye contact and causing her to stumble forward.

"On your knees!" a voice behind me ordered. "On your knees, down! On the ground!"

My knees buckled, crashing to the ground beneath me.

"No," I muttered, loud enough for only me to hear. "No, we have to get her back."

"We'll get her back," Adeline said through gritted teeth beside me. The pain was beginning to subside, but I still felt nothing inside me where that heat of power used to be.

"How are they doing this?" I asked, knowing we wouldn't get an answer. I turned and saw roughly five men, all dressed in black with masks covering their faces.

A singular flash of a silver wing told me these rebels were fae, not humans. Then what had they done with the humans? Where was everyone?

"What do you want with her?" I growled in their direction.

One of the men sauntered forward, a large blade swinging in his hand. I thrashed but invisible hands stopped me, holding me back and pinning me to the ground.

*What was this magic?*

"What we want is this magic. This power." The man took a knee in front of me, coming face-to-face with me.

*Staring death in the face.*

His head tilted to the side, studying me. Sizing me up. I knew that look, I knew exactly what he was doing. I had been in his shoes hundreds of times.

His eyes fell to my black wings. "Dark one," he breathed. "You must be her husband, King of Shadows."

I bared my teeth anyway. "If you think you can beat her, you are wrong. You'll die for this. You'll all die for this."

The man laughed—actually laughed—and I never in my entire life wanted to rip anyone's head off more. "We're well aware of the power the peacemaker possesses," he said. "And don't worry. We'll take good care of your precious wife."

He stood to walk away, but first, he slid his blade forward, grazing my cheek with the sharp metal. Those invisible hands held me there, forcing me into it. Not letting me pull back as the blood began to drip from my face.

The man laughed again.

*He was dead. As soon as I got my power back, they were all dead.*

"Don't come for us," another one of the masked men ordered. "Don't look for her, don't follow us. As long as you follow those rules, your wife will stay alive."

*Yeah right.*

One of my brothers growled on the ground a few feet away, also unable to move.

"You can tell everyone else that power is ours. The peacemaker is no longer welcome."

They sauntered into the forest after the other rebels, after my wife.

The second their magic loosened those invisible hands, my brothers and I were up, charging the space they had followed Jade into. My wings and my feet pumped together, searching desperately anywhere she could be. I even smelled the air as deeply as possible, smelling for the faintest scent of cinnamon.

Whoever those rebels were, they were gone.

And they took Jade with them.

# CHAPTER 24
# *Jade*

Anger flooded my senses. *They had actually managed to suppress my power.*

"Drink this," the man dragging me from the right ordered, pulling a small vial of liquid from his pocket.

"Don't tell me what to do," I spat back, using the free moment to attempt another thrash out of his grasp.

"Fine," he barked back, nothing but rough harshness lacing his words. "You want to do this the hard way?"

I inhaled sharply as the guard to my left gripped my hair in a fist and yanked my head back, pulling my chin down and holding my mouth open as the other man poured the liquid inside.

I would have spit it out, would have done anything to get rid of that damned liquid if it weren't for the hand that clamped over my nose and mouth, holding it shut.

"Swallow it, girl," the men growled.

*Did I really have a damn choice?*

I swallowed the liquid, grimacing as it burned my throat. A few more men yelled from behind me, running to catch up with us in the forest.

Malachi had to be freaking out. I couldn't feel my magic, couldn't feel that tendril of power that had grown to be a comforting warmth over the months.

Whatever the rebels did, it stunted my power. All of it.

*I could really use your help right now,* I thought up to the Saints.

How could they let this happen? Shit, even Eli—who barely knew how to use his power at all—had the *vision* of death.

The Saints said nothing in return.

"We don't have much time," a man from behind us said. I spun to look at him, but my vision blurred. The green forest around me blended and morphed into something that wasn't a forest at all.

"He'll come for you," I tried to whisper, unsure if the words even came out. "He'll come for you all. You won't make it a single day alive after this."

One of the men laughed, low and ugly. "He'll have to find us first."

I blinked my eyes open and tried not to panic. *How long had I been out? How long had it been since the attack?*

"Wha—" I tried to talk, but my mouth dried up instantly. I needed water, I needed–

"Here," someone beside me said, making me jump. "Drink this. Your throat is probably dry as shit right about now."

The masked man to my right handed me a glass of water. I was clearly in no position to refuse, so I accepted it. My muscles ached as I reached forward, grabbing the glass from him and swallowing the liquid.

I took the entire glass down in three gulps.

"Wow," the man sighed, taking the empty glass from me. "You really were thirsty."

"Where am I?" I asked. My damn human eyes couldn't see anything other than the makeshift cot I had been laying on.

"You're with us. You don't need to worry about anything else."

"What do you want from me?"

The fae, with the black mask covering everything but his mouth, tilted his head to the side. "I think you know the answer to that already, peacemaker."

A fresh wave of anger hit me, but I swallowed it down. Anger would cloud my judgment, would blind my vision. I needed a clear, emotionless head.

"Where are the others?" I asked, sounding as casual as possible.

"Your friends, you mean?" he asked. He turned his back and slowly paced back and forth. "They're right where we left them, don't worry. We didn't want anything from your friends. As long as they do what they're told, we won't have any issues with them."

"What they're told?"

"If they come for you, they'll die."

I couldn't bite back the fit of laughter that followed as soon as I processed those words. "Do you even know who you're dealing with?" I asked. "You're going to die," I stated. "It might not be today, it might not be tomorrow. But the others are coming for me. They'll kill you and all of your rebel friends before you can get two steps away from wherever we are."

"Hm," the man grunted. "You have fire. I've heard that about you."

"Well I haven't heard anything about you," I retorted. "Or any of your rebel friends, for that matter."

The man considered these words for a moment before reaching up and untying the black cloth that covered his face.

"Let me formally introduce myself, then," the man started. His dark eyes and sharp features matched Malachi's, equally as fierce and determined, but not nearly as handsome. My chest ached. He held a thick, calloused hand out to shake mine. I didn't move. "My name is Ky. I'm the leader of this organization you all call the rebels, and I believe you and I are going to become great friends."

# CHAPTER 25

# Malachi

"SHE ISN'T HERE!" LUCIEN YELLED FROM BEHIND ME. THAT WASN'T THE first time he had said those words to me, and it wasn't going to be the last. They were all idiots if they thought for even a second that I would stop looking, stop tracking her.

I turned right, eyes scanning the forest around me. "She didn't just disappear, Lucien," I growled. "And we would find her a lot quicker if you actually helped instead of arguing with me."

"Brother," he pushed. *Damn, I really hated Lucien.* I heard his footsteps approaching before he grabbed my bicep and forced me to spin and face him. "Brother!"

Fists clenched and every single ounce of my being on fire, I looked at him. "What?!"

"Jade isn't here in this forest, but that doesn't mean we aren't going to get her back. Come back to the others. We need to learn more about these rebels if we're ever going to find out where they took her."

A tiny flicker of heat in my chest signaled that my power was coming back, slowly, like a tiny stream of water. It wasn't going to be enough, and it surely was too late to be useful.

*Thanks a lot, damned Saints.*

It was gone—that connection that tied me to Jade. That heated presence of her that my magic had grown so used to.

Without my power, our connection was gone.

"Fine," I said, running my dirt-covered hands down my face. "Let's go."

I followed Lucien back to the others, where Cordelia stood in the center of the semi-circle. "I'm just saying," she started speaking to everyone else and oblivious to our approach, "if anyone knows about the rebels, it would be them."

"Who?" I asked. All eyes snapped in my direction. "Who knows about the rebels?"

Cordelia rolled her shoulders back and turned to me. Her jaw was set and determined, but I saw the ounce of pity that flashed across her dark eyes before she answered, "I don't know for sure, but I'm assuming our friends at that inn near Paseocan know something about this."

*The inn.* Cordelia was right. We may have killed the one person who knew anything of certainty, but someone there was bound to know something. The innkeeper, strangers passing by. Someone knew something. And I had a feeling that people near that inn knew more, not just the man who gave us the warning.

"Right," I said. "Then we'll start there. Those who can fly come with me. The others will climb the wall and take the horses back to Rewyth."

I didn't wait for a response, for an argument. My word was final, and the sharpness of my voice told everyone that.

Cordelia had to run to catch up with me. "Don't you want to wait until nightfall?" she asked. "We'll have cover, we can get in and out of that wretched place before anyone sees a thing."

"I can't wait, Cordelia," I said. "They have Jade. They took my wife!" I didn't mean to yell at her, but she flinched backward anyway. In her own way, she knew exactly what I was feeling, knew the amount of fear pulsing through me.

She could also read my thoughts, still, so she knew I wasn't considering waiting. Not even for a second. Those rebels said they wouldn't kill her, but we had no reason to trust them. Saints, we didn't even know who they were.

I didn't wait to see if the others were following. They would catch up. Before we even reached the edge of the forest, my wings pounded in the air, lifting me up and over the trees.

I hated this damned place. It was bad enough that Jade had lived here, had suffered every single day just to feed herself and her sister. But now, when Jade was revisiting the one place she didn't want to return to, she is attacked? All for what? For trying to help people?

"I'm sorry," Eli said from behind me in the air. His silver wings weren't as big as mine, but they carried him just as quickly. "I should have seen this coming. I should have known something wasn't right!"

I clenched my fists, the wind stinging my eyes as we made it over the wall and into the fae lands. If we kept moving, we would make it to the damn inn in a few hours. "It's not your fault, Eli," I said. "We all should have seen it coming. After Fearford, we should have been on the lookout. We all let her down. *I* let her down."

In the corner of my eye, I saw Eli shake his head. "I saw the death, but I...I couldn't see it clearly enough. I still can't focus on what I'm being shown in my visions."

"Well, nobody died yet," I said. "But they will. Trust me, brother. Every single one of those bastards will die for touching her."

His silence was enough. Eli had a soft spot for Jade, he always did. Adonis and Lucien were harder to read, but Eli wore his emotions plain as day on his face. "We'll get her back," he said. "I won't stop until we find her."

"Damn right we'll get her back."

The woman at the inn was just as surprised to see us now as she was the first time she saw us. I, however, did not return the pleasantries.

"Tell me what you know about the rebels," I demanded, bursting through the front door of the rickety inn and slamming my palm on the counter. "And don't think for a second you can get away with lying."

She stammered in shock, putting a wrinkled hand over her chest as she processed the words. "Rebels?" she repeated. "What rebels?"

To my right, in the dining room by the bar, a few men casually got up. Ale mugs half full, they dipped their heads and headed for the back door.

They were two steps from exiting when Lucien kicked that back door in, sauntering inside with Adonis behind him.

Trapped.

*Nobody was leaving this damned inn until I got my answers.*

"So," I announced to the entire inn, clapping my hands together before me. "Some of you may know who I am, but if not, I'll remind you." The men reluctantly looked up from the floor. I saw something there, something dark and defiant lingering in their eyes.

Oh, yes. They knew who I was.

I smiled. "My name is Malachi Weyland. I am the King of Rewyth and the King of Shadows. You decide which is worse."

Adrenaline mixed with anger and a well of emotions that poured into my blood, awakening my power to full force once more. I sent the tendrils of death—more powerful than ever—in the direction of the men, but pulled back right before the magic hit its target.

"Would anyone like to tell me what they know about the rebels?"

"Malachi!" the woman behind the counter squealed. I felt bad for her, I really did. If I would have known she was harboring men who wanted to hurt my wife, I would have killed her a long time ago.

It was a shame, really.

"You don't have to hurt them!" she stammered, clearly shocked by the violence. "Boys, tell the King of Rewyth what he wants to know!"

The two men looked at each other, hands in their pockets and brows drawn together. They knew something alright.

"We don't know anything about any rebels," one of them answered, spitting onto the floor.

"Is that right?" I asked.

They both continued to stare at the floor.

I drew back my power entirely, causing them both to exhale in relief.

*Idiots. All of them.*

"Adeline," I said. She stepped up beside me, a hand on her hip.

"Yes, brother?"

"Perhaps you could entice these men here to help us in our endeavors to find my wife."

She smiled. Adeline and I were not related by blood, but she shared that devious need for justice. I saw myself in Adeline more times than not. "I would love to, brother."

Adeline stepped forward, taking her time as she sized up the men. Their wings were small. Their arms were thin. Saints, Adeline nearly surpassed them in height as she moved to stand behind them.

They both cowered, but did not open their mouths. They did not offer any information about the rebels.

Big mistake. Big, big mistake.

With one swift motion, Adeline placed both of her hands on one of the fae's back and released a rush of her power, her fire. Her grip remained tight on his body, even as he screamed in pain and dropped to his knees. Adeline's smile of satisfaction matched my own. She was learning to wield her powers quickly and efficiently.

Cordelia pushed past me from behind and stopped a foot in front of the men. Her and Adeline together were a sheer force to be reckoned with.

The stories of us together would be told for generations to come.

"Pity," Cordelia said, sending a swift kick between the standing man's knees. He fell to the floor beside his friend. "I thought I was going to miss all the fun."

"Don't worry," Adeline said, finally stepping back from the man as the smell of burnt flesh filled the room. "I saved you some."

"Have they said anything yet?" Cordelia said, turning to me.

"Not a word," I answered. "Claim they don't know anything."

Cordelia smiled and turned back to the men. "Now, now, boys. We're all friends here. We all want the same thing."

The men shook as she approached, her black boots stopping just before them as they looked up at her. "W–we do?"

Cordelia nodded. "We sure do. You see, we want to get our peacemaker back. We want to save the world and fulfill the prophecy of the Saints, etcetera, etcetera. Sound familiar?"

The two boys looked at each other.

Cordelia knelt, gripping the chin of one with her long, piercing fingernails. He squirmed backward, but Adeline was there, meeting him with fire in each hand and a smile of vengeance on her face.

"What do you know about the rebels?" Cordelia asked, any hint of humor or sarcasm now gone from her voice. "Who are they? Where do they come from?"

"I already told you I don't know anything!" The man kept trying to squirm away, but Cordelia only held tighter. Her concerned look morphed slowly into an evil, stomach-churning grin. *Damn, she was good.*

"You don't have to tell me," Cordelia said. "Your mind has already said plenty."

It took the men a second to realize what she meant, but by the time she stood and wiped her hands on the sides of her legs, they were staring with wide eyes and open mouths.

"What do they know?" I asked her.

"They've met a few rebels. They're regulars here and they live nearby. We can't be far from them, which means we can't be far from wherever they took your wife."

I nodded, then tilted my head in the woman's direction.

"No," the woman stammered. "No, please! I'll tell you anything you want to know!"

Cordelia took my hint and stepped toward her. "You already had the chance for that," she said. "My friend here, the King of Shadows, has a tendency to show some people mercy. We share a lot of traits, him and I, but I'm afraid showing mercy is not one of them."

*Really good.*

"I've seen a few rebels here before!" she said, her words coming out like a rush of wind. She pressed her back to the wall behind her with her hands out in surrender. As if that would stop us. As if that would stop me.

"You knew the rebel who came to us the night we stayed here," I guessed. "Who was he? Did you let him in?"

She closed her eyes and attempted to press herself further into that wall. "Please, Malachi," she breathed.

"It's King Weyland," I corrected her, taking a few steps closer and meeting Cordelia. "And it would be wise of you to speak up now. Cordelia here is not very patient."

She shot me a smile filled with vengeance.

"Okay, okay! He was a rebel, yes. They swing by here from time to time to meet in a public place. I didn't know they were rebels at first, I swear! And once I heard the term 'rebel', I had no idea what it meant! I didn't know they were going to hurt your wife, Mal–King Weyland! I swear to you!"

"Where are they?" I barked.

Her hands shook. "I beg of you–"

"WHERE. IS. MY. WIFE?"

"That way!" she screamed. I let my shadows pulse out, grazing her cheek. "That way, that way into the forest! There is an abandoned building hidden underground just past the river. Please, you have to believe me! They would have killed me if I told–"

One pulse of magic, one rapid beat of my heart, and the woman's dead body slumped to the ground, sliding down the wall with a satisfying thud.

Dead.

I turned to the men, once again sending out a heartbeat of power. Two heartbeats.

*Thud. Thud.*

Both dead.

I did not care that I had given in to it, had momentarily let myself lose control. If killing was going to lead me to my wife, then I would kill every damn fae I saw until she was safe in my arms again.

"Let's go," I ordered the others. "It seems we have to pay our friends a visit."

"Dammit," Adeline mumbled, stepping over the two dead bodies. "I wanted to do that part."

"Don't worry," Cordelia said as they exited the inn. "I have a feeling we'll get plenty more chances tonight."

# CHAPTER 26

## Jade

"I'm not putting those on," I demanded, looking at the cuffs Ky held in his hands.

"If you want out of this cramped, dark room, you will. We can't have you igniting your magic at the first whiff of trouble."

I smiled coldly. "Now why would I do something like that? Why would I ever need to use my Saints-given magic in a situation like this?"

He pushed the cuffs further. "Put them on," he said. His voice sounded more final this time, but I still wasn't afraid. Even without my magic, without the one thing I counted on to keep me safe, I was not going to be afraid of this rebel.

"Fine," I said, eventually holding my hands out so he could cuff them. As soon as the metal touched my skin, I flinched. It felt cold and empty and so, so wrong. "What is that?"

"Laced with blocker magic," he said. "Special gift from some of our friends. It will stop you from using your powers, no matter how close to those Saints you are."

He fastened them tightly around my wrists before backing up and taking a long breath. "Let's go," he said. He opened the door and the light flooded in. I had to squint to keep my eyes open.

"If you want me dead," I stated as I stepped out of the tiny, cramped cell, "you should just kill me. You're wasting your own time here, and frankly you're wasting mine."

"I told you, Jade, I do not wish to kill you. That's the opposite of what I want to do with you, actually."

He led me down a long hallway, guiding me toward the light that flooded in from the far end where a staircase appeared. "Then what do you want with me?" I asked. "Because if you think I'm going to help you, you are poorly mistaken."

The man laughed. I clenched my fists further, hating the way those damned cuffs felt. I began to feel a hunger deep in my core, the same place I was so used to feeling my magic and Malachi's.

*I missed that bond so, so much.*

"That's what I'm here to show you," Ky said.

He held his hand out and waved up the staircase. "What's up there?" I asked.

"I suppose you should head upstairs and check it out, peacemaker."

I really hated his guy. He was arrogant and cocky, two things I would wipe directly off his face if I had even a tiny ounce of my magic back.

"Fine," I said. "But don't think these cuffs will stop me if you decide to really piss me off, rebel."

He nodded, but that mask of arrogance cracked for just a second as he sent one final glance down to my cuffs. "Noted."

I ascended the stairs, my legs burning as I took each step. My mind raced with the possibilities of what was waiting for me. Ky was right. If he wanted me dead, he would have killed me when I was unconscious. Then, or when he put these cuffs on my hands.

But he knew I wasn't going to help him. Him, or any rebels, in that case. *So what did he want?* Why go through all this trouble just to keep me alive?

I reached the top of the staircase and turned, finding a long, empty corridor. A few dozen fae seemed to be scattered throughout the room, eating whatever they had in their plain, grey bowls. Everything in the room was grey, actually. Grey and dark and colorless, a mixture of wood and metal combining as the walls ascended upward, sunlight flooding in from dozens of small, rectangular windows at the very top of the walls.

Alarms blared in my mind. Every instinct I had told me this place was bad, was wrong. "What is this?" I asked. "Where are we?"

"This is our headquarters," Ky explained, stepping up beside me as I gawked at the room.

"Are we..." I could hardly get the words out. No, it wasn't possible. We would have heard about this before. This wasn't a simple tent filled with a couple rebellious fae. This was an entire organization. I looked closer, finding weapons strapped to every single fae who sat in the room. Weapons and armor and masks. This had clearly been happening for quite some time, long before I was ever named the peacemaker.

"Yes," Ky said, finishing my question for me. "We're underground."

"It's nothing personal," Ky explained. I had found myself at the end of one of the tables at the far end of the room, listening to Ky and another rebel explain their goal of this entire situation. "We've been expecting the peacemaker for some time now, Jade. We didn't know it would be you, but that changes nothing. Our plan would remain the same no matter who the peacemaker was."

"But I'm not fae," I explained. Ky's story didn't make any sense to me. He told me about how years ago, when a fae began to expect the fulfillment of the prophecy coming, they had built this place. A few fae at first, and then the group grew and grew until a few dozen were coming together almost daily to get the work done, and they all wanted the same thing.

To stop the prophecy before it ever came to fruition.

"I'm nothing like the Paragon, I'm not one of you. I'm here to restore the balance, do you not understand that?"

Ky nodded and looked at his partner. "Yes," Ky said. "We understand that you are not fae, but you must understand our concerns. You're the most powerful person in the world now, Jade Weyland. It doesn't matter who you are or who your husband is, that's the truth. That goes against our ultimate goal. It's as simple as that."

"And what is your ultimate goal?" I pushed. "To have chaos? To let power-hungry, vindictive fae take over?"

"Isn't that exactly what you planned on doing?" Ky's friend asked.

"I'm. Not. Fae." I slammed my shackled hands down on the table. They both flinched, and I couldn't deny the wave of satisfaction that rolled through me.

Perhaps I had a few more fearful qualities than I once thought.

"Right," Ky stated. "We've picked up on that."

"Look," I said, not able to hide my annoyance from my voice, "I understand that you think I'm going to try and take over the world, but I assure you, I am not. I did not want this fate. I didn't ask for it. Saints, if I would have known that all of this trouble came from being this chosen one..." I let my thoughts trail off. "The point is, you've got this all wrong. Did your little friends tell you that I also met the Saints?" They paused. "All of them."

"You met the Saints?" Ky's friend questioned, leaning forward across the table.

I nodded. "It was part of the ritual to become the peacemaker, yes. They speak to me frequently and they guide nearly all of my decisions."

"And where are they now?" Ky pushed. "Your *Saint* friends, where are they? What are they telling you about us, about this situation?"

He raised an eyebrow in a way that sent a rush of fury down my spine. He thought of me as weak. He thought of me as powerless without them. But I wasn't going to admit that they hadn't helped me, even if that's what he wanted me to say. I couldn't give him that satisfaction.

"They don't like you," I blurted instead, slapping the best sarcastic smile I could muster onto my face. Even the small movement made my lips crack.

"Well," Ky replied. "The feelings are mutual then."

I squinted my eyes at him. *Why would anyone not like the Saints? Why would anyone want to be on their bad side?*

The three of us stared at each other for a couple minutes, nobody saying a word. I hated Ky. It's not even that I simply hated him, but it was as if every ounce of my body repelled him. Even with my magic being restrained by those cuffs, I felt a warning deep in my body to stay away.

*Noted.*

Not like I could do much about it now.

"So what?" I asked, breaking the silence. "You keep me here forever? If you don't want me to be the peacemaker, why bother with keeping me alive?"

Slowly, a wicked smile grew on Ky's face. His yellowed teeth flashed against the light coming in from the upper walls. "If I'm being honest with you here, peacemaker," he started. His friend began to smile, too, as they both stared at me. I kept my face free of reactions. "There is another motive I have for your presence with us here."

"Oh really?" I pushed. "Care to enlighten me?"

He nodded, placing his folded hands on the table before him. "Your husband is the King of Shadows." It wasn't a question.

"He is."

"You see, I have met your dear husband before, but of course, he would not recognize me."

My blood ran cold. "You know Malachi?"

"*Know* is not the word I would use for it. But yes, I know of him. We fought against him when he invaded our kingdom and murdered hundreds in cold blood, not caring who was hurt. Innocents. Woman. Children."

*Shit, shit, shit.* "No," I said, leaning forward. "No, you don't understand. That wasn't Malachi's doing. His father forced him to do those things."

Ky sat back in his chair. "I have a hard time believing a fae so powerful would need to take orders from his father. Especially orders so cruel."

"It's true," I pushed. I didn't care that I sounded desperate, I needed him to understand me. I had a deep, sickening feeling as to where this was going. "He isn't the same man he was back then, Ky. I swear to you."

"Either way," he said. "Your husband killed my brother."

Those eyes sharpened, finally hitting me with the anger and betrayal and regret that lurked behind them. I had seen eyes like that; viscous and full of vengeance. Eyes like that would do anything to make that pain go away, to make that anger subside.

*No, I knew what was coming.*

"What do you want with him?" I asked once more.

"A life for a life," Ky said. "Your husband will come for you, Jade Weyland. And when he does, I will kill him."

# CHAPTER 27
## Malachi

"Is this a good idea?" Adonis asked, running to catch up with me. I didn't dare rest, didn't hesitate for a single second before darting in the direction of the river. It would be hard to find, that much I knew. If these rebels had gone undetected for more than a few weeks, they had to be hiding themselves to some extent.

"Is *what* a good idea?" I snapped. "Saving my wife?"

"No, that's not what I mean and you know it. I heard what those rebels said, brother. If you come after Jade, they'll kill her. They'll try to kill you, too."

I snorted. "Consider this me calling their bluff. If they were going to kill Jade, they would have done it back there. They want her for something. They might be draining her magic, sacrificing her in some crazy rebel ritual, I don't know. But I do know I'm going to get her back."

Adonis grabbed my arm and forced me to stop walking. I spun to face him, fist ready to go, before I saw the others standing behind him. They clearly thought the same things he was saying. "You all agree with him?" I asked. My attention slid to Adeline. "Even you?"

"I want Jade back too," Adeline said softly. "But maybe it would be safer if we had some sort of plan first. We can be back in Rewyth before midnight, and we can meet with the others to discuss what might be happening. We can rest, gather more fae to fight with us. Those rebels were strong, Malachi. It would be a risk to run in blind."

"I can't believe this," I muttered. "Jade needs us. She's probably locked up without her magic, waiting for us to bust into wherever the rebels are hiding and kill every single one of them."

"Or," Cordelia said, stepping up. "She knows that we're coming and she's trusting our timing. She has the Saints to help her, too, Malachi. You know she'll be okay."

I hated every single one of them for being right. "Fine," I said after a minute. "We go to Rewyth to gather the others, but I'm not resting until we get her back."

"I would expect nothing else," Lucien mumbled under his breath. "Let's get moving. We can think of a game plan on the way."

I couldn't believe we were so close to her, and we were turning back. I was beginning to feel it, too, that small tether of power that connected us. I had lost that feeling after they had taken her, when whatever shield of magic they were using blocked our power, but it was beginning to reform again. If she was in danger, I would feel it.

At least, I prayed to the Saints I would. They were the ones that had connected us, right? Wouldn't they want me to know if she was in trouble?

My wings cut the air as sharply as a knife, pumping me into the sky with the rest of the group and bringing me home. None of us complained when our backs began to burn, our muscles aching from flying for so long. Nobody said a word when rain pelted our faces, making the flying that much more difficult. They all knew better, and they were on my side, whether or not I wanted to believe that.

We were getting her back.

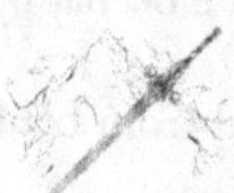

Lenova and the other witches had just made it back to Rewyth when we arrived. Everyone else from the castle looked surprised, to say the least.

My boots landed on the dirt of the kingdom, just inside the gates of Rewyth. Guards circling the castle immediately gave their salute, straightening their backs in shock when they realized who it was.

"Who has seen my mother?" I asked, ignoring everyone and brushing through the gathering crowd at the front doors of the castle. "Where is Esther?"

"Here," Esther said, rummaging through the crowd. "This way, son!" The urgency in her voice told me she already knew what was going on. Witch magic, maybe, or simply her uncanny intuition. Either way, we had no time to waste.

I turned to one of the guards beside me. "Get a small army ready," I ordered. "Anyone with magic gifts, skills, or a sword. Our mission is to save our queen."

He nodded and was off, making his way to the soldiers.

Esther was pulling me through the crowd, leading me to the study where we could talk. My brothers all trailed behind me. "They all had magic," I whispered to Esther. "Strong magic. Enough to put us all on our knees, Jade included."

We filed inside, Esther closing the study door behind us. "Rebels?" she asked. "Have you learned anything about who it was? Where they came from? Surely they were not fae we knew."

"No," I replied. "We were warned that rebels may want to attack Jade, but we didn't possibly think anyone would be stupid enough to actually do it. Turns out, the rebels aren't as stupid as we believed. They absolutely ravished us, Esther."

"What happened?" she asked. "Tell me everything, don't leave out a single detail."

So I did. I relived the events in acute detail, filling Esther in on everything that happened, including the empty kingdom of Fearford and the warning we received at the inn. She didn't interrupt, nor did she seem surprised when I filled her in on the uncanny abilities of our attackers.

"The poison is the only thing I've heard of that limits my abilities that way," I explained. "But it wasn't just that. It was as if someone was weighing us down with invisible ropes."

My brothers, Cordelia, Adeline, and Serefin, waited silently while I explained, nodding along to the details of the attack.

"It wasn't just him," Cordelia added after I was finished. "Even I was stripped of all abilities. I couldn't see into their minds; I couldn't see where they were taking her. It was as if I were a mere human."

"Have you heard of anything like this before?" Adonis asked. "Have you heard of a power that can strip everyone else's? I mean, why would the Saints even allow something like that to happen? And to the peacemaker, of all people.

Esther remained quiet for a chilling amount of time. In the weeks we had been gone, she had changed. I couldn't quite put my finger on why or how, but something was definitely different about her.

"We knew some people wouldn't be happy about the peacemaker's presence. That much is not a surprise."

"Who are these rebels?" Eli asked from behind the group. "What do they want with her?"

"She's a witch, brother," Lucien said. "Not a Saint. She doesn't have all the answers."

Esther smiled softly. I crossed my arms over my chest and waited, trying to ignore the lingering panic that laced every single muscle in my body. It felt so, so wrong to be this far from her.

"They dulled your powers and they took her with them," Esther repeated. "But they didn't kill her. They want something from her."

"What could they possibly want? Her power is hers alone, they cannot take it. They cannot use her power as their own," I replied.

"No, but they can try. Power-hungry individuals do idiotic things all the time. If they think Jade is going to give them a step-up, if they have thought that she can provide them with more power than they ever had before, they'll surely take it."

"And their gifts? I can't imagine how we'll be able to penetrate the rebels' hideout if they have magic like that."

"It could be a shield," Esther explained. "A powerful one. And to hold it against Jade's magic, they must be strong and skilled."

"Well," Lucien added, "I'm sure the Saints' unleashing of magic in the world only made them stronger."

We all took a long breath, glancing around the room.

"I'm open to ideas," I said after a few moments. "If anyone has any thoughts on how to kill the rebels as soon as possible, let me know now."

Again, a few silent beats passed.

It wasn't until Esther stepped forward that our attention resettled on her once more. "Actually," Esther started, "I have something you all may want to see."

## CHAPTER 28

# Jade

"SORRY ABOUT THIS," KY EXPLAINED AS HE SHOVED ME BACK INTO THAT dark room. "With your power, we can't take any risks. This is the only room reinforced with the shielding magic. The longer you stay here, the weaker you'll be."

"Great," I mumbled. "How thoughtful of you."

He removed my cuffs once I was inside, but the weight of the room had already dulled any flare of my abilities I was beginning to feel, stripping me of all connections to my power.

And all connections to Malachi.

I waited until he had closed the dark, steel door behind him, leaving me alone in the room, before I collapsed against the cold wall.

*Kill Malachi?* Saints, I should have known. They didn't care about me! They wanted me dead, just as much as any other power-hungry fae who saw me as a threat. They were going to kill me, too, I was sure of it, right after they eliminated Malachi.

I couldn't let it happen.

He was going to come for me. I knew he would. With any luck, he was gathering an army right now to tear this place to the ground.

"Anything you can do right about now would be great," I whispered, turning my eyes up to the dark ceiling. My human eyes were still adjusting, but I could make out the four corners of the tiny room. A cot, a bucket, and a small cup of water.

*How welcoming.*

The Saints would help me, right? They would have to. They wouldn't put all of this work into creating me as the peacemaker just to let a group of rogue fae end us all, everything we created.

No, I wasn't going to let it happen.

The enchanted force of the wall began to ache in my bones, pulling all of my magic and then some, stripping me of my strength, my fire.

My legs began to ache. My arms felt weak, hanging at my sides.

I couldn't fight anyone this exhausted. I couldn't fight off Ky at full strength, let alone with this damn magic pulling every ounce of force from my body.

I hated it. I hated that I was here, I hated that those bastards blamed Malachi for something that wasn't his fault.

He had killed hundreds before. I knew that. I used to fear that part about him, but now? I knew what it really was. I knew who he really was, and he wasn't a killer. Not really.

He was a king. A man. A husband.

He was given this incredibly dark gift, and had been manipulated into wielding it for so long.

But now? He wouldn't use his power against innocent people. No, he would only use it on those who deserved his wrath.

Ky didn't understand. Malachi may have killed his brother, but that was the old Malachi. The one in pain, the one tied to his father in ways he could never understand.

Exhaustion began to weigh down my eyelids, making it hard to form coherent thoughts.

I would fight. I would find a way out of this damn room and I would fight, if not for myself, then for him, for Malachi. But I was so, very tired. Just an hour of sleep, and then I would feel better. Stronger.

*Just...an...hour...*

I only awoke from my dreamless sleep when I heard the steel door beginning to creek open. I hadn't even made it to the cot, no. I had fallen asleep slumped on the ground next to the steel wall.

The door cracked open quietly, silently.

Much too slow to be Ky. He would swing the door open with the arrogance he couldn't put aside.

"Jade?" a female voice whispered. "Jade, are you in here?"

I shot to my feet, hand moving to my hip where my weapon no longer existed. "What do you want?" I asked, my voice a low growl.

"Saints," the female voice whispered. My eyes were still adjusting, but I made out a female frame as a woman came inside, shutting that steel door behind her.

Wait...I knew that frame. I knew that voice. I knew that girl.

As soon as the steel door was closed, the woman pulled me into her arms.

I hugged her back, finding the strength to lift my arms only for a moment to pull the woman into my embrace. "Sadie," I breathed.

"I can't believe it," Sadie whispered into my hair, not tightening her grip on me for even a second. "It's really you! I never thought I would see you again, Jade. Never, not after..."

"Wait," I said, interrupting her. I used every ounce of strength I had to pull myself from her embrace and look into her shadow-covered face. Any feelings of warmth or kindness I had for my old friend vanished as a new feeling washed over me, one of betrayal and darkness and anger. "You're a rebel?"

# CHAPTER 29
## *Malachi*

Esther walked with a purpose, one I hadn't seen her walk with in quite some time. There was something else lacing her movements, too. *Nerves? Excitement?*

"Where are you taking us?" I asked for the third time.

"You'll see," she answered, also for the third time. She walked us through the dark, nearly empty halls of the castle. Everyone we passed parted ways, gawking at myself and my brothers as we brushed passed. I nodded at a few of them, but otherwise didn't pause.

And then we began heading down to the dungeons.

"Please tell me you haven't been locking prisoners down here," Adeline sighed from behind me. "This place creeps me out."

I hadn't been to the dungeons since, well, since Jade. Since Isaiah and Sadie. To be honest, it creeped me out, too. We rarely had a need for the dark, underground tunnels of the castle, and I couldn't imagine why Esther was dragging us down here.

She had been locked up here once, too.

"This way," she said, turning the corner and taking us down the stiff staircase that led to that dark place.

I glanced back at my brothers. They only gave me a knowing look with raised eyebrows.

And then we followed.

Esther had lit many more lanterns than usual, making the darkness of the dungeons somehow brighter. At least that part was comforting.

We barreled through the underground, following quickly as Esther practically flowed through the dark tunnels.

"Almost there," she said.

"Almost where?" I asked. My nerves, agitation, and slight panic of being away from Jade mixed together in a rush of emotion that was beginning to bubble to the surface.

Esther stopped in her tracks at the end of one of the tunnels and turned to face us, an eerie, lit up smile playing on her lips.

"Dragon."

She waved her hand out, signaling us to head into the last room at the very back of the dungeon.

Dragon? She had locked that poor child up in these dark, dirty tunnels?

With an instinctive hand on my hip, I followed Esther's signal and rounded the corner.

Just as I thought, Dragon sat in the far corner of the room, lit up by the fire in the lanterns around him.

"Careful, now," Esther called from behind us.

My brothers, Serefin, and Adeline filed into the room behind me. Adeline gasped, either from excitement of seeing him or of pure shock from the conditions he was being kept in. Ripped clothes, dirty feet, just as we had found him in the Paragon.

"Dragon," Esther said, filing in after us. "Remember what I taught you. Deep breaths, keep your emotions calm."

Dragon shot up to his feet, his face lit up in excitement. "You're back!" he yelled. "Oh my–Adeline! I never thought I would see you again!"

"What's going on here?" I demanded, my voice booming off the walls around us. "Why is Dragon in the dungeons?"

Dragon began bouncing on his bare feet, barely able to contain the joy.

"Dragon," Esther warned. "Stay back."

"Nonsense," Adeline pushed. She shoved herself to the front of the crowd and dropped to her knees, her arms out on either side of her. Dragon didn't hesitate. His excitement was nearly palpable now as he took the few steps, nearly about to throw himself into Adeline's arms when–

The air in the dungeon shifted. A breeze that should not be possible entered the cramped space around us, blowing so hard I nearly stumbled backward.

"What in the–"

And then, right before my eyes, Dragon began to change. Shift. His features morphed, slowly at first, and then all at once.

He was...he was changing. Shifting into something else, something not fae nor human. I saw the wings first, forming in the wind that gathered dust and blew it all around him. Dragon was lifted off his feet, right before Adeline, and thrust into the air as the change continued.

Someone screamed.

A flash of fire filled the room.

I covered my eyes with my hand as a flash of light, so bright I could have sworn it came from Jade herself, filled even the darkest corners of the deep, underground dungeons.

A few flaps of wings smacked the air, then the stone walls of the room, before a loud, primal, animalistic roar filled the space, wanting me to submit. Wanting everyone in the room to submit, to kneel.

I took my hand away from my eyes.

Dragon had morphed into a...a....

"A dragon," Adeline muttered in awe, still on her knees before him as she looked up at the creature, now three times the size of the small boy. Black wings with sharp talons filled that now much too small corner of the dungeon.

I couldn't move. Couldn't think.

This was impossible. This had to be a dream, a nightmare, a vision. Anything but reality.

And then the dragon opened his mouth. The cool air of the dungeon instantly heated, a small ball of fire became visible in in the back of the beast's throat as–

"Take cover!" Esther screamed from behind us.

But it was too late.

The dragon unleashed the fire that burned within, encapsulating all of us. Adeline, Lucien, Adonis, Eli, Cordelia. Everyone.

I closed my eyes again, shutting them tightly. If I was going to die, I was glad it was by this. By a mystical beast who shouldn't even exist anymore.

But the heat never came. The fire never hit me. I blinked my eyes open again to see Serefin standing in front of us all, an invisible shield of...no, it wasn't glamour. It was something else, like a wall that existed there, protecting us all from the fire that began to fizz out.

Serefin had shield magic.

Dragon was...a dragon.

Everything began to settle as the beast backed itself into the corner, once again calm. Serefin's shield sputtered out before disappearing completely.

"Well," Cordelia sighed from the back of the room. "I think we have quite a bit to unpack here."

*Holy. Shit.*

# CHAPTER 30
# *Jade*

"Jade," Sadie said, holding her hands up in surrender. "Jade, listen to me. Don't freak out, let me explain."

"I don't need to listen to anything you say."

I couldn't believe what I was seeing. After everything I did for her...I trusted her, I thought she trusted me. We worked together, I thought she was on my side.

She knew I was the peacemaker.

And this entire time, all this worry and time spent hoping she was okay, she was one of them. Working with them behind my back.

"I'm not a rebel, Jade!" She whispered in a hushed voice, as if worried that someone would hear her. "I wouldn't do that to you, I wouldn't betray you like that after everything you did for me!"

My anger turned to confusion. "If you're not a rebel—which I find very hard to believe—why are you here? Why are you living with them? Did you know they were trying to kidnap me this entire time?"

"No, Jade! I swear it!"

"Then why?"

Sadie took a long, shaking breath and dropped her hands, letting her shoulders fall and her head hang back. She looked...exhausted.

*No, Jade.* She's *not* exhausted, and you can't trust a single thing she says.

"I made it back to Fearford, after days of running through the forest. Malachi, after what he did to Isaiah..."

"No," I interrupted. "You don't get to say his name. Not after this."

"I found my way back to Fearford and life returned to normal, nobody talked about the peacemaker. Nobody even mentioned the fae. We were simply trying to survive and rebuild ourselves after Isaiah died."

I flinched at the sound of his name off her tongue.

Sadie took a deep breath. "And one day, they came. It was quick and unexpected.

They only had to kill a few humans. The rest, they overpowered with their strength. We didn't stand a chance."

*Okay, maybe she wasn't lying.*

"What do they want? Why would they invade a human kingdom?"

"None of us knew at first. That...that had to be weeks ago, now. We didn't know who they were or what they wanted, just that we had to follow them. Follow them or die. They brought us back here, told us to keep ourselves inside, so that's what we did. That's what we've been doing ever since."

I could hardly believe what she was saying. Correction—I *didn't* believe what she was saying. "You had no idea they were rebels? You conveniently never found out who your captors were the entire time you were here?"

"After a few days, we began to hear things. Whispers of the peacemaker and of her dark husband."

I grimaced.

"But I swear to you, Jade, I had no idea what they were planning to do. I heard yesterday that they had taken you here and had locked you in this cell. It won't be long until they find out I've come to talk to you."

"Then why did you?" I asked. "They could kill you without even blinking, Sadie. Why risk coming down here?"

She stepped forward and placed both hands on my shoulders. I tried not to flinch away. "Because," she started, "you're my friend, Jade. You might not believe it right now, and that's okay. But you saved my life once. So did Malachi. If I can repay the favor in any way, I'll do it."

She smiled at me, and I couldn't help but give her a small nod. Did I trust her? No, not in the slightest. I didn't trust anybody here, human or fae.

But I did need a way out. And Sadie was the only option I had come across.

"Okay," I said. "Do you have a plan?"

Sadie left without anybody noticing, thanks to a guard that had taken a particular liking to her. When she left, though, I found myself craving her presence. The darkness of the steel, magically enforced room grew thicker and more lonely with every passing minute.

I had wondered for so long if Sadie ever made it back to Fearford, ever found peace. Ever recovered from the loss of her friend, Isaiah.

But here she was, living with the rebels.

*At least she was alive,* I told myself. Somebody here wasn't actively trying to kill Malachi, at least I knew that.

And she wasn't alone. She had been talking to the humans, some from Fearford and some from my home. They were all being kept here, being told nothing other than the fact that they were to stay indoors.

If I didn't hate the rebels before, I definitely did now.

I lost track of time in that dark room, not being able to tell if the sun was up or down. Not hearing anything, not even a footstep, from the hallway outside. I had no idea how long it had been since Sadie left, or if an entire day had passed.

I knew nothing.

I tried to keep my thoughts off Malachi. Tried and failed.

He was likely planning a way to storm the place, maybe he was right outside tracking the movements of the rebel guards.

*Keep him safe,* I thought up to the Saints. *If anything else happens, please keep Malachi safe.*

The steel door creaked open.

"Sadie?" I whispered, barely audible. But it wasn't Sadie's lean figure that walked through the door, no.

"Your friend isn't here," a male voice boomed. "You have no friends here, actually."

He left the door cracked as he pushed his way inside. I slid off the cot and immediately backed into the wall behind me, every single instinct alert. Every instinct on fire.

"What are you doing here?" I asked. "What do you want?"

The man became familiar, my eyes adjusting with the filtering light from the hallway. It was Ky's friend, the one who had been with us earlier.

"Ky believes we should leave you alone down here," the man said. "He says you're too dangerous to be messed with."

I held my breath, not daring a response. This fae was twice my size, and without my magic or a weapon...

"I'm here to find out how much of that is true, peacemaker."

I didn't have time to flinch before the fae sent a fist straight into my stomach. Pain and shock both erupted, taking up every single one of my senses. I doubled over, trying to suck in a breath.

But the fae wasn't done.

He sent an elbow into my back, pain ripping through my upper body. I fell to the ground, unable to catch myself as my weak limbs crashed to the cold floor.

"You're not so powerful without your magic, now, are you? Just another dumb, weak human. It's a shame, really."

Another kick to my curled-up body, one I couldn't begin to deflect. I didn't have the energy. Couldn't fight against the erupting pain that now encompassed every single ounce of my being.

*Please,* I thought up to the Saints. *Please, make it stop.*

But it didn't. I thought he would be done after the fourth kick, or maybe the fifth. In fact, I prayed to the Saints every single time that it would be the last.

But it wasn't. Eventually, the pain became too much to bear, too much to hold. So I let it go, let it take over entirely, let it morph with my soul and with my being until all I knew was the pain.

# CHAPTER 31
# Malachi

"HOW IS THIS POSSIBLE?" I ASKED ESTHER. AFTER A LOT OF CHAOS AND yelling, Dragon had finally shifted back to a boy right in front of us. I had never seen anything like it, it was...it was lore, it was not supposed to exist. Yet here he was, right before us.

"I didn't believe it, either," Esther started. "I assume Silas and some of the Paragon knew, hence the name he was given. It suits him, I'll say that much."

"I can't believe this," Adeline breathed. "This whole time, shifters have been real? *Dragons* are real?"

"Dragon is the first I've met, the first I've heard of being real, actually," Esther answered.

"What does this mean?" I asked. "Does this mean other dragons exist?"

"I certainly wouldn't rule it out," Esther replied.

"That explains why I couldn't read his mind before," Cordelia added. "He's not like everyone else." She stepped forward and lowered herself to meet Dragon's eyes. "You're different, aren't you?"

Dragon shrugged. "I guess so. Silas told me not to tell anybody."

"Of course he did," I muttered. "Can you control it? Do you shift often?"

"We've been getting better," Esther explained, "although like most magic, it's difficult to contain with any rush of emotions."

Adeline stepped forward. "Shall we also discuss whatever just happened to Serefin? I mean, he practically saved all of our lives just now!"

We all shifted our attention to Serefin, who stood with wide eyes. "Don't look at me," he said. "I have no idea how I did that."

Esther laughed quietly. "It's shield magic. You protected your friends from Dragon's fire."

Serefin held his hands out before him and looked at them intently. "Shield magic?" he asked. "Are you sure?"

Esther nodded. "After what I just saw, I'm very sure."

Adeline squealed in excitement, and I moved to clap him on the shoulder. "You're a protector now," I said to him. "That's very fitting."

Serefin just smiled. "Always, brother," he replied.

Suddenly, my vision blurred. My body stiffened. I wasn't quite sure what was happening, even my power seemed to stir inside of me, waiting for some sort of attack.

And then there was pain everywhere all at once.

Pain like I had never felt before, burning me from the inside out.

I looked at my friends, but they all seemed fine. Someone shouted my name, but their faces blurred together in my tunneling vision.

Pain in my chest, my stomach, my core, over and over and over again until it stayed.

I hadn't realized I had fallen to the ground, doubled over without breathing, until Cordelia rolled me onto my back.

Someone yelled in the background, I couldn't hear anything over the ringing in my ears.

It hurt, *everything* hurt.

"Malachi?" Adonis yelled over me, leaning across from Cordelia and staring at me.

Saints, I wanted to scream. Wanted to tell them to *go, go, go*.

But I couldn't even take a breath, let alone speak.

I wasn't sure how long I stayed like that. My vision blurred in and out, the darkness taking over for small amounts of time before it all began to fade away.

"Malachi?" Adonis yelled again, shaking my shoulders. "Tell us what's happening!"

"It's her," I managed to get out. I couldn't say anything else, gasping in breaths and fueling my lungs.

Cordelia knew, though. Could see exactly what I was thinking.

Her eyes widened. "It's Jade," she whispered, barely a breath. "They're hurting Jade."

I bent over and coughed again, this time feeling the breath escape from my lungs as if it were my own. And somewhere in the pain, laced deep and deliberately, was a trace of something else.

Something *dark*. Something *familiar*.

Something so filled with her, with Jade's essence, it nearly overtook me entirely. It was our bond coming back full-force, trying to alert me that she was in trouble, that she needed our help.

After a few moments, the pain faded. As soon as I could, I jumped to my feet. "She needs us," I yelled. "We have to go to her! We cannot wait any longer!"

"I'll fetch the others," Adonis said, running back into the depths of the dungeon.

"What about Dragon?" Adeline asked. "He can help us!"

"Only if he can control himself," I replied, "and by the looks of it, I'm not sure he can."

"I can!" Dragon yelled. "I swear to you, I can do it! Let me help her! Let me help get the peacemaker back!"

*Well, I wasn't going to argue with that.*

I nodded and turned on my heel, following Adonis out of the dark hallways.

Serefin's hand fell on my shoulder. "I'm with you, brother," he whispered.

"No," I replied. "You need to go with the others. If anything happens, you can protect them with your shield magic."

"I'd rather protect you. Let me fly by your side, we can find the rebels before the sun rises."

Serefin, not my blood but just as connected to me as anyone who might be my real brother. Serefin was brave, many times braver than me. He had fought directly by my side in battle, had killed for me. Had stood up for me. For years and years of my life, Serefin was the only person I trusted.

But now, I cared about a lot more than my own survival. I had the entire kingdom at risk. I had brothers and friends and... dragons.

Somehow, a handful of witches even fell into the group of people I needed to protect.

"Please," Serefin pushed, sensing my resistance. "You need protection just as much—if not more—than anyone else. I'm not even sure I'll be able to pull my shield out again so soon, but let me try."

I stopped walking and turned to face him, soldiers and witches now running in every direction, around us and through the castle, preparing for our upcoming battle.

"I love you, brother," I started, patting him on both shoulders. "You know I do. I know you want to come with me, I know you want to protect me. But this?" I waved my hands out, signaling to the castle around us, to the people we cared about. To Eli, Adeline, Cordelia, the others. "This is what we've always wanted for Rewyth, Ser. This is what I've fought so hard for. This is what we've always deserved. I want—no, I *need* you to protect that. Protect the integrity of what we've built here. I'll be okay on my own, but them?"

I glanced down the hall where the others waited for us near the castle door. "They need you now, and I need you to protect them."

"They need you, too, Mal," Ser whispered. "We all do."

"You don't need to worry about me."

"Well, I do. You'd do anything to get Jade back, and we know that. But I also know you'd give your own life for hers in an instant if it meant making her safe, if it meant bringing her back home."

His words didn't hurt me as badly as the pain in his eyes. Serefin was great at masking his emotions. He had kept our relationship respectful and professional for as long as he could, only letting me see his true concern or emotion when it was absolutely necessary.

I loved him for that, but I also knew I wasn't going to pull back for Jade.

"Go," I said, nodding in the direction of the others. "That's an order."

Before anyone else could stop me, I ran outside and launched into the air, over the castle wall, over the trees that surrounded Rewyth, over everything I had known. That tug of Jade's power pulled me, guiding me, laced with a pain and a desperation that only made me pump my wings faster and faster.

Jade needed me. I felt it like I felt the air in my own lungs.

And I would stop at nothing to get her back.

# CHAPTER 32
# *Jade*

THE DARKNESS BECAME WORSE THAN THE PAIN.

After the fae left, satisfied with the amount of punches and kicks he had given me, I was left alone in the dark, cold cell.

At first, the hope was the worst part. Hope that someone had heard. Hope that Sadie would come rescue me. Hope that the fae would see he had hurt me enough.

But that quickly faded. Hope was a dangerous, dangerous game, I knew that more than anybody. I tried not to feel it at all, like when I was first sent to marry Malachi. The lack of hope made me strong, made me brave. Forced me to look death in the eye without backing down.

Now, though, hope was around every corner. Every distant sound, every yell echoing off the steel walls.

*Malachi. Malachi. Malachi.*

I placed a hand on the center of my chest. For a split second, when I was sure the fae attacking me wasn't going to stop until I was dead, I thought I felt it; that familiar, magical bond that made him eternally mine.

But now, sitting back in the magically-enforced steel, I felt nothing. Not a shred of magic, not a flicker of power.

I must have been imagining things, imagining the connection being re-formed in my panic of survival.

"Shouldn't the magic of the Saints be stronger than some damn wall?" I whispered to myself.

I waited for a reply, but again, none came.

My breathing, slow, steady, and shallow, became the only sound I heard as I drifted off again, being claimed by the inevitable exhaustion.

# CHAPTER 33
# *Malachi*

Faster. Further. Higher.

My thoughts revolved around Jade and did not stop, not once. The others would catch up, I knew they would. But they wouldn't beat me there.

*Good.* I didn't need anyone trying to stop me. First, we had to find where the damn rebels were camping out. I had a feeling that wouldn't be as easy as it sounded.

*What had that woman at the inn said?*

Past the river and...

It didn't matter. When I got close enough, I would be able to feel her.

And I prayed to the Saints that it wasn't her pain I would be feeling again.

I knew one thing, though. I was going to find whoever laid their damn hands on her, and I was going to rip their head off.

I flew and flew and flew, until every single beat of my wings burned through my body, until I was sure I could not fly any more, and then I finally saw the river.

I dove to the ground without a second of hesitation, my boots grinding against the dirt forest floor. The trees were thinner near the river, creating less coverage for my identifiable black wings.

I crouched near the flowing water, catching my breath. Letting my heart rate slow to its original pace.

I had to focus. Losing focus could mean death, not only for me but for her, too.

*Please,* I thought up to the Saints. *If you do anything else, please help me get her back.*

I wasn't sure if I was half-delirious from the exhaustion of the long flight, or if I truly was losing my mind, but a male voice boomed through my head. *You have everything you need to get her back, King of Shadows.*

I flinched at first, hand immediately falling to my hip where my sword remained strapped. "Who are you?" I said aloud.

*You know who I am.*

Yep, the voice was definitely in my head.

*No, I do not know who you are. If anything, you're a figment of my imagination. You aren't real.*

A rumble of my power flared in my chest, burning my entire upper body in a wavelike flare of heat.

What in the...

"Did you do that?"

*You know exactly who I am.*

"Erebus," I breathed. My mind ran through a hundred different questions for the Saint of death. *Where are you? Why did you give me this gift? What do you want from us, from Jade? Why did you let her get taken?*

But I asked none of those.

"Where is she?" I asked aloud, keeping my voice at a hushed whisper as I scanned the trees around us. Nothing aside from the natural flow of wind caught my attention.

*She's close,* Erebus replied. *Use your gift to find her.*

*I've tried,* I thought back. *It's not strong enough. I don't feel her; I haven't felt her since I got a glimpse of her pain back in Rewyth.*

*You're holding back,* he said, a hint of irritation lacing his words. *Unleash your full power and you will find her. It is the only way.*

*It isn't the only way! You can help her!*

*The Saints can only do so much. We gave you both what you need to live, to take control. Now it is up to you.*

Shit.

*How? How do I unleash the full potential of my power?*

*Stop holding it in, stop fearing for the lives of others. Be unstoppable. Be deadly, if you must, but do not fear who you are, Malachi Weyland. Blood of my blood.*

As those words hit my mind, my body erupted in chills. My power flared up like a wild animal, ferocious and merciless. A newfound energy washed over my body, fueling my muscles with energy and my lungs with breath.

I felt...I felt *unstoppable.*

Is this what he wanted? For me to not hold back, to not worry?

Another flare of my power lapped at the surface, and I didn't fight it. Didn't try to control it.

I was sick and tired of controlling myself, anyway. I knew what rested deep within, I had witnessed it only a handful of times.

Death. Destruction. Power unlike any I had ever seen, besides the one in my wife. It was there, hidden away and shoved so far deep in my soul that I barely remembered its existence.

That was the power that scared me. The magic that turned me into something else, something unlike any other fae.

But I wouldn't hold it in any longer.

I let my head fall back and my palms raise toward the darkening sky as I let go.

Thunder boomed nearby. The vibrations only fueled my power even more. A rush, like unstoppable waves of the sea, escaped from me. I closed my eyes and let it go, let it find Jade. Let it finally move from its resting place deep within me.

And when I opened my eyes again, I saw no sunlight. I saw nothing, actually, even with my fae eyes. Black smoke—no, *power*—rushed from my palms quicker than I had ever seen it, filling the thin forest around me with a dark cloud of doom.

I laughed; I couldn't help it. To feel so free, it wasn't in my nature, not usually. But this? It felt so right.

Black nothingness, black death. I could not even see the glistening river in front of me as I stepped out of my cover behind a thick tree.

Eli had been right with his vision of the future. Death was near.

# CHAPTER 34
# Jade

The entire building shook, rattling from the very steel walls that entrapped me.

*A storm? Someone losing control of their powers?*

I placed my hands on the cold walls and waited for the rattling to stop. No, I knew exactly where that world-shattering boom had come from. I felt it in my soul, even with the exclusion of my magic. I knew it was him.

He was coming for me.

Through the steel walls of my enclosure, I heard panic begin on the outside. Men's voices yelling, footsteps as soldiers began to run.

"They're coming!" someone directly outside my door yelled. "Everyone get ready! Someone get the girl!"

*Shit. Shit. Shit.*

I stood up and backed myself against the wall, as if I could hide from the fae. As if I could disappear entirely.

But a few seconds later, that steel door was bursting open. Not slowly and carefully like it had been opened before, no. Someone kicked the door with such force that it slammed against the wall behind it.

"Let's go!" the same fae who had assaulted me earlier screamed. I hated the way I cowered away, crossing my arms over my stomach for instinctual protection.

But that didn't stop the fae from storming forward with a piercing hand around my neck, his fingers digging into the sensitive skin as he half pulled, half-pushed me out the steel door and into the hallway.

It was not empty like it was the last time I had seen it.

Instead, soldiers ran back and forth, chaos filling the room as orders were yelled, fae panicking and pulling weapons from their belts.

"What's going on?" I asked.

The fae answered by forcing my neck down, causing me to hunch over as he dragged me down the hallway. "You don't speak!" he yelled. Although I could hear the lace of panic in his words.

They weren't expecting this, whatever it was. Did they think Malachi would come quietly? Did they think he would show up without a fight, without a show?

Malachi, the King of Shadows, was not going to show up without a fight.

And they had taken the one thing he cared about the most: his wife.

I was forced down the hall, following the rest of the soldiers filing up the stairs and into the open room of the underground building. I saw a few of them running up another set of stairs.

*That must be the stairs to the outside. That would be my ticket out of here.*

I just had to get rid of this damn fae.

I squirmed under his grasp, trying to loosen his grip, but that only made him angrier.

"Stop moving!" the fae growled, baring his teeth. "You'll only make this harder on yourself, peacemaker."

It was then that I felt it, like the fog being lifted from every inch of my body all at once. It was powerful and hot and forceful, so very *him*. Our magic bond snapping back to life, channeling Malachi's emotions into me.

And mine into him.

And what I felt through that tight bond of magic was nothing less than absolute fury and the promise of death.

*Good,* I thought. *They deserve to die. Every single one of them deserves to die for this.*

"Where are you taking me?" I asked again. "There's nowhere we can go where he won't find me!"

This seemed to piss him off further. He gripped my upper arm, almost piercing my skin, as he began forcing me through the dining hall.

The more pain I felt, the stronger my connection to Malachi would be.

"If you think you can possibly escape," the fae started, "you are sadly mistaken. Fighting will only make it worse. You're coming with me and we're getting away from the building. Now go."

He gave me a harsh shove toward...towards those steps, the ones that led up and out of the building.

*Was he really stupid enough to bring me outside?*

I ducked my head and moved in the direction he ordered, trying not to look too pleased by where we were heading.

Suddenly, all of those lanterns flickered out.

I kept moving toward the stairs, taking the first step on the raised platform when the fae behind me forced me to stop.

A few others began to panic, darkness taking over. Not the type of darkness they could see in, though.

Not the type of darkness even a fae's eyes would adjust to.

*Him.* Death's awakening, darkness looming. It was all him.

*Malachi.*

"What is that?" the fae behind me shouted to someone else.

"I don't know!" the other man yelled back. "Get her out of here and keep her hidden! This is the first place they'll attack when they come for her!"

I bit my cheek to keep from smiling, even as the fae's nails cut through my skin, blood bubbling to the surface where he tightened his grip.

"Keep moving," the fae ordered, growling just inches from my ear. His breath brushed my cheek, I flinched away from the disgusting smell.

I wanted absolutely nothing to do with this fae. If Malachi didn't rip his head off first, I would.

I kept moving up the stairs, one after another, until we reached the top.

And just when I thought the world could not get any darker, could not come any closer to eternal death, I stepped outside.

Darkness swallowed me whole.

# CHAPTER 35
# Malachi

I COULDN'T SEE JADE, BUT I FELT HER. SHE WAS CLOSE. I SENSED IT strongly, pulling me to her with every calculated breath I took.

I needed to cross the river, but flying would be too obvious. Inching out of my hiding spot behind the trees, I crept closer to the flowing water. It trickled quickly but quietly, only making a few splashes as the water fell across the rocks below.

I removed my thick boots and my heavy tunic, dropping them on the ground next to me without a sound, only leaving my trousers and my belt that contained my sword.

And then, with silent motions that not even the closest predator would hear, I slipped into the water.

It was cold and refreshing, igniting every one of my senses as I dipped underneath, pushing the water behind me and propelling myself to the other side.

And when I reached that other side of the stream, I placed both hands on the ground and slid out, as silently as I had slid in.

That power within me lit up again.

Closer. I was getting closer.

The woman at the inn had said something, something about it being...underground?

I took a few steps forward, my bare feet connecting firmly with the cold dirt beneath me. It would make sense if they were underground, hiding away from the rest of the fae that might fly above.

It was the perfect hiding place.

*But where were they? And how would I find them?*

There would have to be some sort of entrance, one likely hidden with glamour if they were smart, like the entrance to the Paragon.

Shadows—my shadows—still spread through the air, pulsing with every breath I took, darkening even the approaching moonlight from any sort of illumination.

I could see, though. Through the shadows that were my very own, I could see even clearer than before. And I searched for only one thing: her.

I crept forward like that for a few minutes—one foot after the other, not breaking a single twig or cracking the smallest leaf. Silent, like a summer breeze passing through the land. But I felt that pull to my wife like I had never felt it before, one of delight and thrill and fear.

She must have known I was coming. Must have sensed it, maybe even seen my shadows. Saints, I hoped she had seen my shadows.

Entirely unleashed, entirely unchained. Coming just for her.

A few footsteps in the distance caught my attention. I halted again, freezing where I stood and sending another wave of thunderous shadows in the direction the sounds came from.

A few fae shouted.

I clenched my fists. That had to be them.

I sent even more of my shadows out, encapsulating every inch of open air with the darkness. Through that magic bond, I felt a flicker of amusement.

Yes, Jade was close. She was here. She knew I was coming for her.

With the shadows covering me, I inched forward. Their camp had to be somewhere nearby, my magic drawing them out of hiding so they could prepare for a fight.

*Like they ever stood a chance.*

I silently pulled my sword from my belt. "Come on, you bastards."

They wanted a fight. I would bring them a war.

I moved forward again, not caring as much about hiding the small snaps of each footstep as I aimed toward where I heard movement.

A few more crunches of forest terrain in the distance.

I raised my sword. I pushed more shadows through the thick, humid air.

"That way!" a voice whispered in the distance, just a few feet away and covered by my shadows. "Spread out! Guard the entrances!"

*Those poor, poor idiots.*

I sent a flare of my power out, pushing toward every being I felt with my primal, instinctual senses. The shadows danced with the looming darkness of the trees, creating a deadly smoke as the first fae body fell, the first victim of my unleashed magic.

And then the second fell.

The third.

Soon, five bodies were down. Five enemies eliminated. Five less fae to hurt her.

I didn't care if they had nothing to do with it. I didn't even care if they hadn't laid eyes on Jade. They were equally as responsible.

I took a few steps forward until I saw the bodies through the smoke. All so young, all so hopeful. I knew what it was like to fight for a cause, but for this? What did these rebels think was going to happen?

"Move!" another fae voice, slightly closer, ordered. I crouched in the shadows, completely hidden by my own darkness. I squinted my eyes to see a small flap in the forest floor pushing open.

A hidden door.

But it was not a soldier that exited the hidden hideout. It was not a fae. It was not a rebel.

*Jade. My wife.*

Any tiny shred of control I had left disappeared entirely, vanishing along with any doubts that I wouldn't be able to get to her in time.

She crawled out of the hidden door, climbing on her hands and knees, looking in awe at the dark shadows twirling in the air around her.

And then the fae from behind her moved, gripping the back of her neck and hauling her to her feet as the door behind them slammed shut.

I could not have controlled the darkness that leapt from me if I wanted to. Thank the Saints that Jade was not affected by my power, because she would have been obliterated, too, as my magic scavenged the several feet between us, landing on their target with a sickening scream.

Jade spun around, watching with wide eyes as the fae behind her loosened his grasp and fell to the ground.

I was on my feet in an instant, half-running, half-flying the short distance to her before I wrapped her in my arms.

"Malachi," she whispered, collapsing into me with a cry of relief. "Malachi, thank the Saints."

I pulled away and held her by the shoulders. "The Saints have nothing to do with this," I mumbled. "It's up to you and I. Let's end these sorry bastards."

Anger fueling my movements, I began to move toward that door.

Jade stopped me with a hand on my chest. "No!" she argued. "No, this is all a trap, Mal! It's a trap, they're going to kill you! You have to get out of here now. Right now!"

"Calm down," I said. "Who's trying to kill me?"

"The leader of the rebels! His name is Ky. He claims you killed his brother in war a long time ago, he's trying to get his revenge."

"That's what this is all about? Some fae trying to get revenge?" I looked back at the door that led to wherever they had kept Jade. "I'm going to kill them all. Then we can go home and we won't have to worry about this again."

"Wait! There are humans in there, innocent ones. Don't kill them all!"

"Saints," I breathed. "They're rebels now, Jade. They deserve to die!"

"Sadie is in there!" The pleading in her eyes made me pause, even if just for a second. "We have to help them, Mal. They're victims here, too."

Deep down, I knew she was right. The humans were nothing but pawns in this fae game. But caring about collateral damage wasn't always my specialty.

"Fine," I said anyway. "The others are on their way. We'll go after who we can, and we'll regroup with them and make a new plan on how to save the humans later. Sound good?"

Jade nodded.

"Are you okay?" I asked her, scanning her face in the darkness.

Through the shadows that danced around us, I noticed the way she held her arm tightly across her torso. Her face had been bruised—freshly, the skin was busted and red and a halo of purple began to color her delicate skin.

"Who did this to you?" I asked, cupping her face with my hand.

"The same people who want you dead. Let's get out of here before they succeed."

I took her hand and guided her through the shadows until we were hidden behind a row of green bushes. We both knelt, hiding ourselves from anyone else who might be exiting that building.

"My power," Jade whispered as we crouched. "It's...it was being suppressed when I was in there. The Saints haven't spoken to me. I haven't been able to use it at all, Mal. Not since we left my home."

"It must be some sort of shield magic," I said. "Which Serefin now has, by the way. It could come in handy later."

"Serefin has shield magic?" Jade asked, a hint of a smile playing on her lips.

I nodded.

"Wow. Of all the power he could possibly get, that suits him best. He'd do anything to protect you, you know."

"And you," I added. "They'll get here soon, Jade. And once they do, we're getting rid of these damn rebels."

"I don't understand," Jade whispered, turning her attention to the forest around us. "They should have noticed your presence by now. Why aren't they attacking?"

"They can't attack what they can't see," I whispered back to her. "Although I wouldn't be surprised if they started battling my shadows with their own magic, soon. If your Saints want to chime in and help us out at any time, just let me know."

*Those damn Saints.*

*We're here,* the low, sultry voice spoke into my mind.

I couldn't help but flinch.

"What?" Jade asked. "What is it?"

"Nothing, it's just..."

*We are connected now, the voice said. Because of your connection. The peacemaker's power will return soon. Keep her out of that damn building.*

"Great, thanks," I whispered to the voice.

"What?" Jade whispered, clearly seeing that something wasn't right.

"I think...I believe the Saints have been speaking in my mind. Only once or twice."

"Is it Erebus?" Jade asked, a wave of hope perking her up from our crouching position in the waves of shadows. "Is he going to help us?"

As she said the words, a rush of strength like I had never felt before washed over me, fueling every single one of my senses. The dark shadows around us immediately began to stir, mixing together in a frenzy of death and chaos.

Someone screamed in the distance, meeting their death by my hand.

Erebus's hand.

A satisfied laugh echoed in my mind.

"I think he already has," I replied.

Jade's smile grew wide and wicked. We actually had a chance of making it out of here alive.

"Come on," I whispered to Jade, pulling my sword out and handing it to her. Saints, I always loved seeing her wield my weapon. "Let's give them what they deserve."

# CHAPTER 36
## *Jade*

I FOCUSED ON THAT SPARK OF POWER THAT I KNEW WAS THERE, I willed it with everything in me to come back. To be strong. To protect me.

But the damn shielding magic that had been in that room lingered, dulling my power and weighing down my limbs. Even holding Malachi's sword took more energy than it needed to, causing my movements to be slow and sloppy.

I followed Malachi as he crouched, walking barefoot and shirtless through the forest as we stalked the perimeter. Aside from a few screams after Malachi's power intensified, we had heard nothing. It was likely they had all gotten spooked off, running into the forest to save themselves.

That, or they were hiding. Waiting, just like us, for the right moment to attack.

Not a single bird chirped in the distance.

Not a single tree waved in the wind.

Death was coming. I felt it in every inch of my being, every ounce of my soul. Eli's vision, the one promising death and retribution, would be coming to light.

"It's too quiet," I whispered up to him.

Malachi's shadows had stilled, too, almost as if in anticipation for what was to come.

He couldn't use his shadows forever. They protected us, yes. They kept us hidden. But they also gave us away.

"Drop them," I whispered up to him. Mal stopped and faced me. "Drop your shadows. They'll think we've left."

He considered this for a minute. "They'll never believe we left without a fight. And the way they haven't come for you yet..."

"They will," I said with absolute assurance. "They'll come for me, Mal. But it'll be you they're trying to kill."

His jaw tightened. "I'll push the shadows toward the way we came," he said. "With any luck, they'll follow the shadows and try to find us. Are you feeling any stronger?"

I nodded. "Yep," I lied.

"I can feel when you're lying, you know," Malachi whispered with a wicked grin. "Even without your magic in full force."

"Fine," I admitted. "But that doesn't mean I'm not ready to fight. Send the shadows. We'll deal with them."

"If you say so, my queen," Malachi muttered, placing a gentle kiss on my forehead. I closed my eyes and took a long breath, trying to take in this moment. Trying to make it last forever.

When I opened my eyes again, the shadows around us were gone, pushing like a cloud back through the forest in the direction we had just come from.

Malachi's pointed ears flickered, no doubt listening for any hint of soldiers moving.

And then, all at once, we were at war.

The first group of fae charged us from our right. With a roar of anger and determination, and with their swords held high, they ran for us.

Malachi quit pushing his shadows out and used all his magic to drop the group of five fae to their knees, screaming in pain.

Malachi was strong, yes, but could he kill every single soldier here? I wasn't sure, but I certainly didn't want to risk it.

Movement caught my attention between a group of trees in the darkness. "Straight ahead!" I yelled. Mal spun on his heel, forgetting the five fae that now cowered on the forest floor and turning his attention to the others.

A crack split through the air. Seconds later, a blazing hot ball of fire whizzed by, narrowly missing my head.

"Shit!" I yelled. "Fire power!"

Another rush of flames came toward us, uncontrolled and chaotic as they came inches from grazing Malachi's body.

"Get back!" he yelled. "Take cover!"

"We have to fight, Mal! They'll keep coming!"

Another ball of fire attacked, even closer this time. Mal and I both ducked to avoid being burnt to ash.

"You aren't strong enough yet, Jade! Get back!" Mal yelled. Something lingered in his voice, something needy and desperate and... terrified.

I did as he ordered, backing up until a few large tree trunks protected me from any balls of fire.

Mal retreated, too, but not as far. He kept his back to me while he took long strides, barefoot and all, and aimed his death power at our attackers.

*Come on, stupid power,* I thought to myself. *Come back any time now, preferably before we're roasted into oblivion.*

Two fae charged Mal from his left. I jumped out from my hiding position, taking three strides toward them with the sword tight in my grasp. I swung once, a battle-cry escaping me as the weapon met flesh, cutting the first fae directly in half at the torso.

"Jade!" Mal yelled. I spun to face him, losing track of the second fae. Mal was on us in seconds, jumping onto the fae's back and snapping his neck in one swift motion.

For two full seconds, Mal and I stood there, eyes wide and staring at each other, our chests rising and falling in unison.

For two full seconds, I let myself feel fear. Fear of not being good enough, of not having my power. *Of Malachi.*

And then I pushed that fear away, swallowing it whole, and tightened my grip on my sword.

Malachi and I turned, back-to-back, ready for another attack.

And before I could take another breath, before I even had the chance of feeling fear again, we were surrounded.

# CHAPTER 37
# Malachi

"It doesn't have to be this way!" I yelled to the circle of fae around us. They all wore black fabric around their faces, with green and black paint smeared across their skin to blend easily into the surrounding foliage.

I tried to push more of my shadows into the surrounding forest, but I needed my strength. I needed all of my damn strength if I was going to make it out of here alive.

Alive, and with my wife.

"Yes," a voice called from the back of the group. "It does have to be this way. Such a pity, really."

Jade's shoulders rose and fell as she breathed deeply behind me. *If any one of these damn bastards touch her, they're dead. They're all dead.*

I scanned the line of soldiers that stopped a few feet away from us.

*Come on.* Come on and attack us already.

In front of me, a couple of the rebels shuffled, creating room for a fae behind them to walk in front.

"Hello, Malachi," he said, crossing his hands in front of his torso. "I would say it's nice to see you again, but it surely is not."

"Who are you?" I asked.

"My name is Ky. I don't expect you to know that, though. I don't expect you to know any of the fae you have gone to battle against."

I waited while the words processed in my mind. *Ky*... this was the fae that hurt Jade.

The one behind all of this.

*The one I was going to kill.*

I stepped forward, only an inch, and looked him up and down. This was the fae behind it all? This was the one who took my wife from me?

*Saints,* I nearly wanted to laugh.

"You harm the peacemaker because of past grievances?" I asked. "Do you know how powerful she is? Your men will not survive a fight against her, I can assure you that."

Ky smirked and tilted his head to the side, as if everything I said to him only amused him further.

"She didn't seem so powerful squirming beneath the fists of my men. I heard her cries all the way down the hall, actually."

*That did it.*

With a single movement, I pulled every last piece of power I had left. I exhaled deeply, pulling and pulling at that heat blooming in my soul and pushing it in Ky's direction, spreading it across the area in front of me. Somewhere in the chaos of darkness, Jade moved from behind me. I heard her say something, but I couldn't make it out over the ringing in my ears.

And I didn't stop. I pushed and pushed and pushed, wishing nothing but death on Ky and his little army of rebels.

*Nobody touches Jade and lives.*

*Nobody even looks at Jade with harm and remains standing.*

*They would all die.*

The sound of metal against metal behind me eventually caught my attention.

Jade was fighting with the others, weapon to weapon. I spun around, not even checking to see if Ky and his friends were dead yet, and began helping my wife.

She had gotten more skilled in combat. So skilled, actually, that she cut three fae down before I even had my hands on one.

"There are more!" she yelled through gritted teeth. "We can't hold them off forever!"

"How is that power of yours coming along?" I asked, snapping the neck of another pale-winged fae.

He fell to the ground before me. I stepped over him before stopping the blade of another, ripping it from their grasp and impaling their torso with the steel.

"Working on it," Jade said, using her black boot to shove a dead fae off her own weapon.

I glanced away for half a second to survey the scene around us.

Jade was right. More were coming. We couldn't hold them off forever, not alone. My power was already depleting. I needed a few minutes to restore it, and that was a few minutes we didn't have.

We kept fighting, fae after fae. Rebel after rebel. Jade's shouts of anger fueled me in my own fight, cutting down as many of those blood-thirsty rebels as possible, until a few began to...began to *run away*.

"What's happening?" Jade asked, not stopping her fight.

A few men screamed as they ran. I looked to find someone pointing up at the sky, past the trees and into the darkness.

I cut one more fae down before following the looks of horror.

Only to find a dragon flying straight toward us.

# CHAPTER 38

# *Jade*

"What is that?" I screamed, my voice hoarse from the effort. Thankfully, nobody else tried to kill me at that given moment. Everyone was too busy running away from whatever monster swarmed the sky above us.

Malachi stared into the sky for a few more seconds before a deep, wicked smile spread across his face. He took a few steps toward me before tearing his gaze away. "Believe it or not, that's Dragon."

I glanced up again, seeing black and red scales lacing the underbelly of the beast. And those wings…those were the things one saw in nightmares. This was the type of beast mothers told horror stories about.

"Dragon is a…"

"Yes," Malachi said, cutting me off. "And unless we want to turn to rubble, we better get out of here. Now."

He moved first, pulling me along with him through the trees. I didn't know which way we were headed, I didn't care.

If Dragon couldn't see us…

"Dragon doesn't know we're down here," I said, more to myself than to Malachi. I repeated it again, louder, so he could hear me. "He doesn't know!"

Malachi was already sprinting, his bare feet practically gliding over the forest floor as he dragged me along with him. The grip he had on my hand tightened. He knew, he had to know. With the chaos going on around us, Dragon was certainly going to…

A loud roar, one that shook the trees around us and vibrated the bones in my body, split through the air.

My stomach dropped. Mal stopped running.

There was nothing we could do but stare at the world around us as Dragon engulfed the entire forest in flames.

# CHAPTER 39
## *Malachi*

I had never been more certain that I was going to die. Maybe once, in the middle of war, surrounded by my enemies without even a sword to fight with. But that was different. There was always a slight sliver of hope, a fraction of a plan that would save my life.

There was always *something*.

Now, with fire coming directly at us from a dragon that shouldn't even exist, I knew death was ours.

I wrapped Jade in my arms and flexed my wings around us, any last shred of hope leaving with my final breath.

And then I waited.

Waited for the heat, the flames, the ash that would surely result from the blow of the dragon.

But it never came. Even as soldiers screamed abruptly around us, until their screams were cut off by something I couldn't see, we were still alive.

I blinked my eyes open, only to find a glimmering shield around us.

"What the—"

"You really should have waited for us," Serefin insisted, standing with his hands held out in the air, a shield of protection stopping Dragon's deadly fire from killing us.

The blaze ceased.

Serefin dropped his shield.

Jade and I both stood, a mixture of adrenaline and relief swarming my body and sending her emotions through our magic tether.

"Saints," Jade whispered as I pulled my wings back from her body. "We almost just died."

"Yes," Serefin said, his face blank. "You did."

"You…you just saved our lives, Ser," Jade stuttered before throwing herself into his arms.

His eyes locked with mine for a split second, long enough for me to see the fear and relief and love swarming beneath them.

Serefin *had* just saved our lives.

"Where are the others?" I asked.

"On their way. They figured they'd wait for Dragon to take out most of the soldiers."

We glanced around the forest. Nothing but burnt tree trunks and piles of ash remained.

"Ky is dead," Jade whispered. "There's no way he survived that fire."

"Then we get the humans and we kill the rest of the rebels. It's the only way."

The three of us locked eyes with a silent promise, one made with unsaid words.

"We might not be able to use our magic in that building," Jade suggested. "It's enforced with something, or one of the fae is working overtime to stop us. And whatever powers they used on us during the attack when they kidnapped me? I'm sure we'll run into them, too."

She was right.

Going into that building to get the humans would be a death-trap. It would be so, so easy to walk away. To leave the humans and return to Rewyth, considering this a victory against all rebels now that their leader was dead.

But that was the dark side thinking, the death and the destruction and the chaos. That was the self-preservation taking over, telling us to run from danger.

The Saints did not gift Jade with this destiny for her to turn away when things grew dangerous. They gave her this power to fight, not just for herself and for Rewyth, but for everyone who may need it.

She met my gaze and nodded.

We didn't have an option.

"The others will be here for backup," Ser insisted. "Do you know how to get into the building?"

"This way," I said, turning to the door that led to the underground hideout. "Get ready."

We walked over the burnt forest floor, my bare feet stepping over the charred bones and ash as we made our way to the hidden door.

The forest grew eerily quiet.

Not a single soldier yelled in the distance. Dragon's wings made no sound now that he was out of sight. No birds chirped. No wind howled.

Nothing.

"Here," I said, bending down and flipping the hatch open to the underground. "I don't know what we're going to find down there, but we can't let those bastards think they've won."

"No," Serefin said from behind me. "We can't."

Jade smiled and stepped forward. "I'll go first," she said. "I know the way."

"Absolutely not," Ser said from behind her, grabbing her arm. "It's too dangerous. I still have the shield magic, I'll go first in case we're attacked."

"Your magic is new," Jade explained. "How can you be sure it will even work when you need it?"

"It's better than nothing," Ser replied. Saints, I didn't want him going first, but with my power depleting and Jade still without the help of the Saints, we didn't have many other options.

"Stay together," I ordered, holding the door open for Serefin. "If anything bad happens down there, we regroup up here and we wait for the others. Understand?"

Jade and Ser both nodded, and *Saints*. I never felt more love for them in my entire life.

I pushed away any thoughts of finality, any thoughts of one of us not coming back up to the surface.

And I followed Serefin down the stairs.

# CHAPTER 40
## Jade

I HELD MY BREATH AS WE DESCENDED THE STAIRS. ONE STEP AFTER THE other, I anticipated the attack. The rush of magic. The deadly force that would certainly be the end of us.

But step after step, it never came.

And before I knew it, we had made it to the end of those dark stairs.

Not a single fae stopped us, not a single fae even lingered in the area.

Maybe we had gotten lucky. Maybe the fae had all left, abandoned the underground hideout and gone to the surface to fight...

But when was I *ever* lucky?

"This way," I whispered. "They're keeping the humans somewhere down here."

Our breathing echoed across the steel walls of the underground fortress. How they even built this place was beyond me, entirely beneath the ground and designed to survive an attack from...well, apparently a dragon.

We walked down the dark hallway, past where I had been kept in that small room. "Hear anything yet?" I asked, motioning to their fae ears.

Mal and Ser both stiffened at the same time, turning to one specific room.

"Over here," Ser ordered. He moved without hesitation, pushing open one of the many doors in the hallway and halting at the door frame. His mouth hung agape, just for a moment, as he surveyed whatever was inside that room.

"What is it?" I asked, pushing forward to see for myself.

I halted, too, unable to form words as I took in the scene in front of me.

Humans, at least a hundred of them, shoved into the small steel room and sitting without even an inch of space between them.

"Saints," I mumbled. Men, women, children. It didn't matter. They had apparently been shoved into this room with no chance of getting out. "How long have you all been in here?"

"Jade," Sadie's voice caught my attention. I turned my head to find her standing from her crouched position in the stale room. "They forced us into here without telling us why."

I pulled her into a hug. Her skin gleamed with sweat. "We're getting everyone out of here," I said. "The rebels won't be a problem anymore."

A few gasps filled the room. "The peacemaker," one of the humans in the back said. "You're real?"

Mal placed a hand on my shoulder. "The peacemaker is very real, and she's here to save your lives. The fae who forced you out of your homes did so wrongfully, and you won't have to live in fear like that. Not anymore. Jade is here to protect you."

I lifted my chin. Hearing Mal say those words sent a fire in my chest, one that flared my power from the inside.

Finally, I began to feel my magic again.

"Can you lead them out of here?" I asked Sadie. "Our people should be here soon. Lead them as far away from this place as you can. We'll find you on the outside."

Sadie nodded and immediately began helping the others stand. Mal, Ser, and I backed up, letting them file out of the dark room they had been held in.

It was inhumane, at the very least.

"I can't believe this," I muttered. "Herding humans as if they are cattle."

Mal's thumb rubbed against the back of my neck. "Never again," he whispered into my ear. "Because of you, Jade. You are their savior."

I relaxed into him, finally letting myself breathe. Finally letting my clenched fists fall. Sadie moved up the stairs in the distance, the file of humans following after her.

We saved them. We actually saved them.

I was finally starting to feel that hidden, dangerous flicker of hope when pain erupted over my entire body. My vision blurred, my legs collapsed beneath me.

*Someone was attacking.*

Mal and Ser both fell, too, onto their knees next to me as pain washed over us, leaving the three of us incapacitated on the ground.

I moved my hands to my head, scratching at the agony, trying to let out that fire inside me.

My body burned, killing me slowly from the inside out.

A scream escaped me, mixing with the torturous cries of the fae next to me.

"That dragon of yours was a surprise, I must say," Ky's voice interrupted my screams. The pain let up long enough for me to glance up at him approaching. "But this fight of ours is not over."

# CHAPTER 41
# *Malachi*

**Ky was supposed to be dead.**

Deader than dead.

Ash on the forest ground that I stepped across with my bare feet.

More pain erupted in my mind, blinding my thoughts. I tried to reach for Jade but could not even manage lifting my hand.

Whatever magic this rebel was using, it was strong.

Serefin needed to use his shield.

"You want to kill me," I managed to cough through gritted teeth, "just do it already."

Ky, the rebel, knelt before me. I wanted so badly to wipe that look off his face with my fist. "And end the fun so soon?" Ky muttered. "That isn't what you did to my brother, you know. He didn't get the mercy of a swift death."

Saints. I didn't have the energy to deal with this again.

Jade moved next to me, just barely. She was moving toward Ser.

*Good.* He could shield her from this. I just had to distract him long enough so they could fight back.

They had a chance.

I closed my eyes, just for a second, and thought about my death magic coming out to absolutely slaughter this man. I pictured the way he would be the one falling to his knees in pain, begging me to kill him just to make the burning inside his body stop.

But when I opened my eyes again, nothing had changed.

Jade let out another scream of pain beside me.

"Let them go!" I yelled to Ky. "They have nothing to do with this!" The rest of my breath was pulled from my lungs, making it impossible to keep talking.

*Pain. So much pain.*

Ky laughed. "And why would I let the peacemaker go?" he asked. "After all the work I've done to get her here?"

More pain split through me, erupting in my chest.

He could kill me, that was fine. But he wasn't laying a finger on her.

Serefin tried to stand and ended up falling, half-catching himself on my shoulder. Ky and Jade both flinched at this movement, but I took the split second of distraction to make my move.

"Get her out of here," I whispered to Ser before releasing him and launching myself at Ky.

It took every last bit of energy I had, every last ounce of strength.

And I launched myself at Ky.

He was shocked, at first. So shocked that he let his magic grip on the three of us falter, just for a second. Long enough for me to throw my shadows at him, full force. He never saw it coming as the darkness pierced his body, radiating all around him.

"Go!" I yelled to Ser. I pushed Jade in the direction of the humans that were still filtering out of the building, now panicking and beginning to shove each other up the narrow stairwell. "Get out of here! Find the others on the surface!"

Ser hesitated, but he knew. He knew I would never forgive him if something happened to her. He knew I couldn't live with myself if she didn't make it out.

It was the only option.

Only, when I turned to face Ky, to finish him off once and for all before he could cause any more trouble in this world, I was met with a long sword through my flesh.

## CHAPTER 42

# *Jade*

"MALACHI!" I RIPPED MYSELF FROM SEREFIN'S GRASP AND TORE MY way back to Malachi, where Ky's blade still impaled him. I felt that sharp pain in my own body, too, through our magic bond that also allowed me to feel his shock as he looked down to see Ky's weapon.

Anger, pain, and pure hatred mixed together inside me, creating a deadly storm of emotions I wouldn't wish on anyone.

And I wanted Ky dead. I wanted him dead more than anything. Mal fell to his knees beside me. I gently lowered him to the ground while Ky pulled the weapon out of Mal's body.

"No," I muttered. Ser drew his own sword, now yelling through his own pain.

Ky might have powerful magic, but he wasn't as angry as us.

My magic rumbled, unable to be contained, begging for a target to relieve some of the pain I was feeling.

And I let it.

I threw everything I had at Ky, at the fae who had hurt Mal, at the one who had caused all this damage. Whatever magic the stupid walls of this place had kept from me was back now, laced with a fiery need for blood. For vengeance.

Serefin yelled something behind me, but I didn't stop. I threw the ball of magic at him until it poured from my fingertips. I wanted nothing but his death, nothing but his bones burning to ash before me.

And so they did.

And I watched in satisfaction as his scream stopped in his throat, his entire body vanishing before my power as I poured and poured and poured.

And just as quickly as it all began, it was over.

I was left panting and sweating, staring at what was just Ky, but was no longer.

I spun around to find Ser half-holding Malachi as his blood poured from his hands. I joined him, dropping to my knees in front of Malachi.

"No," I whispered to him. "Stand up," I ordered. "We have to get out of here and then we'll be able to stop the bleeding."

Mal's eyes were already cloudy, but not from pain or anger. In fact, any anger that had been in his gaze before was gone now.

"You did it," he whispered. "You killed him."

"Yes," I replied, "but there will be more like him. I need you, Mal. This isn't over."

Ser held all of his weight now, grunting under the pressure. The humans were almost all above ground now. Just a couple of minutes, and we could...

"Stay with us, brother," Serefin mumbled. "Jade is right. We need you, Mal. We don't win this war without you."

I gripped Mal's face in my hands. Already so pale, so cold. Blood dripped onto the floor beneath us. "Please," I whispered, ignoring the way my voice cracked. "Please don't leave us now, Mal. We are so close. We are so close to having everything."

Mal smiled. Actually smiled. "I already had everything," he whispered to me. He brought a bloody hand up to brush a tear from my cheek. "I've had it this entire time."

"Don't," I argued. "Don't you dare give up on me now!"

His eyelids grew heavy, taunting me with every blink. This wasn't happening. This couldn't possibly be happening. The mighty, dangerous King of Shadows was not going to be killed by a mere fae, not after everything we'd been through.

Not after everything *he* had been through.

Serefin lost his grip on Mal's shoulders and he fell forward, falling straight into my chest. I fought to lift him up, holding him with all of my remaining strength, which wasn't much.

"It was all supposed to happen this way," Mal muttered, just inches from my face now. I cried violently, tears running freely down my face and dripping from my chin.

"You can't possibly think that," I replied.

"You know it's true, Jade. I was always going to be your downfall. Now, I don't have to be."

He blinked a couple more times.

And then his entire body collapsed.

Malachi Weyland, King of Shadows, died in my arms.

# CHAPTER 43
# Malachi

I HAD MANY REGRETS IN MY LIFE, BUT NONE HURT ME AS BADLY AS seeing the look on Jade's face as I slipped into the darkness.

She had to understand. If it were up to me, I wouldn't leave her. I would *never* leave her. But I tried so hard to fight, to stay awake, to make it through. At the end, as long as Jade was safe, that's all that mattered.

Serefin would protect her. He would get her out.

The pain from Ky's weapon disappeared, leaving me floating in a void of darkness. It did not feel cold or frightening, though. It felt comforting, exactly like I had expected.

A slight breeze caressed my skin, tugging at my awareness.

"Hello?" I called out, though nobody was nearby. I felt that solitude deep in my soul, an expansion of the solitude I felt inside of myself for most of my life.

Until I met her, anyway.

*"I must say, I did not think we would get the chance to meet so soon,"* a familiar voice spoke through the wind.

I did not panic. I had no reason to. I simply turned my head to the side and searched for the source of that voice. "Erebus?" I called out. "Is that you?"

The wind picked up slightly, and when I blinked, I began to see a shape forming within the shadows of the darkness. Not just any shape, but a person.

Erebus, forming from the shadows of night.

*"Of course it's me,"* his gravel voice answered. *"I am the Saint of death, after all. And you're dying."*

"I don't want to die," I answered honestly. "She needs me back there."

Erebus stepped forward in mid-air, walking on nothing but shadows. I glanced around, too, realizing I was doing the same thing within the vast void of emptiness.

*"She's brought you back before, King of Shadows. Anastasia will not grant her this again."*

Erebus's features came into view, sharp and clean. His face was pale, nearly iridescent, actually, which was a sharp contrast from his black curls and grown facial hair. The black linens he wore reminded me of the Paragon, yet when Erebus wore them, they radiated strength.

I suddenly felt the need to bow my head.

"I didn't see you the last time I died," I noted. "Why now?"

A chilling silence passed between us. I felt the weight of his words before he even said them. *"Your last death was not final. I'm afraid this one is."*

I supposed I had already been brought back from death once, when Jade had resurrected me in the trials. Once was already too much.

I was dead. After all these years, after all those struggles. It was finally here.

*"You have nothing to fear,"* Erebus continued. *"Life is a fickle, reckless thing. You will find death to be much more peaceful."*

"Of course you would say that," I muttered. "You are the Saint of death."

The feeling of laughter fell over me before I heard Erebus chuckle. *"And as my descendent, you should feel the same way."*

I lifted my head and looked him in the eye again. As dangerous and terrifying as he was, I recognized something there, a sort of longing I had felt my entire life.

"Was this what you meant?" I asked. "Was this what Anastasia meant when she said I would be her downfall?"

Erebus smirked. *"Welcome home, Malachi."*

# CHAPTER 44
## Jade

It started as panic—pure, horrifying terror that pulsed through my heart, taking over my body, stronger than any adrenaline. More powerful than any magic.

Malachi's body grew cold beneath my hands as I pounded on his chest, begging his heart to start beating again.

The blood from his abdomen had already slowed.

"NO!" I screamed. "You can't die! You can't die, Malachi!"

I hit his chest again.

And again.

"Bring him back!" I yelled, this time to the Saints. "You have to bring him back!"

Serefin leaned over me, pushing onto Mal's wound. As if that would save him. As if that would bring him back, would start his heart again.

Serefin couldn't help. He couldn't bring Malachi back, but I could.

I had done it before, in the Trials of Glory. That was a test, yes, but it was also so, so real. If I could do it then, I could do it again.

I grabbed Mal's face in my hands and closed my eyes. "Please," I mumbled. "Give me the power to bring him back, and I swear I will do no harm. He's my protector. I need him."

The power deep in my chest flickered. Yes, that was it. That was a start. I just needed more, more power, more magic. More life.

And then I could bring him back.

He could come back, yes. I just needed....

"Please," I begged again. "Anastasia, I know you can help me. I just need a little more."

*There is a balance to everything, peacemaker. We have told you this before. It is very delicate, very fragile.*

"I don't care about the damn balance!" I yelled aloud.

Serefin flinched next to me.

"I just want to bring my husband back! Bring him back, Anastasia! I know you can do it! I know you can help me!"

*Just because I can does not mean I will, or that I should. He will be your downfall, Jade Weyland. I have warned you of this fate.*

"NO!" I screamed. "I do not accept this! Bring him back, Anastasia!"

But the Saint of life did not reply.

The panic came back in a wave, crashing over every bone in my chest and tightening, like fingers in a fist. Tightening and tightening and tightening until I couldn't breathe, couldn't think. Couldn't move.

"BRING. HIM. BACK!"

Serefin yelled next to me, still pressing onto Malachi's open wound. The same wound that could have healed by now, could have been healed by now.

"Why?" I asked. "Why did you bring me back but not him? Why now? He's better than me, I swear it! He's stronger and smarter and he's—he's–"

My vision tunneled, everything around me swarming and contorting until I blacked out entirely.

A white light pierced through the darkness. A familiar presence washed over me, warm and welcoming, but somehow still dreaded.

When my eyes adjusted, I saw Anastasia standing before me.

"What am I doing here?" I asked. "I should be with him! I should be, I should be bringing him back!" My breath came in fast, rapid pants, my lungs needing more oxygen than they could handle, than they could take. I clawed at my chest, at my throat.

Anastasia looked at me with a straight face, so different than that comforting smile. In fact, nothing about her was comforting. Not anymore.

*"I can't,"* she said.

"Yes, you can."

She stepped forward, her perfect, smooth forehead wrinkling as she repeated, *"No, Jade. I cannot bring your husband back. Not this time. I warned you of this, I warned you he would be your downfall."*

I shoved my hands over my ears. I couldn't hear this. Not now. Not when everything was at risk.

*"The balance is too far gone,"* Anastasia said. *"Bringing him back will only make it worse. It's not possible, Jade. Not this time. Get yourself out of there before you die, too."*

# CHAPTER 45

## Jade

To my surprise, all pain I felt disappeared. I no longer felt the fatal blow of Ky's sword as if it were my own, radiating pain from my chest and taking over every sense, every thought.

No, all I felt now was a lethal, chilling numbness. One that welcomed me, wrapping me in its arms and swallowing me whole. One that surrounded me entirely, engulfing me within and hiding that pain, hiding those thoughts.

Serefin pulled me away from Mal once I quit screaming.

"Why isn't he coming back?" Ser asked, turning his attention to me. "He isn't waking up, Jade!" Panic laced his words.

"I know," I breathed. "They...they won't let me bring him back."

A silent beat passed.

"What did you just say?"

I met his eyes so he could hear me this time, so he had no confusion about my words as I spoke them. "He's dead," I started, forcing the words out like poison. "They will not revive him, Serefin. They will not let me."

The voice that spoke was not my own. It was a voice so empty, so foreign, that I did not recognize it. I raised my bloody hands in front of me, surveying them. Mal's blood—red and warm—dripped from my fingertips onto the floor of pooled blood next to him.

Malachi was dead.

The thought did not even sound real in my own mind. How could it? The idea of Malachi, of my savior, my everything, being dead was so absurd, I could not even fathom it.

I was the one that should be dead. I was the one that deserved this fate, not him.

It was never supposed to be *him*.

The emptiness inside of me spread until I couldn't feel my own limbs, couldn't hear Serefin talking to me. I saw his lips moving, though, saying something over and over again and trying to get me to hear him.

What was the point?

Mal was dead. This was all over.

My other half.

My king.

*All of it was for nothing.*

I couldn't lead Rewyth alone. I couldn't fight this war, wouldn't be this person.

My emotions became too much, too thick. Too heavy. My power swirled, somehow restored from everything and back in full force, shattering everything around me and somehow literally shaking the ground, rattling the steel walls around us.

"Jade!" Serefin yelled. "Jade, we have to get out of here!"

I couldn't think. Couldn't move.

Serefin shook me hard enough to catch my attention, his fingers digging into my shoulders so hard that I actually felt the pain through my numbness.

Serefin picked up Malachi and threw him over his shoulder. "Come on!" He began running, climbing those stairs up to the surface.

I should have stayed. I should have let the shaking walls crush me, swallowing me entirely. It would have hurt less. Dying would be easier, would be safer.

To face them on the surface would be impossible.

Even so, I watched as Serefin climbed those stairs, Mal's bloody, lifeless body in his arms, and I couldn't help but hope.

This could not be the end. It couldn't.

So I picked myself up, pushed myself onto my weak, wobbling legs, and followed Serefin to the surface.

I climbed the stairs, one by one, somehow finding the strength to keep going, to not give up.

The ground around me continued to shake, matching the turmoil inside, feeding the darkness. We were a perfect match, those crumbling walls and I.

And when we got to the surface, not even the moonlight could have illuminated that darkness.

"Serefin!" Adeline's voice cut through the air. My eyes adjusted, too, until I saw them all. Adeline, Cordelia, Adonis, Lucien, *Saints*. Even Esther. They were all here, and they came with an entire army of fae.

No, I couldn't face them. Not when Serefin carried the body of the man they were all here for.

Adeline ran forward, only to realize the cruel reality of what had happened. She stopped a few feet in front of us. "No," she said, shaking her head. "No, this can't be real. This can't be happening. He's okay, right? He'll be okay?"

I opened my mouth to explain, to make her feel better, to say anything, but no words came out. Serefin pushed past her, toward the army in the tree line.

"Where are the other rebels?" he asked.

"Dead," Lucien called out. "There were only a few, but we took care of them."

"Malachi?" Esther shouted, stepping out of the group and walking toward Serefin, who knelt and laid his body in the ashen dirt. "What happened?" Esther asked, surveying the scene.

She knelt next to his body.

"A sword," Serefin explained. "Jade tried to bring him back, but..."

Esther's eyes found mine. "But *what*? What happened, Jade? Why can't you bring him back?"

I stepped forward, too, not feeling my feet as they moved. "They wouldn't let me," I finally explained. Saints, my mouth barely moved. "They couldn't do it, they said the balance was too delicate."

"The balance?" Esther repeated, her eyes going adrift as she thought. "We can fix this," she mumbled. "Cordelia?"

Cordelia was at her side in an instant, already knowing her next thought. "We can't," Cordelia said, shaking her head. "If the Saints will not allow it, it cannot be done. Jade has already tried."

I stared at them, that numbness growing with every passing second.

No, they couldn't bring him back. Anastasia had been very clear about that. Even if they could, she would not help them.

Cordelia's eyes widened. "Esther, don't even–"

"It's not up for discussion!" Esther yelled back, baring her teeth and straining her neck, making even Cordelia flinch at her words.

"What's going on?" Serefin asked. "Can you help him?"

"Yes!" Esther yelled. "I can and I will. Right, Cordelia?"

Cordelia hesitated for a second, long enough to make me wonder what exactly Esther was going to do to help.

"Right," she said eventually. "We can bring him back."

Cordelia called out to Lenova and the other witches, calling them forward. I stepped back, giving them more room. Adeline hooked her arm through mine, violently sobbing at the sight before us, but I couldn't bring myself to care. To think. To watch.

No, it was all too much.

Having hope would break me, would shatter me entirely.

But together, the witches began to chant.

They held hands, Cordelia and Esther leading the group as they looked up to the moon and begged, pleading in a language I did not understand.

It had to work. Even through the numbness, even though I didn't want to feel any hope, I still held on.

It had to work.

They chanted and chanted around Malachi's body, every single one of the witches speaking in a desperation only someone who had lost so deeply would possibly understand.

*Did they?* Did they understand what was at stake if Malachi did not come back?

Thunder rippled in the distance. Dark and beautiful, reminding me of him.

*Saints.*

It had to work.

Adeline gasped and gripped me harder as Esther stepped forward. I didn't see the dagger in her hand until it was too late.

And before I could even process the scene around me, Esther was plunging the weapon into her own chest.

She fell to the ground beside her son, bleeding out just as he did.

And dying, just as he did.

The rest of the witches carried on, louder now. They had re-formed the circle where Esther stepped out, not a single one even looking away from the moon to witness what happened. Unless I was losing my mind, unless everything I was seeing was simply a delusion.

But the chanting stopped.

The witches dropped their hands, breaking the circle.

And—in a way that absolutely ruined me—Malachi took a breath.

# CHAPTER 46
# Malachi

One entire week passed.

An entire week with no fighting, no battle.

An entire week with no whispers from Erebus, with no summoning from the Saints.

An entire week home with *her*.

Jade and I woke up in bed. I was still getting used to it—waking up beside her. Everything felt surreal, felt like it was too good to be true.

Erebus welcomed me home, and now I was back with Jade.

But Esther wasn't.

"You don't need to keep staring," I said. "I swear to you, I'm fine."

My eyes were closed, but it didn't matter. I could practically feel Jade's gaze burning me with concern. It had been like this the past three nights; every time I woke up in bed, she was already awake, staring.

"I know," she replied. "I just want to be sure."

I blinked my eyes open and rolled over, finding her lying on her side with her head propped on her hand. She always looked so beautiful like that; undone, with her messy black hair falling over her shoulder.

It was hard to find her like that.

Unguarded.

I reached down and grabbed her free hand, pulling it forward and placing it on my bare chest. My heart beat steadily under her warm touch. "See?" I asked. "I'm alive."

Memories flashed through my mind, the same ones I had been trying to suppress for the last three days. Erebus speaking to me, my own mother sacrificing herself.

Jade screaming as the life left my body.

The memories came to me in chaotic spurts of emotion and power, and I still didn't understand so much.

Jade felt the same. I could nearly hear her thoughts through our bond, though that bond had broken before, it was now stronger than ever.

And I felt her fear, her worry.

Just as I was sure she felt mine.

Her brows furrowed as she pulled her hand from my chest, rolling to lie on her back.

"What is it?" I asked. "What's wrong?"

She shook her head as she focused on the ceiling above. "I can't help but feel angry. Sometimes the anger is too much, it's all-consuming. I don't know if I'll ever get past it."

"Angry at who?"

She shrugged. "The Saints. Esther. Everyone. But mostly Anastasia. She held the power to bring you back herself, Esther didn't have to die."

I agreed with her, of course I did. I had hated Esther for a long time, but she had saved Jade's life, too. She was on my side, whether I admitted that in the end or not. There was no denying it now.

But we all knew there was a balance. We could kill and kill and kill, but at some point, there was a line.

We had crossed it one too many times.

"She sacrificed herself for me," I said. Saints, it was the first time I actually said those words out loud. Esther died so I could live, gave herself so I could come back to this world.

I had already lived so much, yet Esther thought I deserved more life.

She was not selfish. She was not cruel or untruthful. At the end of the day, Esther was my mother, and I loved her. She gave her life so I could continue living.

I sat up in bed, running my hands through my mess of curls.

Jade followed. She leaned up and rested her head on my shoulder, narrowly avoiding my relaxed wings.

"It's over, you know," she whispered in my ear. "We've won the fight. We've survived the war."

Saints, I wanted to laugh at that. How many times had I thought that? How many times had I believed I had won, just to be right back where I started once more?

I twisted, wrapping Jade in my arms and pulling her back down on the bed. After a squeal of surprise and laughter, she relaxed into my body.

"I never thanked you, you know," I said to her.

She tilted her chin up to meet my gaze. I would never get over her beauty. "For what?"

"For making me save those humans. For reminding me of my humanity. For always seeing the good in me, even when you can't see it in yourself."

She smiled and reached up, trailing a finger down my cheekbone. "I suppose I should thank you, too," she said.

"Oh, really? May I ask what for?"

The smile slowly faded from her face, the light in her eyes dulling, if just for a moment. She had a way of doing that, of slipping into those emotions that we both fought so hard to avoid. Her brows furrowed as she lifted her chin and answered, "For being the light when I had none."

A knock on the door made Jade jump from her spot in my arms.

"What is it?" I called out.

Serefin's voice replied. "I'm just reminding you of the Sunrise Festival today, your majesties. Wouldn't want either of you to be late."

"Of course not," I replied. "Be right there, Ser."

I waited until his footsteps had retreated down the hall before pushing myself out of bed.

"Can't we just stay in this bed forever?" Jade moaned.

"What?" I teased. "You don't want to celebrate a new world with all of our people?"

"Maybe," she said, dropping herself back onto the bed. "But can't we do it tomorrow?"

"Come on," I said, walking around the tall bed posts and hoisting her off the silk sheets. "It's time we finally had some fun around here."

# CHAPTER 47
## *Jade*

Part of me hated that it all felt so normal; the music, the dancing, the laughing. I mean, everyone was celebrating as if we hadn't just been begging the Saints for Malachi's life back.

Of course, not everyone knew that part. But still. It was eerie to think about.

"You're sulking," Adeline said as she approached. Her floral dress swayed back and forth as she skipped toward me, and two flowers tucked her curled hair back behind her ears. "You're sulking at a party. That's unacceptable, Jade."

"I'm not sulking," I replied. "I'm observing. There's nothing wrong with that."

"Maybe not, but you could use this." She handed me a cup of the fae wine. I took it, sipping on the sweet liquid and looking around at the festival. Malachi stood with his brothers—Eli, Adonis, and Lucien—to my left, all smiling and talking in hushed voices. I didn't remember the last time I saw them all talking to each other that way.

Cordelia walked up to them, placing a light hand on Lucien's shoulder as she casually joined the conversation. She had been upset after Esther died, but I think she understood. Of everyone else here, she would know what Esther was thinking in those last moments. Esther would have wanted us all to be happy, to finally be at peace.

Now, we finally got the chance. The chance to start over, the chance to live this life how we were supposed to live it all along.

Adeline looped her arm through mine as we watched. "You did this for us, Jade," she whispered. "However torturous this fae life has been for you, I want you to know how much of a blessing you were to us."

I put my hand atop hers, fighting the sudden rush of tears. "Thank you, Adeline."

Serefin walked up behind her, placing his hands on both of her shoulders. "Mind if I steal you for a dance?" he whispered.

Adeline smiled, quickly letting go of my arm and letting Serefin guide her to the crowd of dancing fae with an excited squeal.

Serefin met my eyes, too, just for a second, before giving me a silent nod.

We hadn't talked about what happened that day with the rebels. We didn't need to. Malachi was back, and that's all that mattered. Both of us would have done anything to bring him back, but at the end of the day, it was Esther who needed to sacrifice herself.

Not me. Not Serefin.

"So, this is where the fun has been happening," a male voice from behind made me jump. I turned to see my father walking up, dressed in a black jacket and new black boots.

"Father," I said. "I'm surprised you showed up. A fae festival has never really been your version of fun."

"No," he replied, coming to stand in Adeline's place, "but staying cooped up in that castle all day isn't exactly my version of fun, either."

I nodded. "I understand."

"Besides," he continued, "if I want to spend any time with my daughter, I might have to start attending these things now."

I actually smiled, turning to look my father in the eye. He was so different now, so much more clear. "You can see me anytime you want, you know," I pushed. "You just have to send word."

"Yeah, yeah," he said. "When you're not out saving the entire world, I'll let you know."

I smiled again, turning my attention back to the crowd. We stood that way for a while, shoulder to shoulder, taking in the world around us.

"I have to say, this is much better than the worn-down shack we were living in before," he said.

My eyes snapped to his. "You're kidding, right?"

My father shook his head. "Not in the slightest. But I did always know you would be the one to save the world."

I expected him to be joking, but he said all of this with a straight face.

"Well," I replied, "that makes one of us."

I was surprised when my father decided to stick around. The rest of the humans we helped rescue left, journeying back to their lands with a handful of fae to help them rebuild what they had lost.

With time and resources, I was confident we could help them live better lives. Not ones of poverty or scarcity, but lives of abundance.

Humans didn't need to fear the fae anymore. Not while I was here.

My father smiled, his dull, brown eyes actually sparkling for once, as he put a hand on my shoulder. "You did good, kid," he said. "Even if I didn't."

I placed a hand on top of his. He didn't have to say anything else. Neither of us did. I knew what my father meant, what he had said in those few words.

He was proud of me. He was sorry. He was a changed man now.

We both changed.

"Enjoy your celebration," he said, turning to walk back into the castle. "You deserve it."

I watched him walk away, no longer stumbling like I had seen so many times. N limping, not cowering. Simply walking. Like he belonged here. Like he deserved to be here.

My chest welled with an emotion I couldn't quite name.

*He's right,* the soft voice in my head said. I jumped at the sound of it, I hadn't heard Anastasia since the night Mal died. *You deserve this.*

*I thought you were done with me,* I thought back. *I thought you left for good after Malachi came back.*

A tickling feeling of satisfaction filled my chest from her before she replied, *I've had some time to think, to process what happened.*

*You let him come back, didn't you?* I asked. *A life for a life.*

A long beat of silence filled my mind.

*I thought he would be your downfall,* Anastasia admitted. *I thought he would pull you into the darkness, pull you out of the light.*

*What changed?*

*It appears I was wrong, peacemaker. As long as he is at your side, I think darkness bows at your feet.*

I smiled to nobody. *I have to agree with you on that one, Anastasia.*

*Besides,* the voice echoed in my mind, *I think you two have saved enough people. You deserved a little saving of your own. Remember to stay out of trouble next time, okay?*

*No promises,* I thought back.

A warm rush filled my body, illuminating my senses as my power rolled in my veins. I hadn't realized just how much I missed the presence of the Saints until now. The last week, thinking they had abandoned me, was misery.

But she wasn't mad at all.

And she actually approved of this relationship with Malachi.

Finally, everything fell into place.

"What was that about?" Malachi asked as he approached.

I turned to face him. "I don't know, but it was surprisingly pleasant."

Malachi nodded with a raised brow. "Come here," he said. "I want you to hear something."

I took Mal's outstretched hand, letting him guide me through the crowd to where his brothers stood with Cordelia and Dragon.

They were all smiling, clearly excited about something.

"Go ahead," Mal said as soon as I approached the circle. "Tell her what you told me."

Eli stepped forward, his face lit up with a joy I had only seen a few times. "I can see it all," he said, his eyes focusing on something else.

I glanced at Mal, who only smiled back at me.

"You can see what?" I asked.

"The future, everything. Our lives here in Rewyth."

[illegible]waited for him to say more, but he clearly got lost in the thought again, smiling [illegible]nething only he could see.

[illegible]this is a good thing," I said. "And not more death and war like the last [illegible]

[illegible]ly, Malachi pulled me against his body.

"No death," Eli replied. "No war. Just us and, for once, peace."

Even Lucien smiled at this, wrapping his arms around Cordelia's shoulders as Dragon bounced around in front of them.

"Peace," I repeated. "That sounds almost too good to be true."

"Get used to it," Mal whispered into my ear. "Because I think I'm done fighting for now."

I leaned into him, relaxing into his body and watching our friends smile, dance, hope. "Me too."

# Acknowledgments

Thinking about how this series changed my life has truly left me at a loss for words. First, thank you to my mother, Julie, for believing in me. Without you, my writing career would have ended before it ever started. Our business meetings, which almost always required a margarita, were some of the best inspirational conversations I've had, and I surely would not have been successful in this career without your motivation and support. I live my dream now because of you.

Jess and Kenz, you two have been there for me on those late nights and long weeks when I wanted to give up and rip my hair out. You both have always been the ones waving the flashlight toward the end of the tunnel, showing me the light when I needed help to see it. I don't know how I was lucky enough to find you in this life, but I am certain this series would be crumbled in the trash somewhere if it wasn't for your positivity and endless kindness. The universe sent me you two when I needed friendship the most, and I think about how lucky I am every single day.

To my friends and family, who put up with me cancelling plans to stay home and write, thank you for not giving up on me!

And finally, thank you to Jack, who doesn't read my books but still puts up with me talking about fictional characters ten hours a day. This career empties my emotional well on an almost weekly occasion, and you're always there to help me refill that well when I need it.

When I first wrote House of Lies and Sorrow, I thought maybe ten people would read it. I had no idea it would receive the love and support that it has, and it's all because of you—the readers. Every single time a stranger tells me they've loved these books, it warms my heart. Every time. I never take you for granted, and I'm truly floored by the love this series has received.

Thank you for believing in me. Thank you for loving Jade and Malachi. Thank you for taking a chance on an indie author. Thank you for escaping with me into my twisted, dark worlds.

Thank you.

I'll never stop writing for you.

Love,
Em